Magnolias

Romantic History from the Deep South in Four Complete Novels

JACQUELYN COOK

BARBOUR BOOKS
An Imprint of Barbour Publishing, Inc.

For J. N.

ISBN 1-58660-399-X

Cover design by Robyn Martins.

All Scripture quotations, unless otherwise noted, are taken from the King James Version of the Bible.

Published by Barbour Books, an imprint of Barbour Publishing, Inc., P.O. Box 719, Uhrichsville, Ohio 44683, www.barbourbooks.com

ecpa Member of the Evangelical Christian Publishers Association

Printed in the United States of America.

JACQUELYN COOK

Jacquelyn lives in southwest Georgia, near the Florida and Alabama lines. Enjoying hot summer nights, perfumed by magnolias and roses and honeysuckle, how could she write anything but romance?

Jacquelyn and her husband make their home in a small white-columned brick house on a family farm. Their social life revolves around the village church. She says, "What I write about is the 'real' world for me. The cats, dogs, mockingbirds, and butterflies that flit through my stories are real too."

"Thank you, Dear Readers, for liking my work so much that my books have been reprinted in numerous editions."

The River Between

Chapter 1

Uhmmmmm! Uhmmmmm!

The insistent drone of the steamboat's whistle floated up to Lily Edwards in the belvedere atop her father's home, interrupting her daydream. Somewhere, someone waited who could be one with her in mind and spirit as well as heart. She would not be rushed.

Uhmmmmm! The rousing blast drew her irresistibly to the rail. Looking across the treetops at billowing black smoke, she knew she must share in the excitement when the steamer docked. Mama would be angry if she went, but Mama wore a constant scowl these days, because at eighteen, Lily was rapidly passing the age to make a suitable marriage. *Wheet! Wheet!* The short blasts of the whistle, punctuated with black puffs, told her that the paddle wheeler was nearing the wharf.

Lily tossed her long, dark curls, compressed her mushrooming skirt to fit the narrow staircase, and hurried down, singing out, "Emma, Emma, come quickly!" Her maiden aunt was the perfect chaperone for all occasions. Emma Edwards, still unmarried at twenty-five, was dependent for her livelihood upon the bounty of her sister-in-law's family. Young enough to sympathize with Lily's commitment not to marry simply to satisfy social custom, Emma sometimes wavered in her stand because she knew the heartbreak of being an old maid.

"Emma," Lily called again. She left the observatory and negotiated her voluminous crinoline through the attic and down another zigzag staircase to the second floor. She stood for a moment to catch her breath beneath the large, round grate in the hall ceiling. Barbour Hall was a magnificent white-frame mansion built in perfect symmetry of the Greek Revival. Since its construction in 1854, four years earlier, it was considered to be one of the finest examples of Italianate architecture in the South.

"What's the excitement?" Emma's calming voice answered as she emerged from the upstairs sitting room. Her features were set as usual in a placid expression that concealed her emotions as she waited to see what had evoked such enthusiasm.

"A steamboat's coming!" Lily exclaimed, "It's the signal for the *Wave*." Her brown eyes sparkling, Lily tugged at Emma's elbow. "Come with me. Hurry. We can't miss the landing!"

Emma hesitated but she so desired to be part of the crowd flocking to the riverfront. Nervously, she clutched her fists against her chest and twisted her fingers in the faded gray muslin. "You know your mother expects me to make you behave like a lady."

"Oh, Emma, please." Lily's liquid brown eyes became wistful. Her dainty face alight with curiosity about life, she bounded from one foot to the other while Emma considered.

Emma laughed. "You're as ebullient as a soap bubble and just as impossible to keep from floating away. We'll go—but you cannot be seen in that short-sleeved frock," she said in her measured, quiet way. "You must take time to put on a proper street toilet."

"Yes, of course, but do hurry." Lily's lilting voice came in excited bursts as she pulled her toward the spacious bedroom they shared. "At least my hair is already dressed." She looked at her reflection in the mirror over the marble-topped walnut dresser and fingered her dark brown hair that was pulled back from her face with tortoiseshell combs into a cluster of long curls in back.

Whispering conspiratorially, they dressed quickly. From a tremendous walnut armoire in the back corner of the room, Lily chose a green silk dress with wide lace ruffles beginning at her shoulders, meeting in a point to emphasize her tiny waist, and spreading again to flow to her feet over the skirt held wide by her petticoat of stiff crinoline. She especially liked the sleeves with their lacy fullness at the wrists. The skirt Emma chose was elaborately trimmed with braid, and the frayed bodice she covered with a *canezou*, a dainty jacket fashioned with horizontal rows of smocking.

When they had donned tulle bonnets and gloves, they picked up tiny silk parasols against the bright June sun and tiptoed into the back bedroom where a closet concealed a hidden staircase. Silently, they slipped down the dark passageway, hoping they would not meet the servants.

Emerging in the back hallway, they hurried across the wide veranda that spread as gracefully around the house as the girls' billowing skirts. Indeed, Lily often fancied Barbour Hall looked like the belles of the day. The glassed belvedere formed her airy hat; the wooden balustrade, her neck ruffle; the green shutters on the upper story, her *canezou;* and the porch spreading around the first floor, her hooped skirt.

Lily had infected Emma with her sprightliness, and the girls bounced down the steep steps and ran along the cleanly swept path through beds of fragrant summer flowers until they reached the stables.

The buggy ride took nearly half an hour as they proceeded down West Barbour Street, trimmed by China trees. They descended the hill, passed the fine brick storehouses and many churches of Eufaula, Alabama, and continued to the west bank of the Chattahoochee River.

From this high bluff, they could look across the wide, dark blue water into the state of Georgia, which flaunted ownership of the river. Georgia had been one of the original thirteen colonies, but this side of the Chattahoochee had long remained territory occupied by the Creek Indian nation.

Eufaula was a junction of stage lines with six-horse coaches going out into the frontier of Alabama. There were no railroads here, but the bluff, one hundred-fifty feet above the low-water mark, had become a steamboat landing even before the Creeks had been driven out. Because steamboats had plied the Chattahoochee since 1828, Eufaulians were cosmopolitan.

Turning the buggy to the left, the girls followed Riverside Drive past the Tavern, a two-story, English type building with double galleries. Built in 1836, it was the first permanent structure in town. Thus far, it had served as riverboat inn, private residence, and temporary church. The girls laughed about what it might become next as they rode on around the bend in the river and descended the hill to the wharf located at the foot of the bluff just north of the Tavern.

Reining the horse at a high vantage point, they looked down as the tremendous, flat-bottomed boat, fully one hundred seventy-five feet long, belched fire and black smoke from her two towering smokestacks and glided to rest at the wharf. The huge, round paddle box, which covered the machinery of her side wheel, was emblazoned with the name, *Wave,* and above that was her insignia, a painting of a descending dove.

It was evident that Emma had forgotten her fear of Cordelia Edward's wrath. Quivering with excitement, she leaned forward to gaze at the upper deck where Lily was pointing.

"Would you look at that gown!" Lily exclaimed. "Umm, my favorite green. It must be straight from Paris." She laughed as the lady fluttered her fan coquettishly and looked back at the young gentleman who strutted behind her like a peacock. Around them swirled bright colors of silks and satins as the fifty first-class passengers milled about, chattering gaily, waving handkerchiefs, and promenading about the deck. They seemed to ignore the cacophony of piercing whistles, clanging bells, and shouting workmen.

Bales of cotton, piled everywhere along the wharf and on flat-bottomed barges, waited to be poled out for transfer to the steamer when the Italian marble, favored by Eufaula merchants and planters for the imposing mansions they were building in the Bluff City, was unloaded.

Emma motioned toward the police escort for the men carrying huge bags of silver, funds from the sale in Liverpool of the cotton crop that continued to grow larger each year.

Lily, however, was looking at the lower deck just above the water's edge where grizzled, unwashed passengers crowded amongst machinery, crates of merchandise, and all manner of freight. The steamboat mirrored Southern society; there was no middle class. A woman whose hair was stringing about her wrinkled face pulled at four dirty children. Lily thought that her skirt drooped indecently around her limbs without the required number of petticoats.

Lily cocked her head to one side and pursed her lips in puzzled interest as a handsome young man, dressed in light, slim trousers and a dark frock-tailed coat, moved into view behind the tired mother. Lily wondered why he was on the lower deck.

At that moment, a roustabout staggered backwards under the weight of a barrel and bumped into the especially well-dressed gentleman. His tall silk hat fell, revealing a head of neat blond curls. As he whirled around, his chiseled features contorted with a rage his well-tended beard could not conceal.

Lily grimaced, glad that she could not distinguish his words, for they were obviously a curse. Regaining his balance, the young man raised his gold-headed walking stick to deliver a blow. A slightly older man in a dark blue flannel uniform with a gold braid indicating that he was the captain, stepped quickly into the fray. He placed a restraining hand on the uplifted arm. Quietly, his face and manner pleasant, the ship's master reasoned with the hotheaded young man. The cowed roustabout retrieved the hat; and the tall captain, obviously joking, clapped a hand on the petulant fellow's shoulder and guided him down the deck.

Admiring his calm self-assurance, Lily watched him intently as he went striding away. Seeming to feel her eyes upon him, he turned. Swiftly spanning the distance between them, his clear-eyed gaze met hers with a lively interest that made her blink and swallow as he stopped openmouthed and held his breath midlaugh. His smooth, tanned face warmed with a smile, lifting his dark mustache.

Sighing deeply, Lily tilted her head and lowered the silk fringe of her pink parasol. She smiled beneath it in spite of herself, for she responded immediately to the look in his eyes. The pressure of Emma's hand on her arm reminded her wordlessly that this man was far beneath her social station. Knowing she would never again have a chance to meet anyone this exciting, she dropped her thick lashes and shielded her face with the parasol. "Let's go to Papa's office," she said.

Making their way through the jostling crowd past clean-smelling cypress lumber and the less pleasing aroma of salted fish, the girls entered the Cotton Exchange. In spite of the fact that Clare Edwards was surrounded by men all talking at once, he came forward to meet his daughter and sister with doting smiles and affectionate kisses.

Lily hugged her father lovingly. He was fifty-one, and when she thought of his growing so old, it made her sadly vow to keep his last days happy.

"I'm delighted to see my favorite beauties," he beamed, "but you should not be here."

"Oh, Papa, everyone in town is here."

"Yes, yes, but I mean you especially should not be here today." He hesitated. "It will seem forward."

Puzzled, Lily merely looked at her father, who rubbed his hand over his balding head in confusion.

"There's something I should have told you." He faltered. "Come into my private office." He said nothing more until he was ensconced behind the enormous desk that Mama had bought for him. "You know how concerned your mother has been because you haven't. . ." He cleared his throat and hesitated. "Haven't, uh, decided upon one of your beaux. . ."

"They are all just shallow boys!" Lily wailed. "I know Mama wants me to have the proper social position and security." She sighed disgustedly. "But I want more than that. I want a husband I can talk with, enjoy being with. Most of all, he must share my faith in God!"

"I wouldn't trust my girl with less than a Christian gentleman," Papa replied. He cleared his throat again and his voice croaked, "But give this young man a chance."

"What young man?" Lily stirred uneasily, wondering how much longer she could struggle against Mama.

"Well, your mother wrote to her relatives in South Carolina. And if all has gone according to schedule, your distant cousin, Green Bethune, has journeyed aboard the river steamer *Wave*. You must leave quickly now before he comes in and thinks you are here to inspect him."

Chapter 2

The creaking of the buggy made Lily grit her teeth. She clutched the red leather seat, and her stomach lurched with the jerking, swaying motion as she slapped the reins and headed the horse back up the hill toward Barbour Hall.

"You should be happy, Lily." Emma frowned anxiously. She pushed back golden tendrils of hair that were escaping the knot at the back of her head. "I'd be thrilled to be meeting an eligible new beau."

"I know," said Lily. Dread dulled her soft, dark eyes. Her delicate features puckered in a silent plea for understanding and help. "It looks as if Mama is waging an all-out campaign to get me married. It takes all the excitement out of courtship since she's placing a deadline."

"Try to keep an open mind," Emma begged, patting her hand, "and an open heart. Just keep telling yourself that you're about to meet someone special."

A rueful smile twisted Lily's flushed cheeks. "I'll try." Never one to be pressed down for long, she straightened her shoulders and tossed her head so that the coils of her long curls bounced up and down like coffee-colored springs. Her spirits began to rise. "Meeting a man from a faraway place does sound exciting. I love to learn about new things," she said with her usual zest. "If I can just make Mama understand. . ."

"Don't you sass her, now," Emma interrupted in alarm.

As they entered the rear of the wide central hallway, Lily's mother came puffing through the double doors at the entrance. Between them stretched a gracious receiving area made elegant by the fact that it contained only a few carefully selected pieces of furniture. The narrow library table on which Mrs. Edwards now placed her gloves was fashioned in graceful curves entirely from one mahogany log. The two side chairs had been carved especially for this hall. The cool room was filled with the fragrance of roses. Two mass arrangements in matching fan-shaped vases graced the marble shelves set below the murals on each side wall.

Seeing the girls before they could escape, Cordelia Edwards joined them at the back of the hall. She removed her bonnet wearily and said in a tone that indicated that it was she who must attend to everything, "I've been visiting Mrs. Treadwell who is dangerously ill." Sighing, she sank heavily to the hard sofa. Her attention was not upon them as she waited to catch her breath. With a small, self-satisfied smile, she smoothed her hand over the shiny, slick, black horsehair of her sofa with unusual S-shaped legs. A particular treasure to her because this style was made only for a ten-year period around 1783, the sofa was smugly pointed out to visitors.

Standing on a square of the checkerboard black-and-white marble floor like a small pawn, Lily waited. "Lily!" Mrs. Edwards exclaimed. Her double chin shook as she noticed her daughter's outfit. "Why don't you ever do as you're told? I clearly said for you to take a nap this afternoon and look your best for a special dinner tonight." Without giving Lily a chance to reply, she continued, "Go straight to your room and read First Samuel thirteen." She emphasized each syllable with a shake of her finger. "Think about what happened to Saul for being disobedient."

"Yes, Ma'am."

Lily's hands trembled as she dressed for dinner in her favorite pink dotted swiss. Twirling before the looking glass, setting the tiered flounces of her skirt fluttering, she wondered if her cousin was as nervous as she was. Perhaps he did not know the reason for his invitation to visit. Her mother had not divulged a word to her, and she would think the dinner was special primarily because of the delicacies that had arrived from New Orleans aboard the steamboat if her Papa had not warned her.

Dear Papa. He tried to subscribe to the idea of a patriarchal family structure, but it was apparent to everyone that Mama was dominant. Even though his family was of the upper class with a social status equal to Mama's, she had brought far greater wealth into the marriage.

With a final pat to her hair, Lily started down the staircase. When she reached the landing, she heard Mama's artificial greeting voice and realized guests were arriving. From the large oval landing, Lily could look down on the tops of their heads. Mama could not see her because between them hung the crystal teardrops of the crown-of-thorns chandelier. Just in case she might be noticed, Lily pretended to rearrange the flowers in the high niches, the coffin corners. She tried to catch snatches of conversation and prepare for her entrance. When the voice of a stranger rose above the others, she held her breath to listen.

"My dear cousin Cordelia," the voice spoke in cultured tones, "may I present Captain Harrison Wingate?"

Startled at the words, Lily picked up her skirt daintily and moved to the head of the stairs just as the dark head, which was bent low over Cordelia Edwards's hand, lifted. Lily floated like a pink cloud down the grand staircase. The captain's tanned face brightened with delight, and his dark mustache quivered as he drew in his breath and looked at her.

This time Lily met his gaze unashamedly. This was a man who faced life head-on. Smiling demurely with her head cocked to one side, she waited back a pace. She could tell that her mother was struggling for self-control while the blond, curly haired younger man continued speaking.

"Captain Wingate and I have become such fast friends during the trip from Apalachicola Bay that I was certain you'd want me to extend your hospitality," he said suavely.

He turned his head slightly, and Lily recognized his golden beard as the one she had seen on the deck of the steamboat. As she moved nearer, he swung around. His eyes lazily assessing her from head to toe told her that he did indeed know of her existence and of the reason for his visit. With her guard stiffened, she watched in amusement as Mama wavered between indignation that he had brought a common steamboat captain to her dinner party and the desire to establish a good relationship with a possible future son-in-law.

"Yes, of course," Mrs. Edwards murmured. Glancing up at Lily in relief, she continued with more assurance, "May I present my daughter, Lily, Captain Wingate, and this, Dear, is your cousin Green Bethune. Of course you've heard me speak of my darling second-cousin-once-removed, Lizzie Bethune, of the South Carolina Bethunes," she gushed. "This is her youngest son who has just arrived for a lovely visit with us."

Both gentlemen kissed Lily's extended hand, and she murmured polite greetings to them equally; however, other guests began arriving and Cordelia Edwards drew her handsome cousin back to the doorway.

"Green, Dear, come meet one of our most illustrious citizens, Edward B. Young, who built our first bridge across the Chattahoochee, started the Union Female College, established a bank and sawmill and store and, oh, so many things—Mr. and Mrs. Young, this is my cousin, Green Bethune of the Carolina Bethunes."

"Welcome to Alabama, young man," the distinguished gentleman said cordially. He launched into a discussion of business.

Freed from having to converse with Green Bethune until she could prepare herself, Lily looked across the expanse of the entrance hall trying to catch Papa's eye. Standing by the double entrance doors, which were framed by beautifully etched side lights, he was engrossed in conversation with the Reverend and Mrs. Steele and did not notice her. Lily stepped up to greet some of her favorites, Maximilian Wellborn and his wife. The Shorters and the Kendalls were arriving, but she suddenly realized that Captain Wingate was standing back by the stairs—alone.

Embarrassed by her mother's rudeness in not introducing him to anyone, Lily moved quickly to his side and graciously invited him into the parlor. She guided him across the spacious room where they could stand in some seclusion by the white Italian marble fireplace. She had spoken to him to be kind, thinking to put him at ease in an odd situation. It was she, however, who fidgeted nervously. The tall man, in his dark dress clothes, stood casually in command.

She cleared her throat. "Um. You must lead an exciting life, Captain, so fraught with danger—the peril of death at every turning. . ."

She smiled up at him. Her cheeks, radiating the glow from the myriad of candles in the Waterford chandelier, relaxed from the tension of matchmaking as her eyes rested on his calm face.

Harrison Wingate chuckled and answered quietly, "*Oui,* it's exciting, and yes, I enjoy the challenge of what may lie around the bend, but the danger. . ." He shrugged it off with a wave of his hand. "It's not so great if you know the inner depths and precisely where the Chattahoochee conceals her perils." He chuckled again. "Why, just the other day a man fell overboard. I was up top on the hurricane deck when I looked down and saw him floundering. 'I can't swim,' he shrieked. 'Help, help, I'll drown!' " Captain Wingate's eyes twinkled. "I yelled down to him, 'Can you stand?' He gasped that he could. 'Then stand up, man,' I commanded him. He stretched out his legs—we were over a sandbar." He laughed. "He was in two feet of water."

Lily giggled and clapped her hands in delight. The distinctive way he pronounced certain words with an ever-so-slight curl of his lip around a syllable kept her intrigued. He seemed quite nice, not at all the rake she had been led to believe river people to be. "You must be proud of the *Wave,*" she said.

"Yes, she's a beautiful vessel." He nodded. "Didn't I see you when we landed?"

"Shhh, don't let Mama hear you." She pressed her finger to her lips, giggled, and inclined her head closer. "We weren't supposed to go, but I just couldn't miss it."

Harrison Wingate's eyes twinkled and he smoothed his mustache that quivered over an amused smile. "Where is your sister? I haven't seen her."

"My sister? Oh, Emma. She's my aunt and chaperone. Mama probably has her supervising the dinner." She ran her finger over one of the Sèvres vases on the gold-leaf shelving around the huge Belgian mirror that reflected them and studied him surreptitiously. His grammar evinced good breeding, and, although his hands had a strength that showed he had worked, he had the clean fingernails of a gentleman.

Lily and the captain were suddenly bathed in warmth as the last rays of the sun flooded through the lace draperies. A rosy glow washed over the ivory-white walls and even the ceiling mouldings, painted shades of pastel lavender and edged in gold leaf, gleamed. Every window in the house reached from the floor to within a few feet of the eighteen-foot ceilings. Happily, Mama had made only valances in heavy wine velvet. Lily reveled in sunlight.

Relaxed, she wanted to know more about Captain Wingate's travels on the river that gave their kingdom of cotton access to the world. The thousands of bales being shipped down the Chattahoochee to Apalachicola, Florida, not only made it the largest cotton-exporting port in America but also gave exceptional prosperity to Eufaula.

"It must give you a tremendous feeling of power to transport the product on which the lives of everyone in this area depend."

"Well," he laughed self-deprecatingly, "about the time I start feeling like God's overseer on the river, some planter's wife sends me shopping. Right now in my stateroom lies a new gown especially prepared by a shop on Royal Street in New Orleans. The lady gave me orders to use all my energy to save her gown if the boilers explode and the steamer sinks."

Lily was surprised at the pang of jealousy this gave her. "I wish I could travel," she said wistfully. "I'd enjoy meeting interesting new people."

"Many are traveling," he said eagerly. "Europeans are touring our country—and hordes of people are moving West."

"Yes," she agreed. "A number from the Southern Rights group here moved to 'bleeding Kansas' in order. . ." She winced, remembering her mother's repeated warnings that men did not like a woman who was too intelligent. "In order to vote," she finished lamely.

Harrison Wingate apparently did not know that a lady should not talk about politics. He began a lively discussion of the widening gap between North and South.

Exhilarated by the interesting conversation, Lily was surprised by a touch at her elbow.

"Cousin Lily, I'm to escort you to dinner, I believe," Green Bethune said suavely, bowing and offering his arm. "That's a mighty pretty frock you're wearing this evening," he drawled.

She nodded toward the captain, then turned and grasped the proffered arm with stiff fingers. She felt painfully aware that it was intended for her to marry this man, but as they passed into the music room where the square grand piano of carved rosewood was being played, her tension eased and her pink slippers kept time to the lively plinking. Green patted her hand on his elbow and looked at her as if she were the most beautiful creature he had ever met. Lily could see by their reflection in the towering pier mirror behind the piano that they did make a handsome couple. Green bowed gallantly as she preceded him through the sliding doors into the dining room.

Responding flirtatiously to his charm, Lily inclined her head and dimpled her most coquettish smile. "Thank you, kind sir."

The dining room was a place of glittering beauty. Flames from dozens of candles twinkled in the prisms of the chandeliers that hung low over each end of the mahogany table. Their light glimmered in the mirror plateau on the mahogany sideboard.

Lily was glad that the butler had swiftly added a place for Captain Wingate and Emma had hurriedly changed her frock and joined the group as his dinner partner. They brought the number seated at the long, elegantly set table to twenty-four.

As the first course, spicy turtle soup, was being served, Green Bethune smiled ingratiatingly at Lily and said, "Tell me about Eufaula. I thought I was coming to the Western frontier to meet a girl in buckskin or calico at the very least, and here you are a belle in the latest Paris gown."

Lily's laughter filled the air. "Our urbanity is a surprise, I suppose. Being a river port makes the difference. Alabama has been a frontier in constant struggle between Spanish, French, English—and of course, Indians. This county, Barbour, is in a territory that was one of the last strongholds of the Creek Indian nation."

"But you achieved statehood as early as 1819, did you not?" he asked as red snapper court bouillon on mounds of rice was served.

"That's right," she replied, noticing his polished table manners. "But the Creeks remained. Whites began intruding on them and there was a war in 1827—"

"When Carolina was nearly two hundred years old," Green said with a slightly superior sniff.

Lily nodded assent. "The Indians signed a treaty in 1832, ceding their lands east of the Mississippi, but many remained here. . . ." She faltered as she saw Mama glaring at her from the end of the table. Proud of her good brain, Lily thrust out her lower lip and continued doggedly. "One of the tribes was the Eufaulas, which gave the town its original name." Lily paused to take a helping of butter beans. Green nodded laconically, but his attention was on the fish.

"The first white settlement here, called Irwinton, was established around 1835, with men like Lore, Wellborn, Irwin, Iverson, Moore, and Robertson developing the town." Lily could feel the warmth of eyes upon her face. Down the table, Captain Wingate was leaning forward to see and hear her. Quickly dropping her eyes to her plate, she sampled the succulent snapper before finishing.

"Cotton was already being shipped from here." She hesitated, speaking stiffly now, oddly flustered by the captain's gaze. "Even though there was still fighting with the Indians for another year. By 1842, this was a thriving town. Ironically, it was free of Indians by then, but they decided to go back to the Indian name," she laughed self-consciously.

"My, you are an eager young woman," Green replied lazily, turning toward the cinnamon fragrance wafting from the sweet potato soufflé. "I didn't expect a complete history lesson from such a pretty head," he added in a deliberate drawl.

Lily could feel her cheeks turning red. "Our early days have been colorful—but I'm afraid I've bored you with too many facts," she finished lamely.

"Oh, no, not at all." Green's deportment was exquisitely correct, but the glazed expression in his eyes showed no interest in the struggles of the early settlers.

Dessert arrived—rich chocolate molds with butter cream filling and praline topping—and then the ladies were excused. Papa passed cigars and the eminent jurist, John Gill Shorter, launched a political discussion about the Dred Scott Decision. His impassioned words were cut off as the gentlemen moved across the hall to the library. Lily wanted to hear more about the Supreme Court case that had brought the ongoing debate about slave states and free territory to a head and inflamed and divided the nation; but, of course, ladies were excluded from such talk.

"Emma," Lily said softly, linking arms with her confidante as they drifted into the wide receiving hall, "I'm so glad you got to join the party, but Mama was furious because Green invited the captain."

"Well, you made your usual conquest," Emma whispered. "All he could talk about over dinner was your delicate beauty, your superior intelligence, your thoughtfulness. . ."

"No! Really?" Lily's dark eyes sparkled. "I genuinely liked him, too. Why must all of the men Mama considers suitable husbands be so insipid?"

"Didn't you like Green?"

"Oh, he's handsome and charming, but—well, I don't know. He asked me a question and didn't even listen to the answer." Lily felt Mama glaring at her again. The ladies had been seated in the music room where a string quartet had begun a Bach fugue. The girls took seats on the carved side chairs in the hall and politely sipped their demitasse.

When the gentlemen rejoined them, most of them were discussing the cotton crop, but Lily caught Green's hushed, excited voice telling the captain about a friend in New Orleans who had challenged one of the local colonels because of a slight insult and had been shot to death in a duel.

Soon, all of the guests were bidding them a good night. When the last ones had departed, Lily climbed slowly, thoughtfully up the stairs to her bedroom at the front of the house. Putting on her light muslin nightgown, she tried to sort out her feelings. This had been such a stimulating day that she sat for a long while before her rolltop lady's secretary trying to collect the thoughts she wished to record. Gazing unseeingly into the mirror over the small desk, she had just lifted her journal from one of the side bookshelves when the door to her room burst open.

"Lily, my dear child," Mama paused to puff, "I hope you are ready to become a bride."

Chapter 3

Oh, Mama!" Lily wailed. "If you mean Green, we've barely met!" Her face pinched with distress. "Please don't make me decide so soon."

Cordelia Edwards sat heavily on a small, cherry rocker. "Oh, pshaw, you know I don't mean you'd be married tomorrow. I want to keep my baby a little while longer, too. But, Darling, we must plan for your future. What would our friends think if you weren't married before your nineteenth birthday?" She sighed heavily and began loosening her clothing that stretched tightly over her girth.

"But, Mama, it's not that I feel too young to get married," Lily said hurriedly because her mother was obviously about to retire for the night. "I want someone special, somebody who—"

"Green is all you could desire. He's a handsome man!"

"Yes, but. . ."

"He's from one of the first families of South Carolina. He has ample wealth to keep you in Paris gowns."

"There's more to life than Paris gowns." Lily's lower lip thrust out, and she drew shaky breaths as she fought tears.

Mrs. Edwards jerked in surprise. The cherry rocker creaked. "I really must speak to Mr. Edwards about your insolence."

"I'm sorry," she said. "I–I didn't mean to be rude, but you don't understand my feelings." Lily clenched fistfuls of her muslin gown and looked beseechingly at this woman who lived on such a different emotional plane. Her whole world revolved around social functions and friendly gossip. Lily knew she was a fine Christian woman who constantly did works of charity for the sick and the poor, but she somehow remained above them, untouched with love.

"No, I don't understand you," she was saying. "I'm merely telling you to enjoy the courtship of a *beau ideal*. You can have a long period of engagement." She moved wearily to the door, then turned back. "However, be prepared within the month to set a wedding date."

For a long while after her mother had left the room, Lily stood by one of the wide, square windows and looked out at the stars. The realization that her mother would never understand the intensity of her convictions turned the happiness of her day to melancholy. All the while Mama pushed her into marriage and adulthood, she treated her like a child, making little difference between her and her adolescent brother, Foy. Somehow she was afraid that she and her mother would never share the same view of life or the joy of being two adults together.

Sighing, she turned to the soft comfort of her bed. Delicate rosewood posts, rising high above her head, supported a graceful, curved frame and an airy, macramé canopy. The snowy counterpane required a close look to distinguish the white-on-white design of leaves outlined with dainty knots of candlewicking. Satin-stitched grapes added another texture. She always felt secure in its soft comfort. Kneeling on the stool beside the high bed, she folded her hands in prayer.

"Dear heavenly Father, I know that Thy Word tells me to honor my parents and obey them, but please help me now. I know Thou didst create marriage as an extension of Thy love. Guide me to the one who will share my faith in Thee, who will love me better because he first loves Thee. Help me to follow Thy will that I may give my life in service to Thee. In Jesus' name, I pray. Amen."

Climbing into the feather bed, she pretended to be asleep when Emma came into the room, but she knew that the tears slipping down her cheeks would give her away.

Sunlight, streaming through the huge windows and dancing from the bright blue walls to the deep blue and white Oriental rug awakened Lily in a happy frame of mind. She was glad that her room was on the east side of the house, for she loved the early morning. She went into her dressing room to wash her face in the Wedgwood lavatory set in a marble slab. As she grasped the small, porcelain handles of the German silver faucets to cut on the running water, she had to admit that wealth was nice. Papa's own waterworks were a part of the original construction of this house. Water was pumped by a windmill to a cistern in the attic and the drop from the attic, gave pressure.

She breakfasted from an enameled tray brought up the hidden stairs by one of the maids. Hot biscuits, honey, and tea were served on her favorite tea set. The white ridges of the china were studded with pink roses, and someone had added a fresh rose to the tray. Brushing out the tight coils of her hair, she let it float loosely around her shoulders, and she tied a white ribbon in a flat bow on top of her head. After she had dressed in cool, white organdy, she glanced out of the window and saw a dark-suited man rounding the red cedars at the front gate.

"Captain Wingate!" she whispered to herself in surprise. He was no doubt calling to leave his card in the tray on the library table in the entrance hall to express his appreciation for their hospitality. Knowing Mama might be obviously condescending to him, Lily flew down the stairs as swiftly as was decorously possible.

"Good morning, Captain Wingate." She smiled warmly, meeting him on the veranda with her hand extended. The flounces of her skirt billowed frothily around her.

"Miss Lily! What a delightful pleasure." He bent low, taking her small, white hand in his strong, tanned fingers. "I wanted to thank your mother for her hospitality."

"Yes, well," Lily glanced surreptitiously over her shoulder, hoping Mama was not up, "perhaps she's sleeping late. I'll convey your appreciation. Uh, would you like to see the garden?"

"I'd enjoy that very much."

They started around a walk that had been swept with a brush broom early that morning. Everything was fresh with the lush greenness of early June. They strolled in silence past neatly edged flower beds spilling over with a colorful mixture of perennials.

Dwarfed beside a spreading clump of palms, Lily paused and pointed to the huge fans. "This windmill palm was brought a few years ago from Berckmann's Nursery in Augusta, Georgia," she said stiffly, her mind on what Mama would say if she caught her promenading with the steamboat captain. "You'll see several of them around town; they are becoming quite a tradition for Eufaula."

"Nice, but that planting of oak-leaved hydrangeas is more to my liking," he said as they moved on by a pine-shaded bed on the west side of the house. A soft breeze rustled the pine needles on the trees high above their heads and wafted the fragrance of the drooping hydrangea blossoms around them.

"Yes," she agreed. "I really like native plants in naturalized settings, too." She smiled up into his warm eyes that were alive with interest in both her and the surroundings. She was beginning to feel comfortable with him and to forget about Mama. He did not seem to possess any of the less savory characteristics usually associated with the itinerant river population who were said to frequent the taverns and gambling houses.

Not wanting Mama to look down from her bedroom window and see them, Lily led him to the kitchen herb and vegetable garden. Beginning to chat casually, they walked between raised beds of tansy, bee balm, chives, parsley, dill, rosemary, and sweet marjoram. Captain Wingate's foot crushed sun-warmed leaves of mint that had escaped into the path, releasing a clean, mouthwatering fragrance.

"Peach?" Lily asked, suddenly hungry as they passed a small tree bending low with rosy fruit.

"*Merci.*" He smiled.

Peeling back the fuzzy skin, they bit into the soft yellow flesh. Tangy juice trickled down their chins. Laughing, they rounded a clump of pampas grass, which furnished plumes for parlor decorations during the winter, and crossed under the walkway that connected the house with the brick kitchen. Opening a wrought-iron gate, Lily led the way back into the formal garden of boxwood-edged beds.

"Stop!" Harrison grasped her hand with peach-sticky fingers.

Catching her breath at his touch and the soap-scented nearness of him, she turned her eyes from his face toward his pointing finger with difficulty.

Silently, they watched a tiny hummingbird. Its round, green body and blur of wings made an enchanting picture as it darted from one deep-throated orange lily to another. Barely drawing breath, they said nothing until the exquisite creature had flown to the top of a tall pine. Each seemed to feel the other a kindred spirit. She had not realized they were still clasping hands until a hardy voice broke their shared silence.

"Good morning, you two."

Self-consciously, they drew apart physically and turned to see Green Bethune striding toward them from the direction of the guest quarters that were reached from the back porch with an entrance entirely separate from the rest of the house.

"Good morning, Cousin Lily." He inclined his head in a slight bow. "How are you, old chap?" He clapped Harrison on the shoulder and continued exuberantly, "How about me riding back to town with you? I have business with John McNab at his bank."

"Actually, I walked up," replied Harrison quietly.

"All that way?"

"I'm sure Papa would be delighted for you to use the stables," Lily said.

"Why don't you come with me and combine business with pleasure?" Green smiled down at her. "Perhaps you could shop while I set up my banking and make some appointments."

"Well, perhaps," she hesitated. "I didn't realize you had business here."

"Why, of course." He laughed. "I'm a cotton broker for my father's firm. I'm here to buy cotton for shipment directly to Liverpool." He paused, smirked, and added in a deliberate drawl, "This trip was not entirely pleasure." His glazed blue eyes moved over her in a knowing way that reddened Lily's cheeks. "Come along and show me the town."

"All right," Lily agreed. "Why don't y'all wait in the summerhouse while I collect my hat and shawl and Emma to accompany us." She smiled and gestured toward the wicker chairs in a white-latticed, octagon-shaped enclosure festooned with lacy green leaves of wisteria vines.

Lily was always glad to include Emma as her chaperone. Her sweet disposition and calm temperament smoothed any occasion, and her primary pleasure in life came through sharing Lily's happy times.

When the girls returned to the gazebo, Lily's twelve-year-old brother, Foy, was excitedly hopping from one foot to the other as Captain Wingate told him about the cages of circus lions and bears he had recently transported.

As the laughing group headed the carriage down Barbour Street, Lily pointed out the place next door where the distinguished gentleman, Colonel Lewis Llewellen Cato was building a Greek Revival mansion.

"He's a member of the Eufaula Regency, the Southern Rights group I was telling you about," she said, turning to nod at Captain Wingate in the backseat with Emma. "He's a leader in the secessionist movement."

She started to point out to Green how the four important thoroughfares, Livingston, Orange, Randolph, and Eufaula were laid out to spell L-O-R-E in honor of the early leader Seth Lore; however, seeing that her cousin actually cared nothing for learning about the town and its people, she settled back against the red leather seat of the fringe-topped carriage and let Green entertain them with tales of his escapades back home in Charleston.

They left Green at the iron grillwork entrance to the Eastern Bank of Alabama. Wingate strolled with the ladies. They wandered through the apothecary shop and various dry good merchants. At the confectioner's, he bought rock candy.

As they stood crunching the candy, Lily noticed that Green rejoined them from the opposite direction of the bank.

"My business is finished for the morning," he declared. "How about a horseback ride? We've grown soft in that floating hotel of yours, Harrison, old man." He clapped the tall man on the shoulder.

Lily thought that Green, not Harrison, looked soft; but she readily agreed to the exercise because she enjoyed fresh air and sunshine.

Emma was not an enthusiastic horseback rider like Lily. As they changed to riding habits, Lily could tell by the grim expression on Emma's pale face that sometimes being her chaperone was a chore. Lily loved her devotedly and wished Mama did not treat her so nearly like a servant. In their realm of society, there was no acceptable work for a husbandless lady. The only choice was to live on the charity of the nearest relative, reaping few rewards while devoting total energy to another woman's family. Smiling at her as they went back downstairs, Lily was glad that Emma could get out and have some fun with her instead of staying in the back room at the spinning wheel. So many unmarried girls had there earned the name spinster.

While Emma was being helped to mount the gentle mule she preferred, Lily placed her foot in the stirrup and sprang into her sidesaddle unassisted. From the moment her shining black horse felt her weight, he sprang into a lope, lifting front feet, back feet, and speeding away with a long, easy gait. Laughing, her dark hair streaming behind her, Lily knew that the men were surprised. Their horses would probably not reach a lope without first breaking into a trot.

Exhilarated, Lily led the way down the red clay road cut deeply between high banks. Whipping his horse, Green gave chase through the pine-scented woodland. They clattered past a strange-looking field where a spring tornado had snapped off pine saplings waist high. Reining in, laughing, they waited for the others to catch up.

"This field reminds me of one back home," Green said as they walked the horses in pace with Emma's mule. "My brother and I had a yoke made to fit yearling calves. We'd yoke a pair and put small boys from the quarters on their backs. Then we'd run 'em through the stumps. The boys could hang on pretty well because the yearlings could swing their back feet in opposite directions, so we tied the tails together."

The girls looked at him, uncomprehending. Visualizing the scene, Harrison nodded.

Green explained, "They'd start to run, and wham, the yoke would hit a stump. It was great sport to watch who could hold on and who would go sailing over the calf's head." He laughed heartily, slapping his thigh.

"How mean!" declared Emma, her face pink with indignation and too much sun.

"You should've been whipped," laughed Lily.

The four dismounted at a fern-banked creek and drank at a spring bubbling out clear and cold. As they rested in the shade, Lily prevailed upon the captain to tell them more of his colorful river travel. While he talked quietly, she sat smiling. Emma relaxed with her hands in her lap and listened. Her blue eyes showed enjoyment instead of being shuttered against the world as they usually were. The morning passed quickly. Laughing, they foraged along the roadside, plucking a few late plums from the scrubby bushes. The tart, yellow fruit merely whetted their appetites. Clucking to the horses, they galloped back toward Barbour Hall.

When they reached the stables, a servant met them saying that Green had a message. Flinging his reins toward a stableboy, he hurried to the house. Slowly, tiredly, Emma followed.

Holding back with a show of making certain Prince was being properly rubbed down, Lily tenderly stroked the black velvet between his nostrils. Flattening her other hand beneath Prince's huge lips, she let him nip sugar from her palm.

Harrison Wingate stood watching, smiling.

"Um, Captain, won't you stay and dine with us?" she said hesitantly, praying Mama wouldn't explode.

"Thank you," he said quietly, "but I–I've been away from my duties far too long now. I must go." He remained unmoving. Searching her face, he leaned toward her and reached out to pat the horse's nose. "Beautiful animal," he said softly.

Lily held her breath as his eyes locked with hers.

"May I see you again?"

"Oh, I want to, but Mama—I'm afraid she wouldn't allow. . ." She looked into his tanned face, so gentle yet so strong and said softly, "I'll be going to prayer meeting tonight, but I don't suppose that you. . ."

Harrison laughed good-humoredly. "You don't imagine sailors to be religious? God speaks to me in nature—here in your beautiful garden and in the stars when I'm alone at night on the river." His hand was nearly touching hers on the velvet nose. "With the danger from the snags along the river, one must have faith in God's personal care, but I miss the opportunity for the fellowship and strengthening which come from attending church."

Emma was returning to see what had detained Lily. Quickly, Lily whispered the address of the church.

When she entered the house without Harrison Wingate, Green had attended to his business, and the family assembled in the dining room. Lily's appetite leaped when she saw the huge soup tureen on its stand on the sideboard because that meant gumbo. When the top was lifted, she breathed deeply of the pungent aroma. Their cook, Dilsey, had a magical way of mixing herbs in a well-guarded secret recipe. She always beamed and winked at Lily when she turned party leftovers into Lily's favorite dish. Ravenously, Lily ladled a lavish amount of the thick gumbo over the mound of steaming rice in her flat soup bowl.

Cordelia Edwards gushed over their young guest. "You have charmed everyone, Green, Dear. Invitations are pouring in. You two young people are going to a house party next week at Roseland Plantation." She beamed.

"Come with me this afternoon," said Papa. "There's enough cotton stored in the warehouses here to fill all your ships bound for Liverpool and keep those new power looms in Lancashire whirring for a long time." Papa's voice croaked, "Then you'll be free to enjoy yourself."

After the meal, Lily intended to slip to her room by way of the hidden staircase. She had just reached the back hall when she was stopped by a hand on her arm.

"Lily," Green whispered, "I thought I'd never catch you alone."

Lily whirled just as he had anticipated and found herself encircled in his arms. His bristly beard rubbed her face as he tried to kiss her. She pushed away.

"Mr. Bethune! Behave yourself! I'm surprised at you trying to take such liberties. The servants will see." She wrenched back from his grasp in his momentary hesitation and stepped out on the back porch because she knew it would be used by the servants on their way across the high, covered walkway to the brick kitchen.

"You were quick enough to hold hands with Harrison in the garden this morning—oh, I saw you."

"You–you misunderstood. He took my hand to show me something."

"What?"

"It was a humming—oh, you wouldn't understand." She shook her head, and her hair bounced around her shoulders. "I was trying to be nice to your friend, to keep Mama from insulting him."

Green smiled and reached out to squeeze a bouncing brown curl. "You're sure you weren't trying to make me jealous?"

"Of course not! You know my parents would never allow me to have a suitor. . ." She swallowed. "Below my station."

"You really don't know that the Wingates could buy. . ."

Kitty, one of the servants, came along the covered passageway carrying the silver tureen. Green dropped his hand, straightened back away from her, and said nothing more until the tall girl had moved past with her ebony face averted. He resumed the conversation reflectively. "No, I'm sure your parents are careful about your suitors. I guess that's why you sent for me."

"I certainly did not send for you!" Lily snapped, exasperated. "I knew nothing at all about it until after you'd arrived." Her cheeks were flaming.

"Harrison said you were watching the dock. I assumed you were eager to get married. As lovely as you are, we will have beautiful children."

Lily stamped her foot and tears of embarrassment filled her eyes. "I was merely out for a lark. I had no idea you existed. Furthermore, I'm in no hurry to get married," she retorted angrily. "It's all Ma-ma." Her voice became a wail and tears spilled over in spite of all she could do.

"I'm sorry," Green said with genuine contrition. "I really did misunderstand. I'm in no hurry to get married either. Let's just have fun and see what develops."

She nodded, sniffling, and left him to go to her room. Relieved that Papa had requested the young man to accompany him to the Cotton Exchange for the afternoon, she was happier still that he declined her invitation to attend prayer meeting that evening, although she doubted that he would have chosen to ignore her had he suspected that she might encounter Harrison Wingate.

When Lily and Emma arrived at the white-frame church, Harrison already stood on the steps by the gentlemen's door. Of all times, Foy had chosen to accompany them. At least Lily was thankful that Mama and Papa had pleaded weariness and gone to bed early; however, she wondered if Foy had been spying and had suspected that Wingate would be there. She knew that the most glamorous occupation imaginable to a barefoot, southeastern Alabama boy was steamboat captain or river pilot.

His chubby cheeks glowing, Foy rushed worshipfully to Harrison's side and kept them from having a private greeting. Emma glanced at her like a frightened bird and clutched her fists against her chest, but she said nothing as they entered and took their seats on the ladies' aisle.

Reverend Steele spoke eloquently from the book of Acts about Peter's vision while praying on the rooftop. Lily had nearly memorized the story that told of the animals being let down in a sheet and Peter protesting that he had never eaten anything common or unclean; consequently, her mind strayed to the captain. All too often, her eyes lifted from the Bible to look across the church to the men's side at his strong profile that indicated so much character.

After the service she whispered to Emma, "Please stay for choir practice without me. I'll be in the churchyard."

Emma chewed her lips. Doubt played over her features that were made plainer by the fact that her pale hair was parted in the middle and pulled back severely into a knot at the back of her neck.

"Please, Emma!" She squeezed the older girl's arm. "Please."

Emma turned aside wordlessly, and Lily sighed thankfully when she saw Foy darting about with a group of boys in the lengthening shadows of dusk.

"I was praying I'd get to speak with you alone." Harrison stirred in the semidarkness beneath a giant oak.

Lily laughed uncertainly. "I'm afraid I was, too," she whispered as she joined him.

"The *Wave* leaves at dawn."

"Oh."

Emboldened by the small, hurt sound she made, Harrison hurried on. "We're only going to Columbus," he said, referring to the Georgia town that was eighty-five miles up the Chattahoochee at the head of navigation. "We'll reach there tomorrow afternoon and be loaded for return to Apalachicola. I had hoped to stay in Eufaula for a short while, but the boiler on the side-wheeler *Emily* exploded. She was loaded with cargo and furniture, and she burned to the water's edge. We'll have to take the next load that was intended for her."

Lily winced. "Yes, I heard that seven lives were lost. Do be careful. I've heard the Chattahoochee called the longest graveyard in the state of Georgia."

"Don't you worry." He smiled at her tenderly. "I have a good pilot, and I'm trying to put in extra safety precautions and keep the crew watching for logs and snags and sandbars."

"I know it must be an exciting life." She looked up at him with eyes full of admiration. "I always enjoy it when Mama decides we can take a trip."

"The *Wave* has excellent staterooms," Harrison replied eagerly, "and the ladies' saloon is. . ." He stopped and searched her face as if memorizing it. "I'll be back by here in a few days. I have to take a big load of cotton downriver for Green. It will be transferred to his deep-draft sailing ships and go directly to Liverpool. May I call upon you before I leave for the Florida coast?"

Lily's mind blocked out all of the many reasons she should say no. It pulsated with only one word. "Yes," she breathed.

The church doors opened and the chattering choir spilled across the yard. Swiftly, before Lily was swept away, Wingate bent over her hand, pressed a kiss upon it, and whispered, *"Au revoir."*

Floating, she did not remember returning home. Surprised that she was in her room, she dreamily removed petticoat after petticoat, hoops, slippers, and prepared for bed. She opened her rolltop desk, but she was unable to settle down to her journal or to sleep. She climbed through the darkness of the attic and then took the two more short flights to the belvedere. Lily's delight was that Papa had crowned the house with this observatory that was larger than an ordinary cupola. With its three floor-to-ceiling windows on the front and back and two on each side, she felt at one with the sky. When she reached the top, she was disappointed to find Foy there before her.

"Well, Sister!" Foy looked up from the table where he had spread his astronomy books. His round cheeks dimpled a grin and his dark eyes snapped devilishly in the light of his hurricane lantern. "What'll you give me not to tell that you met the captain?"

"There's nothing to tell." She tossed her dark hair and thrust her pert nose in the air. "But I'll give you a mouse ear if you do!" Her angry tone softened to wistfulness. "It doesn't really matter. He's leaving tonight."

Careful not to let him see the tears shining in her eyes, she opened the door and stepped out onto the widow's walk that surrounded the belvedere. She leaned far out over the wooden balustrade, reaching for the stars.

Uhmmmmm! Mournfully, the hum of the steamboat's whistle floated up to her as it called passengers to board. She whispered to the stars, "The river is taking him away from me."

Chapter 4

The treacherous Chattahoochee! Its red, muddy waters swirled with danger. *How many women,* Lily wondered, *have paced landlocked widow's walks and searched the horizon with anxious eyes as they worried about their seafaring men?*

The rumbling blast of the whistle sounded again, drifting through the starlit night to her isolated spot in the high belvedere. Lily could not see the steamboat, but she could visualize the excitement; she longed to be a part of it, to be standing on that deck with Harrison Wingate. Leaning over the wooden balustrade, she imagined herself beside the steadfast man. What fun it would be to take the trip and get to know him better.

"I wish we were going with him."

Lily jumped. She had not realized Foy had stepped out onto the open walkway with her. She looked down at the wistful child. His words, echoing her thoughts, brought her back to reality.

Subdued, she returned to her bedroom. She climbed into her high bed and lay staring up at the airy white canopy. Usually the cheerful blue and white room lifted her spirits, but not this time. She had been as carried away by an adolescent dream as young Foy. Mama was right. It was time for her to grow up. This seafaring man was not hers and never could be. There! She had put it plainly to herself. She must forget about Harrison Wingate.

Sighing, she beat her goose-down pillow and turned over with determination to think about the house party and enjoying the courtship of her distant kin from the fabled aristocracy of South Carolina.

Her dreams, however, were of Harrison. He stood on the cold marble floor of the entrance hall turning his captain's hat in his hands. Hurt etched lines on his face as Emma told him she had gone to Roseland.

Awakening with a start, Lily felt tired, pulled apart by her conflicting emotions. Dressing without her usual care, she wandered listlessly through the garden to the latticed summerhouse. It was a cool and pleasant place. Papa had imported the wicker and rattan furniture from the Orient at her special request when she told him it had become the current rage. Pensively, she sat pulling petals from a rose, rolling them in her fingers, sniffing the sweetness. She glanced up and saw Papa heading toward her. Normally, he would be in his office by now. Had Foy told on her? She tried to mask her apprehension with a smiling greeting.

"Good morning, Papa. You're mighty late going to work. I hope you're not ill?"

"No, no, I'm fine. How's my little girl this morning?" Papa returned too heartily. "Pink is certainly your color." He smiled approvingly as he kissed her high-piled curls.

A servant was following behind him with a silver coffee service and a plate of croissants. Seeing that it was a deliberately staged encounter, Lily steeled herself. Tensely, she buttered a flaky roll and sipped coffee, strongly flavored with chicory. Not really hungry, Lily nibbled and chatted about the weather until the servant left them alone.

Papa rubbed his hand over his balding head and cleared his throat. "Your mother wanted me to talk with you."

"Oh, Papa," she wailed.

"Now, now, don't be upset." His voice croaked as it often did when he was agitated. "How do you like your cousin?"

"I've hardly had time to tell. He's very nice, but. . .I certainly don't love him," she finished firmly, jutting out her chin.

Papa set his thin china cup on the wicker table before he answered. "You will learn to love him as you know him better," he soothed.

"How can I be sure of that with everyone rushing me?" She stuck out her lower lip petulantly.

"I tried to tell your mother that you would rebel at forced arrangements." He sighed. "You must realize that we have your best interests at heart. You are too young to understand yet, but as you see more of life, you will realize the unhappiness that results from marrying out of one's class."

Lily brushed flakes of pastry from the lace at the neckline of her dress and bit her lip, thinking, *I'm always too young on the one hand and too old on the other.*

Clare Edwards's head glistened with beads of perspiration standing out on reddening skin. "Don't you remember my cousin Lucinda who ran away with a workman?" He looked at his daughter with loving concern. "Her life ended in bitterness. She was alone, estranged from her family, deserted by her husband. She. . ."

"I wouldn't do that, Papa," she replied in a wilted voice.

"You have social obligations to be met. You will inherit a great many responsibilities."

"Yes, Papa." She bowed her head and clenched fistfuls of rose petals until her fingernails bit into her palms.

"Now, you best go and see your mother." He sighed heavily and patted her awkwardly. "She has a surprise for you—a new frock to take to Roseland."

The carriage turned in from River Road and stopped at the wide double gates of Roseland Plantation. As the servants rushed to open the white gates, Lily sat back smugly. This plantation was socially prominent throughout the state, and her cousin, who seemed to think nothing here was as grand as in South Carolina, should be impressed. They approached the manor house through a natural woodland of giant water oaks, cedars, and magnolias that still held the last of their huge, waxy-white blossoms and scented the air with heavy perfume. The carriage turned up a broad central walk, two hundred feet long. Sand, white as marble and kept perfectly clear of carriage or horse tread, covered the entire length of this driveway to the white-pillared house that stood resplendent in serene beauty and dignity.

Lily could scarcely contain her excitement as they followed the spirea-garlanded curve of the drive to alight at the wide front steps. General Thomas Flournoy and his wife, who had built this house prior to 1840, graciously greeted the arriving guests. Their daughter, Caroline Elizabeth, rushed out to hug Lily.

"Betty, dear," Lily returned her affectionate greeting, "may I present my cousin Green Bethune from South Carolina."

Betty Flournoy smiled dazzlingly at Green and exclaimed, "Oh, I wonder if you are related to my fiancé, Bethune Beaton McKenzie of Louisville?" She linked her arm in his and ushered him into the house, leaving Lily lagging behind. Miffed, Lily made a show of seeing to Kitty, whom Mama had sent along to take care of her, and to her wardrobe trunk.

"Everybody!" Betty sang out, clapping her hands for attention. "Come meet our guest from South Carolina." She smiled with a smugness that showed she knew this exciting addition would make her house party a huge success.

A cluster of giggling girls turned as one. Their eyes brightened at the perfection of Green's features, and they immediately encircled him.

Green bowed gallantly over each extended hand in turn. He progressed slowly, making polite compliments to each preening girl before he moved to the next.

The faces of the young men, who stood back awaiting their introductions, held mixed emotions. Lily, who was equally unaccustomed to being ignored, watched them in amusement. It was easy to see that some stood in awe of Green's self-assured bearing and stylish clothes while others were plainly jealous of his charm.

That evening, when the lively group reassembled after dressing formally for dinner, Green offered Lily his arm and escorted her into the huge dining room. During the first course of hare and pheasant soup, Green paid her elaborate compliments; however, by the time the entrées of fillet of hare and curried rabbit were served, everyone was turning to him as the center of attention.

"Miss Betty, you and Mr. McKenzie must include Charleston on your honeymoon tour," he said in his cultured accent. "It is quite the center of our *beau monde*. Our local riches have been compared to Peru. Indeed, it has been said that Charleston is to the North what Lima is to the South: capital of the richest province of their respective hemispheres. There are endless balls and galas—and you must see a Shakespearean drama at the Dock Street Theater." He beamed in turn at each one around the table.

Lily squirmed, slightly embarrassed. When the second course was passed, she sampled only the hot, mixed-game pie.

Individuals began chatting to their partners, but Green turned to Elmira Oaks on the other side of him and told her, "You must visit Middleton Gardens someday. It is quite old and famous." He generously helped himself to the third course, roasted fowl.

Lily turned to Betty's rather plain brother and said, "Josiah Flournoy, you handsome old thing, you broke my heart not coming to my last party. What have you been doing lately?" Through all of the side dishes and elaborate desserts, she kept her back to Green. During the evening as they acted out phrases or songs for dumb crambo, she continued to ignore Green. Feigning interest in Josiah, she felt a slight pang for toying with him.

The next afternoon, everyone went outdoors to watch as the gentlemen prepared to go fishing. Roseland Plantation boasted of very good fishing in its creek which emptied into the Chattahoochee. As Josiah Flournoy passed out rods and other fine equipment, he explained to Green that the water was very deep and in some places quite wide for a creek.

Green, in turn, explained to him that on his low country plantation, they controlled their water with sluices to flood the earth and grow rice. Lily hated to hear anyone brag, and she was surprised at how well the other men were accepting him, deferring to his superior knowledge and experience.

After bidding the fishermen merry farewells, the girls went back inside to play with cards or hearts as they chose. They chattered incessantly about Betty's upcoming wedding to her young man, who was from a Scottish family of high rank. Caught up in the talk of love and romance, Lily began to wonder if marriage to Green might not be fun after all. He was fitting well into her circle of friends. He could show her the new sights she longed to see. Suddenly she realized that Betty was asking her about Green.

"Oh, he's from one of the first families of South Carolina," she replied. Wincing, she knew that she sounded exactly like Mama.

"When did you meet him?"

"Are you in love with him?"

"Are you planning to marry?"

Lily laughed at her friends' eager questions. She tried to smile mysteriously as if she really knew the answers but was not ready to tell. "Well," she temporized, "I'll tell you this much; our families would like to see us married."

The girls pressed her for details, and Lily had difficulty changing the subject.

When the gentlemen returned from their fishing expedition, some of her friends stood back in respect of her half-claim to Green, but Elmira Oaks went straight to him and linked her arm with his. Lily sniffed disdainfully because a lady simply did not make the first advance. The party moved to the cool veranda. Over refreshments, the men recounted that the largest bass had gotten away, as usual. While the group laughed over the fish stories and gasped over the killing of a copperhead, Elmira led a willing Green to a double swing at the far end of the porch.

Lily pouted that Green had not come at once to her side. This was supposed to be her courtship, yet he had almost ignored her. Family and friends told Lily she was pretty, but Elmira Oaks was the local reigning beauty. With pearl-like skin, glossy dark hair, and voluptuous figure, Elmira could easily crook her finger at any man. Trying not to look toward the swing, Lily sat gritting her teeth.

"Ohh, Green, you say the funniest things," Elmira laughed melodiously.

"Well, I'm a member of the Laughing Club," he returned. "No, really, it's one of Charleston's many clubs. But I'm prouder of my membership in the Dueling Society."

"Ohh, I love a man who lives by the Code of Honor," she squealed.

Encouraged, Green continued. "Our society is modeled after the old London clubs. Admission is granted only to those who have participated in a duel. A man's rank in the organization is based on the number of his encounters."

Lily fanned rapidly with her hand-painted, ivory fan. Glancing over it at Green, she decided that, although a lady did not allow a gentleman to take liberties, perhaps she had been too stringent in cooling his ardor. She had to admit that he far outshone her former beaux.

That evening she spent a great deal of time on her toilette, deciding that she had better give Elmira some competition and make Green notice her. Because Mama had always fussed that she allowed her skin too much sun, she carefully washed her neck and hands with almond meal to whiten them. Next she softened her lips and cheeks with glycerin diluted with rose water. Frowning at her reflection, she powdered her nose with finely pounded white starch. Kitty was skilled with the curling iron. While she heated it in the fireplace and fashioned Lily's hair into clusters of long curls in back, she whispered excitedly about her budding romance with a strapping stable hand named Lige.

Around them, the bedroom was filled with tinkling giggles and gasps as her friends had their corsets laced to the desired nineteen-inch waist and then fluttered into petticoat after frothy petticoat.

Smiling more confidently now, Lily put on her mother's surprise gift, a creation from the Salon in the Rue de la Paix of Charles Frederick Worth, who was making Paris the arbiter of world fashion. The lovely emerald silk billowed over her widest evening hoops. The dainty décolleté bared her creamy shoulders above short puffs of sleeves.

The orchestra was tuning up, and strains of music drifted from the wide back porch as she pulled on her elbow-length gloves and gave herself a final check in the looking glass. Hurrying until she reached the head of the stairs, she paused and drifted down until Green turned his head and saw her. Smiling, he started toward her, and she moved to meet him without further coquettishness.

Green took her hand, and they joined the group lining up to play twistification. They stood in lines of ladies and gentlemen with partners facing. Then the guitar and fiddle commenced a lively tune. The end couple bowed and clasped both hands as they swung each other around. Still swirling, they grasped the hands of the next in line and continued to swing each person until they reached the end of the line. When their turn came, Lily returned the squeeze of Green's fingers; however, she smiled dazzlingly at each man who swung her down the line. It would not hurt to make Green jealous, too. As she stood panting, waiting for her turn to come as the lines twisted and undulated again and again, Lily was unsure whether her breathlessness came from keeping time to the music or from Green's intimate glances and the pressure of his hands whenever they rejoined as partners.

Twistification was considered a game allowed to those whose churches might turn them out for dancing. Some dances and other games followed.

Resting between sets, the couples strolled the geometric patterns of the formal garden paths. The fragrance of hundreds of roses filled the soft June night. Cardinal de Richelieu and the dainty buds of Champneys' Pink Cluster were the favorites that caused the girls to stop, bend over the clipped boxwood edging, and breathe deeply. Rambling roses draped the fence at the perimeter of the garden. The heady fragrance seemed to pulse to the muted beat of the music. Here and there a large boxwood or American holly cast a secluded shadow, and marble benches offered a spot to rest; however, the young people were never far from the watchful eyes of their chaperones. Green's manner toward her had changed. Responding to her bid for his attention, he made every effort to charm and court her. When he led her through the pergola, a long procession of columns screened by a web of climbing roses, she made only a weak protest as he stole a kiss beneath the romantic bower.

After a light midnight supper of chicken salad, ham, cakes, jellies, and meringues, the dancing continued until three in the morning. Then the groups returned to their various guest quarters. The girls in Lily's room whispered until dawn streaked the sky, and Lily had no chance to sort out her feelings for her suitor.

Before departing for home after brunch the next day, the couples promenaded to Roseland's private landing on a curve of the Chattahoochee. They stood laughing and chatting as they watched the farmhands bringing peaches, vegetables, and meats to be loaded aboard the steamboat for its dining room.

Uhmmm! The whistle of the steamboat around the bend vibrated against Lily's ribs. She held her breath. *Uh-uh-uhmm!* It was not the signal for the *Wave,* but she stood on tiptoe to see.

Green reached for her hand. "How would you like to take a grand tour?"

Lily looked at him in surprise. Was he suggesting they begin thinking of a honeymoon tour? Although his voice was bantering, he was gazing at her quite seriously.

"I—don't know," she faltered, realizing that he had misread her excitement.

"We could sail to Charleston and New York City, and then go to Saratoga and Newport if you like."

"That—would be lovely," she murmured hesitantly. Turning toward the river, she lowered her parasol so that he could not see her face. She had told herself that she had grown up, that she was ready to take her place in society.

The long, flat boat floated alongside, and everyone waved and called out gaily. Lily's hand barely moved, and she said nothing as her eyes sought the vessel, hoping she had mistaken the signal. A huge wheel churned water at the stern. Harrison's steamer had a side wheel. Would she ever again hear a steamboat's whistle or smell the smoke without searching for Harrison Wingate's face?

Back home at Barbour Hall, Lily rushed upstairs to find Emma to share the fun of the house party and the details of Betty Flournoy's upcoming wedding. Emma sat sewing in her favorite spot, the sitting room at the front of the hall. This was the only small room in the house, and both girls enjoyed its intimacy when the sliding doors shut it off from the rest of the hall.

Smiling and nodding, Emma listened patiently to Lily's excited tale. When Lily paused for breath at last, Emma spoke quietly. "Harrison Wingate came soon after you left."

Lily's dark eyes widened and her animated face became solemn. "Was he hurt at my not being here?"

"Well, he's so quiet and dignified," Emma returned, looking at her seriously, "and he doesn't say very much. We had a very nice visit, though. . . ." Her voice trailed away.

Lily looked at her aunt, who obviously had more to say. Emma, however, compressed her lips and made a show of searching for thread in the black-japanned papier-mâché sewing stand by her chair. Lily sat down on the window seat and leaned far out onto the small circular balcony that decorated the porch roof above the entrance doors of the house. She gazed across the grounds that were dappled with sunlight and shade and struggled with the emotions that had sprung up at Emma's words. Emma always listened when Lily spilled out the inmost feelings of her heart; however, she concealed her own desires beneath a placid face and averted eyes. Emma seemed resigned to spinsterhood, but she must long for a better life than she had. Lily glanced back at her through the curtain of her blowing hair, but she could see no emotion revealed. If Emma and Harrison fell in love and she married Green, everyone should be happy. . . . Then why was she fighting so hard to keep back the tears?

She wanted to run out into the garden, to scream and cry like a child. Instead, she concealed her tears and went quietly to her room. She had been telling herself she only wanted the captain for a friend. She enjoyed his lively conversation that recognized her own bright mind. Because she approached life with intense convictions about everything, Harrison's amusing lightness relaxed her tensions. Suddenly, she knew that she wanted more than passing friendship from Harrison Wingate.

Exhaustion overwhelmed her. Stepping out of her crinoline, she climbed into her bed and hugged herself into a tight little knot of despair. Green would be pressing her soon for an engagement. She knew she must do what everyone was expecting of her. If she did not give him a definite answer, he would be turning to other fields. Harrison's face floated before her, and the thought of his smiles turned upon another left her aching. She had no one to advise her now. She was bereft of her confidante.

Betty Flournoy's wedding day was as perfect as only a clear summer day can be. As Lily and Green approached the church, she was proud of her escort's appearance. A high top hat and thin walking stick added to his elegance.

Because the past few weeks since the house party had been such a busy social whirl, Lily had been able to stave off an official engagement; however, she had almost resigned herself to it.

The line of carriages stopping at the church stretched well down the street. Too excited to sit still, Lily suggested that they alight from the carriage and walk the rest of the way.

"Oh, look, Green." She plucked at his sleeve. "I've never seen anything more wonderful!"

She directed his gaze to a strange sight back down the street. An old man, who was apparently quite helpless, sat in a large chair on wheels that was being pulled along by a goat.

"Let's go chat with him and give him some money," she said eagerly.

"No, my sweet, I can't have you looking on such ugliness," Green replied with finality. Taking her elbow, he turned her toward the church.

Lily glanced back over her shoulder. Smiling at the ingenious man, she wished she could do more.

"Lily, Lily," the other bridesmaids called nervously.

She hurried to join them. Swelling music stirred her heart as the bevy of bridesmaids fluttered down the aisle. As they turned and caught sight of the lovely bride in her pearl-encrusted white satin, each girl drew breath as one. Lily's misty eyes sought Green's as she consented to herself to smile a promise to him. He was sweet and protective of her, she realized. Soon she, too, would be dressed in white satin. She should make the best of a situation she could not change.

As the organ trumpeted the single notes and then crashed into the stirring chords of Mendelssohn's "Wedding March" from "A Midsummer Night's Dream," Lily's feet danced to the trills of the recessional. Her heart filled with the music and she moved to Green's side.

With her decision made, she happily participated in all of the wedding festivities and returned home in high spirits.

As she swirled through the double entrance doors of Barbour Hall, she glimpsed a letter waiting on the card tray. With a shuddering sigh, she recognized the seal on it as being the dove insignia from the *Wave.* Her fingers shook as she reached for it, only to draw back quickly.

It was addressed to Emma.

Chapter 5

The letter seemed to move, to taunt her. Lily's trembling fingers flew to her face in a vain effort to hide her emotions. Pleading extreme weariness, she escaped to her room.

She stood at the long window looking out at the stars as they began to twinkle. She must pull herself together and be pleased for Emma. After all, she had Green. He wanted to make her happy, to shield her from the ugliness of life.

Lily could not seem to make a formal petition, yet her thoughts meshed with snatches of prayer. She did not want a perpetual-house-party life, much as she enjoyed fun. She loved attending church and was not pleased that Green usually pled too much business to accompany her. She always left worship services inspired that Jesus had saved her to serve. She did not want to turn away from the twisted old men and goats of life; she wanted to help.

Suddenly, she realized that she did not really love Green. She had been caught up in the romance of the moment at the wedding. She knew that Papa was right that sometimes love grew and flowered after marriage, but now she doubted that would be the case if she married Green. He was handsome. Charming. Perhaps the passion of which she knew so little might flourish for a season, but deep within her she knew they would never be one in mind and spirit.

Sadly, she began to take off her wedding finery.

The door opened slowly and Emma came in clutching the letter to her chest with both hands. The willowy girl leaned against the doorjamb as if she might fall without support. Her face pinched with doubt, she said, "I just don't know what to do."

Lily lifted pain-filled eyes to her friend and waited.

"I know I shouldn't tell you. I should burn this letter and never tell you. Your mother will never forgive me." She sat down in the rocking chair and began to cry softly.

Tortured by the excruciatingly drawn-out revelation, Lily patted her hand and made soothing sounds she did not feel.

"Here." Emma thrust the letter toward her. "Read it."

Lily recoiled. She would be loving. She would be pleasant. But she could not read Harrison's words of love to Emma.

"Read it," Emma repeated. "It's yours."

"Mine? I don't understand."

"Read it," she said again as if to a stupid child. "You'll understand."

June 12, 1858
Apalachicola, Florida

Amie de Mon Coeur,

May I call you that, my darling Lily? I have sent this by your, or may I say our, dear friend Emma, in order not to embarrass you if my love for you is not requited. I was devastated that I missed seeing you, but I quite unburdened my heart to Emma! From the first moment I saw the compassion on your face as you watched the scene on the steamer from beneath your parasol, I have loved you. I dare not hope that you love me as I love you, but it would give me such joy if you would correspond with me so that we can get to know each other better. Send a letter by Julian McKenzie aboard the Laura, *and he will get it to me.*

I anxiously await hearing from you. I do not mean to practice a deception upon your parents, but Emma agreed to accept a first letter until I could be certain of your feelings for me. By her nervousness in the matter, I judge that she fears this may be contrary to her duties as your chaperone, but as I said, she is friend to both of us.

Please do not disappoint me.

Good night. God bless you.

Harrison Wingate

Lily looked up from the letter with shining eyes. "Oh, Emma, thank you so much. I know you risked Mama's ire. And she treats you terribly now."

"Yes. Perhaps that's why I risked this letter," Emma sighed. "Oh, no, I don't mean to spite her," she added quickly. "She is kind to give me a home. But her domineering ways have made my life so miserable that I had to let you decide for yourself if you would follow your heart." She clutched and unclutched her hands in a nervous gesture that made her seem far older than her twenty-five years. "I did not follow mine."

"I've never known why you didn't marry," Lily said softly. "You are the sweetest person I've ever known—and so lovely." She stood over her friend and patted her head of honey-colored hair.

Emma smiled up at her with a look of infinite sadness in her pale blue eyes. "I was very much in love with a young man who asked for my hand. My grandfather refused to allow the marriage because he was not of our faith."

"Well, Harrison is a Christian with a faith even stronger than my own. But would Papa and Mama ever accept him? Papa might, but Mama is so set on Green. . . ."

"What about Green? Do you love him at all?"

"He made me jealous." She laughed sheepishly. "And I thought perhaps I did. The simplest solution to my problems would be to marry him. I want to obey my parents, and life would follow the pattern I'm accustomed to—I can't imagine what sort of life I'd have with Harrison. . . ." She dropped her head in her hands.

Emma nodded and said nothing.

Lily reached for the letter again and held it to her cheek. "But wouldn't it be exciting. . . ?" She sighed.

"You'll answer the letter then?"

"Yes. Whatever the outcome, I'll answer the letter. Even if I never see him again, I'll answer the letter!"

Lily spent a restless night as her tired body pulled toward sleep and her excited mind composed and recomposed her letter.

In the morning, she took her brassbound, rosewood lap desk to the summerhouse. As she unfolded the writing slope, the ardent letters she had envisioned in the night embarrassed her. She thought for a long time before she dipped her pen in the crystal inkwell and began carefully.

June 21, 1858
Eufaula, Alabama

Dear Captain Wingate,

I received your letter and was delighted to hear from you. I would enjoy corresponding with you and hearing about your exciting travels.

I am very sorry that I had gone to Roseland when you returned. The house party served well to entertain my visiting cousin and give me a chance to enjoy seeing Betty Flournoy before her marriage. Her lovely wedding was yesterday. I am certain you would not be interested in that, but I did see something on the way that you would have appreciated. A crippled old man who had rebelled at being bedridden was moving smartly along in a chair on wheels pulled by a goat. How is that for spirit?

Wind ruffled her paper. The open lattice of the summerhouse, partially roofed with swags of wisteria, filtered the sunlight but invited every breeze. Happily, Lily looked up from her writing. With a green blur of wings, a hummingbird hovered over a large buddleia. The glory of its tiny being filled her with longing to be near Harrison once again, to absorb the pleasure in the small things of life that he exuded. She wanted to pour out her heart to him, but she feared being unmaidenly. She contented herself with writing a chatty letter and signed it, "Yours, Lily."

As the summer days sizzled by, Lily drifted in a daze. Chiding herself for constantly daydreaming of Harrison and watching for a letter from him, she was relieved when business took the usually indolent Green by stagecoach to Tuskegee. Her nerves had barely relaxed before they stretched taut again. Mama began to talk about taking a trip to Columbus to visit her sister who had an exceedingly fine dressmaker. Fearing Harrison might return, and knowing Mama had in mind beginning a trousseau, Lily tried to discourage her. Although no one had verbally set a deadline for her, she sensed pressure from all sides to announce an engagement.

Lily and Emma descended the stairs early one morning bound for a walk to the Chewalla bridge. They were hurrying, both to leave before the day became too hot and to escape the scrutiny of Cordelia Edwards. As they slipped softly across the marble floor, the butler placed a letter on the card tray. It bore Emma's name, but a brief nod from her aunt made Lily scoop it up, clutch it to her heart, and run across the lawn like a child at play. Plopping down behind a large bush with her skirt mushrooming around her, she ripped open the letter.

Smith's Bend, Alabama

Dear Lily,

The Wave *will leave here shortly and it's headed your way! Please, please be there this time. I received your letter with joy. Even though you spoke no words of love for me, I could feel it between the lines. I will be in Eufaula only briefly this trip, for the bulk of my load must get directly to Columbus. I must see you. Even if a smile across the water is all you can give, please be there. We should arrive on the tenth of July.*

I love you dearly.

Harrison Wingate

Excuse this pencil note. I am writing hurriedly on an old sideboard to get this off to you.

Lily's footsteps danced along the way to Chewalla bridge, and Emma nervously clutched her fists against her chest as she listened to the girl's daring plan to board Harrison's steamer.

Uhmmmmm! Uhmmmmm!

The steamboat's whistle aroused Lily from her sleep. She bolted upright in the darkness. Jumping off the high bed, she dressed quickly. It had been simple to agree with Mama to take the next steamboat to Columbus to visit with her sister; however, the boat had not arrived that evening as expected. Everyone had finally despaired of the steamer docking and retired for the night. Now, summoned by the wheeting whistle, they hurried to the waterfront.

Burning torches illuminated the scene. Lily pranced along as they alighted from the carriage and joined the others going aboard for Columbus. Cordelia Edwards never noticed details of things she considered beneath her; consequently, she had not guessed that Harrison Wingate was master of this steamboat.

They hastened past the brick warehouse onto the wharf that was overflowing with freight. The night air rang with shouts and laughter as the stevedores hurried to unload the steamboat. Excitedly, Lily eyed the long train of wagons, sent by merchants at Clayton, Ozark, and Abbeville, waiting to haul out the freight.

As soon as they had gone up the gangway, Mrs. Edwards, professing that she felt in a stupor from being awakened, went to her cabin to bed. Giving in to Lily's pleading to stay up a little while, she left her daughter in Emma's care.

The girls stayed on the upper deck and watched the process of unloading and loading. Lily's cheeks flushed with excitement as she caught glimpses of Harrison. He had greeted them all briefly but had immediately returned to his work.

At last, the shouts of the roustabouts stilled, the whistle stopped blasting, and the steamer glided into the dark silent river. The only sound was the water wheel's slow *swish, swish, swish.*

The pounding of Lily's heart slowed to a peaceful rhythm, and she seemed to stop breathing as she watched the quiet man moving steadily along the deck toward her. Emma drifted away to a chair in the shadow of the staterooms.

"I'm sorry I've been so busy since you all came aboard." Harrison smiled down at her as he joined her at the rail. "That you're going with me is more than I dared dream."

"I'm afraid I've been rather devious," she confessed, lowering her lashes shyly. "I let Mama think it coincidence that this was your boat."

Harrison's deep voice chuckled. "I thought she was surprised to see me."

"She'd been wanting to visit a dressmaker and. . ." She hesitated, remembering the purpose of seeing the seamstress. She wished that time could stand as still as the steamer seemed to be doing; but as moonlight played over the shore, the dark bank seemed to move by, and she knew that she could not remain a belle juggling suitors. All artifice vanished as she freed her mind and soul. She lifted wide, honest eyes to his face, and stood waiting, awash with moonglow.

"Oh, Lily." Harrison's laughter stilled. Solemnly, he moved nearer, and his hands hovered close to her shoulders, then dropped to the rail. "You've made me so happy—coming with me. I. . ."

Motionless, scarcely daring to believe the love she saw shining in his eyes, she matched his gaze. Her arms tingled even though his fingers had not quite touched her. Standing so close, breathing the same air he was breathing, she knew he was sharing the same wonder of discovered love. "Harrison," she sighed, as he lifted her hands and tenderly kissed her fingertips.

"You're the loveliest, most beautiful. . ." He looked down at her as if he must make up for the hours that had been so empty away from each other. He caressed her dark hair as it floated on the summer breeze.

Tenderness welled up within her and spilled over as soft laughter.

Gently, he brushed her a kiss. She caught her breath with a tremulous sigh.

"Lily!" A hiss sounded from Emma who had moved down the deck toward them. "Lily, we'd best get to our cabin. Your mother might awaken."

"All right, Emma," she called softly and moved reluctantly away from Harrison, who continued to hold her outstretched hand.

"Until tomorrow," he promised, bending his dark head to kiss her fingertips one last time.

Smiling back at Harrison, she allowed Emma to lead her toward the staterooms that stretched three-fourths of the length of the boat. They shared the small room next to Mama's, and they opened the door from the deck stealthily lest they wake her.

"Lily," Emma hissed again, "I'm afraid."

"Of what?" asked Lily in surprise.

"Shhh. Don't let your mother hear. I'm afraid you're heading for trouble. I should never have helped you deceive her."

"I haven't told her any lies. . . ."

"No, but you didn't tell her Captain Wingate would be on this run."

"Really now." Lily struggled out of her hooped skirt. "I couldn't be sure anything would come of it. He might ask lots of girls to ride, and. . ." She faltered.

"Exactly! You don't know what sort of man he is." Emma's blue eyes held deep concern.

"I think I do," Lily replied with quiet assurance.

"But what do you know about him? Has he told you anything about his background?"

"No, but—"

"Well?"

"He doesn't talk about himself all the time like Green does." Lily was tired now, petulant. "He talks about the present—vital things. Oh, Emma, you're not going to make me doubt him. Now, go to sleep," she said soothingly. "We'll see what tomorrow brings."

Lily lay in her bunk, smiling at the ceiling, warmed by the remembered tenderness of Harrison's kiss. She could hardly wait for morning.

Breakfast would be served on tables set up in the center hallway between the two rows of staterooms, but Lily chose to walk around the rail even though the room opened onto the hall. She was not disappointed; Harrison stood on deck. He smiled and waved, but he was busy directing a stop at a plantation landing to take on food supplies and cordwood for fuel. It was this fat pine and rosin that caused the smokestacks to belch such black smoke. Lily could glimpse a stately mansion on the hill overlooking the muddy water.

Looking down, Lily laughed at a brown mother duck bustling along with five fuzzy babies bobbing intently behind her in a golden-headed knot. Blending into a brown rock, a crowd of turtles sunned lazily.

Every spattering drop of the river sustained some form of life. From a rock outcropping, fern fronds dipped lacy fingers. Yellows, whites, and blues of wildflowers dotted tiny clods of earth. They were closely attended by huge, black bees and brilliant butterflies. A spider crocheted a sparkling web. Drinking in the beauty, Lily felt she might burst with happiness. The steamboat moved back into the channel of the river that was at once peaceful, smooth, sparkling, swirling, eddying. Lifting her eyes toward the eastern shore, Lily marveled at the beauty of maple leaves translucent with sunlight. As the boat labored upstream, the soft, early morning rays filtered and patterned through tall trees laced with vines that swayed and danced to the orchestration of the songbirds. Lily's heart swelled with the music, and she offered up a thankful prayer to the Creator.

Suddenly famished, she went inside to eat. The interior of the boat was well appointed. Chandeliers reflected back from mirrors and ornamented spittoons. Lily smiled approvingly at Harrison's use of greenery, and she noted as she walked down the carpeted passageway that the boat was well kept. The fifty passengers were served in two sittings. Lily joined the second group and ate a bountiful breakfast.

Mama went with a friend to the ladies' saloon to chat. Delighted that she had escaped Mama's scrutiny, Lily stepped back into the sunshine, filled with anticipation. Emma followed her.

"Morning, ladies." Captain Wingate tipped his hat politely as he joined them. "The banks are so pretty along here that I always wish I could sit on them awhile and throw out a line to a bass or crappie." He pointed to the steep slanted bank on the Georgia side. On the west, Alabama rose a sheer bluff. "And the catfish, here—ah." He kissed his fingertips and gestured lavishly. "The best you've ever tasted!"

Lily had never cared for fishing but felt anything would be fun with Harrison. She wanted to tell him so. She winked at Emma and motioned with a nod.

Remaining steadfastly in her position as chaperone, Emma returned a frown. "Oh, look." Emma shivered and pointed as two tremendous alligators slid off a sandbar with a foghornlike bellow at the approach of the boat.

Harrison accepted Emma's presence pleasantly, and he entertained them both, laughing and joking and pointing out landmarks along the steep banks. Suddenly the river narrowed, deepened. Oaks shouldered poplars and gums as they pushed to the water's edge. Rushing to meet the steamboat through this green velvet canyon, the Chattahoochee, revealing itself a little at a time, tempting them toward new delights around the bend always just ahead, flowed clear, dark, cool.

Breaking the spell, a call from the mate, Captain Allen, summoned Harrison. With a flurry of excitement, the passengers moved around the deck toward the shouting.

A slow-going raft of logs lashed together floated downstream just ahead of the unwieldy steamboat. A small tent on the raft sheltered the owner who had chosen this method of marketing his logs. The man waved and motioned apologetically, but he could do little to move from the ship's path.

Lily beamed with pride as Harrison, perfectly calm in the midst of everyone's agitation, maneuvered his ship safely past the raft.

When Harrison rejoined them, he shrugged off the excitement. "Rafts do make our passage difficult, but these men make a handsome profit on their lumber if they can get it safely downstream to a good market." He smiled down at her, and there was a boyish pride and enthusiasm in his eyes as he asked, "Would you like to tour the steamer?"

"I'd love to," exclaimed Lily. Giving them this time together, Emma took a seat in a deck chair.

Foy, however, popped up from nowhere. Ignoring Lily's glaring, he asked, "May I go?"

"Certainly, Son, glad to have you," Harrison said cordially.

The trio climbed to the hurricane deck, a short section of rooms between the smokestacks. "This is where the officers live," Captain Wingate explained. "Henry Shreve, a pioneer in steamboating, named the rooms of his boats for individual states, hence the term 'stateroom.' Many people call this deck the Texas ever since Texas entered the Union as the biggest state of all."

Foy's rosy cheeks glowed with excitement. Lily peeped shyly into the captain's quarters and tried to maintain dignity, but she was almost as excited as her little brother when they climbed to the small glassed-in pilothouse. From here, they could look beyond the fluttering flags to the treetops along the banks or scan far down the river. With a touch of arrogance, the pilot showed them how he made decisions and snapped orders to the engineer and his helpers far below. Of course, Foy wanted to see the huge furnaces being fed. Lily waited for them in a deck chair.

She had never enjoyed anything as much as she enjoyed being with Harrison and watching him move about in his world. She was sorry that Columbus was only eighty-five miles from Eufaula and they were due to land there at two o'clock that afternoon. When would she ever see Harrison again?

They had only gone a few miles when the river made a decided turn south.

Suddenly, the boat stopped with a resounding thud. Passengers caught off guard because of the normally smooth sailing fell sprawling about the deck. Harrison ran to see what debris had been struck. Worse than mere debris, the boat had hit the sandbar at Francis Bend. Like a great mermaid stretching languorously with sunlight glittering off of pure white skin, the bar had lured many ill-fated boats.

When inspection showed that the *Wave* had not torn a hole in her hull but was firmly grounded, Lily whispered to Emma with twinkling eyes, "What a delightful disaster."

Two in the afternoon passed. Lily leaned over the rail, grinning mischievously, happy that all of the workmen's efforts to dislodge the craft were to no avail. As the sun began sinking in a cloud over the water, a mist settled in. Streaks of pinks and golds reflected over and again, sparkling, drifting, lifting in gentle waves. Smiling, Lily went to her cabin.

She emerged wearing cream-colored mousseline de soie. Soft swags around the hem and across the shoulders and bodice were caught up with currant-red velvet ribbons.

Catching sight of her, Harrison motioned to the Italian orchestra on the hurricane deck. Soft strains of music swirled around them as they danced in the twilight. As the moonlight turned the sandbar to softly gleaming silver, other passengers came on deck and joined the dancing; but Lily felt she and Harrison were floating on a cloud, alone.

Dinner was a festive affair. Because they were seated with the captain, Lily eyed her mother apprehensively. Surprisingly, Cordelia Edwards was beaming. Lily realized that Mama quite expected her to be the belle of any situation, and, here, the dashing captain was the one to whom all eyes turned. As many gentlemen claimed her for the dancing that followed the elaborate meal, Mama could not know that Lily glowed because she was falling in love.

The next day, the steamer remained firmly grounded. Food supplies were slightly depleted, but gaiety ran high; and everyone gorged on a load of fresh pineapple. Banjo picking added to the merriment as passengers, who had by now become friends, lounged in deck chairs, chatting. It was cool on deck. The banks on both sides were dense woodland thickly hung with swaying swags of Spanish moss. In Lily's lively imagination, the gay shrouds became Indian ghosts singing with the voice of the wind in the pines. The boat was stopped in full view of an ancient Indian mound, a great oblong shape of red clay some thirteen feet to its flat summit and a hundred feet in diameter. The passengers speculated about the mysteries of the mound.

When Harrison climbed down again to the sandbar, Lily moved to the rail to watch. The eight acres of deep sand were heavily populated with seiners as well as with workmen from the *Wave.* Lily watched them chain their fish baskets to stakes on the sandbar, swim out into the yellow water with their seines, and return with a catch of garfish, carp, cat, and suckers.

A cheer went up. The sweating workmen had freed the vessel at last. Lily sighed in disappointment; however, it was nearly night, and she could enjoy one last evening with Harrison.

Beneath the stars, they danced once more to the singing violins. Spinning with happiness, she did not realize at first that he was whirling her away from the group.

"My lovely Lily, *Je t'aime,"* Harrison whispered against her hair. Taking both her hands in his, he drew back and looked into her eyes. "I've loved you from the first moment I saw you. Each glimpse of you makes me love you more. Dare I hope that you can learn to love me?"

"Yes, Harrison," she whispered softly. "I do love you, oh, I do!"

Placing his arm around her shoulder, he guided her further along the rail to a secluded spot. Cupping her face with a strong hand, he tilted her head and bent down to kiss her tenderly. Shyly, she accepted his kiss. Opening her eyes slowly, wondrously, she looked up at him. The depth of his love was plainly read on his candid face. Moonlight, softly caressing the water surrounding them, reflected in her dark, shining eyes. She entwined her slender arms about his neck.

"I love you, Harrison, and I always will."

He swept her into his arms. She responded to the desire of his kisses until at last, remembering decorum, she eased away.

"I don't mean to rush you, Lily," Harrison said. "I know you deserve a long and proper courtship, but for now I must stay with the steamship line. If I were still on the family plantation, I would perhaps have proper time." He laughed and shook his head. "No, I could never wait for you. I want you to be mine immediately. May I ask your father for your hand?"

"Yes, yes," she breathed. "When we get back to Eufaula, speak to Papa. Don't let on to Mama, for now."

Harrison nodded and reached to draw her close again.

Lily awakened early the next morning and slipped out to the mist-shrouded deck. The dark forest shimmered, blurred. Gradually, she focused on two black, curious eyes. Alert ears pointed upward, quivering. With a sudden flip of a white tail, the deer bounded away. Enchanted, she peered closer and saw an entire deer family feeding quietly, moving silently through the woodland. Led by a quarrelsome gobbler, a flock of wild turkeys jerked and bobbed its way to a rock-bound pool. A fat, white-breasted gray bird dipped its beak quickly and scurried out of their way.

A hand grasped Lily's shoulder, and she turned to find her mother's wary eye upon her. Mrs. Edwards insisted she come in out of the dampness, and they went into the ladies' saloon together. It was a large and lovely room dominated by a Chickering grand piano in one corner. Small writing desks lined the windows. Potted palms and ferns formed the chairs into cozy groupings. Mrs. Edwards selected a large rocker, and Lily took a stool beside her. Dutifully, she began to read the Bible aloud as Cordelia Edwards directed her. Mama reared back smiling and nodding with pleasure as others came in and saw her daughter respectfully at her feet.

They had come to the Book of Ruth. Lily began by merely speaking the words. Gradually, the story gripped her attention. When she came to the sixteenth verse of chapter one and read in her Bible "For whither thou goest, I will go; and where thou lodgest, I will lodge: thy people shall be my people, and thy God my God," the words began to sing. The beautiful love story spoke to her heart and reinforced her joy in her decision to marry Harrison. Breakfast was announced. She put the Bible aside reluctantly, wanting to read about the marriage of Ruth and Boaz. Wistfully, she remembered that they had had Naomi's blessing. She wished that her mother was the sort of woman with whom she could share the deep convictions which were growing in her heart.

After breakfast, the gentlemen passengers came in and everyone engaged in pleasant conversation. Lily listened with half an ear, frustrated because rain kept her from sitting on deck where she might watch Harrison. During a break in the clouds, she took a stroll and had a brief moment with him.

"Lily, Dearest, I'll be staying in Columbus for a few days. You will be going back with me on Monday, won't you?" Harrison asked with anxious eyes.

"Yes." She wiped a spatter of rain from her cheek and smiled radiantly. "Mama never stays away from Papa for very long. I can hardly wait 'til Monday."

"I don't want to wait. Can't I call on you at your aunt's house?"

Lily gripped the wet rail. "Oh, I want to see you! I do. But Mama would be terribly angry if I crossed her in front of her sister. I'm just afraid—"

"Captain Wingate," the mate stepped up deferentially, "we're approaching Columbus."

Distractedly, Wingate nodded to him and searched Lily's face for an answer.

Biting her lip, Lily hesitated. The swishing of the giant side wheel filled her ears, and her stomach churned as she looked at the foaming wake behind it. In the joy of finding mutual love, she had been growing up, changing; but suddenly panic seized her. "You'd better not come," she whispered miserably.

A gust of wind covered her with dirty water from the roof. Harrison Wingate was walking away from her toward duty. With dampened spirits and misty eyes, she shuddered with the certainty that Mama would never change.

Chapter 6

Lily!" Mama's voice summoned her. "Stop daydreaming and get your things together. We must hurry and quit the boat before the storm breaks."

Dazed, Lily turned. The sun was blazing down upon her. Beads of perspiration stood out on her forehead. She had forgotten to put on her hat again. Looking up, she saw an ominous black cloud north of the spot where Cordelia Edwards stood commandingly.

"Yes, Ma'am." She sighed.

Their relatives were waving from the wharf. Emma tugged at her arm and pulled her toward the gangway. Clanging bells and shrieking whistles echoed in her head. She clenched her teeth and let the frenzy of humanity swirl around her.

Looking back over her shoulder, she searched for Harrison. He stood on the top deck. His seeking eyes found hers, and their gaze spanned the distance. For one long moment, sound ceased. Peace filled her heart as they spoke eloquent, if silent, words across the intervening water.

Gashing across the sky, lightning seemed to open the sagging bottom of a thunderhead, releasing a torrent of rain. They ran toward the carriage. Emma and Cordelia kept jumping nervously because of the frightening fireworks of the July thunderstorm, but Lily scarcely noticed. Huddled in a corner, she wrapped herself in dreams of Harrison until they reached Aunt Laurie's handsome, brick house.

The rest of the family met them on the veranda, set off by exquisite iron grillwork, and Lily did not have another quiet moment.

As soon as they could change their wet clothing for afternoon frocks, they came downstairs to the parlor where Aunt Laurie had spread a sumptuous tea for friends who had assembled to greet them. Cousin Octavia was called upon to perform on the piano. Gracefully, she lifted her hoop over the red velvet stool and seated herself with her skirt billowing completely around it. Lily, who always moved too quickly for this type of maneuver and made her hoop fly up in back, was glad that she was only requested to stand beside the square grand piano and sing.

When at last the girls had a chance to sit together on one of the winged love seats, Octavia whispered, "I can't wait to hear about your beau." A frown creased her sweet, round face and she tossed her corn-shuck hair at the wry expression this brought to Lily's face. She continued in a puzzled voice, "One time I look at you, you're terribly unhappy and the next minute you're grinning like a cow eating briars."

Lily laughed. She had always liked her plump-cheeked cousin; however, she was afraid to confide in her for fear she would tell Aunt Laurie.

The next morning, Lily was fitted by the dressmaker. As dainty undergarments, gowns, and peignoirs took shape, everyone laughed and teased her about being a blushing bride. Guiltily, Lily knew her red cheeks and subdued mien came from concealing the fact that she intended Harrison, not Green, to become her groom.

Mama bragged to her sister about Green. Haughtily, she suggested that it was certainly time for Laurie to make a match for Octavia; although she doubted that she could find a suitor with equal financial and social aspects for bringing up her grandchildren. Her words rasped Lily's nerves.

In the flurry of shopping trips and social calls, she finally pulled Mrs. Edwards aside. "Please, let me talk with you, Mama," she begged. "I just don't love Green. I don't want to marry—"

"Nonsense!" Cordelia Edwards patted her hand, smiling absently. "Affection will come." She brushed her aside. "Hurry and get ready, Baby; it's time for the party."

The sweltering July days were frequently punctuated with violent thunderstorms, and the streets were becoming muddy rivers. Octavia insisted, however, that she must show Lily the Paper Factory on Rock Island. Emma did not wish to go so they set off with Kitty in attendance.

As the carriage rolled along the street which paralleled the river, Octavia pointed out the many beautiful homes. "That one has a patriotic flare," she said, pointing to a Greek Revival mansion. "Its eleven columns and two pilasters represent the thirteen original colonies."

"That's nice," murmured Lily absently, lost in the pleasant pain of loving Harrison but being separated from him. She tried to imagine that he was beside her, marveling at the individualistic architecture along this street. With him, it would not be a boring blur. Every detail would become exciting.

Octavia eyed her but said nothing more as they rode through the city of Columbus, Georgia, and out into the country.

Lily found the manufacture of paper to be quite a curiosity. As she listened attentively to the gentleman who conducted the tour, she thought that Harrison would find this interesting, too.

Reverberating thunder signaled another storm. Lily gnawed her thumb as they waited it out. Standing, looking at the rain, she began to tremble. If only

Mama could see how alike she and Harrison were in mind and heart, surely she would accept him. The storm ended as abruptly as it had begun, and the girls hurried to the carriage. Lily splattered a swath of red mud across her skirt, and her face clouded. They climbed into the carriage, but it would not budge.

"Ma'am," said their driver, "the wheels are firmly mired."

With a long, shuddering sigh, Lily released her pent-up emotions and began to sob uncontrollably.

Her cousin looked at her in surprise. "This isn't like you, Lily! The driver can attend to it. What's the matter with you?"

"Oh, Octavia," she gulped. "I'm so much in love."

"Is that all?" Octavia laughed. "That's wonderful. It's marvelous when one can find a love match within the bounds of class."

Lily sobbed harder. As the driver went for assistance in getting the carriage from the muddy bog, she confessed her dilemma.

Shocked, her cheeks quivering, Octavia listened. Nervously chewing a lock of her long hair, she said in a hoarse whisper, "You know girls like us can't marry without our mothers' consent."

Lily nodded miserably.

"And what will you tell Green?" Octavia's eyes widened with fear. "From what you've told me of him, he won't take it lightly!"

Shaking her dark head in despair, Lily sobbed until she felt sick and weak.

Sunday morning they attended worship service. Looking hopefully across the gaslit sanctuary, Lily twisted this way and that, craning to see each face. She whispered to Octavia, "I do wish I'd told Harrison which church we'd attend so you could at least have seen him."

As the choir marched in filling the building with voices lifted in praise, Lily's tense shoulders relaxed. Laying aside her problems and opening her heart, she let the Spirit of the Lord fill her through the music and the reading of the Scripture. Although the sermon seemed unrelated to her situation, a word here, a phrase there, spoke to her with God's promise that the way might be difficult but He would go with her. Leaving the church with joy and strength renewed, she wished that she could communicate her security of salvation to Emma. The dear, sweet girl had made an excuse not to come, as she often did. She seemed to believe that behaving piously and attending church occasionally were simply more duties she had to perform.

When the family left the church, they decided to ride out to look at the Chattahoochee. It was rising rapidly from the constant storms. Columbus was situated on the fall line separating their gentle land in the Gulf Coastal Plain from the swiftly rising Piedmont. Here the river foamed over rocky falls. Watching the patterning of lights and shadows undulating over the pinks, golds, browns, and whites of the rocks and reflecting in the shoals clearly showed why the Creek Indians had name it *chatta*, meaning stones, and *hoochee*, meaning patterned or painted. The angry torrent of water rushing by them indicated that it must have been storming all the way up the course of the sparkling stream to its source at Brasstown Bald, the highest jewel in the Appalachian chain draped around the neck of Georgia. With this much water pouring into the navigable part of the river below Columbus, it would be too dangerous to travel at night.

"We'd best extend our visit."

Lily's stomach churned as her mother voiced the words she had been dreading as she watched the swirling water. "But–but, Mama, if we don't go back with the *Wave*—well, you know Papa will be wanting you home. . . ."

"Yes, I know he will." Mrs. Edwards wavered. "I don't know." She shook her head. "Perhaps we should wait for the next boat."

"But that will be days," Lily wailed.

"The river won't look this bad to you a few miles downstream," Laurie's husband soothed his nervous sister-in-law.

"I guess you're right. And we should be getting home."

Lily sighed in relief.

After they were packed and ready, Cordelia Edwards regretted her decision. "It's just too dangerous on the river," she said with her double chin shaking. "We'd better take the stagecoach home."

"Now, Mama," Lily swallowed hard, "you know how the lurching of the stagecoach ride always sets off your rheumatism, and the trip takes so much longer. On the boat you can stay in bed, and the current will have us home in no time."

Mrs. Edwards finally agreed that the luxury of modern travel outweighed the danger. They bid Columbus farewell at noon on Monday.

Cordelia Edwards remained in her cabin shedding nervous tears, but Lily wrapped a cashmere shawl about her head and shoulders and went on deck to savor the excitement. A young man rode on the bow watching for snags and rocks and changes in the river. Lily leaned far over the rail and watched anxiously as they approached a bridge that had floated off its piers. The day before, the *Cardinal* had struck it. With a hole in her hull, she had gone to pieces and sunk, leaving both submerged and floating debris waiting to entrap the *Wave*.

As the ship's master, Harrison was constantly checking with the mate, Captain Allen, and with the pilot at the wheel, the striker pilot, and the engineer. There was no time for conversation, but Lily reveled in the vitality. Watching a point of interest, and feeling a warmth upon her, she turned to see Harrison's dark eyes smiling his approval of her sparkle.

At suppertime, Lily ate hungrily of the lavish meal. She had repaired the wind damage to her hair and changed to her most becoming street toilet when the *Wave* reached the Eufaula wharf at seven o'clock.

A weary Harrison Wingate was on hand to speak to departing passengers. After he had taken Mrs. Edwards's hand and had been as gracious as possible, Lily extended her gloved fingers and spoke in a loud, firm voice.

"Thank you for a delightful voyage and for getting us here safely, Captain Wingate," she said pertly. Afraid to look at her mother, she continued in a voice that was far too loud, "We must repay you for your kindness. Won't you come and have supper with us tomorrow evening?"

Harrison hesitated, glancing at Mrs. Edwards, who merely pursed her lips and said nothing. Seeing that she was not intending to add her invitation, he squeezed Lily's hand and replied, "Thank you very kindly, Miss Lily. I would be delighted."

Papa waved, and Mama was too absorbed with meeting him and securing their trunks to scold her.

Unfortunately, Green had returned from his business trip inland. That greatly complicated the situation. Lily pretended weariness and stayed in her room all of the next day to avoid both Mama and Green, but she could hardly contain her excitement concerning Harrison.

That evening, she hovered nervously on the landing of the grand staircase, arranging and rearranging the flowers in the coffin niches to remain out of sight below the stairs but be on hand to greet Harrison. Glimpsing him striding toward the house, she floated down the stairs with her face alight with joy.

"Wingate, old man, what a surprise to see you!" Green moved from the corner of the veranda where he had been smoking.

"Nice to see you again," replied Harrison cordially. "I hope you've found enough local planters willing to sell you their fall crop."

Lily joined the men and tried to chat lightly, but nervous tears filled her throat. She squeezed her eyes to slits and looked at them. These were not two schoolboys with whom she was flirting in an effort to keep both interested. Unsuspecting, the friends talked amiably. Seemingly, they had no inkling that they were rivals.

Evidently, Mama had forgotten about her invitation to Harrison. Lily noticed out of the corner of her eye that when Mama was about to call them to supper, she went back to have another place set.

Lily picked at her food. She took little part in the lively conversation that flowed from Green's adventures on the frontier to Harrison's travels on the river. She sighed thankfully when the meal was over and Papa reached for his box of cigars.

By prearrangement, Emma engaged Cordelia Edwards in conversation about a household problem as the ladies were excused. Lily slipped away.

Stationing herself in the back hall near the servants' entrance to the dining room, Lily unashamedly eavesdropped.

Harrison cleared his throat. "Mr. Edwards, there's a matter I would speak with you about quite seriously, Sir."

"Yes? And what is that?" Mr. Edwards soft voice indicated that he was tired, satiated with food, and not ready for dilemmas.

"Well, Sir, I realize that you do not know me—I'll be glad to provide information about my family background, Sir. I. . ."

Lily strained forward, wondering what was happening in the uncomfortable silence. The cigar stench nearly made her retch.

"You see, Sir, I love your daughter very much," Harrison blurted. "I have reason to believe that she returns my affection. I wish to ask you for her hand in marriage."

Something crashed to the floor.

"Sir, I am shocked!" Mr. Edwards's voice rose in power. "You have taken advantage of our hospitality. You presume—surely you haven't taken advantage of my daughter?"

"You insult *me,* Sir!" Green shouted. "You betray our friendship even speaking the name of my intended bride!"

"Your intended? I didn't know. You told me you came here on business," Harrison stammered. "I'm sorry." His voice went limp. "You never mentioned her name. If I had known your intentions in the beginning, I would not have pressed my courtship, but now we are irrevocably in love."

Green growled angrily. "I had not rushed Miss Lily at her request." Green bit off each word with fury. "She said she was not ready for marriage, but I have been led to believe that as soon as she was ready, she would be mine."

"She has agreed to marry me, if you will give your permission, Mr. Edwards," Harrison said with quiet firmness. "I'm sorry my request has taken you by surprise."

Lily leaned her forehead against the doorjamb. Misery gripped her.

"Well. . .you must give me time to think about this, to speak with Mrs. Edwards. . ."

"Surely you wouldn't consider. . ." Green shouted. Then he lowered his voice so that Lily, who was clinging to the wall, could barely hear. "You shall be hearing from me formally, Sir. Through my second."

"Wait, friend." Harrison's voice had regained some of its usual calm strength. "We could not sully Miss Lily's name by anything so public as a duel."

"By no means," Green snarled, "but I say, Sir, that I was cheated at cards on your steamer."

Harrison laughed offhandedly. "And you, Sir, know that I warned you that gambler was a cheat, and you also know that the *Wave* bears a sign saying gentlemen who play cards for money play at their own risk." His voice became placating. "I'm sorry if I offended you—"

"I say you are a liar. This affair is now in the hands of the seconds!"

"So be it," Harrison returned grimly. "Thank you for the hospitality of your table, Mr. Edwards. Good night."

Lily ran into the dark yard and stumbled around the house to meet Harrison as he left, hat in hand. Tears streamed down her cheeks. They walked across the yard stiffly apart, too miserable to speak or to touch each other. When they reached the gate, he looked down at her sadly.

"I knew it would be bad," she sniffed. "But not this bad. I'm so sorry I couldn't prepare Papa, but I had no chance to see him without encountering Mama or Green."

His face blanched. "You should have told me about Green." Obviously feeling betrayed, he spoke gruffly, full of hurt.

"Oh, I should have, I should have, but I don't think of him at all when I'm with you," she wailed. "Believe me. I never cared for him. He doesn't love me. It was all Mama's plans. Papa knew I didn't want to marry him."

"But you let them think that you would."

The dead sound of his voice made her drop her face in her hands. He did nothing to comfort her weeping.

"I was wrong," she gulped, fighting for control. "I see it now. I thought only of myself." She tried to lean against him, but he stood back stiffly. "I have tried to tell them all, but I'm expected to do as I'm told. Oh, I was so afraid for a moment that Green might have a sword concealed in that cane of his. He might have killed you!"

"You are a child." He laughed sardonically. "Nowadays swords are used only in New Orleans—yes, he fancies New Orleans—but the elite do not dive into the fray. The Code Duello is a highly ritualized affair that has only begun. I shall receive a written challenge delivered by his second." He sighed wearily.

"But you can't believe in dueling," she wailed. "For years sermons have been preached, laws have been passed. . ."

"You know very well that all of the laws have carried no more enforcement than the sermons." Again he laughed in bitter irony. "Of course, I don't believe in dueling—but there's nothing that I can do. I must accept his challenge."

"If you left for awhile," she wailed. Even as she said it, she knew she could not bear his going.

"No!" He shook his head grimly. "He might resort to posting, naming me as a villain and a coward in an advertisement in the newspapers. I couldn't have your name. . ."

"I don't care about my name!" she cried out. "I only care about you!" She flung herself against his chest.

Stiffly, his arms closed around her. For a moment he clung to her with longing, then he stroked her hair gently and said as if speaking to a child, "Well-known men fight duels every day. Many of them are bloodless. Duels only become famous if they're fatal—now scoot. Back in the house with you before your father comes after me, too." His laugh sounded false to both of them as he turned her around.

Her steps dragged as she trudged back to the house. The huge, white mansion was ablaze with light. It appeared that every candle in every chandelier and wall sconce was lit. There was no place to hide from her misery.

Chapter 7

Lily stepped into pandemonium. Mama had fainted. Screeching, Kitty ran about flapping her apron. Muttering ugly words, Green stamped down the black-and-white marble hall.

Lily clung to the doorjamb and waited until he had gone out the rear door. Her anxious fingers crumpled her handkerchief as her nerves were shredded.

Papa. Surely she could count on Papa to understand. He sat apart, sunk into his chair with both hands clapped over his bald head. Kneeling beside him, she patted his hand.

"Oh, Papa," she cried. "I should have prepared you, but you were gone all day, and I was afraid that—"

"You knew about this, then?"

"Yes, Papa. I love Harrison. I want to be his wife."

"You're a child. Do you have any idea what kind of men run riverboats?" His voice croaked, then rose in indignation. "They are full of swaggering bravado. They make a noisy exit from the wharf only to round the next bend and meet an ignominious end with everything they own crushed on a shoal of rock!"

"I know that steering a vessel through a twisting channel takes forthright determination," she said through clenched teeth. "But Harrison takes safety precautions and the gamble is worth the risk," she pleaded. "This modern world can't wait to move in a horse and wagon. I like being part of the excitement."

"It's out of the question!" Mama's angry voice made them jump. "No daughter of mine will marry a common riverboat gambler."

"He's not a gambler," Lily bristled.

"What would Laurie think!" Cordelia wailed and feigned another faint. Kitty ran in with smelling salts.

"Papa, Harrison is a fine, Christian man. The kind I want for my husband. I do not want to marry Green!"

"But we have let him think that you would," he answered resignedly. "His personal honor is at stake, and—"

"Surely, you don't condone dueling!" She bowed her head on his knee, then looked up at him with pleading eyes. "You must stop it!"

"Stronger men than I have tried to stop dueling ever since Burr killed Hamilton." He sighed wearily. "But when men in high office—even our presidents—feel they must live by this Code of Honor, what's to be done?"

"Much can be said in its favor." Mama's voice was sharp. Her moment of weakness had passed.

"Mama!" Lily exclaimed, shocked.

"The knowledge that a man will be called to account for false words or affronts to one's character—such as this social climber has made to you—are well guarded by the Code Duello." Cordelia Edwards's mouth was drawn down sternly and her double chins were firmly set. "Most girls your age would gladly risk the loss of a husband to have a hero in the family."

Lily tore at her hair. She turned pleading eyes to Papa, who merely sat there rubbing his hand over his head.

"We will let Green take care of the intruder." Mrs. Edwards spoke with finality. "We shall not speak of it again!"

Lily fled in a storm of tears. In utter loneliness, she lay on her bed. Her wrenching sobs would subside momentarily only to freshen and wrack her again. When she could cry no more, she tiptoed down the hidden stairway and slipped out the doorway to the back porch.

The door to Green's room stood open. Silhouetted in the candlelight, he was cleaning a pair of wooden-handled, long-barreled pistols.

Hesitantly, she knocked, being careful not to further disgrace herself by stepping inside his room.

He looked up in surprise. With a glinty-eyed grimace, he came to the door and waved a gun under her nose. "These pistols were made in London by Wogdon. The balance is superb. Your honor will soon be avenged."

"No, Green, not for me—please." Weak and disheveled, she leaned against the porch wall.

"Your name won't enter in," he quickly assured her. "My challenge," he motioned toward the desk where pen and paper indicated that the note was already written, "merely names him a liar and a cheat."

"Oh, Green!" She fought a wave of nausea. "I'm sorry! I should have explained it to you first." She sighed heavily. "You were gone when I told him to come."

"You told him—you knew?" His sulky face bent close over hers. "You were promised to me."

"No. I never told you. I never said—"

"Not in words. But in actions."

She buried her face in her hands. "Yes, I admit it. It seemed as though we should make a perfect match—but—I can't help it. I fell in love with Harrison."

"You have insulted me." He drew himself up pompously. "I will forgive you if word never gets outside this house that you allowed him to ask for you."

But you would never let me forget it, Lily thought. Sadly, hopelessly, she climbed the stairs to her room. Foy. The thought flickered in her deadened brain. She dragged herself up to the belvedere.

He was there with his hurricane lamp. The fact that he was reading one of Sir Walter Scott's novels of chivalric derring-do made her know he was well aware that the gauntlet had been thrown down.

"One or both of them might be killed, you know," the owl-eyed little boy said matter-of-factly.

"Oh, Foy, I've begged them all. I can't stop the duel. Help me. Find out everything. Maybe I can stop them at the last minute."

"You know that can't be done, Sister," he replied as if he were the elder.

"I know. But I must be there."

The next day, she remained in bed, rising only to receive Foy's reports of the progress of the ritual.

Scratching lightly on Foy's bedroom door, Lily waited only a moment before he slipped out and joined her in the dark hallway. Grimacing, she knew he had slept little during the long night either. She had spent most of it on her knees, claiming her Lord's promise to be with her through trials. Tired, yet seized with a frenzied excitement, she followed Foy down the hidden staircase. In the intense darkness before dawn, they felt their way to the stables and saddled their horses. Forcing themselves to walk slowly, they led the horses down the driveway past their parents' bedroom before they mounted.

"I don't know how I could have stood this without you, Foy," Lily said sorrowfully.

The boy said nothing, but slowly and purposefully he straightened his slumped shoulders and sat erect in his saddle.

The night had cooled little from the hundred degrees of the previous day. Lily's riding habit, soaked with perspiration, felt sticky in the humid darkness. In all of her eighteen years, she had never been so miserable.

Although word of the duel had only been whispered around Eufaula, Foy had easily learned of the appointed place, a secluded clearing on the banks of the Chattahoochee just across the county line. A ring of huge oak trees thickly hung with ghostly gray beards of Spanish moss sheltered the spot from prying eyes.

When Lily dismounted, her knees buckled. With her face as gray as her pearly riding habit, she tethered Prince, who was lathered with salty sweat. Summoning all of her strength, she crept to a spot behind a thick-trunked oak where she could peer out without being seen. Draped on the spreading branches, shrouds of Spanish moss shivered as they breathed the life-giving, humid air. Of matching color with the hairlike plant, Lily blended in a blur, swaying with it.

Flat on his stomach, Foy slithered closer.

A group of men had already assembled. Moving about on springing feet, Green stood out from the rest in his slim, doeskin trousers and white, ruffled shirt.

Harrison arrived. Lily's heart lurched at the sight of his sagging face. Would he ever forgive her for putting him in this awful position? Teardrops rolled unnoticed down her cheeks. Idly, she wondered why he wore such a large, ill-fitting coat in this heat. The two participants stood apart from the rest at the far ends of the clearing.

Captain Allen went forward as Harrison's second to inspect the flintlock pistols. He carried the leather case to Wingate, who deliberated, then lifted one of the pistols that had a barrel fully fifteen inches long. Evidently, Green was granting a trial shot. Allen placed a small paper on a tree. Harrison raised the heavy pistol heavenward then slowly, deliberately aimed and fired.

"Whew!" Foy whistled. He scrambled back to Lily. "He's a crack shot! Maybe we don't have to worry."

Lily gritted her teeth, knowing that speed counted as much as accuracy. Harrison was Foy's unquestioned champion, but a sudden surge of affection for her cousin, heightened by the knowledge that she had wronged him, made her realize that she did not want his blood spilt either.

Clenching both fists over her mouth to keep herself from screaming, Lily watched the ritual proceed with excruciating precision. The seconds flipped a coin high in the air. Green won the toss. He fixed positions. Lily bit her fist savagely when Harrison moved as directed until his black coat was silhouetted sharply against the crimson streaks of dawn as the sun rose behind the Chattahoochee and turned it red as blood. Silently, the adversaries met back-to-back.

"One, two," the giver of the word counted slowly, "three, four." With guns down at their sides, they paced stiffly. "Five, six, seven, eight, nine, ten. Fire!"

Blat!

The short, harsh sound echoed and reechoed through the forest. Eyes shut, Lily swayed. Slowly, she realized there had been only one shot. She opened her eyes. Acrid smoke curled from Green's pistol. She jerked toward Harrison. He still stood. Unflinching, he held his gun down at his side.

Green stared at him, recoiling.

"Back to the mark, Sir!" cried the man who was giver of the word.

Green folded his arms. Head up, he stood defiantly, waiting.

Harrison raised his gun slowly, deliberately. Aimed. There was a hollow "click" as the hammer stopped at half-cock. Swiftly, he lifted it over his head and fired into the air. Lily sank to the ground.

Green was angry, still demanding satisfaction. She knew that the Code Duello allowed three, but no more, encounters. Lying prostrate on the damp ground, Lily felt she could not bear it again. The men returned to opposite sides, and the seconds marched forward.

Green's second shouted his message, "Turn and shoot. Providence will favor truth and right with victory."

Allen spoke quietly but in ringing tones, "Captain Wingate has no desire to harm you. You are entitled to kill him, but he wronged you unknowingly. He does not want your blood on his hands, nor his on yours. He will shoot the sky."

Lily could not breathe as the terrible pacing off began again.

"Gentlemen, are you ready?"

"Ready," replied Green.

"Yes, Sir," said Harrison.

"Fire!"

Blat!

One shot. Lily blinked. Harrison had fired quickly upward. Green snarled, then shot quickly. Harrison's gun dropped. Blood spurted from his arm. Blood was spilt. Green had satisfaction. It was over. Lily retched violently.

The attending surgeon rushed to Harrison's side. Lily longed to run to him, but she dared not be seen. She silently pressed her initialed handkerchief into Foy's hand. The child's crumpled face twitched back tears. He skittered after Harrison, who was departing into the mossy mists of morning. Stiffening in surprise, he took the token, turned, looked back, but could not see her.

Glumly, brother and sister remounted and headed toward Barbour Hall. Halfway home, they dismounted, wept in each other's arms, then finished the ride in silence. With day fully broken, their disappearance had been discovered. Furious, Mama forbade them to leave the grounds until further notice.

Emma came to Lily's bedside, bathed her face with cold cloths, and coaxed her to sip a cooling drink. She reported that Green had exiled himself to New Orleans for a decent interval, but she could secure no word of Harrison.

As soon as Lily recovered somewhat, she thought of Foy and how disappointed he must be in his champion. He might even think Harrison a coward for not fighting more conventionally.

Weakly, she climbed to the belvedere where Foy sat in kingly exile poring over his books.

"Foy, I'm sorry. Were you terribly disappointed in Captain Wingate?"

He surprised her by grinning happily. "I was at first. I wanted him to kill that Green," he said emphatically. "But," he nodded sagely, "that would have been wrong. After I thought about it, I realized that what he did took a lot more courage."

She nodded solemnly.

"And Green—for all his talk of honor—broke his own code."

Lily's eyebrows lifted quizzically.

"Yes. You see, it frequently happens that an honorable man who accepts a challenge will fire into the air." He paused, proud of his superior knowledge. "It is then held scandalous for the other party to fire again."

"Well!" she exclaimed. "But I guess Green just couldn't be satisfied without drawing blood. Oh, Foy, I've just got to know how Captain Wingate is. I must see him!"

"I'll slip out when Mama takes her nap."

"You'll risk a thrashing!"

Foy shrugged.

Harrison's scowl and the grim set of his lips as he moved uncertainly from behind the stables and walked across the back garden made Lily retreat behind a pink fountain of crepe myrtle blossoms and shut her eyes to steady herself. Taking a deep breath, she shyly stepped into view. The air between them shimmered with rising waves of heat, blurring her tearful vision.

A smile lifted his whole body. He caught his breath as he had the first time he saw her. Needing nothing more, she ran to meet him, unmindful of her wildly tilting hoop.

At his side she stopped, suddenly feeling unmaidenly. "Oh, Harrison, you looked so angry with me just now."

"What?" He reached out tentatively to touch her shoulder. "Oh, I just felt awkward—I don't like deception, but Foy said to meet you back by the ha-ha wall."

"I'm sorry." She bowed her head. Shyness overwhelmed her again. "My family was so awful to you. I'm sorry." Gingerly, she stretched out one finger to the sling on his right arm. "Is it bad?"

"A mere nick." He shrugged, and then had to hide the flicker of pain the gesture gave him.

"You shouldn't have gone." His voice was gruff with emotion. "I was afraid you wouldn't want to see me again."

"Why?" she exclaimed, incredulous.

"I'm sure I didn't fulfill your daydreams of a knight in shining armor. And Foy. I know I disillusioned him."

"Huh," she snorted. "Couldn't you look at the sparkle in his eyes and know he thought you're the bravest man he's ever seen?"

He smiled. "And you?"

She cocked her head to one side saucily. "I'm not sure whether I think you're brave or foolhardy. How could you risk your life just standing there taking his first fire?"

"Well." He grinned sheepishly. "I did take the precaution of wearing an ill-fitting coat—hoping he'd misjudge the position of my heart."

"Oh, my dearest darling, he might have killed you." Lily melted against him, burying her face on his chest as the restraint between them dissolved.

Harrison's strong left arm tightened around her. He kissed the top of her dark curls. She lifted her face to him with eyes full of love and stood on tiptoe to meet his tender kiss.

Too filled with emotion to speak further, they silently strolled along the path by the ha-ha wall.

Harrison broke the silence at last. "I understand Green is gone."

"Yes," she murmured from deep within a dream. Rousing herself, she added, "Foy says he broke his own precious ritual by shooting you after you had fired into the air."

"Yes. That went against the code." He stopped and looked down at her and said earnestly, "But, you must understand, I impugned his honor. He belongs to a dueling society. He wanted to draw blood, but he's not as bad as you think." He seemed to want to clear his friend. "He purposely winged me. If he had wanted to, he could have killed me easily. His Code Duello means everything to—"

Lily shuddered. "I'm glad you live by a higher code," she said simply.

Harrison chuckled. "It's one not easy to follow. I wanted to shoot him, sweep you into my arms, and carry you away," he admitted ruefully. "I struggled all night. Loving one's enemy is not impossible, but turning your cheek from an insult—I'd never realized how difficult that is. But I kept on hearing a quiet voice in my head saying, 'Turn the other cheek.' " He laughed self-consciously. "It's hard. Green's insults are still ringing in my ears. But I'll survive that." He shrugged. "I couldn't let him make me a murderer."

"I'm afraid I'll never be as completely submissive to the lordship of Christ as you are."

Embarrassed at her praise, he changed the subject. "What do we do now? Is there any chance that your parents will accept me after this?"

"Oh, there must be, there must be," she cried. "I'll speak to them at supper. Can you meet me back here at dusk?"

Sadly, they parted, knowing that the next few hours would stretch interminably between them.

Unable to eat a bite, Lily pled her love for Harrison.

"It is totally out of the question!" Cordelia Edwards banged her fork vehemently. "You have behaved like a spoiled child, and I will tolerate no more insolence. You will do exactly—"

"We will not discuss it further," Papa said firmly, surprising them both as he stepped into control of the conversation. "Lily, you promised you would not do as my cousin Lucinda did."

"No, Papa." She bowed her dark head. "I won't break with you and Mama. I won't run away and marry without your blessing."

Harrison found her at the back of the garden, crying. He lifted her chin and made her smile up at him. He dropped his lips to hers lightly, tenderly. "Is there no hope?"

She drew a long, shuddering sigh and shook her head.

He stroked her dark, disheveled curls away from her face. "They don't even know me. We rushed them too much! If only we had more time, but I must go away." His usually smiling face sagged with a pain that matched her own.

"Oh, no!" She sank weakly into the curve of his sheltering arm.

"It's best for now. Was your father's answer an absolute refusal?"

"Mama's was, but Papa—maybe he will be more open," she mumbled. She lifted her head from his shoulder and looked into his eyes. "Oh, Harrison, you do understand?" she pleaded. "I love you and I want to be your wife, but I cannot flagrantly disobey my parents. It wouldn't be right just to run away and marry." Her soulful eyes beseeched him.

"Yes," he answered quietly. "It hurts, but I do understand." He drew himself up with a dignity that built a wall between them.

"Oh, Harrison, love me, love me. There must be a way," she wailed. "Give me time," she begged, stroking his smooth, tanned cheek. "They will change. They must change!"

"I'll wait for you, my darling, but each day will be an eternity." He kissed her tear-streaked face.

Silently, hand in hand, they paced the back of the garden. The beautiful view was unbroken as they gazed sadly across the meadow. It looked as if they could walk on forever; nevertheless, they had come to the end of Lily's domain. Even though the view was unspoiled, the ha-ha wall was at their feet. Built down in a ditch so that it was unseen, the wall kept wild animals that roamed loose out of the flower garden.

Harrison took both her hands and pressed kisses upon them. "Please write to me."

"Oh, I will. And you write. In my name. I won't deceive them anymore."

"I must go now. We're scheduled to sail at daylight. You'll come?"

"I can't. But I'll be watching."

He kissed her tenderly, pouring out his heart's longing. The darkness closed around them, and for a moment they existed in the world alone. She breathed a shuddering sigh, and the heavy perfume of the tea olive made the bittersweetness of her love almost too much to bear.

Sunlight, turning the belvedere windows into diamonds, dazzled her swollen eyes. Lily knew that the height made Emma dizzy, but it helped a great deal to have her friend standing with her. Tears streamed down Emma's pale cheeks as she shared Lily's heartbreak and relived her own.

Uhmmmm! Uhmmmm! It had never sounded so mournful. Black smoke, floating above the treetops, drifted down the Chattahoochee.

"Oh, Emma, that graveyard of a river is between us again. Please, God, don't let it be forever." She dropped her head on Emma's shoulder and sobbed.

Chapter 8

Frustrated, Lily paced the garden throughout the lonely days that followed. She would walk as far as the ha-ha wall and stand gazing sadly into the meadow where the cattle and deer roamed wild and free. This unseen barrier was an illusion. It appeared that the garden was without the usual fence to keep out the cattle that foraged at will; however, Lily knew that only her level gaze could continue into openness. Below her feet, a wide ditch had been dug. Wild things could wander in and out of the ditch; but a solid wall, erected against the garden side, defeated them from tasting the flowers.

A bitter sensation rising in her throat made her give up her walks and return to her old haunt above the treetops in the belvedere. There she could see the course of the river punctuated by white puffs from the steamboats plying its muddy waters. With her body rigid, she stood on the widow's walk, but her spirit floated away on a raft of daydreams.

Mama and Papa eyed her warily. Whenever she walked into the room, their bodies stiffened with tension, their hands dropped straight to their sides, and their darting eyes stated plainly that there was no way to bridge the gap.

With their demeanor totally isolating her, she was sustained only by her daily vigil for a letter. At last it came. Feeling alive again, she ran up the six flights of stairs to the privacy of the belvedere before she opened the message from her sweetheart. Kissing the signature, she closed her eyes and imagined him sitting in his cabin on the lofty hurricane deck, smiling with a crinkle around his eyes as he thought of her. Her finger traced his words and, love warmed, stroked her cheek as she read.

July 19, 1858
Along the Chattahoochee

Darling Lily,

I write this hoping I may be able to send it sometime this week by a vessel sailing your way, as I so greatly wish that I could be. My receiving your letters will be uncertain, but please write to me. I will be in the city of Columbia, Alabama, for several days and in Apalachicola, Florida, for as much as a week.

I am terribly lonesome for you. I will not ask you to go against your parents, for I know that would not follow your principles. I love the beauty of your character and soul even more than the loveliness of your face, which always floats before me. Please send me a picture so that I may feel I am touching you.

What can I do to plead my case with your mother? No one could ever take better care of you than I. I love you so much and long for the day that I can call you my wife.

The gentleman who is to carry this letter has just come up and says he must go immediately. Give my love to Emma.

God bless you.

I love you dearly.

Harrison H. Wingate

Reading and rereading his letter, Lily realized that Harrison did not understand the reason for her parents' refusal of their marriage. For this much she was glad. Throughout the day, as she carried the letter about with her, touching it to feel Harrison near, she felt happy and warm. Even though the question of his social class had no solution, she was not of the temperament to give up and spend her time weeping hopelessly. Before she went to bed that night, she kissed the letter again and carefully placed it beneath her pillow. In the morning she read the letter again. Then she surreptitiously lifted the pin that secured the secret drawer in the rosewood lap desk and lovingly placed the letter inside.

Lily eagerly waited for an opportunity to go to the daguerrean gallery to have a likeness taken. At last, her chance to go downtown came when Emma had to visit the dentist to have a tooth filled. Remembering the most approving light in Harrison's eyes had been when she wore the white organdy with its frothy ruffles, she donned that frock and arranged her hair in soft curls. After sitting six times before the big box camera, she got a pleasing likeness. The stiff daguerreotype, on silver plate, showed the fine details of her dress and the printing on the little hymnbook she held in her hand. She could hardly wait to send the picture and the book to Harrison.

Several days later while the girls were shopping, they heard that Julian McKenzie would be leaving on the *Laura* the next morning. Excitedly, Lily hurried home because she knew that she could send her letter and package by him. Tilting her head for a moment of thought, she began to pour out her heart.

July 30, 1858
Eufaula, Alabama

I expect, Captain Wingate, that you have concluded ere this that I do not intend writing. I heard in town that the Laura *will be leaving tomorrow, and I could at last find opportunity to send you the likeness and my love.*

My heart aches that I was such a thoughtless child to allow you to walk into the lion's den unprepared. I should have managed some way to tell Papa. I suppose I expected them to capitulate immediately, seeing that my happiness is at stake. Perhaps I am growing up a little, for after many tears, I am beginning to understand that they think they have my best interest at heart.

Alas! I know not how to change their minds.

You are constantly in my thoughts. So strongly do I imagine myself beside you on the boat that I can almost feel the wind in my hair. I envy you the excitement. My days are quiet. I attend prayer meeting and church services, make social calls in the afternoon, and take long walks. I go frequently to the graveyard beside the little stream that winds its way below our house. 'Tis a lovely, quiet retreat. It offers peace and solitude and seems to fit my mood. While there, I am engaged in reading Grace Truman with much interest.

At night, I vie with Foy for the use of the belvedere. There I pray for you. May the Lord keep you safe from the dangers which beset you. My dearest friend, we must also pray that God will make a way for us to become man and wife.

Good-bye.

Yours, Lily

Lily's spirits rose as she sent the tangible evidence of her love on its way. She was singing, "O Happy Day that Fixed My Choice," when she reentered Barbour Hall. Seated in the parlor, Mr. and Mrs. Edwards looked up in surprise at her sudden merriment.

Snatching at the chance, Lily greeted them, "Good afternoon, Papa, Mama." She nodded politely. "Please, may I speak with you?" Her mother started to shake her head, but Lily hurried on, "I know that you want the best for me, and I appreciate the wisdom of your advice." Her voice trembled. "But I'm old enough now to know what I want to do with my life."

Cordelia Edwards was taking in breath, swelling with indignation. Her husband surprised her by speaking first.

"Marriage is too important to be entrusted to youth, Lily dear," Clare Edwards said gently. "You have been carried away by love and passion just as surely as young Foy has by this dashing figure who seems to lead such an exciting life, but—"

"Matrimony is the royal road to wealth and social advancement," her mother interrupted. "Such essential matters must be left with the parents. We will discuss it no more."

"But, Mama. . ."

"Don't talk back to me."

Lily swallowed, trying desperately to hold a shred of adulthood, but tears seemed to be rising from her toes and filling her whole body.

Haughtily, Mrs. Edwards stood too quickly. Groaning, she clutched her back but continued speaking firmly. "The minute Green returns, we will announce your engagement to him. We must move quickly to arrest any breath of scandal. We cannot have anyone whispering about your indiscreet behavior!"

Stunned, Lily stared at one, then the other; they presented an unrelenting wall. She fled in a storm of tears.

Lily spent many hours sobbing on her bed. Pale and listless, she moved through the ensuing days not knowing or caring what she did. She existed only for another letter. When she received one, her joy turned to sorrow at Harrison's deep hurting, and her eyes were shining with tears as she read.

July 29, 1858
Columbia, Alabama

My sweet Lily,

Another vessel in today and no letter for me. Why have you not written? I am blue, very blue indeed, afraid you might have changed your mind. Do you wish to obey your parents and forget me? I believed you when you said you truly loved me. Oh, how I hope it is merely lack of mail arrangements. Send letters to McKenzie or Atkins & Durrham to be forwarded whenever vessels leave. Numerous vessels have arrived and not one word for me.

I wish that you could see Columbia with me. As the boat docks, the passengers are called to the steamer deck to see the "chocolate layer cake," a huge rock that so resembles one. The rock marks the port of Columbia. It is a hub of the wire grass section. People coming to Columbia for freight and supplies are provided with a camping enclosure for their wagons and livestock. Many sleep in the covered wagons while waiting for their shipments. It is a scene of much activity and excitement that you would enjoy very much.

Do I fool myself in thinking that you would? I know you have been raised a lady, sheltered from the common people. Did I take advantage of your youth and the romance of the moonlight upon the water to dare to kiss you and dream you could be mine?

You will break my heart if you say this is so, but knowing would be better than wondering.

Please write soon.

I love you dearly.

H.H.W.

Frantic at his words and her inability to communicate with him, Lily enlisted the aid of Foy. Daily, she had lessened fighting with him and chasing him when he shot chinaberries at her with a popgun made from a hollowed elder branch. Now she saw him daily as her only ally. The boy had more freedom than she to roam the riverfront. He gladly agreed to take a letter for her and thought he could manage to get it off immediately.

August 10, 1858
Eufaula, Alabama

My heart breaks, Captain Wingate, that you doubt me. Surely you know my love for you is true and everlasting! I long to share your life. How I would enjoy meeting people from different environments and learning more about this world and God's creatures.

I hope by now you have received my letters and are recovered from the "blues." You might have known that I had written. Did I not promise to do so? I will write you every week, but right now there are only two boats running regularly between here and Apalachicola, and very often I do not know when they are here. Brother Foy has come to my aid in getting letters off to you as he admires you more than any man he has ever seen.

Mama is suffering from rheumatism. Papa sent to Hamilton, Georgia, to a physician there, for some medicine that cured a lady worse off than Mama. I do hope that it may have some good effect on her, for I hate to cross her with her suffering so.

Good night.

Yours, Lily

As she reread the letter and added kisses to the signature, she could imagine her mother's reaction if she should intercept their love letters. Although she was not hiding the fact that she was corresponding with Captain Wingate, she knew that her parents would continue to disapprove of him merely because he possessed no wealth or prominence. A person's family name meant everything to Mama.

The temperature was already in the eighties soon after the sun rose. Emma had not tried to comfort Lily during her restless night. Now she looked at her with compassion in her soft, blue eyes.

"Let's slip out before anyone sees us and take a walk," whispered Emma. "This day is really going to steam."

"Yes, I'd like to get away." Lily sighed. She pushed up her long hair that was already wet against her neck and caught it in a silken net. "It's so hot. Don't you think I could leave off one petticoat?"

"No," Emma responded quickly. "If your mother thought I wasn't making you behave like a lady—Lily, the only joy in my life comes from being with you."

Sighing, Lily agreed. Hats in hand, they tiptoed out of the house. They walked in silence as they followed the winding stream until they reached the seclusion of the family graveyard.

"Oh, Emma, what must I do? I love my parents. I respect their advice. I don't want to rush into the wrong thing." She took off her hat and fanned at a pesky swarm of gnats. The heat-heightened colors and scents of the wildflowers and buzzing of the insects seemed to press in upon her.

"I don't know how to advise you," Emma replied. "I only know that my grandfather never relented." She bowed her blond head sadly. Holding onto the cold, marble shaft of a monument, she continued so softly that Lily had to lean toward her to hear. "You can see for yourself what became of my life."

"I don't believe Mama and Papa will ever give their permission either." Lily's voice was flat, devoid of hope. "I promised Papa I would not break with them and marry without their blessing." She had cried until there were no more tears. She felt dry to her soul.

They wandered through the graveyard and back to the stream. Lily cleared a spot on the bank and sat down with her skirt mushrooming around her. The little creek was nearly dry, and Lily had to reach far down to cool her fingers in the sparkling water which bubbled from a nearby spring.

"It's thrilling to be loved by a man who faces his life with so much strength and courage. I enjoy being cherished." Her face was pale and she lifted tortured eyes to Emma. "Do you think I could learn to fit into his world?"

"I don't know." Emma shook her head. She was too afraid of snakes to go near the refreshing water. She stood leaning against the rough bark of a tall pine. Her expression showed concern. "I wish I could advise you, but it really depends on what kind of person you are deep down."

Lily's lower lip trembled. "Knowing my parents won't agree, do you think that if I really love him enough to put him first. . ." She swallowed hard, almost unable to voice the words. "Does it mean I should set him free?"

Emma picked up a rock and threw it into the water. "That was the choice I made," she said bitterly.

"But wasn't your case a little different?" Lily lifted quizzical eyebrows. "For love to last in a marriage, it should be based on both partners' love of God."

"That's true, but if I hadn't been forbidden to see him, might I not have led him to accept Jesus as his personal Savior?"

"Possibly, but important changes in a person's life should come before a marriage commitment is made. I believe God ordained marriage as a permanent basis for building a Christian home. Oh, Emma." She wrung her wet fingers. "As hard as it was, you could not go back on your faith in Christ or your duty to your family. But I can't see what I should do. What changes must I make within myself?"

As they trudged back home, the still, August air lay heavily upon them. Red dust from the road plastered their sticky skin. Kitty had been sent to find them and summon them to Mama's bedside. Lily spoke to her crossly. The long-limbed girl's ebony face drooped with hurt because Lily was usually kind. Lily hurried obediently to do her mother's bidding.

The three presented themselves meekly at the huge master bedroom at the rear of the second floor. Cordelia Edwards lay in a massive bed with straight walnut posts lifting a high, thronelike canopy. All the shutters were swung over the windows, and the girls strained to adjust their eyes to the shadowy room.

Gasping with pain and clutching her neck and back as she tried to sit up among the many pillows, Mrs. Edwards told the girls they would have to take over her duties until the spell of acute rheumatism subsided. She instructed Emma in handling the servants and gave her the set of keys. She did not relinquish this emblem of her domain lightly. Normally, Cordelia Edwards rose from her bed long before any of her servants and rested only on the Sabbath.

Looking then to Lily, she said, "You must make a condolence call for me. Mrs. Pugh has lost a lovely babe, the fourth or fifth she has buried."

"Yes, Ma'am," Lily replied and turned immediately to do her bidding. Her mother was a good woman who was always on hand whenever a need arose in the community.

"And, oh, yes," Mrs. Edwards called after her, "stop by Mrs. Morrison's house. I heard this morning of her extreme illness. She has long been suffering from consumption."

As Lily proceeded toward her sad errands, she foresaw her mother as an invalid who would constantly need her. She would expect Lily to carry out the

Christian service she had begun. Lily well knew that girls in her station were always expected to sacrifice their happiness cheerfully if their parents needed them at home. Sighing, she also knew that the blessing to marry Harrison would never come. Squaring her shoulders, she resigned herself to the life of a spinster, remaining in her mother's house, for she would not marry Green. She would have to stay at home; she must write and tell Harrison. This was the only course open to her. She loved Harrison so much that she must put his welfare first. It would not be fair to keep him hoping. He could find someone else. She had no choice but to write Harrison and set him free.

First, she must do her mother's bidding. After freshening her appearance, she started down the street with Kitty in attendance. Arriving at the Morrison house first, she stood trembling in the circle of friends assembled around the bed. She did not feel prepared to be with this group of older ladies watching Mrs. Morrison's struggles with death. The woman spoke weakly but firmly to them of the great importance of a preparation for death and her perfect willingness to go to God. As she breathed out her life sweetly, Lily left the room sobbing. Released by what she had witnessed, her tears flowed for her own life. It seemed equally at an end.

Feeling that she could stand no more but doggedly determined to do as she was told, she continued to the two-story clapboard home on Randolph Avenue built by United States Senator James L. Pugh. The pall of death was thrown over this home also. Clammy and miserable, Lily walked across the wide porch.

As she started across the entrance hall, a child about eighteen months old toddled toward her. With dancing blue eyes and a smile that spread her plump cheeks, she lifted tiny arms to Lily. Scooping her up spontaneously, Lily was welcomed with a huge hug. She kissed the adorable curls and handed the child a brown-eyed Susan she had idly plucked.

"Thank coo," her tiny voice crooned. She struggled free of Lily's arms and started away in an uncertain, tottering step that made Lily want to help her. "Ma-ma," she excitedly called, "Ma-ma. Flower."

Lily followed her into the twin parlors. Not knowing what to say to the grieving mother, she hoped her presence expressed her sympathy. Even though this visit was also sad, the vibrant joy of this surviving child entranced Lily. She left smiling, but the smile faded as she realized that the only way she would have children to love would be teaching a Sunday school class as Emma did. Emma's life was over. Now, her life was over, too.

Her spirits sank further as she returned past the Morrison house. She would have to go back later to help write the funeral invitations and affix the black ribbons so that they could be hand-carried to friends on surrounding plantations. For now, she must report back to her mother.

Released at last, she went to her room and sat at her desk gritting her teeth. She must write before she lost her resolve to put Harrison's welfare ahead of the happiness she gained from simply knowing he loved her.

Tears splattered the paper as she told Harrison that she would not marry him. She pressed her hands to her temples and pulled at her hair, making it stand out wildly. Ink smeared her cheeks as she wrestled with the longings of her heart. At last, she wrote firmly that she released him from any promises to her. Sealing the letter, she went in search of Foy.

The small boy looked at her with his mouth gaping foolishly and waited for a second command before he replied, "Yes, there's a steamer due in today. I was on my way to the wharf now."

Lily gulped back tears and nodded wordlessly as she handed him the letter. She turned and fled up the stairs to the seclusion of the belvedere. Just as she climbed through to the top, she saw a carriage arriving.

Out stepped Green Bethune.

Chapter 9

"Oh, no. Not now," she wailed aloud. Hoping he had not looked up and seen her, she scurried down the narrow passageway to her room. Her image in the looking glass surprised her. Tear streaks made roads on her face through valleys of attic dust and ink. She washed thoroughly at her lavatory. By the time she had brushed her hair, Emma arrived to say the family was assembled and summoning her.

Sedately, she descended the stairs and extended her hand to Green. Averting her eyes from his, she looked toward the parlor and blinked in surprise. Three wooden barrels were set undecorously in the middle of the room. Their tops had been removed, and straw was spilling everywhere.

"Lily, Honey, I've brought you some wedding gifts from New Orleans," Green spoke exuberantly, his bearded face beaming.

"My goodness," she breathed, moving mechanically to steady herself against the white marble fireplace. The huge Belgian mirror reflected a scene of gaiety, as Mama and Papa opened their presents. Lily traced her finger over the Sèvres vase and tried to grasp the situation. The flattery her parents were pouring as oil upon Green's head and his responsive laughter spoke clearly to Lily. Her life had been decided for her. They had all dismissed her love for Harrison as a young girl's folly.

Emma stood apart from the group. *Harrison would have brought her a present, too,* Lily thought. Knowing she must forget him, she allowed Green to lead her to the small Chippendale settee where he sat close beside her and handed her one package after another. Numb, feeling that she viewed the scene without really being there, she pressed her spine against the carved mahogany leaves and scrolls of the back and gritted her teeth. She opened endless gifts and tried valiantly to show proper appreciation.

Streaks of rose washed over the Georgian silver fruit basket she held in her lap. Lily gazed sadly out of the tall windows. The day had spent itself along with her tears. Her dreams had died. Suddenly her girlhood seemed over. Daydreams must give way to practicality. She felt unbelievably old.

Dinner was announced. The glittering prisms of the chandeliers made her tired eyes ache. The chicken and dumplings did not appeal to her. Green ate voraciously of the heavy, greasy food and talked excitedly of his Western tour. He spoke in the sweeping, positive statements of one accustomed to being told he was right and granted every whim.

Suddenly, she realized that everyone was looking at her expectantly, waiting for her to reply. "Who—what did you say?"

"I said," Green repeated, "that I found New Orleans enchanting. It would be a perfect place to begin our honeymoon."

"But, I. . . ," Lily began. She must put a stop to this, must tell them she preferred not to marry at all.

"New Orleans is especially lovely in the spring," Cordelia Edwards interrupted. All of the ravages of her pain were either vanished or well masked since Green's sudden appearance. "Lily, an early spring wedding would be beautiful. We could far outshine Betty Flournoy's."

"But, Mama. . ."

Foy ambled in at that moment, mumbling an apology for being late. He had gone to the waterfront to take her letter, Lily realized miserably. Her refusal to marry Harrison would soon be in his hands. Foy's hair seemed to bristle as he glared at her.

Green ignored the boy and continued to talk about New Orleans. "You'll like the old French Quarter or Vieux Carre. The dwellings are patterned after the houses of southern France, Spain, and Italy. Heavy doors, directly on the flagstone streets, open into the most delightful courtyards." He took another steaming biscuit and spread it with butter. "I'll take you to an old restaurant, Antoine's, for Pompano Pontchartrain."

No one was allowing Lily to say a word. It seemed no one cared what she thought. Her liquid brown eyes sought Emma's, but her friend would not look at her. As Emma left the table to whisk the cream for dessert, Lily reflected upon the sadness of Emma's existence. The spinster's place was a lonely plane too far above the servants for friendship, too far below the family for inclusion. The sweet girl had so much love to give, yet there was no way for her to escape or do anything else with her life.

The pecan pie, piled high with whipped cream, was far too rich; and Lily feared nausea would overwhelm her. As soon after the meal as politely possible, she pled a headache and escaped to the solitude of her room.

Throughout the night, Lily tossed and turned in the soft feather bed and rehearsed the words she would say to Green in the morning. She planned to tell him firmly that she would not marry him. If she could not marry her true love, she would remain a spinster. Dawn streaked the sky before she slept.

When she washed her face in her lavatory the next morning, she noticed that her eyes were red and swollen. No matter. She sighed. Green never looked into them as Harrison did. Dressing without much care, she went quietly into the hallway.

Creak! A wide floorboard gave her away. Mama looked out from the sitting room at the front of the hall. She used it as her morning room to go over her budget and the ceaseless stream of household activities that accompanied providing for her family and servants.

"Come here, Lily," she called. "I'm making lists for a party to announce your engagement."

"Mama, I'd planned to talk with Green this morning, and. . ." She hesitated. Mama's attention was focused on her lists that scattered over the light beechwood writing table of her secretary. Lily stepped across the room and opened the shutters to the balcony, hoping the draft of fresh air would clear her aching head.

Down below, Green waited. Seeing her, he bowed slightly, tipped his silk hat, and waved it excitedly. "I have the runabout ready," he called. "I want to show you something."

"Green's waiting, Mama," Lily said. The moment she had dreaded all night had come.

"You young people run along." Mrs. Edwards's chins shook as she smiled and nodded. "I'll tell you my plans later."

Lifting her skirt to free her feet, Lily ran down the stairs before her mother could send a chaperone. Surely with their engagement pending, they could be seen alone. She would risk the scandal because she knew a man with Green's pride must be confronted without someone listening.

A lazy smile spread over his perfect features at her apparent enthusiasm. Green helped her into the small buggy with a flourish and headed the horse up College Hill.

"I hope you slept well and are feeling better this morning." Green's pale blue eyes roamed over her with the approval of possession. Without waiting for a reply to this customary, polite greeting, he plunged into his plans. "I wanted to show you a choice of building sites."

"Green, I just really don't know how to. . ." She shifted uncomfortably against the red leather seat that was so narrow that it pressed her too closely against him. All of her planned phrases of the night had flown from her brain.

"Now, now, you just sit back and relax. We'll look at several places, but you don't have to decide today." He patted her hand soothingly. Looking quickly around and seeing no one, he brushed a bristly kiss across her cheek.

The *clop-clop-clop* of the horse's hooves thudded in Lily's aching head. She could think of nothing to say. The creaking of the buggy scraped like fingernails against her brain.

"Whoa!" Green commanded and pulled the horse to a stop near the top of the hill. "I thought you might like this place. Since your mother isn't well, it would be convenient for you to visit her from here."

Lily looked into his handsome face. He was making every effort to be charming. "That's thoughtful of you," she murmured.

"James Kendall is seasoning wood to build up here." He gestured. "I understand he is planning an Italianate design. You might like that also. The tall erect form is majestic on the crest of a hill, and belvederes or even small cupolas afford a view of the Chattahoochee and the green hills beyond. . . ."

Lily shivered in spite of the August heat. "Green, you must listen to me. I could never look out across the river without thinking of Harrison."

A scowl creased Green's brow, and his bearded cheeks contorted as he clenched his jaw. With obvious effort, he controlled his temper. After a long pause, he said between his teeth, "I'm willing to forget our meddlesome friend." Then he continued in a surprisingly even tone, "When I was seventeen, I thought I was in love with someone beneath me, too. Perhaps it's merely guilt because we have so much more than they. I guess it's part of growing up—having a hopeless, bittersweet first love."

"But, Green. . . ," she protested. She grasped his arm, trying to force him to listen, but he was smiling fondly as if she were a two year old.

"You were such a child when I first came. But I've waited patiently for you to grow up. You're much more mature now." His patronizing tone changed to harshness. "We'll never speak of Wingate again—unless we hear of a boiler bursting and the gallant captain going down with his ship." The rumble of his laughter held an unmistakable sound of menace.

Clutching the ivory handle of her parasol until her knuckles turned white, Lily bit her lip miserably. She felt hot and sticky. All of the curls so carefully crimped into her hair with an iron heated in the fireplace were becoming lank in the humidity. Her combs were slipping and hair was sliding down her neck. She wondered why Green was determined to appear forgiving.

Heading the horse down the hill, Green answered her thought. "I left South Carolina with my family's blessing for marrying you. With the blending of our fortunes and our blood, we can build an empire."

At that moment, the buggy rolled past the red-clapboard Pugh house. Lily could almost hear that tiny voice saying, "Thank coo." Rubbing her hand over an aching shoulder, she remembered the feeling of those loving arms in that tight, heart-tugging hug. From beneath the dark fan of her eyelashes, she studied Green. He would give her the beautiful children she longed for and a home to rule as she chose.

Green's tone was gentler, placating when he spoke. "As Mrs. Green Bethune, your life will be such a constant social whirl that you'll have no time to think of little, unimportant people."

Lily well knew that as a married woman she could accomplish things with her life that a spinster could never do.

Green reined the horse in front of a large Greek Revival mansion. The first example of this style in the area, built by Dr. Levi Wellborn in 1839, it rose in templelike grandeur with four massive, round plaster-on-brick columns. A cantilevere balcony ornamented the second story. "Do you like this style? The symmetry and graciousness wear well."

"Yes, I like the straight, clean lines of Miss Roxana Wellborn's house. The balcony without visible support is interesting. . . ." Her voice echoed stiffly in her ears. She hesitated. Her neck and shoulders ached as she tried desperately to accept this turning in her life. "If I had a house," she said slowly, "I'd want tall, round columns like this."

"You shall have as many columns as your little heart desires." Green beamed expansively. "All the way around the house if you want them."

Green continued to drive up and down the town looking at all of the magnificent houses. Riding along the heavily wooded area of Randolph Avenue, he stopped in front of the towering Italian Renaissance mansion just completed by William Simpson. Earnestly, he pointed out the Gothic arches filled with wooden tracery around the veranda and the Gothic windows of the cupola. He began expounding on the air moat built around the lower level to keep it cool and moisture free, but Lily's eyes remained on the cupola. She could imagine Mrs. Simpson up there on the captain's deck watching for the arrival of Mr. Simpson's cotton boats. Green was disregarding what she had said about thinking of Harrison.

"I don't want this style house," she said softly. Her jaw pained sharply from clenching it. Desperately, she tried to focus her attention upon Green. They agreed upon a Greek Revival design with many white columns and a site on Randolph Avenue near the house built by Eufaula's first mayor, Dr. William Thornton. Driving slowly along Eufaula Avenue, they compared the beautiful homes and then returned up the hill to Barbour Hall.

Cordelia Edwards met them happily with her plans completed for the engagement party. Lily glanced over the guest list and mentioned several names her mother had not included.

"I meant to leave them off." Mama sniffed disdainfully. "I'll invite the cream of society—no social climbers."

Papa arrived at that moment and Green explained their house plans. Lily sat apart from them on a stiff-backed chair. The parlor was immaculate again, coolly formal. Their conversation flowed around her as if she were merely one more beautiful object in the room.

That night Lily dreamed that the boiler exploded on the *Wave*. Harrison's face floated in flames. Awakening drenched with perspiration, she tiptoed through her adjoining door into the sitting room. From the window seat she leaned out to the tiny balcony hoping to catch a cool breeze. Feeling someone behind her, she turned to see Emma, who stood with her white gown glistening in the moonlight. Watching her silently, Emma waited, ready to help.

"Oh, Emma, do you think I'll ever get Harrison out of my mind and heart?"

"I don't know," Emma replied, sadly shaking her honey-colored hair that fell in a long braid. "I can't advise you, but I do understand how you feel." Her pale blue eyes ashine with compassion, she put her arm around Lily's shoulder.

Lily knew that her friend did indeed understand all too well. For this very reason, she found it difficult to discuss her problem. She feared hurting Emma's feelings. She could not voice her decision that she did not wish to become like her aunt.

The next morning Green asked in his most charming manner if he might borrow Prince. "I have business out on the Montgomery Road, and I'd prefer going on horseback."

"Well," Lily cleared her throat. "I usually don't let anyone ride Prince except. . ."

"I'd take care of him. I like animals with spirit."

Limply, Lily agreed. Sighing often, Lily moved through the day of dress fittings numbly.

Cordelia Edwards, thoroughly enjoying herself with preparations for the engagement party, was too busy to talk with her daughter. Watching for a chance, Lily finally caught Papa alone.

"Oh, Papa," she wailed, "shouldn't a bride be happy?"

He patted her awkwardly. "Brides are always nervous, Honey," he replied soothingly.

"Papa, are you sure I can learn to love Green?"

"Just give it time; give it time. You see how eager he is to please you."

"Yes, he's charm itself, but does he really care about me?"

Distractedly, Papa mumbled that he must be getting to his office. "Things will work out; you'll see."

Lily sought solitude in the summerhouse. A happy little hummingbird brought memories flooding over her. In her mind's eye, she could see Harrison standing there, his usual vitality stilled. For one long moment that would remain forever locked into her heart, they had been joined in the wonder of one of God's tiny creations. She could almost feel his hand grasping hers. His touch had stirred her whole being. Sadly shaking her head, she hoped that one day she would share her joy in small things with a child.

That evening Green still had not returned. After waiting supper for an hour, they had just begun to eat when the ringing of horseshoes sounded in the drive. Jumping up, Lily hurried to the stable to be certain Prince received proper care.

Whinnying, her pet pushed against her, nipping his big soft lips hungrily at her empty hand. His saddle was in place. There was no sign of Green.

"Papa!" She ran toward the house screaming. "Papa, Prince came back without Green!"

Clare Edwards rushed to meet her. "Prince is used to no one but you," he said soothingly. "Don't you think he probably threw. . ." His voice trailed away and his darting eyes showed that he knew Green to be an experienced horseman.

"He rides to the hounds, and. . . ," Lily began.

"Do you know where Green went?"

"Out on the Montgomery Road."

Edwards quickly organized a search. Foy joined the party without asking. Lily fumed because she could only sit home and fidget. For hours, they waited. Mama sat in the parlor, embroidering a linen handkerchief. Emma's sensitive fingers caressed the mother-of-pearl keys of the rosewood piano with the simple, soothing notes of Beethoven's *Moonlight Sonata*. Sitting, standing, pacing, Lily could not be still.

It was nearly midnight before she saw lanterns flickering through the silent darkness. Running through the yard toward the slow-moving, hushed men, she stopped and gasped.

Green lay on a litter. His face was deathly white.

"Papa!" she screamed. "Papa, is he?"

"No, no, Dear." Papa hurried to meet her. "He's alive. But he's badly wounded. I've sent for the doctor."

Green was taken to his room. Lily was not allowed to go in. On the porch, she questioned Foy.

"He was shot in the back!" The child hopped from one foot to the other excitedly. "Oh, Sister," he whispered, "do you think they might blame Captain Wingate?"

Lily sought a chair. "No, no, surely not." She swallowed. "Anyone who witnessed the duel would know that. . ." Lily thrust both hands into her brown curls and tore at her hair. She well knew that they were still close enough to the frontier for justice to move too swiftly. Many innocent men had been hanged.

"Are you sure he's far away?"

"Well, I thought—what's the sheriff doing with Prince?"

"Checking his hooves," the boy answered importantly. "He was out there doing all kinds of tracking and measuring."

For three days, Green remained near death. Lily sat on the porch nervously watching the comings and goings. Whenever she peered into his darkened room, he lay pale and still. Needing strength, she began to bring her Bible. Pulling the heavy rocking chair to the corner to catch every breeze, she started reading the Psalms. Whenever she read aloud to Mama, her attention was on her diction. At the church, she learned stories and maxims. Now in her need, she read searchingly. With her heart open, the voice of God began to come alive from the pages of her Bible.

Green at last regained consciousness. She spoke to him gently and uttered a thankful prayer. Back on the porch, she was stretching in the sunlight, relaxing taut muscles when Foy bounded up the steps.

"There's going to be a trial," he shouted, "as soon as they know if it's assault or murder."

"Shush, Foy!" She motioned to quiet him lest Green hear. "What have you heard?"

"There's going to be a trial. They've arrested Mr. George Lorring!"

Unmindful of her dress, Lily sank to the steps, dropped her head in her hands, and sobbed. Weak with flooding relief that Harrison was not being accused, she knew with certainty that her heart would never change. The feelings that Green's illness had stirred were merely concern. She would always love Harrison. Through tear-dimmed eyes, she saw Foy standing silently before her. At last she realized he was thrusting something into her hand.

As she took the letter from Harrison, Foy turned without a word and fled. Her heart leaped, but then her hands began to tremble as she remembered her last letter to him. As she read words overflowing with love, she realized that he had not had time to receive her letter saying she could not marry him.

August 29, 1858
Apalachicola, Florida

My sweet, darling Lily,

It is a miserable, dark, rainy Saturday night, and I am alone, thank goodness. The good people of Apalachicola must have retired, for I have not heard a footfall on the sidewalk for over an hour. Silence reigns supreme save for the monotonous dripping of the water in the gutter. I like the stillness because it serves my purpose.

I have said I was alone, but beg pardon, not quite alone. I have two companions, my cigar—not a pipe this time—and a picture of a little blue-grayed person. For the last hour or two, I have been puffing my cigar and talking to the little smoke person as though she were present, trying to tell her how much I love her, though I know it can't be told. I took the little hymnbook, hallowed by her touch, looked for a long time at the name on it, and read several hymns. I intend to read it regularly, and probably by the time I see you again will have read it through. It brings forth confessions of a sinner saved by grace and makes me feel at one with you in spirit.

You have made me the happiest man in the world by your letter, which assured me of your everlasting love and longing to be my wife. I received your letter in two weeks this time although it often takes five. I will not despair again, knowing that your love is true and I will hear again from you if only I will be patient.

It is very late, and my candle is burning low.

Good night.

I love you dearly.

With much devotion,
H. H. Wingate

Lily laid her head on the wicker table and sobbed as she never had before. The tender words pierced her heart. Stumbling, blinded by tears, she ran to the back of the garden. Struggling with her hoop, she sat down on the level, brick ha-ha wall. Dropping into the wide ditch, she was stunned for only a moment. She snatched her skirt from the wild blackberry briars, scrambled up the slope of the ditch, and ran into the meadow until she was sure no one would find her. Throwing herself on the ground, Lily beat her fists and sobbed. How had she ever let this wonderful man go? She had lost him forever.

When she could cry no more, she lay on the grass exhausted. Gradually she realized that no matter how lonely her life might be, she could never marry Green when she loved Harrison.

She left the meadow with strong resolve, knowing that the family would be furious; however, the scene after dinner was far worse than she had ever imagined. She had waited until after the meal. Looking at her parents lolling in their chairs, too well fed to get up immediately, Lily stood shakily to her feet.

"You must listen to me," she said in a quiet, firm voice that turned their eyes upon her. "I know you love me and think you're planning my life for the best—no, wait, let me talk." She flung up her hand as they started to protest. "I've tried very hard to go along with your plans, but I simply cannot do it." Lily's cheeks were growing pale, and she grasped the chair back until her knuckles whitened.

Emma sat clutching her fists, making no effort to hide the tears slipping down her cheeks. Lily looked at her with a shuddering sigh and resumed talking before anyone recovered from shock enough to stop her.

"I have tried to believe you know best," she repeated, "but every principle within me rebels. I cannot—will not—marry one man when I love another."

Mama fainted.

"Lily, you promised me you wouldn't. . ." Papa gasped.

"Yes, Papa, I promised." Lily compressed her lips. "I wrote Harrison that I could not marry him without your blessing. But I will always love him. I will not marry at all."

Mama's eyes fluttered and she moaned.

"You must not tell this to Green in his condition. We will not speak of it again until after the trial," said Papa firmly.

As the lurching stagecoach bumped over the road that wound up to Clayton, the county seat, Lily sank miserably into her corner. Nothing had changed. They were still putting her off like a child who would forget a whim and become docile again. Knowing that she could not go on like this, she shut her eyes to blot out their stern faces and poured her heart out to God. Acknowledging and confessing every sin of her young life, she began to breathe without the painful lump in her chest. A feeling of peace filled her. *Lord,* she prayed, *I commit my life to Thee.*

She climbed down from the stage, filled with a new sense of strength. Tossing back her curls, she lifted her chin, ready to face whatever life brought.

The circuit court session dragged on for several days. Mr. Edwards and others who had been in the search party testified to finding Green Bethune lying facedown, shot in the back, with a large portion, but not all, of his money missing and his papers scattered around him. A witness testified that Green Bethune stopped at the Mitchell residence to ask directions to the Montgomery Road. The witness admitted overlooking the fact that the other road, which appeared to head the same way, went to Lorring's house. Another witness gave evidence of seeing Bethune ride a small black horse up to Lorring's house and that later Lorring rode a large bay in the same direction by which Bethune had returned and taken the other fork.

On the third day in the courtroom, which smelled of tobacco and oiled floorboards, Lily was called to the stand. The prosecuting attorney established that Green Bethune was riding her black horse. "Is it true, Miss Edwards, that your horse was wearing shoes?"

"Yes, Sir," she replied. "I had him shod a few months ago."

"Is it also true that there is a distinctive split in the right front hoof?"

"Yes, Sir."

"And can you positively identify your horse's tracks?"

"Yes, Sir."

"Now, be certain, Miss Edwards. Were these tracks, which were observed, measured, and recorded at the scene of the crime, made by your horse?"

"Yes, Sir."

"Please tell the court when you first saw your horse after Mr. Bethune left you in the morning of the day in question."

"At nine in the evening, I heard Prince cantering up the driveway. I found him at the stable completely lathered. He was very excited and riderless."

"Thank you, Miss Edwards. You may step down."

Lorring's stableman testified that the horse Lorring rode was a large, solid red gelding with a black mane and tail. He was unshod. The man identified the measurements of Lorring's horse's hoof, which corresponded with the tracks seen. The big bay had been found dead back in the swamp and identified.

Tension mounted and people whispered as the sheriff took the stand. Reared back in the chair, he matter-of-factly described how he had measured the tracks from the point where both horses went away from Lorring's house with the bay's tracks coming after the black's. He cleared his throat importantly and everyone leaned forward as he said, "At the point where the assault was committed, Bethune's horse was a little ahead of the one Lorring rode. The black gave a sudden spring forward as though the rider's control over him had ceased the moment when he had started by a sudden affright." He leaned toward the jury. "As from the firing of a gun."

The judge rapped for order.

"Lorring's horse, however, gave evidence of his being under control of his rider. You could readily tell that the bay was frightened because of the deep, though stationary impress from the hoof!"

Again the judge had to rap for order.

"Your honor," the prosecuting attorney said, "I am now ready to sum up this case. The conclusive evidence proves that George Lorring—"

"Stop him!"

"Don't let him get away!"

Lily's bonnet fell awry as she whirled toward the shouts. After a brief scuffle, the culprit was returned to the dock.

"Yes, yes, I shot him!" yelled Lorring, struggling against the men who held him by both arms. "But I only took back what was mine." With every eye upon him, he sneered, "It's that gentleman from South Carolina who is the thief!"

Chapter 10

"Green Bethune is the thief!" Lorring continued to shout. "I recovered what was mine!"

Rapping his gavel to no avail, the judge at last called a recess and cleared the buzzing courtroom.

When court reconvened, Green was called to the stand to identify the stolen property.

Lorring's lawyer deftly led him into giving a full account. "Is it not true, Mr. Bethune, that two days prior to the day in question, you met my client at the Chewalla Hotel and *failed* to pay him exactly the amount of money missing from your person?"

Green answered in a casual tone. "It is true that I met Mr. Lorring and paid him nine thousand and six hundred dollars for 186 bales of cotton."

"Please tell the court what this amounts to per pound."

"Ten cents."

Lily was puzzled and nodded when the judge challenged the line of questioning.

With reassurance that it was pertinent, the defense lawyer continued. "Is it not also true, Mr. Bethune, that as his cotton factor, you wrote to my client six months ago stating that if he would store his last fall's crop until you arrived, you would pay him twelve cents per pound?"

Green squirmed. He cleared his throat. "I did suggest. . . In the fall of 1857, the price had fluctuated from ten to eleven cents. I suggested to Mr. Lorring that because of the new power looms and increased cotton manufacturing in Lancashire, England, the price would probably go up. I said that if he would like to risk holding his crop, I would likely be able to pay twelve cents." He cleared his throat again. "Unfortunately, the market fell back to ten cents."

"Your honor, I would like to place this letter in evidence that Mr. Bethune made a definite agreement."

Lily stood as unobtrusively as possible, but her petticoats seemed to rustle loud enough for everyone to hear as she tiptoed from the courtroom. Seeking a shade tree and a cooling breeze, she did not want to hear the judge's decision. She had made her own.

In her parents' hotel suite, Lily faced them with a bright red spot in each pale cheek. "Papa, Mama, after hearing the evidence, I hope you see that

Green is not the man for me!"

Papa's expression lacked understanding. "Lily, Dear, you didn't wait to hear the decision. Lorring was found guilty of assault and robbery. Green broke no law." His voice croaked. "The letter was not binding—"

"Perhaps not," Lily interrupted, "but in breaking his word, Green broke Mr. Lorring. Time and again, I've noticed him shaving principles that I believe in."

"Don't interrupt your father, Lily," Mrs. Edwards interjected sharply. "You know nothing of business. If a man is to keep great wealth and power, sometimes an end must justify the means."

"Not to me, Mama." Lily stamped her foot. "It is principle that matters. Down to as small an amount as a postage stamp!" Her voice rose angrily. Struggling with her temper, she spoke slowly, emphasizing each word, *"I will not marry Green."*

"What about principles of children obeying their parents?" Mrs. Edwards spit out the words sarcastically. "Of honoring thy father and thy mother?"

"I'm sorry, Mama. I respect you and I want to obey, but I can't keep being a child and a woman at the same time. I know you've planned my life according to custom, but I cannot do something just because everyone is doing it. I have to listen to a higher voice."

"What will our friends think?" wailed Cordelia. Sinking her chin on her chest, she sighed. "How will I ever face Laurie?"

Contritely, Lily realized that her mother actually appeared to be sick. She had to escape them, to be alone and cry. She started toward the door.

"Lily, wait!"

Turning, she looked at Papa, whose face was a frightening purple.

"You promised you wouldn't run away."

"No, Papa." She bowed her head and answered softly. "I realize you love me, and I love you. I would never run away."

The estrangement from her parents left Lily feeling weak and sick. Shedding angry tears, she felt that they did not really care about her or they would understand; yet a growing part of her knew that they did care. Few words were exchanged in the stagecoach back to Eufaula. Subdued, Green said little. Watching him wince at the jolting, she knew the ride was painful. She dreaded their confrontation.

Thankful to be home again and out of her dusty traveling costume, Lily bathed and put on her coolest muslin. After giving Green ample time to rest, she tapped on his door and asked him to walk with her to the summerhouse.

Under the white lattice gazebo, she faced him with quiet resolve. Proud of her self-control, she eluded his reaching hands and spoke firmly. "Green, I've told my parents not to announce our engagement."

"Now, Lily, Honey." He drew her into his arms. "You can't change your mind." He pressed a bearded kiss upon her lips.

Shaken, she pushed him firmly away. "Please, Green, no. Listen. Life with you would be fun. But surface attraction isn't enough. We are too different inside. I can't really give you my heart. You should marry a great beauty—like Elmira—someone to follow you without question. You don't really love me!"

Green looked at her intently, and his eyes showed that he sensed a change in her. He spoke without banner or calculated charm. "I've come to care for you a great deal more than you think. I meant it when I said I like a woman with spirit. Can't we give it a try?"

"No. I believe marriage is forever. Please, Green, don't make this harder. I don't know what's to become of my life, but I'm trying to commit it to God."

Groping through the smothering blackness, Lily crept up the narrow stairs, tiptoed through the attic, and climbed to the belvedere. The intensity of the darkness lessened only slightly when she emerged. Obscuring moon and stars, clouds enwrapped the glassed observatory. Suddenly lightning gashed the sky and thunder shook her high perch. Swirling, beating from all sides, the summer storm lashed her tower hideaway. Below her, the treetops danced madly. Dizzied and frightened, she looked up. Perhaps it was dangerous to be here, but Lily felt she must be alone. Watching the rain streaking the windowpanes, she ruefully reflected that the storm seemed pale compared to the one raging within her.

The evening meal had been an agony as they all tried to shake her resolve. She would not be swayed. Her parents were angry and disappointed with her. Emma sat clutching her hands fearfully. Utterly dejected, Green said bitterly that he would be packed and gone the next morning.

Foy came to her side. He had sat silently through all of the recriminations that had been thrown at her. Now, he did something he had not done since he was a small boy; he kissed her affectionately on the cheek. He seemed suddenly tall as he put his arm around her shoulders and helped her to mount the stairs with a shred of dignity. At the door to her bedroom, he hugged her tightly.

Now as her sighs matched the moans of the wind, Lily remembered the admiring gleam she had seen in his eye. He had said nothing. As she watched the rain streaking the windowpanes, Lily smiled through her tears at the way her young brother had stood beside her. In the middle of the sleepless night, she had sought the solitude of the belvedere. Here she felt totally alone. She would remain so, for she had lost both men.

When at last the storm had spent itself, she sank to the floor and slept, exhausted.

Sunrise flooded the glass-enclosed room with pink and gold and awakened her to a new beginning.

"This is the day which the LORD hath made; we will rejoice and be glad in it." Lily repeated Psalm 118, verse twenty-four, through teeth clenched with determination. She went down the stairs to deal as best she could with her family and the new course she had decided for her life.

In the sweltering days that followed, Lily spent a great deal of time in the isolated belvedere reading. Guilt feelings tormented her. She exhausted herself going over and over the things that had been said and done. She muttered aloud the words she wished she had said from the beginning. One moment she would weep with the deep hurt that her parents had not tried to understand her feelings; the next surge of tears would come from the guilt of not being the obedient daughter they expected. She felt sorry for hurting Green. He had been a thoughtful suitor. There remained one thought from which she did not waver; she loved Harrison. But she had hurt him, too.

She flung angry, questioning prayers at God. "Why? Why?" She took her doubts to Him. "Dear Lord," she prayed, "I have sinned against everyone and against Thee by putting myself first. I know that nothing I can do can save me from my sins, but I know that You have taken them all away by dying on the cross and rising again. I accepted Thee when I was a child and Thou came into my heart. Now as an adult, I want to commit every area of my life to Thee." Filled with the presence of Jesus, she found peace to sustain her through the difficult days.

The tumult within her began to steady, but the longing for Harrison did not cease. Needing direction for her life, she began reading the New Testament.

Harrison seemed to be beside her one morning as she read the tenth chapter of Acts. She was transported from the summer-warm belvedere to the soft, spring night at prayer meeting when they had looked across the church and their eyes had met. Closing her eyes now, she could see him perfectly, sitting there so quietly, yet so vitally alive. She could remember the oneness she had felt watching his ready smile play about his always upturned lips. She could feel the warmth as his eyes expressed love that surpassed mere words. The preacher had been reading this same passage that she now held in her lap about Peter's vision on the rooftop. She had paid little attention that night as her eyes kept lifting to Harrison. Besides, the story of the sheet descending from heaven, filled with beasts and fowls and creeping things, was familiar to her from childhood. Now she read it thoughtfully.

"Rise, Peter; kill, and eat."

"Not so, Lord; for I have never eaten any thing that is common or unclean."

"What God hath cleansed, that call not thou common."

With mounting excitement, Lily read again of Peter's meeting with Cornelius, the centurion of the Italian band. When Cornelius fell at his feet to worship him, Peter commanded him, "Stand up; I myself also am a man."

She began to walk about and read aloud. The familiar words spoke directly to her for the very first time as Peter was lifted from the ancient traditions that it was unlawful for a Jew to keep company with one of another nation.

"But God hath shewed me that I should not call any man common or unclean." She repeated Peter's words over and over and then fell to her knees in prayer.

When she arose, she saw Papa leaving the house. She waved and called to stop him. Clutching the Bible to her, she ran down the endless flights of stairs and out across the yard, catching him just before he left.

"Papa, Papa, I must talk with you at once." Lily's eyes shone.

Mr. Edwards looked in surprise at the animated girl who had been listless and wan. Protesting only slightly that he should be getting to work, he let her drag him by the hand to the summerhouse. The leaves of the wisteria vine that shaded the latticed house were yellowing and dropping prematurely because of the drought. The flowers in the garden drooped their heads like sleepy children ready for a nap. In the midst of them, Lily's face and form were opening like fresh blossoms watered from the fountain springing up within her soul.

Waiting until he was seated comfortably before she began, she said excitedly, "Papa, I've been reading the Scriptures, and I really feel the Lord is speaking to me!" She spread her Bible before him on the wicker table and pointed out the passage.

Clare Edwards smiled at her indulgently as she read again of Peter's vision. Happiness that his daughter was herself again lifted the creases from his brow. Without fully listening to her, he murmured, "Yes, of course I know the story of Peter's beginning to preach Christ to the Gentiles, but what does that have to do—"

"Papa, Papa, it's not just a story. God is speaking to us just as He did to Peter." She brushed back wisps of damp curls. "Listen to verses thirty-four and thirty-five: 'Then Peter opened his mouth, and said, Of a truth I perceive that God is no respecter of persons: But in every nation he that feareth him, and worketh righteousness, is accepted with him.' " She smiled at her father triumphantly with her eyes sparkling and her whole being radiating happiness.

He looked at her quizzically.

"Don't you see, Papa?" She laughed. "It speaks to our ancient tradition of marrying within family groups and class. What matters with God is that a man fears him, serves him, and oh, Papa. . ." She jumped up and danced around him with brown curls bobbing and her skirt tilting and swaying. "Harrison is a dedicated Christian."

Edwards rubbed his hand over his head uncertainly and sighed. He took the Bible from her and reread the passage several times.

At long last, he raised his eyes to his glowing daughter. "Yes, I do see what you are saying. It is basic to building a lasting marriage that both partners believe the cornerstone to be faith in God. However." His voice broke and he looked at her doubtfully. "It is also important to be on the approximate cultural level."

"Yes, Papa," she agreed soberly, standing still and clasping her hands in front of her tiny waist. "That part is so wonderful. Our minds run on the same level—if not always in agreement, at least open to discussion. We are one in spirit, one in mind. All that remains. . ." She blushed at the remembrance of Harrison's touch.

"You have always had a deep faith for one so young," Clare Edwards said thoughtfully.

"Yes, Papa. I've believed as long as I can remember that Jesus is God's Son, that He is my personal Savior, but now I'm trying to grow, to make Him Lord of my whole life. I believe God's voice speaks to us in our minds and from the pages of the Bible to direct even our smallest problems of daily life. God cares about who we marry."

Mr. Edwards cleared his throat. "If you feel this strongly, I will give you my blessing to marry Captain Wingate."

Lily threw her arms around his neck, laughing and crying.

"Wait, wait." He pushed her back and looked anxiously into her face. "Don't get too excited. It will not be this easy to convince your mother not to consider your young man common."

"Yes, we have always thought of this as a problem in the early church," she said seriously, "but I've never shared Mama's view of people. I've never chosen my friends for what their name is or how long their family has had money. I like people for themselves, for what they think, for the ideas we can discuss." She paused and her dark eyes twinkled. "I find merely gossiping about acquaintances not only unchristian but also boring." Her laughter trilled like a mockingbird.

Edwards chuckled, then nodded ruefully. "I should have understood. I should have realized that you have grown into a woman with a mind of your own. But how can I be certain Harrison will take care of you?"

"You can be sure because he is a sincere Christian!" The firmness of her voice and the calmness of her demeanor showed fully that she was no longer a vacillating child.

"All right, Honey." He kissed her a fond good-bye. "I'll have a long talk with your mother tonight."

Happily, Lily gazed after him as he walked quickly away. He was late, she knew, but dear Papa always took time for her. Lily wandered through the garden singing, pausing frequently to savor the beauty. She breathed deeply at a bed of spicily fragrant lemon lilies. She could scarcely contain her joy. The blaze of crimson crepe myrtle blossoms, which defied the heat and drought by shining the brighter, made her smile and hug herself. Laughing at her foolishness, she kissed her hand for Harrison and stroked it across her cheek.

She wanted to remain in the cocoon of her daydreams, but with lagging footsteps she left the garden. Mama's back was better, and Lily had promised to help her make fringe for a counterpane. This was no time to disobey and make her angry.

Several times as the two women bent over the stitched bedcover, Lily opened her mouth to tell of her Scripture reading and her feeling that the Lord was leading her to marry Harrison. Each time she would merely murmur needless answers as Cordelia Edwards chattered on about the latest gossip. Mama gave time, just as Papa did, but she never gave attention. Whenever Lily tried to share ideas, the older woman would wait with a glazed look in her eyes, indicating that her mind was elsewhere while her little girl babbled. Lily tried to content herself with patience. Papa would reason with his wife tonight.

After several hours of bending over the counterpane, Lily was growing tired. Only then did her euphoria diminish. Slowly, she counted and recounted the days since she had received a letter from Harrison. She had released him from his promise to marry her. There was no reason why he should answer the hurtful letter. He was a mature man, ready for marriage. He had probably found someone more willing than she.

At last Mama declared herself tired, and Lily escaped. She went to her bedroom. In her agitation, the four walls seemed to press upon her even though the room was large and airy. Picking up her brassbound lap desk, she headed toward the freedom of the belvedere. As she climbed the stairs, she reassured herself that Harrison still loved her. She would write again, telling him that Papa now gave them his blessing. Pursing her lips, she knew that she did not have her mother's permission, but she could wait no longer to write.

Foy had occupied the belvedere before her. His astronomy books littered the small table.

"Oh, Foy," she faltered, "I wanted to be alone to write to Harrison."

"It's about time you did," he snapped peevishly.

Surprised at his attitude, she replied pleadingly, "Can you get it off for me?"

"I don't know. Maybe not. The river is so very low, the boats cannot run regularly."

Chapter 11

"Boats not running?" Lily looked at him in consternation. "Oh, Foy, I've been so wrapped in misery, I hadn't realized fall was upon us and time for low water."

"You know we haven't had rain, and the cotton fields along the riverbank are drawing moisture. This hot sun evaporates—"

"Oh, I know all that. I just hadn't thought," she interrupted, exasperated. "Foy, we've got to get a letter to Harrison. Papa's given permission."

"Yippee!" Foy yelped joyfully.

"No, wait." She shushed him with her hand. "Mama hasn't, but I must tell him as quickly as possible because—" she bit her lip. "I wrote him that I couldn't marry him. I released him from his promise." She sat down suddenly and dropped her head so that her dark hair tumbled down in a curtain around her face. "He hasn't replied. It's been such a long time. Do you think he's found someone else?"

Foy made no sound. As the silence lengthened, Lily slowly raised her eyes. Foy stood twisting his book and shifting his big feet. His cheeks had lost their rosy roundness, but as she stared at him, the hollows turned beet red. His ears, standing out from his head, seemed almost to flap.

"What is it?" she gasped. "What do you know? It's been so long. What's happened?" She grasped his shoulders and shook him.

"I–I don't know anything," he stammered. "I don't know why you haven't heard. But it's not what you think."

She released him, gritted her teeth, and tried to be patient. "What then?"

"Well, you see, I. . ." He faltered, then finished in a rush. "I didn't send your letter."

"You didn't send my letter!"

"No, I, well, I didn't think you meant what you wrote. You were upset. I knew you'd change your mind." His lip curled. "I didn't want you to marry that Green."

"Foy, have you been reading all our letters?" she demanded.

"No, honest, I haven't, Sister, but that day you'd been crying so much you looked wild. I decided. . ." He took a deep breath. "Yes, I read that one," he admitted. The tops of his ears glowed red. He continued slowly, "I went down to send it, but I just couldn't." He reached into a large book and solemnly handed her the letter.

Incredulously, Lily looked at the paper. Slowly, she unfolded it and scanned the hurtful words of refusal. Thankful that Harrison need never know of her parents' low opinion of him or that she had considered giving in to them and not marrying him, she laughed and cried as she shredded the letter. Leaning far over the rail, she threw the bits into the air.

"You're impossible, Foy, but I do thank you for interfering this time." She hugged him tightly and kissed his cheek. "Now, the problem remains of getting a letter to him. What are we to do?"

"I could take your letter downriver to Columbia." He grinned happily. "The river seldom gets too low for steamers to reach there."

"Mama would never let you make a day-and-a-half trip on horseback. While I'm writing, go to the wharf and see if any boats are running."

He grinned and scampered down the stairs.

Lily sat down at the table, lifted the pin, and opened the secret drawer in which she kept Harrison's letters. Untying the pink ribbon that bound them, she skimmed his last letter. She reread the second paragraph:

> *I have said I was alone, but beg pardon, not quite alone. I have two companions, my cigar—not a pipe this time—and a picture of a little blue-grayed person. For the last hour or two, I have been puffing my cigar and talking to the little smoke person as though she were present, trying to tell her how much I love her, though I know it can't be told.*

Lily smiled and kissed the letter. It made her happy to know that he daydreamed of her as she did of him. She read his last words aloud, trying to hear his deep voice speaking, "You have made me the happiest man in the world by your letter which assured me of your everlasting love and longing to be my wife."

Laying it beside her paper, she began to pour out her heart to Harrison.

> *September 5, 1858*
> *Eufaula, Alabama*
>
> *You surely have despaired of hearing from me, Captain Wingate, but I have just discovered that my last letter failed to get off to you. Now the river is so very low the boats cannot run regularly; and my heart aches that you may be long in receiving this, but I must share my joy.*
>
> *Papa has given us his blessing! When can you come? Could we plan a Christmas wedding?*

Lily put down her carved ivory pen and read over her words. She looked back at Harrison's letter and whispered his closing promise, "I will not despair again, knowing that your love is true and I will hear again from you if only I will be patient." A sob caught her voice. What if his patience had worn thin? It had been such a long time since either had had word of the other. She chewed her pen and then held it up to the light. She squinted into the tiny hole in the carved ivory at the picture of Jerusalem and thought for a long while before she dipped the pen into the inkwell and resumed writing cautiously.

Am I assuming too much? I have not heard from you in five weeks. Have you fallen in love with some Apalachicola lady and forgotten to write?

I tremble to think that I may have lost you in waiting for my parents' permission. I pray that our mail will get through and we will not lose each other forever.

No matter what happens, I will always love you and remain here waiting.

One piece of advice before I close—don't have the blues anymore and quit smoking so much, and I think you will feel better. Don't you wish I would stop talking so? I did love your letter as I will always love you. I shall stop for now and hope this may somehow wing its way to you.

Yours devotedly,
Lily

The next day, Mama remained in her bedroom admitting no one but her personal maid, Kitty. Although the family and the afternoon callers were given word that she was suffering greatly from rheumatism, Papa confided to Lily that he had discussed her ideas with his wife, but she was far from convinced.

Lily had spent the endless morning in the upstairs sitting room, nervously knotting macramé, jumping at each sound, hoping that her mother was about to emerge from her self-imposed isolation to talk with her. After Kitty took her noon meal on a tray, the tall girl reported to Lily that her mother did not feel up to seeing her. Now, with Mrs. Edwards even turning away callers, Lily could endure the house no longer. With Emma accompanying her, she went out into the stifling afternoon.

Heat rose in shimmering waves from the sunbaked road. As they walked, her hope that her mother would grant permission seemed also to shimmer like a mirage floating always before her, unattainable.

They walked down Barbour Street beneath China trees heavily laden with clusters of hard, brown berries. Ahead of them, crowds of tiny yellow butterflies, clinging jealously to a few small damp spots, fluttered up reluctantly just out of reach of their swaying skirts. Turning left, they moved into the cooler, denser shade of Randolph Avenue. Mrs. Simpson waved as they passed her house. Lily felt too morose for idle conversation. She waved but did not slacken her pace. Emma stopped to talk with Mollie Simpson, and the two friends ambled along well behind Lily until they reached Fairview Cemetery. This quiet park suited Lily's mood. It was damp beneath the huge oaks and elms. Idly, she wandered by the tombstones, set at odd angles, that marked the graves of the early pioneers. Here and there clumps of roses, their sweetness intensified by the heat, seemed to heighten her feeling of infinite sadness.

Respecting her need for solitude, Mollie and Emma moved by her to speak consolingly to Mollie's twin sister, Elizabeth Rhodes. Countless times in the last year, Mrs. Rhodes had placed flowers on her little Willie's grave. Sympathetic tears stung Lily's eyes. Fearing that if she began to cry she would never be able to stop, Lily turned from them. The twin sisters were a year younger than Emma, but both of them had beautiful homes and families. Lovely Emma had nothing. Lily must not let herself think about that. Sighing, she walked in the opposite direction along the circling driveway. She stood trembling on the bluff and stared unseeingly down the sheer drop to Cowikee Creek, far, far below, rushing to meet its destiny with the Chattahoochee.

After an unsettling supper for which Mrs. Edwards did not appear, Lily determinedly tapped on her door. Cordelia Edwards emerged grandly attired in black satin. Her hair was elaborately dressed in a youthful style of clusters of curls. Her expression was defiant, but her eyes were puffy and red.

Lily's dark eyes were wide with pleading as she softly begged, "Mama, please talk with me."

"Later," she snapped. "We have guests coming." She pursed her lips. "I've invited a group in for a musical soiree."

The next morning when Lily stepped out of her room, Mrs. Thornton was waiting with her carriage to take them to Mrs. Eli Shorter's plantation to spend the day. Even though their social customs dictated constant visiting, Lily readily saw that her mother was exerting extra effort to keep a crowd around them. As Lily politely greeted Mrs. Len Shorter and Mrs. I. G. Shorter, she could see Mama out of the corner of her eye supervising her prescribed inquiry after their health. Mama's smug smile emphasized the point that proper ladies visited in family groups of mothers with their daughters and daughters-in-law.

Just as they went into the dining room, beautiful Adriana, who had married Henry Russell Shorter, the handsomest of the Shorter men, tossed her long brown hair and asked, "When are you going to announce your engagement to that gorgeous Green Bethune? Someone else might snap him up."

Lily looked down at her plate, and stammered, "We, uh, decided not to marry. He's gone."

Coredelia Edwards popped her lips together. "This baby decided she wasn't ready to get married."

Blushing miserably, Lily toyed with her chicken.

"You won't find another good catch around here." Adriana laughed. "And you're not getting any younger."

Lily tried to change the subject, but the table talk constantly revolved back to marriage.

She sighed with relief when another group of ladies dropped in for a call later in the day. Conversation flowed freely without mention of her problems; nevertheless, she felt a lump of frustration swelling in her chest, threatening to explode like Foy's chinaberry popgun.

Mama sat in the corner talking secretively with Mrs. Colonel Chambers and Mrs. Van Hoose. Lily's breathing stopped when she sensed their subject. She strained forward to listen.

"Yes, my sister in Georgia has a delightful son," Mrs. Chambers gushed.

Desperately seeking escape, Lily discovered that Mrs. John Shorter was leaving to do a little shopping. Getting permission to ride back to Eufaula with her, Lily climbed into the carriage with her older friend and said, "I wanted to talk with you. I need advice on how to convince Mama that I want to lead my own life."

Her friend shrugged expressively and said nothing as her own mother climbed in beside them.

A swelling tide of emotion dashed Lily over the next six rocky days as her mother's dominance defeated her, and she turned more and more to attending the frequent church meetings that were a usual part of Eufaula life. Suddenly, revival broke out in the town. Lily and her friends attended morning and evening prayer meetings. It was a time of high emotion with crowds filling the church. Many came forward to the mourner's bench to confess their sins and need for God. Lily's heart overflowed as she watched the baptism of thirty at one service. Tears misted her eyes as her sweet voice joined the singing of the dear old hymn, "Amazing Grace."

Revival spread to churches of other denominations in the town, too. Lily's group visited everywhere. At a prayer meeting held at the Union Female College, Lily sat watching the shining faces of the schoolgirls. She felt a growing conviction that God did indeed plan a choice of mate for each person just as surely as He destined other purposes for individual lives. Her guilt feelings from disobeying her parents were removed as she drew near to God in the worshipful atmosphere. Much as she longed to please them, she felt a calming assurance that the first thing in her life must be seeking God's will.

Even as Lily rejoiced that the whole town was stirred by revival, she prayed for herself and Harrison. With contrition, she recalled how she had asked God to guide her to the one who would share her faith. That early summer of her girlhood seemed so much more than a few short months ago. Had she really not expected an answer to that prayer? The answer had come so quickly that she had failed to recognize it. Did she have her chance only to lose it? Blinking back tears, she beseeched God that Harrison's heart would not turn cold with their long separation.

The revival opened Mrs. Edwards's heart—but not toward Lily's problem. It only served to keep her too busy for discussion. She was bent on visiting the poor. Dutifully accompanying her to carry gifts of food and clothing, Lily was shocked at seeing the privations of suffering humanity. Her mother kept puffing out her lips and reminding her to count her blessings.

One evening, as she and Emma returned from a concert and dialogue at the college, they sat on the corner of the porch to catch the cooling breeze. Foy loped across the yard waving a small package over his head.

"You've got something, Sister. It came up with the wagons from Columbia."

Smiling at Foy's excitement, she did not reprimand him as he bent over her shoulder eagerly watching her open the package. She took out two photographs, one of Harrison and the other of a beautiful girl. Something else tumbled into her lap, but she snatched up the enclosed note without looking at it.

July 30, 1858
Mobile, Alabama

Ma très chère *Lily,*

I have been home to the family plantation, Greenleaves, to visit. My mother was pleased with all I told her about you, but my sister, Jeanne, was quite surprised to hear I planned to marry you. This is a photograph of Jeanne. You will be great friends, I know.

I am also sending some sea moss. This moss is by some persons, arranged in a highly artistic manner representing landscapes, animals, and so forth. I thought you might enjoy creating something.

I have not heard from you in a very long time. Please send me word that I may come to claim you as my bride before low water renders the river unnavigable.

Your obedient servant,
H. H. Wingate

Glancing at the date, Lily realized that the package had been weeks in transit, and that Harrison's assumption that they would be married was written before the long interval in which he did not hear from her.

Sharing the letter, she said, "It's odd, but his sister looks like a little French doll. Why do you suppose she was so surprised that he planned to marry me?"

"Maybe she was amazed that you would have him," replied Emma.

"But that makes him sound like a cad," protested Lily.

"Maybe he has girls in many ports, and she didn't expect him to ever settle down," contributed Foy.

"Oh, Foy, hush your mouth," she scolded laughingly, but as she idly turned the sea moss that had fallen in her lap, she worried that he might be right. Maybe Mama's permission did not matter after all.

The next evening, they all attended a social given by their neighbors, Mr. and Mrs. Benjamin Franklin Treadwell. As Lily walked across the spacious grounds, she hoped Mrs. Treadwell's daughter, Adriana Shorter, would say no more about her expected marriage to Green. Normally, Lily enjoyed going to the beautiful house which had been designed by the great architect, St. Ledger. Master builders had constructed the tremendous house topped by a cupola with a captain's deck and balustrade.

As the family approached the grand mansion, Papa joined a group of men on the colonnaded veranda who were hotly espousing secession.

"Gentlemen, the South has lost everything by the Compromise of 1850," shouted William Lowndes Yancey. "Secession is the only resort!"

"I agree," thundered John Gill Shorter. "I hope our state will remain separated forever from the Union, as if a wall of fire intervened!"

Lily glanced toward them. Talk of war stirred every gathering now. Wondering what changes were to befall them, she shook her head, turned, and meekly followed the ladies crossing the porch to the beautiful entrance.

Framed by candlelight glittering through the imported sidelights and transom of the front doors, Mary Magdalen Treadwell beckoned the ladies to come inside the hall, which was splendid with frescoes done by the famous mural painter, Sisk. A tall, erect woman of regal bearing and patrician features, Mrs. Treadwell fixed her snapping black eyes upon Lily and said loudly, "Adriana tells me you are not going to marry that handsome young man from the flower of South Carolina society."

"No, Ma'am." Lily ducked her head. Her cheeks flamed as red as the damask draperies hanging from the gold cornices at the long windows. A group of her friends had heard the comment, and she kept her eyes on the heavy carpet of Brussels as she trudged across the room to join them.

"Hello, Lily, guess who I saw?" sang out Mary Elizabeth Brock. "Do you remember that mysterious riverboat captain you were making eyes at in prayer meeting last spring?" She began to laugh as Lily's face matched the draperies again. "Oh, I saw you. Don't deny it."

"Yes, I remember him," replied Lily, trying desperately to speak casually. "Where did you see him? Has a riverboat arrived?"

"No," replied Mary Elizabeth airily. "I just came down on the afternoon stage from Columbus, Georgia."

"You saw him in Columbus, then?" Lily pressed, wishing she could pounce on the infuriating girl and shake a direct statement out of her.

All of the girls giggled and chorused, "We thought you were interested in him!"

"Yes," Lily replied carefully. "He was the most interesting and dashing man I had ever met. Don't tease, Mary Elizabeth. Was he really in Columbus?"

"Oh, no." Mary Elizabeth tossed long, red curls and preened. "Didn't you know? I've been on a grand tour. I saw him in Washington City at a party for senators and congressmen. He was dancing with the most sophisticated beauty I've ever seen."

Lily's cheeks paled as the girl's words flung against them like cold water. Of course, his sister had been surprised that he would marry a silly schoolgirl when he knew accomplished international people.

"He is a mysterious man," contributed Elmira Oaks, interrupting Lily's thoughts. The glossy-haired beauty knew that she was more sensuous and had more worldly knowledge than the rest. She strutted a bit and said loftily, "Why do you suppose he's merely a riverboat captain? My papa says that his family owns an old mansion built facing the Tombigbee River. It's just below Demopolis," she lifted her perfect nose, "and you know what it means to have a plantation in the Black Belt."

Lily knew well what it meant. The so-called Black Belt was a gently rolling prairie named for its fertile black soil. Within this crescent-shaped band covering nearly 4,000 square miles were the largest and wealthiest cotton plantations. Some of the state's most beautiful homes with the most leisurely, gracious living were there.

"With all that," Elmira's knowing voice pierced her thoughts, "you'd think he'd be there. Do you suppose he's done something so bad that he's no longer received?"

"All I know," laughed Mary Elizabeth, "is that I saw him in Washington with a very beautiful woman!"

Chapter 12

"I promise I'll return the favor." Lily sniffed as she stumbled through the darkness of the garden. She squeezed Emma's arm and tried to hold back the tears, but her cheeks glistened in the flickering torchlight. She wondered what she would have done had not Emma stepped into the circle of giggling girls and helped her escape.

Emma had taken her away by insisting that she must walk with her through Mrs. Treadwell's unusually landscaped grounds, which had been inspired by Longfellow's garden at Cambridge. They easily hid themselves from view on the paths that were contoured to outline a seven-chorded lyre and slipped behind the red brick hothouse away from the partygoers.

"Have I lost him?" Lily sobbed on Emma's shoulder. "Did I delay too long in accepting him and make him turn to some woman who didn't have to think and do as she was told?" she wailed bitterly.

"Now, now," Emma soothed, "perhaps it's for the best. I guess Cordelia was right after all." Moonlight and shadows played tricks with her usually smooth face and etched a mask with rivulets of anxiety. "If he's not the gentleman you thought him, it's better to find out now."

"No!" Lily stiffened and drew away. "Emma! How can you say such a thing? I don't doubt Harrison's character! It's his inner self that matters to me, and I am sure of that. It's only," she sniffed, "that I may have driven him to the arms of another woman by not telling him so."

"But, my dear, if his family owns such a large plantation and he's merely a riverboat captain, there's a chance. . . " Emma hesitated.

"I don't care about his family's wealth or social position," Lily declared emphatically.

"But if he's done something to disgrace them, and the people he knows don't receive him. . ."

"But they do," she wailed. "He'd been home when he sent the package and he said his sister—"

"Was surprised that you'd marry him," Emma finished.

Lily fled from her and paced the dark-shadowed area at the back of the garden along the ha-ha wall. Suddenly, she whirled and set her hoops rocking. She stormed at her friend who was pale and drawn with worry.

"No. No! I won't doubt him." She pressed her hands to her temples. "I'm not a child anymore. I won't be told what to think. I won't be a respecter of persons. Harrison stands as a man after God's own heart. He is rich toward God. That's what matters to me!"

Hot, dusty September days inched by as Lily paced out her frustrations in their drought-stricken garden. She seemed to be holding her breath in an agony of waiting. She would not be shaken in her trust of Harrison, but over and over she asked herself if she had grown up too late.

One afternoon, as she sat in the latticed summerhouse staring at a book, pretending to read, she sensed a presence before she heard a step. Whirling, she flung her hand to her throat and gasped.

He came striding toward her. His white suit glistened brightly in the glaring sun, making her squint to see if her eyes could confirm the song her heart was singing. Standing shakily, she stretched out her arms with a joyful cry.

Harrison enfolded her in a strong embrace. Shielded from prying eyes by the drooping, yellowing wisteria vines, they clung to each other. His mustached mouth sought hers. Warmth and peace erased her pain, and she joyfully knew she had been right not to doubt him. His cool, smooth cheek pressed hers as she caught her breath, laughing and crying.

"How in the world did you get here?" she exclaimed at last. "I wasn't expecting to see you because the boats are running so seldom."

"I came down from Columbus, Georgia, on the stage. I've been across the country." He smiled adoringly and dropped a kiss on the top of her head. "It seems forever since I've heard from you. My mail hasn't caught up. You see I've been to Washington City."

"Yes. I'd heard. I didn't know riverboat captains were part of that social scene." Her voice lowered at the remembrance, and she dropped her eyes to her twisting hands. "I heard you were there dancing with a beautiful woman." She suddenly felt hot, sticky, and unkempt in her simple muslin dress.

Chuckles burst forth as he threw back his head and enjoyed a hearty laugh. "How news does travel!" He smiled mischievously and tweaked his mustache, obviously savoring her jealousy.

Lily looked up at him. He had never been as handsome as he was in his white naval uniform. His twinkling eyes were wide with candid innocence and infinite tenderness, yet his tanned face and strong body were unfailingly masculine. Her dark, soulful eyes questioned silently.

"I had business in Washington, very successful, I might add." Grinning, he dropped his teasing tone and explained, "The beautiful lady in question was Senator Atherton's wife."

He was obviously eager to share his business affairs with her. He drew her to the wicker settee, and they sat holding hands and talking.

"A great many lives have been lost," he said earnestly, "to say nothing of four vessels from my family's steamship line alone. So for the past year I've been captain of one of our riverboats to see what could be done." He paused to see if she understood. "I don't like to brag about my family's holdings. We have other boats on the Tombigbee River and a rather large cotton plantation south of Demopolis. I'm certain Green told you all about my background before he introduced me into your family."

"No." She shook her head solemnly. "Green told us nothing." Her face was full of wonder as she said quietly, "I thought you merely captain of the *Wave*."

Harrison's dark eyes searched her face incredulously.

Lily nodded at him with a tremulous smile. She watched his face as the realization spread over it that she had thought to give up all luxuries of life for him. Adoration for her filled his eyes, and he kissed her tenderly, then with a passionate strength that told her she need never worry about another woman again. His life would be completely dedicated to her as her life was to him.

"Well, anyway." He cleared his throat as he made himself pull away and said in an emotion-husky voice, "I've tried to introduce safety precautions, as I had told you, but the real problem is not on the steamboats; it's the river."

"The treacherous Chattahoochee," she murmured. Relaxing in the circle of his arms, she wanted to listen, to share his concern; yet her mind pirouetted to the counterpoint of his deep voice against the melodies of the pines plucked by the fingers of the wind.

"Yes," he continued eagerly. "The Chattahoochee is full of snags, rocks, sandbars, low bridges. It's difficult to induce Congress to provide funds for clearance of the channel. That's what I hoped to accomplish in Washington." He spread his hands. "But, enough of what's kept me away. What have you been doing? Have I waited long enough for your parents to forget the embarrassment of the duel? Pray tell me you are ready to set a date for our wedding."

"Yes, yes." She roused herself, pleased that Harrison had never doubted her. Ruefully reflecting upon her past immature behavior, she breathed a thankful prayer that Foy had not sent her letter of refusal and that Green was out of their lives. Harrison need never know what problems his being too humble to speak about his family's status had caused. "Papa has given his blessing." She took a deep breath. "Mama will soon be persuaded now that you have returned." She shook back her hair and smiled up at him, eyes sparkling. "I'll talk with Mama this afternoon. Can you come back for supper?"

"Yes," he answered simply, and lifted her clenched fists to brush kisses across them.

"I promise to have them prepared this time." She laughed. "You may ask Papa again formally for my hand. Then we will tell them our wedding plans."

"I wish tonight could be our wedding supper." Again his voice was husky.

Lily's laughter tinkled merrily. "Give me a little more time. I must have a wedding gown that will make you proud of your bride."

"I'll always be proud of you. Would six weeks be enough time for you? By then I could arrange my business to allow for a long honeymoon."

"Yes," she answered firmly.

"I can't wait to take you to meet everyone." Harrison's face shone with happiness. "You'll especially love my sister, Jeanne. Everyone says she is very much like my French grandmother."

"French?" Lily lifted quizzical eyebrows.

"Yes. Didn't you know Demopolis was settled in 1817, by Bonapartists exiled because of their claim to the throne of France?"

"Well, I've heard about the Napoleonic exiles, but. . ." She shrugged at her lack of knowledge.

"Yes, well, the refugees' attempt to grow olives and grapes failed. Everything is planted to cotton now, but the riverport of Demopolis is still referred to as the 'Vine and Olive Colony.' "

"That's why you sometimes speak French." She laughed.

"It slips out." He grinned. "I hope you won't mind being out on the plantation. Planters don't build homes in town as much as they do here because our black canebrake mud makes the roads practically impassable during the rainy months of winter and spring."

"I'll love being in your family's home. Wherever it is," Lily said softly, still scarcely daring to believe her happiness.

"I think you'll like Greenleaves. The house looks rather impressive from the river. It's set on a high, white limestone bluff. It was built in 1832 in the plain, Federal style. It was red brick when I left, but by the time we get there I may not recognize it. When I told my mother I was marrying a city girl, she started pestering my father to add a columned front portico and paint everything white to make it the fashionable Greek Revival style."

"I can't wait to see it." She laughed. Joyfully, she looked across the garden. Her eyes focused only on spots of beauty and color. Thinking that all of her problems were behind her, she blurred the things that were withering, dying.

They lingered long in the summerhouse and parted reluctantly even though it would only be for a matter of hours.

Lily immediately went to search out her mother. She was firm in her resolve to convince her that she should marry Harrison without telling her of his wealth and prominence.

Learning that Cordelia Edwards was visiting the sick, Lily ran lightly to the stables, seeking release from pent-up energy and fortification for her nerves. Whinnying eagerly, her spirited horse pranced and nuzzled her. Quickly, she saddled Prince and slipped out through the meadow before anyone could see her. She wanted to be alone. She eased her weight into the sidesaddle and held on tightly as long-legged Prince loped away.

Hatless, dark curls streaming behind, she let the horse run unchecked until they reached the riverbank. Lily jumped down to give Prince a rest and feed him a handful of sugar. Standing on the edge of the cliff, she looked down at the Chattahoochee sunk to its summer level eighty feet below the bridge.

Fancifully, she shook her finger at the thin, blood-red stream lying docilely between the rocks. "You didn't beat me," she said with her eyes twinkling merrily. "You won't come between us again."

When she returned to Barbour Hall, she found her mother in the wide central hallway of the house seeking a breeze. "Mama," she said firmly, "the time has come for us to talk."

"It's too hot, Baby." Cordelia Edwards lolled on the horsehair sofa fanning listlessly.

Calmly, knowing she would neither be put off nor driven to tears, she replied, "No! Harrison is here. He's coming for supper. I must talk with you, now." She looked down at her and softened her tone. "Mother, I love you and respect you. Everyone in town sings your praises as they never will mine. . ." Pinned to the marble checkerboard floor by the piercing arrogance of her mother's gaze, she faltered and her voice trailed away.

Cordelia Edwards sat with her head thrown back, her nostrils flaring, and her lips pressed firmly together.

Clearing her throat, Lily shuffled her feet. "We just don't look at life the same way." She shook her head. "And I guess we never will, but two people can't be exactly alike. It doesn't matter if you like red and I like green." She shrugged. "I've got to live my life as I feel God leading me. I can't be an adult and a baby at the same time."

Cordelia's darting eyes had the frightened look of an animal seeking escape. "I guess that is what I wanted you to do," she admitted. She pinched back tears. "But I'll always think of you as my baby."

"I can't be your baby any longer." Lily's voice was cold as she carefully controlled her temper.

Cordelia's face crumpled. The cloak of haughtiness fell from her shoulders, and she began to cry.

The sensitive girl hovered helplessly over her weeping mother as the sawing blade of her words severed the threads between them. Tears sprang to her eyes as she watched her mother's pain with a sudden stab of realization that the birth-cut between them had been made with a swifter, sharper knife.

Dropping to her knees, Lily gathered her mother's nervously flitting hands in hers. "Mother, I can't be your baby," she said tenderly. "I want to be your daughter. Two women together."

Cordelia began to laugh through her tears. She took her daughter's wet cheeks in both hands, and they kissed each other in loving embrace.

With strong conviction, Lily knew that she would reverence and obey her mother when she could, but she would never again be cast down broken-spirited or feel herself a terrible child. Suddenly, into her mind popped approving words, "Children, obey your parents in the Lord: for this is right." She laughed gently as she remembered how Ephesians six had amplified the commandment.

"Mama," she lifted her shining face and said brightly, "let me show you what I showed Papa." Lily ran to get her Bible and spread it before her mother. Carefully she explained her beliefs as she had to her father.

For once in her life, Mama gave her full attention. She pursed her lips and made no comment as Lily talked. When Lily finished, they sat with silence lengthening.

At last Mrs. Edwards sighed. "I don't see it that way. This Scripture does not say to me what it does to you. I've only tried to do what I think is best," she spoke with an unaccustomed whine. "To provide you with a husband who is your social equal."

Lily waited quietly. She wished that she knew how to convey to her mother the joy she received from knowing her place in heaven was secured by faith in Jesus' sacrificial death and resurrection rather than through keeping laws and doing good works. Sensing that she could press her no further, she held her breath and waited.

Mrs. Edwards looked at her for a long time. Sighing heavily, she said, "If you are determined to have your own way, I won't oppose your marrying Captain Wingate."

Dancing light sparkled in the prisms of the chandeliers above the long dining table and glittered over the blue satin gown of the radiant girl who sat as the center of attention. Mama and Papa had never been more charming. The cook had produced such an elaborate meal that Lily knew all of the servants must be whispering about her romance. The best tablecloth of Italian lace was laid over the gleaming mahogany table. In the center, a silver epergne lifted a pyramid of fragrant pink roses and ferns above the heads of the diners. On either side a tall, five-branched silver candelabra held more lighted tapers aloft. In this festive atmosphere, conversation fluttered like a butterfly over pleasant generalities.

After the meal, the family moved to the parlor for coffee. Harrison cleared his throat. His eyes sought Lily's. She reassured him with a smiling nod. "Sir," he began and cleared his throat again. "Sir, may I formally ask for your daughter's hand in marriage? I love her very dearly and promise you that I will dedicate my life to caring for her."

Clare Edwards reached up to pat Harrison's shoulder. "Lily assures me that you will." He smiled. "Her mother and I give you our blessing."

Foy whooped and then with newfound manhood solemnly shook Harrison's hand.

For once in her life, Cordelia Edwards sat quietly, saying nothing; but a strange smile quirked her lips. Emma looked quizzically at Lily, then shrugged, and served the coffee with a sigh of relief.

As Harrison reached for Lily's hand and squeezed it tightly, she spoke in a strong, sure voice, "We want to be married the first of November."

"But," Mama protested, suddenly coming out from her private thoughts, "that gives us so little time to get ready. A Christmas wedding would be so much more elegant. Wait 'til then," she said firmly.

"But Harrison can take time off for a honeymoon in November. . . ," Lily began hesitantly.

"I would like to end our trip by taking her to my family's plantation for Christmas. All of my brothers and sisters will be returning to Greenleaves for the holidays," he said politely yet confidently to Mrs. Edwards, who acquiesced reluctantly. He turned to smile into Lily's eyes. "Mother's prized camellia garden will be blooming then, and she will take such delight in showing it to you."

"How lovely!" Lily declared in excited anticipation of the new worlds opening to her. "Then we must make it the first of November."

Her parents nodded in agreement; however, their fixed smiles were tinged with sadness.

Harrison noted their emotion and said gently, "I promise not to take her away from you all of the time. I thought next spring we'd start building a home in Eufaula."

Joyful cries met this announcement and everyone began talking at once. Tears of happiness shone in Lily's eyes as plans were made.

When at last she followed Harrison to the porch, she whispered, "I hate for this day to end."

"Many more happy days will begin." He smiled. "We can also build a home anywhere else that strikes your fancy. There is one thing I would ask though," he interjected seriously and looked into her eyes, pleading for understanding. "I find I thrive on the challenge of the river. I want to continue to spend part of my time on the steamship line."

"Of course," Lily agreed. "I know you could never sit around idly."

Blissfully happy days filled the next week. The house buzzed with activity as the servants polished each spot and then shined it again. Plans were made for an engagement party. Emma was everywhere supervising preparations. She wore a constant smile as her loving heart overflowed with gratitude that her darling Lily would never know the loneliness that she had been fated. To Lily's satisfaction, Cordelia Edwards's guest list excluded no one.

The party was a glorious affair. Mary Elizabeth Brock came in nodding, "I told you so." Elmira Oaks tried to start whispers, but no one paid any attention. A few times as she milled about greeting friends, Lily overheard her mother telling people that Harrison's family included French aristocrats and bragging about his recent trip to Washington. Ruefully, she realized that Mama had known, after all, who he was before she gave her blessing. Mama would never change, but Lily tried not to mind.

The next day, Harrison bade Lily a reluctant farewell. "The rapid changes on the river due to the extended drought have caused another disastrous wreck," he told her. "I must see what can be salvaged and settle several other business matters before I return."

"How will you go?" she asked, walking with him as far as the gate.

"There's a small boat, the *Peytona,* leaving immediately. It should get me there—and back," he assured her with a confident smile.

As he went striding away from her, Lily gazed after him, memorizing the way he walked. There was much to do before he returned. Resolutely she started toward the house, then went back to the gate for one last look down the hill, fighting a feeling of bereavement.

Chapter 13

"Where is the mysterious groom?" Elmira Oaks breezed into Lily's blue and white bedroom unannounced.

The circle of bridesmaids, who were clustered around the high, rosewood bed to admire the lustrous white satin wedding gown spread across the counterpane, parted to admit Elmira.

"Isn't this the most beautiful thing you've ever seen?" squealed Mary Elizabeth Brock.

"She'll look like a dream," agreed Elmira airily. "But, really, I thought Captain Wingate was due back a week ago. I wanted to give you a party."

Angry with herself that Elmira made her blush, Lily stammered, "He's—he will be back soon. He had business—"

"This is the prettiest part," interrupted Cousin Octavia. Ignoring Elmira, she directed their gaze to the ropes of pearls that fell in double scallops from below the tiny waist.

"I think I like the sleeves best," admitted Lily with a sudden shyness. "You'll see what I mean when I wear it. I love the way the petals float." She smiled at her plump-cheeked cousin who had come for a two-week visit.

The girls chattered and giggled at once over the lovely bridesmaids' dresses. As maid of honor, Emma would wear a slightly deeper shade of lavender taffeta than they. Creamy lace underlaid the dainty scallops of the necklines and dipped between the deep scallops of the hemlines.

Lily tried to relax. She had not realized that she was so tired. The past few weeks had been exhausting as they prepared for the wedding and packed the huge trunks in readiness for the extended honeymoon trip. She had not heard from Harrison and did not know how to write to him, but she had been too occupied to fret even though he was overdue. Now, Elmira's caustic words made her long for the security of his arms. Wrapped in the warmth of his embrace, she had blotted out what Harrison had tried to tell her about rocks, sandbars and wrecks. They had been mere words, challenges for him to overcome. Now they protruded into her mind as cold, hard foes.

As the group started downstairs in search of refreshments, Elmira turned to Emma. "Do you really think he'll make it back? There hasn't been a boat upriver in weeks."

Emma glanced behind her, hoping that Lily had not overheard the remark, before she replied with false assurance. "Of course, he'll get here!" Then she amended, "You know low water is seldom a problem below Columbia." She hesitated, her smooth cheeks reddening. "Well, I'm sure there are times when it's difficult to reach Columbia by boat, but he will be here the day before the wedding for rehearsal, I'm sure."

"Even if he gets to Columbia, it's a long way away." Elmira tossed her dark mane.

The seeds of doubt sown by Elmira, watered by weariness, began to grow. That night Lily awakened from a dream-troubled sleep. She went to stand by the window and stare at the stars. Had anything happened to Harrison? She brooded, nervously twisting the curtains. What if he could not get back by the third of November, their appointed wedding day? Something stirred and Emma was beside her.

"Don't worry," the older girl whispered. "Everything will work out. Elmira's just a troublemaker. I'm sorry she got *you* started worrying."

Lily looked at her in surprise. The slight inflection Emma placed on her words told Lily that her friend had already been worrying. Although she could not see her clearly in the moonlight, Lily sensed she was in tears.

"Lily, dear," Emma breathed a shuddering sigh, "you know that life on the Chattahoochee is fraught with danger. If something has happened to Harrison, you have known a great love. That can sustain you for the rest of your life, as mine has." She drew back into the shadows and wept in broken sobs.

"Emma, Emma, don't talk like that!" Lily grasped the sleeves of her white muslin nightgown and shook her until her long braid flopped. "Nothing has happened to Harrison. He *will* be here!" she shouted.

She gulped a sigh and whimpered, "I'm sorry, but Emma, he will come." She wiped her eyes and got hold of herself with difficulty. "Dear Emma, your life isn't over." Lily hugged her tightly. "You mustn't say that. Maybe it was for the best that you didn't marry your love. God works all things together for the good to them that love Him and are called according to His purpose. He has a task for each of us. You don't know what lies in store for you if you're ready to serve Him. You can be sure He has some plan for your life."

"No." Emma shook her head. "I don't think that He takes notice of me at all. But I so want your life to be special."

Returning to bed, Lily stared for endless hours at the web of the macramé canopy outlined in the moonlight. Remembering her words of consolation to her friend, she wondered if she had foreshadowed her own destiny. Would Harrison return in time?

As the month drew to a close and all of her preparations lay completed, Lily began again to climb to the belvedere where she was at one with the brilliant blue of the clear October sky. Daily she searched the Scriptures for wisdom. Ruefully, she reflected that she should not have let her joy and the busyness of her life distract her from daily seeking power by reading God's Word.

One evening she sat at her rolltop secretary writing in her journal. "October 31, 1858. Still no message from Harrison. I pray that I may accept whatever comes."

Restlessness overwhelmed her, and she put down her pen and climbed to the belvedere. Clouds scudded across the sky. As she stepped out onto the deck, simultaneous lightning and thunder shook her and made her hang onto the balustrade. Lashed by the wind, her long, brown hair plastered by the rain, Lily wept out her anxiety.

November dawned cold and gray. Wrapped in a heavy shawl, Lily trudged up the stairs to her solitary sanctuary. Heavy shrouds of rain clouds pressed down upon the belvedere. The whole world seemed filled with rain, but the Chattahoochee rose a sparkling stream far, far away in the mountains of eastern Georgia. It must be fed a great deal of rain before it strengthened and stirred again into its mighty self.

Harrison should have been here long before this. The time for rehearsal had come and gone. She knew that everyone in the house was whispering behind her back that the wedding should be postponed. With anxious eyes, she searched the horizon for a puff of smoke that would signal the small boat's arrival.

Around noon, she had returned to her lookout when she saw Foy loping across the lawn, waving his arms like a scarecrow in a windstorm. He was shouting, but the wind whipped his voice away. Running pell-mell down the endless flights of stairs, she met him halfway, in the upstairs hall.

"Sister! Sister!" he screeched. Gasping for breath, he could not get out his words.

Tear streaks on his face made Lily's knees give way.

"King's Rock," he gasped. "King's Rock, Sister!" He collapsed at her feet, buried his face in his arms, and sobbed.

Lily sank to the floor beside him and stroked his hair, his ears. She knew all too well about King's Rock. It lay waiting treacherously, sometimes visible, sometimes not, in one of the most dangerous stretches of the Chattahoochee. The channel narrowed twenty miles north of the town of Chattahoochee, Florida. The anxious river rushed by the rocks at a great rate of speed toward the rendezvous at the town where the Chattahoochee married the Flint. Grief was common at King's Rock where steamer after steamer met its fate.

Emma emerged from the bedroom and stood over them, her face pale, her hands clutched together.

Looking up at her, Lily whispered, "Oh, Emma, I've prayed I could accept whatever came, but I was expecting an answer I wanted to hear." She tried to lift Foy's head. "Foy, Dear, tell me. Tell me."

Fighting for control, the boy wiped his sleeve across his face. "I—" He sniffed. "I went to the waterfront to wait. I knew Captain Wingate would surely arrive today." His voice broke again. "Wagons and carts came in from Columbia," he resumed shakily. "The water is so low. The paddle wheelers can't make it beyond there. The goods were unloaded and they brought the news that the *Peytona* struck King's Rock." He buried his face again.

"Was it grounded or. . ."

With difficulty, Foy straightened up and related the events. "The *Peytona* went smashing into King's Rock! Totally wrecked. She sank! When the wagoners passed by," Foy swallowed convulsively, "they saw pieces of the *Peytona* floating—"

"Surely there were survivors?" Lily gasped.

"Yes, but they didn't know who. It was storming and people washed overboard. Some were lost trying to save others. And you know how Captain Wingate. . ."

Cordelia Edwards appeared and wrapped her children in her ample arms, murmuring soothing words. Kitty stood behind her, wailing loudly.

"Hush, Kitty," she commanded quietly. "Emma, start sending out word to the guests that the wedding will be—"

"No!" Lily shouted. "No, Mama, I won't believe Harrison's dead!"

"Of course not, Dear," she soothed. "We'll merely postpone the wedding. If he takes another boat and makes it past Columbia, there's still Purcell's Swirl. In such stormy weather, paddle wheels are damaged in the whirlpool. You know he can't get here in a day."

Papa came rushing up the stairs. Deep lines in his face told Lily he knew about the accident. As he threw his arms about her stiff shoulders, she cried out, "Oh, Papa, do you know about survivors?"

"No, Dear, I've heard no names. We can only pray Harrison is safe. But, Lily, you must realize he can't get here by boat. A man at the wharf said that the water is so low south of here that you can wade across the river at Fort Gaines. Your mother is right. You must postpone the wedding." He jerked his head meaningfully toward Emma.

"Maybe," Lily admitted sorrowfully. "But, Emma, don't do anything yet." She stood up. "Please. Give me a little time alone." She turned and climbed the attic stairs slowly, like an old, old woman.

Emerging in the belvedere, she collapsed on the floor with her head on a chair. Her tears would not come. Cold, numb, she huddled alone. For long, agonizing moments, she clung to the chair.

At long last, she raised her head. She was not alone. There was one to whom she could turn. Jesus promised His followers they would never be alone.

His Spirit was always there, waiting alongside to comfort, to strengthen, if only one asked.

She stepped out into the cold wind and lifted her face to the sky. "Oh, Lord," she prayed, "if it be Thy will, let Harrison be alive. I know that Thou dost love us and take care of us. I won't worry anymore. I'll leave it with Thee."

Shivering, but warmed inside, she stepped back into the glassed enclosure. She sat holding her Bible and whispered again, "I'll leave it in Your hands."

As peace sent her blood flowing again, she opened the worn Book to Acts ten. She could not put words to her prayers, but the Holy Spirit interceded for her; and as she read God's Word, He seemed to be speaking quietly, clearly in her mind as He had spoken to Cornelius and Peter. She knew with calm assurance that Harrison was not dead. She read on in the second chapter of Ephesians, "For he is our peace, who hath made both one."

When she returned to her anxious family below, she was so strong in her convictions that they could not dissuade her. Even though all of them went about muttering under their breath that it was against their better judgment, they continued the wedding preparations.

On the morning of November third, Lily slowly, deliberately stepped into her widest hoop. The wedding was not scheduled until three in the afternoon, and Emma tried to get her to wait; but she wanted to be dressed and ready. Shaking her head sorrowfully, Emma lifted the lustrous satin over Lily's head, and it settled like a cloud around the slim girl.

Lily watched in the cheval glass while Emma fastened the loops on the satin buttons up the back and the gown closed tightly around her tiny waist. Lily adjusted the flounce of illusion across her shoulders and ran aching fingers along the scallops of pearls embroidered over the bodice. The girl in the mirror looked back with a white satin face and eyes of round, black coals.

"Don't you love the sleeves?" Lily said in a small voice and tried to make the girl in the mirror and the girl straightening the deep flounce around her feet smile. She lifted her arms and the sleeves, fitted to the elbows and then spreading from a ring of pearls into eight petals, floated to her wrists.

Emma laughed softly. "You are a beautiful bride!"

Carefully covering herself with a gray flannel wrapper, Lily compressed her hoops to negotiate the narrow staircase and climbed once more to the belvedere to wait.

Cold and tired, she sat until nearly noon. Passing her hand across her weary eyes, she saw a lathered horse plodding up the hill. When the rider dismounted and started running toward the house, his swinging hands assured her it was Harrison.

Floating down the stairs, she cast away the flannel wrapper. It did not matter if he saw her wedding gown before the ceremony. He must know the depth of her faith in him. He bounded into the entrance hall and swooped her into his arms before her feet touched the last steps. Flinging herself toward him, she laughed and cried.

Kissing her face, her hands, her hair, he murmured words of love and apology. He tried to explain about the accident and his long trip overland.

"Never mind. You're here." She laughed, looking into his eyes that seemed to be sagging in a face stained from the horseback ride. There were streaks of red mud on her dress, too, but the marks only spoke of their dedication to each other.

After Mrs. Edwards had overseen the careful removal of the mud from the gown, Lily had only to don her gossamer veil. Held by a crown of blossoms over her brown hair, it misted around her clusters of long curls. She stood ready, waiting while her groom prepared.

Like lavender butterflies, her bridesmaids fluttered around her. Proceeded by the stalwart Emma, she stepped lightly down the church aisle on the arm of dear Papa. At the altar, Harrison waited, his eyes alight with love.

As the minister's words, "What God hath joined together, let no man put asunder," were sealed with a kiss of commitment, Lily and Harrison began a life of joy which God has promised those who serve Him.

In the happy years that followed, Lily and Harrison were filled with the calm assurance that God walked with them through the trials and challenges of life. Often Lily accompanied Harrison on his travels. Wherever they went, they found ways to spread God's love to those they met; and when Lily chose to stay home with their children, the presence of Harrison's love remained with her. Secure in the commitment of their Christian marriage, they were one in Christ. Never again could the river come between them.

Acknowledgments

When I climbed to the belvedere and looked down on Eufaula, Alabama, as beautiful today as it was in the era of this story, I was transported back in time and could feel the warm breath of my characters. Showing me through the elegant mansion, Douglas Purcell, historian, editor, and Executive Director of the Historic Chattahoochee Commission, made the history of the area come alive. He took me to Fendall Hall which is owned and preserved as a museum by the State of Alabama. Fendall Hall is listed in the National Register of Historic Places. The keeper of the National Register has commented that the parlor and dining room are worthy of exhibition at the Smithsonian Institution. Built by Edward B. Young in 1854, and named for his wife, Ann Fendall Beall, this house merely suggested my story. Barbour Hall and the people who lived there are entirely fiction.

My characters were given added breath, however, when Purcell took me to Shorter Mansion, which is open to the public as a museum, and introduced me to historian and teacher, Mrs. C. E. Mundine. Elizabeth immediately became my friend and helper. She gave me the 1858 diary of Mrs. Elizabeth Rhodes which contained a detailed account of life in Eufaula. I acquired many books to research. Three of the most helpful were: J. A. B. Besson, *History of Eufaula* (Atlanta, 1875); Anne Kendrick Walker, *Backtracking in Barbour County* (Richmond, 1941); and Hoyt M. Warren, *Henry's Heritage: A History of Henry County, Alabama* (Abbeville, Alabama, 1978).

Roseland Plantation and many of the mansions described in the story are beautifully preserved. Some of them are the residences of descendants of the people mentioned in *The River Between.* One of these gracious ladies, Mrs. James Ross (Emma) Foy, invited me into her home and shard love letters written in 1865 by Dr. H. M. Weedon and Mary Young. It was Miss Young who actually lived in Fendall Hall. This correspondence between young lovers separated by the river and the problems delaying their marriage provided a springboard for the correspondence between Lily and Harrison. I cannot thank Mrs. Foy enough.

I greatly appreciate the time Doug Purcell and Elizabeth Mundine gave not only in guiding my research but also in proofing the manuscript to be certain it is historically accurate.

For the visual trip down the Chattahoochee, I thank Marc Doyle of TV

5 WAGA in Atlanta for the use of their beautiful film, "River of Life."

I appreciate the research assistance given by the Lake Blackshear Regional Library, Jane Hendrix, Harriet Bates, and their staff.

Special color for this story was told to me by my friend, John Grover Cleveland Pace, who was born April 21, 1885.

I also thank the many other people who were helpful, especially my son, John Cook; my secretary; Mrs. Glenda Spradley; Mrs. Bill Story; Mrs. Ed Stephens, and Mrs. Lamar Bowen who went from the belvedere to the last page.

Eufaula is delightful to visit anytime; but it is especially lovely the first week in April during the Eufaula Pilgrimage (unless Easter intervenes), when the residents graciously open their historic homes to the public.

The Wind Along the River

Chapter 1

A sudden chill wind snatched Emma's cashmere shawl, threatening to fling it into the Chattahoochee far, far below. Engulfed in loneliness, she had stood too long on the bluff overlooking the river. Evening slipped silently around her, bringing an end to the December day, mild even for Alabama.

Shivering, Emma Edwards glanced at the lowering sky and sighed. She must hurry home to Barbour Hall because her sister-in-law, Cordelia, who thought Emma's only purpose in life was to obey her whims, would be angry again. Lily always said God had a plan for everyone, but Emma thought He had not noticed her. Love had passed her by. At twenty-seven, she had reached the evening of her life.

Blat! Blat! A sharp sound echoed from the hills behind her, seemingly a part of her exploding emotions. Her spreading skirt, weighed down by hoops, and her honey-colored hair, drawn back into a tight knot at the back of her slender neck, remained unruffled by the wind. Her delicate fingers smoothed the lines of her cheeks into an expression as placid as the distant water. She would not allow herself another sigh or frown; but as her gaze dropped to the riverbank at the base of the bluff and to the waves rolling into the shore, lapping, churning, whipping into a white froth, she could feel the same restlessness pounding ceaselessly within her. Surely December 20, 1860, would be a date forever seared upon her brain.

The sun had set behind Eufaula, yet the many mansions of the city sparkled as if their windows were studded with diamonds. They wavered before her startled blue eyes in a haze she knew to be smoke because her throat burned from her sudden gasp. Echoing reports of discharging cannon again assaulted her ears. Squinting to focus the blurred scene, she was able to discern, etched against a blazing bonfire, a buggy rattling down the hill toward her.

"Emma, Emma, come quickly," Lily Wingate's lilting voice called. Her brown hair had slipped from its combs and was streaming in the wind. "Hurry! You mustn't miss the fun of the illuminations!"

"The what?" Emma's relieved laughter bubbled in her throat as she easily negotiated her willowy body into the red leather seat of the runabout. Suppressing her initial reaction of fear, she allowed her heart to respond, as always, with delight to the animation of her niece, just seven years her junior.

"Oh, it's all just too exciting," exclaimed Lily. "Didn't you hear the cannon signaling?"

"Of course," Emma answered.

"The tide can no longer be stemmed!" Lily's voice was shrill with fervor. "Since South Carolina has taken the irrevocable action of secession, the news is coming in that all over the South people are joining in illumination night!"

The buggy swayed as they crossed Randolph Avenue, and Lily struggled with the reins. The horse threatened to rear as the people poured into the street, shouting, waving handkerchiefs. A brigade of soldiers, the Eufaula Rifles, marched smartly around the corner, accompanied by a drum's tattoo.

Emma could not seem to share Lily's exhilaration. As a spinster, she had no real place in Eufaula's kingdom of cotton. While she could sympathize with the local demand for states' rights and a low tariff so that the South could trade its cotton for cheap foreign goods, she had no voice of her own. From this beautiful city, located on a bluff one hundred and fifty feet above the Chattahoochee River separating Alabama from Georgia, cotton was taken on flat-bottomed side-wheelers down to Apalachicola, Florida, and thence to New York and Liverpool. She could easily understand why Eufaula's flourishing economy was based on land, cotton, and slaves; however, she existed only at the beneficence of her late brother, Clare Edwards. Her sister-in-law kept her in a nebulous position—below the other family members but slightly above the servants. Sometimes, only Lily's insistence that Emma had been granted a special gift kept her head erect, her lips smiling, and her heart searching.

Looking at vivacious Lily, Emma wished that she could share Lily's faith and confidence in her own ability to face whatever life brought.

For the last month, the townspeople had been holding their breaths, suspended, waiting for the weight to drop. Immediately after Lincoln's election in November, Barbour County had organized the Minutemen and called for secession and preparations for safety and resistance. Alabama had waited—to see what South Carolina would do. Eufaula's matrons had busily prepared for parties even while the convention deliberated. Drifting on the eddies of the group, Emma had not felt a part of the celebration.

Since noon today, when the news had spread like leaping flames from the Eufaula telegraph office that South Carolina was withdrawing from the nation, flags had been fluttering and young people had been popping firecrackers. Emma had withdrawn from the bustling excitement, feeling acutely that everyone was converging with a plan except her. Now as she looked at Lily, she stiffened her spine against the buggy seat and pulled her old *canezou,* a dainty jacket with horizontal rows of smocking, more closely around her neck. Shivering, glad she had brought the warm shawl, she wondered whether her chill came from night air or from her unreasonable premonition of fear.

Deftly controlling the horse, Lily pulled away from the crowd proceeding up the hill, gathering around Mayor Thornton's house for speeches. Though it was to be expected that their neighbor, Lewis Llewellen Cato, a member of the Eufaula Regency, would be entertaining a large crowd, Emma was surprised to see Barbour Hall ablaze with lights. It had not been so since Lily's father's death last year.

As they drove past the red cedars at the gates, Emma looked up at the magnificent white-frame mansion. Built in 1854 and considered one of the finest examples of Italianate architecture in the South, its floor-to-ceiling windows on both floors and in the belvedere crowning the roof were, every one, sparkling with light.

Lily giggled in delight. "The house looks dressed for a ball. Haven't I always said the glassed belvedere is her airy hat; the wooden balustrade, her neck ruffle; the green shutters on the upper story, her *canezou,* the porch spreading around the first floor, her hooped skirt—?"

"And the trim for her skirt, the pairs of slender columns interspersed with lacy scrolls," Emma finished for her, laughing.

As the merry pair entered through the double doors, Lily's husband, Harrison Wingate, strode across the entry hall floor, a checkerboard of twelve-inch squares of black-and-white Italian marble. His smooth face brightened with a smile that lifted his mustache and radiated from his eyes as he greeted them. "As soon as I put this candlestand by the parlor window," he said, indicating the hand-carved mahogany *torchier* he carried, "and light one last candle, I'll be finished and ready to go. You're coming with us, Emma?"

"The house is already so bright, it could shine all the way to South Carolina," laughed Lily. Then she added emphatically, "Of course, she's coming. She stays alone in this house far too much. I'm not about to let her miss the most exciting thing that ever happened to Eufaula!"

Her face a mask, Emma looked toward the parlor. She dared not venture an answer until she sensed her sister-in-law's mood.

Cordelia Edwards was jovial. She sat close to the crackling fire that had been lighted beneath the mantel of white Italian marble. "Ah, boo, boo, boo," she laughed, jiggling her chins. The six-month-old baby, perched on Mrs. Edwards's stomach, rewarded her with a two-toothed grin. She looked up as the child's father brought in the waist-high stand, and her tone changed to icy sarcasm. "More candles, Captain Wingate? I really thought this room had quite enough light." She glanced meaningfully toward a multitude of candles lending fire to every crystal teardrop of the Waterford chandelier.

"This is the last one, Miss Cordelia," Harrison replied politely as he placed the *torchier* so that the thick, tall candle would shine directly through the lace draperies on the huge square, six-over-six-pane windows. "The crowds are moving up the hill. We must give evidence of our support."

Lily crossed to her mother, dropped a kiss on her baby's dark fuzz of hair, and flopped on the double settee. Cocking her head to one side, she traced her finger over the elaborate Chippendale design of carved mahogany leaves and scrolls which formed the stiff back, and considered her mother before speaking. "Mama, do you feel like playing with Mignonne a little longer? We all wanted to attend the celebration on College Hill."

Emma sniffed in alarm. Lily had said "we." Emma had already been away from the house for more than an hour. Even though the clean, sharp smell of the oak wood invited her to warm her fingers, she had remained standing in the doorway, watching them obliquely in the huge, gold-leaf Belgian mirror over the mantel.

Mrs. Edwards frowned. "You girls know better than to be out about the town alone," she scolded, shaking her fingers until her black taffeta sleeves rustled.

"Yes, Ma'am," Lily replied meekly, "but this time Harrison will be with us."

"Perhaps I'd better stay and help keep. . . ," Emma interjected subserviently and hurried toward the fireside.

"Nonsense; I'll keep her. What are grandmas for?" Cordelia Edwards bounced the baby for another grin. Mignonne watched with thick-lashed eyes, her apple cheeks waiting expectantly for reason to smile.

Quickly, Lily jumped to her feet and gave Emma a push. "Go put on something pretty," she commanded, then added under her breath, "Harrison has a friend I want you to meet."

Emma's cheeks, already as delicately hued as the inside of a seashell, lost all color, but she turned obediently into the hall and fled up the stairs.

In the blue and white room she had once shared with Lily, Emma hurriedly opened the walnut armoire in the back corner. Even though her brother had willed her a small income of her own, the huge wardrobe held only a few frocks. Excitedly, she fingered them with hands that shook at the thought her niece was matchmaking again.

Since Lily had married the riverboat captain two years ago, she seemed to think everyone should be as happily in love as she. But Emma had long ago resigned herself to spinsterhood; only occasionally did she let herself recall her long-ago love, at sixteen, the acceptable age for coming out in preparation for marriage. She had fallen in love with Michael, but her grandfather had refused permission for them to marry because the young man was not of their faith.

Shaking off her reverie with determination, she began to dress quickly. Dropping her daytime hoop, she stepped into a muslin petticoat run through with four steels from below the waist to the hem. The bottom hoop measured two-and-one-half yards around her feet and would keep her skirt extended fashionably. She decided to follow Lily's advice and wear her prettiest frock, a thick velvet in softly glowing pink. A wide band of ribbon and lace encrusted with crystals circled the slight train and rose in stairsteps in front to frame a cluster of crystal on watered silk roses in the center of the billowing skirt. A narrower band repeated the blocked design around the boat neckline and short, puffed sleeves.

Peering into the mirror over the marble-topped walnut dresser, she dusted a little whiting on her forehead and pinched her cheeks for color. Nothing she could do would keep her features from being plain; however, as she did with the rest of her life, she made the best of them. Fastening a necklace of crystals, she smiled. Lily would be pleased. Flinging on a wrap of pink moiré silk, quilted and lined with velvet, she started out, then ran back for her long, white kid gloves.

Glancing out the bedroom window, Emma saw a crowd of singing, shouting people surging up Barbour Street. They moved as if driven with a single sense of purpose. Pressing her hands against her chest. Emma swallowed convulsively. She had no purpose, no place with this moving throng. She leaned her head against the window frame. Maybe she should not intrude upon Lily and Harrison. She had been with them constantly before their marriage when she was needed as a chaperone; now, however, Lily continued to insist that she accompany them by saying that any situation was always smoothed by Emma's calm, pleasant manner.

A rueful laugh choked her. No one seemed to guess that her peacefulness was a sham. She kept her troubles in a tight little knot at the base of her throat and bravely tried to bear them alone. Looking down into the night, she wavered. Perhaps she should not go. She could stay in this room, her one refuge. No one entered here without her bidding—not even Cordelia.

Down below, flaming torches cast eerie shadows beneath the China trees, increasing her foreboding of something moving toward her. Her knees shook. Lily, who faced all of life like a great adventure, would laugh and chide her. Digging her fingernails into the curtains, Emma crushed the creamy lace in her clammy palm. Sparks from the *flambeaux* seemed to be pricking her soul. She breathed a long, steadying sigh. This was a celebration, a new beginning.

With trembling fingers, Emma smoothed her face into an enigmatic smile. She ran down the stairs and followed her family into the dark.

Chapter 2

The blaze of torches illuminated the happy faces of the crowd, thronging out from the Cato house next door and moving up Barbour Street. Emma was swept along as the mass surged across the block to Broad Street and the top of College Hill.

"Freedom from Northern oppressors!"

"Hurrah for a Southern Confederacy!"

Music, beating in stirring rhythm from the colonnaded portico of the Union Female College, spurred marching feet to assemble quickly. Emma noticed the local dignitaries—Judge John Gill Shorter, Edward Young, John McNab, Mayor Thornton, Colonel E. S. Shorter, and others, seated on the porch. With them were two strangers.

The younger man turned as Emma, Lily, and Harrison moved nearer. A smile danced over his even features as he singled them out of the crowd. Briefly saluting Captain Wingate, he continued to look their way. He was staring at Lily, of course. Her marble-browed, raven-haired beauty was the current fashion rage; Emma's cool blondness was quite out of vogue.

Knowing she barely possessed the requisite handspan waist, Emma gave a self-derisive laugh that anyone would notice her. Loving Lily devotedly, gratefully, Emma felt no pangs of jealousy. Her only joy of living came through sharing Lily's family, and she had long ago resigned herself to the fact that her chance of having a life of her own was nearing an end. Sighing, she raised her chin with determination. Without volition, her lashes also lifted in response to the sensing of a stare. Startled, she met with sudden impact his dark and laughing eyes.

Blushing, she turned her attention to Professor J. C. Van Houten as he stood before a group of girls dressed in their brown merino school uniforms. The crimson ribbons on their brown hats quivered with their excitement as they lifted their high, sweet voices in patriotic songs, composed especially for the occasion by their beloved teacher.

Still feeling warm eyes upon her, Emma averted her gaze and tilted her chin. On the college roof she could see the slightly larger-than-life-sized statue of Minerva, goddess of wisdom, science, and the arts, determinedly clutching her wooden diploma. It always amused Emma that the lady's Roman garments had been exchanged for staid, high-necked, long-sleeved, full-skirted garb so that her carved cypress self looked exactly like the schoolgirls below, down to—no, up to—her hair, parted in the middle and fashioned into wooden, long curls at each side. Emma laughed in spite of herself.

The stranger was laughing with her! *Impudent fellow!* How dare he think she was responding to him? Her cheeks blazing, she edged behind Harrison Wingate's substantial back. From this obscurity, she let the impassioned words of John Gill Shorter, the first of the signers of the Minutemen, slide over her shoulders.

Emma looked up at Minerva. *You and I are the only ones not excited,* she thought. *Can anyone really think Lincoln will allow us to have our own nation and not make war?*

As the cheers and applause died down, Emma peered around Harrison's shoulder just as the words of another speaker—Jonathan Ramsey of Georgia, had been his introduction—made the crowd roar with laughter. His entire talk was laced with humor and predictions of how easily the South would whip the North, if indeed the matter should come to war.

Blat! Blat! The twelve-pound Napoleon fired again. Emma jumped so hard her tense neck muscles hurt. The acrid smell of the black powder made her grimace. The cannon had signaled that the speeches were over. The roué from Georgia was shouldering his way through the crowd toward them.

Harrison gave him a congratulatory handshake and turned to the red-faced Emma. "May I present my dear friend and fellow sailor, Jonathan Ramsey from Bulloch County, Georgia."

Emma managed the proper polite bow and pleasant look required by a lady's introduction to a gentleman; however, she narrowed her eyes to convey reproving anger because of his liberties of familiarity. He bowed swiftly and brushed his mustache over her extended hand. "You must be the lovely Miss Emma." He lifted his head and spoke so exuberantly that his dark curls bounced. "Miss Lily does go on and on about you."

Laughing, unable to sustain anger as she looked into his twinkling eyes, Emma said fondly, "She does go on and on about everything."

"I'm as dry as a bone in the desert after all that speechifying." Ramsey chuckled and clapped his hand against his bright cravat as if he were choking. "Let's make a round of the parties. I hear Colonel Chambers is serving eggnog—that is, unless you ladies are hostessing a party. . ." He lifted quizzical, black eyebrows and waited hopefully.

"Oh, no," Lily responded quickly. "We'd be delighted to accompany you tonight—" Her brown eyes darted a look at Emma, and she continued briskly, "but we are planning a grand occasion at Barbour Hall for Christmas. You must join us then, mustn't he, Emma?"

Emma could only nod. This was the first she'd heard of any such plans.

When Jonathan Ramsey's attention was diverted by yet another admirer, Emma hissed at Lily, "Why did you tell him that? He's terribly forward and rude."

"Nonsense!" laughed Lily. "He has zest for life. These times are too exciting to be slow and boring." Cocking her head to one side, she surveyed Emma, whose fingers were working nervously with the neck of her pink cloak. "Just relax. Tonight, let's have fun. . .and, Emma, we must do something about your hair."

Jonathan Ramsey returned to her side with a bow. His apology for the interruption was delivered with such a candid expression on his boyish, clean-shaven cheeks that Emma began to believe she had judged him too harshly. The cut of his dark, frock-tailed coat and the soft material of his slim, tan trousers told her he was a well-to-do gentleman. Although he was not as tall and dashing as Harrison and lacked the captain's quietly mysterious depths, Jonathan was quite the most fun of anyone she had ever been around. His warmth soon had her giggling like a schoolgirl.

They strolled down Broad Street, a boulevard with a wide median planted with towering magnolias and oaks. Greek Revival and Italianate mansions, each with its own distinctive architecture, graced both sides of the street. While most planters in southeastern Alabama and southwestern Georgia built their houses on their plantations, the planters and merchants of Eufaula built side by side along the town's boulevards. For the past twenty years, thousands of bales of cotton had been shipped down the Chattahoochee to Apalachicola, Florida, the largest cotton-exporting port in America. This exceptional prosperity lent a fairyland opulence which tonight twinkled as though thousands of fireflies fluttered to keep every house ablaze with light. White-coated butlers bowed the laughing couples through double doors of one house after another.

Each hostess seemed intent upon outdoing the other. Light suppers of oyster patties, lobster, chicken salad, cakes, jellies, ices, shrimps, meringues, tongue, and small hams were arranged in elaborate beauty on gleaming mahogany sideboards ashine with silver.

"I can't eat another morsel," laughed Emma, "—after this." She reached for one more Spanish wind cake. She bit into the meringue which had been slowly baked to a delicate crispness. "Umm," she murmured, savoring the whipped cream filling. Lastly, she popped the pink meringue rosebud into her upturned mouth.

"It's as hard as stealing cream from a cat to get a smile out of you," grinned Ramsey, "but it's surely worth the wait."

"Let's go to the Treadwell house for dancing," interrupted Lily.

As the merry foursome made their way through the torchlit garden, they were stopped by Henry Clayton.

"May I speak with you gentlemen for a moment? Beg pardon, ladies." He bent low with a sweeping gesture.

As the men stepped aside under the sheltering shadow of a glossy-leafed magnolia tree, Emma turned to Lily. "Why did you tell—him?" She swallowed, too insecure to speak Jonathan's name aloud just yet. "Why did you say we were having a big celebration? You know your mother is not feeling well and wants us to have another quiet Christmas in mourning."

"One Christmas in mourning is quite enough," Lily answered firmly. "Papa would want us to celebrate for his grandchild." Suddenly drooping, she pressed her fist against her mouth and whispered, "Oh, I wish he could've seen my pretty one."

Sympathetic at the tears shining in Lily's wide, dark eyes, Emma sighed. She had known neither peace nor joy since her brother, Clare Edwards, had died. She existed alone with Cordelia and Cordelia's adolescent son, Foy, in Barbour Hall.

"I'll come home first thing in the morning and help get started with the work." Lily's voice drew her back.

"You know it isn't the work I'm worried about." An unaccustomed frown creased Emma's forehead. She pulled her quilted moiré wrap more tightly around her slender shoulders and clutched it to her chest with both hands. "I don't know how we'll get ready in four days—I'll manage somehow." She looked down at Lily. "But it's your mama. Most of the time she has me keep the keys, but I can't really do anything without her telling me."

"I'll manage Mama." Lily's voice lacked confidence as she leaned over to incline her ear toward the magnolia tree.

Clayton was speaking urgently. "Gentlemen, we all certainly hope that we can become a sovereign nation which can export its own goods without interference. We pray this will not come to war. If, indeed, it does, we have no army."

"Except the local militia groups," interjected Ramsey.

"But worse," continued Clayton, "we have no navy!"

"A navy will be vital," nodded Harrison. "We have no hope if we cannot navigate our rivers and keep our seaports open. We must have a navy!"

"Then we can count on you gentlemen?" Clayton lowered his voice and stepped further under the tree.

"A navy," gasped Lily, her face paling in the torchlight. "I had not thought—surely Harrison would never have to go to war. . ."

"Come on, ladies," Jonathan Ramsey called gaily. "Hurry. The orchestra's playing the 'Tallahassee Waltz.' "

Drifting through open French doors, the lilting popular music soothed Emma's frown. Bass notes set their feet sliding to three-quarter time, but the treble trilled up the scale as daintily as a minuet. Unaccustomed to dancing, Emma feared her feet would be as wooden and useless as Minerva's, but, oh, how she longed to dance! His black brows raised quizzically, Mr. Ramsey bowed before her with an exaggerated wave of his arm. Lifting her clear, sweet face to his, she stood motionless for a moment, hands raised, lips parted, eyes wide. Slowly, she stretched out her hand and let him lead her to the dance floor. He seemed not to notice the questions in her innocent blue eyes or the fears pulsating the veins beneath her crystal necklace.

Sweeping her along in the confident curve of his arm, he guided her forward to the right, forward to the left, then sliding backwards. Laughing, she stumbled through the reverse steps.

"Relax." He chuckled good-humoredly. "Just float where I—and the music—take you."

Whirling, swaying, her hoop tilting her pink velvet skirt to the rhythm of the music and making the iridescent beading shimmer, Emma began to feel as happy as a schoolgirl, as giddy as a child on a swing.

After several dances, Jonathan brought two punch cups and ushered her to the coolness of the garden. Walking silently through the sharp-scented borders of black-green boxwood, they settled on a marble bench invitingly placed before a blossom-laden camellia bush.

Her breath coming in quick gasps, her cheeks flushed, Emma said, "I don't know when I've had such fun!" Golden tendrils were escaping around her damp forehead, and she tried in vain to secure them.

"Miss Emma, how lovely you are," Jonathan said softly. "You are as delicate and perfect as these camellias." He plucked a waxy pink blossom and gently presented it to her, gazing at her for a long moment. Then he said seriously, "You didn't seem to second Miss Lily's invitation for Christmas. Dare I hope that you might welcome me?"

"Oh, of course, of course," Emma responded quickly with her eyes sparkling. "We couldn't have you spend such a special day in a hotel, Mr. Ramsey. Besides, it wouldn't seem a party without you." She dropped her lashes, and her cheeks flushed pinker for letting this slip out.

If she had thought him forward, what would he think of her?

Jonathan Ramsey laughed heartily. "Then, of course, I'll be there."

Emma's glow remained as they returned to the dancing.

When at last the evening had to end and they left her at Barbour Hall, her euphoria continued. Putting on her flannelette nightgown, she hugged herself and laughed softly, as full of anticipation as a child about to hang up her first stocking. She climbed the needlepoint-covered stool onto the high, rosewood bed, laid the camellia on the pillow beside her cheek, and snuggled into the feather mattress. With her mind flitting, whirling, dancing, she lay staring happily at the airy white mesh which covered the lilting curve of the rosewood canopy.

A sudden gust of wind lengthened the shadow of her candle. The loose knots of the diamond-patterned macramé canopy became a giant spiderweb against the ceiling.

Quickly blowing out the candle, she closed her eyes, exhausted. Just as she dozed into a pleasant dream, a rasping voice snatched her back.

"Emma! Em-mah!"

Chapter 3

"Emmaaa. . . ," Cordelia Edwards whined.

Sighing, Emma climbed down from the bed, threw a blue flannel wrapper over her gown, and padded across the drafty hall to her sister-in-law's large, square room at the rear of the second floor.

Enthroned upon a massive bed with straight, walnut bedposts holding aloft a walnut canopy, Cordelia Edwards parted the wine velvet bed curtains and peered out as Emma set her candle on the marble-top bedside table. Her face pursed into a pout, she said, "I didn't think you'd leave me for so long. You stayed out half the night. My rheumatism is paining miserably." She sank weakly against the goose-down pillows. "You'd best make me a mustard plaster."

Emma complied as quickly as possible, making apologies, even though she knew that Mrs. Edwards's personal maid, Kitty, could have mixed the hot water, dry mustard, and flour as well as she.

Spreading the sour-smelling paste on a clean cloth and folding it carefully to keep it from oozing, she applied the poultice to Cordelia's broad back. She refilled the copper kettle at the Wedgwood lavatory in the dressing room and replaced it on the hearth. She sighed, thankful that her brother had been far ahead of his time and installed a cistern in the attic which was filled by a windmill for a ready supply of gravity-forced, running water. She sat shivering by the banked coals until the poultice had sufficiently reddened Cordelia's soft flesh and she could remove it. Dawn was streaking the sky as she climbed wearily into bed.

When Emma awoke, it was with a slow luxurious stretching and a smiling remembrance of her pleasant evening. Suddenly she sat bolt upright. Sunlight streamed through her eastern window, danced around the blue walls, and hopscotched over the blue and white Oriental rug. How had she slept so long? Cordelia Edwards's voice rumbled from the morning room.

Jumping down from the bed, Emma ran to her dressing room, grasped the German silver faucets of the lavatory, and splashed cool water on her face. Hurrying into a faded calico, she hesitated to open her door into the small sitting room which adjoined. Instead, she stepped to the wide, central hall and peeped through the sliding doors that closed off one end to form the morning room. She stood stiffly, trying to determine her sister-in-law's mood and adjust herself before she entered.

Laughter surprised her. There sat Lily bubbling with good spirits and actually eating eggs and greasy sausage. Emma slipped quietly into the cozy room and queasily took only coffee from the laden breakfast tray. Lily, feeding Mignonne, who sat beside her on the small sofa, had already convinced her mother that what she needed to make her feel good again was a joyous Christmas celebration. Cordelia relaxed against the comfortable upholstery of the gracefully curving Louis XV style furniture and rapidly formulated menus.

"Foy and I will be in charge of decorating." Lily smiled fondly at her fourteen-year-old brother, who sat with his long legs dangling over the window seat.

"You bet," he croaked excitedly. His childhood chubbiness had melted into hollows and angles. Although he tried to move with dignity befitting his advancing years, his natural exuberance overcame him. He hopped down and started for the door with his dark eyes sparkling. "I'll find a perfect tree—and I know where some mistletoe—"

"You be careful climbing treetops after mistletoe," warned his mother, as she finished her buttered biscuits and fig preserves. "Take Lige with you."

"Yes, Ma'am." Foy grinned, leaving the room with his long arms and legs flapping like an excited scarecrow.

Emma sat at the small French secretary of light beechwood and made lists at Cordelia's direction. The fluttering in her stomach calmed and her anticipation grew. When Lily rose to leave, her words brought a blush to Emma's smooth face.

"I must go home and dispatch Harrison and Jonathan on a turkey hunt."

"Emma and I will start cooking," answered her mother. Paying no attention to Emma's pink cheeks and downcast eyelashes, Cordelia led the way downstairs and across the suspended, covered walkway to the separate brick kitchen.

The cook, Aunt Dilsey, scowled when Mrs. Edwards shunted her aside to make her own special cake. Aunt Dilsey soon recovered her authority, and her broad face beamed beneath her red bandanna as she put the young girls to various tasks of seeding raisins, cutting orange peel, and chopping the candied citron. Disdainfully setting aside the pecans, which could be picked up in the yard and eaten anytime, she directed two girls in cracking and picking out the almonds, English walnuts, and the Christmas favorite, Brazil nuts, which had come up the Chattahoochee on the steamboats returning for more bales of cotton. With everyone working, Dilsey herself began cooking sweet potatoes in a huge iron pot hanging on an arm over the open fire. Soon she had turned them into a custard which filled the small building with the fragrance of cinnamon.

"No hog-killin', no Chris'mus, seems to me," pouted old Patience.

"Too hot for that. We'll have to make do with cured ham from the smokehouse," laughed Emma, pushing wet curls from her forehead with a sticky forearm. She and dark, long-boned Kitty worked together over a wide, earthen bowl. Orange juice dripped over their hands into the bowl as they cut sections, carefully removing seeds and membrane, and mixed in coconut. Sprinkling on sugar, Emma stirred and tasted the ambrosia. "Perfect." She smiled at Kitty with a self-satisfied glow, glad that she had purchased the oranges and coconut when the last steamboat came up from the seaport of Apalachicola. Celebration or not, it would not be Christmas without ambrosia.

Aunt Dilsey had evidently felt that way about fruitcake. Gleefully, she produced a covered box and let them all have a sniff of the dark, rich cakes she had made weeks ago and set to ripen.

Red-faced from the warmth of the kitchen, Mrs. Edwards laughed and joked with her servants as she placed her cake, made delicate with stiffly beaten egg whites, in the oven built into the brick wall by the fireplace. She did not yet trust the new iron cookstove in the corner for baking.

When Cordelia and Emma left the kitchen at last and walked back across the high, covered walkway to the house, they heard Dilsey's mellow voice pouring forth in song:

"There's a star in the east on Christmas morn.
  Rise up, shepherd, and fol-ler;
It'll lead to the place where the Savior's born,
  Rise up, shepherd, and fol-ler."
The younger servants answered in rich harmony:
  "Fol-ler, Fol-ler, rise up, shepherd, and fol-ler,
Fol-ler de star of Beth-le-hem,
  Rise up, shepherd, and fol-ler."

They stood for a moment on the porch to cool and catch their breath and to listen as one group chanted a line and another echoed back the refrain.

"Leave yo' sheep and leave yo' lambs,
  Rise up, shepherd, and fol-ler.
Leave yo' ewes and leave yo' rams,
  Rise up, shepherd, and fol-ler.
Take good heed to de an-gel's word,
  Rise up, shepherd, and fol-ler,
You'll forget your sheep, you'll forget your herd,
  Rise up, shepherd, and fol-ler."

As they stepped into the house, the sharp fragrance of freshly cut pine filled the wide central hallway. Cordelia flopped on the sofa of shiny, slick, black horsehair. It was her favorite piece of furniture because the style of its unusual S–shaped legs dated to 1783 and had been made for only a period of ten years. Declaring herself too tired to move farther than this spot at the rear of the hall, she leaned back and surveyed her children's handiwork. Lily had returned, and she and Foy had made ropes of black-green pine, which they hung in swags from the chair rail down both sides of the long hall.

"Come look!" Lily pulled a weary Emma across the black-and-white marble floor, threw open the double entrance doors, and pushed her onto the veranda. Pine garlands also hung in each interval between the pairs of white columns.

Grinning from ear to ear, Lige carried in a stepladder. Foy followed, carefully holding a branch of waxy, delicate green leaves with tiny white berries. With great ceremony he climbed the ladder and fastened the mistletoe to the crown-of-thorns chandelier, a unique ring of six-pointed stars, stabbed with crystal thorns and hung with varying crystal teardrops.

"It was so high in the treetops that I had to shoot it down," Foy said proudly as he jumped from the ladder and looked up at his prize. "That gives me the honor of claiming the first kiss." With a bony arm he swiftly pulled Lily beneath the mistletoe. His ears stood out beet red from his bristly hair as he planted a shy kiss on her cheek.

For the next two days, the house rang with laughter, singing, scurrying footsteps, and rattling paper. Foy joined Harrison and Jonathan in the hunt, and they came in with quail and dove to supplement the turkey and ham. With each trip from the woods, Foy brought more holly until every spot, even the picture frames, glowed with green leaves and scarlet berries. Cordelia Edwards had taken back the huge ring of keys which denoted authority over the house, but only when Emma was very tired did the old feeling of not belonging overshadow her happiness. She tried to remind herself that Mr. Ramsey was a stranger passing through, and she should not let her heart beat faster at the thought of him; but the sound of Jonathan's laughter, even if from another room, always brought a peaceful smile to her face.

Food baskets were packed for the poor. "All my dear Mr. Edwards's good works must be continued, of course," his widow declared with a catch in her voice and tears shining in her eyes.

Each evening after supper, they settled contentedly in the parlor around the fire. Mrs. Edwards was careful to shield herself from the heat by using the face screen, ornamented with a picture of English ladies and gentlemen, worked in gold, silver, and china beads. She could not allow the paraffin she used to conceal wrinkles to melt. They took turns reading passages from Charles Dickens's *Christmas Carol.* When Emma's time came to sit by the fine Argand lamp and read by the sperm oil flame, she was extremely conscious of Jonathan's warm eyes upon her.

Lily and Foy strictly forbade anyone's entering the music room until Christmas Eve. When Lily arrived at first dark with Harrison behind her quietly carrying Mignonne, she signaled Foy and called to her mother, "Come on, Mama, it's time. Now, you're going to hang up your stocking, too!"

Ceremoniously, she slid open the doors of red Bohemian etched glass and revealed a tremendous cedar tree standing in the center of the room, with myriads of candles twinkling from its branches.

"Look, Baby, see the pretty tree."

Mignonne gazed at the flickering lights in wonder and stretched out dimpled hands. Harrison held her close to see the various ornaments—a spun-glass swan, a dog carrying a golden basket in his mouth, a bunch of green grapes imported from Germany when Lily was an infant, and other crystal or tinseled treasures. Then he handed her to his wife and stationed himself in the corner near the buckets of water, just in case of fire.

Oblivious to the fact that she was gowned in sumptuous emerald velvet especially ordered for her from the Paris Salon of Charles Frederick Worth, Lily sat on the floor beside the tree. Candlelight glistened on her creamy bare shoulders and the magnificent diamond and emerald necklace which had belonged to Harrison's French grandmother. Rivaling the tree for sparkle, Lily showed Mignonne the Christmas garden. Set amid cotton snow were miniature houses, shepherds, and sheep. Lily lifted the tiny manger and told her infant daughter about the baby Jesus. Harrison read aloud the second chapter of Luke.

"Now it's time to 'hang the stockings by the chimney with care,'" quoted Foy.

"Why, where is yours, Emma?" Lily demanded of the girl standing in the shadows. "Go to your room and get one this minute!"

After Emma had complied obediently, she was directed to the square piano which had been pushed awry so that the tree would be reflected in the towering pier mirror between the floor-to-ceiling windows. Carefully she lifted her skirt of shimmering, ice-blue taffeta around the piano stool. Her fingers moved lovingly over the mother-of-pearl keys of the beautifully carved rosewood instrument. When she was playing beautiful music and lifting her clear soprano in song, she came nearest to grasping Lily's belief that God smiled with love upon each individual.

A stirring in the hallway interrupted "Hark! The Herald Angels Sing." Jonathan Ramsey had arrived. Voicing jovial greetings and filling the room with laughter, he smiled appreciatively at Emma's gown, which was trimmed with a fichu of creamy lace. She had no sparkling jewels, only a cameo nestled in the lace and opal earrings; but she had tied a blue velvet ribbon midway on her slender neck. Taking Lily's advice, she had loosened her honey-colored hair from its usual severe knot into soft masses of ringlets.

Emma had spent a great deal of time on her toilette; now, however, she nervously clutched her cameo. She should not have presumed to dress for a dance until she secured permission to go. Her blue eyes darted toward her sister-in-law who was wearing her most put-upon expression.

"Uh," Emma cleared her throat, "don't you think I'd better stay with you and Mignonne—and Foy? All of the servants have left for the setting up at their church—you know, to watch for the coming of Christ as they always do on Christmas Eve. . ."

"Has everyone gone?" Cordelia queried brusquely.

"Yes, Ma'am," Emma replied meekly. "Even feeble old Patience said she must not let her Lord catch her in bed on the night when the very cows fall on their knees."

"Don't you think you can manage, Mama?" interjected Lily. "Everyone who is anyone is going to the party in John Clark's new building."

"I'll play with Mignonne 'til she gets sleepy," volunteered Foy with a crooked, loving smile toward his aunt.

It was agreed upon, and Emma went for her wrap. When she descended the stairs with a rustle of crinoline and a drifting scent of lavender, Jonathan was paying no attention to her. He and Foy were engaged in a grinning, motioning byplay. As she stepped down onto the marble floor, Foy edged her beneath the crown-of-thorns chandelier, and Jonathan reached a swift arm about her slender waist and brushed the merest whisper of a kiss across her lips.

Stiffening in surprise, she gasped and stared with wide blue eyes. He grinned and silently pointed to the mistletoe. Cordelia's face puffed in shock, but for the rest of the evening, Emma tingled with a notion of floating two inches above the dance floor.

Mysterious rustlings awakened Emma. A smile twitched about her lips, but she pretended she was asleep and kept her eyes squeezed shut.

"Chris'mus gif'!" shouted a voice as her bedroom door was thrust open. "I s'prise you!"

"Oh, you caught me," laughed Emma, sitting up in the bed. She handed over silver coins from a pouch beside the bed.

Kitty chuckled and Tildy squealed in delight. Emboldened, they crossed the hall to Cordelia Edwards's room and burst in, repeating the cry, "Chris'mus gif'!"

Smiling that the day was properly begun, Emma went to the window and parted the lace curtains. The sun was well up, but the air was crisp and cold. *Good,* she thought, *this is more like Christmas.* It would also be more comfortable for the last-minute cooking, she knew. Humming as she dressed, Emma secured the leather pouch to her belt in preparation for further surprises.

The pungent aroma of coffee drew her along that walkway to the kitchen. Aunt Dilsey had already fried the salty, cured ham and was pouring coffee in the grease to make the red-eye gravy. Biscuits, baked in the Dutch oven surrounded by hot coals on the hearth, waited, crusty brown on the outside, fluffy on the inside. A large platter was heaped with oysters.

"Wait to cook the eggs until Lily arrives—oh, I hear them now!" Emma hurried out to get a hug and kiss from Mignonne before Cordelia claimed her.

After breakfast, Foy lighted the candles on the Christmas tree and importantly distributed the stockings and gifts. Delighted exclamations and thanks followed each opening of books, lace collars and cuffs, silver dishes, and so on. Then the happy group trouped out to see Lily's present from Harrison, a pretty carriage with a perfectly matched pair of ponies. Emma turned toward the kitchen.

"Martha, Martha, don't be cumbered about much serving,' " quoted Lily, frowning when she saw that Emma was not going to church with the rest of the family. "Really, Emma, you must also feed the soul! Worship and fellowship can refresh and strengthen you for your tasks. . . ."

Emma shrugged Lily's hand off of her shoulder and stood firm. She wished that Lily would not press her. Attending church was simply one more obligation in her duty-filled life. Cordelia did not care whether she was included; certainly God could not care about her insignificant life.

After completing dinner preparations, she went upstairs to change into a pale pink wool frock. Wide navy ribbon banded the two-yard hem and rose at intervals halfway up the skirt in a club design. This was repeated on the matching knee-length jacket which she laid carefully over the bed. Returning downstairs, she heard a commotion on the front porch.

"Chris'mus gif'. I seed you first!"

She watched through the sidelights of the door as Jonathan delivered a coin to a small boy with mock surprise and protestation. "That's not fair. You only caught me because you slipped up barefooted as a yard dog." He laughed.

Emma opened the doors, laughing, and Jonathan made her an elaborate bow.

"Please, don't think me forward," he said quite seriously. "I know we've just met, but do accept a small token of my esteem." He held out a nosegay of violets and geraniums.

Accepting the bouquet with a flush of pleasure, Emma ushered him into the parlor where they chatted until the family burst in.

A glow of happiness radiated from Emma's face as it had not in the years since she had earned the title "spinster". The snowy damask gleamed, the polished silver sparkled, the best Spode china basked beneath perfect food. The turkey was delicately browned; the doves, delightfully crisp; the vegetables, perfectly seasoned—each in turn drew exclamations of "Best I ever tasted."

The meal was eaten slowly with a great deal of happy talk. At last, they moved to the parlor and languished by the fire, half-dozing while enjoying comfortable silences and idle chatter.

Popping firecrackers roused them at last. While Lily bundled the baby, Emma ran to her room where she donned her pink coat and added a hat made of navy ribbon. Burying her face in the nosegay, she sighed with the happiness of blossoming love. Carefully pressing a geranium leaf and a violet between the pages of her new book, she plucked three more violets and pinned them to the neck of her jacket.

When they rejoined the men, Harrison wore a Spanish costume with red trousers and a tremendous hat while Jonathan sported a clown costume of yellow. With his mouth pursed in mock seriousness and his eyes popping, he tipped a hat as small as a teacup and escorted Emma to the wagon.

Foy, in the funniest costume he could improvise, peered with snapping eyes through his dough face, a papier-mâché mask. He had decorated the wagon and even put crepe paper on the mules. He handed out drums and bugles, and they piled aboard and drove into the street to join other wagons and outlandishly costumed, masked riders on horseback in the annual celebration known as the Fantastic Rides. The noisy merrymakers moved about the streets in an impromptu parade, then headed north toward Roseland, the plantation owned by Colonel Toney and his wife, who were renowned for elaborate entertainments. Long before they reached the house, guns answered with joyful blasts their noisy announcement in lieu of church bells that "Christ is born!"

After refreshments with the Toneys, the group returned more quietly into town. Shadows were lengthening, and Emma shivered with a sudden chill as they met first the Pioneer Guards and then Brannon's Zouaves out marching in full force. Oblivious to the usual Christmas merrymakers, the militia groups drilled seriously.

"We'd better get out of these costumes," said Harrison under his breath to Jonathan. "Captain Baker is entertaining the Eufaula Rifles and we're expected."

Lily's dark eyes were wide and liquid as she clutched Emma's flowing sleeve.

"Yes," agreed Jonathan, "they will want you there. With your knowledge of the Chattahoochee and the depths of Apalachicola Bay, you will play an important part in defense—"

Harrison frowned and shook his head.

As they entered at the rear of the hall, the happiness of the day seemed to be cracking and breaking into jagged pieces like a broken mirror.

Harrison lifted Mignonne high into the air to make her laugh before he kissed her good-bye.

As the men started down the steps, Jonathan's voice drifted behind his departing back. "This might be the last Christmas as we know it for a very long time. Seeing you with Mignonne makes me realize, too late, that I should have spent it with my daughter."

Chapter 4

His daughter! Aghast, Emma flung one clutching hand to her chest and with the other stifled the thought that threatened to become a scream. Paralyzed for a moment, she wrenched her feet from the floor and ran across the back hall. No one saw her as she escaped up the hidden staircase.

Slamming through the door to her bedroom, she snatched the violets and geraniums from their vase and threw them across the floor. "How could you? How could you?" she whimpered through clenched teeth. She stamped around the room with her kidskin slippers grinding each blossom and leaf into the blue and white rug. From below, Mignonne's cries bellowed forth, alerting everyone, punishing everyone who did not immediately rush to her aid. Gulping tears, Emma wished she could make someone attend to her hurting. Shivering like a puppy which had been patted on the head and then kicked, she stood in the center of the huge room, small and forlorn.

Reprimanding herself, she fought for control. Her tears congealed. Looking down at her feet, she winced. Angry purple and red and green smears stained the valuable Oriental rug. Sighing, she realized that the nosegay had meant nothing to such a worldly man. She had judged him a roué from the beginning; why had she not remembered? Dry-eyed, she jerked back her head and flung her arms, cross-wristed, upon it. The kiss—merely a prank under the mistletoe.

A rattle at the window caused her to part the lace curtains and peer through the wavery glass. The shiny carriage with its prancing ponies was moving away.

"Oh, Lily, how could you?" she whispered in anguish as she leaned her forehead against the cold windowpane.

Lily had said, "Have fun, just for tonight." She, of course, did not know that Emma's twenty-seven-year-old spinster's heart beat as foolishly as any schoolgirl's.

Suddenly bone-cold and weak with exhaustion, Emma crawled beneath the quilts, coat and all. Piling pillows over her head, she sobbed as she had not allowed herself to do since she was sixteen.

Emma was glad that Lily did not visit during the next two days. She imagined herself lashing out at her with angry words; however, when she heard Lily's lilting voice floating up the staircase, she knew that she did not want to face her niece and tried to escape her by running down the hidden back stairs which the servants used. But Lily saw her.

"Oh, Emma, there you are. Fort Moultrie has been burned—why, whatever is wrong with you?" She stared in surprise at Emma's face which was pinched and blue.

"N–nothing," replied Emma. "Nothing's wrong," she said in a weak whine. Her shoulders slumped dejectedly.

"Something is wrong!" Lily stamped her foot. "Are you ill? What's the matter?"

"Why didn't you tell me?"

"Tell you what?"

"That he—Jonathan's—married."

Lily's dark eyes filled with sudden understanding and sympathy. Taking Emma's hand, she pulled her into the blue and white bedroom and led her to the wing chair by the fireplace. Looking down at the older girl, she said solemnly, "He's not married."

Emma, huddling miserably between the sheltering wings of the chair, watched Lily throw kindling on the fire and poke it into a blaze before she spoke. "Yes, he is," she said sadly. "I heard him mention his daughter."

"No, he isn't," Lily said firmly. She drew the carved cherry rocker close and chafed Emma's cold hands. "He was. His wife died in childbirth. Two years ago. He owns a tremendous cotton plantation over near Savannah. But he hasn't stayed there much since she died—" She bowed her shining, dark hair and said softly, "Oh, Emma, I'm sorry. I didn't think to tell you."

"It's all right." Emma's voice rang hollowly in her ears as she fought for composure.

"No, no, it's not. You've been miserable, and it's all my fault. I didn't stop to think—I only meant for you to enjoy the parties—the holidays. . ."

The fire crackled merrily. Color returned to Emma's cheeks as relief flowed through her. Now it was Lily who drooped dejectedly.

"It's all right," Emma repeated, patting her lovingly.

"I'm not too sure." The younger girl threw back her curls and looked into her aunt's eyes with worry. "Are you falling so much in love?"

"Yes." Emma laughed shakily. "But if he's not married, what's wrong with that?"

"Well, he's always here, there, or the other place. Since Betty died he's been rambling the world. I'm not sure he's over her. All his joking might be to mask his emptiness. And besides that—with all this war talk, men are too occupied to have time to think of love," she finished in a rush.

Emma sat silently, trying to still her fluttering hands. The muscles of her pale face twitched as she struggled to erase the pain.

"Everything about the secession has seemed so exciting," Lily reflected slowly, "but since I've heard about Fort Moultrie's being burned, I've begun to feel that a huge black net is hanging over us, just waiting to drop."

Relieved to change the topic from her own problems, Emma coughed and brought her voice to its normal melodious register. "I've had a strange, uneasy feeling ever since last October when we were in Montgomery, while Douglas was campaigning for the presidency. Do you remember the torchlight procession when Douglas was egged? I can still see that short, square figure with eggs breaking against it."

Lily laughed shortly and chattered on. "Yes, but the picture that comes back to me is of Janie's wedding party when a man rushed in saying, 'Lincoln is elected.' The words fell like a pall. You could see the Southern spirit as it leaped into the eyes of the men. It seemed thrilling then to have our honor defended, but I was really frightened that night with all the men out, armed and equipped, expecting trouble." Lily paused and searched Emma's vulnerable face with a frown.

When she resumed speaking, her words came slowly, deliberately. "Then the threat of riot seemed to blow over, and everyone began to say we could declare our sovereignty and independence; it became exciting—but, oh, Emma," she wailed, "this is not the time to fall in love!"

Icy drizzle chilled New Year's Eve. News was received of the resignation of the President's cabinet at Washington City. At dawn on the first day of 1861, the temperature plummeted to twenty degrees. The unaccustomed ice killed the flowers.

Cordelia took to her bed against the damp cold. Waiting upon her, Emma was closely confined. Each day she stood peering out her lace curtains, her heart beating with the drums which assembled the Eufaula Rifles and Pioneer Guards for drilling. She tried not to focus on the unaccustomed sight of jagged icicles dripping from the eaves. They seemed too much to mirror the painful, useless thawing within her breast.

" 'Not the time to fall in love,' " she whispered against the cold, wavery glass. "He hasn't given me another thought."

The temperature crept back up above the freezing mark, but then cold, gray rain fell for several days without letup. Shivering, unable to get warm in the high-ceilinged house which was designed for the three seasons of hot, humid weather, the family speculated on the disasters which would result if the temperature again dropped to freezing.

At last, on the tenth of January, the sun shone brilliantly and the blue sky sparkled. Emma was setting the big pots of ferns back on the front porch when she glimpsed a figure rounding the red cedars at the gate. Pressing her hand to her heart as if she could still its beating, she tried to force herself to be calm.

She turned slowly and said as coolly as possible, "Good morning, Mr. Ramsey."

"Good morning," he called cheerily, bounding up the steps to the high porch. "You're as blue and gold and lovely as the day." He smiled, taking her hand.

Lowering her eyelashes shyly, she looked down at her faded gray dress and knew he was complimenting her eyes and hair. A small, pleased smile touched her lips.

"Everything is coming to a head," Jonathan said seriously, plunging into conversation with no apology for his failure to thank her for Christmas dinner. "Have you heard the news today?"

Solemnly she shook her golden curls. She could not tell him that all her thoughts had centered on him. The way he moved, with rapid, jerking gestures, and talked, in quick bursts, told Emma he had been far too busy to think of her.

"Mississippi passed her Ordinance of Secession yesterday! They made provisions for a state army and appointed the Honorable Jefferson Davis her major general." His eyes flashed with excitement. "They seized the fort on Ship Island and the U.S. Hospital on the Mississippi River—and at any moment a telegram should come saying Florida has seceded."

"What of Alabama?"

"The state convention is in secret session. The vote will be taken tomorrow." He paused, his eyes gentle upon her face, as he said softly, "Will you do me the honor of accompanying me to the celebrations when it is announced?"

"You're sure, then, of the outcome?"

"Of course!"

Emma snapped a dead frond from the fern and crumpled it in her hand. He had mentioned the river installations, but her questions about his part in all this lodged in her throat.

Jonathan stood waiting. His dark curls bobbed as he earnestly asked again, "You'll come with me?"

"I don't know—I—you know Cordelia. . ." Her face was clouded with uncertainty.

"But the main party is to be given by Lewis Llewellen Cato. Surely she will want to go to her neighbor's house."

"I don't know. I just—can't—say. We'll see."

"I'll be here to get you," he said confidently. Squeezing her hand as he bent swiftly over it in a perfunctory bow, he hurried away. He turned at the gate and waved. " 'Til tomorrow," he called.

She sat on the steps in the pale sunshine with her chin in her hands. What should she do? It was clearly evident that Lily was right. He had merely been seeking diversion for the holidays. His only interest lay in the silly politics. She could protect herself if she used her sister-in-law as an excuse and stayed safely in Barbour Hall. She wanted to be near him, to absorb his vitality, to laugh at his funny stories, to feel the warmth of his twinkling eyes, to touch—she choked on the surging emotion and dropped her head to her knees. Numbness hurt less.

Jerking her chin up, she gritted her teeth. She would not let him make her cry. She simply would not go. When Alabama's fate was decided, he would leave Eufaula and she would never have to see him again.

"Em-ma," Cordelia's voice summoned, unsettling her completely.

On January 11, the sun blessed the day with warmth. Everyone moved about quietly, expectantly. Waiting. Suddenly at two in the afternoon, church bells began to toll. Rejoicing, the people filled the street, shouting, "Great news! Alabama has left the Union that would make slaves of us!" Spreading the lace curtains at the window where she stood, Emma was struck with the sobering thought that their state was now sovereign and independent.

"The old bonds are broken." Cordelia voiced her thoughts as she thrust her head in at the bedroom door. "Come, it's time we were going to the Catos'."

Emma lifted troubled eyes to her sister-in-law's face. As usual, her plans were decided for her. "I'll hurry and change," she replied soberly, but she remained immobile, staring out of the window. "I know they are defending what they believe to be their rights, but many of them are so young." She sighed and pointed down to the group called Brannon's Zouaves, mere boys parading in Turkish-style costumes.

"Much of the best blood of our boys will be spilt, I fear," said Cordelia, peering out. "I can't help being glad that Foy is too young to volunteer."

As they stood bound in spirit for a moment, Foy came loping across the lawn with arms and legs flying. He joined a group of boys shooting fireworks. Sighing and shaking their heads, the women turned and began to prepare for the party.

Half-sorry, half-glad that she could not wait for Jonathan Ramsey, Emma accompanied Cordelia down the street. Just as they reached the Catos' hitching post, the cannon blasted. Emma steadied herself by hanging onto the iron horsehead. She twisted her nose at the acrid smell as the cannon fired one hundred rounds in honor of the occasion. Halfway through, she could bear it no longer and clapped her hands over her ears. At last the nerve-racking blasts ended, and she opened her eyes.

Jonathan stood beside her, laughing. Taking her by the elbow of her pink wool coat, he guided her down the central walk to the house. On each side, angled pathways invited strolls though boxwood-edged diamonds and triangles of formal, symmetrical flower beds. Her steps lagged as she looked toward a display of spring bulbs.

"Hurry," he said. "Colonel Cato is about to introduce Yancey." His springing step bespoke his excitement as he pushed her to a spot in front of the white clapboard Greek Revival mansion.

William Lowndes Yancey came through the double entrance doors and stood on the wide porch, majestically set off with thirteen square, white columns across the front and around the sides of the house. With a great show of oratory, he expounded the Southern Rights' position.

Standing amid the cheering crowd, Emma had never felt so alone. She wondered why Jonathan had asked her to join him. He had given her such flattering attention during the Christmas festivities; now, he scarcely noticed her presence. Throwing back her head, she looked up at the large, pillared observatory set high atop the steep roof. This cupola was an exact replica of the first story.

I'm like that, she thought. *A fake. A shell with no life stirring within me.*

Clapping vigorously, Jonathan led a cheer. When the din had subsided, he smiled down at Emma with his eyes gleaming and said enthusiastically, "The South can never be conquered!"

White-coated servants began moving among the guests with huge trays of refreshments. Jonathan declared, "I'm famished," and led Emma to a laden table set beneath a huge oak. Demurely she accepted a tall, slender goblet of syllabub, a fashionable dessert made by churning milk, cream, and cider, and nibbled a petit four. Watching Jonathan pile a plate with dainty party food, Emma wondered why she had ever thought him less handsome than Harrison. His face was always set in such a sweet expression; his dark eyes always twinkled. And that curl of dark hair tumbling over his forehead— She sighed, breathed the sweet fragrance of the narcissus which had recovered from the cold and bloomed again, and longed to reach up and smooth the curl back in place.

"You're mighty quiet today." He smiled down at her.

"Yes," she replied shakily. "It's all so—so overwhelming. I—I—just. . ." she stammered. Afraid that he would see the longing in her eyes, she dropped her eyelashes and concentrated on tracing the blocks of navy ribbon on her pink skirt.

"Yes, everything is moving swiftly now," he said briskly. "I'll wager Georgia will leave the Union by next week."

"Oh?"

Jonathan paused with a pecan tasse midway to his mouth and considered the small, hurt sound.

"I guess that means you'll be going home?" She lifted her eyes to memorize his face.

Delighted, he popped the bite-size pie into his mouth, crunched, and laughed. "Then I take it you'd miss me?"

"Why should I?" She turned away, angry with herself that she had betrayed her emotions. "I've hardly seen you enough to miss you." She started down a path between tall nandina bushes laden with large clusters of red berries.

"Wait!" He caught her shoulders and turned her toward him. "I'm sorry I laughed. I wasn't laughing at you. I thought perhaps you feel as I. . ."

Her face still clouded, Emma tried to shrug off his grasp.

"To answer your question," he said candidly, still holding her firmly, "I won't be going home. I have to make another quick trip to Montgomery—that's where I've been." He pulled her closer. "I apologize for not coming by since Christmas to thank you. I've been so busy. We're working to form a Confederacy of Southern States. . ." He paused, inhaled, breathed softly, sweetly against the golden ringlets escaping around her forehead. "Lovely Emma. I do care. If we only had more time!"

She ceased her struggle. Gazing into his face as it moved down toward hers, she tried to read his eyes, tried to see if her love was mirrored there.

"Ah, Ramsey, there you are."

Jonathan dropped his hands from her shoulders and turned toward the brusque voice. Her face blazing with shame, she stumbled backward.

"I must speak with you," the man continued. "The revenue cutter, *Lewis Cass* and the tender, *Alert,* belonging to the lighthouse establishment, were seized at Mobile by the state. We must get volunteers together for a navy to man. . ."

Emma wandered away, unnoticed. Their lovely moment had been shattered. Plucking a shriveled brown bud from a camellia bush, she threw it savagely, wishing she had never met Jonathan Ramsey. The promise of winter flowers had been spoiled by the unexpected freeze. Biting her lip and fighting back tears, she pulled the dead buds and wished that she could have remained as she was, moving through life with outward calm, never allowing herself to feel. That was better than being raw, bleeding.

Lily was bouncing toward her, eyes flashing and cheeks rosy from the crisp air. Unable to bear gaiety at the moment, Emma sought to get away.

"Does Cordelia need me?" she asked with a quiver in her voice. She turned toward the house and tried to pull a smooth mask over her face.

"No, no, Mama is sitting by the fire with Miss Martha Jane and the other ladies." Lily's attention was on retying the green satin streamers of her bonnet. "Come join the party. Professor Van Houten is assembling the orchestra in the gazebo." She tugged at Emma's hand, which was cold in spite of the kid gloves. "Relax. Have fun."

Unable to escape, Emma followed her through the grandly formal garden toward the gazebo in back. J. C. Van Houten was tapping his way ahead of them with his gold-headed cane. Just as the blind musician lifted his baton to start the orchestra, Harrison and Jonathan joined them.

For the rest of the party, Jonathan remained at her side, laughing, joking, charming her. Unable to stem the love spilling over the moss-covered dams of her heart, she smiled at him adoringly.

It was only when the celebration ended and evening's chill began to fall that fear and turmoil, churning within, caused her to have difficulty swallowing.

Chapter 5

The rousing blast of the steamboat's whistle startled Emma, and the porcelain bowl in her hand crashed to the floor, showering her with fragments. She had thought that she was ready to face this day. Now she knew that she was not. The insistent drone drew her outside. From the porch she could see black puffs of smoke which punctuated shortened blasts. Clutching her fists to her chest, she shivered. The past weeks had flown so swiftly that she had not had time to dread today.

Emma had been swept into the excitement which had gripped Eufaula from the moment of Alabama's secession. Since the Catos' party, men had filled the streets, drilling; women had sat by the fire, sewing. Emma's hands had moved swiftly as her heart pulsed to the rhythm of Jonathan's words, "I do care."

Suddenly alive, a part of the world, she happily participated in the outfitting of the first troops that marched in uniforms provided by Mary Magdalen Treadwell. Helping to make the banner for the soldiers, Emma had been too busy to dwell on their leaving. Whenever Jonathan and Emma were not working with their respective groups, Jonathan had been constantly at her side. The war preparations and imminent departure accelerated their urgency to talk. They spoke in quick snatches, hopping from one subject to another as they tried to find out minute details about each other's thoughts and lives.

Suddenly, they fell silent. As they attended a party for departing soldiers, Jonathan's humor became forced. Emma's throat constricted, stifling speech. They stood stiffly in a corner with smiles frozen upon their faces. The back of his hand brushed hers. She looked up at him, her eyes filled with love.

The next morning, February 2, 1861, two companies from the county, the Pioneer Guards and the Clayton Guards, left to join the service of the state in the First Alabama Infantry. Emma watched with tears in her eyes as they marched away, proudly bearing the ladies' banners. Dangling on a slender thread of emotion since Jonathan's declaration to her, she wavered between glorying in the men's upholding their honor and fearing the unknown path ahead.

On February 9, Jefferson Davis was elected President of the Confederate States of America. The town's own company, the Eufaula Rifles, was mustered into the service of the State of Alabama and prepared to leave as part of Davis's escort to Montgomery, where the Confederacy formed. Jonathan Ramsey, Harrison Wingate, and Edward Bullock were going also.

The twelfth had dawned brilliant with sunlight. Now as Emma stood on the porch, a balmy breeze blew, tantalizing with false spring as delightful as only February could be. Scarlet flowering quince and yellow daffodils emblazoned the street down which she watched people, brought out by the sonorous hum of the riverboat, pour forth in parade. Looking at the black puffs above the treetops, Emma had only one thought: *Jonathan is leaving.*

By the time she could brush her hair and fasten it with tortoiseshell combs, she heard the prancing feet of ponies and hurried out to climb into Lily's carriage. Even Lily had lost her voice. As they rode to the Pope home at the foot of Broad Street, their silence intensified the jingling of the reins.

Jonathan came to stand behind her under the huge oak tree. His breath was warm upon the back of her neck as Miss Ella Pope presented the colors to Eufaula Rifles' Captain Alpheus Baker. Jonathan smiled down at Emma with an odd light in his eyes as the speeches were made. When John Van Houten lifted his violin with soft, white hands and scraped his bow in a plaintive cry, she looked at Jonathan through a mist of tears and wondered why his expression had changed. Around her, women wept as the sorrowing violin unleashed their pent emotions. Jonathan brushed against her, and she drew a shaky breath.

When the ceremony ended, Jonathan lightly grasped her elbow in a tingling touch and helped her into the carriage. They rode slowly behind the soldiers as they marched to the wharf.

The tread of the marching men and the beat of their drums pounded in Emma's temples, and she could not think.

No laughter sparkled in Jonathan's eyes now as he looked at Emma's flushed cheeks. He cleared his throat and spoke haltingly. "Van Houten amazes me. Uh—has he—was he born blind?"

"No, um—I think he was. . ." Emma coughed and blinked back tears. She struggled to get her voice into its natural range. "He was fourteen—had sore eyes. . . The doctor's treatment—uh—destroyed his sight."

"I see." On the seat between them, his fingers brushed hers, twined, gripped. "What a pity. . ."

Emma swallowed. The warmth of his gaze and the softness of his voice made his words, to which neither was listening, float around her like a love song. She could feel her cheeks flaming in response to the pressure of his hand, and she looked quickly toward the front seat of the carriage. Lily's and Harrison's erect backs evidenced their endeavors to ignore them. Turning questioning eyes to Jonathan's face, she tried to continue speaking casually so as not to say the words of longing shouting from her heart. "He—he turned it for the good. He went to Weimar, Hungary, and studied under the great Franz Liszt. . ."

Uh! Uh! Uhmmm! The steamboat's mournful blast enveloped her. They had reached the end of the street. The carriage rolled by the Tavern. She sighed as they descended the hill and stopped at the wharf.

The steamer, *Ben Franklin,* waited impatiently, its boilers hiccupping steam. People were surging up the gangway, filling both decks of the flat-bottomed boat, waving, shouting. The band struck up a tune and men hanging over the rails and women answering from the banks joined in lustily singing "Ben Bolt" and "Lily Dale." Many leading citizens were accompanying the soldiers on the first leg of the journey upriver to Columbus, Georgia.

Jonathan lifted Emma tenderly from the carriage. Saying nothing, he retained her hand and hurried her away from the crowd to a spot where the forest marched down to the muddy water.

The crisp breeze kissed her cheeks with color as she followed silently. Stepping into the cold shadow of a giant oak which sheltered them from prying eyes, she trembled violently.

Jonathan's strong arms enwrapped her. Weakly, she clung to him and relaxed against his warmth. He held her for a long, lingering moment. Gently, he pushed back the bonnet which shielded her face from him. He looked questioningly at her and then drew her close again and spoke lovingly with his lips against the golden ringlets escaping around her forehead. "Lovely Emma. Darling Emma. Why did I wait until I had to leave to realize I don't want to part from you? Everything has been moving so fast. My duties are pressing. . ." He caressed her hair.

"Oh, Jonathan, Jonathan," she breathed. "I do understand," she whispered, gazing adoringly at his face, close above hers.

"I should have told you about—" he said earnestly. His face creased in a worried frown. "I want to ask you. . ." He ceased to struggle for words and said simply, "I need you."

Her smiling lips lifted to meet his. The tenderness of his kiss softened the last time-calloused edges of her heart.

Wheet! Wheet! A shrill whistle and white puffs of steam signaled last call.

"I must go." He held her away and gazed at her radiant face. "I'll return as soon as—you'll wait?"

"Forever." She smiled. The shroud of her fear fell from her. Straightening her bonnet, she stepped back into the sunshine of the river path with only a glimmer of a thought of how angry Cordelia would be if anyone had observed her scandalous behavior.

Jonathan ran up the gangway. It lifted. *Clang! Clang! Clang!* bells signaled importantly. Slowly the huge paddle wheel strained. Lifting a sparkling cascade of water, it strengthened into a rhythmic *swish,* swiftly propelling the steamboat away.

"I do declare, Emma," Lily greeted Emma, cocking her head to one side and laughing, "if I didn't know you were a lady, I'd say you had on rouge."

Emma's blush deepened, and her smile seemed to animate every inch of her body.

"Tell, tell!"

"He loves me," she sighed.

Lily squeezed her hand delightedly. Together, they looked across the intervening water at their men waving from the upper deck.

"I remember as if it were yesterday the first time I saw Harrison," said Lily softly. "We were sitting right here. He was so quiet and strong. In command of the situation."

Emma laughed. "And so totally inaccessible to you with your mother's demanding that you marry within your class," she said nodding. "And your vowing not to marry anyone unless he was a Christian."

"Oh, it does matter," Lily responded seriously. "When marriage is based on the love of God, your love just keeps on growing!" She frowned at Emma and said in a concerned tone which made her seem the elder. "What about Jonathan's faith?"

"I don't know." Emma stopped with a sudden flare of anger. Trying to shrug off the question, she concentrated on waving one last time before the white wake of the steamboat churned out of sight. From the corner of her eye, she could see by Lily's bowed head and clasped hands that she was praying. She knew Lily thought God cared about every detail of her life. Defiantly, she threw back her head and looked at the sky. Under her breath she queried, "If You do care about me, God, bring Jonathan back."

The kinswomen said little until they reached Barbour Hall. Then Emma asked haltingly, "When do you think they'll return?"

"I'm afraid it will be awhile. Didn't he tell you why they were going?"

"No."

"To organize a navy."

On Saint Valentine's Eve, Foy attended a party at Cordelia's prodding. Even though the tall, thin boy groaned and protested in a hoarse croak that it was silly to have to draw a name and be someone's valentine, Emma noticed a sly gleam in his eye. Smiling, she looked down from her bedroom window as he loped across the yard and realized that the years were passing and her small charge would soon be grown. She wondered if he had a special girl. Chuckling, she stood looking out at the moonlight patterning her lace curtains, remembering Ophelia's song from *Hamlet:*

Tomorrow is Saint Valentine's day
All in the morning betime,

And I a maid at your window,
To be your Valentine.

Throughout the next morning, she stood idly with her hands poised over her tasks. Only when Cordelia began to eye her suspiciously did she realize that she was daydreaming as much as Lily once had. Late that afternoon, Emma noticed an envelope bearing her name placed in the card tray on the narrow, mahogany library table near the entrance doors. She opened the envelope with shaking fingers and lifted out a lovely bit of red satin and white lace. Clutching it to her heart, she ran up the stairs to her room before she looked at it and read the verse:

When first I saw thee,
Thy placid face,
With all the charms,
That play about it
I *loved* thee.
From J.

As the days passed without further word, Emma occasionally climbed the stairs to the attic and rushed up the two more short flights to the belvedere. No telltale puffs of smoke appeared above the treetops to promise the arrival of a steamboat. Because she could hardly bear the closed feeling of the dark, narrow passageway and because the belvedere, with its three floor-to-ceiling windows front and back and two on each side, made her feel a bit dizzy, she abandoned the lookout and tried to keep busy. She removed the plumes of pampas grass which had decorated the parlor for the winter and went out into the side yard to cut forsythia branches and daffodils.

March was roaring in like a lion, and the wind whipped her hooped skirt and snatched her hair from the knot at the back of her neck. Intent upon shielding her basket of fragile, yellow flowers, she did not realize anyone had entered the garden until she looked up into the dark and laughing eyes of Jonathan Ramsey.

"Oh," she gasped with her free hand flying to her throat.

"I'm sorry I startled you," he apologized quickly. "You make such a picture that I hated to stop you. I wish I were a painter."

"The title would be 'Dishevelment,' no doubt," she returned wryly, dabbing futilely at her hair. "Come, let's see if the gazebo will give us a little shelter from the wind." Keeping a decorous distance between them, she led him to the white-latticed summerhouse. The octagon-shaped enclosure was festooned with gnarled wisteria vines, covered with limp buds, full of promise.

"Have you heard the exciting news?" he asked. Vibrant with enthusiasm, he seemed almost to dance from one foot to the other.

"No," she replied evenly. Placing her basket on the wicker and rattan table, she felt suddenly shy in his presence and chose to sit in one of the wicker chairs instead of on the double settee.

"The Confederate Navy is now formally constituted under the direction of Stephen Mallory." He strode back and forth, speaking in a voice pitched high with excitement. "We have sent peace emissaries to the United States with a formal demand to turn over Fort Sumter and Fort Pickens since they lie within our territory." Suddenly he stopped his pacing and stood before her. "With this show of strength, we will surely avert war."

She had never seen him this agitated. Emma sat quietly, while silence lengthened. She gazed up at him expectantly.

"Uh-um." He cleared his throat. "Now that these affairs are settled," he resumed softly, "I feel that I can speak what is in my heart." He dropped to sit in the other wicker chair and scraped it across the marble floor until he was close beside her. His smooth face drooped with seriousness. In a doubtful tone he said, "I want to ask you to be my wife."

Emma's breath caught in her throat at the suddenness of his proposal. She opened her mouth, but words could not form; and her delicate face paled.

"No, wait." He waved a shushing hand. "Don't answer yet." His forehead creased with worry, and he swallowed before he continued. "There's something I should have told you— Would it matter to you terribly that—that I've had a wife?"

Emma gazed into his eyes, open wide like a wistful ten-year-old boy's, and smiled reassuringly. Ever so gently she brushed her fingertips across his smooth cheek and whispered, "No, that cannot affect the depth of my feelings for you."

Swiftly, he grasped both her hands in his, kissed them, then bowed his head upon them. "There's more. I have a child. A daughter."

"I know," she murmured. "Lily. . ."

"Of course. Then—dare I hope?"

"I love children," she said quietly, tenderly. "My arms have longed for one of my own. . ." Color rushed back into her cheeks.

His eyes searched her face. "Yes. Well. . . You see—Luther Elizabeth died when the baby came. I was devastated—I've wandered—I hardly know my child—she doesn't know me." Blinking back tears, he bowed his head upon her hands. "I promised myself that I would never fall in love again."

Pulling one hand free, she gently stroked his springing, dark curls until he raised his head and smiled happily. Catching her hand, he tenderly kissed the palm.

"You are so like my Betty, all pink and blue and gold with the wide-eyed innocence of a freshly scrubbed child." He chuckled.

Emma stiffened ever so slightly.

He hurriedly added, "Oh, no, I'll never compare you. You, dear Emma, are a caring woman. I enjoy your mind. I want to experience life with you."

Seeing how closely he was attuned to her feelings, she spoke confidently, "I do understand. At sixteen, in love with life—wanting to be in love—I thought I was terribly, painfully in love, but. . ." He was moving nearer and his breath was sweet and warm on her face. Pushing her hand against the rough material of his coat, she could feel his heart beating. "No, wait, I want to tell you—now that I've met you, I know what I felt then was not really love at all."

His arms closed around her, strong, warm, shielding her from the damp March wind. She met his kiss ardently, sealing their love.

"I know you'll want a proper period of engagement," he said at last, "but don't make me wait too long. I'm eager to take you to my plantation. It's in Bulloch County, Georgia, over near Savannah."

She nodded, too full of emotion to trust her voice. Shivering as the wind blew colder, knowing Cordelia would be looking for her, she reluctantly told him she must go.

As she entered the hall, Cordelia accosted her. "You're seeing entirely too much of that man!" She eyed her suspiciously. "Are his intentions honorable?"

Surprised, Emma blurted, "Why, yes, they are. He asked me to marry him," she said with unaccustomed sharpness.

Cordelia Edwards drew herself up with a haughty sniff. "Why—why, you know nothing of his background," she spluttered.

"I know enough," said Emma firmly between clenched teeth. Miserably, she wished she had not let her sister-in-law bully her into this admission before she could announce it joyfully.

Deflated, Cordelia sank to the horsehair sofa. Her voice a whine, she said, "But surely, you're not thinking of leaving me in my old age." She projected a pitiful, heavy lump, sliding down on the shiny, slick surface, but her next words carried an edge. "Not after all these years that I've provided you a good home."

Lily, of course, was delighted. On the fourth of March, the family, including Jonathan, went to the Wingate home on Eufaula Avenue. The modesty of the old, cottage-type house was characteristic of Harrison Wingate and reminded Emma of the way his humility had caused Cordelia to refuse him her daughter's hand because she had thought him a poor riverboat captain below their social strata. The small engagement party was proceeding with great gaiety until an agitated knock sounded at the door.

Harrison's face creased with deep lines of worry as he relayed to them the message from the telegraph office. Lincoln's inaugural address earlier that day had not answered the questions burning in Southern minds. "His wording casts serious doubt on the negotiations for peace," the tall man said, sadly shaking his head. "I believed with our leaders that when Lincoln saw us arming, he would surely back down and let us peacefully form our own nation."

With the spontaneity of the party spoiled, the guests departed early. When only the family remained, Foy turned to the captain, whom he idolized. "What will you do," he asked with owl-eyed seriousness, "if it comes to war? You didn't believe in dueling—would you fight in war?"

"Yes, Son," Harrison answered quietly. "I'll defend my home and my country."

"But–but," the boy stammered, "it's hard to understand." His ears turned red. "In the Old Testament, King David fought in wars, but in the New Testament—you always quote 'turn the other cheek'. . . ."

"From a personal insult, yes." Harrison rubbed the creases in his forehead. "Perhaps it will help you to turn in the Bible to Paul's letter to the Romans, especially chapter thirteen. He says, 'Let every soul be subject unto the higher powers.' Paul explains that government is ordained by God." He clapped Foy's shoulder. "And don't forget, he was saying this even though at the time the rulers were very evil."

The next weeks weighed their spirits with waiting. March scampered away like the proverbial lamb. As peace hung in the balance, Emma felt her own fate dangling.

"If there should be war," Jonathan declared solemnly one afternoon as they sat in the gazebo, "of course, we will have to postpone our wedding plans."

The wisteria, dripping off the gazebo in lavender cascades, filled the air with a heady fragrance which seemed to increase the ache in Emma's heart. Even though they would not have married anyway until after a proper period of engagement, the finality in his voice tightened her nerves.

"War. What a terrible word." She sighed. "And civil war—unthinkable."

He squeezed her hand and spoke reassuringly, "Even if there's war, it won't last long."

April unfolded gently, fluttering from her chrysalis with poetic beauty. Jonathan called for Emma in a runabout, and they drove along the Chattahoochee. Ferns and wildflowers crowded the narrow roadside. In the woodlands, wild azaleas flamed. Beneath tall trees, dogwoods stood in pristine beauty like diminutive brides in airy veils. Waiting.

They rode beneath the watercolor sky through lacy trees of gentle, yellow-green, their fingers twined on the red leather seat. The pleasant smell of freshly turned earth filled the air. Singing floated across the dell as field hands dropped cotton seed into the bright red clay waiting expectantly to burst forth with bounty. Occasionally Jonathan said amusing things, but Emma smiled wistfully because his eyes held a faraway look.

Cordelia fussed because Emma had gone out unchaperoned. Perturbed, Emma flared that she was hardly a debutante.

Then, on April 12, in Charleston Harbor, the thing they had been dreading happened. A gun thudded. A shell whined across a mile of water. War began. From the moment the news of the bombardment arrived, the men of the town remained milling about the telegraph office.

Surrender of Fort Sumter had been denied. Beauregard had fired the shot. By the next day, Major Anderson had surrendered the fort for the Union.

Emma sat at the rolltop ladies' secretary in her bedroom and recorded in her journal:

Great excitement prevails in Eufaula with the surrender of Fort Sumter. All communications between us and the North have stopped. Telegraph wires are pulled down and even the express news has been discontinued. Preparations on both sides are being made for war.

Putting down her pen, she wept into her folded arms. She could not bear to write her anguish at what this might mean for Jonathan and her.

A few days later the cannon boomed again from the bluff, heralding celebration at the secession of Virginia.

A week after the Confederates took Fort Sumter, Lily bounded into Barbour Hall, shouting, "Emma, have you heard the terrible news?"

Chapter 6

"Terrible news?" Emma paused, openmouthed. "What could be worse news than war?"

"Lincoln has blockaded our ports." Lily stamped her foot. "Our gateway to the world just clanged shut!"

"She's worried about no more Paris gowns," Harrison teased laughingly.

"Well, I do have a little sense," Lily flared, tossing her dark hair. "All we have around here is cotton, cotton, cotton. If we can't get manufactured goods or mineral resources from the North, they can't cut off our supplies from Europe. . . ," she snapped fierily.

Jonathan had come in behind them. *He always seems to catch me in a faded dress,* thought Emma ruefully. However, if he noticed her clothing he never commented. Nodding a greeting, he looked directly into her eyes and smiled dazzlingly.

"What we came to tell you, Emma, is. . . ," Jonathan's excitement seemed a tangible thing bouncing from wall to wall, "is—well, good-bye."

Emma's blue eyes widened in alarm. "What?"

"Oh, not for long," he continued quickly. "They've closed the biggest ports first. We're heading for Apalachicola as quickly as possible before they realize the importance of the Chattahoochee River."

"The *Wave* has been pressed into service for the Confederate Navy," explained Harrison in his usual quiet way.

With shaking hands, Emma began to set the cart for afternoon tea. She had just gathered a small pail of strawberries and whipped a bowl of cream to smother biscuits made flaky with a great deal of lard. As she worked, she surreptitiously searched Jonathan's face for signs of the wanderlust of which Lily had warned. He, himself, had told her that he had not planned to fall in love a second time. He almost danced as he helped her push the mahogany tea cart to the parlor where Cordelia Edwards waited beside a low fire. His movements showed Emma his eagerness for adventure.

Mrs. Edwards helped herself to an extra dollop of cream and said, "I know President Lincoln and President Davis have both called for army volunteers—" She savored a bite of tart, juicy strawberries. "But do you think they'll actually go to war?"

"Yes, Miss Cordelia," replied Harrison. "I'm afraid both sides are as eager for battle as two young hotheads calling each other out for a duel."

"In fact, Ma'am," Jonathan added, "news of bloodshed came today. Seems there was a fight in Baltimore with the Seventh Regiment New York and a Boston company attempting to pass through the city on their way to Washington at Lincoln's command." He spread a square of white damask across his leg and grinned as he took a plate from Emma. "But don't you fret. This war will be as temporary as—as a napkin on a fat man's lap!"

War talk was forgotten as they laughed together and enjoyed their tea. Looking down at her hands, trembling as they lifted the silver teapot, Emma was struck for the first time by their bareness. She had given only passing thought to the fact that he had presented her with no token of betrothal; now, however, she could not stop staring at her bare hands. Bent on merrymaking, the men urged her across the hall to the music room. They lustily sang "Old Zip Coon," "Dan Tucker," "Oh, Susanna," and "Old Uncle Ned" while Emma played the grand piano with plain, bare fingers.

The next morning, April 20, Emma rode with Lily to the river. As they drove through the busy storehouse area, crowded with Saturday shoppers who had come into town from the surrounding cotton plantations, the women were forced to stop several times until wagons, loaded with provisions already becoming scarce, could pass. The steamboat's impatient whistle made Emma clutch nervously at her yellow plaid skirt.

Lily patted her. "Don't worry; Harrison wouldn't leave without saying good-bye."

Intense excitement surrounded the *Wave* as the stevedores loaded the last of the freight from the wharf. The tremendous, flat-bottomed boat, fully 175 feet long, was Harrison Wingate's pride and joy. Fire and black smoke belching from the two towering smokestacks told Emma the boilers must be fully stoked, ready to depart. The busy captain honored them by singling them out of the crowd, beaming and saluting them from the pilothouse. Some fifty-odd passengers, milling along the rails of both upper and lower decks, made a colorful blur; consequently, Emma could not distinguish which one was Jonathan. She focused on the gleaming, round paddle box emblazoned with the boat's name and, above that, her insignia, a painting of a descending dove. The huge water wheel beneath the paddle box seemed to shiver, as eager to leave as Jonathan. Shrieking whistles and clanging bells rasped Emma's nerves, and she wished she had not tried to say good-bye.

"I wish we were going with them," Lily declared as she led Emma up the gangway. Jonathan suddenly appeared beside them, and, with his touch, Emma's tension lifted. Elated that he had been watching for her, she smiled up at him, handsome in a doe-colored waistcoat and slim, dark trousers. Gaily, he tipped his top hat and whispered an endearment, causing both to laugh. They could hear nothing but the shouting of the roustabouts. He guided her to the upper deck and found a spot where the staterooms kept the wind from snatching at her fanchon. Pushing down the streamers of the bonnet, she noticed that Lily had gone to Harrison's cabin for a private farewell, for, of course, no emotion should be displayed in public.

Trying to smooth the anxiety and longing from her face, Emma stood as relaxed as possible, but her knuckles were white as she grasped the rail.

Inches away, Jonathan shifted from one foot to the other and lifted his hands toward her shoulders, then dropped them uncertainly. Under her yellow lace mantilla, the hairs on her arms tingled, and she shivered.

The mixed emotions on his face made her struggle for words to ease their tension. How she wished she could say she would miss him. Instead, she avoided his eyes, stared at his bright cravat, and heard herself saying, "Be careful. This river's so dangerous! The whirlpools—" She bit her lip. "The hidden obstructions. . .so many boats have sunk."

"Don't you worry." He laughed and smoothed the crease on her forehead with the tip of his index finer. "Wingate's had plenty of experience on this—what do they call it? The longest graveyard in the state of Georgia? But he knows where the hidden dangers lie." He bent closer and breathed sweetly against her face. "Don't you worry," he repeated tenderly as to a child.

His eyes twinkling, he lifted his head and laughed.

"Why, just the other day, Wingate was regaling the passengers with a story of a man who fell overboard several years ago. He was floundering and struggling in a swift current, calling loudly for help and 'bout to drown. Captain Wingate yelled from the pilothouse, 'Put your feet down! Stand up!' Finally the man did." Jonathan chuckled. "He was over a sandbar. The water was not waist deep!"

Laughing, Emma relaxed her tight fists and stood smiling at him radiantly.

"Emma, I—the war has interfered or I would have—"

Uhmmmmm! Uhmmmmm! The low growl of the whistle shook them. Passengers jostled for positions at the rail.

Hurriedly, Jonathan pulled a long narrow package from his waistcoat pocket and pressed it into her hand. A high piercing shriek signaled last call, and she could distinguish only, "a token" and "forget me."

"No, I'll never forget you," she whispered into the wind.

Lily hurried her ashore, where they watched the tremendous waterwheel on the side of the boat begin to turn. Dizzied by emotion, Emma wished for a share of the calm acceptance evident on Lily's face. Through swirling mists, Emma took one last look at Jonathan.

When they had climbed into the carriage, Emma opened the small package eagerly. Solemnly, she lifted a folded fan from the box and fingered the long, narrow ebony sticks, inlaid with gold. Slowly spreading the ribs apart, she held her breath for a long moment and looked at the beautiful painting on the soft, kidskin covering. With a long, shuddering sigh, she suddenly began to weep in shaking sobs.

"Why, it's exquisite! Whatever is the matter?" asked Lily in surprise.

"I expected—" Emma sniffed. "I hoped—it was a. . ." She began to cry again.

Clucking to the ponies, Lily slapped the reins and hurried them away. The open, fringe-topped carriage afforded no protection from curious eyes. "You're disappointed in the gift?" she inquired after they had moved beyond the crowd around the Tavern.

"No, no, it's more than that." Drooping dejectedly, Emma dried her face on the lace mantilla. "He said a token—not to forget him. He hasn't given me anything to seal the engagement. From the shape of the box, I'd hoped this was a necklace."

They rode up Barbour Street in silence. Then Emma continued brokenly, "He said he wanted to marry me—to take me to his plantation, but then—but then—"

"The war. And, yes, I can answer that question in your eyes. He likes to move about."

"But if he'd just wanted a mother for his child—most men marry the first wife's sister or kinswoman. . ."

Concern showed in Lily's dark eyes. For once, she seemed at a loss for words.

Forlorn, Emma refused to attend church with Lily the next day; however, at ten o'clock Monday morning, she did go with her to the citywide prayer meeting. The business houses closed and some nine hundred people crowded into the church as the Reverends Cotton, Reeves, and McIntosh, representing various denominations, led in meditation and prayer to God in behalf of their beloved country.

Emma suppressed her cross mood with difficulty, remaining tensely silent during the long afternoon of assisting Cordelia's entertainment of her callers, Mrs. John Shorter and Mrs. Eli Shorter. The visit of Elizabeth Rhodes and her twin sister, Mollie Simpson, friends her own age, helped Emma relax a bit. But when Mrs. Dent and her daughter Lizzie bustled in, flushed and excited from a day in town shopping for Lizzie's upcoming wedding, Emma's throat constricted. A heavy lump in her chest and a throbbing headache made pleasant responses difficult.

"You'll just die when you see my bridal gown, Emma," Lizzie gushed. "You are coming out to the wedding, now?" she urged as they left for Fendall Hall to spend the night with the Edward Youngs.

"Yes," Emma answered quietly, "if I can get a ride."

Emma felt quite sick the next morning and was glad to get out of the house into the crisp morning air to gather strawberries. The melancholy which had hovered around her over the past days had gone unnoticed because every woman in town was saddened by departing soldiers.

She could not discuss her problems with Lily because Mignonne was running a high fever, and Lily sat bathing the child's brow and consulting in worried tones with Dr. Thornton during his several visits. Doggedly, Emma attended the frequent prayer meetings for their country with Cordelia, but she merely sat with clenched teeth, unable to pray, finding no comfort.

When Lizzie's wedding day, May 2, 1861, dawned cloudy and unpleasantly cold after April's summery heat, Emma's spirits sank lower. Her head ached and a slight sniffle made her wonder if she could stay at home, pleading a cold.

A quick footstep on the front porch caused her to catch her breath and look up from where she knelt adding a finishing touch to the arrangement of poppies and larkspur on the wall shelf in the receiving hall. Knowing Kitty had gone upstairs to help Cordelia dress for the wedding, she did not hold back her emotion. Her feet scarcely touched the black-and-white marble as she flung herself across the room and into Jonathan's outstretched arms. Crushed against him, unable to breathe, Emma let her hopes soar. The ardor of his kiss seemed to say that the separation had also been difficult for him.

Discreetly, she led him into the parlor where they could enjoy a moment of privacy. When she told him of John Horry Dent's daughter's wedding, he declared himself delighted to be her escort.

Her cold forgotten, she bounded up the stairs two at a time like Foy. Hurriedly, she donned a frock of pink organdy, with five tiers of flounces fluttering around the skirt and yet another ruffle across the bodice and sleeves. Did she look too much like Mignonne? Turning anxiously toward the cheval glass, she breathed a pleased sigh and smiled at her image. With her pink cheeks and unlined face, she did look young enough to be a bride herself. Radiantly, she descended the stairs to be met by Jonathan's smile of approval at the fluffy pink cloud around her.

Because Harrison had not returned and Lily chose not to leave her sick baby, Cordelia rode alone in the backseat of the carriage to the Dent plantation. But Jonathan answered Mrs. Edwards's grumpy questioning about his family background with patience and good humor.

The sun smiled forth upon the assembled Bleak House Plantation guests. Lizzie Dent, serenely lovely, emerged in a gown of lustrous white satin, made for her in New York several months before. As she and Whitfield Clark exchanged vows, Emma stole glances at Jonathan; surely he would see weddings need not be postponed because of war.

Afterward, as they mingled with the guests on the festive grounds, Emma realized that the subject of the war crept into every conversation. *Men,* she sighed, *were less readily affected by beauty and love.*

John Horry Dent stood in the yard with a group of farmers. As Emma and Jonathan approached, she heard him saying in his slow, deliberate way, "As our country is at war, I'm thinking I should plant less cotton and more corn and provisions."

Others nodded and someone agreed, "Yes, we'll not be importing corn, and flour, and bacon for a while."

While they sat eating their barbecue, succulent pork swimming in the Dents' secret sauce, young Horry Dent came over to talk navy with Jonathan.

"Secretary Mallory has ordered me to New Orleans for duty on the steamer *McRea,*" Horry said.

"You'll be under Captain Rosseau," returned Jonathan in a congratulatory tone. "Fine man. He'll know how to run the blockade."

"Yes," replied the smooth-cheeked young man seriously. "The Mississippi is where the important naval battles will be fought."

"Maybe," drawled Jonathan, "but I think I can find enough excitement on the Chattahoochee." He gave Emma a broad wink.

On the ride back into Eufaula that evening, Emma's emotions fluttered from the romance of the day. She felt certain Jonathan would ask to marry her before he returned to duty. She smiled up at him, handsome in his gray naval officer's uniform. A glance over her shoulder rewarded her with a view of Cordelia's nodding head. A snore indicated she was dozing, but Jonathan continued a noncommittal banter. Sighing, Emma tried to enjoy merely being in his presence. She contented herself with the promise in his wink.

But Jonathan left as suddenly as he had appeared, and Emma remained a spinster, joining other women as they waited for an occasional furloughed soldier or sailor to return. Lonely, uneventful days passed slowly. Cucumbers, beans, peas, and squash busied their hands, while Emma's mind winged along the river. Was Jonathan entertaining some other wide-eyed innocent girl with his stories?

On an afternoon in late May, Elizabeth Rhodes and Mollie Simpson called with exciting news. A dispatch had come from downriver that the U.S. warship, *Crusader,* was sailing toward the bay, with the express purpose of recapturing a schooner taken by the people of Apalachicola and burning the city. A company of fifty men left, taking all Eufaula's ammunition to help at the batteries being erected on Saint Vincent's Island to defend the bay. Fearfully the women waved as they steamed away.

Emma felt as limp as a bedsheet hung on a line, parched by the sun, whipped by the wind, as she waited for news of Jonathan. None came.

The soft, warm beauty of June went unnoticed. Business was nearly suspended as people waited for word of the war. Anxious lookouts watched the river from belvederes and cupolas, fearful that the enemy might break through the defenses at Apalachicola Bay and come steaming up the Chattahoochee.

On Mignonne's first birthday, June 11, 1861, Lily climbed, over and over, to the belvedere to scan the sky, stubbornly maintaining that Harrison would come to join in the celebration. Only after dark when her sleepy child could stay awake no longer, did Lily give up and wish her daughter a happy birthday. On noon of that day, they later learned, the screw steamer USS *Montgomery* had sealed the entrance to their port.

On June 13, the townspeople filled the churches in answer to President Davis's request that the Confederate States observe a day of fasting and prayer. Emma chafed at the inactivity of the long Thursday, quieter even than a usual Sabbath.

Business resumed slowly with people soberly admitting that they were in for a long and bloody siege. Too long, they now realized, they had been solely agricultural, depending upon the North for everything else. Confidence was still voiced by some that the South could win—if the war did not last too long.

Emma joined eagerly the newly organized Ladies' Aid Society, anxious to do any small thing she could to speed this conflict to a swift conclusion. Mrs. B. F. Treadwell had personally outfitted the first soldiers leaving Eufaula. Now more help was needed. Their neighbor, Mrs. L. L. Cato, accompanied by Mrs. Alpheus Baker, called at Barbour Hall to solicit contributions for the boys at the front. A few days later, Captain Baker himself, home on leave from Fort Pickens at Pensacola, Florida, spoke to the society, telling them what they needed to do first. Mr. Young donated meeting rooms above his store, and work began in earnest. Even though cutting and sewing heavy pants was exhausting, Emma relished the satisfaction of helping and went to the sewing rooms whenever Cordelia could spare her.

On Sunday the sky blazed with the tail of a comet, and moanings and whisperings about evil omens filled the servants' quarters. The comet gave Emma no cause to fear; but the next day, a small envelope bearing her name caused her to clutch both hands to her chest, almost too afraid to reach out and take it from the library table by the front door. A cryptic note, hurriedly scribbled in pencil, read:

Apalachicola Bay
June 12, 1861

My dear, sweet Emma,

Blockade a farce. Painted my schooner and slipped right through.

A neutral ship was outside the Sound with a special prize I had been expecting.

See you soon as a cat can wink his eye.

My love,
J.

Time passed slowly. Emma helped cut soldiers' coats and paid a social call with Cordelia on Mrs. John Gill Shorter, at home from Montgomery, the state capital, where Eufaula's own Mr. Shorter was governor. During the last few weeks, she told them, since the moving of the capital of the Confederate States of America from Montgomery to Richmond, Virginia, changes had been brought about.

When, on a Monday morning, church bells began to toll, Emma rushed into the street to join the throng heading for the telegraph office. Rumors had spread the day before, at church, that a tremendous battle was taking place.

The clerk cleared his throat and began to read the dispatch, "Night has closed on a hard-fought field called Manassas. After a day-long battle, our forces are in possession of the field after a glorious victory."

Cheers rang out. The clerk stood waiting with his paper shaking with excitement.

"The numbers engaged were 35,000 Federals. The enemy was routed. They fled, abandoning a large amount of arms, munitions, knapsacks, and baggage."

Cheers interrupted him again.

"The ground is strewn for miles," his voice changed timbre, "with those killed. Confederates killed number 385. Federal dead estimated to be 450–500. The farmhouses are filled with wounded, 1500 Confederates and 1100 Federals."

A hush fell over the crowd as he continued to read praise for the gallantry of the troops and the resolution offered by the Confederate Congress. "We deplore the necessity which has washed the evil of our country with the blood of so many of her noble sons. We offer their families our warmest, cordial sympathy. . . ."

Emma turned away, but she could not shut out his words, "a dozen of our men have been captured. We have taken 1300 prisoners." Walking slowly toward home, she heard snatches, "Recognize the hand of the great high God. . . Sabbath service of thanksgiving and praise. . ." Before this, the war had been mere skirmishes with only an occasional man killed. Suddenly the specter of death loomed large.

Celebrations continued for this major victory. More messages brought the news that many people from Washington City had gone out to watch the battle in the Virginia village of Manassas, twenty-five miles southwest of the capital, for a Sunday excursion, and to cheer their attacking combatants with the cry, "On to Richmond!" General Thomas Jackson's brigade held firm, so firm that, in the afternoon, when General B. E. Bee arrived with reinforcements he declared, "There is Jackson standing like a stone wall." The Federals were driven back across a small river called Bull Run; and the spectators fled, with the new knowledge that the war would be more than one brief battle.

That afternoon, black puffs of smoke preceded the signal from the whistle of the *Wave.* The resulting happy reunion caught up even Cordelia in the excitement. It was decided that the family would attend the cotillion victory celebration.

Surveying her meager wardrobe in the walnut armoire, Emma sniffed disgustedly. She would have to wear the same pink organdy she had worn to Liz's wedding. Cordelia magnanimously offered her a valuable pair of dangling earrings of Etruscan gold. Even though the style was currently popular, Emma decided they did not flatter her and declined.

When they arrived at the hotel on Broad Street, a crowd of men gathered around Harrison and Jonathan for news of the blockade. Emma greeted the other ladies vaguely, straining to hear the men's conversation.

"Why, the blockade's a farce," laughed Jonathan. "The Federals sent in a 787-ton screw steamer, the USS *Montgomery."* He chuckled. "How they ever thought they'd get something so huge in that shallow bay, I'll never know. Like trying to float a watermelon in a saucer." He grinned, and was rewarded by laughter from the crowd. "They tried to sound the water, but the ship almost ran aground," he continued. "They finally brought her into position. They do command the main entrance to the port."

"But they can't lock us in with oceangoing vessels, and they don't have any shallow-draft steamers—yet," added Harrison. "We can still slip our schooners through the shoal water because their big screw propellers can't maneuver in the narrow, intricate channels. They'll never apprehend all our blockade runners since there are four passages to watch at once."

"You know how the semicircle of islands separates Apalachicola from the Gulf of Mexico," Jonathan continued.

Emma leaned forward, aware that he was drawing with his finger, but uncertain of what he was outlining.

"They have blocked West Pass between Sand Island and Saint Vincent's Island and stopped neutral ships from standing off Saint Vincent's Bar to be relieved of cargo by the lighters from the wharves. But!" He waved his index finger and continued gleefully, "We can still slip through Indian Pass between

Saint George Island and Indian Peninsula and—well, just the other night I made it through East Pass between Saint George and Dog Island."

Awed murmurings hummed over the group of men.

"But how can you stay clear of the *Montgomery*'s guns?" queried Foy, shouldering his way into the crowd as Emma wished she could do.

"By a simple trick," Jonathan replied. His dancing eyes met Emma's over Foy's shoulder, but he continued his story, "I painted my little schooner, the *Hollycock*, white."

"White?" chorused the men. "Not black?"

"No. A dull white. Properly painted, she is absolutely indiscernible at a cable's length. Of course, all the crew must wear white at night. One black figure on the bridge would betray an otherwise invisible vessel. Not even a cigar is allowed."

A thrill of vicarious excitement stirred the less daring.

"The *Hollycock* is an extremely fast sailor." Jonathan was enjoying playing to an audience now, and he warmed to his story. "She has a very low hull and slender spars that make her particularly hard to see in darkness. On foggy or moonless nights, we lower her sails and drift with the current right past the blockaders." Grinning, he paused in his story as the listeners nodded and laughed, visualizing the daring of his scheme. "Time and again we've eluded detection. Even though we could see the blockaders, they couldn't see us. But the other night," exhilaration vibrated in his voice, "we had cotton in every space—bales even in the cabin and—"

"Is it true," Foy interrupted breathlessly, "that you scatter a few barrels of oil in the hull and connect a fuse in case—in case of capture?"

"Yes." Jonathan nodded. "We couldn't let so valuable a cargo fall into the hands of the enemy. We'd have to burn it. Anyway," he continued his story, "the moon came from behind a cloud just as we drifted by, and the lookout spotted us. The *Montgomery* steamed in pursuit. We ran up our canvas, but we lacked the speed to outrun them."

Ears pricked, Emma leaned forward, not caring if it was unladylike to join the group of men who were now hushed expectantly.

"Suddenly the wind becalmed. Their bullets played 'Ole Dan Tucker' around my ears." He paused and smiled with every eye upon him. "It seemed we were lost."

"What happened?" several chorused.

"A great gust filled her sails. We ran for shore seeking the safety of the shoals. The *Hollycock* is a centerboard schooner. That means that an adjustable blade, pushed out through her flat-bottomed keel, maintains her perpendicular. We drew up the centerboard to reduce the draft." He shrugged his shoulders, expressing ease. "Went right over a bar in only four and a half feet of water. . ." He motioned outwardly with both hands. The men guffawed at the image of the big steamer's being foiled.

"On the Atlantic," Harrison said, "blockade-running is a science. Here on the Gulf, it's a gentleman's game."

Emma turned away at the sound of their laughter. Jonathan had described his exploits as though he had been running his yacht in the America's Cup race. The sudden realization of danger sickened her.

Sawing scrapes on the violin as the orchestra tuned up made Emma wince as she stumbled across the room blinded by tears. The tune of a cotillion filled the ballroom, and many couples joined in the brisk dance. Emma sat miserably on the sidelines. Still surrounded, Jonathan continued to talk. When the cotillion ended, Van Houten tapped his baton and indicated three lively beats. Emma smiled as they struck up the lilting "Tallahassee Waltz." Hidden by her hoop skirt, her feet began to dance in place.

Jonathan bowed before her. With twinkling eyes, he said, "Our waltz is becoming very popular. It's such a light and dainty tune that the moment I hear it, I think of you." He took her hand and led her to the floor. Danger was forgotten.

At first, her toes tripped instead of gliding, and the flounces of her pink organdy fluttered as her hooped skirt rocked upward, forward to the right, forward to the left. The steadying of his hands made her relax. She glided smoothly in the backward steps and began to float on the joyful rhythm of three-quarter time.

Laughing, flushed after several Strauss waltzes, Emma begged for air. Jonathan led her from the heat of the ballroom to a corner of the veranda where a cool breeze wafted the fragrance of honeysuckle. Other couples crowded the porch and there was little privacy; but the tenderness of his face as he gazed at her made her feel she had been kissed.

"I told you I captured a special prize," said Jonathan, like a little boy who had just caught Santa Claus. "I'd sent a message home—I'd been waiting. . ." He took out a long, narrow package shaped like the one that had held the fan and pressed it into her hand.

With shaking fingers, she lifted the top of an ebony box. Sparkling against the white velvet lining, a necklace of rubies cast a pink glow. She drew a deep breath. "Oh, it's so lovely," she gasped. "Oh, I never expected to have anything so beautiful!"

"You grow more beautiful every time you smile." His face shone with candid emotion.

Emma could not resist brushing his smooth cheek with her fingertips.

"I'm glad you're wearing pink tonight." He laughed softly, as if slightly embarrassed at the tremor in his voice. "The first time I saw you, you had on pink velvet. Your radiance made me think of the pink rubies which belonged to my mother," he said gently as he took the necklace from the box in her hand and fastened it about her slender neck.

Unable to speak, she pressed the cool jewels against her porcelain skin and looked at him through misted eyes.

"I wanted to wait for the perfect gift for you—one that would have special meaning." His voice was tender as his eyes held hers for a long moment before he added laughingly, "but I almost lost it when the Yankees blocked the port." Lifting a matching ruby ring from the box, he slipped it on her finger. Grasping her hand tightly, he whispered, "You haven't changed? You'll still be mine?"

"Oh, Jonathan, of course," she breathed. "Always." With shining eyes, she looked up at him. "You know—I'm sure you do—that I have little dowry—I couldn't have a fine wedding, but I'm sure the Reverend Reeves will. . ."

Jonathan dropped her hands and grasped the porch rail. "Emma—" He hesitated. "Dearest Emma, please understand. I don't want to risk. . ."

Her lashes fanned back from anxious eyes.

"I didn't mean this for a wedding gift. I can't marry you now. I must leave." His voice cracked. He swallowed hard. "I just meant this to pledge our engagement. Please understand," he repeated. "The C.S.A. is dependent upon people like me to slip through the blockade."

"People like you!" Her voice rose shrilly and her lower lip trembled. "You're a worse daredevil than that hot-air balloonist who came through. You risked your life for these rubies and then—and then. . ." She flung out her hand and the hard stone clanked against the column. "I thought you'd finished your childish adventuring. Blockade-runners—" The necklace followed the heaving of her chest.

"Blockade-runners are f–f–foolhardy!" she sobbed.

Chapter 7

Jonathan drew back red-faced. Glancing at the other couples, he took the weeping woman by the elbow, led her off the porch, and hurried her down the walk. Pushing her behind the shelter of a thick magnolia, he stood apart from her, stiff with anger and embarrassment.

Burying her face in her hands, she sobbed uncontrollably.

"Don't," he whispered miserably, "please, don't!"

"Why must you continue to take such foolish chances?" she snuffled. "Cotton bales can stay in a w–w–warehouse. We can do without Paris gowns and Italian marble."

"Is that what you think?" he spat out disgustedly. "Maybe I did risk my life for your jewels—which you don't seem to appreciate—but. . ."

"Oh, Jonathan, of course I do!" She wailed and clutched the necklace in both hands, "I love my—my engagement gifts. It—it seemed so much that I thought it was—a wedding gift—I misunderstood." She gulped. Forlornly, she dropped her head.

Gently, he kissed the golden curls on the top of her bowed head.

"I'm so ashamed!" Her words wavered on a sigh. "I'm frightened."

"Little one, don't cry." Jonathan enfolded her in his arms and stroked her hair as she wept into the rough gray material of his uniform. "I understand," he whispered. "I know your friends are marrying, but. . .I don't want to risk—leaving you in—a family way—alone. . ."

Emma snuggled in the tight circle of his arms and dabbed at her eyes. "I wouldn't be alone. Lily's here. . .You're here often. I'm not afraid of—that. . ."

He pulled her roughly against his chest and buried his face in her hair. "I saw Betty die. Be patient with me, Emma." He hugged her convulsively. "Please wait 'til I'm here to stay."

Almost unable to breathe, she sighed. "Oh, Jonathan, I'll wait." She raised her lips for a lingering kiss to seal their betrothal.

"I want you to understand," he said at last. He guided her to a bench in the garden and began to explain. "The cotton in the warehouses in Apalachicola alone is worth a million dollars even if you only count it ten cents a pound." He held both her hands in his and continued urgently. "What you must realize is that everyone in southwest Georgia and southeast Alabama is entirely dependent upon the sale of cotton for the necessities of life. Cotton is the only thing the Confederacy can sell for gold or trade for weapons of defense!"

Drooping dejectedly, Emma looked at her hands and said nothing.

Jonathan continued in a strained voice. "The South has few factories. Our soldiers have few arms except what they can capture. We are sealed off from our supplies of guns and ammunition from Europe. We *must* run the blockade!"

"Yes," she sighed. "I see what you mean, but—you're not a sailor. Can't someone else. . . ?" She pulled her hands from his and clenched and unclenched fistfuls of pink organdy ruffles. "I thought you were a farmer."

Jonathan laughed halfheartedly. "I'm learning. The Confederate Navy has outstanding officers. Many resigned their commissions in the United States Navy. We have many British naval officers, the very cream of the English Navy, who have temporarily become captains of blockade-runners. Perhaps the rest of us are farmers—but we are learning."

The moon was high, and many of the older people were leaving. Emma stirred uneasily, knowing Cordelia would be looking for her. Jonathan rose slowly, as if he were carrying a heavy weight, and smiled sadly down at her. She felt too weak-kneed to stand.

"The Confederacy must have cloth for uniforms—buttons, thread, boots, shoes, stockings," he said disgustedly, "iron, steel, copper, chemicals—medicines—salt. Can't you comprehend that I must. . ."

"Yes. Yes, I see. I'll wait for our wedding."

She gave him her hand. Silently they rejoined the dancers, but the melody seemed muted. Emma accepted compliments on her jewels and congratulations from Lily, Elizabeth, and Mollie; but her heart felt as cold as the glitter of the rubies.

Wait. Wait. Wait. The cruel word pounded often in her temples in tandem with a raging toothache, complicated by several trips to the dentist. Dr. Plant filled the offending cavity, but an ulceration at the root necessitated his removing the filling. Pacing her room, holding a rock heated in the fireplace against her cheek, she agonized over her silly behavior as much as over the pain in her mouth. She must not rush Jonathan to marry her or she would surely drive him from her.

Her love and yearning for him had grown stronger, but he had drawn away. Did his distant attitude indicate that he regretted his proposal? She flung the rock into the coals. He had said he needed her. He had never actually voiced the words of love she longed to hear. Hot tears of pain and anguish burned down her cheeks.

The Confederates were trying to reinforce their hold upon Apalachicola from the batteries on Saint Vincent's Island, but their supply of guns and ammunition was pitifully small. Emma did not try to discuss her resulting fears with Lily—who was totally enthralled with teaching Mignonne to walk.

The post office was still receiving mail by stage; she checked daily, fruitlessly, for a letter from Jonathan. An unusual amount of rain for August further dampened Emma's spirits. She spent the gray days straining her eyes over the stitching of soldiers' trousers. Working with the Ladies' Aid Society busied her hands, but her mind seemed deadened, and she stabbed her needle with a growing sense of hopelessness.

September shimmered in on a blast of dry heat. And with its bright sunshine, Emma's heart brightened with the sound of the pulsating whistle of the *Wave*.

The dining room of Barbour Hall was the site of as festive a meal as Emma could prepare with growing shortages. Despite Mrs. Edwards's remonstrations, Foy could not wait for polite dinner conversation and pestered the men until they revealed what had been happening.

"Well," grinned Jonathan, generously helping himself to Emma's freshly dug sweet potatoes, "it has been pretty exciting. We continued to slip by the *Montgomery* with no trouble, but the USS *R. R. Cuyler*'s joining her tripled the number of men and guns against us."

Foy's reddened ears seemed to quiver as he held his fork in midair and leaned forward.

"The *Cuyler* is another screw steamer—the Union still doesn't have vessels suitable for operation in shallow water. On the night of August 26. . ." Jonathan's voice became low and deliberate as it always did when he was spinning tales. "Five Yankee boats went out on reconnaissance from the *Cuyler* and *Montgomery* and discovered the supply ship *Finland* and the schooner *New Plan* at anchor in the bay." Jonathan took a bite of fried chicken and smiled at Emma in a way that communicated only his pleasure in the meal—nothing more to ease the slight restraint between them.

"Did they get away?" Foy croaked.

"No," contributed Harrison evenly. "The Yankees captured both of them easily. They made the crew of the *New Plan* take an oath of allegiance to the United States and then released them. They took the *Finland* as a lawful prize, but the Union seamen had trouble trying to remove their prize from the bay." He laughed and his eyes fastened on Lily's face in that special way in which they seemed to exchange thoughts. "The winds and tides were unfavorable, but the Federals attempted to tow the *Finland* to the blockading station at East Pass." He paused and grinned. "She grounded on Saint Vincent's Bar."

"And there she stayed all night 'til we came along about dawn." Jonathan gestured with his chicken leg. "The night was dark but dangerously clear. All hands were on deck. The sails were down, of course, and we were crouching behind the bulwarks when. . ."

Emma's attention had been on passing hot biscuits. Staring wide-eyed at Jonathan, she set the plate down with a *whack*.

Turning toward her, he explained, "Harrison, in the *Wave,* was towing my schooner, *Hollycock.* We were creeping down the river heading into Apalachicola. We had no lights. Not a sound could be heard save the regular *beat, beat, beat* of the paddle wheels which, in spite of our snail's pace, was dangerously loud."

"I was in the pilothouse, straining my eyes in the darkness," Harrison picked up the story, "when I saw the dim white outline of the surf. Suddenly, Burrus gripped my arm and pointed to the *Finland* on our starboard bow. . ."

"I had nine men from the Apalachicola Guards on the *Hollycock.* A centerboard schooner can pivot and navigate small circles with ease. We came around and fired a broadside." Jonathan chuckled with glee. "You should've seen those Yankees scatter. They set fire to the *Finland* and took to their boats."

"You mean you routed the Union Navy with only nine men?" Foy clapped his hands. "Nine men and courage! I've got to go with you next time!"

A snort of alarm came from Cordelia, who had been eating while the others talked.

Jonathan laughed. "We sent 'em running. Didn't even injure one—but we hurt their pride! And we got back our supplies," he continued quickly. "Our detachment boarded the burning *Finland* and recovered the lifeboats, salvaging two hundred sacks of coffee, four hundred revolvers, a number of rifles, dirks, a six-pounder fieldpiece, five hundred thousand percussion caps, and a quantity of fruit."

"And the Yankee ships were too big to enter the bay and stop you?" Lily asked.

"Yes, Ma'am. We got away from them one more time." Jonathan patted his full stomach in satisfaction.

Emma twisted the ruby ring on her finger and asked timidly, "You look so tired. Can you stay awhile?"

"Wish we could." Harrison shook his head. "We must leave tomorrow morning for Columbus. This load must get to the supply lines. Low water will prevent our reaching Columbus before long."

"Have you heard much talk," Jonathan inquired, "about Columbus's being the nucleus of the Confederate Ordnance Department?"

"Columbus?" squeaked Foy, surprised that the nearby Georgia town was of any importance to the war.

"Yes," Lily interjected, "I'd heard it called the largest industrial center south of Richmond. And since it's connected by railroad with Montgomery, Atlanta, and Richmond. . ."

"Sometimes I think this war's being waged by railroad men," grumbled Harrison bitterly. "The Union's choking off the waterways and laying rails."

"I'm going with you," said Lily suddenly. "A trip on the *Wave* is always such fun, and it looks like the only chance to see you."

Harrison smiled and nodded assent. "It will be a quick trip. I'll pick up a load of uniforms and tents from the cotton mills, and fifes and drums from the music store. . ."

"Please go by the mill and get me a barrel of meal and a barrel of flour," interrupted Cordelia.

Emma could not subdue the lights dancing in her eyes. Remembering how Lily and Harrison's romance had blossomed on the beautifully appointed steamboat with the orchestra playing and moonlight dancing upon the water, she held her breath, smiled shyly up at Jonathan, and asked softly, "Are you going, too?"

Jonathan's tone indicated the seriousness of his business. "Yes, I'm going to the Naval Ironworks to confer with Chief Engineer Warner about getting some vessels built to move down the river and raise the blockade. We must work quickly before the Federals ascend the river and attack Columbus." A frown pursed his usually jolly face. "They know of the swords, rifles, and ammunition produced there. We only hope they don't know we're building a torpedo boat."

Emma slumped in her chair, toying with her food. Jonathan was too worried about defending the river to consider her. Powerless to go or do unless she was told, she leaned her head back against the tall chair.

"I've heard that with so many industries running day and night, even some women are working," said Lily, obviously fired with enthusiasm. "I wish I could do something useful."

"Lily!" Cordelia Edwards exclaimed and fanned herself in shock.

Lily laughed and finally caught Emma's pleading glance. "Um, Mama, why don't you and Emma come along and visit Aunt Laurie?"

Emma dared not breathe or look at her sister-in-law.

"Well, maybe," Mrs. Edwards replied slowly. "If you'll have done with foolish talk."

Hurried preparations were made for the trip. Even though Cordelia feared wrecks from snags and obstructions in the shallow river or fires from boiler explosions, the luxuries of water travel on a floating hotel such as the *Wave* and the anticipation of seeing her sister finally outweighed the dangers. All was in readiness when Foy caused an explosion of his own.

Standing by the front doors amid trunks and carpetbags, Foy declared, "I've packed all my belongings, Mama. I won't be coming back," he mumbled, head down and eyes averted. Suddenly, his chin came up with a defiance which equaled Lily's fire. "I'm joining the navy!"

"No!" Cordelia shrieked. "You're still a baby! You can't go." Then she whined, "You can't leave me."

Cordelia's shouts and cries during the carriage ride to the wharf proved to no avail. Foy's mind seemed made up.

Emma sat wringing her hands, allowed no voice in the destiny of this child she loved so much. She had watched him fearfully of late as many of his friends, lured, no doubt, by the colorful, braid-trimmed boleros and bloused Turkish trousers copied from French light-infantry uniforms, joined Brannon's Zouaves. Foy had even secured a *kepi.* She had seen him wearing the cap, running, and pretending to shoot from behind bushes.

With nothing resolved, they reached the wharf. Even though he was extremely busy, Captain Wingate was summoned. Although she always hated to admit her son-in-law's merits, Cordelia turned to him in despair.

"Wait a little, son," said Harrison with quiet firmness.

"I'm old enough! I've heard of drummer boys as young as ten," Foy flared defiantly.

"Yes." Harrison nodded. "You're right, but to become a midshipman you must be proficient in reading, writing, and the rudiments of mathematics. I'll help you every time I'm home. If you hope to be a naval officer, you must continue your schooling until you're sixteen."

"You promise I can go then?"

Harrison held out his hand and nodded solemnly.

Foy looked him in the eye and shook hands. Then he ducked his head to hide tears.

Cordelia sat down heavily, moaning, "Emma, we cannot travel. Foy has given me a brow ague! Unload the trunks. We'll go back home."

Emma's forehead dropped to her fist. Squeezing her eyelids, she realized she would not even be able to say good-bye to Jonathan. Sick with disappointment but knowing she was dependent upon Cordelia for a home, she had no choice but to obey.

"Summon Kitty and help me to bed," Cordelia ordered. "Then get me thirty grains of quinine."

Emma well knew that while the cure for Cordelia's aching head was taking its slow effect, she would be in no condition to supervise the many servants, to instruct and reinstruct them at each task. Emma was accustomed to running the household on these occasions while the quinine caused her sister-in-law to lose her equilibrium. Cordelia would clutch her head as if to ascertain its size and declare it filled with a dozen drums and roaring ocean waves. Although Emma did not taste the dose of quinine upon her own tongue, a bitterness filled her mouth, invaded her brain, spoiled her countenance, and stiffened her movements.

Early in October, when Elizabeth rushed in bubbling with the news that

Mollie had delivered a son, Emma went with her to the magnificent, towering, three-and-a-half-story, Italianate mansion that William Simpson had built for his wife, Mary Ann, affectionately called Mollie, on North Randolph Street next to the home of her sister, Mrs. Chauncey Rhodes. The sisters had even had double weddings and, as Elizabeth tenderly bathed Mollie's face, Emma felt shut out by the twins' closeness and her own spinsterhood.

In the nursery, Mollie's three little girls crowded around her as she lifted William Thomas Simpson, Jr., in her arms. Pressing the tiny body to her heart and kissing his soft, sweet head, Emma was overwhelmed with longing.

Waiting on Mollie and holding the precious bundle became a daily joy and torment. As Emma walked back to Barbour Hall through the Indian summer afternoons with her skirt sweeping the dry, rustling leaves around her, she ached with the knowledge of her age—twenty-eight. Would Jonathan ever decide the time was right to marry? He never spoke of his daughter. Possibly he did not want other children.

Shrinking into a lonely shell, Emma made excuses to stop going to choir practice. She gave up teaching her Sabbath school class and pressed her hands over her ears when ringing bells called townsfolk to the services.

Lily eyed her warily but compressed her lips and said nothing until one hot afternoon as they sat in the big rocking chairs on the wide veranda of Barbour Hall. "Emma, Dear, are you all right?" she began hesitantly. "You haven't been to prayer meeting with me in weeks."

"I'm tired," Emma snapped. Her face was set in tense lines and her eyes defied Lily to enter her thoughts.

"Feeding on God's Word rests and sustains me." Lily spoke gently.

Emma said nothing.

Lily sighed. Her soft, dark eyes were moist as she tried again. "Let me help. Have you and Jonathan quarreled?"

"No," Emma replied shortly. She opened the top button on the high neck of her white shirtwaist and fanned. "Well, not really." She looked at Lily, who leaned forward, eagerly trying to share her sorrow. Relenting slightly, she let out her breath and spoke in a wavering voice, "I'm beginning to think he won't ever be ready to—to marry. . ."

"It is a bad time," Lily replied quickly. Running her fingers through her dark hair, she said haltingly, "Try—to see his side of it. Don't shut him out. Share your thoughts." She sat for a moment looking down into the garden. "When I pray for Harrison, I am one with him across the miles. Come with me tonight. You'll feel better if you'll let God. . ."

"No!" Emma flung out. Dry-eyed, her whole body drawn with misery, she clutched the arms of the rocker. "Why do you think God cares? The whole Confederacy is praying to Him. Maybe the Union is, too, but all we hear is report after report of bloody battles—death—disease!"

"Emmaaa!" Cordelia's coarse voice wailed from inside the house.

Jumping to her feet, glad for once to answer Cordelia's summons, Emma fled Lily without a backward glance.

The cold, wet wind that brought in November increased Cordelia's aguish neuralgia. Lily was dispatched to the drugstore to get more quinine.

Emma was in the upstairs hallway making certain that the round iron grate which conducted the summer heat up the grand staircase and out through the belvedere was now securely closed. Looking down on the landing below, she was surprised at the way Lily was dragging up the stairs.

"There is no more quinine," Lily said in hushed tones. Her face ashen, she bit her lip. "There will be no more."

Staring into Lily's frightened eyes, Emma gasped, "Whatever is the matter?"

Chapter 8

They're evacuating the fort on Saint Vincent's." Lily's brown eyes were wide with alarm. "More vessels have been added to the blockade. Five schooners cleared the port in late November, but only one could get back in. The Federals have captured the rest and taken their loads of cotton and turpentine!"

"Jonathan?" Emma gasped, clutching her fists to her chest.

"No, no, he's all right. The *Hollycock* wasn't among them," Lily assured her. She sank to a chair and continued in a frightened voice. "I had a message from Harrison. They're withdrawing up the river."

Gurgling in Emma's throat bubbled out, half laughter, half tears.

"What will become of us," Cordelia Edwards wailed, "if the Yankees attack up the Chattahoochee?" She fell back, fanning rapidly.

As Lily turned to reassure her mother that many miles of fortified river still lay between them and the enemy, Emma went to the window and looked out through a blur of tears. Slowly a smile spread across her face and she lifted her shoulders. Jonathan could no longer run the dangerous blockade and risk being shut out of the country. Perhaps—probably—he was coming home.

Humming "Joy to the World," Emma hurried out to the kitchen to consult with Aunt Dilsey. "There will be no fruit for ambrosia. What can we have?" she queried.

Emma's high hopes and good spirits infected everyone. Happily, the servants speeded their pace, and Barbour Hall soon rang with laughter. The smell of Christmas filled every room.

Cheeks flushed, her hair escaping its knot into golden ringlets around her forehead, Emma was adding a final bit of holly to the central hall when a footstep on the veranda made her heart leap.

Turning joyfully with outstretched arms, she smiled into the dark and laughing eyes which had filled her dreams.

Bursting through the door without waiting for a formal invitation, Jonathan grasped her shoulders and beamed at her. "Oh, Emma, dearest Emma, how I've missed you!"

They stood grinning foolishly, each renewing the joy of the other's face. Then he pushed her backward, making her blink in surprise. Shoving her beneath the crown-of-thorns chandelier, he crushed his lips upon hers.

Blissfully, she returned his kiss, exalting because he had known without looking that she had covered the crystal teardrops with mistletoe.

Joy seasoned Christmas dinner. Ringing laughter filled the void left by unavailable delicacies. As if by unspoken rule, the war went unmentioned until all the traditions had been observed. Only after they had settled around the fireplace in the parlor did Jonathan break the drowsy silence.

"I have news I can't hold any longer," he exclaimed. "We've stopped running the blockade like so many puppies worrying an old cow. We're moving upriver to Saffold, and. . ."

"Aww," pouted Foy, disgusted that he had missed the sport.

"Why Saffold?" Cordelia Edwards roused from her dozing. "The Saffolds and David Johnston are old friends of my dear departed Mr. Edwards."

"It's on their plantation—not far from that old mule-powered cotton gin—that the navy yard is building a gunboat."

"Where," Emma's voice squeaked. She cleared her throat and asked timidly, "Where is Saffold?"

"It's on the Georgia side of the river, down in Early County, less than a hundred miles from here."

Emma's eyes sparkled, and she drew in her breath delightedly as she beamed at Jonathan. A clear promise shone back from his eyes. With only a third as much of the river separating them as it had been to Apalachicola, they could often be together.

"We've merely tried to defend ourselves long enough," Jonathan spoke emphatically. "We're on the offensive now. Work was begun back in October on a gunboat named for the river, the *Chattahoochee.* I'll be at Saffold supervising completion, and training the crew, and. . ."

Extending his upturned hand toward Emma, he smiled at her tenderly. She could feel his warmth, and his yearning gesture told her that he, too, wished propriety allowed them more time alone.

"With a vessel such as this, we'll soon raise the blockade," he continued slowly, deliberately. His voice dropped and he leaned closer. "The war will soon be over and we can be married."

"How big is the gunboat?" Foy interrupted excitedly.

"Well," Jonathan turned. "She's a beauty. One hundred thirty feet long, thirty feet across at the beam, two engines to power two propellers—"

"What about you?" Lily turned worried eyes toward Harrison.

"Now that the river has risen, I'll be passing here constantly." He inclined his dark head toward hers and smiled reassuringly. "Florida's Governor Milton has ordered that no more cotton vessels be allowed to attempt leaving port because the Yankees are capturing too many prizes." He shrugged his shoulders expressively. "My work is reversed. Instead of taking cotton downriver to the sea, I'll just be going down as far as Saffold, loading bales from the plantation landings and taking them upriver to supply the cotton mills at Columbus. Uniforms, tents, and so on are being shipped out of there by rail."

Lily's brown curls bounced as she bobbed about the room. "And you'll be nearly empty going down, and we'll all—" Her voice rose to an excited squeal. "Oh, Mama, don't you want to visit Mrs. Johnston?"

Jonathan's spirit leaped across the crowded room and locked with Emma's as vivacious Lily bubbled over with plans for them to visit Saffold. Emma sat with her head buzzing as dizzily as if he had actually whirled her in a waltz.

Even though the holidays were wet and cold, the family enjoyed pleasant, quiet hours by the fire. Embracing with smiles, Emma and Jonathan played backgammon or dominoes at the corner game table. In the adjoining library, Harrison helped Foy with trigonometry. Cordelia toasted her feet by the hearth and dictated the necessary letters to Lily to advise their friends of their upcoming visit. Since The Pines would be nearby, it was decided that they would also visit there.

"Oh, Emma!" Lily exclaimed. "You're going to love the Shackelford girls. They're delights."

"Real beauties, you say?" Jonathan perked up, feigning interest.

Emma merely smiled. Sustained by the loving warmth of Jonathan's presence, she wanted to savor each hour and not worry about the future.

They welcomed the New Year, 1862, buoyed by Jonathan's confidence that the Confederacy's new weapons would soon win the war. Eufaula celebrated and the band played "Home Again" as the *Chewalla* steamed into sight, bringing the Clayton Guards, the Pioneer Guards, and the Eufaula Rifles home after their twelve month's enlistment.

Jonathan and Harrison left with the promise that they would be reunited shortly; however, weather and circumstances created nerve-racking delays. Severe cold in January kept Cordelia in bed moaning with rheumatism. Terrifying thunderstorms shook February. Lightning struck a neighbor's house and raging fire consumed it.

The men came in March, bringing the dreadful news that the city of Apalachicola was in danger of falling. If the Confederates retreated, the Union raiders would begin pressing up the Apalachicola River, which flowed out of the Chattahoochee. The girls kept this news from Cordelia, Emma hoping steadfastly for their trip downriver. As yet the Yankees had not reached the Alabama line.

One morning when it seemed she could endure no more waiting, Emma walked into the garden and stretched her arms upward to a fresh-washed, watercolor sky. The trees, dressed in the yellow-green lace of young leaves, danced in the gentle breeze. In the distance, a low hum floated on the soft air. Gradually, the hollows of her loneliness began to fill until her very arms and legs reverberated with the sound of the steamboat's whistle.

Uhmmmmm! Uhmmmmm!

"Lily!" she screamed, running toward the house. "Lily!" she gasped, "The *Wave!*"

It looks like a floating wedding cake, Emma thought, smiling, nodding, and hugging herself as she approached the vessel, seeing it as if for the first time. The flat-bottomed boat, with its huge, side paddle wheel, rose in tiers of decks trimmed with white railings. Stained-glass windows sparkled like spun sugar in the hurricane deck. The tiny, airy pilothouse crowned the top. Emma laughed as she assisted Cordelia up the gangway. Normally, she was not fanciful; but then, she was usually going along as companion or chaperone. This trip was different. She was going to meet Jonathan.

Cordelia sniffed disdainfully as she hurried across the main deck just above the water's edge. Neither the cackling chickens nor the squealing pigs, waiting to be killed and served along the way, caused her to twist her nose. Rather, the frizzled and unwashed folk who crowded to the lower deck, ate the leftover grub stock, and scrambled ashore to help wood up the hungry engines twice each day, offended her sensibilities. Puffing, she climbed to the upper deck, where she settled back in a chair and prepared for a pleasant visit with friends.

Emma moved quietly through the group of broad-skirted, narrow-bonneted ladies and top-hatted gentlemen who crowded the deck so like a plantation gallery. The air tingled with anticipation as one huge paddle wheel reversed and the other turned forward. The tremendous boat backed smartly from the wharf and headed downriver. Lily and Mignonne were already established in the captain's stateroom. Emma need do nothing but lean against the rail, stare out at the green water shimmering in the sunshine, and dream of Jonathan and a home of her own.

The *Wave* floated gently, smoothly down the Chattahoochee, which was here smooth, there swirling swiftly over shoals, and always just ahead, turning through a green tunnel of trees shouldering their way to the water's edge. The crest of the high banks was guarded by ancient, dark green oaks. The bright red of infant maple leaves glistened along the slopes. Between them an impenetrable forest laced together with swags of vines blossoming with fragrant, yellow jessamine. Emma leaned over the rail to look at the undulating green water. Wavering, she clutched her head.

"Dizzy?" asked Lily, joining her at the rail.

"Yes," admitted Emma ruefully. "I don't know why. There's no feeling of movement underfoot."

"Look straight ahead until you adjust," Lily advised. "It won't take long—

oh, would you look at those sycamores stretching their arms out over the water. That white bark is so beautiful!"

Enchanted by the mystery of what lay beyond each turning, Lily leaned far out, pointing and admiring. Each time they reached a clearing, she waved vigorously to children running to see the steamboat pass and exclaimed that this imposing manor house was more beautiful than the last. Emma fretted because they stopped every few miles at yet another plantation landing to take on passengers, food, and cordwood for fuel. Would they never get to Saffold?

As the lazy day drifted to a close, they watched the colors of the sunset reflecting in the water over and again, rippling, sparkling, drifting, lifting. Relaxed, Emma suddenly realized that her dizziness was gone. Stretching and laughing, they got up from their deck chairs to dress for dinner.

Harrison and Lily presided over the festive meal. In the central hallway between the staterooms, long tables were set for fifty passengers. Chickens had been fricasseed; pigs had been roasted. Thick soups, heavily sauced Creole dishes, and platters of game were consumed by businessmen heading for the bustling river town of Columbia, Alabama; visiting ladies; and sundry other travelers. At the close of the meal, a rustle of ceremony claimed the attention of the diners. Two waiters carried in a tremendous birthday cake. Foy reddened with embarrassment and pleasure. At last he was sixteen.

The Italian orchestra was no longer traveling with the *Wave* because of the war; however, the congenial group went into the ladies' saloon, and Emma obliged by playing waltzes on the Chickering grand piano.

Excitement pounded in Emma's temples as they completed their unloading and pulled away from Columbia at last. The scenery began to change. Limestone outcroppings made the river more dangerous with hidden shallows. The hardwood trees gave way to towering, black-green pines. Their spring growth made them look as if their branches were set with golden candles.

When at last they reached their destination and prepared to leave the steamer, Foy grinned at Emma. "I wish we could go straight to the navy yard," he whispered.

"Me, too," she replied, "but we'll have to be patient a little longer."

The family climbed into the carriage which had been sent to meet them, and rode a short distance through piney woods, before the sandy road suddenly turned.

"Oh!" Lily drew in her breath in delight. "Oh, I'd forgotten how beautiful the live oaks are." She sighed as they drove down the long, cool avenue.

Dressed in the glistening, dark green velvet of tiny evergreen leaves, hoop-skirted trees lifted their arms and intertwined their fingers over the roadway. Each spreading arm and dipping elbow was draped with gray lace shawls of

Spanish moss. "They look like ladies-in-waiting for a bridal procession," Lily declared.

Emma blushed but said nothing.

"These coastal live oaks are one of the main reasons that the shipyard is here at Saffold," Harrison said. "Their strong, yellow wood is very durable underwater."

"Surely they won't cut these!" Lily drew up indignantly.

"Well, not the *allée* to the house, I'm sure," he laughed.

At the end of the lane, the Johnston home glistened whitely. Lofty, round columns of heart pine marched across the spreading portico where Mrs. Johnston graciously welcomed them.

By midafternoon Emma was nervously fidgeting, wondering how she could ever politely ask to see the gunboat.

Mrs. Johnson looked up at her with her plump face wreathed in understanding smiles. "We're all invited to a little tea aboard the *Chattahoochee* this afternoon, my dear. We frequently entertain the officers and the young ladies of the neighborhood; consequently, they are returning our hospitality."

Stiff with disappointment because of her failure to spot Jonathan as the party went up the gangway to the *Chattahoochee,* Emma followed the group about. Awestruck, she threw back her head and looked straight upward at the three towering masts of the 130-foot vessel. The first lieutenant conducting their tour explained that while the masts would be sail rigged, the light-draft vessel was also steam-driven by a double propeller.

Misery overwhelmed her and she could scarcely feign attention as they watched workmen mounting the battery, which would consist of four broadside cannon, and forward and aft pivot guns. She gave up trying to look wise and hurried below to the officers' quarters. Surely Jonathan would be there arranging the tea.

Surprisingly, flowers in great profusion filled the wardroom. Three exquisitely gowned young ladies were introduced to her as some of the Shackelford girls who had come down from The Pines. Their mother had sent the flowers, a great market basket of strawberries, some cream, and a pound cake. She murmured small talk as she nibbled the rich dessert, but her eyes kept straying to the doors of the officers' cabins on both sides. Her mind struggled to decide if she had misunderstood. Jonathan *was* stationed aboard the *Chattahoochee,* wasn't he?

The hair on the back of Emma's neck prickled and the space between her shoulders burned. Turning quickly, she saw him as he climbed down from the gun deck. Laughing, shaking hands, he made slow progress across the crowded wardroom, but his twinkling eyes were upon her.

Glowing, Emma stood waiting. At last, he reached her and bowed formally, kissing her hand.

"Miss Edwards, how lovely you look in my favorite pink." His charming smile became a boyish grin as he whispered, "Emma, Dearest, how I've missed you!"

"I was beginning to think I'd misunderstood," she answered softly.

"I'm sorry I wasn't here to meet you," he apologized. "I've only just arrived from the Naval Ironworks at Columbus. I was ordered to bring down a raft loaded with machinery and cannon." He squeezed her hand and jerked his head in the direction of the door, but he continued speaking formally. "We have some very valuable weapons. Have you seen the Dahlgren?"

Happily, she followed him up to the gun deck and stood looking at the dark curl which fell over his forehead as he excitedly showed her the shiny pivot-mounted gun.

"There's none better for naval action," he exclaimed enthusiastically. "The *Chattahoochee* is a first-class gunboat. Even unfinished, she could hold off the Yankees." He led her along the deck of the square-rigged schooner, and she wondered if she were about to receive another tour. When they reached the secluded shadow of the towering smokestack, he leaned close above her and whispered. "Darling Emma, this war will soon be over. With these new weapons, we'll lick the enemy. Then I can give myself completely to you!"

She could only whisper, "I love you."

Jonathan gazed down at her with an intensity which reddened her cheeks and made her shiver like a puppy. He kissed her with heightened urgency. His voice husky with emotion, he promised, "Soon, we'll be man and wife!"

Standing at the rail with her golden head as close to his dark curls as they dared without raising everyone's eyebrows, they discussed wedding arrangements and whispered endearments. All too soon the group was spilling around them, babbling excited plans for the evening. Incredulous that the way was prepared for them to be together, they learned that the officers and ladies were all invited to visit The Pines.

The Shackelford plantation covered three thousand acres, many miles of which stretched along the Chattahoochee. From the moment they approached the house and saw candles twinkling from every window upstairs and down, and laughing couples drifting in and out through French doors onto the wide piazza, Emma sensed a welcoming atmosphere, a quiet peace far removed from the ugliness of war.

Even though Jonathan and his fellow officers wore uniforms resplendent with gold braid and brass buttons, they faded into insignificance beside the exquisite gowns of the ladies. While some of the men wore Confederate gray, others were attired in dark blue flannel. These officers formerly had been in the United States Navy, and they preferred to continue to wear the color they deemed universal for men of the sea.

Jonathan had just introduced Emma to his friend, Cowles Myles Collier, when the handsome, former West Point cadet's attention became riveted upon the curving staircase. Two beautiful girls, identically gowned in apricot silk, matching the highlights of their spiraling auburn curls, floated down. Identical smiles puzzled onlookers as to which twin was Hannah and which was Georgie. When Collier hurried to bow before one of them, Jonathan whispered, "That must be Hannah."

A beautiful girl with a crown of brown curls drifted down the stairs with a quiet elegance, to be identified by Jonathan as Ellen. Emma quickly searched his face for signs that he might be interested in this quietly restrained girl.

Some of the older Shackelford girls and their husbands also joined the group which assembled in the dining room, a seeming fairyland of white and gold. Massive arrangements of white iris and sprays of bridal wreath spirea were reflected in the gleaming mahogany sideboard. Their delicate perfume filled the room. The long table was covered with snowy white linen and set with gold-banded white china. Candlelight gleamed on the silver, twinkled in the crystal, and sparkled in Emma's eyes as she basked in Jonathan's full attention.

Supper was bountiful. Emma noticed only a slight flat taste from the scarcity of salt and lack of foreign spices. The food was delightfully aromatic with herbs from the kitchen garden. Because the plantation raised most of the food, the fare did not look as meager as their table in town where the supply in the stores had become alarmingly short. Pleasant conversation flowed as they remained long at the table eating course after course.

When at last they moved into the parlor, Hannah and Georgie captivated the party by singing duets, accompanied by Ellen on the piano. Then, as the group separated into playing chess, writing letters home from well-supplied desks, reading books by oil lamps, or talking with their host, James Shackelford, in his invalid's chair. Jonathan grasped Emma's elbow and guided her quietly through a French door to the piazza. Saying nothing as they moved along the wide veranda, Emma could feel her face glowing in the moonlight. She touched her fingers to her cheeks and sighed rapturously.

"All through the meal I dreamed of the time when you'll be hostess at our table at Magnolia Springs." Jonathan smiled down at her, holding her hands tightly. "But—" He arched his black brows and asked anxiously, "After being accustomed to a cosmopolitan place like Eufaula, can you be happy on an isolated plantation?" Then he added quickly, "If you wanted to visit a city, we're not far from Savannah."

"I can be happy anywhere as long as it's with you," she breathed. The tightness in Emma's chest from her long-stored love released in a flood of happiness. "I'd adore plantation living. The easy pace, the quiet simplicity. . ."

Satisfied, Jonathan drew her into the shadows and slipped his arm around her shoulders to shield her from the chill night air. Time was softly suspended. It seemed only moments before the servants appeared to signal family prayers.

Then the guests were shown to their rooms where high feather beds were turned down and servants stood smiling, ready to supply every need.

Emma wanted to relive each lovely moment, but she drifted into peaceful slumber only to be awakened by neighing and whinnying. Looking out of her window, she saw horses being brought to the block. Jonathan was among the early risers joining Ellen Shackelford and a group of riders for a brisk canter along the bridle paths of The Pines.

Smiling, stretching, enjoying the luxury of not being at the beck and call of Cordelia, who had remained with Mrs. Johnston, Emma leisurely completed her toilette. She chose a white dimity sprigged with delicate sprays of pastel flowers. Nodding at her reflection in the looking glass, she confirmed that this simple, fitted bodice, with the detailing on the sleeves from elbow to wrist and lace falling around her expressive hands, suited her and the occasion better than a multitude of ruffles. She brushed her hair and let it fall loosely. There was no use trying to contain it in the March breeze.

At midmorning, the party climbed into carriages and buggies. Followed by a wagon loaded with picnic hampers, they drove through woods of slender, sharp-scented pines along roads of deep, shifting sand. Sharp bayonets of palmetto, crowding beneath the tall evergreens, threatened the dainty dogwoods' snowy lace.

Soon after they turned south from the River Road toward Glenn Springs, the overpowering smell of rotten eggs made Emma want to hold her breath. Her wry face provoked much laughter as the group reached the picnic area by a spring which bubbled out of lime rock. Finally, they persuaded her that it was the healthful thing to do to drink sulfur water, especially in the springtime. She turned down her mouth and shuddered. The water tasted fully as bad as it smelled.

Setting up an easel, Myles Collier began to paint the elfin Hannah as she posed by the spring. Ellen sat on a stump and strummed her guitar and sang "My Nannie O." Sitting about on quilts, the group joined dreamily in singing Stephen Foster's "Jeanie with the Light Brown Hair."

Floating on the melody, Jonathan and Emma strolled the woodland on a brown, pine-needle carpet. Meandering hand in hand, smiling softly at each other, they wandered beneath the whispering pines high above them in the restless wind and listened to the endless tunes of the mockingbirds. The dogwoods, completely covered with white blossoms, made Emma think of brides and bridesmaids. Filled with longing, she wanted to tell Jonathan that she had changed her mind about preferring to be married in Eufaula. Nowhere could be lovelier than Saffold just now, and she felt certain that the motherly Mrs.

Johnston would be delighted to give her a wedding.

Looking up at Jonathan, she failed to watch where she was going. Piercing swords of palmetto stabbed her drifting dimity skirt, halting her progress until Jonathan cut her free with a pocketknife. As she sat down on a mossy log to work the prickly pieces loose from the sheer material, Jonathan cut a branch of dogwood over her head and sat down beside her.

"Dogwood always makes me think of the Resurrection," he said. "The petals form a cross, with the rusty notches of the nail prints in the tips and the crown of thorns in the center."

Soberly Emma took the flowers he offered. This was Jonathan different from his laughing, joking self. Sensing that it was not the time to rush him about a wedding, she was content as they talked of their thoughts and feelings and got to know each other more fully. With his arm around her shoulders and his head so close to hers, she joyfully discovered what Lily had meant by being one with a man in mind and spirit. Tenderly, lovingly, he kissed her before they rejoined the other couples for a gay picnic by the spring.

Suddenly, a damp, chill wind snatched at the tablecloth. They had not noticed a black cloud rolling in. Large, cold raindrops pelted them as they scurried about, packing, running, hitching the horses, jumping into the carriages, becoming thoroughly soaked by the time they reached The Pines.

Young Horry Dent was there with a summons for Jonathan. Standing waiting for him in the hallway, Emma frowned at her bedraggled skirt as she noticed for the first time the spot of blood where she had cut her finger on the palmetto. When Jonathan came at last to her side, his eyes were glittering. His relaxed posture had suddenly become stiffly, militarily erect.

"I must return to duty at once," he said briskly. "Horry Dent has been transferred here as assistant engineer. He just came down from Columbus on a raft loaded with hardware, and he brought tremendous news!"

To Emma his eyes seemed suddenly as hard and impenetrable as his brass buttons. She could no longer follow his thoughts. "What news?" she asked meekly.

"Everything has changed." He swallowed excitedly. "The whole of naval warfare has been revolutionized!" He sprang from one foot to the other, eager to leave. "Catesby Jones is coming to take command of the *Chattahoochee*. Things will start to pop." He nodded his head. "It won't be long, Emma. We'll be married just as soon as the South wins the war!"

Chapter 9

"Catesby Jones? Who is he? How can one man—make such a difference?" Emma stammered. "How can everything change so quickly?"

The excitement in Jonathan's voice had carried around the entrance hall. The men pressed closer. The ladies paused, draped along the staircase, dabbing at dripping curls.

With all eyes upon him, Jonathan explained. "Jones is a hero of one of our greater Confederate victories! It will be handed down in history as one of the prime achievements of this war," he declared in ringing tones. "The first battle between ships of iron!"

"Iron?"

"Iron ships?"

Curiosity buzzed through the group. Some of the girls shrugged and continued up the stairs to change their rain-soaked frocks, but Emma remained. Clinging to the banister, she strained to see Jonathan's face. A sickened feeling that this news held portent for her life with him made her clutch her hands together as he shared news he had received.

"As you all know, when the United States Navy left the Grosport Navy Yard across from Norfolk when Virginia seceded, they didn't have time to take all their vessels so they set some afire. There was one, the USS *Merrimack,* which burned to the waterline and sank." His dark eyes were gleaming with excitement. "Our men have raised her hull, cut off the sides, and covered what was left with iron plates. They renamed their armored warship the CSS *Virginia.*"

Emma plucked at the wet dimity clinging to her throat and held her breath. Jonathan had completely forgotten her presence.

"Can't you just imagine what she looked like?" He gestured wildly. "The five Yankee vessels dozing in the harbor at Hampton Roads must have thought a giant turtle had risen from the sea sprouting guns. The *Cumberland* opened fire; but the shells bounced off that hard shell, and the *Virginia*—or *Merrimack,* if you please—took one snap at the *Cumberland*'s wooden sides and sank her, then burned the *Congress* with red-hot shot from her guns."

A cheer resounded through the entry hall.

"Lieutenant Jones was the executive officer—wait. . ." Jonathan held up his hand to stifle another cheer. "There's more. The next morning when they returned to finish the job, an iron raft came out to meet them, the Federals' ironclad, the *Monitor.* She was only a quarter the size of the *Virginia* with only one gun set in the center like a big, round cheesebox, but. . . ," he paused for effect, "it revolved—making it a hopeless target."

"The battle lasted four hours," Horry Dent piped up from the doorway, unable to control his excitement. "Thousands of people stood on the shore cheering them on."

"When Admiral Buchanan was severely wounded, Jones became commander and dueled the *Monitor,*" Jonathan continued. "They finally withdrew. Neither could do much harm to the other's iron sides."

"All the old navies of the world will be useless," shouted Myles Collier above the ensuing clamor. "We'll have to discard wooden vessels and build ironclads—" He started for the door as if ready to begin, then stopped short, "What will this mean for the future of the *Chattahoochee?*"

"I don't know," replied Jonathan. "But plans for building an ironclad based on the *Virginia* are being made at Columbus. With such a ram we can easily cut through the blockade. . ."

The men were leaving, walking out into a reverberating thunderstorm, as oblivious to the lion's roar of the March wind as to the anxious, longing looks of the ladies.

War had scraped its horrid finger against the surface of their placid haven. Everything changed. No longer was it difficult to differentiate between the twins. Hannah was in constant tears. Myles Collier had asked for her hand in marriage before he shipped out, but her father refused permission. Even though Collier was from one of the first families of Virginia, James Shackelford had a deep-seated prejudice against soldiers and sailors. Lily sympathized with Hannah, recalling her own dilemma when her parents refused to let her marry Harrison. Emma, however, had difficulty swallowing bitterness. No one had refused her permission to wed—except the groom.

Stony-faced, refusing to give way to tears, Emma packed her trunk. Even if they could have imposed longer upon their hosts, Jonathan had no time for her. He was totally occupied with drilling the seventy-eight men required to man the guns of the *Chattahoochee.* Since the vessel was so nearly finished, it was decided to complete her before putting all efforts into constructing the ironclad with the yard name *Muscogee.*

With their lovely idyll ended, Emma rode back through the avenue of live oaks, head down. She could not bear to look at their graceful ladies-in-waiting. Reverberating cannon blasts assaulted her ears when they reached the wharf. Jonathan was so intent upon the target practice that he did not notice her when she climbed the gangway to the *Wave.*

Uhmmmmm! Uhmmmmm!

At the departing signal Jonathan turned, threw his hand high and smiled across the water.

Emma wanted to throw herself upon her bunk in a fit of weeping, but she had to stand over the prostrate Cordelia. If Jonathan had asked her to remain behind as a bride, it would have been difficult to tear herself from her sister-in-law. Cordelia was inconsolable because Foy was not returning to Eufaula with them. Sixteen now, suddenly tall, looking like a walking broomstick, he joined the crew of the *Chattahoochee.*

The women arrived in an almost-deserted Eufaula. The men of the Clayton Guards had plowed their lands for spring planting, but with the acceleration of the war they returned to service. The Eufaula Rifles had disbanded. Now, the Eufaula Light Artillery was organized and moved out on March 26. Two days later the older men of the town organized the Minuteman to provide the women and children some protection.

Prowling the house each night, Emma bolted doors. Barbour Hall echoed hollowly without the constant antics of Foy and his friends, now all enlisted in the army or navy. Emma moved woodenly through her nursing chores with a loneliness that enveloped her soul. Jonathan's preoccupation with mounting an offensive seemed to have shut her out.

The frightening report came that Apalachicola had been evacuated on March 14, Emma's twenty-ninth birthday. Groups of women and children had snatched up what they could on short notice, leaving in a deluge of cold rain. The rising river threatened to carry them away, but they reached a low bluff upriver and lay in the mud until late the next day when rafts and flats arrived to take them over the flooded countryside.

Nervously, Emma and Lily joined the throng in town awaiting news. Finally they heard that on April 3, Commander H. S. Stellwagen had landed the *Mercedia* at Apalachicola and demanded the remaining secessionists surrender. The Confederate troops had withdrawn fifty-seven miles upriver to fortify Ricko's Bluff. In April, the steamer *Jackson* somehow made it through the blockade. When it passed Eufaula headed for Columbus with a load of ten thousand rifles for the Confederacy, Emma sank into silence with sickening certainty that the war would not soon be over but had settled down to a long and bloody siege.

One sunny morning in mid-May Lily arrived, as effervescent as usual, with Mignonne talking excitedly about the birds' nest her mother had showed her. Lily's brown eyes sparkled as she waited for her daughter to finish her tale before speaking excitedly, "The *Wave* is headed for Saffold. Do you feel like going, Mama?"

"No, no, I don't feel like it," sighed Cordelia, pale against the pillows of her massive bed. "But," she rose heavily, unplaiting her hair, "if I'm to see Foy, I must."

Emma began to breath again.

Everything in Saffold had changed—no tea parties. Formerly flirting seamen now moved purposefully about assigned tasks. Emma eyed each uniformed back, but she did not see Jonathan. Although she almost felt his beloved boat was her rival, she laughed at herself and admitted the freshly painted *Chattahoochee* was beautiful with her slender, stone-colored hull and sails now swelling in the breeze.

Even Cordelia went on a tour of the gunboat this time. Following Foy, she negotiated her hoop skirt down the ladder into the crew's quarters with difficulty. Grinning until his ears seemed to flap, Foy showed them the berth deck and pointed out his hammock, a canvas only two feet wide fastened at the ends, onto hooks driven into the deck beams.

"They knew I was green, and they strung up my hammock as tightly as they could." Foy laughed. "I climbed in and tumbled right out. All that first night either I or the mattress was falling out, but I learned to bag it in the middle so the sides turn up. Now, I have no trouble sleeping in my dream bag—except getting enough time in it."

Cordelia declined going down in the hold area, but she did take a quick look at the engine room with its huge boilers. Lagging behind, Emma drew back from the menacing sound of hissing steam.

"Don't worry," Foy calmed them. Proud of his knowledge, he explained, "We're waiting for more iron to close a hole in the smokestack before we can get up sufficient steam to turn the two propellers."

Trailing Cordelia about the gun deck, Emma kept glancing around in hopes of seeing Jonathan. Idly she asked Foy why the boxes of sand had been placed there.

"Oh, that's so we won't slip on the blood on deck during a battle," he said casually.

Cordelia gasped. Emma paled. What had happened to the assurances of bloodless war?

Turning, Emma saw Jonathan at last. He was striding across the deck to greet her. "Catesby Jones hasn't arrived," he said without even asking how she was. "We can't seem to get the *Chattahoochee* completed and ready for action." He spoke agitatedly as he moved back and forth between Emma and a workman fitting a rifled cannon. "We must get on the offensive! But we can't secure the iron to complete the engines, and we're running out of time!"

Emma murmured noncommittally. She saw that he had no room left in his thoughts for loving words.

"All plans are at variance," he complained to her. Distraught, he raked his fingers through his black curls. "The small garrison on Ricko's Bluff has a battery of only ten guns." He shook his head. "Pitifully inadequate protection for an area where eighty thousand bales of cotton were stored. Many of our officials are calling for obstructions to be sunk in the river to block the Federals' sailing upstream."

Emma looked at him with her blue eyes wide, questioning. She did not grasp his meaning; but the frantic note in his voice indicated that he did not know which way to turn, and she longed to comfort him.

"Don't you see? When the *Chattahoochee* and *Muscogee* are completed, we must be able to get downstream if we are ever to attack and break the blockade!"

The heated argument among the Confederate officials about whether or not to stop passage on the river by filling it with impassable objects was not settled by the time the *Wave* was loaded. Their party had to board the steamboat without knowing what was to be done.

By the time the whistle signaled departure, people had arrived from all directions and crowded onto the decks of the *Wave*, many of them refugees from Pensacola or Apalachicola, drawn together by the sudden realization of the horrors of war. Bit by more terrible bit of the bloody battles as the Federal Army tried to take the Confederate capital Richmond, Virginia, had filtered in.

One young woman, attired in black taffeta and heavy mourning veils, fainted from the intense heat, unusual for early June. Making her way through the crush of passengers, Emma reached the woman's side with a basin of water. As she pushed back the veil and bathed the ashy face, the woman spoke.

"My name is Mary Allison," she said. "I've been riding all day through the pine woods to get here. I know all of the staterooms are occupied, and I shall have to sit up all night; but, oh, I just must try to claim my husband's body." A sob wracked her. "We've been married a year, but we only spent one month together. Oh, this is a hard, cruel war!"

Emma knelt beside Mary and watched helplessly as uncontrollable weeping overwhelmed her. Around them flowed anguished stories of relatives going to Richmond to visit wounded brothers or husbands. The whole town of Marianna, Florida, was in mourning since the news had come of the appalling slaughters on May 31 and June 1, south of Richmond at Seven Pines and Chickahominy.

A country doctor, who confessed he had never extracted a bullet or dressed a fractured limb but was going to offer his services to the army, knelt beside Emma and took Mary's hands.

Noise and confusion reigned until at last Harrison arranged for the gentlemen to rest as best they could in the saloon and the ladies to appropriate all the berths.

Emma lay awake far into the night thinking of poor Mary Allison. Jonathan would say they should not have married. But they had had one month to remember. Hot tears soaked her pillow before she slept.

The next morning the ladies waited amiably to make their toilettes as the stewardess passed from one room to the other with the only handbasin left on board. Once the *Wave* had been famous for the elegance of her fittings; those who knew this were able to shrug off the inconvenience.

The sun had risen, a ball of heat. Seeking relief on the shady side of the boat, Emma found that Lily had made friends with an Englishwoman who had been governess to Florida Governor Milton's children. Frightened by the war news, Sarah Jones had been unable to leave through the blockaded Gulf ports; consequently, she was heading north in hopes of escaping to England through Richmond. Lily and Sarah Jones were drawn together by their love of nature. They stood at the rail admiring the luxuriant foliage on the banks. Emma looked at the blood-red blossoms of vines which strangled some of the tallest pines and could not share their enthusiasm. She had never been in such a crowd, yet felt so alone.

The seemingly interminable trip dragged on with stops at nearly every plantation landing. "Great cotton speculations are going on," Lily explained to the foreign visitor. "The planters are hurrying to ship the cotton to the interior where it is being bought up by speculators for fifteen cents a pound."

"Oh, but it's wasting," cried Miss Jones, gesturing up the rugged precipice as cotton bales slid down a wooden chute to the river.

Feeling dazed by the hot, west wind burning her cheeks, Emma silently looked up the cliff where Miss Jones pointed. Giddily she felt that she, too, was poised on a precipice about to plunge.

"Why build six-story warehouses way up there?" the Englishwoman demanded indignantly, her face florid beneath carroty hair. She ran along the deck where a bale, with casing torn and cords broken, was spreading apart, whitening the muddy stream. "Oh," she cried again, "my countrymen in Liverpool and Lancashire are starving in penury, out of work without cotton. Oh, the unattainable path of cotton on Rebel waters, floating away on the windings of the river!" Miss Jones turned back angrily to face them. "Has no one ambition to build at the water level?"

Patiently, Lily pointed to the water marks on the warehouses and trees sixty feet above their heads. "The Chattahoochee has sudden and excessive rises by season," she explained. "In summer the bridge at Eufaula is eighty feet above the river, but once the water was so high a steamboat passed round the side of the bridge over the cotton fields."

Emma felt little patience with Sarah Jones as she complained over dinner that the Southern heat was making her ill and the very plate and fork were burning her hand. Emma laughed to herself at the stocky, robust girl and paid little attention as she expounded at length on how the war should be settled.

Emma's blue eyes glazed as she let her mind drift to Jonathan. Suddenly she blinked and focused, aware that Sarah Jones was addressing her directly.

"Why do you make obeisance to that domineering Edwards woman?" she snapped. "Are you her servant?"

"Um, well, no, uh," Emma stammered, shocked.

"Emma's my aunt," Lily interjected quickly, her liquid eyes not leaving Emma's hurt face. "In our realm of society, one lives with the nearest relative if—if. . ."

"If you're unfortunate enough to be a 'maiden lady'," Emma finished bitterly.

"Why don't you get a job?" Miss Jones puffed herself to her full five feet. "You should do as I do. I've been a governess all over your country." If she had made the connection between Lily and Mrs. Edwards, she was not embarrassed. She stared at them haughtily as they both opened their mouths but said nothing.

"Well, you see," Lily faltered, "there's just no job acceptable to a lady—here—and. . . ," she finished brightly, "Emma's engaged to be married." Lily smiled sweetly and lifted Emma's rubied hand.

"We're just waiting for the war to be over." Emma's voice was flat and her face felt too pinched to smile.

"Humph! You're mighty old to start a family," Miss Jones retorted.

"Not really. I long for children," she answered softly.

"I teach children." The governess tossed her carroty hair.

"I used to teach at Sabbath school," said Emma, wondering why she kept replying. Wincing, she realized that she had given up the pleasure of being with the children when she stopped attending church because she felt God did not care.

With the meal over at last, Emma withdrew further and further into a shell of silence. By Sunday afternoon when they scrambled up the steep bank at Eufaula, with Sarah grumbling about the idle men's failure to build steps, Emma felt incapable of words.

Looking up, she saw Kitty and Lige grinning at her, crossing the bridge to Georgetown, Georgia. She knew they frequently took the train to Americus to attend the church where they had been baptized, and she merely nodded to them in her misery.

The servants, however, were bent upon attracting their attention; she mustered the energy to compliment Kitty who was dressed in a new crinoline-stiffened skirt of the latest western style but had wrapped her head in a turban of the East. Resplendent in heavy gold rings and neck chains, Lige stood holding Kitty's fan and parasol. Emma admired his fancy cravat, and he smiled broadly so that his gold tooth sparkled in the sunlight.

They seemed to know so little of the bloodshed. Emma tried to smooth the frown from her face and not spoil their carefree gaiety. Sticky-hot, dirty, feeling tired and very old, she could not manage a smile.

Riding through Eufaula on the way to Barbour Hall, Emma sighed over the melancholy effects of the war and the blockade. She realized how forlorn their proud town must look to Sarah Jones. Jagged glass turned the drugstore window into an evil grin, the few remaining bottles looking like scattered teeth. Boards closed most of the shops. The *clopping* of their horse's hooves resounded in deserted streets, peopled only by the hotel guests. Could Lily's prayers and Jonathan's new weapons save them?

The echoing emptiness of the marble floors of Barbour Hall seemed to mimic the hollowness of Emma's heart. It seemed scarcely to beat until news came that the *Wave* had been summoned to return to Saffold.

Chapter 10

My beautiful *Wave* a warship," wailed Lily. Throwing back her head, she clung to the rail and looked above her at the hurricane deck where once the orchestra had played. She wiped tears and spoke in a strained voice. "Oh, Harrison! How different times are now than when we danced in the moonlight on the decks of this boat of dreams. Will we ever again have beauty and peace and loving our neighbor?"

Harrison's arm enclosed her in a safe little world of their own. "One day." He smiled down at her with tender understanding. "*Ma chére,* one day our world shall sing again." He stroked his hand along the ship's rail. "I love her, too, but she must be armed to protect our home and our pretty Mignonne."

Standing on the deck with Harrison and Lily, yet terribly, unbearably alone, Emma thought bitterly that the *Wave* was part of their oneness. The *Chattahoochee* seemed a rival, a wedge between her and Jonathan. Glancing at them out of the corner of her eye, she watched their rapt expressions. Emma's longing for this kind of love, love that had grown deeper with time, was more painful than when she had stood in the shadows playing the part of their chaperone. Then, she had had no hope of a life of her own. She had shut up her heart and moved through her days doing what was required of her. Now, since she had opened her heart to Jonathan, fear that he might not really love or marry her tore at the ragged, bleeding edges.

Arriving at the Saffold Navy Yard, they stepped into a scene of intense activity. The muscles in Emma's legs ached with tension as she followed the Wingates up the gangway on the *Chattahoochee.* A smile quivered on her cheeks, and she stood openmouthed as Jonathan came striding purposefully across the deck to meet them. How alive he looked, how handsome—with his feet stepping quickly to the rhythm of the wind in the rigging and his eyes dancing with excitement. Her yearning heart reached out to him, but he greeted them hurriedly. His smile brushed over her, and he turned and gestured.

"May I present Captain Catesby Jones," Jonathan said enthusiastically. "Now that he's taken command, we'll clear our river of the enemy for sure!"

Captain Jones bowed graciously over their hands. He moved with military bearing and self-assurance, but he rubbed his hand over his balding head and spoke self-deprecatingly. "We'll do our best, but we're frustrated at the delays in finishing the boilers because of the lack of iron. The Union is building with iron by the ton while we receive fifty pounds at a time, melted down from church bells and other cherished objects."

Emma stood trembling, trying to listen to the men's brisk discussion of their problems. Coherent thoughts were blocked by her longing to reach out and touch Jonathan's cheek, gone slack with inadequacy, to brush the dark curl from eyes now filled with worry. Suddenly Jones gave some command. Jonathan bowed over her hand and was gone.

Disappointed, hurt, she rode unseeingly up the avenue of live oaks. Somehow, in spite of the shortages, the amazing Mrs. Johnston continued to entertain them all graciously, planning that evening's dinner party to include the officers of the gunboat. Emma dressed with shaking hands, then sat nervously in a corner of the parlor. She half-rose at the sound of Jonathan's voice in the foyer, but two local girls rushed to his side, coquettishly fanning and flirting. They chattered incessantly about riding with him down the river on an expedition to lay torpedoes.

Stinging with jealousy, Emma gritted her teeth. How could she convey to them that her ruby necklace and ring were engagement gifts from Jonathan Ramsey? Sulkily, she sat waiting for him to cross the room to her. It seemed forever before he disengaged himself from the local belles. She picked up a stereoscope and pretended to be interested in the photographs.

"Darling Emma." Jonathan smiled down at her. "Time begins again now that you are here!" He squeezed her hand as he bowed over it and kissed it, then held it lovingly to his cheek.

Blood rushed to her face, and she drew the first relaxed breath she had had in weeks. "Oh, Jonathan," she whispered, "time doesn't move at all when I'm away from you." She nodded eager assent to the jerk of his head and stood quickly to follow him into the sanctuary of the garden. Before they reached the French door onto the piazza, a commotion in the entrance hall stopped them.

An arrogantly handsome young man in a sharply pressed, dark blue flannel uniform entered the parlor, immediately focusing the attention of everyone in the room upon him. Emma's lovely moment shattered at her feet. With her hand at her constricted throat, she saw the glitter of excitement in Jonathan's eyes as he turned back to be introduced.

"Beg pardon a moment." Jonathan nodded absently to her. "We've been awaiting Lieutenant George Gift. He's fresh from a brilliant and successful engagement of the sloop of war *Arkansas* in the battles on the Mississippi near Vicksburg. She's an ironclad ram such as the *Muscogee* will be." He left her side and joined the men gathered around Gift to hear his tales of action they eagerly awaited.

Dejected, yet trying to maintain a smile, Emma blotted out the bloody details until she heard him say the *Arkansas* had blown up and he had escaped by swimming. With his story ended, Gift's eyes lighted on Ellen Shackelford, seated at the far end of the parlor. Waving his hand at the men to indicate that they had talked enough of battle, he strode across the room to Ellen's side and bowed before her.

Only then did Jonathan and Emma step out into the garden. As they strolled paths sharply scented with boxwood, he continued to talk of war. He explained that Captain Jones and Gift, his first lieutenant, were Annapolis graduates who had served together in the U.S. Navy.

Her emotions as tremulous as the moonlight, she merely nodded, afraid to speak. Fighting tears, she lifted her chin defiantly and tried to steel herself. She had gotten along alone all these years. She could do it again. She needed no one, nothing. Clearly, this man was too enthralled with the war to need her as she longed for—no, she would not give way. She straightened her drooping shoulders and concentrated on his voice, which was pitched high with enthusiasm.

"With two officers so experienced in battle, we shall soon engage the enemy and break their blockade. Then, Emma—" He took both her hands and dropped a gentle kiss on the golden tendrils on her forehead. "Then, my darling Emma," his voice became a horse whisper, "our time will come at last."

In the peaceful beauty of the garden, paths beckoned in all directions. Guiding her behind the dense screen of a magnolia, Jonathan suddenly swept her into his arms. Hungrily he kissed her. Responding with all her pent-up longing, Emma twined her arms about his neck, knotted her fingers in his springy, black curls, and returned his kiss joyfully. Breathlessly, she pushed back at last and laughed softly.

He did not release her. Keeping his arms tightly around her, he kissed her eyes, her hair, as she gasped for breath. "Emma, dearest, dearest Emma," he whispered against her ear, kissed it, laughed as she shivered. "Soon, soon we will be married!"

Doubts and fears forgotten, Emma lifted her shining face to his. Unable to speak through her flooding happiness, she tiptoed and answered him with a kiss.

Approaching footsteps and murmuring voices told them that other couples were joining them in the garden. Discreetly, they pulled apart to stroll contentedly hand in hand through the moonlit garden, unnoticing of fall's nip in the air. Late roses wafted intoxicating perfume around their happy faces. Needing no communication save the touching of hands, they said little. Suddenly they realized that the garden had become quiet. The moon had scudded across the sky; the lovely evening was over. Tenderly, Jonathan lifted her chin, smiled, kissed her. They reluctantly crossed the piazza and rejoined the other couples in the parlor.

George Gift's animation gave evidence of the fact he was completely smitten with the dainty Ellen. As the guests departed, Gift and Jones conferred briefly. The captain rubbed his hand over his balding head, pulled his beard, then smiled.

The dashing Gift turned, bowed gallantly, and said, "Ladies, we would like to invite you to join us tomorrow for an entertainment aboard the *Chattahoochee!*"

Cheering went up from the men in the rigging as the ladies' carriages arrived at the riverside. Fluttering banners welcomed them with the stars and bars of the Confederacy flying at each masthead and the colorful Spanish, French, and English flags at the end of the gaff.

Beaming, Jonathan took Emma's pink parasol and squeezed the ruby on her finger as he helped her aboard. Standing beside him, she relaxed happily and enjoyed the crisp breeze on her face as the *Chattahoochee* floated down her namesake. No one mentioned the fact that she had to be towed by a small steamer because her own engines were still incomplete.

"Fire the broadsides rapidly!" With this shout, the crew began the exercise. Firing by divisions, single guns, all guns, and the cannon blasted. Delighted clapping by the ladies followed each burst. Emma shuddered at the noise, but she smiled when Jonathan pointed as a shot ricocheted, skipping and bounding up the river, throwing up beautiful jets at every contact with the water.

"We plan to invite some ladies from Columbus down to observe gunnery practice," Jonathan told her. "They tended members of the crew in the Soldier's Home Hospital there, and the officers want to show their gratitude."

"Don't show them too much gratitude." Emma pursed her lips, only half teasing.

"Ahha, you know all the ladies love me!" Jonathan cocked his head to one side with a devilish gleam in his eye. Seeing the solemn expression on her delicate face, he tilted her pink silk parasol to shield them from view and slyly kissed her cheek.

"Behave, Jonathan. Someone will see you," she murmured, giggling, feeling like a schoolgirl again. She spent a happy afternoon basking in Jonathan's attention as he whispered, teased, and found every excuse to squeeze a helpful arm around her waist or surreptitiously touch her hand.

Back at Saffold, Emma stifled a yawn. Pleasantly drowsy from the brilliant sunshine and the wind along the river, she closed her eyes from the constantly rippling shimmer. Like cold water dashed in her face, new orders were flung with a shout from the wharf. The gunboat must report to a new station fifty miles south at Chattahoochee, Florida. There at the Alabama boundary where the Chattahoochee became the Apalachicola River, work would be completed on her engines. Even though the *Chattahoochee* was helpless to maneuver, she would stand guard against the advancing enemy with her guns.

Cheers went up from men anxious for a chance at action. Suddenly chilled and drooping wearily, Emma anxiously listened to snatches of George Gift's daring plan to attack the enemy.

The dinner party that evening at The Pines was overshadowed by the fact that the *Chattahoochee* was leaving the next day. A cold, wet wind kept the guests grouped around the fireplaces. Distractedly, Jonathan and the other officers attempted light banter; however, it was obvious that their minds were upon their impending duty. Only Lieutenant Gift retreated to a quiet corner to talk earnestly with Ellen.

After the men had returned to the gunboat and the girls were braiding their hair for the night, Ellen shyly confided to Emma that George Gift had declared his undying love and proposed marriage.

"Oh, how wonderful!" Emma exclaimed. Noting Ellen's placid look, she added, "What did you tell him?"

"Well, he rather surprised me—our acquaintance has been so brief," Ellen replied quietly. "I told him about my father's prejudice against army and navy men. If he makes himself better known to my parents, who can tell? I asked him to wait a year and propose again." Ellen knelt beside the high bed in prayer; then she climbed on the step and blew out the candle.

Submerged in the soft feather bed, Emma stared through the darkness at the canopy over her head, wishing she could share Ellen's wisdom and patience. She must control her fear that love would again slip through her fingers as it had when she was young and her grandfather had refused to let her marry Michael. Her days stretched long with loneliness; her life held no purpose. She tried to recapture the joy of her day on the river, but a brooding emptiness overwhelmed her and a hard lump lodged in her chest. Dawn streaked the sky before she slept.

Tired and tense, she rubbed her neck as they reached the wharf the next morning. Pretending they felt secure from enemy attack, the ladies bid their champions good-bye and waved until the colors of the *Chattahoochee*'s flags blended with the autumn leaves drifting down the stream.

Harrison was to remain with the *Wave* at the navy yard for her plating and gun installation. Lily supervised the removal of the Chickering grand piano and some other treasures; then she patted the huge steamboat and told her good-bye. Clinging to Harrison's hand until the very last minute, she whispered, " 'The LORD watch between me and thee, when we are absent one from another.' "

Boarding a sailing vessel, *Kate L. Bruce,* bound northward to Eufaula, Lily and Emma hung over the rail and fluttered their handkerchiefs at Harrison and the *Wave* until they were out of sight. Falling into each other's arms, they burst into tears.

Panic rose in Emma's throat, and she gripped the rail fearfully as they rounded a bend. Ahead, three connected boats stretched across the river. Suddenly the boats began to tip. Passengers rushed to the rail shouting, gasping in astonishment as the muddy waters swirled over the three boats, sinking into the channel.

Jostled from her handhold, Emma barely avoided falling as the large sailing schooner lurched and careened nearly into the barrier. A thrill of fear rippled over the passengers. It had been believed that the enemy was held off downriver, but popping up along the riverbank were over a hundred men. Suddenly the colors of the Confederate Engineer Corps waved. Those who had, moments earlier, relaxed weakly, surged forward toward the captain.

"Have no fear," Captain Theodore Moreno shouted, waving his gauntlet. "We have the situation under control. I'm a civil engineer sent to partially obstruct the channel. At all costs we must keep the enemy out of Columbus, but I'll get you through." He climbed to the pilothouse, pointing out a narrow channel for the huge schooner's passage.

Word buzzed along the decks that Moreno had constructed several batteries at Columbus and another at Fort Gaines, which lay just ahead. Forewarning about the battery did little to dispel the fear produced by the sight of the body of twenty-four-pound cannon and the wagons and artillerymen.

"It's good to know they're here to protect us," Lily said in a small, unconvincing voice as she patted her mother's hand.

Cordelia had come on deck when they stopped. The bristling cannon made her swoon. "Is the enemy really advancing up our river?" she cried.

"Oh, Lily." Emma shivered. "I felt so cut off from Jonathan when the river was too low to pass this summer. Now I understand his frustration about the placing of obstructions. Will we be cut off from them for good?"

Silently, Lily shrugged and shook her head.

"Harrison has been wounded!" Lily came running into Barbour Hall with the terrifying news. "The messenger assures me his wounds are slight. Oh, but I must go to him at once!"

"What happened?" Emma gasped.

"The *Wave* was severely damaged in battle with a Federal blockader," Lily replied. Her face paper-white against her dark hair, she continued breathlessly. "She's being towed up from Apalachicola Bay." She saw Emma's hands clutching, twisting against her chest and added, "The *Chattahoochee* is returning to Saffold for repairs. They have Harrison."

Even though the trip was becoming increasingly dangerous from the war and obstructions in the river and the onset of winter storms, Lily began hurried preparations to catch the next steamer, and Emma began to fear being left behind.

She sat beside Cordelia feeding her ginger tea for her headache, nervously awaiting her decision. Finally, Mrs. Edwards decided that she would remain, but Emma should take some warm clothing and blankets to Foy.

Cold rain was falling when their steamer reached the Saffold Navy Yard. Noticing guards on the *Chattahoochee,* they ran down the wharf.

Wet, shivering, Emma did not care who saw them as Jonathan threw his arms around her and helped her aboard the gunboat. Even though she always hated going below the waterline, she welcomed the wardroom's shelter from the wind. Lily hurried to Harrison, who lay in one of the officer's cabins.

Jonathan and Emma sat in the officers' mess drinking sassafras tea. The Wingates joined them at the oak table, Harrison pale from loss of blood.

"It's nothing," he declared of his injured shoulder. "Glad as I am to see you both, I'm sorry, too." He sighed and shook his head. "Lily says she must see it through to the end."

"You've told her then?" queried Jonathan.

Emma lifted puzzled eyes to his face. "What?"

"The thing we've been dreading," Jonathan replied. "General Howell Cobb has taken command. He says southwest Georgia and southeast Alabama are now the granary of the Confederacy. That plus the sword factory in Columbus, and all the cotton—and—well, he's ordered Captain Moreno to obstruct the river—completely." He dropped his head in his hands and raked his fingers through his curls. "To keep the enemy out, we will bottle ourselves up."

"But they don't have to know we're bottled up," said Harrison firmly. "It's rumored that the reason they tried to capture the *Wave* is they still need light-draft steamers to engage and sink the *Chattahoochee.* We must keep them in fear of her."

Lily's liquid brown eyes overflowed with tears. "The *Wave* is what Moreno means to use," she answered Emma's questioning look.

Catesby Jones came down the ladder and greeted the guests. Rubbing his hand over his balding head and tugging at his beard, he reluctantly agreed to let Lily and Emma accompany them downriver.

Emma and Lily boarded the *Chattahoochee* in darkness, having left Mrs. Johnston's warm beds at five o'clock in the morning. The crew hurried things forward, bundling cumbersome traps aboard. The anchor came apeak at sunrise; the topsails were sheeted home, and the cry rang out, "All hands make sail!"

The women had barely gotten warm below deck when they were thrown from their chairs with a sudden slam. The gunboat had run ashore, twisting and straining the ship aft.

"She's leaking! Hawsers out! Man the pumps!"

The doleful *rattle, rattle, chuck, chuck* of the pumps made Lily and Emma clutch each other's hands.

Jonathan and George Gift ran the hawsers. The large ropes secured the ship while the pumps lowered the water. After about an hour the ship was freed, but by that time the wind had risen treacherously; consequently, the sails were lowered and the boilers fired.

As they steamed ahead uneventfully, Jonathan laughed and told Emma, "The crew is grumbling that we had no right to expect good luck."

She raised her eyebrows. "Because of us women on board?"

"No," he chuckled. "Because we started on Friday."

"King's Rock!" A shout rang out from above. "King's Rock!"

At this spot, twenty miles north of the town of Chattahoochee, Harrison's steamer, the *Peytona,* had been completely destroyed on the rocks when he was hurrying to his and Lily's wedding. Only Lily's deep faith that he would come had kept her family from sending the guests away.

Jonathan hurried topside again. Harrison clasped Lily's hands and joined her in prayer.

Retreating from their oneness, Emma threw a heavy shawl about her head and shoulders. If she and Jonathan were married, at least she would have a brooch, with a lock of his hair, upon her breast to hold onto. She climbed to the deck to watch as the men ran lines ashore and dropped for about a mile. Winter rains made the water deeper than when the *Peytona* and another steamer, the *Apalachicola,* had been completely wrecked; but she knew that many steamers had come to grief here regardless of depth. Water rushed through the narrow channel past menacing rocks. Looking fearfully at the threatening walls of the channel, Emma shivered.

For fifteen seemingly interminable hours, officers and crew remained on deck. When finally the danger was past and they came below, their throats were so sore from yelling that they could barely speak.

The *Wave,* tied to the wharf, listing badly and with great hunks of her wedding-cake trim missing, was the first sight they saw when they reached the town of Chattahoochee, Florida.

"Oh!" Lily's voice was like the cry of an injured bird.

Theodore Moreno met them. "I've heard there's a large chain left lying on the wharf at Apalachicola," he said. "I'm going to slip into the city under cover of night and—steal it!" He gestured offhandedly as though it would be quite simple.

Jonathan's experience in slipping silently by the Federal war vessels anchored in the harbor made him a likely candidate to accompany Moreno. They and thirteen other daring men left in a small scow schooner.

Emma spent a sleepless night in the hotel, pacing the floor, visualizing the poised guns of the enemy, ready to blow the scow out of the water as if it were a bug.

The next day when the *Chattahoochee* had been refueled and scrubbed fore and aft, everyone reboarded. At the point where the river became mightier, as the Flint River, red with the mud of southwestern Georgia, poured into the Chattahoochee to become the Apalachicola River, the engines failed and no amount of work could get them going. Finally, they hoisted sails and, with guns ready, reached a series of horseshoe bends known as the Narrows. There they waited, a floating battery to guard this area on the level with the Florida capital of Tallahassee. No one dared voice the fear that the raiding party would not return to meet them.

At last the schooner sailed into sight. Fifteen men waved and shouted exuberantly.

Jonathan related their adventure gleefully. "We approached cautiously. The lights of the Yankees boats glittered on the water. We let our scow float slowly by, drifting on the current, holding our breath that they wouldn't see us. We crept up on the wharf, shouldered the chain, lowered it into the scow. *Clank!* Dropping on board, it sounded loud enough to wake the dead!" He laughed heartily.

"I'll never forget the sound," chuckled Moreno. "They must have been in their cups or they would've heard it. But we slipped right under their noses with our prize!" he said proudly.

Around the bend limped the *Wave.* Lily knew the sad moment had come. Harrison positioned the beautiful paddle wheeler across the narrowest part of the river. The prized chain was carried through her dining hall. Harrison brought out the ship's wheel. Weak from effort, he leaned on Lily as they stood on the bank. Clinging together, they watched with ashen faces as the chain was fastened.

Even while the engineers worked to hook the chain to the opposite shore, George Gift begged Captain Jones, "Don't let them block us in! When the *Chattahoochee*'s engines are repaired, we can recapture Apalachicola! We must be able to get downriver," he pleaded, "to guard the mouth against the Yankee marauders!"

Sadly, Jones pointed upward to the thirty-two-pounders being placed in a battery along Rock Bluff. "These obstructions are the main defense of the river." He shook his balding head. "There is little hope of resistance above if the enemy breaks through here!"

Crash! Crash! Crash! Emma jumped, clutching air. Felled trees crushed the *Wave*'s pilothouse, splintering the lacy hurricane deck. More timber gashed her side. The river, swollen by winter freshets, violated her decks. The crew stood at attention and saluted with Captain Harrison Wingate the sinking lady who was giving her life for their country.

Later, when Harrison silently handed Lily Captain Moreno's voucher—$1,325.35 for the *Wave*'s hull—Lily wept again.

Through icy winter rains, Harrison once again carried cargo up and down the Chattahoochee as captain of the steamboat *Alice.* Lily frequently accompanied him, leaving a lonely Emma to remain with Cordelia.

The *Chattahoochee* was formally commissioned on January 1, 1863, with Jonathan a part of her proud crew. She steamed up and down the river scanning with her guns, marking time as each side laid plans to attack the other.

Emma's days passed in a blur until the roaring March wind reminded her that on the fourteenth she would turn thirty. Elizabeth and Mollie were only a year and a half younger; yet they were respected matrons with lovely homes and beautiful children. As much as she wanted to forget her advancing age, she was a little hurt that no one remembered her birthday.

A letter from Jonathan brought a smile back to her delicate face.

CSS Chattahoochee *in Florida waters*
February 15, 1863

My Darling Emma,

I miss you so much. We are having a life of laborious inaction. I would sooner have the privilege of shying a shell at the rascals occasionally. When we get our ironclads finished, we shall trash them all. We have made plans for an entertainment for the ladies of Columbus who had given our men such good care in the hospital. They are to come down by steamer. They will stop at The Pines *to pick up the ladies there. I will let you know the definite plans so that they can pick you up when they pass Eufaula.*

Can't wait to see you,
Jonathan Ramsey

Emma washed her best frocks and made arrangements to have her hoop skirts repaired, as no new ones could be bought. The lace curtains in her room would be long enough to make a wedding dress, and she had found bits of old lace trimming in the attic. There were no buttons, but she began collecting persimmon seeds to substitute. Eagerly, she found excuses to be in town whenever mail was expected. At last her vigil was rewarded in late April with a letter.

CSS Chattahoochee *in Florida waters*
February 25, 1863

My Dearest Emma,

Catesby Jones has been transferred and we have a new commander, Lieutenant John Julius Guthrie. He is agreeable to go ahead with our plans for entertaining the Columbus ladies. I will let you know. We have been visited by some delightful local ladies. But you know where my heart is. George Gift has proposed a daring plan to fit up a steamboat with cotton and go down to the Apalachicola bar and pick up a Yankee craft. If his elaborate scheme works, we shall recapture Apalachicola!

Your obedient servant,
Jonathan Ramsey

Worry lines creased Emma's forehead. She feared Gift's harebrained schemes. She always shuddered when he bragged of the many ships sunk from under him while he swam for his life. She went to town each day in May but received no word. On the last day of the cool, wet month, she was surprised at the numbers of people she saw, all taking excitedly.

"What's happened?" she asked breathlessly.

"The *Chattahoochee* exploded! Many are wounded! Fifteen are dead!"

Chapter 11

"Do they have the names?" Emma gasped, her voice echoing hollowly against the buzzing in her ears. No one seemed to hear her question. Shimmering spots before her eyes blinded her. Groping, she found a box and sat heavily. When finally she thought she could stand without fainting, she plucked at the sleeve of the man who had brought the terrible news.

"Please, please, Sir." She swallowed and wavered again. "My husband-to-be was aboard—do—do you have—" Her delicate face went beyond pallor to blueness. "Do you know the names of the wounded—the—the—dead?"

The big, gruff man looked down at her, grabbed off his hat, and replied, "No'm, ain't heard who's dead. Only know fourteen—maybe fifteen—was killed when the thing blowed up. Three drowned." He brightened. "I hear tell Lieutenant Guthrie, he run about the deck administering baptism to the dying. Was he. . ."

Emma shook her head.

"Dr. Ford give aid t' th' scalded."

Again she shook her head, unable to speak.

"Them's the only names I heard." His ruddy face broke into a hopeful smile. "But many of the wounded abandoned ship—jumped right overboard afore she sank. Happened on May twenty-seventh at high noon. 'Tis said they laid on the muddy banks in the pouring rain from then 'til midnight when that old steamer *William H. Young* came and carried 'em away."

"Carried them?" Emma swallowed. "Carried them where?"

"Well, Ma'am." He twisted his hat in his hand. "The dead was taken to Chattahoochee for burial. Some wounded—" he scratched his head and spat tobacco juice— "might be at Saffold, but lots of the worst 'uns was taken to that there hospital in Columbus. You know, the Soldier's Home."

"Thank you," she whispered and turned away. Her tears frozen, she staggered toward home, her knees giving way again and again as she climbed the hill to Barbour Hall. Stopping several times to rest, she tried frantically to decide how to tell Cordelia; but her thoughts bumped against the hard, cold hollows of her insides, and she could not capture them.

As gently as she could, she explained the tragedy to her sister-in-law. Crying in each other's arms, they tried to decide whether to go upstream or down. They agreed to go to Saffold; then, they doubted their choice. If only the Wingates had been at home—Harrison would know how best to travel; Lily would pray for guidance. Finally, they decided time enough had passed for the steamer to have reached Columbus with the load of wounded. Holding fast to the hope that their loved ones were alive, they chose to go first to the hospital, last to the cemetery.

The slowness of the journey tortured Emma. She sat in a little heap, congealed into numbness. Trying to shut out the sound of Cordelia's fits of loud blubbering and her piteous recounting of the tale to every stranger they met, Emma thought the trip would never end.

When they arrived at the Soldier's Home on the southwest corner of Broad and Thomas Streets, they walked past carriages jamming both avenues that led to the wooden building. Going through the first floor, pressing her fist against her mouth and swallowing convulsively, Emma looked from one man to another, burned almost beyond recognition. *Jonathan and Foy are alive. They must be alive,* she told herself over and over to fill the emptiness of her soul.

Blinking tears, fighting nausea, she grasped the loose flesh of Cordelia's elbow and helped the puffing old woman upstairs. "Why?" Emma cried bitterly. "Why does God let things like this happen?"

"Mama!" A weak gasp stopped them midway through the upper floor.

With tears of joy, Cordelia sank to the cot and gathered Foy in her arms.

"Oh, Mama," Foy sobbed against her shoulder, "my friend Mallory's feet and hands are crisped; his face is badly scalded." He snuffed and struggled for control. "But he's so cheerful. He'll make it—he was a hero on the *Virginia*—he must make it!"

Shivering, Emma waited to be certain Foy was not critically injured before she asked about Jonathan. Scrubbing his finger under his nose, he pointed to a corner.

Jonathan was sleeping. Emma thought he had never looked so beautiful. His matted curls shone darkly against the pallor of his face, gone slack like a small boy's. Shaking with relief, she collapsed to a stool and sat quietly beside him, content to watch him breathe.

"Ma'am," a weak voice whispered from the cot behind her. "I'm Duffey," he gasped as she turned. "Fireman—*Chattahoochee*—please—read." Then he rolled his eyes in the direction of a small table.

Emma picked up the Bible he indicated and began to read Psalms. Her lips stiff with the horror of his burns, she merely called the words. Soothed, he fell asleep.

She sat gazing at Jonathan. No burns marred his skin. Her hand hovered about him as she restrained her longing to touch him. She leaned over to examine his left foot, wrapped in a bloody bandage.

Jonathan's eyelids fluttered. Noticing her, he sat bolt upright. "Oh, Em—

I hate for you to see. . ." Weakly, he fell back. "It's too—it's too terrible." Jerking wildly, his hand groped for hers.

Quietly, she caught his hand in both of hers and whispered soothing words. Brushing a quick kiss across his fevered brow, she looked up and saw a well-groomed woman smiling at her. Gratefully, Emma reached for the bowl of milk and bread she held out. She had heard that the ladies of Columbus were feeding their own families corn bread and saving their precious store of flour for the soldiers' bread. As she tenderly fed the warm milk to Jonathan, the edges of her heart began to melt.

Strengthened by the milk toast, Jonathan talked wildly, as if ripping the words from his brain. "It was so terrible," he repeated, wiping his arm across his eyes. "Those scalded men ran—ran about—about the deck, frantic with pain, leaving the impression of their bleeding feet—sometimes flesh—the nails and all—behind them." He gagged. "After the boilers exploded, we. . . thought the magazine would blow, too. Men were going over the side." He choked.

"Don't think about it." Emma patted him. "It's over. It's over." She pushed him back against the pillow and wished that she could gather him in her arms as Cordelia had done Foy.

"I wouldn't mind so much if we had taken out the enemy." He raised toward her on one elbow and would not let her soothe him back. "Let me tell you. The schooner *Fashion* was loaded—it was loaded with cotton—trying to run the blockade—Indian Pass. Captured, and we tried. . . ," he coughed but kept talking jerkily, "to cross the obstructions, give aid. The river was too low to cross Blountstown Bar. We waited. Waited for the river to rise. The order was given to raise steam, and then—and then. . ."

"Was this Mr. Gift's plan?" Emma wondered frantically how to get Jonathan's mind off of the horrifying scene.

"No." He swallowed hard and recovered himself. "No, George had gone to General Cobb's headquarters for approval. We could have recaptured Apalachicola." He gasped and fell back weakly, "but now the *Chattahoochee* is no more." Tears slipped between his tightly squeezed eyelids.

"Rest now. Rest," she soothed. "We're going to stay with Cordelia's sister, Laurie. I'll be here." She wet her handkerchief and washed the offending tears, smoothed back the damp curls. "Sleep now. I'll be here every day. Just sleep."

"They're burying Duffey in Linwood Cemetery." Jonathan sighed, reaching for Emma's hand when she returned the next morning. Foy wept quietly. His fellow midshipman, Charles Mallory, had also died.

Emma felt that Jonathan would have recovered his strength more quickly if she had had salt to season the food she cooked daily and brought to him. It angered her when she heard that the enemy had learned that the *Chattahoochee* had sunk and had attacked the saltworks on Alligator Bay, east of Dog Island, scattering two hundred bushels of salt along the shore.

One afternoon Emma looked up from reading to her listless patient to see Lieutenant Gift, greeting everyone cheerily, bouncing across the room, stirring disheveled, disconsolate men to life with his immaculate uniform and exuberant manner.

"Great news, men," he sang out. "We're raising the *Chattahoochee!*"

Hoarse voices cheered.

"I placed the Dahlgren," he said as he moved beside Jonathan's cot, "and one of the thirty-two-pounders as a battery on the riverbank where she lies. Just in time, too." He gestured excitedly. "The Union heard she was out of commission. They tried to pass the Narrows," he nodded at Emma, "where the *Wave* lies." He paused until the effect of the enemy attack soaked into opium-dazed brains. "General Cobb dispatched a force to strengthen us. The Federals didn't expect the *Chattahoochee*'s guns to be breathing down upon them from the bluff," he laughed. "We sent 'em packing!"

The room filled with clapping and cheering.

"You can salvage her, then?" Jonathan's eyes lighted with interest, and he raised on one elbow to question his friend.

"Yes," Gift assured him. "The job's tremendous, but David S. Johnston is towing her to Saffold for overhauling. We'll have her back in service in no time."

Jonathan struggled to regain his strength. Floundering weakly, he finally mastered heavy crutches. Though she worried over the cause—his foot remained a bloody, draining, putrid-smelling sore—Emma rejoiced that he was unable to be transferred to Savannah with the uninjured of his crew. When the Saffold Navy Yard repaired the damage to the *Chattahoochee*'s timbers, she was to be brought to Columbus for replacement of machinery and boilers. Jonathan would still be there.

Nervously, she watched his color improve and his strength increase; however, she searched in vain for the return of his high spirits and unflagging good humor. Thinking that sunshine would help him, Emma proposed a carriage ride. As they left the hospital behind and she threw back her head and breathed deeply of the fragrant summer air, Jonathan squeezed her hand in his old loving way. For so long he had clutched it, as if silently begging for strength she did not have to give. The dreadful fear that he would not recover melted slightly, but her face felt stiff as she smiled at him. Words would not come, so they rode silently. Lost in whirling worries, she did not notice their direction until he reined the horse at the Columbus Naval Yard.

George Gift waved to them. Although she murmured protests, Jonathan struggled with his cumbersome crutches and made his way across the yard, panting.

"Our ram is progressing!" exclaimed Gift, tipping his hat to Emma as they joined him. "The boilers are in and the engines are ready to set." He smiled at Emma and explained, "The *Muscogee* is patterned after the *Merrimack/Virginia.* When we get her launched, the enemy will know we'll give 'em a fight."

Emma looked at the wide, flat boat made of square, green pine and tried to understand as he showed her that it was placed solidly instead of in ribs like an ordinary boat. A great many men were pounding huge iron nails, while others were busily caulking. Her spirits lifted on the swell of Gift's enthusiasm.

"The iron for plating is scarce, so it might be November before we launch." Gift shrugged. "But soon as our ironclads on the Alabama are finished and in action, we'll easily repossess New Orleans. The news coming from the Mississippi River is good!" Eyebrows raised, he bobbed about as he spoke. "Many think this is the turning point of the war. The campaign at Vicksburg will close gloriously for us." He threw up his hand dramatically. "I'd say, within the next ten days!"

Jonathan straightened on his crutches. A broad smile spread across his face. His dark eyes came alive again. Laughing for the first time in weeks, he looked at Emma tenderly and renewed his promise with a slow and deliberate wink.

Emma's spirits soared.

Declaring a crushed foot could not keep him down, Jonathan resumed his duty. Reluctantly, Emma told him good-bye. With Cordelia and the convalescing Foy, she returned to Eufaula.

They found the population swelled with refugees from Vicksburg, speaking with the same optimism George Gift had voiced. Emma cleaned Barbour Hall in happy preparation for a celebration visit from Jonathan.

With total shock they received the news from Vicksburg. On July fourth, the Confederate stronghold, which had controlled the Mississippi River, had fallen. The Confederate States were divided.

The fall of Vicksburg plunged Eufaulians into despair. Emma stood in the marketplace washed in a pitch and yaw of anguished words. The townspeople had believed the city to be well supplied with food and ammunition. Now, four days after the fall, they learned the brave garrison had lived for two weeks by eating their horses and mules, finally surrendering because men were dying of starvation.

She was asked to help nurse several of the refugee children, victims of whooping cough, who had come to Eufaula. They died; despair had no end. The summer of 1863 seemed blotchy with measles and smallpox, blotting out worry about the increasingly bad war news.

"Why does God let these horrible things happen?" an exhausted Emma flung at Lily as they sat on the porch one steaming afternoon.

Lily closed her eyes for a long moment before she replied. "God doesn't cause the evil in the world," she answered softly. "Men do. With their sinful, greedy ways."

"But Christians suffer just as much—sometimes more." Emma dropped her head between sweaty palms. "Don't you ever wish you could just run away?"

Lily tried to hug her, but Emma's shoulders remained stiff. "Darling Emma, Jesus told His disciples they would have to face trials and tribulations, but they could live victoriously if they would completely commit their lives to trusting and obeying Him."

Emma glared at her; a muscle twitched in her cheek. She did not reply because Lily simply could not understand; she thought that everything could fit into what she called the lordship of Christ.

"We couldn't do much good if we ran away—if we withdrew from the world." Lily continued to speak sweetly, ignoring Emma's silence. "A boat must be in the water to be of any use. Each Christian is given a task to help others find safe harbor in the storms."

A contemptuous laugh twisted Emma's mouth. "Well, my ship is tossing on a mighty stormy sea."

"But, don't you understand? If you'll just ask, God will send His Spirit, the very presence of Jesus, to walk beside you, to guide and strengthen. Oh, Emma, don't try to live your life alone!"

Emma turned away from her and walked into the dry, wilting garden. She had always walked alone. It seemed she always would. Jonathan remained at Columbus supervising the repair of the *Chattahoochee* and the building of the *Muscogee*. She knew that his foot refused to heal. It still drained and caused him pain, but he hobbled about on crutches. His letters remained full of plans for an offensive. Columbus, the head of navigation in the Apalachicola-Chattahoochee River system, was the last stronghold in Confederate naval installations. Emma knew with a sickening dread that Confederate naval efforts could be driven in no farther north than Columbus, Georgia.

Christmas scented the air. Jonathan's eyes sparkled, and his voice held its old excitement as he arrived at Barbour Hall to take Emma to the Christmas Eve party at Roseland Plantation. "We're ready to launch the *Muscogee!*" he said. "We're only waiting for the river to rise, and from present appearances that won't be long!"

Smilingly Emma listened, enjoyed being near him, and reveled in the fact that they could sit side by side for five miles through the clear, star-filled night. When they arrived at Roseland's gates, Emma noticed that many other officers and soldiers were in the buggies and carriages circling the glistening, white sand driveway. Colonel and Mrs. Toney, who now owned the beautiful white house, greeted their guests with aristocratic manners and urged all to make merry.

Emma did not mind sitting at the edge of the room while others danced; however, the lilting rhythm of the "Tallahassee Waltz" made her feet step and glide automatically beneath her hoop skirt.

"We could make it a threesome—you, my crutch, and me." Jonathan's face contorted with the first bitterness Emma had seen him show.

"How in the world do you suppose they were able to load the table with so many delicacies?" interrupted Elizabeth Rhodes, sitting down beside them with her beloved Chauncey. "I really do not approve of giving such entertainments with our country in such dire distress." Elizabeth sniffed disdainfully. "Christmas Day will be sad with so many chairs left vacant with occupants fallen on a bloody field. . ."

Emma's wan smile became a mask, and she shut out her friend's sad pronouncements. Her happiness could not be dampened, because the launching of the *Muscogee* was near, and Jonathan had invited her to come.

Icy wind cut through Emma's cashmere shawl and scratched its fingers under the frayed bands of navy blue ribbon in the club trim on her faded pink coat and skirt. The wool was shiny now, wearing thin, and Emma had difficulty trying to keep her teeth from chattering as she stood with the crowd on the banks of the Chattahoochee at the Naval Ironworks in Columbus for the launching of the *Muscogee*. The river had risen rapidly since Christmas, ten feet just yesterday, and now on New Year's Day, 1864, the boisterous crowd waited for the ironclad ram to float from the blocks.

"Cold enough for hog killing, for sure," said the man on her left. "It's. . ."

Suddenly a brass band struck up, "When Johnny Comes Marching Home Again." Toes began to tap and scattered voices took up the popular new song, shouting out when they came to "Hurrah, Hurrah!"

Emma's eyes were on Jonathan. Proudly, without his crutch, he limped about as the crew tried to slide the *Muscogee* off the building ways and into the water. The freshet had raised the level of the water around the vessel. The added rainwater formed, pushed. For a long breath it seemed the ram must lift. The *Muscogee* held fast. The river fell back, too weak, too low. A moan went up from the crowd.

Disgusted muttering rumbled with the steamer, *Marianna*, as she was brought about to tow the ironclad into the water. Emma clutched her fists to her chest and leaned forward, still hopeful. The flat, iron ram refused to budge.

"It'll take a second flood to lift that slantin' p'cu'lar-lookin' craft," scoffed a young man wearing a badge from the *Columbus Daily Enquirer*.

Shivering, Emma waited silently for Jonathan after the crowd had dispersed. He limped toward her. The sparkle in his eyes had been replaced by grim determination.

"We'll have to extend her hull to add buoyancy," he said. "We may even have to reduce the casement to remove excess weight." He sighed heavily. Forcing his sagging face to lift, he grinned crookedly at her. "But we'll do it! Have faith in me, Emma. We'll break the blockade. Then I'll get you a wedding gown from Paris."

"Oh, Jonathan, I–I don't need—I have curt. . ." Her hands flew to her throat. "I have faith in you." Emma smiled sadly. Her eyes went beyond him down to the wharf to the wreck of the *Chattahoochee* listing badly to port.

Confederate victories in the spring campaigns had Eufaulians talking optimistically again, but to Emma, the failure to launch the *Muscogee* seemed an ill omen. Jonathan wrote her enthusiastic letters about the repair work on both vessels. Excitedly, he reported that Lieutenant Gift had been transferred in March to command the *Chattahoochee.*

"With Gift in charge, we can be sure of action," he wrote.

Coping with shortages filled Emma's waiting. The "coffee" she made by roasting sweet potatoes and okra seed was as unsatisfying as her pretense at living. Woodenly waiting upon Cordelia, she existed between letters, until April gowned herself in dainty bridal wreath spirea and tossed on honeysuckle veils. The love songs of the birds, as they worked companionably on their nests, struck a responsive chord in Emma's heart and plucked forth embarrassing spasms of tears.

The green velvet skirt of May mushroomed around Barbour Hall as they stepped onto the porch early one morning. Emma strained forward as she heard a muffled shout.

"A gunboat!" The words trembled on the breeze.

"A gunboat! At the wharf!" echoed through deserted streets.

"A gunboat! The Yankees!" gasped Cordelia, sagging in a swoon.

"A gunboat! The *Chattahoochee?*" shouted Emma expectantly. Leaving Cordelia to Kitty, she ran to the stable and hitched the pony to the buggy by herself. Wielding a whip with one hand and clutching the careening buggy with the other, she reached the wharf completely disheveled; but she did not care.

The stone-colored gunboat lay smartly at the wharf with flags flying. Beaming, Jonathan saluted Emma from the gun deck. Dabbing her hair into place, she hurried to meet him at the gangway.

How she longed to fly into his arms, but crowds of people were converging to gawk at the *Chattahoochee.* Jonathan's hands hovered close to her shoulders, and the transmitted warmth told her he shared her yearning.

As if to restrain himself, he quickly grasped both her hands. Vibrant again, he smiled into her eyes with the impact of a touch and whispered, "Emma, my darling!"

"Oh, Jonathan," she breathed. "Jonathan." Speaking his name brought such joy. For one long moment they existed alone. Then jostling elbows made her look around at the scrubbed deck, the replaced cannon. "Oh, is she repaired?" Her voice came out a high squeak. "Are you on the way to break the blockade at last?"

"Well, yes," Jonathan grinned sheepishly, "and no." He guided her to a less crowded spot beside the smokestack before he explained. "She's repaired—but empty." He turned his palms up expressively. "We have no iron to build engines or boilers. We just let her drift down the river. We got her here safely only through Harrison Wingate's expertise as pilot. We kept her in the channel by using sweeps."

"Sweeps?" Disappointment flattened her tone, and she sagged against the smokestack.

"Long oars. To turn her bow into the current."

"Oh." She turned away so that he could not see her face. "Then why did you leave Columbus?"

"The river above is almost dried up. The water level is so low we were afraid she'd break her back. We planned to go farther, but she grounded twice, and we'll have to leave her at Eufaula until another rise in the river."

"Then you're going. . ."

"Gift is in command." His eyes glittered with excitement. "George has a daring plan to break the blockade—but come below where it's quieter."

As Emma stepped below deck into the wardroom, Ellen Shackelford emerged from the captain's cabin. Emma's shock could not be disguised. "Ellen—I–I didn't know you were here," she stammered.

The dainty girl blushed. "Then you haven't heard the news?"

Emma shook her head.

"Mr. Gift and I were married at The Pines on the tenth of April."

Emma hugged her friend; but jealousy's icy steel plunged hard between them, muffling her good wishes. She had heard that Hannah had married Myles Collier last September. All the officers were finding time for marriage—except Jonathan.

That evening, she brushed her hair until it shone, then donned her pink organdy and Jonathan's rubies. Smilingly, she gave him her hand when he called for her to attend the frolic on board the *Chattahoochee*. Pleasantly, she laughed at his jokes as she nibbled refreshments. Sweetly, she joined in the singing of "The Last Rose of Summer," "Home Sweet Home," and "Annie Laurie."

But the high vibrating whine of a Jew's harp floated plaintively on the still air, making it impossible to keep back her tears any longer. Perhaps Jonathan did not really love her. She moved down the deck from him, unnoticed. With a shuddering sigh, she let the thought escape which she had fought to suppress. Jonathan had never actually said the words, "I love you." She sank into a chair. The music stopped.

"Here's the plan," George Gift announced exuberantly. "Our valiant lady cannot take us into the fray without her boilers." Waving his hand over his head, he shouted, "But her crew will win her honor! Tomorrow at dawn we leave for the bay, taking all of the ship's boats and. . ."

Emma turned questioning eyes on Jonathan, but he was watching Gift.

"My force will consist of 130 men and officers," Gift was saying. "I shall bring all my young men back lieutenants," he boasted. High-spirited shouts applauded him.

"We will attack at East Pass," he continued in a lower conspiratorial voice. "The coast is blockaded by the U.S. steamers *Somerset* and *Adela.* In our ship's boats, we will slip up on one, man her, and capture the other. Then, we'll run the vessels into Mobile—or burn them!"

Feet stamped; hands clapped; cheers sounded.

In lonely silence, Emma sat with fear pounding in her temples. Feeling she must get away from the noise, she moved to the bow of the boat. Jonathan followed.

"What a daring—and dangerous—scheme!" she breathed fearfully.

"Isn't it?" Jonathan grinned delightedly. "We're a crew without a ship. What else can we do?"

"Nothing. But you can't fight with courage alone," she said flatly.

"We have incendiary materials, rifles, muskets, shotguns, revolvers, and cutlasses. . ."

"Oh, yes," she said sourly, "you have guns." She laughed bitterly. "And what did they say the *Somerset* had—ten cannon?" She turned away from him. Angry with herself that she could not stop the tears streaming down her cheeks, she gritted her teeth. "You'll attack a giant warship with a rowboat!"

"Don't you worry your pretty head," he said gently, turning her face toward him. "We can do it with surprise on our side. They'll never expect it!" He caressed her cheek and stroked away the tears. "I'll soon be back a hero—and then. . ."

Pain seared her inside, and she could not keep it out of her eyes as she searched his face. For so many years she had ached with emptiness. No one cared about her. Oh, why had she let herself love him so desperately?

Jonathan dropped a light, teasing kiss upon her trembling lips. When she neither responded nor fussed that someone might see, he studied her thoughtfully. "It's more than our mission, isn't it? I thought you looked angry and hurt with me when you found out George and Ellen were married." He plunged his fingers into his hair and squeezed his palms against his forehead.

For a long, silent moment they stood motionless, with distance growing between them. Then he began to speak slowly, deliberately, "I'm not like him. George flies off in all directions at once. In the midst of all this, he's been on a daring adventure on the *Ranger* from Bermuda to the Wilmington Bar. He survived another wreck and came back feeling wealthy."

He snorted and looked the other way. Continuing in a gruff voice he said, "I have nothing. No money at all. My funds are tied up at my plantation. Anyway, I guess I can just handle one thing at a time." His voice dropped despondently. "We have so little left to fight with. We've got to break this blockade or all is lost." Throwing up his hands, he set his dark curls standing up on end. "Can't you give me just a little more time?"

"Yes." Demurely she bowed her head, and moonlight washed her hair with silver. "I'm sorry I was so. . .I. . ." Fragile as the moths fluttering about the ship's lantern, she quivered and seemed about to fly away.

Jonathan pulled her into a shadow and wrapped her in his arms. The passionate strength of his kisses was all of the promise she needed to set her heart hoping again.

The next morning at dawn, Emma stood on the wharf watching. The crew marched off the proud *Chattahoochee,* turned, saluted. They ambled aboard the riverboat, *Marianna.* Her yawls and those of the steamers *Young* and *Uchee* and one metallic boat were tucked beneath her wings. Dragging behind her were the two boats belonging to the *Chattahoochee.* Like a mother hen taking her biddies to attack the hawk, this pitiful fleet left the dock.

"Foolhardy!" snorted Cordelia.

Saying nothing, Emma leaned forward, hand stretched out motionlessly toward the gay flags fluttering from the *Marianna.* Jonathan shouted something, but behind him the band was playing. She stood until the last sad notes of the trumpet sang, "I'll take my stand, to live and die in Dixie. Away. . ."

The steamboat rounded the bend. Silence engulfed the wharf. Silence filled the days. Silence and an agony of waiting.

Chapter 12

Shipwrecked! As our whole nation is, it seems." Harrison Wingate sat in the parlor of Barbour Hall with his head in his hands.

Emma had never seen the vital man defeated. Her emotions churning, she sat silently, fighting for outer calm and biting her tongue to keep from shouting her questions as he related their disaster with agonizing detail—but her mind was screaming.

"We tried valiantly," he resumed slowly. "The *Marianna* took us to the obstructions. We carried our small boats overland around them, then drifted down the river to the bay. Muffling our oars, we landed in the night at East Point near the U.S. steamer, *Adela*." His eyes, dark hollows in his strained face, searched theirs for understanding. "Our only hope of capturing her was to board in sudden surprise. We hid our boats and waited—" he swallowed— "waited for a dark night. But every night was clear. The sea was so smooth, so phosphorescent, that when we dipped the oars into the water, they emitted a luminous light which shone brightly across the bay."

Again he dropped his head, and the ladies waited for him to resume his story. Emma wanted to cry out Jonathan's name, but her throat constricted with a burning, bitter taste. Harrison Wingate's failure to mention him inflamed her fears.

"Waiting for a stormy night to cover us," Harrison continued wearily, "we ran out of provisions. Our scouts slipped into Apalachicola. Some of our men were captured, but one scout made it back to tell us a spy had alerted the enemy of our planned attack."

Emma remembered with bitterness George Gift's loud bragging. Harrison's voice thumped dully against her roaring ears.

"Without surprise, a handful of men in rowboats had no chance," he sighed. "We pushed across the sound to escape upriver. Part of our boats hugged the shore. One under command of Midshipman DeBlanc and one I was in under Gift pushed directly across the sound. The enemy drove DeBlanc's force back into the swamps. Some were captured; most escaped. Part of the men went right up the river road because the Yankees mistook them for their own command." He laughed ironically.

Emma could bear it no longer. "What of Jonathan?" she squeaked.

Harrison nodded gravely. "A launch gave chase to us, but our boat was swift. We escaped the Yankees only to be caught in a stormy gale. Jonathan's boat was swamped."

Emma drew in her breath. Two red spots shone in her cheeks.

"Gift turned back to rescue them."

She exhaled, leaning forward, and clutched at Harrison's hand to drag the story from him.

"Jonathan and nine others clung to the side of our boat. Seventeen were already inside. The sea washed over us—nearly swamped us. Gift became ill. Midshipman Scharf took command. Our only hope of safety was to turn 'round and go to sea before the wind. We had to lighten the boat, so guns, water casks, supplies were thrown overboard. Five who were exhausted were taken in." He nodded at Emma. "Jonathan among them."

Lily shrank close beside Harrison.

"As we headed our boat for the Gulf of Mexico, a large wave struck under her quarter. The breakers were roaring over the beach. We threw off our clothing preparing to swim. Somehow Scharf beached us on Saint George Island."

Cordelia sighed and murmured.

"And Jonathan?" Emma managed weakly.

"Exhausted!" he exclaimed. "For two days we starved, eating palmetto cabbage, alligators, and oysters. The old wound on his foot opened up and. . ." He shook his head sadly. "He's back in the hospital in Columbus."

Emma scarcely listened to the rest of the tale of DeBlanc's search of the islands and the rescue. They had escaped upriver, sunk their boats, and traveled overland to join their party above the obstructions. Gift was back at work repairing the *Chattahoochee* and planning to try again to take the Bay, but Jonathan and a few others were in the Soldier's Home. Alive. Not dead. He was alive but very ill.

Emma prowled the room, fiddling with small objects. *How,* she wondered, *can I manage to get to Columbus?* Even though the war had relaxed some social standards, a maiden lady could not make such a trip alone. Morning sickness had plagued Lily lately, suggesting that another confinement was upon her. Emma loved Lily too much to envy her, yet the thought of another baby increased her depression that she would never have one of her own.

"How long, O Lord, before this ends?" Cordelia's wail broke through Emma's thoughts.

"What do the men say now?" asked Lily. "Those who thought this war a duel which would soon settle an affair of honor and principle with little shedding of blood?"

"Even men like Gift who were trained for warfare are saying we must arbitrate more intelligently." Harrison sighed. "War is so futile—settling a dispute by who can kill the most men solves nothing. No one ever thought there could be such a long and bloody war!"

No word came from Jonathan. On the seventeenth of June, the *Uchee* came to tow the *Chattahoochee* back to the Columbus. Emma endured the waiting, the hoping, for two more weeks before going to ask Elizabeth Rhodes to journey with her to the hospital. Elizabeth, however, was all astir over another trip. A train trip to Georgia was planned, with Colonel Shorter and his family, to visit Mrs. Shorter's brother who was in command of a brigade at Camp Sumter at a village called Andersonville—it was said that twenty-seven thousand Yankee prisoners were confined there—and to call upon Sophronia Bearden at Looking Glass Plantation.

One hot afternoon, Kitty announced that Dr. C. J. Pope and Dr. W. H. Thornton had come to call upon Emma. Puzzled, she hurried into the parlor.

"We need you, Miss Emma," said Dr. Pope immediately. His well-mannered tone made a request, but his substance and self-assurance gave import of command. "We need you as a nurse."

Astounded, Emma stared at him. "Uh—" She fidgeted with her collar. "Uh, do—be seated, gentlemen." She sank to a chair.

"Wounded are pouring into Eufaula." Dr. Thornton nodded his graying head. "We've heard you helped out at the Soldier's Home. We beg your aid. The Tavern on the bluff has been turned into the ward for the blood poison cases."

"Blood poison?" Emma's stomach turned. She stared glassily at the frock-coated gentlemen and stammered. "I–I'm afraid you misunderstood. I only visited a patient. I'm not a nurse." Remembering how she could not look at Jonathan's wound, much as she loved him, she swallowed bile, "I–I've only nursed sick children." She passed her hand over her eyes. "I really get quite queasy. . ."

Dr. Pope pursed his lips. "Perhaps the rheumatism cases at Bell Hospital," he interjected hurriedly. "All our Confederate surgeons are transferring their chronic cases here. Surgeon H. V. Miller is treating them with a good galvanic battery and using colchium and iodide of potassium as standby remedies. We really—"

"Emma! Em-ma!" Cordelia's voice called.

Glad to hear Cordelia's summons for once, Emma rose, dismissing them. "Thank you for thinking of me, gentlemen, but my sister-in-law needs me constantly."

"Yes—ahem—do consider it," said Dr. Pope.

"We really do need you, Ma'am," agreed Dr. Thornton, hat in hand.

A letter from Jonathan came at last:

Columbus, Georgia
July 5, 1864

Dear Emma,

Don't come to Columbus. Works have been erected and every able-bodied man enlisted for the city's defense. The population has swelled to 12,000 because refugees are pouring in from north of here. Women and children are sheltered in huts and in abandoned rolling stock along the railroad. They are living on cornmeal supplied by the state.

A battery of four guns has been placed on the William H. Young, *and some of our crew are using the old steamer to defend the river down at Chattahoochee, Florida. The* Kate L. Bruce *has been sunk as another obstruction.*

We are cheered by the progress on the Muscogee *which is nearly ready for launching. Two boilers have been sent from the wreck of the* Raleigh *at Wilmington and are being placed on the* Chattahoochee. *She will soon be ready for action. Every preparation is being made for a raid on the blockade.*

Again, do not try to come here.

Your obedient servant,
Jonathan Ramsey

Emma read the letter over and over again, finding none of Jonathan's usual humor, no words of affection. Reading it yet another time, she realized he had not mentioned his wound or said where he was or what he was doing.

Her reverie was interrupted by visitors at the door. Kitty announced Mary Elizabeth Young and Dr. Hamilton Weedon.

"Emma, Dear," Mary said breathlessly as she entered the parlor with a swishing of petticoats. "May I present to you Dr. Weedon, who's been serving as chief surgeon with the Fourth Florida Regiment," she gushed, "and has just arrived to take charge of the military hospital which has been set up in the Tavern."

A slightly built man with closely cropped hair and a mustache bowed correctly over Emma's hand. He murmured polite acknowledgments and then fixed her with piercing dark eyes and spoke intensely. "I see immediately, Ma'am, that Miss Mary is correct in telling me your pleasant smile and calm manner would serve greatly in nursing desperate men."

Flustered, Emma sat down suddenly and stammered, "I'm—not at all sure that I could. . ."

"Competent nurses are hard to find," Dr. Weedon continued briskly. "So many don't know castor oil from a gun rod or laudanum from a hole in the ground."

Emma laughed shakily.

"Women make better nurses than the enlisted men." His snapping eyes assessed her, and his crisp voice demanded attention. "I'm certain you are familiar with the work of Miss Florence Nightingale during the Crimean War. When she arrived in Turkey, she cut the hospital death rate from 42 percent to 2 percent."

"I understand that she still campaigns for hospital reforms from her invalid's bed," drawled Mary, preening her brown hair. Her eyes sparkled when she looked at Dr. Weedon.

His smile softened upon her, but he whirled back to Emma. "You'd help morale. These men have wounds that will not heal. They are facing amputation—or death."

"My sister-in-law suffers terribly from rheumatism, and I spend a great deal of time nursing her. . . ," Emma whispered, wondering desperately how to defend herself from this intense man.

"Yes. Well, you have more experience for the cases at Bell Hospital." He cleared his throat. "But we can use older ladies there." He shrugged. "Those who'd get emotional or faint at the Tavern."

Cordelia Edwards swept into the parlor at that moment. Introductions and polite comments were made. When Cordelia was apprised of the situation, she shocked Emma by saying, "Of course, you may go. We must give our all for the war effort." She smiled benignly, and her chins shook importantly.

"Thank you, Miss Cordelia." Dr. Weedon bowed gallantly. "May I beg your aid? The use of your flower garden?"

Puffed with pride, she replied, "Most certainly, but how. . ."

"As you know, the Union government has declared medicine and surgical instruments contraband of war. Our blockade-runners are no longer getting through with quinine, chloroform, morphine, paregoric—" He turned his hands to suggest emptiness. "None of the things we need so much."

Cordelia clutched her head at the mention of the lack of quinine but did not interrupt.

"Our druggists have compounded a tincture of dogwood, poplar, and willow barks mixed with whiskey as a quinine substitute." He shook his head and clucked his tongue. "It is inferior; however, the opium we've extracted from red garden poppies does help relieve the suffering. We're asking the ladies to grow them."

Emma's mind rushed on frantically as they discussed native roots and herbs Cordelia could contribute. As soon as the guests left Barbour Hall, Emma hurried to Lily's house. Pale and wan, she sat holding Mignonne and the huge family Bible.

"You're not trying to teach a four year old to read the Bible, are you?" Emma asked scornfully.

"Not yet," laughed Lilly. "I'm teaching her letters from the large capitals at the beginning of passages. But don't scoff, Emma, Dear. If you'll just listen, the voice of God will speak to you from the pages of the Bible."

Ready to change the subject, Emma explained Dr. Weedon's request. Pacing about the room, she spoke distractedly. "I've read that Florence Nightingale felt that God called her to devote her life to nursing—that she even refused to marry a man she loved because it would interfere with her dedication to duty." Her stomach gurgled and she shuddered. "I'm not called!" Her mouth twisted sourly.

"Possibly not," agreed Lily, "but your sweet, calm manner. . ."

"My calm manner," Emma laughed bitterly, "is a farce. My insides are tossing, churning—oh, Lily, I wish I had some of your inner strength," she wailed.

The next morning, Emma reported to the Tavern on the bluff high above the Chattahoochee. Shaking, she stepped across the narrow porch and stood in the doorway with her willowy body wavering as if she would fall. The three large rooms which ran across the front of the old riverboat inn were filled with cots on which lay maimed men. Low moans came from dim corners. The odor rising on waves of the intense July heat filled her mouth with bitter, sickening juice.

A large, motherly woman bustled toward her. "Good morning." She smiled. Wiping her hands on a white apron stained with blood, she reached out toward Emma and said heartily, "You must be Emma Edwards. I'm so thankful to see you, my dear. I'm Sorie Stow."

"Yes, Ma'am," Emma whispered. She swallowed hard and managed, "Mrs. Stow, I'm really not a nurse—I. . ."

The kindly woman gently guided her back onto the porch and fanned her with fresh air. "You'll get used to it, Dear. The gangrene hospitals are the worst."

"But, how do you keep from fainting—from—" she gagged— "being sick?"

Mrs. Stow looked at Emma's blue face thoughtfully and replied, "Well, I guess none of us accept it naturally. It's just something you have to fight. At first it's hard. There's a war going on between the two natures within you. But you can do it because you know it's expected of you."

Emma sighed doubtfully.

"You'll do fine." She patted Emma fondly. "Just get a smile on that pretty face. I'll let you start by taking the stronger patients out on the upstairs porch for fresh air and lemonade."

In a state of numbness, Emma stumbled through the morning with a false smile and shaking hands. She wished for Lily's comforting presence, but, of course, she would not be allowed to look on anything as terrible as this for fear her baby might be marked. Chewing her lips, Emma wondered if Harrison was avoiding her. He had brought her no word about Jonathan.

Sick in mind and body, Emma struggled to do what was expected of her. Cordelia insisted she go each day; however, when she was at Barbour Hall, her sister-in-law's demands upon her increased, and she was already weary when she reported for duty. One morning a dying man asked her to read the Bible to him.

"Read the Gospel of John," he rasped. "It's the easiest to understand and the most comforting."

Her own voice was becoming hoarse by the time she had read to the sixth chapter. "And when even was now come," she said softly, aware that men all about her had stopped their thrashing to listen, "his disciples went down unto the sea, and entered into a ship, and went over the sea toward Capernaum. And it was now dark, and Jesus was not come to them."

Emma looked at the men, many of whom were seafarers, and continued, "And the sea arose by reason of a great wind that blew. So when they had rowed about five and twenty or thirty furlongs, they see Jesus walking on the sea, and drawing nigh unto the ship: and they were afraid."

She tried to moisten her mouth. "But he saith unto them, It is I; be not afraid. Then they willingly received him into the ship: and immediately the ship was at the land whither they went."

Around her, stillness remained. Suddenly, a man behind Emma began to shake. Quickly she covered the feverish man with all the blankets she could find.

"That chill like to shook me clean out of the garrison," he said through chattering teeth.

Dr. Weedon came to her side. "Many of these mariners have malaria from the miasmas emanating from stagnant water," he said. "We must have some of the quinine substitute. Miss Emma, please go and see if the bark has been collected."

Glad to escape, she turned away.

"And bring some carrots for poultices," Dr. Pope called after her.

When she returned, the boy had died. The older man who had the chill told her, "He went whispering, 'It is I; be not afraid.' "

Tears stung her eyes. She turned without a word and stumbled blindly to find Dr. Weedon.

Wearily he shook his head as he accepted what she had brought. "It's bad enough to try to treat wounds with herbs and bark instead of medicine," he sighed, "but worse, we can't get surgical instruments through the blockade. I'm amputating with a carpenter's saw. I've made a pair of retractors from the iron bale of a water bucket. I'm even reduced to using knitting needles and common table forks for surgical instruments." His briskness gone, he sat for a few moments, then stood, seeming to move each part of his body with a separate effort. "Mrs. Stow took sick. You'll have to help me. Come."

Emma knelt in bloody water, fighting nausea as a patient clutched her hand while Dr. Weedon cauterized a gangrenous sore and cut away black, dead tissue. He washed it out with whiskey and plugged the wound with raw cotton soaked in turpentine.

Dizzily, she dropped in a corner. Utterly exhausted, she hung down her head and fell into a doze. Seconds later she jerked awake. Her wild eyes lighted on a smooth-cheeked boy. "Michael!" She knelt beside him and pushed damp hair from a thin face that could have seen no more than fifteen summers. Shaking with a chill, she realized this lad could almost have been her child. Teeth chattering with the impact of how many years had passed since she had seen Michael, she stumbled outside. Under the magnolia tree she wept. The evening of her life had come. A gnawing at her brain warned that she had lost Jonathan even as she had lost Michael. As this awful war was drawing to its bloody end, her life was drawing to a painful close.

She could not go back into the Tavern. Without seeing where she was going, she walked the long distance to Lily's house. In a trancelike state, she played with the joy-filled Mignonne, lifting a tiny, china cup to her lips in a pretend tea party.

At last, she lifted pain-filled eyes to Lily's lovely face and said in anguish, "I can't go on. I just can't stand it anymore! I'm not a Florence Nightingale."

"I wish I could relieve you awhile," said Lily. "But everyone refuses to let me take a turn. Perhaps you are wrong in thinking it was easy for Miss Nightingale. I've been reading more about her." Lily brought a book and placed it before Emma's unseeing eyes.

With the back of her hand pressed against her lips, the pale girl sat unmoving.

Frowning anxiously, Lily continued earnestly, "Miss Nightingale seemed a model of compassion, but she had no joy. It was not self-forgetting service, but the attainment of proud self-satisfaction. After her Crimean height, she wrote that her lamp showed her own utter shipwreck on the rock of self-willed pride in her devotion to duty. Only after years of bitterness did she pray for forgiveness and submit herself to God's outstretched hand."

Too exhausted to sleep, Emma tossed fitfully throughout the night. When she stepped into the Tavern yard next morning, she clapped her hand to her mouth in horror. There, awaiting disposal, strewn about like so much cordwood, lay several amputated limbs.

She ran.

Down the river she ran until she was totally alone. Flinging herself prostrate on the edge of the bluff, she vomited into the muddy red Chattahoochee. Her body wet with sweat in the hundred-degree heat, her heart beating rapidly, her emotions churning, pulling, tugging in every direction, she cried out to God. "Why, why, Lord, why?"

She rose shakily to her feet and thrust both fists heavenward. Wavering, nearly falling into the chasm of the summer-low water far, far below, she did not really care if she fell. Suddenly the wind began to whip her skirt, to snatch her hair from its confining knot. The rushing wind whirled round her, dipped down, and whipped the sleeping river into a choppy sea.

Lowering around her, the black sky suddenly split. The clap of thunder which followed the lightning's gash shook her to her knees. Huge drops of rain pelted her, merging with her tears.

"Dear Lord," she sobbed, "Lily says You care about every person. Do You really care about someone as worthless as I?" She looked up into the stormy sky, bursting as only July's intensity could explode.

"Forgive me, Lord. I know You created this world—and You created me as I am for some purpose. I've always known Jesus died for the sins of the world, but I didn't want to believe He died for my sins. I thought I had to earn a place in heaven. Was that what Lily meant about Miss Nightingale? Forgive me, Lord. Forgive me for hardening my heart against You!"

Suddenly, into her mind rushed the words which had eased the young man's dying. The disciples had just been shown that Jesus is the Bread of Life; yet, they had headed their ship across the dark sea without Him. They were afraid.

Speaking clearly in her mind, a voice said, *"It is I; be not afraid!"*

Emma's breathing slowed. Her gurgling stomach quieted. Her clutching hands which had torn the old muslin at the neck of her dress lay still in her lap.

"Come into my heart and take control of my life, Lord Jesus. I cannot go on alone," she said aloud.

Sitting quietly as the sun came out again and dried her clothing, Emma felt warmed by an inner peace. Her tears ceased. Stretching, inhaling the storm-cleansed air, she looked upward into the glory of the firmament. The greatness of God, Creator of this splendor, yet Lover of her individual soul, filled her with overwhelming joy.

Again in her mind the voice of the Holy Spirit spoke clearly. *"Go, I have prepared you for the task of proclaiming My love to these young men, of making of their deaths a victory. You can do it in My strength, for lo, I am with you always, even unto the end of the world."*

An inner calm now matched her placid smile. "Lead me, Lord," she prayed. Certain now of love and strength and purpose, she walked back into the hospital.

During her absence, a new load of patients had arrived. On a cot in a far corner lay Jonathan Ramsey.

Chapter 13

Blinking, trying to adjust her eyes to the dim light, Emma rubbed them. Perhaps the trick of vision, mind, and heart that had played upon her nerves a false Michael was tantalizing her again. Slowly she moved across the room. The hair on the dirty pillow curled black as a bird's wing; the brows etched a frown against skin which shone like wax in a slanting ray of sunlight. "Jonathan," she gasped, dropping to her knees beside him.

His eyelids fluttered. Weakly he raised a trembling hand to the damp, golden strands frizzling upon her forehead, glowing in the sunbeam. "Are you real?" he rasped. "Is that a halo? Are you an ang—"

"I'm real, oh, I'm real and here with you!" she cried, laughing, weeping, grasping the shaking hand and smothering kisses upon the back, the palm. She turned so that the light behind her would show him her face.

"Oh, Emma. I didn't want you to know!"

"Jonathan, I love you. Of course I must know. I love you." She clutched his hand to her cheek and washed it with her tears. Tenderness and love for him overwhelmed her. "I love you!" she repeated, not holding back merely because he did not speak the words to her. How desperately she had loved him, needed him to give her a sense of importance and self-esteem. Now, her love leaped from such narrow confines and enwrapped him, nurtured him. "My precious Jonathan, how long have you been this ill?"

"Since the shipwreck on Saint George Island," he mumbled. "My old wound reopened. The infection is in the bone, they say. The open sore has grown from one inch to three. I didn't want to come here." He pulled his hand from hers and dropped his arm over his eyes. "All they seem to know is amputation. . . I won't have that! I won't!"

"Sometimes it's necessary," she soothed, "the only thing to save a life. But there's other hope. Dr. Weedon makes a healing salve of alder pitch and blooms." She patted him and spoke with a confidence which belied what her eyes told her. "We'll soon have you well."

"How calm you are, how sweet," he sighed. "I feel stronger already."

Happily, she bathed his face and hands and brought him water. She searched out Dr. Weedon and attended him as he treated Jonathan's greenish, running sore. When Jonathan fell into a peaceful sleep, her joy gave wings to her feet. Soul singing, she hurried to share the wonderful events with Lily.

Days followed swiftly as Emma ministered to Jonathan and the others with a new sense of purpose. With her focus no longer inward but upward, outward, she moved among them without her old, paralyzing fears that someone would whisper behind her back, or laugh at her, or worst of all, snub her. Often she needed to quote Lily's favorite verse, "I can do all things through Christ which strengtheneth me," to get through a gruesome ordeal. Reassured that she was no longer alone, constantly sustained by prayer, she read the Scriptures and brought peace to the dying.

With her head throbbing from the stuffy sickrooms, Emma left the Tavern one morning for a walk along the bluff. The air smelled clean from the reviving rain of the night before. The cool breeze roughened her arms into goose bumps. She paused to look below her at the green river.

Wearily, she let her gaze drift down the mighty Chattahoochee as it stretched forth to meet the glorious canopy of fresh-washed sky. She lifted the tired lines of her face into a smile. For a moment she freed her mind from care as she absorbed the beauty. The magnitude of God exhilarated her senses.

Breathing a thankful prayer for the greatness of the Creator, she felt her soul filling with His presence. "Thank You, God, for loving me and caring what I do, for giving me a purpose to share Thy love with others," she breathed.

Bong! Bong! Bong! A lone church bell sounded. How had she forgotten the Sabbath? She must hurry to make her patients comfortable before she slipped away to church. Great as was her sense of God's grandeur in the beauty of nature, she needed to be in His house to lift her voice in praise and worship. And, oh, how she needed the strengthening fellowship of Christian brethren.

Gaily, she began to sing the old hymn, "Brethren, We Have Met to Worship." She continued to hum the tune as she moved through the Tavern infirmary.

As she drove the pony and buggy up the hill toward the church, Emma reflected that the whole town of Eufaula, safely separated by the river from the scenes of battle, had become a hospital. She passed sheds, erected south from Broad Street, which overflowed with sick and wounded from the Army of Tennessee and the Army of Virginia. Emma shook her head ruefully. She knew that many a swooning belle had plumbed her inner strength and resolutely become a nurse.

Sunday evening, Dr. Pope called upon them at Barbour Hall. The handsome man's pleasant features dropped with exhaustion as he spoke ingratiatingly to them. "I know you ladies are sacrificing greatly," he said, pursing his prominent lips, "and I hate to ask another thing, but the courthouse and the O'Harro House Hotel can hold no more wounded. We're beginning to fill private homes. Miss Cordelia, could we—" He cleared his throat. "May we use

Barbour Hall for convalescent cases?"

Indignantly, Cordelia drew herself up and puffed out her ample chest. "Common soldiers—with goodness knows what diseases in my home? Certainly not!" she declared emphatically.

"Think about it, Ma'am," Dr. Pope pleaded. "We need to get some of these patients away from the hospital gangrene lest they be reinfected. You've always been known to attend every church service and to render good works."

Pride inflated Cordelia's cheeks. "Thank you for your kind words, Doctor, but Emma and I are women alone. We have no gentlemen relatives with us."

"You have your servants and many lovely rooms. There will be no scandal in these sad times."

Cordelia Edwards shook her head doubtfully.

"You should do it, Mama," said Lily, entering from the parlor doorway. "Pray about it."

"I'll let you know, Dr. Pope." Cordelia stood haughtily, indicating that he should leave.

After the doctor's departure, Lily turned her liquid brown eyes upon her mother. "Mama," she began hesitantly, "you and I have never looked at things the same way. You believe that salvation comes through righteous living and doing good works." She paused and drew in her breath. "I believe we are saved by Jesus' death for our sins—not by what we do—except repenting and obeying. Then the good we do is a joyful giving to Him by loving others. If we love Him, we must do for the least of these brethren."

Emma smiled at her. "How long did I hear this with my ear before I opened my heart to His Spirit?"

Cordelia Edwards whirled angrily and left them without a word. After a long interval, they heard her coming back down the stairs. She reentered the parlor with tears in her eyes.

"You were wiser than I, Daughter," Mrs. Edwards said in a voice filled with humility. "I have asked forgiveness for my pride in what I did for God and thankfully accepted what He has done for me."

The three women embraced, sisters in Christ.

"Run now, Emma, and tell Dr. Pope to send his patients. Quick!" She caught herself and chuckled. "Please."

Because Mrs. Edwards's room on the west rear of the house was shady and cool, she had her massive bed moved out and cots set up for a dozen patients.

"I'm putting you in charge of convalescent cases," Dr. Weedon told Emma, piercing her with his gaze for a long moment. "I'm also releasing Jonathan Ramsey to you. Have no false hope!" He shook his head. "He needs amputation, but he refuses. Indeed, he's too weak to stand the shock. What you must do is build his strength, and then. . ." He shrugged and turned to his patients.

In the pleasant atmosphere of Barbour Hall, the disheartened men improved. Daily, Emma applied the alder pitch salve to Jonathan's wound and prayed. Mrs. Edwards and Kitty worked diligently to care for their charges. Cordelia suffered her own illness without her former grumpiness, and sat with the men for motherly chats. Old Aunt Dilsey grumbled about cooking for so many men, but she set the children searching for eggs and sang lustily over the cook pots as she concocted light fare for delicate stomachs. Emma moved about with a sweet smile and a look of deep contentment in her eyes.

She noticed that Jonathan's restlessness was assuaged when she played the piano in the long August evenings. Her fingers caressed the mother-of-pearl keys in the deliberate, soothing notes of Beethoven's Sonata Number 14, "Moonlight." With an eye to Jonathan's crutch, she avoided waltzes and played Chopin's romantic nocturnes. The music flowed like liquid silver through the candlelit house.

Sitting on the porch to catch the cooling evening breeze, Jonathan smiled sadly at her with longing in his eyes. "Seeing you bustling about domestic duties makes me dream that you are my wife and mistress of Magnolia Springs," he said wistfully. He reached for her hand and clutched it.

"That happy day will surely come soon," Emma replied with her eyes full of love. "For now I'll enjoy just being near you, seeing you get better day by day." Her accepting love held him gently. No longer thinking of herself at all, she relaxed and savored their private moment.

"How can you be so content?"

"God loves me; you love me; I have purpose in life," she laughed. Seeing his face cloud with misery, she drew back regretfully, knowing she had said the wrong thing.

"And I have none!" he flung out bitterly. "I sit here a cripple while the *Chattahoochee* is nearly ready to fight again."

"If she recovered, so can you! Even as a crippled ship, she had use keeping the enemy at bay."

"What use have I?" He raked his fingers through dark curls grown shaggy and unkempt.

Emma's pale blue eyes searched his face in the moonlight. Realizing how deeply depressed he had become, she said softly, "You're of great use to me. You couldn't know how lost and alone and desperate I'd become that day when you arrived at the Tavern. Let me share. . ."

Tenderly, he took her face in both his hands and seemed calmed by her peacefulness. "Dear Emma. Lovely Emma," he whispered and kissed her lightly.

Jonathan tried valiantly, but fever drained him. He seemed to have forgotten all his funny stories, and he smiled only when Mignonne was there with her trilling laughter and unending chatter. The beautiful tot would run by him with her dark eyes flashing and her long brown curls bobbing, demanding that he grab at her and tease; then, she would plop her sturdy little body into his lap for a story. Lily brought her often. Although it was considered unseemly for anyone as great with child as Lily to be seen in public, she declared Barbour Hall was home; and she must be allowed to come and help with these recovering men.

One afternoon as Emma stepped onto the porch for a breath of air, she saw a handsome young man swinging across the yard as if he owned it. Lean, virile, vastly different from her lifeless charges, he bounded up the steps and smothered her in a hug.

"Foy!" she exclaimed joyfully as he lifted her in a whirling jig.

The family gathered around the table where Foy ate. "The *Muscogee*," he told them, "is almost ready for launching!" Beneath heavy brows, his smoldering eyes met Jonathan's. "The iron supply's still low." He shoved in another spoonful. "She's been armored only at the knuckle, but six, seven-inch rifles from Catesby Jones's Naval Foundry at Selma are in place." He gulped buttermilk. "Officially she's been named the CSS *Jackson* after the Mississippi capital." He laughed. In a deep, resonant voice, he added, "But we'll always use the yard name, *Muscogee*."

Bringing all of the food that was left in the pie safe, Emma looked at the sun-bleached hair tousled around his ears and smiled. With a pang she realized he was now eighteen. *When did our flop-eared, owl-eyed little boy become a man?*

Foy's whirlwind visit increased Jonathan's longing to return to duty; however, his health did not improve. Dr. Weedon came, accompanied by Mary Young, whom he was now affectionately calling by her pet name, Molly. The doctor frowned and shook his head at Emma when he examined Jonathan's foot and drained the wound.

For diversion and relief from the heat of the stifling stillness of September, Emma hitched the runabout and took Jonathan to visit Fairview Cemetery, where his friends from the hospital rested in their graves.

Moving slowly on his cumbersome crutch, he walked with Emma to the grassy bank, where they stood looking down the cliff into Chewalla Creek, rushing to meet its destiny with the Chattahoochee.

Yearning to take Jonathan in her arms and kiss away his tears as she would Mignonne's, Emma looked at the defeated man with tender compassion and prayed for wisdom to help him.

"Jonathan," she began hesitantly as they sat down on the bank, "I was struggling so desperately until the voice of God spoke to me through the Scriptures as I was reading to the patients. . ."

He patted her hand absently, but his eyes roamed far down the flowing river.

"What helped me most," she continued shyly, "was the story of the disciples out on the stormy sea. They were helpless, afraid. Jesus came walking to them saying, 'It is I; be not afraid.' " Between Jonathan and Emma, the sultry air hung lifeless, still. Jonathan continued to stare unseeingly at the water. She took a deep breath and plunged on. "The minute they let Him into the boat, they were at the land where they were going. Let Jesus into your heart. It will help you through. . ."

He turned to her and lifted her hand to rub it against the stubble of his beard. "You're so sweet," he said sadly. "I accepted Christ and was baptized when I was ten. It was meaningful to me then. Bible stories are helpful for teaching a child and for easing a dying man. You're doing a good work, Emma." Reaching for his crutch, he struggled to his feet, shrugging off her help, dismissing her.

A week after its occurrence they heard the terrible news that on September 2, 1864, Sherman had captured Atlanta. Rumors abounded that he had begun a march to the sea.

Excitement leaped again on the twenty-second of December. Jonathan hobbled into the kitchen to find Emma. Whooping for joy, he shouted, "The *Muscogee*'s been launched! They say she glided into the water so smoothly that the motion wouldn't have shaken the water in a tumbler," he exulted. "Emma, send for Dr. Weedon. I must get back to duty! Even the *Columbus Daily Enquirer* calls our ironclad a crowning achievement. The Union is shaking in fear. They've increased the blockade, but our ram will break it."

Clutching her frayed cashmere shawl about her shoulders as she started her search for Dr. Weedon, Emma realized that Jonathan did not know the strength of the blockade. No supplies were getting through. Christmas dinner was made up of make-dos, substitutions for the regular holiday fare. No eggs, no chicken—they were reserved for the very ill. The hogs had subsisted on what they could forage in the streets and were too thin to kill.

Worst of all, with no way to market cotton to bring in cash, Lily had sold her best Paris gowns to provide necessities. If she had had gold, there was nothing to buy for Mignonne. Tearfully the four year old was told that Santa Claus could not get through the blockade and must save his toys for next year.

Dr. Weedon drained Jonathan's foot again. He would not consent to the sick man's returning to the navy.

When Kitty and Tildy burst into her bedroom on Christmas morning with shouts of "Chris'mus gif'," Emma had nothing for them. She buried her head under the covers and cried.

Mignonne played happily with toy animals which Lily had fashioned from rags and chicken feathers, but the family's day was crowned with bitterness when the word passed around Eufaula that General W. T. Sherman had wired Abraham Lincoln, "I beg to present you as a Christmas gift the city of Savannah," after having taken the city on the twentieth of December.

New Year's Day, 1865, brought the delayed news that since September, Sherman had been marching through Georgia, ravaging a swath sixty miles wide across the state from Atlanta to the sea, and Magnolia Springs Plantation had fallen victim to his pillage. There was no word on the whereabouts of his family, but crops in the fields, barns, outbuildings—everything had been set ablaze. The beautiful house had been looted, torched. Nothing remained of the house but two blackened chimneys. Crushing the letter savagely, the disease-ridden man could not hold back his tears.

Emma could not bear to watch him. Disconsolately, she laid her head upon his knee.

"All that's left are Mother's rubies," Jonathan said at last. "I'm so glad I sent for them." His voice seemed to be coming from a great distance. Idly, he plucked at her hair. "They are yours. Keep them. I release you from your vow. I cannot marry you now!"

"No, Jonathan, no." She lifted her head aghast and looked at him wild-eyed. "I've never had worldly goods. It doesn't matter to me that you have no fine house to take me to." She grasped out to embrace him. "All I want is to be your wife!"

"You've lived in luxury," he replied curtly, drawing away from her reaching hands.

"As a servant. Until now. Cordelia treats me like a sister lately." Her aching, empty arms hugged about her own shoulders.

"Yes." His voice sounded harsh, hollow. "I've noticed the change in her. She'll take care of you. I cannot marry you with nothing!" He hobbled away.

Like winter's unrelenting cold, Jonathan's impersonal gaze froze Emma in its icy grip. Even the joy of Lily's delivery of Harrison Wingate, Jr., on February 22, 1865, was diminished because his father was not at home. Somberly, Emma stood over Lily, reflecting that an eon ago, before the war when Mignonne was born, she had been sent away from the house because she was a maiden lady. *Now I'm a nurse,* she thought.

Panting, sweating, gripping Emma's hand, Lily cried, "Oh, I wish Harrison was here!" She tried to laugh. "In times like this I wish Mama had been right when she used to tell me you found babies out in the cabbage patch!"

Emma smiled halfheartedly. She, too, wished for the security the quiet man's presence always gave, but he was on a downriver expedition on the *William H. Young*. The threats of a few such steamers and the *Chattahoochee* and *Muscogee* still held the river safe.

But the enemy advanced from the west.

General James H. Wilson's cavalry galloped through Alabama like a spring tornado. Captain Catesby Jones's Selma Naval Foundry was his first target. The niter works, the powder mill and magazine, the whole industrial town of Selma which was forging half the Confederacy's cannon, making two-thirds of the fixed ammunition, exploded and burned with sulfurous black smoke like Dante's *Inferno*.

Bugles blaring, Wilson's troopers charged down upon Montgomery, torched eighty-five thousand bales of cotton worth forty million dollars, threw sixty thousand bushels of corn into the flames, rode on through the pall of smoke, and stopped short at the banks of the Chattahoochee River swollen by spring rains, swirling at flood stage.

With shaking hands, Eufaulians read reports in April 14's *Columbus Daily Sun* and murmured encouragement to each other because the newspaper stated, "Everything is in readiness for battle. Let us keep calm." Unsure of Foy's whereabouts, the women of Barbour Hall remained on their knees in prayer as reports filtered through of two brigades moving up to attack Columbus.

Breathlessly, the city waited. Bulging with refugees from Alabama, fleeing Wilson, and from Georgia, fleeing Sherman, the river city trembled with only old men, boys, and walking wounded to protect her. Georgia's General Howell Cobb rushed in, but he had only two thousand unseasoned troops to guard the bridges. Frantically, the Confederates rendered the northernmost bridge unusable, tore up plank flooring of the southernmost, Dillingham Street Bridge, and settled into two forts at the Fourteenth Street Bridge. With four, ten-pound Parrots bearing on the road, they waited.

Wilson swept through Girade, Alabama, and massed for attack. Surprisingly, the bugles blew "Water Call." As the Bluecoats tended their horses and rested, Columbus waited. On the morning of April 16, Columbus prepared. At two in the afternoon, Yankee troopers were visible on the hills. Confederate batteries shelled ineffectually. No answering fire came. They waited.

Night descended, clear, moonless. At eight o'clock, the still, quiet blackness as of midnight was shattered by a shot, another, ten thousand more. Flashes puncturing the dark shroud pinpointed Confederate strong points.

Yelling, "Selma, Selma, go for the bridge!" Union troops charged.

In chaos of darkness, men fought, struggled on the bridge, confused friend with foe in the utter blackness of the covered wooden span. The smell of turpentine flared nostrils. A Confederate match was struck, shot down. At eleven o'clock, General Wilson rode into Columbus.

Panic ensued. Women and children ran through the streets. The confused sounds of flight rumbled through a night suddenly bright as midday. One hundred thousand bales of cotton bloomed at midnight in a fiery blaze. For miles the earth trembled as explosions rocked the arsenal, the Naval Ironworks,

Haiman and Brother Sword Factory. Vowing to destroy everything, Wilson wrecked the railroad and burned the quartermaster depot.

Capturing the *Jackson/Muscogee,* the Union troops set fire to the vessel, cutting her adrift. The formidable ram careened down the Chattahoochee and sank on a shoal with her armor melted.

By the end of the seventeenth, Columbus lay in ashes. The paper mill, the flour mill, the Eagle Textile Mill, the bridges—everything was burned. The *Daily Sun* and the *Columbus Times* were wrecked. The *Memphis Appeal* which had fled from city to city ended its wandering publication. Only the *Daily Enquirer's* presses remained intact, but Wilson forced the paper to cease publication.

No further word reached Eufaula. At Barbour Hall, no message came from Foy.

Then one morning a rumpled, disheveled young man with singed hair and eyebrows walked stiffly across the yard. "I lit the match to the *Chattahoochee.*" Foy grinned ruefully.

"No!" his family chorused. "What happened?"

"It was the first time I ever saw shelling at night." He sat with arms hanging limply. "A beautiful but awful spectacle. Every second our eyes were blinded by the blue light of shells exploding around us. Grape and canister came whistling by." He shook his head sorrowfully and rubbed the stub of his eyebrows.

"Wilson's raiders captured the *Muscogee,* stripped her, set her burning." He nodded at Jonathan, knowing how proud he had been of the *Chattahoochee.* "We couldn't let 'em ravish our lady. We escaped as far as Race Pass. There was nothing else to do." He swallowed bitterness. "Our crew wet her decks with kerosene, ignited slow fuses, and retreated by the firelight." He dropped his head in his hands.

Jonathan lay on his cot submerged in despair. Hatred of Sherman and Wilson and the unnecessary devastation they had wrecked poisoned his soul even as his wounded foot poisoned his blood. Again and again he went over the awful story with Foy, lamenting, cursing the destruction that had taken place a week after General Robert E. Lee's surrender to General U. S. Grant, April 9, 1865. It made him feel no better that Wilson, coming in from the west, had known neither of the armistice nor of the fact that on April 14, the Stars and Stripes were raised over Fort Sumter; and on that night Lincoln had been shot.

Except for a few last skirmishes in the west, the April 16 battle for Columbus was the last. The long, agonizing War Between the States was over.

Emma gave Jonathan all her loving care, praying for him constantly and asking Lily's and Cordelia's prayers, too. He had lost the will to live; she tried to resign herself to the fact that he was dying.

Emma felt she had to get away, if only for a moment, to escape the sick, the dying. Not wanting even Kitty with her, she hitched the runabout and drove out the road west of Eufaula. Flexing her shoulders in the warm morning sun and inhaling the fragrance of honeysuckle, she found it hard to believe that her favorite month, April, had passed in such a blur, but, yes, it was the twenty-eighth day. Beneath the dark pines, sparkling white dogwood turned the woodland into a fairyland. She tried to let the beauty lighten her spirits, but something was missing. There was no music. At first she thought that melody was merely absent from her soul, but as she began to look around uneasily, she realized that the birds had hushed their singing. No squirrels played along the ground.

Slapping the reins, she urged the pony toward Oak Hill Plantation. She entered the gates with a sigh of relief.

Her friend, Matilda, greeted her delightedly. Gray had streaked her hair since word came that her husband had died at Seven Pines, but her face, still young, wreathed in smiles as she poured tea made of rose hips and other odd, unsatisfying ingredients. They settled down to chat.

Galloping horses pounded into the yard. Sloshing their tea, Emma and Matilda rushed to the open door as a bluecoat officer stamped onto the porch with a clanking of spurs.

"Set food out," he demanded in an accent harsh to their ears. "My men are hungry."

Matilda looked around her yard at the dozen men. "We can give you a little bread, but that's all we have," she said with her head held high. She turned and nodded at a trembling servant.

The man glowered at her and snorted.

A sudden realization flooded over Emma that these men, like Wilson, might have been beyond communication. She quickly stepped forward. "The armistice has been signed," she said, proud of her firm voice. "You can do us no harm. The war is over!"

"We've not heard of an armistice," he replied curtly.

"Lee surrendered to Grant. Johnston to Sherman. Lincoln's dead!" Then she repeated firmly. "You dare not harm us."

He recoiled in shock. Grimacing, he took off his forage cap and scratched red hair. Eyeing her suspiciously, he snarled, "You might be telling the truth—but Lincoln dead?" He dropped his hand to the Colt pistol in his belt. "No! No such message has reached us. We've received no parcel of change of orders. We're advance guard. Must hurry on. If—if it's true—" he threw them another puzzled look and shrugged— "I can afford you no protection. The command will soon be passing."

Taking the food Matilda proffered, he clanked down the steps. Greedily eating cold cornbread, the men whirled their horses out of the yard. Breaking branches off the trees, they threw them on the ground to guide the advancing army.

"Quickly, quickly." Matilda clapped her hands and directed her frightened household. "Bar the doors!"

Emma reached outside the windows, closed the green shutters, and fastened them. Matilda worked swiftly behind her removing the sticks and lowering the glass. With everything as secure as possible, they stood peering through the cracks in the wooden shutters, waiting.

A lone figure struggled up the lane. Recognizing the white-haired lady in faded silk as their neighbor, Matilda threw off the bars, and they hurried to meet her just as her knees buckled.

"I escaped—across—the fields," she panted. "They burned my house. Destroyed everything!"

With the younger women on each side half-dragging her, they moved slowly toward the porch. Looking around frantically, they lifted, pushed her inside, rebarred the door. Waited.

They heard them coming from afar, the unmistakable tread of marching men. Like a mighty, rushing water, the sound grew, pouring over them with drenching sweat. For an hour there was no break in the lines. They passed, a steady, solid stream of bluecoats, tramping by, leading weary, sore-footed horses.

Silently the women peered between the cracks, praying the army would march on without molesting them. Suddenly a sharp command was given. Mounted cavalrymen whirled into the yard, drew rein, turned carbines fixed with sabers upon the house. In the soft spring sunshine, they presented an unbroken line of glittering steel.

A pounding on the heavy front door and a shout, "Open!" echoed through the house. Mutely, the women shrank back. *Crash!* The ruby glass of the sidelight shattered against their skirts. Through the gash, the ugly nose of the Spencer carbine brandished its wicked bayonet.

"Ahhh!" Matilda clapped her hand over her mouth to stifle her scream.

Emma leaned close to the jagged hole and shouted, "Stop that at once. There's been an armistice. We will not open the doors. You dare not break them down. Lee surrendered to Grant! The war is over!"

Cursing, threatening to torch the house with them in it, the Yankee demanded they open the door.

"We will not!" She looked around at the women and children. "Your advance guard took all we had." Mustering all of the authority into her voice that she could, she shouted the information she had given the guard and ended with a command. "The hostilities have ceased. You dare not harm us or burn this house!"

For an endless moment, all was silent. Emma stole a quick look through the sidelight. The huge man stood deliberating. He reached into the paraphernalia banded across his body and brought out a twist of tobacco as long as his hand. He chomped into the horrid brown stuff and gnawed off a cheekful. Chewing thoughtfully, he turned and stalked off with the metal scabbard of his low-slung saber dragging, scraping the floor, leaving an indelible scar. He stopped to bark at his men. He turned back. Emma shrank fearfully from her peephole.

Hesitating curses, shuffling feet, clapping, clanking arms, told her they were leaving the porch. Exhaling at last, she dissolved to the floor in a pool of sweat.

With tears streaming down their cheeks, the women ran from room to room, peering through the cracks in the shutters and watching the hams and bacon taken from the smokehouse, the dairy house emptied, the stock turned from the barn, and the corn cribs dumped. Doors were wrenched from their hinges, gates kicked down. And all the while the detachment wreaked their devastation, the column of the army trod relentlessly down the road.

For two hours they passed. Dusk gathered before the enemy was out of sight and all was silent again.

"I must get home." Emma's flat, determined voice startled them as she broke the silence.

"No, Emma, it's too dangerous!" shrieked Matilda.

"I must warn them. The bluecoats are headed for Eufaula. They'll burn our beautiful town. I told you what they did to Columbus. Foy said some of the soldiers even took the ladies' dresses and made feed bags for their horses."

Matilda stood openmouthed, soundless with horror.

Emma looked at the exhausted old woman behind them and the crying children pulling at Matilida's skirts. "I hate to leave you," she told her friend, "but there's only a handful of old men and boys with all those women and wounded. No one to stop them before they come in shooting and burn the town. I must warn them. I must!"

They were afraid to open the door. Tiptoeing into the yard, they found the small runabout, its silver mountings missing; the red cushions, slashed. The pony was nowhere to be seen. Matilda's horse and carriage were gone.

"You can't walk!"

"I'm not a good rider anyway." Emma laughed shakily. "I'll have to go catty-cornered through the woods to head them off."

Hugging Matilda, she started resolutely across the rough ridges of a plowed field. Fearful that more soldiers might be coming down the road, she glanced behind her, stumbled, fell flat. With her breath knocked out of her, she lay condemning herself for stupidity. Hearing a noise, she clambered on hands and knees without looking back until she reached the dark safety of the woods. Snatching her skirt free from the blackberry briars which ringed the field, she lunged into the thick forest.

Stepping carefully now, she tried desperately to concentrate on direction, to avoid the grasping arms of vines, to watch for snakes, to listen. . . . Jingling reins and whinnying horses told her she had strayed too far north toward the road. She stopped, pressing herself flat against an oak. The cavalry was mounted now; rested horses trotted faster toward Eufaula.

Exhausted, her feet aching from paper-lined shoes, she huddled behind the tree until sound ceased. Wearily, she dragged to her feet and hurried on. Running, walking, hobbling, frantic now, she feared she would lose her way as darkness leaped before her, thwarting her like a big black gnome.

Catching her foot on a log, she fell and began to cry. She thought of the tales of Wilson's march—how he had left the road from Selma through Montgomery black with the smoke of burning mansions and putrid with the stench of dead horses and mules. Women had been made to give up their jewels, and trusted servants had been threatened with death if they did not help to burn and destroy.

Emma had confused one soldier briefly, but when the officers arrived they would destroy without asking. *Beautiful Eufaula,* she wept, *where Lily and Mignonne waited alone without Harrison, where only Cordelia tended Jonathan and the wounded.* "Jonathan," she sobbed. Struggling to her feet, she pressed onward, praying for strength.

At last, she came out of the forest and stood at the top of the hill looking down upon Eufaula, candlelit, peaceful. With her last strength, she hurried to Dr. Pope's house on Broad Street. But Dr. Pope, Eufaula's mayor, was not there. Staring in amazement at Emma's torn, dirty clothing and scratched face and hands, Mrs. Pope listened to her tale. Helping Emma into her buggy, she whipped the horse and raced toward the Tavern.

Patting Emma as she talked, the doctor pursed his lips and nodded absently at the details, which poured from her lips as though unbidden. Finally, he stopped her story and began snapping orders. Able-bodied men were few. The townsmen had not yet returned home from fields of battle. He sent two teenaged boys, Edward Young and Edward Stern, galloping westward waving a white flag of truce.

Emma sank gratefully upon her bed while her warning passed around the town like leaping flames. Frantically the women buried their silver in their gardens, and hid their precious sugar and flour between the ceilings and roofs of their houses.

At dawn on the twenty-ninth of April, the youthful couriers galloped back into town. Shrugging that they had not found the enemy encampment, they innocently explained that they had stopped at a house and spent the night. Exasperated, Dr. Pope sent them out again down the Clayton Road to present the white flag and delay the attack while he gathered the prominent, older men who were city councilmen to go with him to face the enemy.

Emma had rested only a few hours when a small boy brought a cryptic note from Dr. Pope.

Dress in your Sunday best. Go at once to my house. We have a plan to save the town. I'm relying upon you.

C. J. Pope

Puzzled, she washed her face and put on her best pink taffeta frock. She had not worn the rubies since that unspeakable day when Jonathan had said he could not marry her. For some defiant, unfathomable reason, she put on the necklace and the large ruby ring. Carefully she arranged her hair. She fastened the green shutters, barred the doors, and hurried out into the silent streets.

When she reached the house at the foot of the hill on the north side of Broad Street, she found Mrs. Pope, bustling about, preparing a fine meal. "Here, Emma, set the table with my finest china and silver." Mrs. Pope laughed ironically. "It makes my Southern blood boil to have to serve them." She wiped a wisp of gray hair from her damp forehead and shrugged. "But Dr. Pope insists that this is the only way to save us from the torch. We must entertain them like gentlemen and keep them occupied until they can receive their orders to prove the war is over."

All morning, the ladies of the town helped Mrs. Pope and her daughter, Ella, not daring to think what would happen if the plan failed.

Just before noon, they heard the sound, the rattle of sabers, the jingling of reins, the clopping hoofs of hundreds upon hundreds of horses. The regiment crested the hill, the muffled drumbeat livened, was joined by fifes, and the jaunty tune, "Yankee Doodle," echoed through the streets.

Emma clapped her hands to her buzzing ears. She shook her head, unsure, but, yes, she heard the plaintive notes of a violin. A frightened moan escaped her lips as she saw Professor J. C. Van Houten across the street on the steps of Miss Sarah Shorter Hunter's house. The blind musician had tucked his violin beneath his chin. How could he be so defiant? He was playing "Dixie."

The band blared the louder as it passed. Next came the entourage, Dr. Pope and the councilmen escorting the gold-braided officers into the yard and onto the porch. Emma retreated behind the lace curtains to watch as the officers in alien blue deposited part of their weapons on the porch.

The majestic man with epaulets must be the general. While some of the men swaggered with the four-foot scabbards slung from their left hips and dragging the ground, he walked smartly with his saber carefully fastened up with a hook. Lean, hard-muscled, he wore a short blue jacket resplendent with brass buttons and, tucked into knee-high boots, light blue trousers with a yellow stripe down the leg. With dignity, he handed over his saber and holstered pistol to his guard. As he carefully folded his gauntlets into his wide leather belt, Emma knew the moment had come.

Pressing her fingertips against her stiff cheeks, she put on a pleasant smile as she stepped into the entrance hall. The tall man removed his slouch hat and gave a slight bow as she and the other women swished forward. Hope rose that he was a gentleman.

"Ladies, may I present Brevet Major-General Benjamin H. Grierson," said Dr. Pope with false heartiness.

Acknowledging him with a gracious nod, Emma was startled at the appraising look he swept over her. Just then the strains of "Dixie" emanated so strongly from across the street that she feared he would become angry. Scarcely knowing what she said, she greeted the general with chattering charm as Lily would have done. The tall man smiled down at her sardonically.

Dr. Pope explained that he had directed General Grierson to send his men across the Chattahoochee River to Harrison's Mill near Georgetown, Georgia, where a spring would provide water for their camp.

Mrs. Pope welcomed the officers to her table, pitching her voice higher than usual against the unending sounds of clopping hoofs, jingling reins, and marching feet in horrifying counterpoint to the spirited mingled rhythms of "Yankee Doodle" and "Dixie." Using all her ingenuity to stretch her meager supply of food, she served many courses. Over after-dinner coffee, made of roasted grain, she tactfully pointed out to the general the heartbreaking conditions in the South brought about by the war. Then she invited the satiated men into the music room.

Against the discordant noise outside, Emma played several selections on the piano. John McNab's little daughter was brought in to sing. General Grierson, who had said little but had conducted himself like a gentleman, lifted the child to his knee and asked for a kiss.

"No, Sir." The little girl shook her head. She kicked his slick, black boot. "I won't kiss a Yankee!"

Emma's hand fluttered toward her chest, but then she stretched them toward Grierson placatingly. "Please excuse her, Sir." She laughed lightly. "She's just a child."

The general smiled with the lower half of his face only, set the tot down, and winked at Emma.

She held her breath fearfully as he gazed at her. What would he do? It was readily apparent that young and old of Eufaula would bend but not bow their spirits to their conquerors.

Suddenly he roared with laughter. "It seems I'm not the only one who doesn't know that the war has ended!" He stood up, obviously ready to leave. "I'll take your word." He nodded. "I'll accept your hospitality. I'll keep my men in camp and allow no foraging of the town until I receive my parcel with orders from General Sherman."

For twelve long hours, one company after another of men and horses appeared at the top of Broad Street and continued down upon them in a slow, tired march until four thousand cavalry had passed. Only when the last bluecoat had disappeared into the shadows of the covered wooden bridge spanning the Chattahoochee and stepped out of his adopted state, did the old man from New Jersey stop sawing the sad notes of "Dixie" and lay down his violin.

Exhausted, her nerves jangled, Emma dragged wearily back to Barbour Hall. Finally awakening Lige, who was guarding the door, she tiptoed in and lit a candle to check on the wounded men before she went to bed. Jonathan was not on his cot. Searching the huge house with rising fear, she fought far worse panic than the enemy had caused.

Jonathan was gone.

Chapter 14

Jonathan!" she called out softly.

The flame from her candle etched eerie shadows against the walls, spider-webbed the high ceilings as she tiptoed from room to room, searching. He was not in the house. The belvedere? Surely not. The stairs would be painfully impossible, unless. . . She could not bear the thought that he might jump. Perhaps he had heard she was entertaining the Yankee general. Her knees jelly, she climbed the endless flights. He was not there.

Stumbling back down the passageways, she ran out into the yard. "Jonathan! Jonathan!" she called. Through the paths and gates and enclosures of the gardens, she searched. Empty. She peered fearfully up and down the deserted street. Leaves rustled behind her. Whirling, she glimpsed a night predator scurrying away. Letting out her breath, she realized she must not venture into the dark streets. The occupying army was everywhere, everywhere.

She could barely stand. Creeping to her bed, she lay with exhausted tears slipping out, soaking the pillow. Sleep came in snatches as she listened throughout the night for a sound to indicate that Jonathan had returned. She feared this final indignity of the conquering army had been more than he could bear. Since the Yankees had burned his plantation, he had slipped into a far place in his soul from which she could not lift him. He had lost the will to live.

As dawn streaked the sky, Emma rubbed swollen eyes and saw with surprise that she still wore her best pink taffeta. No matter now. She slid down from the high bed and hurried through the half-light to the stable. Cordelia's horse and carriage were gone. Whether they had been taken by Jonathan or by the invaders, she could not know. She stood with her hand trembling on the gate. Her eyes darted about, straining to see if anyone hid behind trees, around corners.

Seeing no one, she ran down the hill toward the river. Panting, she stepped into the dimly lit Tavern.

"Well, Emma, you're just in time." Dr. Pope looked up absently. "I'm in need of a dedicated nurse."

"No, Doctor, I—I can't stay—now." She labored for breath. "I'm looking for Jonathan Ramsey." She pushed back stray wisps of golden curls which were clinging to her damp forehead. "I thought maybe—is he here?"

"Um." He pursed his lips. "No. Haven't seen him." He shook his head.

"Wait, Emma," he called out as she turned away. "Thank you for being such a great help yesterday. The Yankee, Grierson, was quite taken with you."

Emma nodded mutely, turned, and fled the Tavern, recoiling in horror as she saw bluecoat soldiers with axes raised. Crashing down, the axes split the heads of wooden barrels. Whiskey, which had been carefully hoarded for medicinal use, might now cause drunken rioting. Amber liquid gushed from the broken barrels and poured in streams into the ditch at her feet. Shoving her aside, men fell to their knees and lapped the whiskey from the ditch. Stumbling backward over a razor-backed hog, she sprawled in an undignified heap. Squealing, the hog pushed from under her hoop skirt. A herd of oinking pigs rooted between the men guzzling liquor. The pigs swilled until they staggered away as drunk as the men.

Stunned, Emma sat amazed. Suddenly she began to laugh hysterically. Tears streaming, she struggled to her feet and stumbled to a secluded spot on the riverbank. As she looked down into the mists of morning, her breathing slowed, her hiccupping ceased. The wind, chilled from the long night, made the tear trails on her cheeks as icy as the fear made her heart.

Lifting her face into the wind, she prayed, "Strengthen me, O Lord. Help me to bear whatever comes. Help me not to waver from serving You." Then she began to sob. "Please, help me find Jonathan before it's too late."

Fairview Cemetery. The thought popped into her mind. He had gone there frequently of late to sit by the graves of his friends.

Walking, trotting, tripping, wondering if her lungs would burst and her feet in their worn, kidskin shoes would bleed before she covered another mile, she doggedly pressed onward.

There was no mistaking Cordelia's carriage. The horse was tethered by the graves of Confederate dead. The lemon-green lace of a weeping willow shivered around her. The slender branches danced frenziedly, whipped by a stiff breeze. She looked through a mist of tears and focused her eyes upon him at last. He was standing on the brink of the cliff.

Slowly, quietly, lest her sudden appearance startle him and make him jump, she crept forward.

Jonathan turned, raked his fingers through his black hair, looked at her blankly for a moment; and then he smiled. Slowly, as from a great depth, the smile spread over his face and lighted his eyes. As if from a century ago, she looked again into the eyes she loved, the dark and laughing eyes of Jonathan Ramsey.

He stretched out his arms. "Emma, my darling, you're always near when I need you. I love you. Oh, how I love you!"

Laughing, crying, not waiting to wonder why at last he said the words she had longed to hear, she flung herself into the haven of his embrace.

Kissing her hungrily, he stroked her flying hair and murmured again, "I love you."

A red ball of sun peeped from behind the dark green trees on the opposite shore. The tranquil black mirror of the Chattahoochee dazzled their tear-filled eyes with sparkling pinks and golds. Emma gazed wonderingly into his radiant face. He laughed and stopped her questioning with a smothering, passionate kiss which dizzied her, burning away the last mists of fear. Golden-green with new life, the trees around them housed orchestras of awakening birds. Melodies filled the April breeze. She leaned back at last, begged air, and looked into his dear face. Reaching up, she squeezed his curls and pushed back the lock from his forehead. Suddenly her knees gave way from her long searching and she swayed. Jonathan smoothed a place, and they sat on the grass beneath the sheltering arms of a blossoming dogwood.

Clasping the ruby on her hand, Jonathan smiled. "You never gave up on me, did you?" He fingered the heavy necklace, stroked her tender throat, and tilted her face for a gentle kiss. Looking at her adoringly, he said, "I must tell you—I know you've been praying for me, and I read the Bible where you marked it and left it by my cot." He paused, plucked a dogwood blossom from above their heads, and traced a thoughtful finger over the rusty holes in the cross the white flower formed around a crown of thorns. He cleared his throat. "I told you I accepted that Jesus died on the cross for my sins when I was a child. Unfortunately, when I reached my teens, I fell into what I thought were good times. As an adult, material possessions became my god."

He pulled her close. Peacefully, she nestled her head on his shoulder. He kissed the golden curls on her forehead before continuing huskily. "God continued to bless me, but I worshiped money. My pride was my beautiful wife, my home. When she died—" He shook his head sorrowfully. "I turned to humanism, indulging myself. Even though I was yearning for spiritual things, I couldn't possess them. My soul was panting, but it couldn't rest. I was seeking but never finding, journeying yet never arriving. . ." His voice choked.

Gently Emma lifted her head and kissed his cheek. Happily, she knew that she could share her innermost thoughts with him, her spiritual depths, but for now she would sit quietly and let him talk.

"When I met you," he continued, "I blamed God for my problems. I couldn't love Him or myself—and much as I wanted to, I was afraid to love you. Afraid I'd lose you as I did Betty." He caught the hand which stroked his chin and kissed the palm. "Threatened with the loss of my foot—knowing you had to face the invaders alone—I was ready to throw myself into the Chattahoochee."

"What happened?" she whispered in awe.

"Your prayers, the dogwood, the message of Easter. Jesus suffered more than I. He arose. He lives! Suddenly I remembered that God is more powerful than all the evil in the world. I turned my whole life over to Him. I bowed before Him as my Lord." The weary lines of his face had vanished. His smile radiated his whole being. "You were right. The moment I let Jesus into the ship of my life I was at the land whither I went!"

The sun rose above the clouds, and morning burst brilliantly around them. Restlessness and searching ended, Emma sighed with deep contentment and tranquilly nestled against his shoulder. "I know now that God has a purpose for our lives," she said blissfully, "and that He will be with us and never let us bear our burdens alone."

"Yes," he answered quietly. "I'm not quite sure just yet what He wants me to do. Perhaps it's to share this message with others. It won't be easy. Our whole world is collapsing. I don't know what tomorrow will bring, but we'll trust God to provide our needs. With you and our children at my side, I can face each day rejoicing in doing God's will."

The smell of freshly turned earth was strong on the wind along the river as it caressed their joyful faces with the promise of a new beginning.

Acknowledgments

Truth, it has been said, is stranger than fiction. Many events in this book would not be believable were they not true. The background characters were the heroes of the day. This book begins where *The River Between* left off and chronicles life in Eufaula, Alabama, during the Civil War and actual struggles for control of the Chattahoochee River. Only the center stage figures who people Barbour Hall are fiction. The house itself is suggested by Fendall Hall, built in 1854 by Edward Young. Presently owned by the State of Alabama, it is open to the public.

Again, my appreciation goes to Douglas Purcell, director of the Historic Chattahoochee Commission. His superb fund of knowledge guided me at every turning. Emma (Mrs. James Ross) Foy transported me back in time with innumerable small details. She, Jane Dempsey, and Hilda Sexton of the Eufaula Heritage Association (located in Shorter Mansion and open to the public) transcribed the diaries of Elizabeth Rhodes, which not only gave me the chronology of the events but the minds of those who experienced them.

The Confederate Navy came alive through the enthusiasm of Bob Holcombe, curator of the Confederate Naval Museum in Columbus, Georgia. There one can see the remains of the gunboat, *Chattahoochee,* and the ram, *Muscogee,* which were raised from their watery graves one hundred years later in 1965. Holcombe graciously schooled me in nautical matters and provided numerous references.

The recognized authority on the naval war on the local scene is Dr. Maxine Turner. She was very helpful to me, and her book, *Naval Operations on the Apalachicola and Chattahoochee,* became my guide.

The love letters of George and Ellen Gift, collected in *Hope Bids Me Onward,* provided details of life aboard the *Chattahoochee* and the fact that ladies were often on the boats. Sarah Jones's journal, *Life in the South,* gave colorful details as did Bradlee's *Blockade Running.* Kane's *Christmas in the South* added validity to my knowledge of local customs, many of which remain to the present. Countless old books about the Confederate Navy and about medical problems of the era gave a sentence here and there. My thanks goes to Harriet Bates of the Lake Blackshear Regional Library for securing them from all over the Southeast. One day when we had cross-checked a contradictory fact for the umpteenth time, I said, "My readers will skim over this without ever realizing the trouble we've taken to be accurate." She replied, "But aren't we having fun!"

Dr. Robert A. Collins assisted with medical matters and the Reverend James D. Eldridge was helpful with the spiritual side. The music of the "Tallahassee Waltz" was unearthed in the Florida Collection of the State Library of Florida by librarian Linda Gail Brown. Thanks also go to Carolyn Nicholson, Marilyn Story, and Glenda Spradley.

Eufaula, Alabama, was spared the invader's torch just as I have described it from old memoirs. Especially poignant were "Other Days: A Transcript on Vellum" by Anne Kendrick Walker, and Mattie Thomas Thompson's *History of Barbour County, Alabama.* Eufaula's historically preserved mansions are graciously opened to visitors each April and October.

River of Fire

Chapter 1

Sunlight kindled red and gold flames in the curls cascading down Adrianna's back as she strolled along Eufaula Avenue, happily noting that store windows contained merchandise from around the world now that the war was over. She paused to admire millinery for the fall of 1874 in the window of Stern's Temple of Fashion.

Suddenly she realized the street was quiet, deserted. Shops were closed. Did everyone in Alabama take a nap after the noon meal?

She swallowed nervously. She had noticed soldiers in the hotel. Now there was no one in sight, and she had completely lost direction.

Out of the corner of her eye, she glimpsed a lean young man moving toward her with hard-muscled strides. His fine nose and chin and his confident carriage bore the mark of a gentleman, even though the cut of his waistcoat was outdated. As he neared, Adrianna looked quickly away.

Twirling her lace-trimmed parasol over her shoulder, Adrianna stepped along Hart's Block. The feel of eyes upon her back made her shiver. Even though she practiced ignoring people who stared at her brilliant hair, especially against her bottle-green street costume, she could not resist a peep at the vigorous man.

He had broken into a lope. Her tense frown smoothed into a tender smile as she saw within the man the image of a small boy, arms and legs flapping.

"Wait!" he shouted as he neared her. "You must—come with me—before. . ."

Snapping her head away from him, she quickened her pace. His strong hand grasped her shoulder.

"Please," he said, panting. "Listen, Ma'am. I'd never hurt you. You must let me take you back to your hotel. You're walking to the polling place, and—"

"Certainly not, Sir," she said icily. "We have not been introduced."

For a moment he stared in consternation, then a slow smile filled his lean face. Doffing his high silk hat, he bowed low and intoned, "May I present Foy Edwards, Esquire."

Giggling in spite of herself, she responded, "Hello, I'm Adrianna Atherton."

Clapping his hat back on his head, he grasped her elbow. "That's done. Now come on," he said urgently and headed her down the empty street in the opposite direction.

Shrill piping and menacing drumbeats shattered the stillness. An angry roar of voices clashed against the music. Wrenching around, Adrianna saw the street filling with armed men.

She shrieked, and her knees buckled.

"Don't play Lot's wife. Come on!"

His arm shot around her trim waist. As he half-carried her, she felt the hard outline of a pistol against her ribs. Behind them rang the shouts of the mob.

"Who?" she gasped. "What?"

"That's the Radical Party, and—" Scuffling sounds behind them increased his pace. "Run!"

A shot echoed and reechoed against the brick buildings. For one long moment there was deathly silence. Then hundreds of shots rained down from the upper floors of the storehouses.

"That's the Democrats. We're 'bout to the hotel. Oh, good grannies!" He jerked her to a stop.

Adrianna blinked at a wall of blue-coated soldiers.

"And that's the Federal Occupation Army!" He spat out the words.

Her parasol dropped with a clatter as they darted into an alley. Running blindly, she had begun to think she could go no farther when he stopped abruptly, leaped astride a horse, and swung her up behind him. Sitting side-saddle as they galloped away, Adrianna held tightly to the back of her rescuer with one hand and clutched her hat with the other.

When they reached a quiet street lined with China trees, he slowed the sorrel to a trot. Clucking to the horse, he turned in at a gate and rode up a drive past huge red cedars.

Adrianna stared at the tremendous house spreading before her. Wildly overgrown shrubs screened the veranda. Her eyes moved up to the balcony on the second story and higher still to the glassed belvedere and widow's walk which crowned the roof.

"Welcome to Barbour Hall," he said as he dismounted. Lifting her from the sorrel's back, he observed, "You're a young lady of contradictions. Your hair looks like maple leaves in autumn, yet your perfume. . ." He sniffed experimentally. "Ah, the first breath of spring." He beamed down at her as he reluctantly dropped his hands and stepped away.

"It's French hyacinths." She swallowed and her blue-green eyes gazed wonderingly at him.

He cleared his throat, turned toward the house, and frowned.

Watching his brows knit together as he looked from her to the house, Adrianna could tell he was realizing for the first time how shabby it had become. She wondered why such a magnificent mansion had been neglected. If her grandfather's wealth had diminished since the war, she had not realized it.

Looking at his home, the serious young man said ruefully, "My sister used to say she looked like a hoop-skirted belle dressed for a ball, but now she's a dowdy old dowager."

"Your sister?" She pressed one finger to her lips to suppress a laugh.

"No," he said, chuckling. "She's grown more beautiful with maturity. I meant the house."

"Well." She pursed her lips. "Hoop skirts are out of style." She saw what he meant about the delicately trimmed, spreading porch. "But a house would look funny with a bustle." She laughed delightedly at the thought, then said more seriously, "Pruning the shrubs and painting the house would work wonders."

"I hadn't noticed how badly she'd gone down since Mama died three years ago." He removed his hat and pushed back thick hair. "I really must get some work done on her, but I haven't been able—I can't ask you in."

"Oh, that's all right. I don't mind a little dirt." She started up the steps.

"No." His voice was a deep rumble. "I'm a bachelor. It wouldn't be proper for you to go in unchaperoned."

Adrianna pursed her lips and said, "That's old-fashioned. I can certainly trust the man who saved my life."

"No." The determined set of his chin stopped her midstep. "I would not sully your reputation. Come. We'll sit in the summerhouse until it's safe to take you to the hotel."

Meekly following along the boxwood-bordered path, she broke the silence. "Seriously, I do thank you for coming to my aid. It's a good thing you happened along."

"I didn't just happen along." He looked down at her. "I was waiting in an upstairs window—no, not for you." He grinned at her mock surprise. "We were expecting trouble. That mob was marching through the county, voting at every precinct under a different name."

"I noticed you're armed. Are you a law officer?"

"No. The marshals and policemen had tried to intervene, but volunteer police had to be summoned." He lifted a swag of wisteria vine, which drooped over the open doorway of the white-latticed gazebo.

"How do you know so much about me—that I'm at the hotel, and. . ."

With a deep chuckle he said, "I was born and bred in Eufaula, Alabama. I know all the young ladies in town—"

"I'll just bet you do!" She tossed her head coyly as she arranged her skirt on a graying wicker settee.

Ignoring the flirtatious honey in her voice, he folded his long body into a chair across from her.

"I would say. . ." He studied her in amusement. "That you're Senator Atherton's daughter."

"Granddaughter," she corrected. "But how—"

"Sixteen years ago my sister, Lily, was made ragingly jealous upon hearing that Captain Wingate was seen dancing with the most beautiful lady in Washington City," he said, laughing. "You must look exactly like your grandmother."

A smile twitched about her lips at the clever way he had complimented her without being impolitely forward.

"The lady in question doesn't take very good care of you," he continued. "You should not have been on the street unchaperoned—and not at all on election day."

"Actually," she looked down, "I came to Alabama to look after Ma-ma. Her health is failing. We arrived last evening on the train from Macon. I slipped out while my grandparents were resting for the Wingates' anniversary party, and—are you? What did you say your name was?"

He laughed and looked at her with intense brown eyes. Flustered by his probing gaze, she waited.

"Foy," he said at last. "Foy Edwards. But you can forget it again," he said, teasingly. "I plan to pretend we've never met."

"Then my grandfather. . ." She stammered, unable to breathe as she watched the change his slow smile brought to his face. "Came—came here to consult with. . ."

"With Harrison Wingate and me." He reared back in his chair, seeming imperceptibly to pull away from her. The soft intimacy of his voice became more businesslike. "Years before the war, Harrison tried to induce Congress to clear the channel of the Chattahoochee."

"That beautiful green river we crossed on the trestle coming into Eufaula?"

"Yes. It's always been dangerous. Narrow, winding, full of rocks, sandbars, snags." Foy gestured with his long arms. "And since the war—with all the sunken boats and obstructions—even a good captain like Harrison is risking his life at every turning. If we're to join the industrial boom, the river must be cleared!"

"Yes!" Her eyes sparkled as she caught his excitement. "Back East, men are becoming millionaires overnight. Factories, new machinery, marvelous inventions—oh, I love trying modern things!"

"Yes, well," Foy said seriously, "I can't approve of some of the new methods—believe in old values and principles myself." He shrugged. "But I am excited by new challenges." He leaned forward, his eyes snapping. "Harrison and I are partners in building a new steamboat. She's modern, all right, sleek, beautiful, the most luxurious appointments." He tipped the chair back with his arms behind his head and grinned at Adrianna with small-boy excitement.

"How exciting!" she exclaimed, bringing her fingertips together under her dimpled chin. "Oh, I do admire anyone who knows exactly where he's going in life. I don't know what I'm—"

Suddenly the sun, which had warmed them through the latticed roof, moved behind a cloud. A crisp breeze warned them that the November day was speeding past.

Consulting the small gold watch pinned to her bodice, Adrianna exclaimed, "Mercy! It's three o'clock. Ma-ma will be waking and—"

"Yes, young lady, it's time I was taking you home." Foy flopped the chair down with a thump. "Wait here." He got up. "I'll hitch the runabout and conduct you back more properly."

"You think the riot is over?"

"Downtown, yes, but out troubles are just beginning. We've been warned of ballot stuffing at Spring Hill, eighteen miles from town."

"You'll be at the anniversary party?" Her voice was small as she tried to hide her hope.

"No." He shook his head. Worry etched his strong features. "I told Lily I couldn't make it. I'm expected to help guard the ballot box until the vote is counted. We've had a scalawag for a judge. Until we put an end to lawlessness and get a government with a strong foundation, we'll never get our world on course."

He turned at the open doorway. "I hate to miss the fun, but I'm afraid the troubles of this day are just beginning."

Chapter 2

A rainbow of silks and satins spread over Adrianna's room. It was time for the party, and she still could not decide what to wear. Eyes dancing, she held up pink, then turquoise. She chose the more sophisticated.

Foy Edwards needs impressing, she thought, as she fastened her tightly laced corset. Buttoning on the corset cover and stepping into the bustle skirt with its steel hoops protruding behind her, she wavered. She did not want him to think her worldly. She shrugged into a cambric petticoat. Neither could she let him think her a child. Foy Edwards was older, fully his own man. Shivering as the turquoise taffeta rustled over her creamy shoulders, she realized that made him exciting.

Rousing herself, she hurriedly brushed her red-gold hair. Dear Ma-ma's rheumatism-twisted hands could no longer manage tiny fastenings. She would be needing Adrianna. Leaving a pouf of curls on her forehead, she combed the rest of her hair back demurely and caught it at the nape of her neck with a white silk rose.

"How about that, Mr. Edwards." She tapped the dimple in her chin and grinned impishly at her reflection.

Foy had said he was not going to the party. For a moment the thought mocked her. Of too sunny a nature to worry, Adrianna laughed. Foy Edwards would somehow arrange to get there. Humming happily, she whirled out of the room on a cloud of fragrance.

When the carriage drew up to the Wingate home, Adrianna thought the house far less impressive than Barbour Hall, but as she followed her grandparents up to the wide, square-columned porch, she felt enveloped by unpretentious warmth. A tall man rushed out to meet the Washington visitors.

"It's a great pleasure to welcome you to Alabama, Senator Atherton," Harrison Wingate said in a deep voice. He shook hands with his imposing, white-haired guest. Then he bowed to kiss the gloved hand of Isadora Atherton. "And you, my lady," he said cordially. "My wife has heard so much of your beauty," he grinned, "that she feels she knows you."

Adrianna suppressed a giggle as she noticed the sidelong glance Wingate flashed at his wife. Remembering what Foy had said about Lily's jealousy, she studied her grandmother. Gray had washed Isadora's hair to a faded pink, but her voluptuous figure and beautiful bone structure still gave claim to her being a great beauty.

"We're delighted to have you," responded Lily Wingate. "Do come in out of the damp air." As she graciously welcomed her guests into the wide, central hall, Lily tossed her rich, dark hair and wrinkled her nose at her husband's teasing look.

"And this is our granddaughter, Adrianna," Samuel Pembroke Atherton said in the booming voice he used to show her off from a political platform.

"You look startlingly like your grandmother, young lady." Captain Wingate bowed elegantly over her hand.

"Why, thank you, Captain Wingate," Adrianna answered with a smile in her voice. Accepting the obvious compliment, she fervently hoped she would never be as vain as her grandmother.

"I had expected you to be a child." Lily laughed uncertainly. "A friend for Mignonne, but. . ." Her voice trailed away. "What a delightful fragrance! Lighter than jasmine."

"Hyacinth." Adrianna smiled. "Are you a connoisseur of perfumes?"

"No, no. We haven't had French perfume here lately. But I love flowers. Growing them is my favorite pastime."

Acknowledging introductions as Lily guided her about, Adrianna let her eyes drift. She quickly assessed the people to be a bit provincial. She wondered why. From what Grandfather had told her, Eufaula had been a prosperous riverboat town for fifty years. Cotton from surrounding plantations was shipped down the Chattahoochee River to the Gulf of Mexico, and goods were brought back from all over the world. Planters as well as merchants had filled the town with mansions.

As her family had driven along the streets, Adrianna had been impressed by the aloof grandeur of the homes, yet as she moved through the Wingates' home, she noticed that the windows had old lace curtains instead of fashionable draperies. Most of these ladies still looked like walking mushrooms in the hoop skirts of the prewar era.

Adrianna smoothed her taffeta skirt, proudly aware that it fell stylishly straight to her toes in front. Yards of matching satin swirled tightly across her stomach and puffed elegantly behind her in a bustle.

"I understand you played a great part in saving the town from the invaders' torch, Mrs. Ramsey." Senator Atherton's voice filled the room. "The cotton in the warehouses was saved, too, I presume?"

Adrianna turned casually, then blinked in surprise. The heroine he addressed was a placid, middle-aged woman with white-blonde hair. She acknowledged the senator's remark with a self-deprecating murmur. "I really didn't do that much—"

"Emma's swift action made the difference," interrupted a man whose devoted smile indicated that he must be her husband. "We were fortunate that her warning saved Eufaula from being burned and looted as so many parts of Alabama and your state of Georgia were, Sir."

Emma Ramsey smiled with contentment as the jovial man squeezed her shoulder. "We were lucky that General Grierson was a gentleman," she said in a quiet voice, "and waited for proof that the armistice had been signed."

Jonathan Ramsey raked his fingers through thick, iron-gray curls. "In answer to your other question, Sir, Grierson was not quite as kind as we first thought. On his march through Alabama, he saw three hundred thousand bales of cotton which he was good enough not to destroy." He laughed bitterly, but the crinkles around his eyes showed his unflagging humor. "When the war was over, however, Grierson jumped on our cotton like a duck on a June bug. He said he was determined to break the spirit of the town's aristocrats and their finances as well."

"We tried to help young Foy," interjected Harrison Wingate.

Adrianna gave her full attention.

"Help get his father's Cotton Exchange on its feet," he explained. "Foy had served two years in the Confederate Navy and, like all leading Southern men, was accused of treason and disfranchised. Ironically, some of us were given back the right to vote sooner than Foy because he held more than $20,000 in taxable property—held it briefly, that is. Grierson and the federal government confiscated every bale of his cotton."

Tears stung Adrianna's eyes as sympathetic understanding of the decay of Barbour Hall flooded through her. She looked toward the still-empty hallway. Their meeting no doubt had meant nothing to him, but she could think of no one but Foy Edwards.

Munching a tangy shrimp mousse offered to her by a butler, Adrianna turned back to the conversation. Harrison Wingate was explaining how his steamboat, *Wave,* had been deliberately sunk across the Chattahoochee to block the advance of the enemy.

Behind her ivory fan, Adrianna's cheeks blazed as she listened to the captain explain how he and Foy Edwards were building a new steamboat while fighting to get the river cleared. She had misjudged these people as behind the times. Now she listened with growing admiration for the spirit with which they endeavored to rebuild their lives. She wished she had not flaunted her expensive dress direct from the Paris salon of fashion leader Charles Frederick Worth.

Over her fan, Adrianna peered across the parlor to the doorway. She sniffed disgustedly. Foy was not coming.

Solicitously, she turned to help Ma-ma with the thin china teacup, which shook in her swollen fingers. Behind them raged a heated discussion about unbearable tax burdens. In some places, they had been increased by 500 percent. Talk of taxes meant little until she heard her grandfather's question.

"I say, Ramsey, don't you own a plantation in Georgia?"

"I did," he replied heatedly. "In Bulloch County. Everything at Magnolia Springs was completely destroyed during Sherman's ravaging march. The last I heard, it was being held for taxes. As if taxes had not been raised enough, I can only redeem my plantation by paying double the tax!"

Emma explained softly to Isadora and Adrianna, "His six-year-old daughter, Elizabeth, was there at the time. We could never find a trace of what happened to her."

Having been a child at home with her mother in Madison, Georgia, a town uniquely spared by General Sherman, Adrianna had thought little about the War Between the States in which more than half a million men had died and another half million had been wounded. She had never realized that these last few years of Reconstruction had been far worse for the South than war.

Again, her eyes drifted to the door. She saw that someone else was watching. Across the hall in the music room stood a petite beauty with hair as black and shining as a bird's wing. Attired in glowing pink velvet draped in a more fashionable polonaise, the girl looked like a French porcelain doll. Beneath flirtatious bangs, her snapping dark eyes guarded the door.

"We had hoped, Senator Atherton, that perhaps," Harrison Wingate's quiet voice demanded attention. "Perhaps, since Georgia has had three years with conservative government reestablished—and since honest voters have returned you and you've finally been reseated in the Senate—" Everyone in the room turned toward him as his voice shook with emotion. "If we don't have an honest election this time, maybe you could start a congressional investigation." Harrison turned his hands eloquently. "Being under a Federal Army of Occupation is not the bitterest pill, nor even having our elected officials controlled by Northerners come South with all their worldly goods in small bags made of carpet. The worst problems are from our corrupt city court judge, Elias Keils. Our crooked government is enriching a few and giving no protection to life and property. We fear for the safety of our families!"

Lily turned to Adrianna and her grandmother. "I do apologize, ladies, for having the party in the midst of a furor. I guess I'm just too sentimental. Our wedding day, November 3, 1858, was so special that I wanted to have our anniversary party today even though it was election Tuesday."

"That's quite all right, my dear." Isadora Atherton smiled regally. "We napped. We slept right through the disturbance."

Adrianna felt a blush rising and fanned rapidly. The quick calculation that the Wingates had been married for sixteen years surprised her. From the moment she had stepped into their home, she had felt their love.

The house of her childhood had been an echoing emptiness of chilly silences. Her parents had finally separated, and she had been shunted around among them and her grandparents.

Wistfully, Adrianna watched the tall, quiet man smile across the parlor into the lively eyes of his vivacious wife as if they were newlyweds. Folding her fan in her lap, Adrianna let her longing eyes assess them openly. Even as their harmony enveloped their guests, they seemed set apart by a special closeness. Adrianna's full lips quivered with desire to share that kind of oneness with someone special.

Laughter rippled around her. Adrianna shook herself and tried to listen to Jonathan Ramsey joke about the riot.

"And old Lige said that when the shooting started he eased up close to E. M. Bounds. 'I figured,' " Jonathan mimicked, " 'if they was any man in town the Lord would take care of it 'ud be the Reverend Mr. Bounds.' "

Chuckles broke off as his story was interrupted by a commotion in the entrance hall. The door burst open. A disheveled man entered and shouted the news: "There's been trouble at Old Spring Hill. The bullets found their mark in an innocent young man. He lies dying!"

Adrianna stiffened in horror as she saw Lily fling her hand to her throat and mouth the silent word, "Foy."

Chapter 3

Foy!" Adrianna inhaled his name. Wingate calmly moved through the room. Clapping his hand upon the man's shoulder, he gave a quiet command. "Get hold of yourself, Samuel. Slowly now. Who's wounded? What happened?"

"The boy. Not his father." Samuel shook with emotion. "Little Willie Keils."

Adrianna sank back against the settee, thankful that it had not been Foy. Taking a bracing sip of tea, she listened to the man's tale.

"The polls closed at five o'clock. Foy and I and several others were guarding—trying to help the Spring Hill folks keep the peace. Old Judge Keils had gone out there—"

"Yes." Harrison stopped the flow of details. "Just tell us what happened."

"Keils barred the door. The managers began counting the ballots. Suddenly a group of men made a rush, firing double-barreled shotguns as they ran. A clerk unlocked the door. They rushed in—knocked out the lamp. It was black as midnight. Shots were flying. I could've hit Foy myself."

"What?" Harrison shook him. "Foy's hurt?"

"Just nicked. He's all right. Doc Weedon's patching him up."

A collective sigh was released.

"It was Keils they were after. Some say little Willie threw himself in front of his father. It was easy to mistake a boy for such a slightly built man in the dark. Four bullets rained into the child. When the lamp was lit, the ballots were burning. Elias Keils was cowering in a corner with some of the mob ready to hang him. He begged Mr. Wallace as a lodge brother to save him. They respected Mr. Wallace—him and the pistols he held in each hand."

Samuel gulped another breath. Seeing Harrison's meaningful glare, he finished his story. "Bad as his lodge brothers hated his crookedness, they saved Keils by escorting him to jail. But I'm afraid little Willie's dying."

Adrianna had not heard the door open again, but suddenly there stood Foy. His left arm rested in a sling. Rising quickly, she started toward him.

The petite brunette who had also been watching stepped swiftly from the music room. She softly kissed Foy's cheek.

With an aching sigh, Adrianna drew behind a fern stand and watched miserably. No wonder he knew about French perfume.

"I'm fine, I'm fine!" Foy's deep voice assured Lily, who hurried to him and brushed his thick hair from his pale face with a trembling hand. "It's just a scratch. Really," he said, embarrassed.

Adrianna could read loving concern on the plain face of Emma Ramsey. *So all the women love him,* she thought. Adrianna wished she could touch his lean cheeks, smooth his furrowed brow. Surprised at this longing, she chided herself that Foy surely charmed every woman who met him. Adrianna leaned forward to catch Foy's words.

"Let's not disrupt your party, Lily," he said, forcing a smile. "Introduce me to your guests."

Adrianna could feel her cheeks betraying her as he crossed the parlor.

"I say, this must be the young man I've been hearing such good things about!" Her grandfather's voice resounded in Adrianna's ears as he stepped in front of her with his hand outstretched. "Distinguished career in the navy, I understand."

Foy shook the proffered hand and replied sardonically, "I'm afraid my most memorable act was striking the match to burn our gunboat, *Chattahoochee,* before the enemy could take her. But I did gain a love for the river," he continued earnestly. "We appreciate your coming, Sir. We have great plans." His voice rose with enthusiasm. "We hope you'll have time to see the steamboat we're building. She's a real beauty!"

Foy grinned at his own exuberance. "There's a promise of a good cotton crop this year, and if you can send us engineers to help clear the channel, this section of Georgia, Alabama, and Florida can make a comeback."

Adrianna struggled to regain her poise as her grandfather discussed the situation with Foy. At long last he turned to Isadora, who preened as the young man bowed before her.

"It's a great pleasure to meet you, Mrs. Atherton." Foy brushed a polite kiss over her majestically extended hand. "Word of your great beauty preceded you."

When Foy finally was presented to her, Adrianna managed to gaze disinterestedly at him.

"How delightful to meet you, Miss Atherton." His deep voice was coolly formal, but he pressed a genuine kiss upon her hand. His eyes twinkled merrily at her discomfort. With a sly wink, he asked, "Did I hear that you are a horsewoman?"

Adrianna's cheeks twitched as she tried to keep from laughing.

Foy turned and bowed again to Isadora. "Would you trust a stranger and accord me the honor of escorting your granddaughter on a ride about our city tomorrow afternoon?"

"I'd love to!" Adrianna blurted. Her high spirits bubbled as Isadora considered, then nodded. Meeting his warm gaze, Adrianna said mischievously, "I find staying in a hotel room quite confining." A giggle escaped and she looked away to control her mirth. The black-haired beauty stood clingingly behind Foy.

Realizing she had appeared anxious, Adrianna amended, "Perhaps another time." Biting her lip, she hesitated. "Your arm?"

The girl nudged Foy. Adrianna frowned, thinking her far too young for him.

"A scratch," he said, shrugging. "Shall I call for you at three?" He looked down at the girl who was pinching him. "Have you met Mignonne?"

"No," she replied coolly.

"Minnie, may I present Miss Adrianna Atherton."

"It's so exciting to meet you, Miss Atherton," she said, stretching her words into floating syllables like molasses sliding over a stack of hotcakes. "Living in Washington must be just marvelous."

Adrianna's jealousy melted slightly at the sincere admiration in the younger girl's manner. But she was not pleased when dinner was announced and she was seated with Mignonne far down the table from Foy and her grandfather. Making the best of it, she chatted pleasantly and answered the girl's endless questions.

Mignonne kept staring at her hair. "Whatever do you put on your hair to give it that stunning color?"

"Nothing!" Adrianna retorted. "Why would anyone want to dye their hair flaming red?"

Mignonne's dark eyes filled with tears. "I didn't mean to be rude, Ma'am."

Adrianna laughed lightly and patted the girl's hand. "That's all right. I'm sorry I sounded annoyed. It's just that I'm asked that so much! I should be used to it by now." She took a bite of candied sweet potatoes. "This is certainly a delicious meal."

She tried her best to be nice to Mignonne, but her attention kept drifting to Foy. She caught only snatches of conversation as he told the senator how he had drawn a detailed map of the river showing where hulls of sunken boats prevented passage. The men planned a morning meeting at the river to discuss securing an appropriation from Congress to clear the channel of the Chattahoochee, and the evening came to an end.

Adrianna donned her smartly tailored, brown riding habit early and prowled the hotel suite nervously. Gray mists had shrouded the morning with foreboding. She feared that Ma-ma would not allow her to go out on horseback if the weather did not clear.

A brisk knock sent her scurrying across the room. She threw open the door with a wide, welcoming smile.

There stood Mignonne.

"I hope," Foy said, peeping around the plume of Mignonne's riding hat, "that we haven't kept you waiting. Harrison, Senator Atherton, and I had so much business. Good afternoon, Mrs. Atherton. You're feeling well, I trust?"

Turning aside to hide her disappointment, Adrianna had no need for words.

Isadora swept forward from the adjoining bedroom.

"Yes, thank you," she cooed, as she commandingly extended her hand for him to kiss. "I find the atmosphere of your fair city as pure as mountain air." Her voice and intimate smile made it seem he had created it especially for her.

Putting on her narrow-brimmed hat and kid gloves, Adrianna watched her grandmother. Isadora had dressed in a becoming afternoon frock which matched her hair. For the first time, Adrianna suspected that Ma-ma used dye. Her artifice seemed lost upon Foy. Responding seriously, he explained he had brought Mignonne so that Mrs. Atherton need not worry they would be unchaperoned. He assured her that the disturbance seemed over for the time being.

Adrianna swallowed her resentment. Foy's apparent attraction had fooled her. His feeling toward her had been as shallow as everyone else's in her young life. The warm camaraderie between Foy and Mignonne spoke with swift eloquence that they cared about each other. Her cheeks pale, her green eyes wistful, Adrianna morosely followed them into a day which remained as gray as her mood.

Foy bowed elaborately as he helped them mount their horses. "And now we begin our tour of the famous Bluff City."

Mignonne chattered incessantly, pointing out beautiful churches and telling Adrianna about the people who lived in the various mansions.

Subdued, Adrianna commented on the beautiful Greek Revival houses, but she was accustomed to seeing such houses in her native Georgia. As they walked their horses beneath dripping trees along Randolph Avenue, she watched this pair so eagerly trying to entertain her. Of course, Adrianna was the granddaughter of someone important to Foy's business. He had amused himself yesterday by playing Sir Galahad.

With a sigh, she pulled her eyes from his strong, sharp profile and glanced up, up three stories to a cupola surrounded by a captain's walk. "This one's different," she said, struggling to be pleasant. "One doesn't expect to see Italianate architecture in the middle of the countryside."

"Actually, we're quite near the river," said Mignonne. "The Simpsons could watch their steamboats from up there. My mother—"

"I'm so glad you like this style," Foy interrupted, beaming at Adrianna.

"Yes." She felt warmed by his smile.

"Italianate architecture was in vogue during the 1850s when Eufaula was a flourishing shipping point." He spoke eagerly, openly relieved that she was interested again. "Cotton went to Europe, and returning boats brought French and English furniture and Italian marble. If we can just get a few problems resolved, it will be that way again!"

"You'll manage," she replied. "I've never known anyone as sure of what he wanted to do."

A slow smile spread over his serious face. "Come on. I want to show you Barbour Hall." He kneed his horse to a brisk canter.

Feeling safe with the sureness of his leading, Adrianna followed, the ribbons of her hat streaming as they rode along the river bluff. Exhilarated by the speed, she was sorry when they turned the corner at Barbour Street and slowed again.

"That's the Keils's house," Mignonne said in a stage whisper. "It has hand paintings on the walls and silver doorknobs!"

"And gold window cornices which match the pier mirrors," said Foy. "You can build in a grand manner when you're stealing tax revenue." He spat out his words bitterly.

Adrianna glanced up to the cupola.

Following her gaze, Foy said, "It's rumored there are holes in the cupola for rifles to shoot through. And see that door under the front steps? I've heard there's a secret passage on the first floor, and—uh-oh."

A woman's figure stirred in the high bay window.

"Let's move on. Everyone knows I was at Spring Hill. Mrs. Keils can't help her husband's bribes and crooked schemes. I sadly regret that the little boy is wounded."

As they approached Barbour Hall, small, cold drops of rain stung their cheeks. Foy spoke in a melancholy tone. "For ten years we've lived with lawlessness that has made gun-toting a necessity. My life has been standing still!"

The earnestness on his face melted the reserve Adrianna had thrown around her heart at the threat of Mignonne. Now she knew why so desirable a man had remained unmarried. Entering his home, she resolved that if he wanted nothing more, she would give him friendship.

"Oh, how beautiful!" she exclaimed in genuine appreciation as she stepped into the elegant spaciousness of the central hall. "It must be wonderful to have a place preserved through generations. I've never had a permanent home." For a moment she thought of all the places and people with whom she had stayed. She had never felt stable or secure. She shook off her wistfulness and smiled. "This marble floor is so dramatic!" She gestured across the black-and-white diamonds, which stretched the entire length of the house.

"I like the crown-of-thorns chandelier," said Mignonne softly. She pointed up to the ring of six-pointed stars stabbed with crystal thorns and hung with teardrops.

Casually Adrianna glanced at it, thinking that these people were a bit provincial in the way they brought religion into their everyday life.

She followed Foy to the right into the music room. "How lovely!" She clasped her fingertips together in delight. Crossing to the square, rosewood piano, she rippled a tune on the keys. "Who's the musician in the family?"

"Emma's the most accomplished." Foy smiled down at her, obviously pleased that she liked his home.

"Emma?" She paused, struggling to remember. "Ramsey? Your family?"

Foy laughed. "Of course. She's my aunt. She was Lily's chaperone. My nursemaid. Everyone loves Emma."

"Well, I declare," she murmured. As she absorbed the reason Emma had looked at Foy so lovingly, happiness swelled within her. With a flood of tenderness, she smiled at the thick hair curling around his ears.

Pointing at the crystal chandelier over the long mahogany table in the dining room, Foy stopped talking midsentence as if he could feel her eyes upon him. He turned, mistook her hands clasped to her heart, and said, "But you must be cold. Come to the fire."

Mignonne disappeared into the back hall as Foy ushered Adrianna across to the parlor.

Sitting gracefully on a small settee close to the white marble fireplace, Adrianna smiled at Foy as he dropped to one knee on the hearth. Dry oak logs lay smoldering, giving no warmth.

From a brass basket, Foy took a splinter of fat, lightwood kindling. "This fat li'dard will get a roaring fire going." He touched a match to the pine splinter. It flared. Quickly poking the blazing sliver between the logs, he sat back on his heels with satisfaction as rich pine tar sizzled fiery trails over the dry logs.

"I should have realized you'd be cold and wet." Foy looked up at her, his lean face full of concern.

"I'm fine," Adrianna assured him. Spreading her hands toward the flickering blaze, she leaned toward Foy. Leaping blue and yellow flames filled the fireplace and roared in her ears. Aromatic steam rose from the wet wool at Foy's shoulders. "I'm just. . .fine." Her voice dropped to a whisper.

"I'm sorry I didn't realize sooner that. . ." His breath caught as his dark eyes searched hers.

Tremulously, she met the force of his gaze. For a suspended moment, they remained dangerously close to the popping, crackling fire.

Shaken by the feelings setting her face aglow, Adrianna drew back from the blaze. She swallowed, tried to speak. "Really, I. . ."

Foy's face was close beside hers as he remained kneeling before her. He breathed deeply of her perfume. "I've questioned. . ." He gazed at her wonderingly and his hand lifted, trembled inches from her cheek. "Why my life has been suspended. Perhaps—" His voice broke huskily. "Perhaps, without knowing it, I've been waiting for you."

Motionless, Adrianna stared at him. Surely, she had misunderstood his whispered words. But, no, she could not mistake the feeling of his eyes caressing her face.

A rattle, a thump sounded from the hallway. Neither of them moved, but Adrianna slowly lifted her eyes to the image in the gold-leaf mirror behind Foy. Pushing the mahogany tea cart as if she owned it, Mignonne was speculatively eyeing them.

Sighing, Adrianna took the cup of tea that Mignonne poured with practiced skill. Bowing her head over the steaming brew, she took comfort from it as the scent of cinnamon and apples bathed her face. She must control her turbulent emotions. She had only known this man for twenty-four hours, yet she was falling in love with him.

"I have a surprise!" Foy's eyes twinkled as he set his cup on the mantel. "Something both you girls will love. Adrianna's grandfather has agreed to take a trip up the Chattahoochee! We're all going to see—"

"Ohhhh," cried Adrianna. "It sounds so exciting, but—" She sighed and gestured as she talked. "Ma-ma will never go."

"Yes, she will. Never fear. Foy is here."

Adrianna's eyes danced. It was not friendship she wanted from this man. It was love. The uncharted course before her might be as filled with rocks and hidden shoals as the treacherous Chattahoochee, but she was eager to face the dangers.

Chapter 4

Your grandmother will surely want to go," Foy said, "when I tell her that 'Le Sphinx,' starring Alice D. Lengard, will be opening at the Springer Saturday night."

Adrianna hesitated. "The Springer?"

"The Springer Opera House," he said quickly. "It was only built three years ago. Already it's known as the finest between New York and New Orleans. Harrison has reserved a box."

Mignonne clapped delightedly.

"However did you know that theater is the one thing Ma-ma could not resist?" Laughter bubbled in Adrianna's voice.

"I guessed." Foy smiled at her pleasure.

Companionably, they helped themselves to pastries and settled around the crackling fire to plan their trip. At last, Lige was summoned to bring around the carriage. They rode to the hotel through a downpour of cold, gray rain, but Adrianna's heart was filled with sunshine.

Rain continued the next morning. Cross from the pain the weather gave her, Isadora Atherton kept Adrianna jumping to satisfy her whims. By afternoon, Isadora had become peevish that no one was according her attention. When at four o'clock a knock sounded at the door to their suite, Adrianna was delighted to admit Lily Wingate.

After the customary small talk, Lily inclined her dark head and said sadly, "I've come from visiting Mrs. Keils."

"You did?" Adrianna asked in surprise.

"Sometimes you have to turn the other cheek," Lily said self-consciously. "I felt so sorry for her. Little Willie died just now. Our son, Harrison Junior, is nine. When I think how she must feel. . ." Her voice choked with sympathy. "Isn't it sad how often wrongdoing makes the innocent suffer?"

"What will happen to the scalawag?" asked Adrianna. "Or have they already strung him up?"

"Adrianna!" exclaimed Isadora, shocked.

"That's all right." Lily's tone assured her that she was not offended by youthful directness. "He's been taken to Montgomery where they'll begin impeachment proceedings."

Isadora patted her perfectly arranged hair disinterestedly and murmured,

"I'm sure there will be a congressional investigation. The senator will—" She broke off.

"Yes. Well." Lily nodded. "A fine, honest man, General Alpheus Baker, one of our war heroes, was running against him. Harrison says that when he is declared judge. . .maybe now our lives can begin again."

Foy's voice seemed to whisper in Adrianna's ear. *"I've wondered why my life has been suspended. Perhaps, without knowing it, I've been waiting for you."*

Slowly, she traced his initials on her cheek with the tip of her finger as she listened to his sister explaining the plans for the trip to Columbus, Georgia, at the head of navigation of the Chattahoochee.

"There has been plenty of rain upstream," Lily said in her bright, vivacious way. "The river is high and reasonably safe. You need not worry." She laughed lightly. "The year Harrison and I married, there was a drought. The river dropped so low that he had a terrible time getting here for our wedding."

Adrianna noticed how often and how lovingly Lily spoke her husband's name. She marveled again at the closeness of their marriage. It was hard to believe this young-looking woman had been married sixteen years and had a nine-year-old son.

Friday morning dawned crisp and clear. Thumbing through her extensive wardrobe, Adrianna decided to don the same bottle-green costume she had worn on Tuesday. She hoped it would remind Foy of their first meeting.

Excitedly, she helped her grandmother board the omnibus, which would take them to the steamboat landing. As they swung around the curving road, which descended the steep bluff, the *clang* of the bell and the high-pitched *wheet-wheet* of the whistle made her lean forward.

"They won't leave us, Adrianna." Senator Atherton laughed.

Suddenly they reached the clearing, and she could see the tremendous, flat-bottomed boat with its lower deck just above the water's edge. Other decks mounted up like stairsteps. Above all towered the smokestacks. Swinging between them, a sign proclaimed the name *New Jackson*. Passengers surged across the clearing, scrambled down the bank, and sprawled over the lower deck, heedless of the stevedores who strained bulging muscles to load the last of the freight. Separating from the group, Mignonne leaned far out over the rail and waved her handkerchief.

Uhmmm! Uhm! Uhmmmm! The deep, rumbling blast of the steamboat's whistle made Adrianna jump.

She felt his presence and turned. Foy smiled and said something that was swallowed by the whistle echoing and reechoing around them. They laughed. They had no need for words. Foy's eyes lighted as he drank in her appearance. His slight nod as his glance flicked over the vibrant green dress told her he remembered. Glad she had no need to speak, she mentally recreated the sensation of their flight on horseback, when she had been held tightly against him.

The crowd parted as her handsome grandparents moved grandly toward the gangplank. The distinguished-looking senator towered six inches above most of the men, whom he greeted with quick handshakes. Isadora Atherton's voluptuous figure, laced into an extremely full bustle, showed to perfection. Her high-billed bonnet completed the odd, goose-shaped fashion of the day.

Forgotten by her kin as usual, Adrianna lagged behind. Foy stepped closer in the crush of chattering people, grasped her elbow, and helped her over the gangway and up the stairs to the first-class deck.

The huge waterwheel at the stern of the boat strained, reversed, and backed the craft into the channel. Settling in to a rythmic *swish, swish, swish,* the wheel threw rainbow mists into the air and left a foaming white wake behind.

Dizzied by the movement and exhilaration, Adrianna grasped the wooden rail. Foy's hand brushed hers, as if accidentally, then settled two inches down the rail, far enough for decorum, but close enough to make the hairs on the back of her hand tingle.

"Direct your eyes straight ahead." He spoke softly as the boat glided in peaceful silence.

"Oh, it's glorious!" Enchanted, Adrianna stretched both hands toward the huge golden leaves of the sycamores, which knelt at the water's edge. Behind them, deep red sweet gums clung to the slope. Stalwart brown oaks lined the crest of the bluff that was Alabama. "There's a mysterious feeling," she exclaimed. "Like floating through fairyland."

Smiling at her with satisfaction, Foy replied, "Nothing quite matches the feeling of a paddle wheeler on a beautiful river. Look," he said, pointing. "Speaking of matching. . ."

She turned toward Georgia. The huge red ball of sun rising behind bottle-green pines set fire to translucent maple leaves. Tenderly, Foy reached one finger to brush a red-gold strand tumbling over her forehead. "Maple leaves in autumn," he whispered. "Springtime in my heart."

Adrianna glowed from the sunlight of happiness rising within her.

Weaving toward them from the bow of the boat, Mignonne came all achatter. Foy dropped his hand to the wooden rail. "Our steamer will have brass rails," he said enthusiastically. "White fretwork trim. Even a mahogany dance floor!"

"And guess what?" Mignonne interposed. "She's named for me!"

Adrianna felt as if the deck had collapsed. Voices sounded muted, hollow.

"I can't wait to get to the ironworks and show her to you!" Foy exclaimed.

"I'll bet Foy'll never call her Minnie." Mignonne stuck the tip of her pink tongue out at him. The conversation continued, but Adrianna had withdrawn into her own misery. Evidently, she had mistaken Foy's natural warmth and little-boy sweetness for romantic interest. If his boat were named for Mignonne, they must be engaged. Suddenly, she realized that they were watching her expectantly.

"I . . .uh," she stammered. "I guess I'd better. . . Ma-ma will be wanting me. Please excuse. . ." Head high, Adrianna walked quickly toward her grandmother. Even though the boat glided smoothly, she felt dizzy. Numbly she planned her only course. She would compliment their boat. She would attend the theater party. Then she would catch a train at Columbus and go home.

Mother wants me. That's what I'll say. She clamped her teeth resolutely. She could not bear a return trip near Foy in the romantic aura of the river if he were pledged to another.

She joined Isadora, who was reclining on a wicker chaise longue in the ladies' saloon.

"Mother has written for me to come home." The lie rolled from Adrianna's tongue, hot, bitter.

"I need you," Isadora snapped, obviously annoyed at the inconvenience it would cause her.

Trying to keep their tense voices from carrying to the other ladies, they argued. At last, Isadora consented to Adrianna's plan to leave from Columbus.

With both hands to her aching head, the girl realized miserably that her mother might not want to be bothered with her.

Just as she rose, murmuring that she wanted to lie down, Adrianna was thrown back. The steamer lurched. Wood splintered; women wailed.

"We're sinking," Isadora shrieked and fell back in a swoon.

Adrianna ran to a window and saw burly Captain Fry rushing below, his arms piled high with pillows and blankets.

"Mark my words," a sharp-faced woman beside Adrianna said with a sniff. "You will never feel safe with a Fry as captain!"

Startled, Adrianna raised quizzical eyebrows.

Thus encouraged, the woman continued in a gossipy voice, "Yes, my dear, didn't you know the Fry brothers were accused of being Yankee sympathizers?"

The boat dropped slightly and settled with a shudder. Adrianna rushed back to waft smelling salts beneath Isadora's nose. Should she take her grandmother to her cabin and loosen her corset? Frantically, Adrianna looked toward a large, motherly woman who smiled reassuringly.

"I think, ladies, that we should move outside to the rails in case quitting the boat becomes necessary," she said.

The sharp-nosed woman looked at the prostrate Isadora and sniffed disdainfully. "Don't upset yourself. The river here is shallow enough to wade. As I was saying, the Frys had their licenses suspended during the war. I always wondered—"

"Now, Gussie," interrupted another woman. "The Frys proved themselves innocent."

Adrianna was amazed that the seasoned travelers seemed interested only in gossiping. Conversation stopped when Dan Fry reappeared. "No cause for alarm, folks," he shouted. "She struck a snag, but we staunched the hole. Praise be, we're now grounded on a sandbar, and we'll have her fixed in jig time."

Astounded that the captain had saved his boat with mere feathers, wool, and sand, Adrianna noted the inadequacy of her own knowledge. Perhaps she could hold Foy's interest better if she knew more things outside herself.

Long after the hole was repaired, the *New Jackson* remained stranded in the shallow spot in the river. Plans were made to transfer the passengers to the *GWE Wiley*. Suddenly the river rose slightly from a freshet upstream, and the flatboat lifted from the sandbar.

That afternoon, with the boat under way, Lily joined Adrianna and Isadora on the shady side of the deck. Her rosy-cheeked son, whom everyone called Beau, asked permission to go to the pilothouse. Watching his bobbing, sun-streaked hair as he scampered up the stairs, Adrianna thought tenderly that his Uncle Foy must have looked like him.

Breaking her mood, Mignonne plopped into the chair beside her.

"I'm so glad Papa let me stay out of school," Mignonne said. "It's the first time I've ever met anyone sophisticated like you."

Adrianna laughed. The girl would be surprised to know just how unsure of herself she felt. "School?" she murmured. "I thought you'd finished." Her eyes came into focus on the beautiful girl, and she asked, "How old are you?"

"Fourteen."

"I'd guessed sixteen, you're so lovely—seventeen, even."

"She is blossoming early," said Lily.

For a moment Adrianna's hopes rose. Clearly, Mignonne was too young for Foy. But he could have fallen in love with her and be waiting for her to make her debut, to present herself at the marriageable age of sixteen. Obviously there was warmth between them. She rubbed her glare-dazzled eyes and tried to turn her attention to where Lily was pointing.

"Look, look!" Lily gestured as the steamboat nudged through a tunnel of trees and slid beside a clearing. " 'Look on the fields; for they are white already to harvest.' " she quoted. Then she added softly, "But the laborers are few."

Puzzled, Adrianna moved to the rail to see. She stared across a field of cotton. It was snow white, certainly, yet many workers moved through the rows.

"Don't mind Lily." Foy's deep voice vibrated behind her ear. "She knows a Scripture for every occasion."

Adrianna could see fondness and pride in the look Foy gave his sister. She coughed to cover her embarrassment that she had not known Lily was quoting the Bible. This family's faith seemed such a deep and abiding part of their lives that she feared their derision because of the little religious training she had received.

Foy joined her at the rail, and together they leaned toward the entrancing view. Pickers passing down rows on one side of the field began a chanting song. An answering melody came from deep, rolling voices in another group, and the chant rippled back and forth across the field. The music drifted over the water and encircled the young couple.

Smiling up at Foy's face, Adrianna said, "I wish I could paint that scene."

"You're an artist?"

"Oh, no. But I'd like to be. Perhaps I should study. I just haven't decided."

Foy smiled down at her and said lightly, "It's important to have a goal." He laughed and gestured. "Of course, I probably have too many. But when I see a field of cotton like that, I have hope. Some of the planters are getting land that was overgrown during the war back in shape for a bumper crop. If I can buy and store their cotton and then ship it myself as well—"

"I thought the *Mig,* er, your steamer, was for luxury travel."

"That's just the cream." Foy laughed. "It's shipping freight that pays the bills. You see, if we can get into both sides of the business. . ." Foy's eyes burned as he shared his plans and dreams.

That evening at dinner, the senior members of the party sat at Captain Dan Fry's table. Adrianna, Mignonne, and Foy joined a younger group. Adrianna bit into crisply battered fried chicken. Roasted venison was passed next. Oysters were served in abundance. She lost track of what she ate as, through the many courses, Foy joked and teased.

After dinner, the laughing group moved into the grand saloon for dancing. With Foy's arms whirling her giddily in a waltz and music filling her senses, Adrianna forgot Mignonne, forgot everything but the thrill of Foy's touch and his strong hand holding hers.

At last, breathlessly, they went onto the deck to cool. Stars twinkled magically around them. The boat tugged slightly at her mooring.

"Your eyes are like the Chattahoochee," Foy said softly. "Ever changing. At supper they were as blue and soft as your gown. Now they're dark as the night river." He leaned closer.

His breath was warm and sweet against her face, for moments measured by moonbeams. The melody of the rushing river as it paused to play among the rocks intensified her longing for his love. Her innocent lips trembled as she lifted her face toward his and hoped for his kiss.

Voices drifted around them. Foy straightened, moved away.

"But this morning," he said and laughed shakily, as time began again to tick. "This morning your eyes were like the river at its clearest—green!"

"Green as envy," she laughed ruefully, "when I heard you'd named your boat for Mignonne. Don't you think—" She frowned, suddenly angered that the enchanted moment had been shattered by people spilling around them.

"That's silly!" Astounded, Foy stared at her. "I couldn't know I'd meet you and fall—"

"That fourteen is too young for—" The tart sound of her voice surprised her, but it continued. "You must be all of twenty-five."

"I'm twenty-eight," he said between stiff lips. "And you?"

"Eighteen, nearly nineteen!"

Surprise showed on his face. "I thought you nearer my age. You're so sophisticated."

A harsh laugh rattled in her throat as he used Mignonne's term. "Oh, I've traveled a lot." *From one parent to another,* she thought bitterly. Fighting tears, she seemed unable to keep her manner from chilling into haughtiness. Like a falling star, their shimmering closeness plummeted, extinguished.

"Foy. Foyee, come on." Mignonne was tugging at his hand. "Miss Adrianna, they're wanting everyone to line up for a cotillion."

The next day Foy joined Adrianna on deck. "We're nearly to Race Pass," he said with a serious expression, which seemed to shut her out. "I'll show you the grave of the *Chattahoochee*."

"The river's grave?" Puzzled by his words and his distant attitude, she lifted her eyebrows.

"Our gunboat," he said in a voice of deep melancholy. "We had to sink her to keep the Yankees from taking her."

Suddenly the huge paddle wheels shuddered to a stop. Adrianna leaned over the rail to peer through the muddy water. She could see only a tip of the sunken hull, and she watched breathlessly as the *New Jackson* grazed slowly by it with a horrifying scraping sound.

"Whew!" Adrianna whistled. "I hadn't understood what you meant about the dangers of obstructions. I do now!"

"She's waiting to drag another streamer down with her, all right," Foy replied dourly.

"How did you get away after you sank her?"

"Escaping the Yankees was no problem. We were a crew with no ship." He rubbed his furrowed eyebrows. "Some of us went west to try and join General Nathan Bedford Forrest. We didn't know the war was over. I was gone when

Emma needed me most. I always seem to have bad timing." He regarded her with an unreadable look and repeated, "Bad timing."

That evening in the finest hotel in Columbus, Georgia, Adrianna dressed with care. Wanting to restore the light in Foy's eyes, she chose a lavishly draped gown of lustrous pink satin. As she brushed perfume on her warm skin, she was glad that the pink from too much sun had faded to a golden glow. Pulling on elbow-length, white kid gloves, she appraised herself from every angle. A small tiara was fastened into the crown of sparkling curls piled high upon her head. She looked taller, older. Her reflection in the looking glass pleased her until she leaned closer and noticed six new freckles marching across her nose.

When she entered the hotel lobby, Foy's face lifted in delight.

"Good evening, fairy princess." Foy inhaled appreciatively and bowed to kiss her fingertips. As he slowly lifted his head, his dark eyes touched lingeringly on each new freckle with the feel of a kiss. He chuckled softly.

"Good evening," drawled a honeyed voice.

Reluctantly, they turned. Mignonne bobbed a curtsy to Adrianna's elegance. Her long curls bounced like coffee-colored springs.

" 'Lo, Miggie," Foy said. He reached out and tugged a curl.

"Not Miggie," the girl wailed in mock horror. "Minnie's bad enough!" She wrinkled her pert nose at him.

Adrianna withdrew from them into her soul. As she moved mechanically to the waiting carriage, she felt achingly alone. Whenever she and Foy snatched a private moment, she felt certain that Foy was as overwhelmed with passion as she. But an intangible snag seemed to jut between them each time they drew near. If he were pledged to Mignonne, the only honorable thing for her to do was leave. *Tomorrow,* she thought resolutely as she stepped from the carriage in front of the Springer Opera House.

Emerging in their private box, she looked about the theater and exclaimed, "Why, it's just like Ford's Theater in Washington!"

"I'm so glad you approve," Foy said. Holding a velvet chair at the brass rail for her, he then seated himself close behind.

Adrianna tried to concentrate on Mrs. Lengard's fine acting, but each time Foy leaned forward to comment, his breath was warm against her bare shoulder.

As the first act's crisis gripped everyone's attention, Adrianna had the uneasy sensation someone was watching her. Looking down into the darkened theater, she could distinguish no one; however, outlined against the gold box by the lights from the stage, her bright hair and pink dress were clearly visible.

When the houselights came up at the end of the act, she saw him just as his gaze turned toward Lily. His features had the chiseled perfection of a Greek statue.

Adrianna noticed Lily blushing, her poise obviously shaken. Adrianna's own skin reddened when the man's attention returned to her. His eyes roamed lazily over her, causing her to feel that he could see the flowers embroidered on her corset cover. Flapping her ivory fan angrily, she snapped her head around.

Harrison Wingate, always unperturbable, acknowledged the man with a quick salute, but when his hand dropped to his side, his fist clenched.

Mignonne's response was innocence, Isadora's experience, Senator Atherton's a jovial façade. Foy Edwards puzzled her most. The reddened tips of his ears and the knitting of his heavy brows betrayed anger.

Adrianna heard none of the second act. Although she kept her face coolly turned toward the stage, she could feel the man's eyes often upon her. She kept wondering who this irritating, fascinating man could be who had everyone in their box sitting on a razor's edge of emotion.

When the houselights came on for intermission, he had disappeared.

Chapter 5

Gaslights illumined the theater. A babble of voices floated up to their silent box. The private door opened. He entered.

Tension crackled. After a long moment, Harrison leaned around his wife, offering his hand. Ignored, his big hand seemed to hang suspended.

The man's golden curls bobbed in a curt nod. He laughed. "Harrison, old man, still trying to be the stalwart steamboat captain, I heah." His cultured voice had the unmistakable accent of Charleston. He laughed again and swiftly thrust out his hand to shake Harrison's now-limp fingers.

Quickly he turned his gaze upon Lily. "Why, Lily, Honey," he said, grasping both her shoulders and holding her back in genuine admiration. "What a beautiful woman you've become!" He kissed her warmly on the cheek.

Obviously flustered, Lily stammered, "Why, Green, how—what a surprise! I. . .we'd heard you were no longer in cotton—"

"No, cotton factoring is not the most lucrative. . ."

"Humph!" Foy snorted close behind Adrianna's ear. "The way he practiced it, filthy lucre is more the word!"

Over her concealing fan, Adrianna noted the man's elegantly tailored clothes. Although he was a few years older than Foy, he remained trim. Only a slight puffiness around his eyes and a glazed look indicated dissipation.

He finished answering Lily and turned toward Adrianna.

"I'm forgetting my manners," Lily said quickly. "Senator and Mrs. Atherton, may I present my distant cousin, Green Bethune." Her voice flattened. "From South Carolina."

"Senator Atherton, I'm honored to make your acquaintance, Sir." He shook hands quickly, then interrupted the senator's reply to bow over Isadora's fingertips. "And yours, beautiful lady. And this must be your daughter."

Isadora's delicate face could not hide her gratification at the compliment to her agelessness. "Adrianna, Dear." She slipped her arm around Adrianna's waist and imperceptibly shoved her forward. "Mr. Bethune."

"Miss Adrianna!" He kissed her hand correctly. "What a lovely name!" He smiled familiarly as he squeezed her fingers in private greeting.

A thrill of excitement quivered over her at his obvious interest and the tangible jealousy from Foy who stood fuming behind her. Adrianna flashed her most dazzling smile and cooed, "How do you do, Mr. Bethune. Don't I detect the voice of Charleston?" She withdrew her hand.

"Do you know our city?" he replied eagerly. "She's suffered greatly, but she's still the center of our *beau monde!*"

"Oh, I quite agree, Sir," Adrianna said coyly. Batting her eyelashes in an inviting glance, she thought that if this charming older man paid her court, Foy should reconsider his concerns about their age difference. Searching for something to hold Green's attention, she let honey drip from her words. "I do adore Charleston's fine old houses and gardens. It's just marvelous they weren't destroyed in that awful war—"

"Green," Lily interrupted. "You do remember Foy? And this—"

"Well, well, he's grown a yard since I've seen him." Green Bethune laughed mirthlessly as he nodded to Foy. His eyes slid past him to the beautiful girl.

"And this," Lily repeated, "is our daughter, Mignonne. Young Harrison is at the hotel—in bed, I hope."

Mignonne extended her hand prettily, but her lip protruded petulantly at Green's words.

"What a pretty child," he said. "So like your mother when I knew her."

Gaslights dimming signaled the last act was about to begin. Bethune turned quickly to include the whole group. "You all must be my guests for a late supper after the play. No, I insist." He waved down their protests. "I won't take no for an answer." As he left their box, Green Bethune's eyes once again swept over Adrianna, devouring her.

Thankful for the darkness, Adrianna sank miserably into her chair. She had led him on. Deliberately! It was as if she had imitated Isadora. Hot color drained from her cheeks as she realized what she had let jealousy do to her. From the corner of her eye, she could see Foy's fist clenching and unclenching. Mignonne's proprietary air over Foy had made her feel threatened. She had seen Mignonne as another woman. Peeping around her fan at Mignonne, she now saw a pouting child, a child with a crush on an adored uncle.

Squirming, she thought the show would never end, yet she feared its conclusion. She had begun a flirtation with this worldly man that she lacked experience to handle.

Adrianna's long fingernails bit into her palms. She felt certain that Foy had been falling in love with her. What must he think of her now?

In the fashionable restaurant, Adrianna sipped coffee and toyed with rich, chocolate pie. Green Bethune had managed to seat her beside himself. She gazed beseechingly at Foy, but he sat with Mignonne at the far end of the table.

Most of the conversation flowed between Green Bethune and Senator Atherton, both of whom were accustomed to dominating any gathering. Saying nothing, behaving as inconspicuously as possible, Adrianna was careful to turn no inviting glances upon Green. She barely listened until he raised his voice to claim everyone's attention and explain his reason for being in Columbus.

"Of course, I still have my shipping line to Liverpool," Green said. "But until cotton regains its kingship, I'm dabbling in insurance, helping out a firm from New York City."

"How did that come about?" asked Harrison, trying to ease a noticeably tense situation.

Green laughed. "Since the War of Northern Aggression, some Northern insurance companies have given positions to Southern war heroes." He paused to let his audience absorb his intimation. "To create goodwill in the South. It's taken a great deal of work to pay off claims on Confederate dead and reinstate lapsed policies."

Adrianna noticed Foy muttering something to no one in particular. She tried to catch his eye, but he would not look at her. Sitting stiffly with a false smile fixed upon her face, she jumped as she heard her name mentioned.

"Mrs. Atherton, may I have your permission to call upon Miss Adrianna tomorrow?"

Isadora responded to Green's charm. "I would be delighted for such a fine gentleman to call." She tilted her head coyly. "But this independent child is leaving us tomorrow."

Stricken, Adrianna sat staring at her plate. She scarcely knew how she endured the rest of the evening.

As they left the restaurant, Foy brushed against her. "You're leaving? I thought you promised to see my steamboat!"

"I did. I'm going to," she answered in a small voice. "Foy, I must explain."

Suddenly everyone was moving purposefully, saying good night, sweeping them apart.

Feeling that winter had descended, Adrianna dressed warmly in aquamarine velvet with white fur trim. Weak and sick from crying, she peered in the mirror at her red, swollen eyes and blotched face. She would never see Foy after this morning, and this was how he would remember her. If he remembered her.

"Oh, Foy, I love you so much!" she whispered.

Images of his face when first they met moved slowly as she savored the bittersweetness. He had felt the same impact. He had fallen in love with her, but in anger and jealousy she had retreated into icy silence.

How often had her father taken her by the shoulders and said, "Adrianna, you're becoming moody again. You're holding things inside and your attitude is growing worse each day. Let it out."

They would talk out her problems. She would cry, feel better, be her sunny self again. If only she could talk with him now. The rest of the family loved her in their own ways, but her father listened. Since her parents had separated, she did not even know where he was.

The rattling of a table being rolled into the sitting room told her breakfast had arrived. Time was running out.

The sitting room was filled with Senator Atherton's voice as he conferred with aides. Isadora lounged in a French negligee, seemingly unperturbed that everyone else was dressed to go out.

"You're not going?" asked Adrianna, suddenly fearful that she would miss seeing Foy this last time.

"It's just another steamboat." Isadora shrugged.

"But I promised to. . ." Her voice broke.

"Oh, you can go with your grandfather," Isadora said brusquely, noticing Adrianna's crestfallen face. "But I'm entirely too fatigued to wear myself out further when I won't be having you to—oh, my poor, poor fingers," she wailed and displayed a trembling hand.

"Oh, Ma-ma, let me stay with you! Oh, not this morning. I mean, stay. You need me—I'll telegraph Mother that I'm not coming, and. . ."

Isadora eyed her thoughtfully. "I'd like to have you." She wavered. "But, no. She's expecting you. Arrangements have been made. Your traveling companion, Mrs. Cristie, will be here at noon. I'm sorry, Adrianna, but you're always changing your mind and now it's too late!"

The steamboat floated like a white palace. Emblazoned between towering black smokestacks was the name *Mignonne Wingate* and the emblem of a descending dove. Adrianna bit her lip.

Hand high over his head, Foy waved. He bounded over the gangway to her side. "You came!" he cried. "Tell me you're not leaving."

"I—" She searched his face. If only he would speak the words she longed to hear. "I asked Ma-ma to let me stay." She swallowed. "But she said arrangements. . .I want to stay with—I want to ride the *Mignonne*—Oh, Foy, I've acted so silly! I thought you were engaged to her, and—"

"What?" He twisted his face incredulously. "Good grannies, Woman!" As the senator's group came on board, Foy gestured wildly, sorely torn. Jerking a nod toward Harrison, who escorted the men down the deck, Foy grasped Adrianna's elbow and muttered, "Let's go somewhere we can talk. I'll show you the pilothouse."

Silently, they climbed the tiers of decks to the glass tower. Alone at last, they stood a pace apart not knowing what to say.

Foy broke the painful silence. "How could you think I was engaged to a child I've loved and cared for since birth?"

"I could see you loved each other, but—"

"You know Lily is my sister."

"She's so young-looking. Mignonne is so beautiful. Remember, I met you all during the riot, and with her hanging on your arm all the time and—and the boat named for her, how could I know she was your niece? I assumed you were betrothed. That's why I had to lie about—"

"Lie?" Foy's brows, which had begun to relax with understanding, knitted again.

With tear-filled eyes, Adrianna searched his serious face. If only he would gather her in his arms and let her cry out her heartache as Papa had done. Miserably, she looked down at her clasping hands and mumbled, "I had to get away. Loving you. . ." She swallowed. "Seeing you pledged to another—I had to make up that my mother had sent for me."

The wind whistled through the door of the pilothouse. Adrianna shivered, leaning hopefully toward Foy. He said nothing. Slowly she raised her head. His hands hung limply at his sides. Unreadable emotions played over his face. She longed to trace his cheekbone with her fingertips, to kiss the reddened rims of his ears. In his smoldering eyes, she saw pain.

His voice broke huskily when at last he spoke. "We need time—time together. I've got such plans. Can't you. . ." Hesitantly, his hands came up and grasped her shoulders. He looked down into her face and said urgently, "Can't you explain? Stay here!"

"The arrangements are made. My grandfather is a benevolent Santa Claus at times. At others, he's as hard and unyielding as—God. He'd make me go to punish the lie."

Foy frowned. "I don't agree with your concept of God. But, Adrianna, any lie is always wrong, always causes hurting, and—"

She wrenched from his grip. "What is truth?" She twisted her mouth scornfully.

"Truth is—Adrianna, don't get off on a tangent. I can't quote you chapter and verse like Lily does, but I know Jesus said, 'I am the way, the truth.' There are so many things we need to talk about." Foy's strong, tanned hands cupped her trembling cheeks as he whispered, "Oh, my beautiful Adrianna, please—"

"Good morning, you two," a cheery voice sang out from the deck below.

"Green!" Foy spat out the word as he dropped his hands.

"Who is that man?" Adrianna stamped her foot.

"Mama had arranged for Lily to marry him, but Lily had the good sense to choose Harrison. Green shot Harrison in a duel!"

Shocked, Adrianna recoiled. Foy's sharp features were frozen in fury. His heavy brows were drawn down, shutting her out. She began to shake as she realized she had told Foy she loved him, yet he had made no such declaration. With a flip of her veil, she turned her back.

As the door opened and Green Bethune entered the pilothouse, Adrianna smiled, smiled far too much. Because Foy seemed to hate this man, she put a false warmth into her voice. "Good morning, Mr. Bethune!"

He doffed his round, hard hat and bowed over her hand, kissing it lingeringly. "How delightful to see you. I rose early this morning hoping to catch you before you left. Your hat and gown remind me of the waters and warmth of the gulf. Have you taken the cruise down to the bay?"

"I—no, I haven't seen it." She withdrew her hand and tucked it into her white fur muff. "I'd hoped to take an excursion while. . ." She peered over Green's shoulder, beseeching Foy.

The tautness of his skin over the sharp bones of his face bespoke hurt pride, cold anger. Suddenly he whirled, stalked to the door, and stamped down the steep stairway.

She would not want Foy shot in a duel, but she was disappointed that he was not staying to fight his adversary. Speaking loud enough to carry, she flung out, "I think perhaps I'd rather go to New York."

"Winter in the city is a cultural enrichment." Green nodded. "Perhaps I could escort you to the theater."

Foy dropped from sight.

Edging uneasily away from Green Bethune, Adrianna stared down at a lone dogwood tree on the riverbank. Green followed her to the window, but suddenly his intimate manner changed. "I admire your independent spirit," he said seriously. "You call to mind Susan B. Anthony, and I thought—"

Flattered, Adrianna turned. Perhaps this man understood her. "She is my idol. How did you guess?"

Smoothly, he preened his side whiskers. "I suspected as much. As a champion of women's rights, she works against laws which keep women from achieving financial independence. A friend of mine sold her a life insurance policy back in 1855."

Adrianna looked at him in surprise. "I didn't know women bought life insurance."

"Few realize the power of this avenue to money, the available collateral. I felt that if apprised of the opportunity, you would want to buy a policy."

Adrianna's mouth dropped open as he quickly took papers from a case. *What a vain and foolish creature I've been in thinking his interest personal!* She laughed harshly. "I'm sorry to disappoint you, Mr. Bethune, but I have no funds whatsoever."

"You jest." He touched a finger to her fur collar. "Let me explain how—"

"Mr. Bethune, I have no money at all. My grandfather lavishes presents to bring credit upon himself. If I want something, I have to justify—"

"That is exactly the reason women need—"

"Mr. Bethune," she said icily, "I don't have a penny to call my own." She stepped from the tower with as much dignity as she could muster.

Cold wind whipped her veil. Clutching her hat as she descended to the hurricane deck, Adrianna headed toward the sound of her grandfather's voice. Trailing after his party, which Foy was now leading, she said nothing. When she occasionally looked out from the icy recesses of her soul, the proud indifference she saw on Foy's averted profile chilled her to the marrow.

Like a sleepwalker, Adrianna moved through the rest of the morning until she found herself at the train depot. Suddenly, a hiss of steam swirled around Adrianna's skirt. She had stumbled too close to the iron locomotive. A flying cinder seared her eye. Crying out, stopping to dig at it, she was tugged through the train depot by Mrs. Cristie.

"Wait. Wait. Please wait," she begged. Looking back over her shoulder, she ached to see Foy, to hear one word that would give her hope. Dragging her feet, she was jostled by the hurrying crowd. A rattling baggage cart ran over the end of her skirt. Was that Foy she saw?

The conductor lifted her elbow, propelling her aboard.

Hands and nose pressed to the window, she peered out. Joyfully, she saw that it was Foy striding toward her! Behind him a dark head—Mignonne? No, Lily. Suddenly he stopped. Adrianna rose. With a great screeching, the train jerked forward. Slamming into the unyielding seat, she cried out in pain. Tears unleashed, she peered again through the vibrating window. She saw Foy growing ever smaller, arm held high, waving good-bye.

Chapter 6

Foy banged his fist against the baggage cart. "What an idiot I've been," he growled. Shaking his smarting hand, he looked despairingly after the train.

Lily stood quietly beside him until the roar and rattle subsided. With warm sympathy in her eyes, she replied, "Yes, little brother, I'm afraid so. Tell me now, why did we come to see Adrianna off and not speak to her?"

"I don't know," Foy said miserably. He plunged both hands into his sun-streaked hair. "I've never felt so. . ." He let out a disgusted snort, and his voice deepened reflectively. "From the moment I looked down at that blazing red hair and saw her walking down the street into danger. . ." His ears reddened and he grinned ruefully. "I'll admit I was smitten." He shrugged. "But then I realized I'm way too old for her. It's best she's gone."

Foy grasped Lily's elbow to guide her through the bustling depot, but she stood firmly. "You're not that old, Foy. You just never had a chance to be young. You were a child when you went off to war. It was seeing so many men die that makes you feel—Foy, you didn't let Adrianna go without telling her you love her?"

Foy groaned noncommittally. "But do I? One minute she's so warm, so full of humor." He turned from Lily. "Then she slips away into—" He lifted tense shoulders in puzzlement, then dropped them in defeat. "I can't tell what she's thinking. I want to believe she feels what I feel. But then she turns a smile on Green that would melt an avalanche."

"She loves you," said Lily with conviction. She laughed lightly. "I was beginning to think my baby brother would never fall in love."

"Yeah." He ducked his head. "I'd steeled myself against the local belles. I can't afford to get married. Not with every penny tied up building the *Mignonne*."

"I know." Lily sighed and patted his arm. "And I'm sorry about the confusion over Mignonne. To us she's still a child. It's time we realized."

"I thought I was doing the right thing taking her along." Foy smoothed his wild hair. "Thought I was providing a proper chaperone, but Adrianna's probably too worldly to—"

"No, I doubt that."

"You like her, then?" Foy looked at Lily eagerly. "I was afraid you—she's been raised so differently."

Lily laughed delightedly. "Of course I do. You know I love people for the good I see in them. The poor child's been spoiled and confused. Anyone who had to live with that Isadora Atherton. . ." Lily's voice became an icy hiss.

Foy chuckled. "Still jealous!" He wagged a teasing finger, then sobered. "I suppose it doesn't matter what we think. Adrianna's so wealthy and I. . . Sister, I can't even afford her fancy French perfume!"

"What she needs is love she can count on, love that won't be snatched away," said Lily sadly. "She has a natural *joie de vivre* that I found charming, but the loneliness in her eyes hints that she's never found the joy of committing her life to the Lord. I'd welcome the opportunity to counsel her. You know how strongly I feel that a Christian should marry a person who is Christian if the marriage is to have a lasting foundation."

Silently they walked out of the noisy depot.

Foy made a harsh, sorrowful sound. "You want to save her soul and I want. . ." He shook his head disgustedly. "We let our chance go by. The one love of my life, and I'll never see her again!"

Pacing the deck of the *Mignonne Wingate,* Foy tortured himself for all the things he could have said. He had let Green Bethune's wealth diminish him to the speechless anger he had felt sixteen years earlier when Green had tried to captivate Lily. Witty words crowded Foy's mind now that it was too late.

He crossed the freight deck and stepped down into the engine room where workmen stood laughing and talking.

"Hey, boys, we've got to get these boilers installed." Foy tried to push pleasantly. If the steamboat had been more nearly completed, he would have felt freer to offer Adrianna his love.

Frustrated at the slow progress, Foy climbed to the pilothouse. He gripped the seven-foot wooden steering wheel until his knuckles whitened. Foy had longed to be a river pilot from the moment Captain Harrison Wingate had fired his twelve-year-old enthusiasm with the challenges of unexpected adventure on the river. Even the boiler explosion on the gunboat *Chattahoochee* had not shattered his dream. Because Jonathan Ramsey's wound sustained in the disaster had led to the amputation of his foot, Foy felt pleased to give him the job of managing the Edwardses' Cotton Exchange.

Free to follow his dream, Foy had learned the pilot's craft at the hand of a master, Bose Marcrum. Eager, intense, Foy had advanced quickly from the apprenticeship known on this river as a striker pilot. For top certification he had been required to draw from memory a detailed map of the river from Columbus to Apalachicola Bay. Now he looked with pride at the wall where he had hung his license.

He was ready to live his dream. If only the workmen would keep the hammers banging. Frustrated, he plunged his fingers into his hair. *And still the river needs clearing!*

Sighing deeply, Foy seemed to smell the lingering scent of hyacinths in the small enclosure. His brows drew down in a frown. Could this life ever make a sophisticated woman like Adrianna content?

Sometimes Adrianna seemed so happy. Her voice sounded like a smile. Suddenly he remembered its painful tone as she confessed her lie. "I had to get away," she had said. "Loving you. . ." Loving you! He leaned his head against the wheel and groaned. With nothing to offer her, he had left her precious words floating between them, unanswered.

Disgusted with himself, Foy pounded his fist against the wheel. *Then that bragging idiot Green oiled his way between us like he did Lily and Harrison!*

Distraught, Foy stamped down to the grand saloon where the mahogany dance floor had just been finished. Throwing aside his coat and rolling up his sleeves, he dropped to his knees and briskly rubbed in beeswax.

Exhausted by bedtime, Foy felt calmer. He wrote a long, ink-stained letter to Adrianna pouring out his desire to marry her when he could become established. Satisfied, he fell asleep. At midnight, he awakened and ripped the letter to shreds. At two o'clock, he wrote a careful, chatty letter, merely signing it, "I love you." At daybreak, he realized he could not mail it. He did not know where Adrianna had gone.

Lily passed breakfast ham to a downcast Foy. "Senator Atherton and Isadora have returned to Washington," she said.

Harrison looked at him seriously. "The senator's arranging for us to testify at a hearing. He feels certain the time is right for a Congressional appropriation to clear the channel."

"Y'all go," Foy mumbled without looking up. "I'll stay and try to push some work out of the men."

"You might need this while we're gone," Lily added.

Foy unfolded the paper she thrust into his hand and read the Madison, Georgia, address of Adrianna's mother. He grinned at his sister. Lily never moped and moaned. She made things happen.

After posting his letter, Foy threw himself into work with a fury. Daily his hopes rose at mail time. Daily he was disappointed.

On the eighteenth of December, a telegram came. Fearful that some mishap had befallen Adrianna, Foy ripped it open.

FIRE. WAREHOUSE TEN. 750 BALES LOST. COME.
JONATHAN

Foy moaned. Dangling his hands between his knees, he sat staring into space. That warehouse had been his insurance against disaster.

Throughout the journey back to Eufaula, Foy berated himself. Perhaps he should decide if he were a cotton factor or a river pilot. Should he stay behind his father's old desk and be ready to take advantage of the constantly fluctuating market instead of following his dream of the river?

When he reached home and came in sight of the Cotton Exchange, Foy's shoulders lifted and his chest swelled with pride. He would not let the frustration Green had caused sway him from his goal. He would remain a cotton broker, buying bales from the farmers. One day he would be more than just the middle-man. He would also own the river packets on which the bales were taken to Apalachicola Bay to be transferred to oceangoing vessels bound for the cotton mills of Lancashire. Determined, Foy strode into his father's old office.

Jonathan sat slumped behind the enormous desk. Seeing Foy, he said bitterly, "I've failed you, Boy!"

"Nonsense! What happened?"

"I thought if J. G. Guice could come back from the war with his good right arm gone and become one of the South's best samplers and graders of cotton, that surely I. . ." He wiped his red nose. "I'm no good as a cotton factor. Maybe the Lord is trying to tell me something!"

"Fires happen. You know how often cotton will catch fire at the gin and smolder from the inside of the bale for weeks before air strikes and it flames."

"Yes. . ." Jonathan blew his nose and struggled to control his emotions. "That's what most folks tell you, but. . ."

"Did you try soapy water? It will penetrate when plain water will roll off."

"With this fire we didn't have a chance. Come on. You might as well see for yourself."

The distinctive smell of burning rags assailed Foy's nose long before he turned the corner and saw Warehouse Ten, a pile of still-smoldering wreckage.

"Whew!" Foy whistled between his teeth. He had known the cotton would be damaged, but he had hoped to sell some for salvage. Every bale was completely gone.

"Every able-bodied man in town was passing buckets," said Jonathan. "The E. B. Youngs got here with their hand engine. The best they could do was save the other buildings. I've never seen such a flash fire. Bales were blazing!"

Foy began to kick the charred remains.

"Could have been the weather," Jonathan mused. "It was one of those drastic changes, hot one day, then extremely cold, sleeting like everything. The cotton froze."

Foy leaned over a blackened corner post and sniffed. *Coal oil!*

"Expanded," Jonathan continued. "Burst a steel band. It could have struck a spark, started a fire in the jute bagging."

"Not this time." Foy knelt to smell a brick pillar.

"You're right, Foy." A deep voice intervened.

Foy turned and nodded grimly to Dan Rowlett.

"I told the boys when we were fighting the fire, 'Boys,' I said, 'this don't look right to me.' "

"Arson?" Jonathan gasped.

Rowlett's head jerked curtly. "Fire was blazing from three different spots."

"Who?" asked Foy.

"I've got me ideas," Rowlett answered, "but I can't prove a thing."

"Well, Jonathan," Foy said with false heartiness as he clapped the distraught man's shoulder, "it's my fault. Not yours. Every carpetbagger and scalawag in town knows my part in the Keils affair. They are out to get me!"

On Christmas Eve in somber spirits, Foy picked up his gun and whistled for his dog. He set out on his annual tramp through the woods in search of game for Emma's Christmas dinner. He missed Harrison, who had not returned from Washington, and Jonathan, who could not hike with his artificial limb.

Usually Foy felt peace in the freedom of nature, but after an hour, his game bag remained empty. His tension increased as he stepped into a clearing and surveyed abandoned fields. Once-green acres were choked with vines and scrub.

Adrianna is just too young, he thought. A mere child when the war ended, she could not understand the devastation.

Even after the armistice had been signed, General Grierson's men had seized horses and livestock at will while scouring the country looking for Jefferson Davis. After the Confederate president was taken prisoner, the war seemed really over, and weary soldiers plodded home. How galling it had been to watch federal guards stop proud men and force them to show paroles before they could cross the covered bridge which spanned the Chattahoochee.

How doggedly we fought for our homes and our belief in the inalienable right of local self-government, Foy thought. He was proud that Alabama had contributed 122,000 soldiers to the Confederate Army, saddened that 35,000 fell before the musket and disease. Foy had returned from naval duty to a Eufaula filled with wounded and dying men. With capital gone and labor scattered, the returning heroes were subjected to Federal Occupation troops and disfranchisement.

Getting rid of Keils will help, Foy thought. *We can snap back with a little more time. Time! Will Adrianna wait?*

Looking as if through Adrianna's eyes at a once-palatial mansion, unpainted, crumbling, he wondered how he could ask her to wait. His farmer friends, small and great alike, struggled to maintain themselves by planting meager patches instead of great fields of cotton.

How has Green maintained his wealth? I can't compete with him.

Trudging down a muddy lane, Foy reached a crossroad and entered a frame building. Speaking to a group of men heatedly discussing farming and politics, Foy stretched cold hands toward the potbellied stove. Dipping his hand into a big wooden barrel for a dry cracker, he overheard a once-proud matron bartering eggs.

"Oh, you must make it one more orange," she pleaded. "One for each child's stocking." Softly under her breath, she added, "It's all they will have for Christmas."

Foy's fingers separated the few coins in his pocket. He must leave one each for Kitty and Lige, who seemed not to realize that Christmas would never be the same. They still awakened him with shouts of, "Chris'mus gif', I seed you first!"

Stepping around an open tub of corned mackerel, Foy ducked back and grinned as a brown stream of tobacco juice barely missed him. He looked over his head. At least the stores had Christmas merchandise again. Toys were suspended from the ceiling among the lanterns, horse collars, and buggy whips. He moved to where a huge bag was spilling out rough brown coconuts. Since boyhood, it had been his job to ceremoniously place a nail in the eye of a Christmas coconut and hammer a well-placed blow. He would drain the thin, white milk and drink it before he whacked the coconut to split it. How juicy were those first morsels Emma grated for her special cake!

Happily, Foy selected a perfect coconut and a hoop of ripe-smelling cheese for Emma and Jonathan. Feeling certain that Lily would not miss Christmas at home, he bought Brazil nuts and Malaga grapes for her and Harrison and rock candy for Mignonne. Foy then turned to the counter where a wooden box lined with red paper seemed to draw him. Excitedly, Foy rummaged among the Chinese firecrackers for the ones which would make the most noise. For Harrison Junior he picked a torpedo. Beau was at the age to enjoy slipping up on a group of girls and throwing it at their feet to make them squeal. For Emma and Jonathan's son, Wingate Ramsey, Foy bought a Roman candle. It would light up the heavens with its fiery balls and delight Win's eight-year-old heart.

Whistling as he left the country store, Foy almost missed the covey of quail flushed by his bird dog. Bagging one bobwhite, he became more watchful.

Stepping softly over a carpet of pine needles and leaf mold, Foy was swallowed into the dark forest. Sunlight broke through on the top of a poplar, turning it to shimmering gold. Suddenly a deer leaped, bounding over the path with her white tail flagging. She disappeared into the undergrowth. All was quiet, at peace.

The sharp-scented air cleared his thinking. A worshipful feeling of God here with him filled his being.

"Thank You, God, for creating such beauty," Foy prayed.

"Thank You that my war wounds are healed and I have strength to forge ahead. Help me to know if Adrianna is the wife You've chosen for me."

Adrianna. Her name seemed to float tantalizingly beyond the next turning. His feeling for her had exploded so intensely, so suddenly that he had tried to dismiss it as infatuation. Picking up a purple sweet gum leaf, he smoothed the starlike surface and knew that the longing he felt was love. He gathered some of the hard, prickly burs. Would Adrianna ever like anything so simple as dipping sweet gum burs in silver paint to decorate for Christmas?

A turkey mounted up before him on strong wings. Foy cupped his hand around his mouth and called, "Gobble-gobble-gobble."

"Gobble-gobble." The wizened head of another turkey popped from behind a bush.

Bang!

My luck is changing, Foy exulted as he picked up the heavy turkey. Even wild game had been scarce since the war.

Striding back through Eufaula toward the Ramseys' small, homey cottage, Foy rounded the corner. Just as he had anticipated, the Wingates had arrived.

"Christmas!" Lily shouted as she ran toward Foy with arms outstretched.

Harrison clapped him on the shoulder. "Great news! Washington says the Chattahoochee channel will be cleared!"

When they all went to church on Christmas morning, the world seemed right again save for Foy's wistful dreams of Adrianna's bright red head added to the family circle.

On the coldest day of January, it arrived: a letter which smelled of springtime.

Abington Hotel
New York City, New York
January 20, 1875

Dear Mr. Edwards:

I shudder to know what you must think of me for being such a tardy correspondent, but your letter followed me from Georgia to Washington, where I stayed only briefly before my grandfather sent me to New York to further my education. Your nice letter finally caught up with me here.

I'm afraid I must have appeared an empty-headed ninny among all you purposeful people. I'm studying philosophy to help get my feelings more properly controlled by reason.

Don't you find all these modern ideas like Darwin's exciting? Next I might study art.

I spent my first Christmas with snow. It was lucky that Grandfather and Ma-ma's present was a warm fur, because I enjoyed walking the snowy streets. The city was bustling with shoppers buying elegant gifts. The lights were bright and the music gay. But don't you find sometimes one gets lonely in a crowd?

Please write and tell me all about your new steamer. I promise to answer quickly this time.

Your friend,
Adrianna Atherton

Foy held the letter against his face and breathed its sweet fragrance. *Lily is right,* he thought. *Wealth and furs don't warm the heart.* Closing his eyes, he could picture Adrianna's face bubbling with cheerfulness, then becoming wistful when she thought no one was watching.

How he longed to gather her in his arms, to kiss her, to show her she was loved! With an ache in his throat, he took out his leather writing case and carefully composed a letter telling her that work was to begin on clearing the river. "The *Mignonne* is almost finished," he wrote. "I can't wait for you to see her."

Foy sat back and wiped sweaty palms. Could she read between the lines his desire for her to share his life? As yet he dared not declare his intentions.

Adrianna's reply came quickly. Chatty, the letter held no clue to her feelings for him. Foy puzzled over a passage about art:

The first Impressionist exhibition in Paris last fall was laughed at as a grotesque Bohemian joke, but some of my American friends are assimilating it into "luminism." I like their use of a blonde palette and long to go to Paris to see this new work of Claude Monet and Auguste Renoir.

Panic-stricken, Foy feared that Adrianna would go to France and be lost to him forever. He wrote back immediately:

I don't understand a word you are saying about art, but I'm proud of your growing talent. Darling, please don't go to Paris. Couldn't you paint the flowers in Eufaula?

Exhausted from long, trying hours at work, Foy relaxed by writing to Adrianna before he went to bed. The letters often took several nights to finish.

Her long, sweet replies and the interest she took in things that mattered to him delighted him. He felt she had gone astray on philosophy when she wrote:

The new currents of thought coupled with technological and industrial advances have everyone questioning old values and searching for new means of adapting to the rapid changes in the economic and social environment. I'm interested in the new pragmatism. It is so much easier to live with than the old idealism.

They argued through several letters. She thought he was dogmatic in his assertion of the unchanging principles of the Bible.

In spite of these disagreements, the chain of letters spanned the distance through the early summer and forged a bond of friendship. Their first infatuation deepened into love as they learned more about each other, but each feared to reveal their feelings.

Columbus, Georgia
July 15, 1875

The Mignonne *should be finished in two weeks! The stained-glass windows have been installed and I can't wait for you to see them.*

Foy sat, pen poised. Now he was ready to declare his dreams, ask her to return. As he hesitated, a hot west wind warned him to wait. It signaled disaster.

Drought!

The burning wind continued. The sun scorched everything green into brittle, lifeless brown. Each afternoon, temperatures reached 100, 105, 110 degrees. Strong men collapsed, even died.

Eufaula, Alabama
August 21, 1875

Dear Adrianna,

There are no beautiful cotton fields for you to paint. The plants stand stalwartly surviving, but without rain, they produce no fluffy white bolls, only useless stalks to be mowed down.

I thought I was building two empires, but both of them were dependent on cotton. Cotton and weather. Even if I had a load to haul, we couldn't get the Mignonne *out of Columbus. The drought has nearly dried up the lakes and rivers.*

Putting down his pen and pacing his room, Foy wondered if he should try to explain that he had no money to ask her to marry him. No. He banged one first against the other. City people never understood why farmers could suddenly be overwhelmed by debts through no fault of their own. Could he make Adrianna understand that the economy of the whole region was tied to agriculture?

He dipped his pen in the ink and shook his head sadly as he finished his letter without a proposal:

At least the low water helps efforts to clear the channel of the Chattahoochee.

I love you,
Foy

Eufaula, Alabama
October 2, 1875

The rains came too late. There were no spring or summer crops. The farmers are doggedly saying next year will be better and are preparing to plant for winter.

At least the political drought seems over. I can see Reconstruction coming to a close and Eufaula becoming safe for young brides again. With the Radical Party in control and Elias Keils giving safe asylum to thieves, we have lived in constant danger.

You'll be happy to know that Keils has fled the state. A new constitution this year will spread the voting to precincts. There should be no more riots, but then you do meet exciting people during riots, don't you?

Only the threat of fire remains. Some are natural from city growth, but some are still being set.

Foy's confidence improved when the price of his stored cotton went up again. Joyfully, he paid his bills and settled old debts.

Eufaula, Alabama
November 4, 1875

My Darling Adrianna,

I can't believe it's been a year since the wonderful day we met. It seems like yesterday, yet like forever, and I long to see you! I'm sending you a Christmas present. I hope your family will feel I have courted you long enough for you to accept. I am only waiting now for the river to rise.

Winter rains drenched the mountains, and once again the Chattahoochee became a mighty river hurrying to the sea. The family returned to Columbus for final work on the *Mignonne*. Foy began a letter that would be his carefully rehearsed marriage proposal.

Columbus, Georgia
January 5, 1876

The Mignonne *is afloat! We've taken her on a few runs to try her machinery. She's ready. . .*

A brisk knock sounded at his door and Lily burst into the room.

"Guess what?" she exclaimed, waving two letters under his nose. "The Cleburne Fire Company wants to hire the *Mignonne Wingate*. They plan to raise money for a new engine by selling tickets for a spring charity excursion to Apalachicola Bay. It'll be a grand occasion! We'll be filled to capacity. Oh, Foy!" She regarded him with liquid brown eyes. "This is the beginning!"

"How about inviting Senator and Mrs. Atherton and honoring them since he got Congress to clear the channel?"

"And Adrianna?" Lily teased.

"And Adrianna, of course!"

"This other letter is from her." Lily gave him a hug as she left the room.

Eager to write his letter, Foy scanned Adrianna's words inattentively until she mentioned one man's name.

I'm not as lonely now. I've been seeing the latest plays and all the sights, including the construction beginning on the new Brooklyn Bridge. You'll never guess who looked me up. That nice man you all introduced me to, Mr. Green Bethune.

Foy crushed her letter and hurled it savagely at the wall.

Chapter 7

Adrianna wandered aimlessly down the crowded New York street through swirling April Fool's Day snow. Snowflakes clinging to her eyelashes merged with tears as she agonized, *Have I done the wrong thing? No,* she thought, *I should not have written Foy about Green.*

Sighing, she shrugged her fur-trimmed jacket more tightly about her neck. She should have been satisfied with their growing friendship, but every time she had felt Foy's letters warming to love, he had seemed to draw back. How foolish she had been to think she could push him into proposing by using Green to make him jealous. She must have hurt him—or angered him. He had not replied.

Turning into the wind, Adrianna trudged toward her hotel. At first, winter in the city had exhilarated her senses, but now she longed for the warmth and perfumed flowers of the South as much as she ached to feel Foy's arms.

"Well, not quite as much," she whispered to herself, giggling.

Adrianna had been closely supervised in New York yet lonely. She had remained on the edges of the sophisticated groups who avidly discussed the confusing new theories for living lives of self-gratification.

Then, without warning, Green Bethune had appeared at her hotel. He had presented her with an insurance policy paid for by Isadora. Adrianna had started to turn away, but her homesickness responded to the soft Southern sound of his voice. She had eagerly accepted when he invited her to dinner and the theater. The charming man had made certain that the cuisine was superb, the play witty and intelligent.

Adrianna had settled easily into being squired about town. Green had showered her with attention and would fit well into the political arena that was her family's life. Even though she had fallen more in love with Foy with each letter from him, she must be realistic. It was time to admit that he had made no commitment. She must forget Foy and decide on Green.

With her chin high, Adrianna entered the Abington and walked past the hotel desk. It had been so long since she wrote Foy, hoping to push him into a proposal of marriage by making him jealous of Green, that she was beginning to realize he must be too angry to reply.

Her dimpled chin trembled. Yes, this was one more time she had been wrong. She gritted her teeth. Didn't one of the philosophies she was studying say it was all right to do the wrong thing for the right reason? But was it?

At the elevator, Adrianna turned back to inquire for messages. The desk clerk handed her a letter. Ripping it open, she let her eyes dance over the words.

Eufaula, Alabama
March 3, 1876

The Mignonne *is afloat! We've taken her on a few runs to try her machinery. She's ready! We've made some freight hauls, but her formal introduction into service will be a grand excursion trip to the bay as a charity fund raiser for the Cleburne Fire Company. We are inviting Senator and Mrs. Atherton, and I hope very much that you can be here April twenty-seventh.*

Your friend,
Foy Edwards

Her delight burst radiantly upon the dazzled clerk. "Get my bill ready, please," she said. "I'm going. . ." Adrianna paused. How could she explain? Then the word rang out with certainty: "Home!"

The crashing of cymbals and the *oompah-pah* of a tuba underscoring a lively brass band echoed up Eufaula's bluff as Adrianna's carriage descended toward the riverside. The *Mignonne Wingate* floated regally, dazzling white against the dark Chattahoochee. The music was coming from the hurricane deck where a big bass drum was emblazoned with the name, Professor Ryan's Sunny South Brass Band. Crowds of people milled about laughing, calling greetings.

Adrianna's breath caught in her throat. She clasped her fingertips over her open mouth in sudden fear of her long-anticipated meeting with Foy. She swept the passengers with appraising eyes. Self-confident ladies, every inch as stylish as those on the streets of New York, promenaded in lavishly draped bustles of every hue. The men wore jackets of muted blacks, browns, and blues. Most of them had given up the old-fashioned high top hats and replaced them with the new round hard ones.

Sighing, Adrianna wished she had anticipated the crowd and written Foy which train to meet. In her excitement about seeing him, she had not considered how formal his invitation had been. Adrianna fought tears. Perhaps Foy simply wanted to add her to the crowd.

Should I go back? she wondered. *Have I come only to break my heart?*

Wiping a tear, she lifted her eyes to the pilothouse. Foy! Arm straight up, he waved frantically, then bounded down endless flights of stairs.

There is some use to red hair, she thought, giggling nervously as she slipped and slid down the hill.

Foy's feet hit the gangplank in three rocking bounces that threatened to tumble him into the water. "You came," he shouted. "You're alone!" It was a joyful cry.

"Yes." Adrianna stopped, waiting as he scrambled up the slope. Puzzled by his intensity, she asked, "Aren't my grandparents here?"

"No, they—" Foy stopped short. "I was afraid." His brows came together, and a muscle twitched in his set jaw. "I didn't know whether to invite you or not. Mrs. Atherton was frightened of the river. I debated a long time."

Adrianna's sensitive face paled and her lips trembled. Tension crackled between them. She searched his scowling countenance with troubled eyes.

"I was afraid," he repeated low in his throat, "that you might bring Green!"

"No!" Adrianna gasped. "Oh, Foy, I shouldn't have teased. I wanted to make you—" She lifted her hand toward his face and leaned yearningly closer. "I hoped you'd invite me back." She snapped her fingers and said, "I don't care that for Green."

Foy laughed in relief. Looking at her hungrily, he stepped as close as he dared and whispered, "You are more beautiful than my dreams." He breathed deeply and rolled his eyes heavenward.

Adrianna's laughter rang out as she watched him react to the warm waft of her perfume. Love was plain on his tender face. How she regretted that she had hurt him! She longed to fling herself into his arms, yet even if they had been betrothed, decorum permitted no such public display.

Meeting his eyes, she said lightly, "Hello, I'm Adrianna Atherton."

"Foy Edwards, Esquire." He grinned and tipped his pilot's cap. Proffering his elbow, he escorted her across the gangway. "May I present the grandest steamboat on the Chattahoochee, the *Mignonne Wingate.* She is named, of course, for my partner's daughter."

Adrianna laughed ruefully. As they reached the lower deck and were sheltered slightly from curious eyes, she said, "Oh, Foy, you look so. . ." She swallowed her flooding emotions. "Wonderful! So tanned and strong." Her bare ring finger lightly tapped his hard-muscled arm, and her eyes caressed his high cheekbones. "So confident."

"You've changed." Foy laughed huskily. "You're exquisite!"

Foy's dark eyes devoured the perfection of her trim figure encased in the slim column of white silk. Wonderingly, he brushed the back of his hand against her cheek, which had lost some of its roundness.

"Have you been eating enough?"

"Just lost my baby fat." She laughed again, pleased at the impact she had made upon him. "Foy, I'm sorry that—"

Uhmmmmm! Uhmmmmm!

The growling blast of the whistle made her jump. Shattering their private moment, the sound signaled a final flurry of activity. *Uhmmmmm! Uhmmmmm!* Echoes bounced from bank to bank. Chanting more quickly, the deckhands reached for the last of the freight from the sweating men who had carried it down the steep bluff. With a shout, the shoreman lifted the loop of heavy rope from the post and tossed it to the deck. The whistle kept blasting as the gangplank folded upward. The great paddle wheel at the stern shuddered. Turning slowly, it churned a white wake.

Foy was swept away by a call. Across the crowd of passengers, Adrianna sought him with her eyes. They exchanged wordless promises for later.

Warmed, ecstatically happy, Adrianna turned to find Lily at her side. Foy's sister introduced her to several people. Then she showed Adrianna to her private stateroom.

Glad that Foy had not assigned her a berth in the ladies' sleeping cabin, Adrianna retreated gratefully. Stretching luxuriously on her bed, she savored each moment of meeting Foy. Mentally, she kissed his straight nose, the heavy brows which shielded his smoldering eyes, his hollow cheeks, his lips. Shivering with delight at her dreaming, Adrianna was glad she had dismissed Mrs. Cristie when she stopped at the hotel to rest and change.

From Foy's invitation, she had expected her grandparents to be along. She had thought she would be amply chaperoned. Biting her lip, she hoped no one would gossip that she was traveling alone, but she did enjoy solitude. She felt suddenly shy.

Changing to a demure, billowy, pink cotton set off by lace and wine velvet bows, Adrianna picked up her sketchbook. Determinedly, she stepped out into the warm April sunshine.

She seated herself on deck and was immediately struck by the solitary feeling of a dead pine clinging to the bank. She tried to capture the emotion of the scene with charcoal.

Suddenly Foy was bending over her, nodding approvingly. He said, "Ready for your tour?"

Adrianna smiled and followed him down to the lower deck past freight neatly stacked and bales of cotton on which the deckhands lounged. Foy guided her closer to the big boilers and the steam engine which turned the paddle wheel. Grimacing, she put her hands over her ears against the roar as firemen fed the hungry firebox under the boiler with long sticks of cordwood.

They climbed back to the elegant grandeur of the upper deck and leaned over the rail to let the spring breeze cool their cheeks. Adrianna's eyes sparkled with excitement as she said fervently, "The *Mignonne*'s a beautiful boat."

"Isn't she?" Foy grinned. "She's as slim and restive as a thoroughbred race-horse."

Proudly, Foy showed her through the inviting lounge. Next, they peeped into the dining room. White-uniformed waiters were setting tables covered in immaculate linen.

"We'd better hurry," said Foy. They sniffed at the spicy odors already filling the room and their mouths watered.

Grasping Adrianna's elbow, Foy helped her up the steps to the hurricane deck where he tapped on the door of the captain's office.

Harrison Wingate welcomed the smiling pair. The rich, dark woods in the room were set off by gleaming brass. "We're pleased you've joined us, Miss Adrianna. Seems as though April 27, 1876, will be a banner day for the Wingates and the Edwards."

"I'm delighted to be part of your first excursion, Captain Wingate," Adrianna replied warmly. "It certainly is a success."

"Yes," he agreed. "The Cleburne Fire Company turned out in full force."

"Firemen?" Adrianna queried. "So refined, so elegantly dressed?"

"They are the cream of Eufaula society." Harrison laughed at her astonishment.

"The volunteer firemen," Foy explained, "are the leading men of the town. They're organized to protect their homes. We have several different companies. They practice precision drills, sort of like the old militia groups."

"Are there still so many fires?" asked Adrianna.

"Bad fires average one every six weeks," replied Harrison gravely. "Some are a natural result of congested city growth, but many are set by arsonists. In 1872, whole blocks of our business district burned."

"Things are better since Dan Rowlett became chief of the Eufaula Fire Department," Foy said. "They have one hook and ladder company, and there are two hand engines, but we need more. The Cleburne Company put on this charity excursion to raise money for an engine and a firehouse. I must introduce you to the ladies who planned it, Mrs. G. L. Guice and Mrs. Wells Bray. You'll especially like Miss Islay Reeves. With all their enthusiastic work, we'll soon have better fire protection."

The happy couple continued their tour of the steamer by looking in quickly on Lily. Since she was already laying out evening clothes, they scampered up the stairs to the pilothouse. Foy introduced Adrianna.

"This is our pilot, Mr. Trimmer, and his striker, Ben."

Friendly, but with unmistakable arrogance, Trimmer let Adrianna watch. The big boat yielded to the slightest turn of the large steering wheel and followed the main channel safely around a bend.

From his spot on the lazy bench, Ben, the young apprentice steersman, gaped at Adrianna. Foy grinned smugly and squeezed a possessive arm around her shoulders as he helped her down from the pilothouse.

That evening when Adrianna stepped into the dining room, she remembered the gawky lad and wondered if the boat were safe in his hands. She saw the arrogant pilot in a corner, and Foy was striding toward her.

Adrianna's red hair danced on her bare shoulders and floated down the back of her elegant, pink satin gown.

Foy's deep-set eyes widened in delight as he drank in her appearance. He proudly offered his arm to escort her to the captain's table.

Harrison Wingate was the image of quiet dignity in his dark blue serge suit with brass buttons. Foy's navy blue uniform was less grand. The men guests wore dinner jackets and black ties. The ladies wore ornate gowns and jewels. Adrianna noticed Lily's emeralds, but what astonished her was Emma Ramsey. Seated at the next table, Emma moved in a pink glow from a huge ring and an elaborate necklace of rubies.

Relaxed, happier than she could ever remember, Adrianna enjoyed each course proffered by waiters in spotless white uniforms. She felt much more at ease than she had on her first visit.

"Everyone in New York," she said enthusiastically, "is discussing Charles Darwin's latest book, *The Descent of Man*, and debating his theory of evolution."

The table fell silent. Lily scowled. She had opened her mouth to retort when her son's high-pitched young voice brought an embarrassed red spot to her cheeks.

"I'd like another piece of custard pie, please," Beau called loudly to the waiter.

With a steady hand to his wife's scolding finger, Harrison quietly nodded to the waiter to bring the boy more pie. Chuckling, the handsome captain launched into a funny story of old days on the river.

Thankful that attention had been diverted from her attempt to flaunt her newfound knowledge, Adrianna retreated within herself. Too late, she realized that by introducing such a controversial subject at the dinner table, she had been as childishly rude as Beau. With the end of supper, Lily invited the passengers to the front deck to watch the sunset on the water. Some of them remained, impatiently waiting for tables to be cleared for cards. Not wanting to be caught in a game of whist, Adrianna looked about frantically for Foy.

Her seeking eyes spotted his strong profile etched against the flickering lamplight as he spoke earnestly with Mr. Trimmer. He flashed her a smile and started across the crowded room.

"It's time for my watch," Foy said in his deep, serious voice.

"Oh." It was a small, defeated sound.

"Would you like to watch the sunset?"

Not wanting to encounter Lily, Adrianna started to shake her head.

Foy leaned closer and whispered, "From the pilothouse?"

"Yes!"

Giddily, she climbed the stairs, feeling she was ascending to the turret of her fairy castle.

While Ben murmured to Foy of changes in the river, Adrianna smiled down at the darkening water. Clouds reflected against its black, mysterious depths. The trees seemed to stand on tiptoe on their separate shores and reach their arms toward each other in vain. The boat glided smoothly, silently down the stream. There was little sound save for the soft *chu-choooo, chu-choooo* of escaping steam.

"Oh, look how pretty!" Adrianna broke the silence. Pointing to a waterfall which leaped in joyous abandon to make its creek one with the river, she turned to share the beauty with Foy.

Tall, strong, Foy held the wheel with a light touch. Not taking his eyes from her to look where she pointed, Foy wrapped her in his warm gaze.

Adrianna's eyes swept the bench, the confines of the glassed tower. Ben was gone. They were alone, at last.

"Do you think that you could learn to love. . ." Foy's voice broke huskily. "The river?"

"Yes," she whispered. "I already do. . ." She turned her back so that he could not read the hunger on her face. "Love your river."

"But do you understand." He cupped her chin with strong fingers and turned her delicate face toward his eager gaze.

Trembling, Adrianna waited. She must chart her course more carefully this time.

"You understand—" Foy cleared his throat. "That the Chattahoochee's always plotting ten ways to kill a steamboat. Harrison and I want to rebuild his steamer line, and Jonathan. . ." Gently, he drew her nearer as he searched her face with worried eyes. Clearing his throat again, he said eagerly, "Jonathan is getting the Cotton Exchange on its feet. You could restore Barbour Hall. It would always be home." His long arm dropped tentatively around her slender waist.

"I've never had a real home," she whispered close to his chest.

Foy's arm tightened. Smothering her against him, he buried his face in her flaming hair. "Oh, Adrianna, I love you. I never knew it was possible to love anyone so much! Or hurt so much," he said in an agonized voice. "You tortured me with thoughts of you with Green!"

Wriggling free, Adrianna looked up into his dear face. Twining her fingers in his sun-streaked hair, she pulled it playfully. "You ninny!" She laughed.

"It's you I love!"

Lifting her lips, Adrianna met his kiss joyfully.

Kissing her with rising passion, Foy threw both arms around her, crushing her against him.

Scarcely able to breathe, Adrianna let her mind light upon one brightly glowing word: *Home!* she thought. *Now I have a home. It is in Foy's arms.* Someday she would tell him. For now her whole being must respond to the urgency of his kisses.

Plop! Plop! Plop! Whirring, flopping, the wheel spun madly out of control. Foy grabbed it, hauled it around frantically, too late. With a shuddering quiver, the *Mignonne* struck a hidden outcropping along the shore.

"Half-speed, Mr. Murphey," Foy said, leaning over the speaking tube to instruct the engineer far below.

Gently, carefully, Foy urged the huge, flat-bottomed craft off her grounding. She grazed the reef, slid by, sailed on smoothly.

"Good grannies, that was close!" exclaimed Foy, wiping his forehead. He grinned sheepishly as a scowling Mr. Trimmer appeared at the top of the stairs.

They followed the sighing sounds of music to the grand saloon where Lewis's String Band was playing. Smiling, too filled with emotions to speak, Adrianna accepted Foy's hand and stepped onto the dance floor. In each other's arms, close in the only way propriety allowed, they waltzed to their inner music. When they were separated by the intricate figures of a cotillion, Adrianna smiled vaguely at her other partners. She seemed to breathe only when she rejoined Foy's arms.

When the dancing ended, Foy lingered at her stateroom door. Emma and Jonathan walked by casually but with the watchful eyes of chaperones. Foy brushed a kiss on her temple and whispered with a voice full of promise, "Tomorrow."

"Tomorrow!" Adrianna sighed happily.

Sunlight streaming through her cabin window bathed Adrianna in a rosy glow. "Home," she whispered and hugged herself, pretending she was in Foy's arms. Stretching dreamily, she savored the joy of being loved, then bounded out of bed, anticipating a day with Foy.

Foy was nowhere to be seen at breakfast. Not daring to climb to the pilothouse, Adrianna decided to take her easel to the front of the boat. As she sat back, trying to capture the new techniques of Monet, Adrianna suddenly felt someone behind her.

Lily, her face clouded by an unaccustomed scowl, was bearing down upon her. "Adrianna," Lily snapped, "I simply must speak with you about last night!"

Chapter 8

Adrianna clapped her fingertips to her flaming cheeks, heedless of the paintbrush which scattered yellow oil across her dress.

"Yes, Miss Lily?" she replied meekly. Ducking her head, she dabbed at the flecks of paint and wondered, *Did Mr. Trimmer tell Captain Wingate my being in the pilothouse endangered the boat?* She lifted troubled eyes to the angry face of Foy's sister.

Lily was obviously struggling to control her temper. Pressing her lips together, she glanced at Adrianna's canvas. Distracted, she spoke in a strained voice. "Why, that's lovely! You've captured the light shimmering on the water in such a different way."

"It's a new technique," Adrianna replied warily. "You use pure color and try to capture the light and atmosphere, the sensation of the moment."

"I like it very much," Lily said.

Her frown deepened and again her voice was intense. "It's not that we here are against change, Adrianna. I've always fought against anyone saying that we must do something a certain way simply because we've always done it."

Adrianna's eyes darted about frantically. If only Foy would come to her rescue.

"Your mind has obviously been broadened by travel and study," Lily said. "But as hostess here, I must point out that one simply does not bring up anyone as controversial as Mr. Darwin at a social dinner table."

"Oh!" Adrianna's mouth remained round, and she felt hot and cold at the same time. "I'm sorry. I—" She had realized she was wrong, but something in Lily's tone made her jut her chin and speak defiantly. "I only meant to introduce stimulating conversation. I realize that for years these different theories of evolution have aroused tremendous conflict between science and religion. Even between Mr. Darwin and his wife and children, I've heard. But don't you think parts of the Bible are simply lovely myths?"

"Myths?" Lily exploded. "I certainly do not! Myths are fables written by people to explain gods. The Bible is God's Word written at His inspiration to reveal Himself to His people."

Hurt by Lily's dogmatic attitude, Adrianna became sarcastic. "Do you really believe all this," she said, waving her paintbrush at the passing woodland, "was created by God in only seven days?"

Foy's deep voice rumbled close behind her. "I do." He smiled warmly as she turned toward him, then he tenderly wiped a smudge of paint from her cheek. "But the Bible doesn't say twenty-four-hour days." His tone was gentle as he looked pleadingly from Adrianna to Lily. "Where does it say one day is with the Lord as a thousand years, and a thousand years as one day?"

"It's in Second Peter," replied Lily more evenly. "Peter was quoting Psalms and telling about creation and the end of the world."

Harrison, who had walked up with Foy, dropped a calming arm around his wife's tense shoulders and said, "It's the sudden surge in scientific thought that has fooled people into thinking they must choose either science or religion." Spreading his hands he continued in a quiet, firm voice. "Having spent much of my life alone with the stars, I know how unchangeable God is. As He reveals more to scientists, they will one day discover our world is larger and He is much greater than our little minds now grasp."

The angry churning of Adrianna's stomach was put to rest by Harrison's calming presence. Foy wrapped her in a loving glance, and she basked in the glow.

Lily had nodded agreement with her husband, but she persisted. "In the beginning, Darwin believed in God and was going to be a clergyman. I read that he said he did not in the least doubt the strict and literal truth of every word of the Bible. He himself never makes evolution a religious issue or takes part in all the silly debates that would make men monkeys. But," she flung out earnestly, "people are not brute beasts. God creates persons with souls to commune with Him."

"Darwin is beginning to leave God out as I once did." Emma's placid voice broke into their discussion.

Adrianna looked up in surprise as Emma and Jonathan joined their circle.

"I agree that God created man with a soul and made apes as separate creatures," Jonathan said. He began to chuckle. "Of course, you've gotta believe in some evolving when you see how much bigger this rascal's grown than our generation." Jonathan reached up to slap Foy's shoulders. Even Lily laughed.

Looking at each one in the loving group, Adrianna knew she wanted to become part of this family. Even in their slight differences of opinion, they could be understanding and supportive of one another.

"Seriously though," Jonathan continued, "it's not the question of evolution that matters, but if you place God first. Back in 1859, in his first edition of *Origin of the Species,* Darwin spoke frankly of God as director of evolution. Sadly, his book was received with such enthusiasm by the German materialists that Darwin became intoxicated with his success. In the second edition, he cut God out."

Adrianna's conscience made her think for a moment that Jonathan was chiding her for becoming so impressed with her knowledge that she had left out God. Then she realized with some surprise that he was speaking of himself.

"We often start with faith," mused Jonathan. "But we end in folly because of our pride."

Passengers were filling the deck now. Some joined in discussions of the Social Darwinism that was sweeping the country. Others drifted away intent upon relaxing and forgetting cares.

Foy whispered close to Adrianna's ear, "Would you like to come to the pilothouse?"

Sparkling, she nodded and hurried to put away her paints.

Ben grinned as the laughing couple entered the pilothouse. Adrianna greeted the lanky boy pleasantly.

"Thought I'd starve afore yo' watch came." Ben chuckled and gladly relinquished the wheel to Foy.

As soon as Ben's scruffy head disappeared, Foy said softly, "Come here."

Adrianna's rosy face glowed like sunlight on water as Foy's dark eyes enveloped her with his love. She moved into the shelter of his arms. Bending, he kissed her tenderly. He kept her close as he turned his attention to the wheel. Remaining nestled against him, she gazed at his strong, sharp profile as he peered at a distant point of land.

"If you'll be good," he said huskily, "and let me keep half a mind on my business, you can stay awhile."

Adrianna's laughter tinkled. "I love it here," she said. "We're looking down on the world, and you are master of our fate."

"Well, God is master of our fate. . ."

Adrianna stiffened. Would Foy preach to her, too, or chide her about her argument with Lily?

"But," Foy continued, "He expects me to take serious responsibility for the lives of those on board, and today we'll be passing through the river's most dangerous parts."

Startled, Adrianna drew back a discreet distance. She thought of the people on the deck below pursuing pleasure with no thought of danger.

"How can you tell?" Adrianna asked. "Why, everything looks exactly the same."

Foy laughed. "No. Not really." He thought for a moment. "The main hazard is shallow spots, bars."

Adrianna nodded, remembering being stuck on the sandbar on the way to Columbus. Foy's serious tone reclaimed her attention.

"We're coming to a perilous spot none of us will ever forget—King's Rock. I was a kid, but I'll always remember the gray November day when Harrison wrecked." He shook his head reflectively. "Lily was waiting for Harrison to return for their wedding. There was a bad drought. The river was so low Harrison's boat, *Peytona*, smashed into King's Rock. Many lives were lost.

"We all gave up hope that Harrison had survived—except Lily," Foy continued. "Somehow, she knew Harrison was alive and would come to her. She has a strong belief in prayer and that God speaks to her to strengthen and guide." Foy fell silent, remembering.

"You really love your family, don't you?" Adrianna asked softly.

"Of course." Foy shrugged.

"I'm sorry I offended Lily. I'll try to be more careful. I want her to like me."

"She loves you," said Foy simply. Smiling down at her, he added, "We all do." His long arm hugged her rib-crushingly. Then he gently pushed her away and put both hands to the huge wheel.

Suddenly, the wide, gentle Chattahoochee funneled into a cut between walls of rock. The pent-up water gushed forward, striking hidden reefs. Foy's full attention was upon keeping the boat centered in the narrow passage. Wide-eyed, Adrianna nodded as he pointed out King's Rock. There had been no recent freshets, no mud to cloud the water. Today the water ran deep, and the flat-bottomed boat skimmed laughingly over the menacing rock.

Watching Foy steer carefully past, Adrianna wondered how much of a barrier Lily might be. Would Foy not ask her to marry him if Lily did not approve? She had hoped he might actually propose when she spoke of her longing for family; but now he was preoccupied, and she knew she must be satisfied with his words of love and seeming assumption of a future marriage.

Piercing, unearthly cries made her jump. "What?" she mouthed as she clapped her hands over her ears. Foy could not hear her above the din. The wail ran up the scale like a human in distress. She could see that Foy was laughing.

"What in the world?" she asked when at last there was such silence that the surrounding woodland seemed to stop reeling and crouch in waiting.

"That demoniac yell," Foy said, laughing between words, "is the new steam whistle of the *Amos Hamilton*. Be glad you're not closer. She's coming down the Flint River trying to beat our schedule into the town of Chattahoochee."

"Well, I greatly prefer your whistle." Adrianna laughed, shivering.

"We'll be stopping for awhile," Foy said. "We're in Florida now, and some tourists always want to take a look at the state penitentiary." As he guided the steamboat to the wharf, he spoke gruffly. "Many of my buddies died when the *Chattahoochee*'s boiler exploded and she sank. I never pass here without visiting their graves."

Adrianna felt good stretching her legs as she walked with a silent Foy. When they reached the graveyard, she waited quietly as he took off his cap and stood in sad contemplation.

"Oh! Susanna, oh, don't you cry for me." Voices of people lining the wharf raised to join the lively, if slightly off-key, notes of a brass band playing from the hurricane deck of the *Amos Hamilton*.

Adrianna's spirits lifted with excitement as another whistle sounded. With flags flying, the *G. Gunby Jordan* floated smoothly to the wharf.

"She's the pride of the People's Line," Foy explained as he took Adrianna's elbow and hurried her forward. "Competition between the lines is becoming fierce."

Adrianna saw that a stream of people laden with picnic baskets was hurrying to meet the *Jordan* while only a small group approached the *Mignonne Wingate*.

"Oh, Foy!" Adrianna exclaimed. "They're taking all the business!"

Foy laughed. "It's all right this time. Islay Reeves did such a good job selling tickets to raise money for the fire engine that we have a full load. But the Wingate Line is going to have to scratch for a share of the trade. Fortunately, everyone likes Harrison. The newspapers influence trade by the stories they carry about how various captains manage their steamers."

Whistles were signaling departure.

Wheet! Wheet! The *G. Gunby Jordan* tooted impatiently, lifted her gangplank, and sailed on.

Adrianna and Foy ran aboard their own boat and joined a party on the deck. Hours flitted by unnoticed. Isolated from the world, the boat drifted through flat, coastal plains forested in cottonwoods. The joyful *plink, plink, plinking* of a banjo set everyone's toes tapping as they listened to the well-known entertainer Matt O'Brien. They looked at each other in amazement as his small son, Master Marc, picked up a large guitar and began accompanying his father. Then father and son urged the whole group to join in singing popular songs.

Adrianna's voice rose happily as she sang, "Listen to the mockingbird, listen to the mockingbird, the mockingbird calling for its mate." She turned to smile meaningfully at Foy. He was watching the shoreline in tense-jawed silence.

"What's wrong?" she whispered, suddenly realizing the boat was moving slowly and turning frequently.

"Oh, nothing." Foy knit his brows and shook his head. "Just Moccasin Slough. It's a new channel caused by obstructions placed in the main river during the war."

"I thought the government had cleared. . ."

"They've improved it some, but it's still dangerous."

"Do you need to go to the pilothouse?" she asked half-fearfully, half-hopefully.

"No." Foy shook his head. "It's really shallow here. Old Trimmer says he's the only one who can take a steamboat over mud." He laughed and surveyed her with a warm gaze. "I hear the string band tuning up inside. It's still fifty miles to Apalachicola. Would you like to dance?"

"Of course!" Adrianna's eyes sparkled. "How long do we have?" she asked as they stepped onto the mahogany floor.

"Four hours," Foy said softly as he took her in his arms and breathed against her hair.

After the set, Adrianna and Foy went out to the deck to cool their faces. Adrianna noticed Lily and Harrison standing alone with their shoulders hunched in misery. Suddenly, Harrison drew his wife into the shelter of his arms and kissed her. She sank forlornly against him.

Surprised because a public display of affection was considered improper, Adrianna looked at Foy questioningly. "Whatever is the matter?" she whispered.

Guiding her around the corner, Foy explained, "We're passing through the Narrows. During the war we had to block off the river to keep the enemy from attacking. This is where they sank the *Wave*."

Adrianna's eyes misted with understanding. She would never forget being in Foy's arms on his first boat. She peeped around the corner of the staterooms and saw Harrison tenderly cuff his wife's chin and whisper a laughing word to lift her spirits. Lily smiled wanly and wiped her tears.

Adrianna smudged a sympathetic tear and gazed up at Foy. "Now I understand a little more what the *Mignonne Wingate* means to you."

Foy rubbed his fingertip over her nose and chuckled.

"What? What?" she demanded, stamping her foot.

"Since our walk this morning, you have six new freckles." She made a wry face and tried to twist away.

"I want to kiss each one!" He bent nearer.

"Someone will see," she protested weakly as he kissed her cheekbone. She shivered deliciously as his kisses followed the spots dancing across the bridge of her nose.

Darkness had fallen by the time the *Mignonne* moored at the wharf in the town of Apalachicola. The next morning when Adrianna started out to breakfast, she was surprised to find everyone gathered at the rail chattering and exclaiming in dismay. Looking over Islay Reeves's head, Adrianna gaped at piles of brick and rubble, a scene of utter desolation.

"I was here two years ago," said Islay. "Then, it was the brightest, busiest, most prosperous city on the Florida coast. There were fine brick stores, expensive warehouses, elegant dwellings."

"What happened?" Adrianna gasped.

"The hurricane of 1874," Islay replied. "It did worse damage than the Yankees!"

For a moment the young women watched as supplies were loaded from the wharf; then, arm in arm, they went in and breakfasted on ham, eggs, grits, biscuits, and syrup. They barely noticed when the steamer left the mouth of the river to begin the cruise across Apalachicola Bay.

It was nine o'clock when Adrianna started down the central hallway to her stateroom. Suddenly, she grabbed at her stomach, which seemed to be falling to her toes. She lurched to the opposite side of the hallway. Her breakfast bounced as the boat rolled. Dismayed, she stumbled outside. Several ladies hung onto the rail, seasick.

The flat-bottomed river craft tossed giddily as ocean waves roughened Apalachicola Bay in spite of its protective chain of islands.

As the boat slowed and the choppiness calmed slightly, Adrianna adjusted to the pitch and yaw. Enraptured by the spectacular scenery, she gazed at the coastline of Florida. The beaches glittered white like poured-out diamonds. The restless water sparkled like a brilliant aquamarine set in a ring of whitecaps.

Foy's strong brown fingers closed over her delicate hand. Seeming to sense her mood, he said nothing. They remained together as the steamer approached Saint George Island.

When the boat beached on a narrow slip of land, they walked two hundred yards across hard-packed wet sand to view the splendor of the Gulf of Mexico. Overwhelmed by the magnitude of the ocean, Adrianna felt her soul swelling out across the vastness. Reverence filled her as she remembered what Harrison had said. He was right. To have created this ocean, God was far greater than her mind had ever grasped.

"Would y'all like to go in bathing?" A timid voice broke her reverie.

Adrianna turned to see Mignonne standing shyly back.

"Oh, I'd love to." Adrianna's voice lifted with a smile. Eager to make amends with Foy's beautiful niece, she whispered companionably, "I brought the very latest bathing suit from New York."

"Mine is French," Mignonne confided.

Agreeing they would swim after lunch, Mignonne and Adrianna joined the ladies. They had exchanged their formal gowns for sportswear, which differed from street clothes only in that the skirts did not drag on the ground. Adrianna blended happily in with the women and girls collecting shells.

Squeals of delight and cries of, "Come see the different shape of this one," or "Listen in this one for the sound of the ocean," wafted across the beaches as the ladies filled their baskets. The small boys ran shouting in barefoot abandon, enjoying the freedom of one-piece, striped, knit bathing suits.

Wondering where Foy had gone, Adrianna glanced up the shore. The older men and women sat beneath canvas umbrellas. She laughed at the incongruity of the men in dark business suits and hats and the ladies in bonnets and blankets to protect them for the sun.

Suddenly she saw Foy smiling down upon her proudly. He had never looked more handsome. A blue silk scarf tie fluttered at his neck, and his light trousers and shirt were accented by a matching blue silk cummerbund. Foy waved a salute.

Adrianna tilted her head and beguilingly twirled her parasol. Foy strode forward purposefully, as though ready at last to give her his undivided attention.

Strolling away from the crowd, they suddenly came to a stretch of beach completely covered with flat gray shapes.

"It looks as if a giant coin purse has spilled," said Adrianna.

"They are live sand dollars," Foy answered. He picked up one of the thin, flat sea urchins the size of a silver dollar. "God has made some wondrous creatures," he said. Turning it over, he rubbed off a bit of the velvetlike skin to show her the five-pointed pattern of holes for tube-feet.

"How can you tell it's alive?" Adrianna asked laughingly.

"Those are dead." Foy motioned to some of the wafers further up the shore, which had bleached to bone-white. "Look closely at these," he said. "You can just see the hairlike particles moving."

Leaning closer, Adrianna cupped his hand to steady it, bringing it nearer. Her breath caught in her throat. "It's fascinating," she began. Openmouthed, she looked up into his dark eyes. Shivering in the heat of his gaze, she waited, unmoving, even though the warm Gulf waters rushed in around their feet. Gently Foy kissed her upturned lips.

"Adrianna, my darling!" Foy's deep voice roughened with emotion as his arm came around her waist and he pulled her against his thin shirt. "Don't ever run away from me again," he pleaded. "I must have you for my own!"

Turning her parasol to shield them from prying eyes, Adrianna pressed her body tightly against his chest and met the fire of his kisses. Around them gentle wavelets ebbed and flowed. Oblivious to the white froth swishing their ankles, they stood enthralled by the wonder of their love.

Suddenly, they realized that the earth was moving beneath their feet. Allured by the tide, sand was swirling out from under them. Laughing, they hopped through egg-white waves toward higher ground.

"Mr. Ed–wards," called a croaking voice.

They turned, blushing, to see Ben standing above them on a sand dune they had thought protected them from view.

The boy cupped his hands to his mouth and called louder. "They're wantin' you to crank one o' the ice-cream churns."

"Ice cream!" Adrianna exclaimed. "Way out here? Where will the ice come from?"

Laughing, Foy looked at her and licked his lips as if to say she was more delicious than ice cream. "Didn't you see those big blocks loaded at the Apalachicola wharf? The ice came from a ship just in from New England." Foy took her elbow and they reluctantly followed Ben.

The ice cream was made with great ceremony. Curiously, Adrianna watched Foy's family.

"When I live with Senator Atherton and Ma-ma, we mostly eat in restaurants," she said. "I've never had the fun of making ice cream before."

Her appetite whetted when Emma poured a thick, creamy custard into various ice-cream freezers.

"It's a cooked custard made rich with eggs," Emma explained. "We'll leave some plain vanilla. When it's nearly frozen, we'll add wild strawberries to one, mulberries to another." Emma smiled warmly at Adrianna, as if trying hard to make her feel included. "This is our family's favorite, sherbet made from strong, sweet lemonade. Lemons grow here in great abundance."

Jonathan took the filled churns from her, placed them in wooden buckets, and attached cranks.

Beau and Win were playing with a miniature churn. Adrianna watched in surprise as Lily filled it with custard.

"I thought it was a toy."

"Oh, no," replied Lily. "It really freezes cream. Making cream is one of the simple pleasures our family enjoys."

Adrianna made no reply. She felt chilled by the wariness in Lily's eyes and the slight edge to her voice. Not knowing how to help, she sat down on a crate to watch.

Foy's muscles bulged as he rotated one of the cranks. He turned and smiled up at her. She shivered delightedly. She knew that Foy was the only man she would ever love. Green Bethune had flattered her, but she had not loved him as she did Foy. She sighed as the spring breeze kissed her cheek.

"We'd better not let you stick yo' finger in the ice cream," Jonathan said, laughing. "It would make it too sweet."

She focused her eyes to see Jonathan adding layers of ice and salt around Foy's spinning churn. Jonathan grinned at Adrianna and winked. "Takes brains instead of muscle to add the salt. Too much salt causes a skim to freeze too quickly at the edge."

Feeding Foy a piece of ice while he puffed and changed arms on the crank, Adrianna sighed with pleasure. As other men offered to turn the freezers, she noticed a mischievous gleam dancing in Foy's eye.

"Yeeeek!" she screamed. "You rascal!" Shivering as a cold globule slid down her spine, she clapped at the ice he had slipped down her back. Playfully, she chased him, whacking him with her parasol.

When the churns began to stall, they were opened. After the salty ice was carefully brushed away, the paddles were removed, and Jonathan packed ice and paper over each churn to keep it frozen until after lunch. Everyone vied for the paddles. Heads close together, Foy and Adrianna licked the fluffy ice cream from the blades. Next they sampled the lemon sherbet.

"Be careful," warned Foy as he wiped the tangy juice running down her chin. "The sherbet will freeze the roof of your mouth and knock the top of your head off." He bent closer and whispered, "Like you do me."

Adrianna smiled wistfully at Foy and longed to touch his face, so fun-loving, yet serious. She knew that she enticed him, but her tumultuous feelings had gone far beyond mere attraction.

"I'll bet you say that to every girl you take on an excursion," she said, flinging out the words coquettishly. She tried to be saucy and bright, but the fear that he romanced other girls stabbed sharply. When the party was over, she must go—but where? After being with Foy every day, she could not bear the thought of leaving him.

"Adrianna," Foy whispered so close behind her that his breath tickled her ear. "You don't know how special you are. My life hasn't had time for love." He inhaled against her fragrant hair. "I meant it when I said I'd been waiting for you. But your life has been so full."

"No," she whispered. "It's been empty without you."

Inches away, his arms hovered. Tingling from Foy's nearness, she ached to feel the security of his embrace, to pour out the hurts of her lonely childhood. Shc must assure Foy of her need, her lasting love.

Foy's tanned face paled beneath his sun-streaked hair. "I still don't have much to offer, but—dare I hope. . ." Obviously shaken by the emotions playing over her delicate face, he took her elbow. "Come. Let's get away from the crowd."

"Lunchtime!" Lily's voice called them back. "Adrianna, Dear," Lily smilingly summoned. "Come tell Minnie Bray and Mattie Walker about your new painting techniques. All we know how to do is sketch and make watercolor daisies."

After lunch, Adrianna excused herself to return to the steamer and don her new American bathing suit, a dress of light blue flannel with bands of navy braid around the square neck and short puffed sleeves. The skirt was daringly cropped to her knees. The scalloped hem revealed tight, matching bloomers caught with a frill of scallops just below her knees. Black cotton stockings clung to the calves of her long, slim legs.

Stepping into rubber slippers, Adrianna hurried back across the beach toward Mignonne. Struggling through the deep sand in ankle-laced, high-heeled shoes, the girl also wore a blue, braid-trimmed flannel dress. Adrianna's eyes widened as she noticed that Mignonne's bustle-style skirt fell well below her knees, and below that long, bloused bloomers covered her calves.

Apprehensively, Adrianna jerked around so quickly that her blue bandanna slipped off and her flaming hair tumbled from its pins. The older ladies were wrapped in voluminous, ground-sweeping capes. Lily was concealed by a peplumed jacket over full-length trousers. With her cheeks burning, Adrianna swallowed hard. Islay and Minnie had bared their forearms, but Adrianna's calves in their clinging black cotton stockings were the only visible limbs.

Adrianna blinked at the glare-dazzled scene. As she drew back, she had an impression of shocked faces, cold with condemnation. Suddenly, she focused on the fire snapping from Lily's eyes.

Chapter 9

Adrianna remained the focal point in the silent scene of shocked disapproval. Panic-stricken, she suddenly heard an artificial chuckle penetrating the silence. Foy! She had hoped to escape before he saw her. Frantically she clapped her hand to her tumbling hair. Scooping up her fallen bandanna, she prepared to flee.

"Come on in; the water's fine," Foy said with false heartiness.

"I—maybe I shouldn't get too much sun," Adrianna stammered. She pulled her elbow away form his grasp.

Foy's voice dropped to an intimate whisper. "I love to count new freckles. Come on."

Running lightly into the warm Gulf waters, they splashed through foaming waves until they stood waist deep. Through the crystal water, Adrianna's black-stockinged calves were clearly visible. Looking like a little boy in his striped, short-sleeved suit, he grinned at her mischievously. She let out a relieved breath that she was screened from the view of those on shore.

Spanning her waist with strong hands, Foy lifted her gently as they jumped to ride the gentle swells. Adrianna wished she could stay in Foy's embrace and never have to walk back up on that beach.

Squeals of laughter came from Mignonne and her group of friends playing nearby, yet Adrianna and Foy felt joyfully alone. When a sudden breaker foamed over her head, Adrianna coughed and spluttered, tasting salt.

Gleefully, Foy pulled her out to deeper water, higher waves. As the roaring surf arched over them, he pulled her close. Cradled in the curve of the wave, they clung, kissing as the whitecap cascaded over them.

Breathlessly exhilarated, they rose and fell with the gentle surf. Adrianna's bandanna was snatched away by the changing tide. Her long hair floated about her laughing face. Her muscles were tiring, but Adrianna hated to see summoning arms motioning them back to shore.

They paddled back to shallow water. On her stomach, Adrianna walked her hands on the white-sand bottom and let her legs float behind in the foam at the tips of the waves. How could she stand up? The wet stockings stuck to her long legs. She lay limply, dreading the staring eyes of all those she must walk past to reach the steamer. The tide pushed her upward, scraping her stomach on the sand.

Childish shrieks drew haughty faces around. Beau and Win shouted with delight as the incoming tide filled their moat. They screeched with horror as the relentless waves washed away their sand castle.

Adrianna wished she could wash away clear to China. Snatching the moment of distraction, she stood. Her shaking legs were too weak to run. An arm closed around her shoulders and wrapped her in the concealing folds of a ground-sweeping cape. Surprised, she looked down into Mignonne's eyes.

"I'll never forget this," Adrianna whispered. Thankful tears trickled through the salt on her cheeks. Pulling the dark blue hood over her flaming hair, she clutched the flapping cape around her quivering legs. "I'll love you forever!"

Smiling in silent satisfaction, Mignonne walked across the island with Adrianna and up the gangplank. The girls turned to look back, sorry to end the enchanting day.

Adrianna had hoped Saint George Island would be remembered as the place Foy pledged undying love, but she had made another silly blunder. Sadly, she knew herself to be her own worst enemy.

As the tide swallowed the island, the romance of the day washed away. Foy had disappeared in the bustle of departure. Yawning drowsily, Adrianna thanked Mignonne again and bid her good night. As she turned toward her stateroom, she lifted drooping eyelids to see Foy gazing down at her with a look that said he, too, hoped for a good night kiss.

"I thought all day we'd get to talk alone," he breathed against her face. He guided her toward a shadowed spot across the moon-washed deck. "I wanted to ask you—but every time. . ."

"Scientists say the moon. . ." Jonathan's jovial voice broke in upon them. "The moon's going down much quicker nowadays."

Surprised, Adrianna looked over Foy's shoulder at the white satin moon which seemed near enough to touch.

"I'm sure you'll agree, Foy," Jonathan continued into their silence. "It's going down lots faster now than when you were a lad waiting for darkness so you could hide and shoot your chinaberry popgun."

They all laughed. Catching Emma's meaningful look, Adrianna bid them good night. *Were the chaperones merely clearing the decks of dream-struck young people?* she wondered. *Or are they scandalized and trying to keep Foy away from me?*

Drowsy from sun and sea and sand, Adrianna immediately fell into heavy sleep, but when she awoke next morning, she lay brooding. She dreaded to go on deck. She imagined all the things people must be saying behind her back. There was no other way to see Foy; and at last, dressing gingerly because of her sunburn, she ventured out. Foy did not appear. She sat miserably fanning her hot face imagining reasons why. Adrianna finally sought out Mignonne. With evident pleasure that her friendship had been accepted, the girl readily left her group. She came quickly back with the news that Mr. Trimmer, complaining bitterly that fish and ice cream had made him sick, had retired to his quarters. Foy was standing double watches.

Not daring to go uninvited to the pilothouse and give tongues more reason to wag, Adrianna had started back to her cabin when Jonathan Ramsey called to her from his deck chair.

"Come join me," he said, patting the chair beside him.

Normally, Jonathan's twinkling eyes and lively expression made his lined face comfortably pleasant, but his eyes probed too deeply and his voice dropped a shade too intimately as he said, "I'd like to talk with you." Unable to think of an excuse, Adrianna sank glumly into a chair beside Foy's uncle. Her eyes became icy gray as she withdrew inside herself, shutting away the expected scolding.

Jonathan settled an open book on his knees. "Adrianna," his voice softened with words meant only for her ears. "Meeting you has changed my life."

Adrianna stiffened warily. If her skimpy attire had made him misconstrue her character, she certainly had never suspected this side of him.

"You're a brilliant as well as beautiful woman," Jonathan continued slowly. "Emma turned my life around. She helped me through the bad times of losing everything I thought mattered; my child, my home—even my foot, which I can get along just as well without." He laughed shortly. "But something was still missing."

Gazing deeply at the discomfited girl, he laid his big hand restrainingly on her arm and continued earnestly. "Until I met you, I thought I'd given my life to Christ's lordship. I've been making lay talks, trying to help myself and others overcome the bitterness of losing our homes and our fortunes to the War of the Sixties, but. . ."

Dismayed, Adrianna drew back. She exhaled thankfully as she noticed Emma approaching from the far end of the deck.

"You're intelligent," Jonathan repeated. "Pursuing varied interests is fine to a point, but—" He cleared his throat. "Since the war, so many new theories and religions have arisen that I don't wonder you're confused. You need the certainty of truth."

Embarrassed, Adrianna jerked her chin defiantly. "What is truth?"

Jonathan smiled tenderly. "Jesus said, 'I am the way, the truth, and the life.' " Jonathan flipped the pages of his book—she saw it was the Bible—from John 14 to First Corinthians 3. He held it for her to see as he read the eleventh verse.

" 'For other foundation can no man lay than that is laid, which is Jesus Christ. Now if any man build upon this foundation gold, silver, precious stones. . .' "

Adrianna bristled, wondering if he was saying she built her life on materialism.

" 'Wood, hay, stubble,' " he continued. " 'Every man's work shall be made manifest. . .it shall be revealed by fire.' "

Jonathan beamed at her as if she should understand, but Adrianna felt thoroughly confused. Relief flooded her as Emma joined them. Placid Emma always seemed to make pleasant any situation.

Rising to greet her and take flight, Adrianna was again restrained by Jonathan's hand on her arm.

"I was telling Adrianna," he said as he smiled up at his wife, "that watching her struggle to find direction has changed my life. I've told God to take my life and do with it what He will."

Emma waited in quiet expectancy.

"I believe God is calling me to preach," Jonathan said firmly. He smiled enthusiastically at Adrianna and then looked into Emma's face. "I believe God wants me to help lead this confused generation back to the Bible. They must be told that the teachings of men may seem right, but they will prove to be very wrong. God's Word will stand forever as a foundation for life and a guide to joyful living. What would you think about being a preacher's wife?"

"I think that would be wonderful!"

As Emma's silver-blonde head came down in an unaccustomed public display of affection, Jonathan raised his face to receive her kiss.

Slipping away from the pair, Adrianna went to her stateroom.

The *Mignonne Wingate* sped all too swiftly upstream, ending the excursion. Adrianna remained closeted in her stateroom, nursing both her sunburn and her feeling that everyone was talking about her.

I must be a terrible person, she thought morosely.

When she did join the group, everyone seemed sunburned, drowsy, and subdued. Moments alone with Foy were few because Mr. Trimmer remained off duty, and Foy feared leaving his steamboat too long in the hands of the young striker.

They shared a few snatched kisses in secluded corners, but a lump remained in Adrianna's throat. Did Foy merely enjoy kissing her and having a good time? Or had he drawn away because his family did not approve?

She was sitting on deck beside Islay Reeves one afternoon when Islay broke their companionable silence.

"What are your next plans?" she asked. "It must be fun to move about the world. Are you going back to Washington?"

"Ummm," Adrianna responded. She sighed. *What indeed?* she wondered. She had no excuse to stay in Eufaula. She must telegraph Isadora. She lifted troubled eyes to her new friend. "What did you say?"

"I said," repeated Islay, "that you must stay until after the drills and the ball."

"Drills?" Adrianna repeated distractedly.

"Fire drills." Islay nodded enthusiastically. "Every spring, fire companies from Alabama and Georgia gather for the annual convention. Eufaula has an ongoing rivalry for the silver cup with Americus, Georgia. Next week's picnic and ball will be the highlight of our social season. You simply must stay!"

"Of course she must!" Foy's deep voice made them jump. He had appeared from nowhere. His cheeks seemed slack with relief when Adrianna gravely agreed to stay.

He settled down beside her with a grinning report that Trimmer had insisted upon taking the boat through Moccasin Slough. Suddenly Adrianna felt alive again. She had one week's reprieve.

All too soon they were back in Eufaula.

Islay had invited her to spend the week as her houseguest, and Lily had insisted that she stay with the Wingates. Fearful of time alone with Lily, Adrianna declared that the Central Hotel accommodations were fine and that the host's wife, Mrs. Billings, took personal care of her. She would stay there until she contacted her grandparents.

Even though Foy looked tired and unkempt from his double watches, he insisted upon escorting her as she checked into the Central Hotel. Deep in her own thoughts, Adrianna scarcely noticed where she was going as Foy guided her across the hotel lobby.

"Ooof!" She coughed as his elbow rammed her sharply in the ribs.

"Good grannies! What's he doing here?" Foy growled.

Befuddled, Adrianna followed Foy's glare. Green! How could she ever contend with these two at once?

Muttering under his breath, Foy pulled her behind a potted palm. Too late. Green came striding across the room and clapped him on the shoulder of his rumpled suit.

"Foy, old boy," Green said with insufferable politeness. "So sorry I missed that grand excursion on yo' little steamer." Then with a sweeping bow, he kissed Adrianna's trembling hand. "Miss Adrianna, you are positively glowing like a golden goddess."

"A bit too much sun." Adrianna giggled nervously. "Whatever are you doing here, Mr. Bethune?" She withdrew her hand and reached for her ivory fan. Retreating behind it, she fanned rapidly.

"Why, I'm here for the Volunteer Firemen's Convention. What better time to sell fire insurance?" Green beamed at her. "I lie." Green dropped his blond, curly head in mock abjection. "My business is merely an excuse. New

York became boring without you. I could not wait for you to return."

From the corner of her eye, Adrianna saw Foy's jaw muscle twitching. She spoke coquettishly to turn aside the force of Green's words. "Sir! You do go on—charming every lady in sight."

"No, really," Green said sincerely. "I hear there's to be a picnic after the competitions. You must do me the honor of accompanying me—"

"She's agreed to go to the ball with me," Foy interrupted gruffly.

"I. . .um," Adrianna stuttered. Foy was merely assuming. She looked from one to the other. "Gentlemen." She sighed with genuine weariness. "You simply must let me check into my room and get some rest." When they both voiced protestations, she said firmly, "Mr. Bethune, I shall be delighted to attend the picnic with you. And Mr. Edwards." She turned upon him her most dazzling smile. "I'll go with you to the ball."

Crashing cymbals and stridently tooting cornets drew Adrianna to the window of her hotel room. Looking down into the street, she saw a brass band rounding the corner and knew the parade was about to begin.

The climax of the fun-filled week was upon her. Sighing, she placed a small pink hat squarely on her head. Studying herself in the mirror, she reflected that she had not tried to use Green to make Foy jealous, but Green seemed to have nothing but leisure to pay her court. She tilted the hat saucily over her right eye. Securing it with two six-inch hat pins, she remembered how Foy had seemed to be working day and night. He had looked tired and tense when he took her to the skating tournament and had said very little when they attended the Eufaula Library Society musical soiree.

Adrianna was at once glad and sorry that her visit was concluding. She twirled before the looking glass for one last check of her appearance and picked up a parasol that she would surely need against the hot June sun. Fortifying herself with a long, deep breath, she went out to meet the day.

Adrianna threaded her way through the chattering crowd in the hotel lobby. Reaching the appointed place on Broad Street, she found Foy's family. Emma introduced her to her special friends, Mrs. Chauncey Rhodes and Mrs. William Simpson.

Adrianna looked from one to the other in confusion. They were identical twins.

"Don't worry if you can't keep them straight," said Jonathan, chuckling. "They had a double wedding and—wasn't it Mr. Simpson who tried to escort Elizabeth from the church instead of his bride, Mollie?" Laughter pulled their group into a companionable circle. Adrianna relaxed. She would not worry about Foy and Green today. She would simply enjoy the excitement.

Her attention was upon the ceremony naming the Cleburne Fire Company's new engine for Islay Reeves. Watching her friend Islay, Adrianna did not see Foy as he approached. His hand brushed the shining hair spilling down her back, and she turned a sparkling smile upon him. Foy inhaled and rolled his eyes heavenward.

Engulfed in whistles and cheers as Mayor Wells J. Bray led the parade before them, Adrianna gave half attention to the first group bearing the banner, "E. B. Young Fire Company," and pulling a handsome engine and hose reel. As they marched smartly in their dark blue coats and black pantaloons, she thought about the two men in her life. Green noticed and complimented everything she wore while Foy scarcely said a word. *But, oh, his reactions,* she thought and backed a fraction closer to him as cheers rose again.

"Peep through here," Foy said, pointing. "I don't want you to miss the 'Oceanics' from Brunswick, Georgia. They claim to give the impression of the Atlantic Ocean with their uniforms, and—" Adrianna caught a glimpse of the blue caps, white shirts, blue pants, and red stockings just as the banner, "City by the Sea," began to shake.

Next came the Phoenix Company, marching with a whirling display of Japanese parasols; the Chattahoochee Number Five; another brass band; and companies visiting from across Alabama and Georgia. Last of all came Eufaula's hook and ladder company.

"Most towns have engine companies and hose companies," said Foy. "But only a few have a rig like this," he added proudly.

His voice was drowned out by cheering as the parade ended with the carriage of the Eufaula fire department chief, Dan Rowlett. Riding triumphantly around him were six tiny girls waving the colors. Laughing, Adrianna joined in the clapping.

Foy squeezed an arm around her in the press of the crowd moving toward the Firemanic Tournament.

The Mechanics of Americus came first in the reel contest. The reel was stationed one hundred yards from the engine. The men stood at attention. A sandbag dropped on signal. The squad ran, carrying the reel to the engine, and began attaching hose.

"They look so serious," commented Adrianna.

"It's an important drill; a matter of honor, and two hundred dollars in gold are at stake," Foy explained. "But their time is too slow, and see, they didn't play their water all the way to that flagman."

Adrianna was tiring by the next set of contests, but Foy urged her to watch a little longer.

"You must see the Phoenix Company," Foy said, laughing. "We call them the 'Toe-nails.' "

"Why?" She cut her eyes flirtatiously from under her pink hat.

"Just wait," he said teasingly.

She watched the company fill their tank at the cistern. The men took their positions, then removed their shoes and socks. The chief shouted through a silver megaphone as the men dug their feet into the ground and attacked the hand pump madly.

"The 'Toe-nails' say they pump better because they get a good purchase on the ground with their toes." Foy laughed. "Listen to the German jeweler, Schrieber."

Adrianna followed his pointing finger to the little man who held the hose nozzle. Straining forward, she caught his agonized shout.

"Vater, vater, gif me vater!"

She turned her face into Foy's shoulder to hide her giggles.

"It's a local byword among us boys." Foy chuckled. "But I'm sure bud thirsty. Let's duck into Besson's Drugstore for a strawberry soda."

"You have sodas here?" Adrianna clapped her hands.

"Sure, we do," he said, looking hurt at her surprise. "We've had a mineral water factory for ages, and soda water—" He shrugged. "Maybe five years."

Adrianna grimaced, sorry that Foy had caught her implication. In New York City, Green had frequently taken her to soda fountains, but she had not expected to find the treat this far from—the word which popped into her brain was *civilization*. She was thankful she had not spoken it aloud.

Why did I have to think about Green? Adrianna moaned inwardly as she looked up and saw the handsome man had followed them into the drugstore.

Green pulled up another wrought-iron chair and joined them at the small, glass table without being asked. "Good morning, good morning," Green said heartily. "You have sodas," he said, raising his eyebrows, "here?"

Foy glowered but said nothing.

"I didn't expect the custom to have spread this soon." After all of his exclaiming over their sodas, Green ordered a ginger ale.

"It isn't—is it t–time for the p–picnic?" Adrianna stammered. She had thought she had overcome her stuttering, but the animosity between the two men shook her.

"There are lots more contests before the picnic." Green beamed at her. "Right now, I'm doing a little wagering. How 'bout it, Edwards?" Green turned to Foy. Whipping out a leather wallet, he extracted a thousand-dollar bill and waved it tantalizingly. "This says Eufaula's E. B. Youngs will lower the record of the Wide-Awakes from Americus."

Adrianna gasped. She had not known such a large bill was printed. Understanding Foy had no money to spare foolishly, she touched his arm restrainingly. He grinned crookedly at her and shook his head.

Green raised his voice loud enough for everyone in the drugstore to hear.

"I understand those two teams are the big rivals—but is this too rich for your blood?"

Foy snorted disgustedly. "I work too hard for my money to—"

"I know you don't carry cash around," Green interrupted. "An IOU will do fine. Miss Adrianna will hold the bets."

"No!" Foy spoke with calm firmness. "I'm not a gambling man," he said pleasantly. "It's against my principles." Turning indifferently away, Foy finished his soda. "Come on. We're missing the fun."

They went out into the rapidly heating day to watch the next contests.

Cheers arose when the famous Alabama company, the E. B. Youngs, appeared on the tracks. They stood at attention as the sandbag dropped. Then they ran down the track shouting, "Hurrah!"

Adrianna watched in amazement as the runners dug quickly to the wooden water main made of hollowed logs squared and beveled to fit together. A hole had already been drilled in the pipe and plugged with a small slick of wood. The designated plugman snatched out the wooden fireplug.

A man with a stopwatch yelled, "Run to the plug: 12:15."

Standing uncomfortably between Green and Foy, she waited as the pipeman made the connection with the hard rubber hose and water began to draw. As the men pumped frantically, she watched Foy's jaw muscle twitch and realized Green had not only tried to push him into betting because of her, but betting against his friends.

"Water to the flag," shouted the timekeeper. "Twenty-four!"

Next came the Pulaski Number One. They made a pretty run to the plug, but the pipeman fell down as he reached the engine. They failed to make connections and the shout went up, "A burst."

The Wide-Awakes from Americus came forward amid great cheering.

The timekeeper shouted, "Run to the plug: 12:20!"

Fanning tiredly, Adrianna felt hot and slightly sick as her two suitors watched the frantically working firemen.

"Water to the flag. . . ," came the shout. "Twenty-six!" Eufaula had won. Whistles, shouts, and stamping feet created pandemonium. Green went smilingly off to collect his bets. Foy would have lost if Green had forced him into betting. As the Youngs received the coveted silver cup, Adrianna hid behind her fan and wiped perspiration.

Listlessly, she followed Green to the picnic. Although he was at his charming best, she did not know what he said or what she ate.

The moon rose full and clear for the great complimentary ball given by the Cleburne Fire Company on Saturday night. Moving the kerosene lamp closer to the chevel glass, Adrianna frowned at her reflection. Green would know her gown was the latest Paris style, but would it be too different from the other ladies? She had chosen pure white satin which shone with the luster of fine pearls. Trimmed only with narrow net ruching on the scooped neckline and sleeveless armholes, the dress emphasized her innocent beauty. Craning to see the back, she knew it would capture all eyes because the satin was softly crushed into cascading poufs from the bustle to the train. She pinned a pink rose in her hair as her only adornment, pulled on elbow-length white kid gloves, and went down to meet Foy.

Adrianna searched Foy's serious eyes in vain for a sign that he thought she looked like a bride. She had never known him to be so tensely silent. Had she somehow disappointed him again? An odd expression made him look like a lost little boy dressed in black tie and tails.

As the orchestra tuned up and began Mr. Strauss's latest waltz, Foy wordlessly held out his white-gloved hands. Moving into his arms, Adrianna clung wistfully to his shoulder as he whirled her to the music with his long black tailcoat flapping and her white train swishing. Swaying close enough to feel the beating of each other's hearts, they spoke no words. Frightened that something between them seemed lost, Adrianna struggled to pull her charm into place when Foy's friends claimed her for occasional dances.

Suddenly Green appeared and asked her for a dance just as a polka began. Tripping over her train on the lively, jerky steps, she apologized for weariness.

"Of course you're tired," Green replied solicitously. "Let's go into the garden to cool."

Adrianna agreed without thinking.

The warm June night, heavy with the fragrance of roses, closed around them as Green led her to a secluded bench.

"You have never been more lovely, my dear," he said sincerely. Daringly, he kissed her bare neck. "You might have stepped from a painting by Renoir."

Pleased in spite of herself, she smiled softly. Green was, indeed, a highly cultured gentleman.

"I don't believe you understood. . ." He took both of her hands in his and squeezed them until she looked at him with attention. "What was I trying to tell you at the picnic is that my own plantation near Charleston is prospering again. But more than that—" He dropped a kiss on her nose and lifted her chin, urging her to look at him. "My fleet of ships will again be carrying cotton to Liverpool. How would you like to see London and Paris?" His voice rose excitedly. "I want to show you the world!"

Adrianna drew back, mouth agape.

"Beautiful creature!" Green dropped to one knee beside her. "Will you do me the honor of becoming my wife?"

Shocked, Adrianna looked at Green kneeling humbly before her. Then her eyes narrowed and hardened to a cold gray. She knew that the time had come for her to grow up. Jonathan had told her to set a course for her life and stick to it.

"Green, I—" Her voice squeaked. "I'm flattered. You're such a cultured gentleman. Seeing the world with you. . ." Trembling, she knew she would fit far better into Green's realm than in this small town with these overly religious people. "I'm all aflutter." She pressed her hands against her chest, turning back the acceptance which formed on her lips. "Please. . ." She tried to appear demure. "May I have until tomorrow to answer? Tomorrow night?"

Green kissed her palms. "Only 'til Sunday night, my lovely. I'm leaving for New York on the Monday morning train."

"Yes," she murmured. "I must leave, too—to visit my mother." Sighing, she knew that she no longer had an excuse to stay in Eufaula. Her dreams of being a fairy princess in the castle tower of Barbour Hall were ebbing away as swiftly as the tide had destroyed the children's sand castle. The ball was almost over. Foy would be claiming her for one last dance, then taking her home. *Telling me good-bye?* Twisting her feet in their white suede dancing shoes, she thought ruefully of glass slippers and Cinderella. Yes, she must hurry and leave Eufaula, because her carriage was turning into a pumpkin.

Chapter 10

Foy pummeled his pillow. This should have been one of the happiest nights of his life. He had planned to propose to Adrianna after the ball. She had looked so beautiful, so like a bride, and he had not even told her. He had endured the dance, repeatedly rehearsing his speech. The hour was upon him when Adrianna returned from the garden with Green. She had seemed remote, unattainable.

Green! Savagely, Foy flung the pillow across the bedroom. *It's all Green's fault!*

No. He dropped his head in his hands. Green was not on the boat. But Lily was and. . .

He had thought he was communicating his love and his desire to make Adrianna his bride. Every time they had been alone and he had primed himself to extract a promise from her, they had been interrupted. He suspected Lily had planned some of the diversions.

Oh, Lily had been broad-minded enough about the bathing suit, but Adrianna's flippant attitude about the Bible had made Lily argue long and hard that he should try to bring Adrianna to Christ before they married. Her impassioned words rattled in his brain.

"Foy, you know that Paul says we should not marry just to be marrying, but to marry 'only in the Lord,' " Lily had insisted. "Remember that Second Corinthians 6:14 says, 'Be ye not unequally yoked together with unbelievers: for what fellowship hath righteousness with unrighteousness?' "

"But Adrianna is a sweet, good person," Foy had replied.

"Darling Foy, you know being a Christian does not mean being a good person. It means acknowledging that we have sinned by missing the mark of the high calling of God. We can never be righteous enough on our own to bridge the separation from Him. Only as we accept Jesus' death on the cross as payment for our sins and believe in His resurrection as the evidence that we have eternal fellowship with God do we become children of God."

Lily had reminded him of people they knew whose lasting marriages were based on the love of God. She pointed out some unhappy acquaintances whose shallow faith played no part in governing family relationships. She had cautioned him on the futility of planning to change a partner after marriage.

Acknowledging Lily's godly wisdom, Foy had agreed to take time pursuing his courtship. But Green had intervened.

Foy paced his bedroom. Perhaps Adrianna did fit better into Green's world. Miserable, Foy trudged to the thick blackness of the attic, wrestling with his problems as he climbed the familiar stairs. Emerging in the glassed belvedere, Foy saw the rosy streaks of dawn lighting the sky. His spirits lifted. Suddenly he thought what he could offer Adrianna: love, a permanent home, tenderness, and caring. *I can offer more than Green,* he thought. *I love her very soul!*

Adrianna had agreed to a brief visit on Sunday afternoon. Foy's hands shook as he opened the double doors and ushered her into Barbour Hall. He knew that his time had run out.

"What was it you wanted to show me?" Adrianna asked coolly. Fear, anger, pride, and jealousy tumbled like a kaleidoscope in Foy's brain. Love and desire filled his throat, stopping words. He ground his teeth resolutely. A navy man could not give up without a try. Silently, he bowed his head over Adrianna's delicate hand and kissed her fingertips. Then he pulled her up the curving staircase to the second floor.

"This way," Foy indicated, leading her upward again through the dark passage of the attic. They remained silent until they stepped through the opening into the belvedere.

Adrianna's expression lifted with delight as she emerged in the sun-filled room. Foy watched in relief as she was drawn out of her silence.

"What a wonderful view! It's like owning the world!" Adrianna exclaimed as she turned from one windowed wall to the other and looked out across the tops of trees along the winding river.

"This has always been my special place," Foy said with small-boy eagerness. "Mine and Lily's." Seeing her smile slide, he hurried on. "I'd hoped it might be special to you. When I was a lad and Lily and Harrison were in love and struggling against the world to get married, I dreamed that one day I would be a pilot on the Chattahoochee, and, and. . ." His deep voice choked with emotion. "And my wife would be here watching for me."

Foy's voice dropped so low he wondered if she had heard. She had turned a rigid back to him. Sunlight set her hair ablaze.

Overcome, Foy crossed the small room in a step and buried his face in her hair. Hopefully, he wrapped long arms around her and held her close.

"Why would she have to stay here?" Adrianna asked in a strained voice. "Why couldn't she go with you?"

"Well." Foy laughed shakily. "I'd always imagined her at home with the house full of children, but. . ." Hopelessly, he slackened his grip. He could not bear to ask for her only to be told she was marrying Green. Releasing her, he stepped back.

Adrianna turned. Wistfully, like a love-starved child, she looked at him, saying nothing. Foy crushed her in an embrace and kissed her trembling lips. Letting his love flow, urging her to love him, he suddenly realized Adrianna was responding joyfully.

Encouraged, he drew back and took her dimpled chin in his shaking hand to lock her gaze with his. "Adrianna, I'm crazy with love for you. I'd hoped if I waited, I'd have more to offer. I can never give you what Green can, but I love you. Dare I hope you'll be my bride? Will you marry me? Now?"

For answer, Adrianna's arms went up. Twining her fingers in his hair, she spoke with her smile singing in her words. "Yes, oh, yes, Foy!" Then her voice trembled tearfully. "I. . .I've never known real affection, only approval when I did right. My wildest dreams weren't as wonderful as you loving me."

"Do you want time to think about it?" Foy asked. "Can you be happy in Eufaula? In Barbour Hall?"

"I don't need to think—unless you're not sure," she said teasingly. Then she spoke seriously. "I've never had a real home in one place." Shyly, she raised her face for his kiss. "Home, my home, is here in your arms."

"And here you'll stay." Foy swept Adrianna to a special corner. With one arm securely around her, he added to the other inscriptions preserved on the wall, "Adrianna and Foy, June 5, 1876."

Then his face clouded doubtfully. "As for the house, you'll have your work cut out for you. Not one thing has been moved since Mama died. Come on. I'll take you for an inspection tour of your dilapidated mansion. I asked Kitty and Lige to be here to protect your—"

"My reputation?" Adrianna's laughter pealed. "You mean I still have one after the episode of the exposed limbs?"

Foy feigned a wicked leer. "You were delicious. But Lily, at least, took it in stride."

Adrianna looked at him with near disbelief. Then she followed him to the upstairs sitting room. Long-boned Kitty, with a self-conscious look, was puttering about the small morning room.

"Kitty," Foy said excitedly to the woman who had been his childhood nurse, "meet Miss Adrianna. She has agreed to marry me and become the new mistress of Barbour Hall."

"I'm so glad to know you," Adrianna said. "And to have you to help me with this huge house." She whispered conspiratorially, "You'll have to teach me all the things Foy likes and doesn't like."

A pleased expression spread over Kitty's face. "I been taking care of him since he wuz this high." She extended her hand. "This house been needing a lady like you."

Kitty opened the door into the adjoining blue and white bedroom which

Lily and Emma had shared. She let Adrianna peep into the huge master bedroom at the rear, but she kept the door to Foy's room firmly shut. As the women conversed about the running of the house, Foy stood back in dazed happiness.

Hand in hand, the happy couple walked through the main floor. Foy suddenly realized how badly everything needed painting.

"What I'd like here is some new murals," Adrianna suggested as they stood in the spacious central hall.

"Anything your heart desires," Foy said, lifting her hand to kiss it.

"And the curtains. . ." She stepped into the parlor. "These are really old and out of style." Frowning, she ran her fingers over the carved mahogany leaves and scrolls on the stiff-backed, double settee. "In fact, there are several things in here I'd like to change."

"Sure." He shrugged.

They strolled through the wildly overgrown garden where Adrianna met Lige. She charmed him with her smile.

In the white-latticed gazebo, Foy and Adrianna sat nestled silently, savoring the joy of shared love. At last Adrianna spoke. "I suppose I must leave tomorrow as I had planned."

Shocked, Foy straightened. "I don't ever want to be parted from you again!"

Laughing lightly, she kissed his ear and said, "But I must go home to tell Ma-ma. A bride has so many things to do!"

"But, but," Foy spluttered. He had not thought of wedding preparations. "Well, you can't leave before June eleventh," he said triumphantly. "Mignonne will be sixteen, and she'd never forgive you if you missed her coming-out party!"

Reluctantly, they left their haven and went to the Wingate house to share their news. Lily hugged Adrianna with welcoming arms and apologized for not being able to give an immediate engagement party.

"Oh, I couldn't take away from Mignonne's big day," Adrianna said, smiling at her young friend.

"I have the perfect solution," Harrison interposed. "There's to be a grand celebration for our nation's hundredth birthday. Senator Atherton has promised to be the July Fourth speaker. Perhaps your parents could come, too, and we'd have—"

"The wedding in July?" Foy leaned forward.

"No, no!" Lily laughed and patted him fondly. "The engagement party. You must do things properly if you expect local society to accept your bride."

When Lily invited them to stay for supper, Foy saw Adrianna's cheeks become pale. She twisted her hands and declared that she must return to the hotel.

"What's the matter?" he demanded when they were alone in the buggy.

"I promised Green that—he's waiting to—I'm to have supper with. . ."

"What?" Foy exploded. "If you're engaged to me you can't be meeting him!" Tears filled Adrianna's eyes and he relented. "I'm sorry." He patted her hand. "You didn't know we'd be engaged. But it won't hurt him to wait and wonder." Her chin trembled and he cupped it tenderly. "Send him a note."

"No. Foy, Green's going back to New York tomorrow. It's only right that I meet him and tell him about us."

"I'll go with you."

Adrianna shook her head. "Green's a proud man. I must see him alone and—tell him good-bye."

For the next few days, Foy found every possible excuse to look in at Barbour Hall. Laughing and chattering, Adrianna and Kitty were cleaning every nook and cranny.

With careful thoughts of her reputation, Adrianna had belatedly accepted Islay's invitation and moved in as her houseguest for the remainder of her stay. Foy and Adrianna had shared the news of their forthcoming marriage with close friends; and Islay, Emma, Mignonne, and Lily came over daily to help get the house prepared for another bride.

One morning Foy found Lily stamping about the parlor. With her eyes flashing, she snapped, "Mama's mahogany double settee! It was Chippendale!" Her voice rose in a wail. "A finely carved design made in 1820. Adrianna said she was replacing 'that old handmade piece,' " Lily said mockingly, "with 'modern, factory-turned chairs.' "

"Adrianna didn't know," said Foy soothingly. "Don't push her, Lily," he pleaded. "Help her. Lead her gently into the fold like you've done the rest of us."

With tears streaming down her cheeks, Lily stared at him. "No, I guess she doesn't know about the things that set gentry apart. She's going to break you!" She stormed out the door.

Foy looked around uneasily. He hoped Adrianna had not heard. She entered a few moments later and kissed him delightedly.

"I've engaged the famous French mural painter, Monsieur Le Franc, to come and paint palm-filled urns on the central-hall walls," she said gleefully. "And just wait until you see what I've planned for the music room!"

Foy felt old recalling how Mignonne had looked at her ball. No longer an adorable child, Mignonne was a stunningly beautiful woman. Adrianna had delighted him by asking Mignonne to be her maid of honor.

Since his confrontation with Lily, Foy had been edgy. He was tired of the disruption that Adrianna's nesting instincts had brought to his bachelor quarters. He was almost relieved that she was spending a few weeks at home with her mother.

Without Adrianna, however, Barbour Hall seemed empty in spite of the wooden barrels which began arriving. He opened one. Spilling out straw packing, he found a set of china which was far more elaborately decorated than the set already filling the dining room.

Suddenly fearing the cost of having a wife, Foy retreated from the barrels and set out with long strides for a walk. Ambling aimlessly, he ended up at the fairgrounds and racetrack.

"Good grannies!" Foy bumped his head with the heel of his hand when he rounded the horse barn and spotted Green Bethune.

The arrogant man saw Foy. His mouth curved up in a one-sided smile.

Foy managed a gruff greeting. "Sure didn't expect to see you in the sticks again."

"Couldn't resist the temptation to challenge your local horses." Green beamed with friendly charm. "Care to wager against your town favorite, Strawberry Jack?"

Foy frowned. "I wouldn't bet against Strawberry Jack. His owner brought his know-how straight from Kentucky. His coat of arms is S.S.S.—Speed, Safety, and Style."

Green's blue eyes narrowed knowingly. "Let's stir the sporting blood. What will you wager," he said, "on whom the fair Adrianna will be to wife?"

Taken aback, Foy stammered, "That bet would be taking candy from a baby, Sir. She'll marry me and that right soon."

"What wager?" Green taunted.

Foy laughed hollowly. "I'd stake my life." He shrugged. "Anything. The *Mignonne Wingate*."

Green chuckled and turned as if to walk away. "So certain are you?" Suddenly he whirled and put his face near Foy's. "She told me you asked her to marry you. She's coming back to make a formal announcement after the fair. But who will it be?"

Feeling reduced to the small-boy fury which had defeated him when first he met Green Bethune, Foy ground his teeth and said nothing.

Green sneered at Foy and added, "I'll see your bet on the *Mignonne Wingate* and raise you. Obviously, she didn't tell you I also proposed! I'm meeting her here for her answer. That little redhead's choice just might be your Fo'th of July fireworks!"

Chapter 11

Adrianna alighted from the train in the Eufaula depot. Eagerly, she searched for Foy's sun-streaked hair above the milling crowd.

The people converged on Senator Atherton. Adrianna stood uncertainly with her parents. They remained unnoticed as all attention focused on the distinguished statesman and his elaborately costumed wife.

Chattering, Adrianna tried to bridge the distance between her parents.

"Oh, there he is," she squealed at last. "Come meet Foy!"

"Foy," she cried ecstatically, "this is my mama." She smiled down at the small woman. "And Sam Atherton, my papa! He came for our engagement party, too!"

"How do you do, Sir?"

Sam Atherton stepped forward and shook hands cordially. "I'm pleased to meet Adrianna's young man."

Adrianna held out her hand, longing for Foy's touch, waiting for his gaze to wrap her in love.

Foy did not look at her.

"I'm so excited they. . ." Her voice trailed as she watched Foy's stern face. "That they could come for. . ." She swallowed. What could be wrong? "Our formal announcement," she finished in a whisper. She stared at him. "You're still—when is Lily planning the party?"

Adrianna waited.

"She couldn't send out invitations." Foy cast her a sidelong glance.

The four stood like the corners of an empty room.

"Lily had to have a final word from you." Foy shoved the words into the void.

"Oh."

"I expect she wants to know the wedding date," Mrs. Atherton contributed softly.

Foy jutted out his chin. "Uh, yes, Ma'am. Something like that." He gestured them toward a carriage.

Their conversation was stiff and formal as they followed the parade to the fairgrounds. Adrianna shifted uncomfortably. Foy had never been shy about meeting strangers. She did so want her parents to love him, but he seemed determined to give them a bad impression.

As they passed through the exhibits and her mother lingered at the canned goods, Adrianna hissed, "What's wrong with you?"

"Nothing's wrong with me."

"Ohh, look at these beautiful pianos." Adrianna stepped forward quickly because Ma-ma was watching with a puzzled frown.

"We don't need a new piano."

"No. But Foy, I would like some of these Brumby rockers for the porch." She pointed to the next exhibit. "They're big enough for rocking ba—"

"Prefer the old family furniture myself."

Adrianna turned to her father, who was conversing with a Mrs. Parker about the display of her novel pets, Texas anteaters and horned frogs.

Linking her arm with his, Adrianna lifted her chin icily and left Foy to bring her mother. The crowd moved toward the speaker's platform and Senator Atherton's booming voice.

Watching Foy's rigid back, Adrianna wiped beads of perspiration from her upper lip. Grandfather was intoning every detail of America's hundred years. Patting her hands soundlessly when the closing applause finally came, she thought that surely now she could have a moment with Foy.

A man with a megaphone announced the performance of the daring equestrienne Nellie Burke, and the crowd swept them along to the white-fenced track.

Adjusting her jostled hat, Adrianna looked up to see Foy giving her a cold look. Pushing back the straw brim, she saw Green Bethune across the track.

"Oh, no!" she wailed. "I'd hoped we'd never have to see him again!"

Foy glowered. "Don't tell me you didn't expect to see Green. He said you were coming back to choose between us. That you told him to meet you here!"

"And you believed him? Oh, Foy." She turned close against him. "You know it's you I love. I told him I was marrying you."

"Miss Adrianna, your beauty increases with each passing day."

Adrianna jumped as Green's voice penetrated her misery. Somehow he had pushed his way through the crowd. Adrianna managed to introduce him to her parents.

Green put on his most charming manner. "Mr. Atherton, you must place your bets on the best horse, Charleston's Pride!" He chuckled. "Unless you want to lose your money on the local favorite—what was that little ole horse, Foy, Strawberry Jack?"

"Foy! You didn't gamble?" Adrianna asked anxiously behind her fan.

Foy's retort was drowned out by cheering for Nellie Burke's barrel racing, but when Adrianna tugged at his sleeve, he repeated, "I can depend on Strawberry Jack."

"Didn't you think you could depend on me?"

Foy ducked his head and rubbed a crimson ear. "I—wasn't sure. Grannies, Woman, you're driving me crazy. If you really love me, let's get married as soon as possible." He slipped his arm around her.

"As soon as possible." She nodded solemnly.

Wild cheering rang out again as the harness racers trotted on the track. Relieved to find the source of Foy's strange behavior, yet frightened at Green's continuing interference, Adrianna folded her fan and gnawed it nervously.

Swaying in the heat, Adrianna did not feel a part of the roaring crowd. She did not understand the source of the frenzy over Strawberry Jack until she looked at Green's angry face. He was not accustomed to losing.

The Atherton party was next ushered to Hart's Hall where the old families of Eufaula were celebrating with a great Centennial Tea Party. Green did not follow, and Foy behaved more normally as he introduced her parents to his family. Jonathan offered his arm to Adrianna's mother saying, "You must have a delicacy from each food table. The ladies have outdone themselves decorating. See, there is fruit from Georgia, palmetto and rice from South Carolina, minerals from Pennsylvania, pines from North Carolina. . ."

Relieved that her mother was thus escorted, Adrianna thought to escape for a moment to make things right with Foy, but her grandmother caught her arm.

"You must carry my plate," Isadora said, critically surveying the room. "I'm glad to see the ladies have become cognizant of fashion."

Adrianna looked about her. The dresses were styled with the latest cord-pleat trimming and gophering, and the tremendous hats were adorned with gold-colored silk velvet flowers, gold-spangled plumes, or fruit ornaments.

"You need not trouble yourself about my lack of society, Ma-ma," Adrianna said. "These people are of fine old families. Now, admit it, you've never seen more elegant diamonds, and the coiffures are *à la Grecque*."

"I suppose so," Isadora agreed reluctantly. "But your young man exhibits an uncouth gruffness. You must polish—"

"It's just that we've had a—a slight misunderstanding."

Adrianna's anxiety increased with each passing hour. The two family groups dined at Rowlett's Restaurant, conversing nervously.

Night fell at last, but the heat of the day did not cool. Neither did Foy's temper. As the party left the restaurant for the hotel, he silently guided Adrianna to a small runabout. They had a moment alone at last.

As the horse clopped into the darkness, Adrianna dropped the cloak of reserve she had clung to all day. "Oh, Foy, how could you think I'd—"

"Why should Green lie?"

"Because Green is Green!" Adrianna lifted her chin defiantly, then sagged. "Perhaps I should have told you. But. . ." She nestled against him. "It didn't seem worth mentioning."

Foy did not respond.

Straightening, she blurted, "Yes, he asked me to marry him. I can't help that."

Tight-lipped, Foy stared unseeingly ahead of the horse. "Green," he said, spitting out the word. "Green said you'd choose between us when you came for the Fourth."

"That's not true!"

Reaching out with trembling fingertips, Adrianna turned Foy's hurt face close to hers. "I've loved you from the moment I saw you, but I didn't know you loved me. And I allowed Green to court me, but. . ."

One finger stroked his red-tipped ear. She thought back to that Sunday night when she had given Green her answer and shivered at the recollection of the angry scene.

"Green proposed before you did. I asked him to give me time to answer. No, wait," she begged as Foy stiffened and turned away. "I had given up hope that you'd ask me. But don't you remember? When you did ask, I said yes instantly!"

Foy relaxed slightly.

"I met Green on Sunday night because I'd promised an answer. I told Green that I would marry you. That we'd announce it formally when I came for the Centennial Celebration."

"That was your mistake." Foy slapped the reins at the barely moving horse. "You shouldn't have let him know that. Never give Green an inch."

"He won't come between us anymore." Not worrying about an unladylike advance, Adrianna kissed his ear. "It's you I love and you I want to marry—if you still want me."

Saying nothing, Foy directed the buggy beneath an ancient cedar and dropped the reins. Wrapping Adrianna in a crushing embrace, he kissed her, pouring out despair and longing. His soul filled with joy as she responded.

"Tomorrow, let's set the date for the engagement party and the wedding," he urged when it seemed he could trust his voice.

"Tomorrow," she promised.

Adrianna beamed at her parents as she and Foy showed them through Barbour Hall the next morning.

"Quite impressive," said Sam Atherton as they crossed the black-and-white marble floor of the central hall.

Foy proudly showed Sam the pine timbers, which had been cut on the property and allowed to season three years before the house was built in 1854.

While the men were occupied, Adrianna showed her mother some of the modernizing she planned. In the back hall, she pointed to the black couch with S-shaped legs and said, "I want to get rid of that horsehair sofa with those funny legs and put in a new Turkish divan."

Lily joined them in the parlor. Graciously putting the Athertons at ease, she related her plans for the engagement party. "I told Foy that to set the wedding sooner than three months after the engagement was formally announced would be improper."

Disappointed, Adrianna nodded meekly.

"October then?"

Mary Atherton nodded in agreement.

"You'd better check the senator's schedule," Sam Atherton said sardonically.

"Where will we have the wedding?" Lily asked tentatively.

Adrianna panicked. Knowing that the bride's home was customary, she looked from one parent to the other, thought of her grandparents, and wondered, *Where is my home?* She stared at Lily and found understanding in her eyes.

Lily said, "Since your family is so. . .cosmopolitan—perhaps Eufaula? Our church is—"

"Oh, yes!" Adrianna clapped her hands delightedly. "Eufaula, since our family's so scattered. Can't you," she said, looking pleadingly from one parent to the other, "come back to Eufaula?" Receiving their nods, she ran into the hall. "But not the church. Here. Right here. I want to come down that beautiful stairway." Her voice rose excitedly. "Can't you just picture that, Foy?"

"Perfectly."

"And the reception. Oh, it must be in this lovely dining room. Come, you haven't seen the most beautiful part of the house!"

Tugging at her parents' hands, she hurried them into the music room. "Mr. Le Franc has moved into the house for three months to hand-paint the walls. It's quite elaborate, I know." She felt suddenly uncertain. "But he uses such delicate hues that—"

"It's lovely," murmured Mrs. Atherton, testing the paint of the fleurs-de-lis stenciled on the walls.

Sam Atherton threw back his head to see the ceiling. It looked like a blue sky filled with clouds and butterflies. He grinned and said fondly, "It looks like you, Pudding."

"Thank you, Papa. And you will give me away?" Tears of happiness filled her eyes as he squeezed her hand in assent. Adrianna turned their attention upward.

"Mr. Le Franc brings in the flowers from the garden to paint. See, each corner is different." She pointed to lilies, pansies, roses, and tulips.

"He's a very fine artist," replied Lily. "The hollyhock on that door panel has such depth."

Adrianna met Foy's eyes across the room and reveled in their oneness. "Look at the dining room," she babbled. "Mr. Le Franc was intrigued with the design on the silver, and he added that to this ceiling and wall. Didn't Foy tell me that y'all buried this silver in the garden when the Yankees came? And, oh, Mama, can't you just see a wedding cake on this beautiful mahogany table beneath that glorious Waterford chandelier?"

The cake was magnificent indeed as it waited beneath the chandelier for the wedding to begin. Emma had claimed the honor of making it from the recipe she had used for Lily and Harrison. Admiring the towering masterpiece, Adrianna could smell the aroma of fruit, mace, and nutmeg through the glistening white frosting.

When Adrianna and her family had returned to Eufaula for the wedding, moved up to September 17 to accommodate Senator Atherton's schedule, Barbour Hall had turned into a fairyland of roses. Foy explained that their neighbor, Mrs. Kendall, had sent bouquets of long-stemmed beauties from the thousands of bushes in her garden. Smiling, Adrianna knew this gift from the grandest mansion in town gave their marriage a stamp of approval from local society. She inhaled the sweetness and drifted up the stairs to the sunny bedroom where she was to dress.

The time had come at last. Adrianna fumbled with the tiny satin buttons from the neck to the pointed waist of the closely fitted bodice. She had chosen a simply styled wedding gown to set off her dazzling hair. The brocaded satin skirt showed the embossed roses only in a glimmer when she moved.

Mignonne helped her drape an airy lace overskirt down one side. Silently, she placed the gossamer veil over Adrianna's flaming hair and blushing face.

Mignonne tiptoed out to peep down the stairs.

"It's time," she whispered as if afraid to break the spell. "Everyone is assembled in the parlor." She handed Adrianna a bouquet of white roses and dainty tuberoses and clutched her own nosegay of pink that matched her pink bridesmaid dress. "I hope you and Foy will live happily ever after." She went out to take her place.

Papa joined Adrianna in the upstairs hall. Gripping his arm, she walked down the short flight to the landing and paused.

The soft notes floating from the music room ceased. Emma struck the stirring chords of the "Wedding March." Adrianna floated down the remaining stairs and paused for a moment beneath the chandelier's crown of thorns.

In the parlor, an altar of glossy magnolia leaves and delicate lanceleaf smilax was banked before the white marble fireplace. Jonathan waited, an open

Bible in his hand. Beside him, Harrison stood stalwartly as best man. Beau and Win, in sailor suits, wore grins as wide as the collars flapping on their shoulders. They flanked either side, holding satin pillows bearing rings. Mignonne waited expectantly. Sweeping them in a brief, loving glance, Adrianna looked at Foy. Elegantly handsome in his trim, naval uniform of Confederate gray with his sword on his hip, Foy waited with his face alight with love.

Releasing a tremulous breath, Adrianna drifted toward Foy.

"Dearly beloved," said Jonathan in a warm voice. "We are gathered together here in the sight of God, and in the face of this company, to join together this man and this woman in holy matrimony." He paused to smile, and his twinkling eyes eased Adrianna's trembling. "Marriage was divinely instituted when Jehovah God spoke the nuptial words to Adam and Eve in the Garden of Eden. Jesus of Nazareth honored its celebration by His presence at the wedding in Cana of Galilee, and chose its beautiful relations as the figure of that union between Himself and His church. Into this holy estate, these two persons come now to be joined." Jonathan's voice gentled. He was asking for Foy's vow. "Wilt thou love her, comfort her, honor and keep her, in sickness and in health; and, forsaking all others, keep thee only unto her, so long as ye both shall live?"

"I will!" Foy answered strongly.

Jonathan turned to her. "Adrianna, wilt thou have this man to be thy wedded husband, to live together after God's ordinance, in the holy estate of matrimony? Wilt thou obey him and serve him, love, honor, and keep him in sickness and in health; and forsaking all others, keep thee only unto him, so long as ye both shall live?"

"I will," whispered Adrianna.

"Who giveth this woman to be married to this man?"

"I do," Sam Atherton said, and he gave her right hand to Jonathan who placed it in Foy's.

With Foy's strong handclasp, Adrianna's fear vanished. Steadily, she pledged her troth and smiled at him as he slipped the ring on her finger. He received her ring.

Jonathan was praying, joining their right hands, intoning, "What therefore God hath joined together, let not man put asunder. I pronounce that Foy and Adrianna are man and wife in the name of the Father, and of the Son, and of the Holy Ghost. Amen." Jonathan smiled. "You may now kiss your bride."

Foy lifted the veil covering her face and folded it back. Their eyes met. Whispering, "Mrs. Edwards," he bent toward her lips, and she met his kiss. Cheers and congratulations, then hugs and kisses overwhelmed the happy couple and swept them into the dining room.

Ceremonially, Foy unsheathed his naval sword and handed it to Adrianna.

Her arms shook as she lifted the long sword. Foy's strong hands closed over her delicate fingers, strengthening her as together they cut the first slice of cake. Laughing, she fed the rich cake to Foy.

For the formal wedding portrait, they moved to the mahogany secretary where Foy sat in a stiff-backed chair with his arm propped on the small desk. Adrianna stood slightly behind.

Poof! The photographer's black powder went off with an acrid smell and a blinding flash.

"Fire," a coarse voice yelled. "Mr. Foy, Mr. Foyeee!" Lige tumbled into the back hall. "Yo' warehouse afire!"

Chapter 12

Adrianna stood unmoving as Foy kissed her and ran after Ligc. As news of the fire rippled across the room, all the men rushed out.

Adrianna tried to smile and move graciously among the ladies who stood about chattering nervously. Lily whispered for her to cut souvenir pieces of the wedding cake for the guests. Although Lily tried to keep her movements from looking like she was sending the guests away, Adrianna sensed her tension.

Old Mrs. Robbins followed Adrianna about, giving her streams of advice on marriage. "Now let me show you how to seal up a piece of cake to keep for wedding anniversaries," she said. "I still had crumbs to feed my husband on our golden wedding day."

Clanging bells interrupted her spiel. Everyone rushed to the window. The E. B. Youngs were assembling.

Another fire alarm bell rang. "That's the signal for the Chattahoochee Number 5," said Emma in a hushed voice. "It must be a terrible fire!"

Adrianna turned to Lily and whispered, "Oh, we must go—" Her voice broke.

"Yes," Lily agreed.

With trembling hands, Adrianna removed her veil. The grim women climbed into a buggy and headed toward the warehouses.

The smell of burning rags made Adrianna's nose twitch by the time they reached the bottom of the hill. Smoldering bales surrounded the Cotton Exchange.

"Oh." Adrianna turned at the small sound from Lily.

"It's Number One warehouse—where all the best cotton is—was stored," Lily explained as she struggled to guide the jittery horse close to the fire.

The wood-shingled roof of the long, brick building blazed from both ends.

The "Toe-nails" stood staunchly dug into the wet ground as they pumped frantically. Holding the hose nozzle, Mr. Schrieber cried, "Vater, vater, gif me vater!"

Adrianna shrieked as she saw Foy coming out from the smoke-filled building with another bale on a hand truck. With a roar, the fire met, and the roof exploded upward, then collapsed into the thick-walled shell.

Lily's hand restrained Adrianna from running to Foy as he sat on the ground with his head in his hands. "He's all right."

"I'll never get that uniform clean," Adrianna said in a voice wavering between laughter and tears. The sudden realization that Foy's personal care was now her task sent a thrill of joy through her.

At the far end of the warehouse, she saw the Cleburne Company's new engine training its hose upon the carriage factory. Men were tiring. In the lull as they left their engines, and fresh crews stepped up, fire burst out in several places.

"Oh, the wind is spreading it everywhere!" Adrianna wailed.

"There's not much wind," Lily replied flatly. "It's starting in too many places."

"You mean. . ."

Lily bit off the word, "Arson."

"No! Green?"

For a long moment they sat clutching each other's hands, thinking of the proud man who had suffered so much indignity at the hands of their family.

"Surely not Green." Adrianna broke the silence first.

"Surely not," Lily agreed. "Green doesn't live by the same principles as my Harrison, but he does have his own code of honor. No! He couldn't have done anything this dangerous, but who can tell what he might—what he may do?"

Night was falling when the fire companies finally contained the fire. Foy's face was streaked with smut, and his eyes sagged when at last he came to speak to Adrianna.

"We've controlled the spreading." He smiled and winked. "Go on home and bid our guests good night. I'll be there soon."

"Home," Adrianna whispered. She blew a kiss gently toward him.

Barbour Hall was empty at last. Well-wishers, friends, dishwashers—all were gone. Adrianna stretched in the cool emptiness of the marble-floored hall. The heavy perfume of roses filled her with longing. She picked up an extravagant bouquet of yellow roses and climbed the stairs, loving each step possessively. She placed the roses on the marble-top table beside the massive bed in the master bedroom. Dreamily, she untied the wine velvet curtains from the straight walnut bedposts which held aloft a thronelike canopy.

Carefully laying aside her wedding gown, she lavished her French hyacinth perfume on her pulse points and slipped into a white nightgown of delicately embroidered linen. She sighed in pure happiness. Everything was the perfection she had always imagined for her wedding night.

Bam! The front door slammed and footsteps clattered across the hall.

"Wife! Where are you?"

"Here," she called, running to look over the balcony rail.

Foy's face had been scrubbed. He bounded up the stairs, and she flew to meet him halfway. On the landing, he smothered her with kisses, then held her back to drink in her beauty.

"My wife, my wife," he whispered. Scooping her up in his arms, he carried her up the remaining steps and over the threshold. Gently, he closed the door.

Adrianna awakened smiling. Foy's long arms were wrapped tightly about her. Shifting slightly, she lay watching him. When he stirred, she playfully kissed his ear; and he grabbed her, tussling, nuzzling.

Thus began the pattern of September. Adrianna felt no lack of honeymoon trip. Reveling in being together, she and Foy rode through the woodland, picnicking, swimming, boating.

Suddenly, September days grew short. Work was calling Foy. Adrianna polished Barbour Hall until it shone to match the radiance of her face. Foy bounded back into the house at every possible moment, eager to enjoy their peaceful home. Only when he encountered Monsieur Le Franc did he frown.

"Shush, he'll hear you." Adrianna forestalled his complaints. "You can't rush art. Besides, the guest room has a private entrance on the back—"

"I hate having another man in the house," Foy grumbled. "And you never did tell me what he's charging."

Adrianna bit her lip. She was beginning to worry, to tell the Frenchman the walls and ceilings had reached perfection, but he kept insisting upon one more rosebud here or apple there.

Adrianna was shocked when at last Mr. Le Franc produced his bill. She was afraid to show it to Foy. Surely he would have more money soon. Work had begun intruding upon their long, lovely nights.

More and more often, Adrianna waited alone in the big bed or read by the fire smoldering on the bedroom hearth. Noisily Foy would appear, declaring, "You'll never make a fire that way. You're too stingy with the fat li'dard." Swiftly he would poke the aromatic splinters beneath the smoking logs. With a crackling roar, the fire would light his face as he turned to take her in his arms.

Smiling secretly, Adrianna knew she had no need of lightwood. The whole house became warm and bright the moment Foy entered.

Warm, dry days meant harvest. Wagons loaded with cotton bales squeaked and groaned their way into Eufaula. Foy was kept busy sampling and grading.

Since Southern ladies had worked diligently as volunteer nurses during the war, it was now acceptable for them to take paying jobs in a few respectable positions. Adrianna begged to be allowed to help at the Cotton Exchange, but Foy, like most men, still thundered, "No wife of mine will ever work!" Yet he rationed out the money for her household expenses.

With hours to spend alone, Adrianna turned to her painting. The brilliant blue of the cloudless October sky drew her to the belvedere one day and out to the garden the next.

On a Sunday afternoon so beautiful she had begged to go for a drive, Foy had left to work at something he said could not wait. Wandering listlessly in the garden, Adrianna paused to watch a pair of cardinals twittering together in a weigela bush. Summer's last trumpet-shaped blooms nearly matched the scarlet birds they encircled.

Excitedly Adrianna made a thumbnail sketch, working swiftly to get her values right. Cadmium red mixed with just a touch of alizarin crimson seemed perfect. Quickly, she wet her paper and carried it to her easel in the garden. Striving to keep her work transparent, she put in the lighter parts of the bush, let the first work dry, then stroked in the darker stems. Letting out her breath, she sat back smiling, waiting for the precise moment to paint in the crimson blossoms.

"Adrianna," Lily's voice called from the porch.

Adrianna hated to be stopped before her creation was complete. "Here," she called grudgingly. The frightened birds flew to the top of a pine tree. "Come around here, Lily."

"Oh, there you are." Lily rounded a turning in the path. "I'd hope to see you two at church this morning. Don't you think it's about time you—"

"We'll go when we get older," Adrianna said crossly. "We're too busy now." She reached out with a wet, shaking brush; and her colors ran, obscuring the brown female. There was no way to save it, so she tried to take advantage of the accident by swirling in a few dead leaves.

"You've really become very good," said Lily sincerely. "You could have painted the friezes in the dining room yourself."

"I almost wish I had." Adrianna sighed. "I might have done the stenciling, but I'm not nearly good enough for the freehand flowers Mr. Le Franc painted."

"Is he finished?"

"Yes," she replied tersely.

She turned to face Lily but looked beyond her to the house. Narrowing her eyes at the peeling white paint and shabby green shutters, she spoke in a chilly voice. "I have no more workmen engaged except to paint the outside of the house."

Lily nodded at the obvious need, then said slowly, "I came through the back hall. Mama's sofa—her most treasured piece—I should have mentioned to you sooner about giving things away. I hope you didn't—the S-shaped legs were made for only a period of about ten years, around 1783. Besides sentiment, it was quite valuable."

"I know. I didn't give it away. I sold it."

The two women sat so silently that the birds returned.

"Honestly, Lily," Adrianna said miserably. "I didn't know I was spending more than Foy had. He won't tell me things. All of this," she said, waving her hand, "seemed limitless to me. He let me go on and on spending before he exploded about having no liquid assets." She pressed her trembling lips together and admitted, "I dismissed Mr. Le Franc. I sold the couch to pay him."

Pain played over Lily's face. When at last she spoke, her voice shook. "I understand. I was afraid you two weren't happy."

"We're fine," snapped Adrianna. Defiance melting, she spoke wistfully, "Do you really think I'm good? Could I sell some paintings?"

"Perhaps," said Lily kindly. "But I'm afraid that nothing we do will bring in enough money to help. Being patient will help the most. I know you get lonely with Foy working such long hours. I miss Harrison, too. He's been gone so much on the *Mignonne*. But remember, Dear," she said gently, "they're doing it for us—trying to get their business going again."

Adrianna made no reply.

"Harrison usually tells me everything. We had our problems before we married because of his humility and my parents' pride, but we worked things out before the marriage—which is the best way to prevent mistakes. Of course, we had the same values."

Adrianna capped and uncapped her tube of paint.

"Harrison and I have been through some hard times, but always we've had each other to depend on."

Adrianna still did not reply. Lily rose to leave.

"Foy and I have always been close," Lily said softly. "I know how much he loves you, and I want to help you. But there's something bothering Foy that you and I don't know about. I've an uneasy feeling. . ." Lily shivered, was gone.

Adrianna sat staring at her painting. She longed for the kind of lasting relationship Lily and Harrison had, but she didn't know how to reach for it. Remembering the chilly echoes of her childhood home and the fearful time when her father had gone away for good, Adrianna shivered.

"Pretty, pret–ty, pret–ty," the cardinal sang over her head.

"Am I only pretty to him?" she asked the bird. If Foy loved her only when she did right, she could not survive. Making unending mistakes, she seemed to be her own worst enemy.

Sadly, she picked up her brush and added the focal point of her painting. Determined not to stop again before she finished, she ignored Foy's horse clattering up the driveway. She heard Foy moving through the house, banging doors. Stroking slowly, deliberately, she continued to paint until she felt him behind her, glaring at her work.

"You let the fire go out in the stove," Foy complained. "A dutiful wife would have—"

"A dutiful wife?" Adrianna exploded. "You think I should have waited and waited and sat there poking in wood—"

"I know. I'm late—again," Foy admitted ruefully. He came up behind her and hugged her close. "Have you got anything good? I'm starved."

Adrianna twisted away and went into the kitchen. She brought out tepid food from the pie safe. Silently, she sat beside him watching him wolf down congealed peas and clammy corn bread.

Foy gave her a lopsided grin. "Did you have a lonely afternoon? I had to get my books straightened out while everything was quiet." He reached for a second helping. "Cotton will be pouring in tomorrow. This is the first really big crop since the war."

"I'd have rather been alone." She picked at a crumb. "Lily came scolding." She lifted clouded eyes to his serious face. "You'll be getting enough cotton to pay your bills, then?"

"Well." He sighed. "It doesn't work that way. Right now I'm buying cotton. You see, a cotton broker buys from farmers. I warehouse it until I can resell, and—I might as well tell you—my fire insurance hasn't been renewed."

Adrianna looked at him blankly. "Have you tried another company?"

"The only other agency in town is owned by Green Bethune."

"Oh," she replied absently. "Will he be coming back? Maybe he could take my watercolors to New York to sell—"

"You stay away from Green." An unaccustomed arrogance twisted Foy's lips. "I can afford to finance your little painting."

"Finance my little painting!" Adrianna erupted. She stamped into the kitchen and threw the dirty dishes into the dishpan, breaking two.

Cold fury sealed Adrianna's lips as she and Foy went about preparations for the night. Without a word, she took her pillow and started from the master bedroom.

"What're you doing?" Foy gripped her wrist.

"I don't want to sleep in here tonight," she flared. She withdrew her hand, and her chin jutted out. "I'll try Lily's old bed tonight."

"Well, just maybe—" he shouted. "Maybe I'll rest more in my old room."

Staring at the spider-web patterns cast by the moonlight through the macramé canopy of Lily's bed, Adrianna lay shivering miserably. The nighttime temperature had suddenly dropped, and she felt as cold, lonely, and unloved as she had in childhood. She had been a bride for one beautiful month. Scrubbing at tear-wet cheeks, she thought that her honeymoon was over. Had her marriage also ended?

Far into the night, Adrianna tossed and turned. She went to the window and looked out at a spectacular harvest moon. The beauty of silhouetted branches filled her with excitement. Here was another moment of time she must capture and preserve for those who looked but did not see. Foy thought her painting was something with which she frittered away time. Art meant everything to her, and she must make him understand.

She tiptoed into his room. Sprawled diagonally across the bed, Foy snored in exhausted sleep. There was no room for her.

Creeping back to the front room, Adrianna gazed out the window. She had sensed a growing professional quality about her work which Lily had confirmed. She would sell some paintings and have money she didn't have to beg for. *I'll show Mr. Foy he won't have to finance my little painting,* she thought bitterly. She climbed into bed and cried herself to sleep.

Throughout the week, Adrianna remained red-eyed, and Foy went about in a daze. Although they had kissed and made up one night, by daylight they seemed more and more estranged. Foy's moroseness made Adrianna fear his love for her had run its course.

A respite came from an unexpected source. Low water kept the *Mignonne* stranded. Since Lily had made the trip with Harrison, Adrianna merely had to cope with a worried husband.

She busied herself supervising the painting of the house. Peeling white paint was scraped away. Adrianna watched with pleasure as the workmen smoothed burnt sienna on the walls of the spreading house.

The sun was straight overhead before she realized it, and Foy appeared for dinner.

"Brown!" He exploded. "You're painting Mama's house brown?"

"I like it," Adrianna said coolly. "Besides, I thought it was my—our home now."

Foy ducked his head sheepishly. "It is. I'm sorry. But—brown?"

"Wait 'til it's finished," she pleaded. "The shutters will be a darker, richer brown and the dentil trim and up there around the belvedere will be light cream. It will set off the architectural details."

Foy frowned. "I don't know. Lily always said she looked like a belle dressed for a ball, and—"

"Well, she's an old dowager now, and brown velvet suits her—and me." Suddenly her temper flared. "I doubt there's anything in your precious Bible that says a house has to be white!"

Foy winced. "Adrianna, don't be flippant." He reached for her hand. "I should have been a better witness. Lily told me I should lead you to become a Christian before we married. I understand her reasoning now. With so many new things to adjust to. . ."

"I'm just as good as you are." She jerked her hand away. "I was raised by the Ten Commandments."

"Of course you're a good person, Darling," Foy said, trying to put his arms around her. "But being good and following the commandments doesn't save us from our sins. We are saved by grace through faith in Christ, and—don't you remember how the rich young ruler went away sorrowful?"

"I don't know what you're talking about. But don't call me a sinner," she snapped. She turned away coldly. "You'll have to get something to eat at Rowlett's. I'm busy."

She felt a pang of guilt as Foy left without another word. While she was not hungry, she knew that Foy was accustomed to his biggest meal at noon. Remorseful, she spent the afternoon making his favorite pie. With cheeks red from the heat of the woodstove and hair plastered to her forehead, she carried the pie across the porch from the separate kitchen and entered the house. As she stepped into the back of the hall, her hands shook. The pie dipped, slid. Suddenly, the whole thing splattered on the black-and-white marble floor.

At that moment a face appeared at the front entrance. "Hello," the woman called cheerily. "I'm Mrs. Williams, Foy's Sunday school teacher."

Adrianna paced the garden. She had obviously hurt the well-intentioned visitor by snapping that she was not in the mood to attend church, but that had been nothing compared to the scene when Lily arrived and repeated Foy's words, "You've painted Mama's house brown?"

Wringing her hands, she felt that she could never do the things needed to please Foy's family. She could not please Foy enough to make him love her. Neither could she go back to her grandparents and admit her marriage was a failure.

Collapsing into a wicker chair in the gazebo, she dropped her face in her hands, sobbing. A heavy footstep lifted her hopes and she held out her hand. "Oh, Foy, I—"

"You're much too beautiful to cry," drawled a familiar voice. "Tell me what's the matter."

Taking both her hands in his, Green Bethune knelt before her.

Chapter 13

Green!" Adrianna tried to withdraw from his grasp.

Green kissed her hands tenderly before he released her. Raking out a fine linen handkerchief, he dabbed at her tear-splotched face.

Fresh sobs shook her with the fear that Foy would find them.

"Tell ole Green what's the matter. Is the honeymoon over so soon?" He cocked his head to one side, and his blue eyes began to glitter devilishly.

"Are you ready to come away with me and see the world?"

Adrianna blew her nose on the proffered handkerchief. Frightened, she called up every shred of poise her grandmother's training had instilled.

"Not at all, Mr. Bethune." She lifted her chin as regally as Isadora and conveyed a coolness which put distance between them.

Green's assurance faltered, but he sat down, uninvited. He stroked his muttonchop whiskers and watched her.

"Every bride must shed a few tears." She managed a smile and spoke as brightly as possible. "What are you doing in—the country?"

Green's features relaxed into sincerity as he said, "I had to see you again. To be sure before I returned to New York." He leaned toward her, reaching out.

Adrianna stopped him with stiff-backed reserve. "Oh, you're going to New York? Would you do me a favor?"

"Anything."

"Could you take some of my watercolors? Perhaps my old teachers would display them, and maybe. . ."

"Sell them?" He finished for her. "You need money, then?" He slid his hand inside his expensively tailored jacket. "Let me—"

"No, no!" she said quickly before he could bring out his wallet. "I'd like to become established as an artist, that's all. Lily thinks I'm good enough—and. . ." Suddenly she slumped, defeated. "Yes, I do need money. I've run up too many bills to present to a new husband." She tossed her head as again he reached inside his coat. "No, I couldn't accept a loan from you, but if you'd take the paintings. . ."

"Consider it done, fair lady. But have you thought about your insurance policy?"

"What about it?"

"You can use your insurance policy as collateral for a loan."

"Oh, really?" Adrianna clapped her hands delightedly.

Green leaned forward. "You see, you still need me to be your friend. Put on your hat, and I'll take you to the hotel for tea. When you're feeling better, I'll introduce you to my agent. . ."

"Green, thank you for your help. I'm very glad you're no longer angry with me, but. . ." Adrianna stood and held out her hand in a gesture of dismissal. "A married woman cannot, must not, try to carry on a casual friendship with another man."

Green started to protest.

Striving to be pleasant yet firm, Adrianna touched a finger to his lips and said, "No, Green, I love my husband very much, but even the most happily married woman could not allow herself to be around a man of such irresistible charm as you."

Gravely, Green clasped her fingers to his lips. He left without a word.

Adrianna realized, too late, that she still clutched his handkerchief.

Excited at the prospect of having money to pay the painters, she hurried upstairs and washed her tear-streaked face. Rinsing out the embroidered handkerchief, she laid it over the silver faucets to dry. She would leave it at the insurance office.

Dressing hurriedly, she began a frantic search for the forgotten policy. At last she found it. She was already downtown when she remembered she had left Green's monogrammed handkerchief on the lavatory.

Chapter 14

Foy rubbed his neck as he unfolded his long frame from the leather couch in his office. It had been a miserable night.

I behaved like an idiot, he moaned to himself. From the moment he had found Green Bethune's handkerchief, he had ranted and raved. He believed Adrianna's tearful explanation, but he had reeled from the blow to his pride. Anger seared him again as he thought of how she had told his worst enemy she needed money instead of confessing it to him.

Balling his pillow and afghan to throw them into a chest, Foy jerked around and saw a grinning Green Bethune.

"New housing accommodations, I see."

"Uh." Foy cleared his throat. "Working late and fell asleep," he muttered. "Gotta sell cotton, you know. You buying today?"

Green smiled sardonically.

Shifting uncomfortably in the malignant silence, Foy waited.

Green stroked the back of his hand along his whiskers. When at last he spoke, his voice was low. "I think you know. I'm here to call in our bet."

Foy snorted. "What I recall is a casual conversation—a declaration of faith in my wife. Which, by the way, hasn't changed."

He tried to turn away, but Green's piercing blue eyes held him.

"What I recall, Sir, is a definite wager. I asked, 'What will you wager on whom the fair Adrianna will be to wife?' " He jerked his thumb toward where Foy had stowed his bedding. "I remember your exact words." He mocked. " 'She'll marry me and that right soon. I'd stake my life. Anything. The *Mignonne Wingate*.' "

Foy struggled for control. "But surely you jest. A little tiff doesn't—"

"A man's word is his bond, Sir." Adopting the manner which charmed the unwary, Green laughingly said, "I wouldn't simply take the *Mignonne Wingate*. I prefer racing—and high stakes." Suddenly, he leaned down with palms flat on Foy's desk. "I'll give you a sporting chance. We'll set up a race. If the *Mignonne* is fast enough to rendezvous with my ship, we're square. If not, she's mine. That is, if she survives the trip. If not, I wouldn't want her anyway."

Foy opened his mouth to refuse, but Green continued.

"Let's make it interesting. See how many bales you can carry. Since you need money, I'll double the price per pound on the day you deliver. I do want the fair Adrianna properly fed. Of course, we'll let the lady herself decide which of us—"

Furious, Foy spoke between clenched teeth. "I have faith in my wife and my steamboat. What are your exact terms?"

Foy covered the distance to Barbour Hall in long strides like a horse running for the barn. His mind galloped faster still as he moved from wounded pride at Green's discovery of his problems to despair at the thought of losing the boat for which he had worked so long. Too agitated to tell Adrianna, he greeted her gruffly.

Sunday dinner with Lily's family could not be avoided. Harrison served the roast beef and discoursed on local businessman building a cotton mill in Eufaula.

"Of course, it's the thing to do," he said, "but I'm afraid too many have returned from the war with nothing but missing limbs and tattered uniforms. I don't know where the ten or eleven years have gone since the war, but I expect it will be ten more before they can raise enough capital to buy spindles and looms."

Foy mumbled a noncommittal sound.

Harrison eyed his morose guests but kept talking. "John Tullis and the Lampley brothers are shipping more cotton to New England mills, but don't you think we'd best keep shipping directly to Liverpool?"

Foy said nothing.

Lily looked at the blanched faces around her table and tried to bridge the conversational gap. "I don't know how you all ever know what to do about selling with the price so low and the constant fluctuations." She stood up to begin clearing the table.

"I know a way we can get double the price." Foy's voice echoed in his ears. "From Green."

"Is he back? I wish he'd stay in South Carolina!" Lily clanked the silver in the plate. "He doesn't ever quite break laws, but he shaves principles," she continued. "Don't deal with Green!"

As if that settled it, she picked up the platter and started to the butler's pantry. Adrianna and Mignonne followed with the plates.

"Lily," Adrianna said hesitantly, "do you want that canopy bed in your old room? Grandfather is sending me a modern one."

"Yes, I'd like it for Mignonne," Lily replied. "It's a Sheraton. I always loved that room because the morning sun pours in."

Hearing Lily through the open doorway, Foy's face burned because the concern in Lily's voice told him that Kitty had gossiped. Lily knew they had moved from the master bedroom.

Not catching the meaning Foy had, Adrianna spoke glumly. "I promise not to dispose of any more of your mother's things. Green took some of my paintings to sell, and—"

"Have you been seeing Green?" Lily's voice shrilled. "I was wondering if Foy were sick or mad. Here, Mignonne, take the scuppernong cobbler to the dining room to dip."

Foy ducked his head as the girl brought in the pie. The women's voices, echoing against the crockery in the hall-like pantry, became angrier.

"It was just a petty argument. Green came looking for Foy on business, and. . ." Suddenly, she shouted, "Of course, I'm not seeing Green. I may not understand your precious Bible, but–but. . . ," she spluttered. "I'm good enough to be true to my husband." She began to cry. "Even—" She snatched a sob. "Even if he leaves me."

Suddenly the narrow passage was filled with bewildered faces.

"What's going on?" demanded Harrison sternly.

"She accused me of seeing Green!" Adrianna buried her face against Foy's chest.

Foy stood stiff-armed. "She's not seeing Green," he said in a cold monotone. "But how did he know. . ." He backed away from her. "That you moved out of my bedroom?"

"I don't know." She sobbed harder.

Lily tried to shoo the children outdoors. Beau scampered out, but Mignonne obstinately remained.

"Green knew plenty. He came snooping at the office early this morning." Foy threw out his arms. "Y'all will have to know. He caught me sleeping at the office. He'd goaded me into saying something and. . . Well, Green's called in a bet." Foy dropped his head in his hands. "He says I no longer have you 'to wife,' so I forfeit a wager I made. He says we have to win a race with the *Mignonne* or lose her."

"You risked my namesake?" squealed the dark-haired girl.

"How could you doubt me?" Adrianna's fiery mane flew wildly with her rage.

Foy jutted his chin at her. "That was the problem. I thought I could depend on you."

Mignonne tugged at his arm and shrieked, "No, no, you can't! Papa! Stop him!"

Distractedly, Foy shook her off and faced Adrianna. "I thought I could depend on you. In this family we believe " 'What God hath joined together let no man put asunder.' "

"Maybe God hasn't joined us," Adrianna flung out the words and shrank back into a corner, weeping.

"Now, now." Harrison waved his hands in a calming gesture. "Quiet down, all of you. A race might be great sport. We have a fine craft. I, for one, would like to see what she can do."

"You can't condone a race!" exploded Lily. "The Chattahoochee is too narrow for two boats! The rocks—no! It's too dangerous!"

"Dangerous, yes." Harrison tilted his head boyishly. "But not impossible. Two boats can't race side by side, but there are other ways to race. Let Foy talk."

Relieved at Harrison's attitude, Foy felt his blood flowing again. "The race will be against time and the obstacles in the river. Green has it all figured out: how fast a time we must make, how many bales we must carry. We'll have checkpoints."

"We'll turn his trick to our advantage!" Harrison rubbed his hands together exultantly. "Just think what good publicity this will be. If we're the fastest, it will help us get business, Lily." He grinned sheepishly. "If steamboats are to compete with all these new railroads, we must increase our speed and improve our ability to keep to a schedule."

"We're to leave Thursday morning. If we meet Green's ship at Apalachicola Bay before it leaves for Liverpool at dawn on Saturday, he'll pay double the going rate for the cotton. You've got to take some risks in life or lose everything." Foy shot a meaningful glance at Adrianna, who still cowered in the corner.

"Are you saying we'll lose. . ." Mignonne's lip trembled.

"I know it's not fair to you, but he didn't give me much choice. If we don't make it in time," Foy mumbled without looking at his niece, "Green will get our steamboat."

Mignonne began to shriek again.

"You must stop this, Harrison," Lily demanded against the din.

"Now, Lily, I know only too well how Green can get a fellow involved in something he doesn't want to do."

"But, but—" Lily sobbed. "Nobody's ever raced on the Chattahoochee. Least if they did, they didn't live to tell the tale!"

Chapter 15

Uhmmmmm! Uhmmmmm!

The steamboat's whistle floated up the Columbus, Georgia street, grating Adrianna's nerves. She wanted to run away, yet she must be a part of this foolhardy race.

Adrianna tried to lengthen her strides to keep up with Lily, but her slim skirt restricted her. She glanced gratefully at her sister-in-law. Against the men's protests, Lily had declared the women would face the trip with them no matter what the dangers.

Lily's brown eyes still flashed with anger, but her springing step bespoke excitement as she glanced over her shoulder.

"Emma, Emma, come quickly," Lily sang out. "We stayed far too long settling the children with Aunt Laurie."

"I don't—hurry as fast I used to," Emma puffed. Smiling at Adrianna's taut face, she spoke reassuringly, "Everything will be all right."

Uhmmmmm! Uhmmmmm!

The rousing blast drew them down to the wharf where the steamboat, emitting black puffs of smoke, quivered as a thing alive.

Wheet! Wheet! From the lofty pilothouse, Foy saluted them with the whistle.

Harrison paced the deck with his watch in his hand. Excitedly, he swung the watch chain fastened to his belt as he spoke. "It's nearly time to leave. We've lightened the load all we can." He grinned and brushed back his graying temples. "I even got a haircut."

Adrianna laughed and matched his frivolous tone. "Well, I'm traveling light. I left my trunk. Do you believe I can survive with just one frock? Can't I take two?" She glanced at the steamer's furniture, which had been moved to the wharf. "You've made me plenty of room."

Everyone laughed and started on their separate ways. Crossing the empty freight deck, Adrianna went to the upper deck and squeezed past burlap-wrapped cotton which arrogantly crowded what was normally passenger space. When this race was over, she would go back to her mother, but for now she continued to climb toward Foy.

Singing called Adrianna's attention to the banks. In astonishment, she saw a huge crowd along the riverfront and others watching from the upper windows of the Columbus Ironworks. Green Bethune's agent strutted up and down the steep roadway like a cock of the walk.

Bong! Bong! A clock struck. *Bong!* Adrianna ran up the remaining steps to the pilothouse. *Bong!* Friday. *Bong!* November 3. *Bong!* 1876. *Bong!* Eight o'clock. *Bonggg!*

As the last note reverberated on the misty air, Harrison saluted Green's man. Gangplanks fell upon the hardened deck. Lines let go. With a deep, hoarse puff, the *Mignonne Wingate* swung back and shot straight from her mooring. Green's man stared at the watch in his hand and his jaw fell.

Foy chortled. "We gained three minutes on his time already. He thought we'd back outstream."

"I wish we didn't have to stop to load at Eufaula," said Adrianna. "I understand that you want to top off the load where the water is deeper, but as long as it took us to get to the bay before, I don't see how we'll ever make it from here by Saturday dawn."

"Well," said Foy, "if I hadn't lost so much cotton in the fire, we would have had three thousand bales in the warehouse. But Green probably would've demanded we load some at Columbus, anyway, since it's the head of navigation." He shrugged.

Ahead, the morning fog seemed to be an impenetrable wall. Adrianna could barely see the river. As she strained her eyes to see, Adrianna remembered tales of fiery wrecks and lost lives. Not wanting to distract Foy and feeling too estranged to sit quietly beside him, Adrianna wandered to the ladies' saloon.

Lily sat with a big book in her lap. Beside her lay a Bible and two books by Charles Darwin. She looked up and laughed as Adrianna entered. "If Harrison saw these books, he'd say I'm making the boat draw more than its allowed twenty-two inches." She patted the velvet settee beside her in invitation for Adrianna to join her. "Adrianna, I'm afraid I've been dogmatic with you. I realized I needed to read all this and do what I've told you—think for myself."

Adrianna sat on the edge of the couch and glanced at the geology time scale Lily tapped with her finger.

"Way before Darwin, the English geologist Lyell named these eras. Look." She spread the Bible open to Genesis. "The Bible doesn't suppose to be a science book, but amazingly, it gives the order of creation—plants, fish and fowl, then mammals, exactly as recently discovered."

"Uhmm-huh."

"I wouldn't find too much disagreement with *Origin of the Species* if Darwin hadn't cut out, 'In the beginning God,' but. . ."

Adrianna did not really care. When the race was over, she would move in with her mother, who pressed her only on the most trivial matters.

Lily raised her voice and pulled at Adrianna's arm to claim her attention. "But when I tried to wade through *The Descent of Man,* I was upset by how Darwin tried to explain away God Himself."

The *cluck, cluck* of the waterwheel slowed to a *swish, swish.*

"Citing ways he thinks animals are just as good as man, Darwin tries to explain away the fact that people feel God in their hearts and have morals—duty to one another."

Not seeming to notice the boat's lack of progress, Lily continued. "Of course, God can create through any means He chooses, but personally, I see it the way Archbishop Whately tried to point out: Man came into the world a civilized being; savages have undergone degradation just as nations have fallen away in civilization, lapsing into barbarism."

"Yes, I see what you mean." Adrianna nodded.

"I pray for Mrs. Darwin. I feel so sorry for her."

"Why?" Adrianna looked startled.

"She is well-known to be a Christian. She must have been proud of her husband's scientific thinking in the beginning, but how it must pain her that he now declares himself agnostic!"

"What does that mean?"

"One who says he doesn't know about God because he can't prove Him."

"But we can't prove God," Adrianna exclaimed.

"We don't need to," said Lily. "He proves us. We can feel God's love filling our souls, see it demonstrated in the lives of true believers, taste it in the glories of nature."

Bam! The boat stopped with a groaning of wood. Precariously balanced, Adrianna hit the floor.

Lily helped her up and they ran to the deck.

"Whew!" Harrison blew out his cheeks. "We're in a stretch of low water," he said grimly. "Grounded on a sandbar."

"But Lily." Adrianna plucked her sleeve. "I thought that was why we left Columbus with a light load—because of low water."

"Yes, Dear," Lily said soothingly. "We'll top off the load at Eufaula because the water is usually better there. This is just one of those things that happens."

They leaned over the rail to watch. Men jumped off on the white sand and began to shovel it away from the boat. Others grabbed long poles and tried to push the boat from the bar.

Precious minutes pounded away.

"Oh, Lily, what—"

Lily shook her head resignedly. "Sometimes we can only sit for a freshet, a rain upstream which makes the river rise."

The red globe of the sun had burned away the early mists. Streaming through the trees on the Georgia shore, the sunlight cast flames through translucent maple leaves. The beauty seared Adrianna's heart as she recalled Foy's words, "Maple leaves in autumn, springtime in my heart." Overcome with weeping, she went into her stateroom and threw herself on her bunk.

Adrianna did not know how long she cried or how the steamboat got under way again. She only knew she could not face Foy's family. She lay staring at the sign on her stateroom door, "Should anything happen to the boat, remove this door and cling to it. It will float and save your life." *I need more than that,* she thought and began to weep again.

Hot sun beat on her head and dazzled her eyes when at last Adrianna emerged at four in the afternoon. Looking up at the Alabama bluffs, she could see Eufaula.

The *Mignonne* landed smartly. By prearranged plan, stevedores sprang up from the wharf and set to work loading.

A huge man sang out, "You's making mighty good time, Cap'n Harrison."

Adrianna brightened. The watch pinned to her white shirtwaist showed five o'clock when they departed from Eufaula. Her blood singing again, she ran lightly up to the pilothouse.

"Open that throttle, Mr. Murphey," Foy said into the speaking tube which connected with the engineer far below. "Keep those gauges to the top, Jonathan." He grinned at Adrianna. Wrapping his arm about her waist, he pulled her close beside him.

Watching his profile as he stared intently downriver, Adrianna thought, *He doesn't know how badly I'm hurting.*

At eight o'clock with the night turned crisp and cold, they swung into the landing at Fort Gaines, Georgia. The crew had lapsed into relaxed routine. Now every muscle tensed. Commands were shouted through megaphones. The crew shouldered cordwood waiting on the dock, and paraded back, laughing, joking.

When once again the *Mignonne Wingate* was slipping silently through the night, the family sat down to supper. Harrison pulled a small package from his pocket. "Happy anniversary." He looked adoringly at Lily as if she were a bride.

Lily kissed him soundly in spite of the watching group. Before she opened her gift, she hurried out and returned with a cake she had smuggled aboard.

Tears misted Adrianna's eyes. She could not see the present Lily was exclaiming over. She did not taste the flavor of the cake Harrison was declaring his special favorite.

When the men had gone back to their posts, the three women went into the ladies' saloon. Adrianna cried in anguish, "Oh, Lily! I hadn't realized today was your anniversary. I'm so sorry. I've ruined everything. You'll probably lose your boat." She sniffed. "Maybe even our lives."

"After eighteen years, I don't need a party—but what could be more exciting than this?" Lily laughed. "Besides that, we will not lose our boat, and our lives are in God's keeping."

Adrianna bowed her bright head and spoke in muffled sobs. "You're still in love after eighteen years, and already Foy—I'm afraid he'll leave me like my father left. . ." She began to sob uncontrollably.

Lily wrapped Adrianna in her arms and stroked her hair. "Darling, I love you. We all do. Foy will never leave you."

"How can you be sure of that?" Adrianna clung to Lily.

"I know because he's a Christian. His love for you is based on his love for God. Whether we are good or bad makes no difference. God loves us. God sees infinite worth in every person He created in spite of our sin."

Adrianna stiffened, but Lily continued earnestly.

"Foy will never stop loving you and trying to do what is best for you. He will cherish you, no matter what. But we must start at the beginning. I've tried to dive into the middle, to tell you what I think you should do, and I haven't been the help I want to be."

Adrianna sniffed and scrubbed at her cheeks. She sat back and looked into Lily's concerned face.

"Long ago I gave my life to the lordship of Christ. I've wanted to bring all my family to this wonderful joy, but. . ." She laughed ruefully. "Sometimes I'm too eager for everyone to let God's love fill their spiritual emptiness. I push too hard. But Emma. . ."

Lily paused and patted the placid woman who sat quietly beside them in an attitude of prayer.

"Emma has shown me that I needed to stop and confess my own sins."

"But you're not a sinner! Everyone talks about what a wonderful Christian you are."

"I'm a Christian because I've accepted on faith that Christ died to pay the penalty for my sin. Paul tells us that all have sinned, missed the mark of the high calling of God, and deliberately stepped over the boundaries God has set. But through God's *grace*—that word means unmerited favor—we are set free from our sins simply by faith in Christ Jesus. I'm sure of my salvation, my place in heaven.

"We are not saved as a reward for being good—we could never do enough good works to reconcile ourselves to God. We are saved as a gift because we are spiritually needy. To demonstrate this change, we are to do good for others in the Savior's name. We must confess our daily sins and then build our lives on Christ. But wait. Let me show you."

Lily returned with her Bible and thumbed quickly to First Corinthians 3:11. " 'For other foundation can no man lay than that is laid, which is Jesus Christ. Now if any man build upon this foundation gold. . .hay, stubble. . .' " She ran her finger down the verses. " 'It shall be revealed by fire; and the fire shall try every man's work. . .' "

She looked up at Adrianna. "We're constantly tried by fire, tested, but if our lives are founded on Christ, if our marriages have this basis—"

"But if Foy would talk to me, explain—then I would. . ." Adrianna looked at her hands twisting in her lap.

"Fine, you need to talk things out. But I'm not speaking about compromise—'I'll give in on this, if you do that'—I mean having God's kind of love for each other. The Greek word for that is *agape*. It means always seeking the highest good of the other."

Adrianna sat for a long moment considering the difference. "I've never read the Bible," she admitted. "It's such a—difficult Book."

"I used to think that, too," said Emma softly. "It's because the Bible came from unlimited God to limited man. You cannot understand the Bible with your natural mind as you understand philosophers. The Bible is spiritual, and you must be born of the Spirit or it will remain a difficult, closed book."

"Oh, that's too hard!"

"No, it isn't, Dear. For long, painful years, I wouldn't listen to what Lily was trying to share. I attended church when I had to—as a duty. Then one day I opened my heart to God's Holy Spirit. Now I want to be in God's house every Sabbath to find peace for my soul and strength for the week ahead. I hear God speaking to me when I approach the Bible praying that the Spirit will teach me."

"Start with the Gospel of John," Lily said, smiling. "It has the deepest theology, yet it's also the easiest for a beginner to understand. It will show you that sinners cannot get right with God through their own efforts. Calvary's cross was necessary."

Adrianna was rescued from having to answer the earnest women because Harrison came in to tell them that they were exactly on schedule. Feeling confident that they would easily win, the women decided to retire for the night.

Tossing fitfully, Adrianna suddenly sat upright. The steamer pitched and yawed, and it seemed the *Mignonne* would break like a matchstick.

Barefoot, Adrianna clambered to the pilothouse. She watched Foy wrestling the flopping wheel. Confused by the blackness of the night, Adrianna sensed they were crosswise, straining against the current. The *Mignonne* trembled, fought Foy, tried to turn back upstream.

Fearing to speak, Adrianna waited helplessly. At last, Foy gained control and they once again headed downstream.

"Grannies! That was close!" Foy threw her a quick look over his shoulder.

"I didn't think you knew I was here."

Foy laughed. "You don't know how you fill the place with springtime—with more than just your perfume." He scooped her close for a quick kiss, then released her and held the knobs of the wheel with both hands. "I'd have hated to have lost her through stupid carelessness!"

"What happened?"

"For the past year there's been a dog chained on a bluff one mile north of Purcell's Swirl. He lets out a deep woof when he hears a packet on the river." Foy scrubbed his arm across his sweaty brow.

"I'm sleepy, but I'm sure I wasn't dozing." He nodded at her ruefully. "I took a chance on going on even though there are no stars to steer by, but the old hound must've broke his chain. Tonight he barked close to the water—and immediately, we hit the rapids and flung into the whirlpool."

"You need some coffee." Adrianna lifted the pot and found it empty.

"I'd sure love a cup, but the steward is late. He'll probably come around shortly."

"I want to get it for you myself." Adrianna ran down, stopping long enough to pull on cotton stockings and halfway button on her shoes. As she climbed back up with the steaming pot, she remembered previously thinking that Lily waited upon Harrison with slavelike devotion. She had been holding back until Foy did something equal for her. Now she absorbed the warmth of seeking another's good.

Companionably, they watched the dark water as the boat sashayed over the next six miles. When they docked at Columbia, Alabama, Adrianna was surprised at the crowd watching for them.

Foy flexed his shoulders, and Adrianna massaged his neck while they waited for the crew to wood up and load supplies.

"You can bet there's someone telegraphing Green," Foy growled as they headed back into the stream. "Go back and get some rest. Things will be uneventful for awhile." He kissed her, let her go, then pulled her back for a long, stirring kiss. "Mr. Trimmer will take the watch at two," he promised.

Happier than she had been in weeks, Adrianna snuggled beneath the blankets and slept until she felt Foy's cold body climbing into the warm bed.

Adrianna awoke suddenly. Foy was gone. She had not known when he left. Smiling, remembering, she blinked her eyes as the first light of a new day filtered into their cabin through stained-glass windows. Stretching luxuriously, she roused enough to realize what had awakened her. Silence.

Her ears pricked. The stillness alarmed her. The rhythm of the paddle wheel had slowed, yet she had a sense of rushing forward.

Everyone was up. Lily stood gripping the rail.

"What?" Adrianna gasped.

Her eyes dark coals in her pale face, Lily whispered, "King's Rock."

It seemed the boat was standing still. Walls of menacing rock rushed past. Hurtling through the tunnel of their old nemesis, they dared not breathe. When they passed through, victorious, Lily uttered a thankful prayer.

As she went about her toilette preparing for the day, Adrianna remembered how carelessly she had ridden the steamboat before. A stop had only meant an adventure at a new place. Now, every change in the sound of the machinery gave cause for alarm. Sighing, she gazed across the black water. The scene was no longer a romantic picture to paint.

A splintering crunch wrenched her around to the stern. Adrianna gaped down on the straining paddle wheel. A log entangled the paddles, bursting several of the wheel planks into jagged fragments. As she watched, men converged.

"One engine damaged beyond use, Sir."

"One engine damaged beyond use, Sir!" The shout was relayed to convey the message to Harrison.

Extricating the log took an hour. Then the men set to work replacing broken planks.

"The buckets can be repaired under way while we limp along on the other engine," Foy explained. "She'll just be hard to steer."

Drifting perilously for the next twenty miles, they finally reached the River Junction landing serving the nearby town of Chattahoochee, Florida. It was nine o'clock Saturday morning. The first twenty-four hours were behind them. They had covered 223 miles. In less than another twenty-four hours they must go 146 more to keep their rendezvous at Apalachicola Bay.

When they moored at the wharf, a brass band struck up. Clapping, cheering, a crowd converged upon them with congratulations. Excitedly chattering people called their fast schedule a cannonball run.

Enthusiasm renewed, Adrianna greeted people in the crowd as she walked along the wharf to steady her legs from the constant motion of the steamboat. Spotting a kindred spirit, a young woman with fiery red hair, Adrianna smiled and spoke. "Oh, may I see your baby?"

"Of course." With a friendly smile, she pulled back a pink blanket to allow Adrianna a peep at the puckered face.

"Oh, how precious! I hope I'll have one someday."

Uhh-uhh-uhmmmmm! The *Halli Belle,* a small steamer, blasted a warning call.

"Captain Brown's ready. Good-bye. Good luck," the redhead said and hurried aboard the *Halli Belle*.

Adrianna fidgeted. Time was fleeting. This was their longest stopover. At this point, the murky green Chattahoochee and the muddy red Flint became one, and the mightier river was called the Apalachicola. Ahead of them was the Narrows where the *Wave* had sunk. Venomous Moccasin Slough lay waiting to meet them. Although Foy and Harrison were already congratulating themselves, Adrianna noticed that Jonathan told no jokes or funny stories.

When at last they were under way again, Adrianna paced the deck. The sun warmed away the mists of morning and promised a beautiful day. Lily sat exclaiming over flora and fauna, but Adrianna was too nervous to paint or sit still.

Not wanting to talk, she stood alone on the bow even though the wind chilled her. Black smoke and sparks showered her as they rounded a bend and caught up with the *Halli Belle*. The small steamer blocked the narrow channel. They could not pass.

Adrianna fumed. Surely their captain knew of the stakes in the race. Upriver and down, people were wildly enthusiastic, pulling for them to set new records. Suddenly, she realized the *Halli Belle* was racing, trying to be able to brag about outdistancing the *Mignonne*.

Landmarks slid by. They were losing valuable time. With her red hair whipping, Adrianna leaned far out from the bow like a ship's figurehead. She motioned aside the intruders.

The channel widened. Grazing the shoals, the *Mignonne* pulled even.

Gauging the distance between the two racers, Adrianna sighted the railings and beat her fist. "Jonathan, fire that boiler," she muttered between clenched teeth.

The *Mignonne* pulled ahead, passed, took control of the channel. Blasting her whistle, she rounded a bend, leaving the *Halli Belle* a puff of smoke and sparks above the treetops.

Ka-boom! An explosion rent the air. *Ka-boom!* Balls of fire shot over the trees.

Clang! Clang! The *Mignonne*'s bell echoed against the banks. Horrified, Adrianna recognized the pilot's signal for backing.

"No, no, we can't go back," she screamed as the boat shivered to a stop and reversed the paddle wheel.

Flying wildly up the steps, Adrianna ran into the pilothouse and clawed at Foy's arm.

"No," she cried. "Don't go back, Foy. Someone else will come along to help." Tears streamed down her cheeks. "We'll never make up the time we've lost already. We'll lose everything."

"No, Adrianna." Foy's voice was cold as he pushed her out of his line of vision. "We won't lose the important things. Haven't you listened to what Lily's always saying about storing your treasures in heaven?"

"But–but," she blubbered.

"I knew when I met you that our values were different." His voice had a frightening, dead sound. "I let you tempt me to lie abed instead of worshiping on Sunday mornings as had always been my custom. I've let foolish pride make me strive for money every sort of way. I've risked this boat that isn't fully mine." He sighed heavily. "I won't compromise my principles again. I won't leave those people."

Foy backed the *Mignonne* around the bend. Adrianna stared at him wordlessly. The steamboat stopped. Adrianna clapped her hands over her face at the sight. Fire swept from the boiler room, consumed the racks of cordwood, leaped across the deck of the *Halli Belle*. Alarms clanged.

"Man the pumps; man the pumps!" Captain Brown shouted through his megaphone.

The deckhands turned from him in panic. Diving into the river, three burly men splashed and spluttered, trying to swim. Six others scrambled to lower a lifeboat. Not waiting for passengers, they all jumped at once, rocking, tilting, dumping themselves into the water.

Horror-stricken, Adrianna watched the *Mignonne*'s officers lower their own boat and row to the *Halli Belle*.

Rushing to Captain Brown's aid, they manned the pumps. They struggled with a pitiful stream of water against the roaring blaze. Swirling, windswept flames enveloped the cabin, beat them back. Captain Brown rushed into his office, ran back clutching record books and money just as the flaming door lintel fell.

Screaming people jumped overboard. The water was shallow, and they waded to dry land.

Tipping precariously, the flame-gutted *Halli Belle* laid her pilothouse into a treetop. The young pilot scrambled out onto the branches and climbed down the tree.

Numbly, Adrianna trailed Lily as she gave directions for the bedraggled passengers to be brought aboard the cotton-filled decks of the Mignonne.

Moaning, weeping people were laid on the mahogany dance floor on the grand saloon. Picking her way among them, Adrianna realized Harrison had concealed three with sheets.

Over the babble of voices, two men hurled curses at Captain Brown. They railed at the foolhardiness of racing until the *Halli Belle*'s thin boiler burst.

Fighting hysteria, Adrianna remembered the redhead and her baby. Joining others who searched for loved ones, she found the mother with the beautiful child sleeping peacefully in her arms.

Emma attended cuts and bruises. Jonathan worked to make those scalded by the steam as comfortable as possible. Burns were coated with flour to seal out air. Those of the *Halli Belle*'s crew and passengers who were unhurt retold the incident in strained, high-pitched voices.

Suddenly sickened, Adrianna ran outside to the rail, clutching her turning stomach.

Sobered by the accident, Foy called for less speed from the engineers, and they proceeded carefully downriver even after they had transferred their unexpected passengers to another steamer at the next landing. With the boat winding slowly through low, flat country, the family seemed to take on an unspoken resignation to failure. Adrianna became sick with inner turmoil, adamant that they must not lose.

Moccasin Slough taunted them next as it devoured the river into its fabled breaks in the channel. They entered the mouth. Gracefully as a swan, the *Mignonne* turned this way and that, easily making every point through the writhing trickle.

Adrianna sighed in relief when they reached the tail end of the slough. She claimed victory too soon. The hull of the *Barbara Lee* lay sunk in water over her boiler deck.

The *Mignonne*'s bell rang to pull alongside.

"Must we stop again?" Adrianna cried to Harrison. "Look! They're all right. Everyone's smiling and waving. Please, let's go on. You people give up too easily!"

Harrison's voice, gentle yet firm, reproved her. "Adrianna, when I decided to be master of the *Mignonne,* I linked my destiny with her destiny. It is my duty to forget self in the interest of those whom I serve."

"But, but," Adrianna spluttered. "What about duty to. . ." Her voice rose angrily. "To us?"

"Adrianna!" Lily broke in. "This is what I've been trying to tell you about Darwin."

"What?" Adrianna exploded. "Why on earth are you bringing up his name at a time like this?"

"His name is linked—perhaps unfairly—with Social Darwinism in business: the competitive struggle, the survival of the fittest. What would you have us do just now?"

Adrianna stared at her wild-eyed.

"I don't pretend to understand pragmatism and all of the other 'isms' which draw people in all directions," Lily said flatly. "But I know that to say 'whatever works is good and true' is wrong. God is unchangeable truth. It is not right to do the wrong thing for what you consider the right reasons. The

Bible clearly sets forth good and evil, right and wrong."

Face perspiring, cheeks flaming, Adrianna felt suddenly cold inside. "Your fundamentals—your precious principles—" She choked. "Are they more important than losing the *Mignonne* to Green?"

"Of course. Our defeats are merely punctuation, commas in God's plan for us. Let Green have his money and power. What we have is. . ."

Adrianna fled.

Flinging herself upon her bed, she wept her misery. How Foy and his family must hate her! Everything was all her fault.

Persistent knocking at her cabin door penetrated her sobs. Foy and Lily called, pleaded. She would not let them in.

Darkness fell. Everything seemed lost.

Chapter 16

The smothering blackness of the night merged with the darkness in Adrianna's soul. None of them would ever forgive her. There was nothing to do but leave. She had taken so many wrong avenues, thinking she had plenty of time to find her way. Now, totally alone, she had completely lost direction.

She slipped to the floor. Bowing her head on her bunk, she began to speak aloud. "They can't forgive me. But if You'll forgive me, God, only if You'll forgive me, can I live! I told Foy I was not a sinner. Now I know I am, and I can't redeem myself."

Repentant, Adrianna confessed all the sins of mind and heart in her young life and turned away from all she had been seeking.

Her sobbing ceased. The turbulent raging within her quieted. The blackness of midnight wrapped her in a warm, velvet blanket with its blessing of rest. The room seemed filled with the person, power, and presence of God.

"Oh, dear Jesus," she prayed. "Now I know You are alive! I thankfully accept the gift of Your loving sacrifice for me."

Knowing that God's love would go with her no matter what happened, she stopped trembling. She lit her lamp and thumbed to the Gospel of John in the Bible Lily had given her.

" 'In the beginning was the Word.' " She smiled. The Holy Spirit was already helping her to understand. The Word is Jesus. " 'In him was life; and the life was the light of men.' " She read through the fourteenth chapter. " 'I am the way, the truth, and the life: no man cometh unto the Father, but by me.' "

Wonder filled her. She had questioned how to find truth. Now she saw that she must begin with truth, Jesus Christ, and not deter from that. She had searched everywhere for a guide for her life. The Bible had been right here at her fingertips.

As God's voice spoke to her from the pages of the Bible, Adrianna knew she would never again withdraw from those she loved. The love bubbling up within her needed to be shared. She must see Foy.

Quickly, she washed her face and brushed her red hair. With her hand on the door, she turned back and lavished on the scent of hyacinth. Her delicate face sparkled in a confident smile as she climbed the stairs to the starlit glass house.

"Hello, I'm Adrianna Atherton." Her rising inflection transmitted her smile. Her voice dropped low as she added sincerely, "But I want to be Adrianna Edwards."

Foy turned. The painfully serious set of his face lifted as a slow smile appeared. He doffed his braided cap, bowed low, and intoned, "Foy Edwards, Esquire, at your service, Ma'am." His dark eyes twinkled and his firm mouth twitched mischievously. He wrapped his arms around her and pulled her close beside him at the wheel.

"I love you. I was in love with you before we met." He nuzzled her fragrant hair. "You'll be Adrianna Edwards, always and forever." He sealed his words with a fervent kiss.

Trembling with the wonder that Foy's God-given love had continued even when she had gone astray, Adrianna nestled in the warmth of his arms.

"I'm so sorry, Foy. I've been awful—but tonight I've committed my heart to Christ's lordship. From now on I'll base my life and our marriage on His love."

Foy hugged her so tightly that she laughingly protested the safety of her ribs.

"One thing, though." She pushed back to look at him. "Please talk to me. Explain. I was only spending money like my family has always lived. I don't really care about money, but make me understand."

"I'm sorry. I've been as wrong as you. Pride got in my way. Adrianna, don't shut me out. You get so quiet when you're mad. I want to share your hurts as well as your joys."

Adrianna nodded and kissed his red-rimmed ear. "I'll start banging on the piano when I'm mad," she said, laughing. "I know now I can let you into my soul and you'll love me, no matter what."

"Lily thinks one reason she and Harrison stay so happy is that they never go to bed angry."

Adrianna laughed. "I may keep you up fighting 'til dawn, but I won't go to sleep without being in our bed and kissing you good night." She stroked her finger over his straight nose and firm chin. "I've been so afraid that you'd take your love away to punish me, like my family does, that I've been my own worst enemy, pushing you away when I needed you most. Now I understand the depth of your love, but will you stay in love with me?"

"You bet I will!" Foy grinned at her with a gleam in his eyes. "It's a funny thing, but a really caring, Bible-based love keeps the fires of passion aflame."

Soft night sounds rippled round them, filling their glass tower. Silently, they stood watching the surrounding stars, feeling the wonder of being joined by God. Foy whispered a thankful prayer against Adrianna's fragrant hair.

Blissfully, Adrianna murmured, "Fairy tales do come true, but with a little work instead of a magic wand."

Suddenly, she stirred in Foy's sheltering arms and asked fearfully, "Oh, dear! What about Lily and Harrison? How will they feel about me?"

"Darling, you've touched their hearts from the beginning. Lily hurt for you because you had never been given love and affection. She wanted to help you find her Savior." He kissed her gently. "And they, of all people, understand about Green."

Green. The thought of him brought them back to the earth. They looked down. Flaming torches showed figures moving on the shore.

"Uh-oh," Foy said. "I almost missed our most important landing." Releasing her, he gave orders into the speaking tube and eased the boat toward shore.

"What? You mean we still have a chance?"

Foy grinned. "We had allowed some time for getting by King's Rock that we didn't have to use. Didn't you notice we stopped awhile back?"

"Yes."

"Harrison telegraphed ahead." Suddenly Foy was dancing from one foot to the other in excitement. "Just you wait."

They climbed down from the peaceful isolation of the pilothouse. Adrianna hugged Lily and shared her joy.

"Last night I accepted Jesus as my personal Savior. I thought that I was a Christian because my name was on a church roll and I tried to be morally upright. I didn't know what for until you showed me. Thank you, Lily."

"I'm so very happy," replied Lily with tears shining in her eyes. "Keep studying, growing, learning everything you can, but remember: Always let philosophy fit into your faith instead of making faith fit into your philosophy."

"And test any idea by the measure of Christ," Emma added, kissing her cheek.

The silence was suddenly shattered. Hammers pounded; boards splintered as workmen stripped the steamer of excess poundage. Spars, doors, windows were carried down the gangplank.

Adrianna, Lily, and Emma pulled their chairs out of the ladies' saloon. Furniture from the main cabin and staterooms was placed on the dock.

One crew marched out removing weight while another boarded, stuffing the *Mignonne*'s hold with fuel. Ratty-looking men, lounging about the waterfront, slapped their knees and swapped racing tales as they watched six barrels of rosin being rolled aboard. Their eyes bulged as barrel after barrel of kerosene followed. When huge burlap bundles of fat pine stumps thumped onto the cargo deck, they declared they had never seen such a load of hot fuels.

The bell clanged; the whistle blasted. The last man jumped ashore. The plank lifted. The *Mignonne* pulled swiftly away from the landing. Cheers rose from the crowd as well-wishers waved their arms above their heads.

Black smoke belched from the two tall smokestacks. Cinders fell unnoticed on the women clutching the rail, watching the dark river.

Lily staunchly declared she trusted Harrison's judgment, but Emma remained silent with her lips pressed tightly. Watching Emma's pale face, Adrianna knew she feared for Jonathan, who had lost his foot to a boiler explosion.

Unable to remain still, Adrianna ran below to see the engine room for herself. Her eyes widened at the sight of the boiler, glowing red.

Wiping sweat from his dirty face, Jonathan watched the boiler gauges. Roaring flames leaped from the open doors of the huge furnaces. Two burly men poked the fire with long rods, stirring kerosene-soaked wood. Her nose burning from the fumes, Adrianna stepped back.

Squeezing through a break in the teetering cotton bales, Adrianna crept to the edge of the lower deck. They were traveling far too fast to be safe. Surely there was something she could do to help.

Pulling, tugging, she dragged a bundle of the lightwood knots toward the boiler room. Wordlessly, Lily joined her.

Bam! The *Mignonne* struck solidly, stopped. Scurrying back through the crevice, Adrianna saw the bow was mired in mud.

Clang! The pilot signaled for backing.

They pulled her out. Undamaged, the *Mignonne* steamed on.

Squinting, rubbing her eyes, Adrianna saw the sky was lighter even though rain was falling. "Oh, Lily!" she panted. "Day is coming. What if—after all this—Green's ship doesn't wait until eight o'clock? What if he leaves before dawn?"

"No." Lily laughed ruefully. "He won't do that. One of Green's fatal charms is his sense of honor."

Swish, swish, swisssh. The paddle wheel was slowing. The firemen were burning the empty rosin barrels. In their excitement at making a burst of speed, they had used it all. Wood racks were empty. The spluttering gauge was stopping slowly.

The *Mignonne* floated toward shore. The gangplank splashed down, bounced as serious-faced men ran down, shouldered wood, hurried back. No laughter or joking sounded this time. Suddenly a chanting song began, steadying their rhythm.

"Oh, can't they carry more than one piece at a time?" Adrianna checked her watch and glanced at the grave face of Lily, who seemed as determined as she to remain at the center of activity in spite of the rain.

Lily shook her dark hair. "You don't know how heavy cordwood is." She let out a long sigh and pointed to a nattily dressed man sheltered by a big, black umbrella as he paced the dock. "That must be Green's agent. This is our last stop to wood up."

As they pulled back into the stream, the rain became a downpour. The lovely boat seemed to cough tiredly, unable to gain momentum as the rain-soaked wood sputtered, smoked, went out. Kerosene was added liberally, but the fire burned disinterestedly.

Foy clopped down from above. Trusting Mr. Trimmer with the wheel, he joined the boiler room crew.

"This wood's no good!" Jonathan shouted. "It's waterlogged, but—worse—it's not the porous red oak we ordered. If I throw on enough kerosene, it will finally burn, but it will never make a hot fire. It's deadwood!"

"Do you think Green had rotten wood placed there?" Adrianna gasped.

"It's the kind of thing he would do," Lily replied.

Foy's eyebrows knit in a determined scowl. "The kerosene won't last at the rate you're using it. Bring all the li'dard." He grabbed an axe. Muscles rippling beneath his wet, white shirt, Foy split the knotted wood into splinters. Adrianna picked up a piece. The pungency of turpentine penetrated her senses. The stumps, like so many oily-backed ducks, yielded tender insides streaked red-gold, dry.

"Reminds me of your hair." Foy winked.

"Not now." She laughed and dabbed at the loose strands clinging wetly to her dirty face.

Family and crew worked, endeavoring to kindle the deadwood with the rosin-rich pine. Each added splinter blazed, elicited a brief glow from the logs, consumed itself, was gone. The supply of fat lightwood was exhausted, yet the smoldering fire refused to burn.

Bedraggled, the whole family stood on the boiler deck and clasped hands.

Foy patted the *Mignonne*'s side as if to tell her good-bye. "I'm sorry. I'll make it up to y'all somehow."

"So near," said Harrison, pointing.

Etched against the streaks of morning lay the skyline of Apalachicola.

"It's almost light." Foy raked his hands through his hair. "Light," he repeated. "Light!" he shouted. "Adrianna, Emma run! Gather all the candles from the cupboards. I'll get the crates of 'em from the storeroom."

"Lily," said Harrison, catching Foy's excitement. "Take a crew to the kitchen. Bring the slabs of bacon, all the fat side meat and grease. We aren't beaten yet!"

Scattering like mice over the huge boat, everyone snatched up combustibles. The candles, flung atop the wood, dripped inflaming wax. Fat meat sizzled, igniting wood. Kitchen grease burst into flames. Resisting no longer, the deadwood leaped into blazing gold and blue, then banked into hot, red coals.

With a mighty belch of fire and smoke, the *Mignonne* shot forward into Apalachicola Bay.

Green flags flying identified a majestic ship riding at anchor on the ocean swells. A signal flag fluttered as they were sighted.

Cheers rang out from the exhausted crew of the *Mignonne*. The family gathered on the upper deck, and Harrison offered a prayer of thanks.

Adrianna and Foy leaned eagerly out at the bow, facing joyfully into the wind. Rivers of testing fire lay behind them. Safe in each other's arms, they needed no words. Bracing as the riverboat hit the rough waves of the sparkling, blue-green Gulf, Adrianna breathed salt air. The magnificent vastness of God's creation enraptured her. Times were changing. They were moving out from their small world; but God was out there, too, bigger than the universe, in control of all history.

Foy hugged Adrianna close and nuzzled his face into her brilliant hair. A new day was dawning; beyond the horizon lay a new century. With a sure course charted, they were ready to meet the challenge.

Acknowledgments

The steamboat days of the 1870s on the shallow, shoal-ridden Chattahoochee River between Alabama and Georgia were brought to life for me by Edward A. Mueller, author of *Perilous Journeys: A History of Steamboating on the Chattahoochee, Apalachicola, and Flint Rivers, 1828–1928.* Mueller shared his extensive collection of firsthand accounts, many of which were extracted from microfilm of Columbus, Georgia, newspapers by T. J. Peddy.

The boats, excursions, landmarks, and disasters are all true; however, I have compressed dates and fictionalized. Mueller helped me make a fictional composite which is as accurate as possible to this particular time and river.

Some of the best articles which I drew from were: "Steaming on the Chattahoochee," by W. C. Woodall, *Georgia Magazine,* Aug./Sept. 1969, "Romance along the Alabama Rivers," by J. H. Scruggs, Jr., *Weekly Philatelic Gossip,* Sept. 19, 1953, and "River Steamboats Were Way to Go," edited by Ed Mueller from the Bainbridge, Georgia, newspaper of 1877, printed in the *Tallahassee Democrat,* July 10, 1966.

The Cannonball Route was actually set as the fastest schedule on the Chattahoochee in 1886 by the steamer *William D. Ellis* of the People's Line.

The Reconstruction Era came to a close in Eufaula as I have described it with the riot on Lily and Harrison's anniversary. Facts came from "The Eufaula Riot of 1874," by Harry P. Owens, *The Alabama Review,* July, 1963, pp. 224–237. Much other information was gleaned from Anne Kendrick Walker's *Backtracking in Barbour County* (Richmond, 1941).

I would like to thank Fleming H. Revell Publishers for use of material about Darwin in "Cut Out God" from *Tarbell's Teacher's Guide,* 1983–84, p. 247.

Thanks goes to Mimi Rogers, chief curator of the Jekyll Island Museum, for permission to draw from a wedding exhibit, and to P. J. Thomas, manager, Springer Opera House Arts Association, Inc., for information on a play which opened there November 7, 1874.

Douglas Purcell, executive director of the Historic Chattahoochee Commission, searched out information and took me to Fendall Hall which inspired my Barbour Hall. On the National Register of Historic Places, Fendall Hall is preserved as a museum by the state of Alabama. The painting of its parlor and dining room was actually done by Monsieur Le Franc about 1886. This beautiful house is open to the public several days each week through the auspices of RSVP of Eufaula and Barbour County in cooperation with the Alabama Historical Commission.

Florence Foy Strang introduced me to the delightful events of the Volunteer Firemen. Some of the firemen's artifacts are on display at Shorter Mansion where Hilda Sexton has been very helpful. Other details of the Firemanic Tournaments came from microfilm of the May 15, 1886, *Americus Times-Recorder.*

Americus, Georgia, Fire Chief Morris Smith provided helpful information on fire fighting. Mrs. James T. West, Sr., of DeSoto, Georgia, was at one time the only woman east of the Mississippi who was a licensed cotton sampler and weigher and warehouse manager. Her reminiscences gave life to the scenes of cotton fires.

Again thanks goes to: Lake Blackshear Regional Library and especially Harriet Bates who can unearth the most obscure fact; to the Reverend James Eldridge, Hinton Lampley, Marvlyn and Bill Story, Sandra Bowen, Glenda Calhoun, and Ginny Hodges.

Although the background characters and events are true, the main characters and story are fictional.

Beyond the Searching River

Chapter 1

Cinder-laden smoke spewed from the locomotive and obscured the scene of the wreck. Dazed, Libba Ramsey lay against the bank of red, Georgia clay like a rag doll tossed aside by a careless child. She scrubbed the turquoise ring on her clenched fist against an offending trickle of water tickling her cheek.

I never allow myself to cry? she questioned. She fought to remember. She had been sitting on the observation platform of the president's coach buttoning her shoe when the ballooning smokestack and pointed cowcatcher of a locomotive loomed through the haze of the September morning.

Blackness reclaimed her. She sank against the unyielding clay. Dreaming, she smelled, not clean woodsmoke, but the sharp, penetrating odor of turpentine. Her dry eyes burned with the branding of the image of pine trees skinned by railroad tracks knotted around them like pretzels.

"That snake-eyed Sherman. I'll never forgive him!" Libba struggled up against the restraining hands of a young man bending over her, squeezing water from his handkerchief.

"Wake up. The war is over, done," he said in a softly drawling voice. "It's Friday, September 15, 1876. Remember?" Gentle fingers soothed her thin shoulder. "One must forgive, forget."

Like a hurt puppy determined to get up, Libba wriggled, raised her head, forced open intensely blue eyes. She did not lie in a flat, pine swamp. Hills covered in oaks and poplars surrounded her. The railroad tracks lay straight, sure of their destination rather than being grotesquely twisted.

The young man blinked gray-blue eyes as if he had just awakened and was delighted with what he had discovered. His tousled dark hair was streaked with gray, but as she watched an engaging grin chase the concern from his innocent, round face, she knew he could be only slightly older than the almost eighteen she thought herself to be.

Blushing, she straightened the bustle bent beneath her and raked her fingers through her wild tangle of curls, which were as sooty black as the smut he had just washed from her face.

"For a minute I was six years old again," she explained. "Sherman's men burned Magnolia Springs. I fled through the piney woods to Savannah."

"You are no doubt fleeing from Savannah this time. The yellow fever epidemic? No wonder you're so plucky. You've done a lot of escaping for one so young." He waved his arms in wide gestures as he talked, adding further punctuation to his expressive voice. "Who are you? Where are you running *to?*"

She shook her head. "Nobody," she said huskily. Choking on emotion, she could say no more. She could not tell this kind young man that she barely knew who she was. She lowered thick, dark lashes lest he see the secret pain that blinded her from her uncertain searching.

Daniel Marshall thought her clear blue eyes the most enchanting he had ever seen. They dominated a face white as porcelain. Her pointed chin trembled momentarily only to firm with determination. When he had jumped from the train to take her out of harm's way, he had thought her a child. Indeed, she probably weighed less than ninety pounds. When he scooped her into his arms, he felt her shoulder blades protruding, fragile as a bird's wing. But she was unmistakably emerging into womanhood. Daniel was surprised at his longing to continue to hold her, to shelter her from whatever it was that he had glimpsed in her eyes.

Suddenly self-conscious, he slapped short fingers to his face, pulling down the corners of his eyes and mouth to make a mask of tragedy. Lowering his voice to a comic exaggeration, he intoned, "You'll feel better if you cry."

Libba jutted her chin. "I never cry. What happened?" Glazing her eyes against him, she slid her hand over a patch on her skirt while he absorbed her rebuff before replying.

"The car at the end broke loose from the rest of the train. The freight following slammed into it. The jolt must have thrown you clear. Where were you?"

"Oh! Is everyone all right? I must help." Forgetting herself, Libba tried to stand, but her knees gave way when she saw that the locomotive, W. M. Wadley, was spewing steam into the colonel's private car.

Its brass bell belatedly tolling brought chattering passengers spilling from the coaches. Men dressed in long, flapping coattails discussed the delays of the rail accident, still a common occurrence in these modern days.

Women, upholstered in the odd, goose-shaped silhouette of the day—narrow skirts pulled back into heavily adorned bustles and enormous, plumed Gainsborough hats—were excitedly taking part in the scene as they exercised their new freedom, both from cumbersome hoop skirts and from restrictive prewar mores. All, however, were properly hatted and gloved even at this early hour. Libba was suddenly aware that she was not, and, worse, she was allowing a strange man to talk with her.

She forgot herself again when she spotted the striking figure of a broad-shouldered man, calm in spite of the confusion of everyone else. Laboring along with the crew to right the wreck was the man for whom the engine was named. Unhatted, crowned with thick white hair, Colonel Wadley towered above the rest. With the erect carriage of his six-foot, one-inch frame clothed in perfectly tailored, plum-colored alpaca and with his aristocratic bearing, William Morrill Wadley was a man in charge. He was oblivious to the escaping steam hissing around his ankles from behind the cowcatcher of the locomotive, built to honor him more than twenty years ago when he was merely superintendent of the Central Railroad and Banking Company. In a crisp, New Hamphire twang, he barked curt orders which he expected to be followed to the letter. Abruptly, he turned and came striding toward them.

Daniel's graying eyebrows lifted at the corners as he spoke in an awe-struck whisper. "Do you know who that is?" He hurriedly smoothed his rumpled, threadbare, blue serge suit. "He's Colonel Wadley, president of the Central. He's been called the ablest railroad official in the South. He was superintendent of the railroads of the Confederacy." He deepened his voice to a rumble, and the outside corners of his eyebrows went up as he made a wry face and added, "Even though he was born a Yankee." Changing back to his natural grin, he added respectfully, "He's the man who put the railroads back together after the war."

Libba stood on wobbly knees as Wadley and his statuesque, auburn-haired wife approached.

"Luther Elizabeth, are you hurt?" Mrs. Wadley reached out to Libba. The pupils of her bright, yellow-hazel eyes enlarged at the bump on Libba's forehead. "Mr. Wadley," she said to her husband in formal address, reflecting her Savannah upbringing. "This child is hurt!"

"I–I'm fine, Miss Rebecca," Libba stammered.

Daniel Marshall opened his mouth in surprise. Puffing out his smooth cheeks, he let his vulnerable face fall slack as he moved aside deferentially for the patrician gentleman. If this girl was Wadley's daughter, what chance did he have to woo her? He had only a crumbling mansion and a mother to provide for. He had sprung into manhood early in those terrible days during the Reconstruction. People knew that the war was over and something must be done to make a living, but there was nothing with which to start. From his mother he had received a good brain and a strong faith which enabled him to reach deep within himself for the strength and courage to continue when the future held no promise. Now, faced with the commanding presence of Wadley, whose name was in the South equivalent with that in the East of New York Central tycoon Cornelius Vanderbilt, he felt his courage draining. Castigating himself for cowardice, Daniel Marshall backed away.

Wadley bent to examine Libba's injury, thankful that his wife's latest object of charity was not critically hurt. Wadley had been sitting at the rear of the car when he looked up and saw the engine coming. He remembered nothing else until he found himself on the side of the road, not knowing how he had gotten out. The loose car had been stopped by the action of automatic air brakes, but the freight train which was following had smashed nearly to the berths where his family lay sleeping.

With a soothing touch, surprising in so large and muscular a man, Colonel Wadley assisted Libba back aboard a Pullman car.

A dense cloud of black smoke rose above the waiting passenger engine, R. R. Cuyler. Two long blasts from the whistle, the signal to release brakes and proceed, jarred Libba's teeth and made her wonder if the whole earth were shaking. The bell began to clang. She turned to say thank you, but her Good Samaritan was gone.

Lying in a berth, lulled by the soft *choo-choo-choo* of the rolling train, Libba submitted gratefully as Rebecca Wadley sponged her cuts. Gazing soberly at this plain woman who had such laughing eyes, Libba reflected on her good fortune in meeting these wonderful people when Wadley had come as the president of the Union Society, the charitable club which oversaw Bethesda Orphanage for boys. His wife had meanwhile inspected the girls' branch, the Savannah Female Asylum. Libba had lived there in austere poverty with her mind mercifully blotting out her past.

In the strict, religious atmosphere, she had survived. She had tried to put a little fun in the other orphans' existence. Something in Libba's indomitable spirit had captured the attention of the motherly Mrs. Wadley.

Yellow fever had broken out in August of 1876. By mid-September, the cemeteries could not hold the corpses with emaciated frames and strangely yellow faces. No one knew the cause of the dreadful scourge. Whispering that the epidemic must have come in on filthy foreign ships, people fled the seashore.

Libba had thought only that the young usually survived and she would again—but for what? From some unsearchable distance, God had perhaps ordained that fortune smile for a time upon her. The Wadleys had invited her to visit their cotton plantation in the uplands of Monroe County, Georgia.

The swaying of her berth lessened as the *bum-bump, bum-bump* of the train over the rails slowed. The whistle blasted one long, mournful *ummmmmm* to indicate it was approaching Georgia's central city, Macon. It was only an overnight trip from the seacoast since Colonel Wadley had consolidated lines and accelerated passenger service. Built during the slow, easy romance of the steamboat era, Macon had seen its river trade dwindle; however, town planners had moved quickly to push rail lines beyond the river, north above the fall line, southwest through cotton land. Now the rail center of the whole southeast, Macon recognized William Wadley as the unquestioned genius behind its economic power.

"Macon! Ma–con, Ge–or–gia," called the conductor.

Ssssst! With steam escaping, the train rattled, jolted to a screeching stop. Looking out of the window, Libba saw the young man. With springing steps and laughing asides to fellow passengers, he bounded away.

Oh! She thought. *I didn't thank him. I don't even know his name. I'll never see him again!*

With a longing emptiness, she remembered the way the outside corners of his eyebrows had gone up from his little-boy eyes as he talked in funny voices trying to make her laugh. Sighing forlornly because love was an unknown quantity in her life, she dabbed at a blur in her eye. Turning her mouth down bitterly, she mumbled resolutely, "Just a cinder."

Rolling over painfully, she saw that Rebecca Wadley was putting away her washbasin, sponge, and salve.

"Bolingbroke is only fifteen miles north of Macon." Mrs. Wadley's soft voice drawled the words into extra syllables. "Are you able to get up?"

"Yes, Ma'am," Libba said staunchly.

Carriages waited at the depot in Bolingbroke. Libba was swept along with a flurry as passengers and baggage were transferred. A short distance from the railroad, they approached a simple, dignified entrance guarded by massive, acrid-smelling boxwoods. Wrought-iron gates swung wide, welcoming them into Great Hill Place.

The carriages swayed along a winding lane through the cool greenness of damp, natural woodland. Libba breathed fragrant cedar, cleansing after the smoke from the woodburning locomotive. Towering over everything were the oaks. Accustomed to low, spreading live oaks of the coast, Libba gazed up, up at these stalwart sentinels which seemed to echo the Wadleys' promise of beneficent protection.

With her cloak of stoic acceptance sliding from around her, Libba was transformed by the tranquility. Thirstily, she drank in the beauty, the peace, the vibrancy. Pines whispered. Mockingbirds trilled melodious tunes. Squirrels and chipmunks scampered unafraid over the rustling brown carpet of pine straw. Slender hardwoods trembled in the newly cool breeze, waiting eagerly for a finger of frost to stroke them into living flames.

The joy of homecoming made the family lean forward as they approached the house through a lane of black-green pyramids of magnolias glistening in the setting sun. Silence burst as dogs came loping from all directions, barking a welcoming chorus. Fine hunting dogs wagging tails, huge mongrels wagging bodies, and one tailless mutt hopping gamely on three legs were joined by whooping children to form a parade to the house.

"Ahhh!" Libba glimpsed Great Hill Place. She had feared overwhelming grandeur; instead, the white-frame house shouldered sheltering oaks and spreading camellias and stood as contentedly among the surrounding boxwoods as stately Mrs. Wadley now stood with grandchildren nudging her skirts.

A gabled stoop extending from the porch gave an odd, friendly look. Suddenly more sons, daughters, and various spouses spilled around them. The Wadleys had had nine children, seven now living, and Libba laughed helplessly at trying to sort them out. The warmth of their greeting made Libba feel, for the first time in her life, at home.

Supper was a feast. Salty-peppery fried ham and meat-seasoned peas and beans awakened Libba's taste buds. She thought the meat course was completed, but the white-haired man who served the table offered her a huge tureen with chunks of chicken and dumplings swimming in butter. Declaring they must fatten her up and put color in her cheeks, everyone pressed Libba to take second helpings. When hot scuppernong cobbler with whipped cream sliding into melting pools was placed before her, she ate slowly, resting between spoonfuls.

"Enough!" Libba held up her hands in defeat. "It's wonderful, but I can't eat another bite!"

Her smile included the butler, Prince. He returned her look with a scowl that bristled the white eyebrows standing out from his dark face and soured his bulldog jowls. Plainly he thought that she was not the social equal of this family whom he had remained a part of in spite of the Emancipation. Libba's wariness returned. Even here, her mettle would be tested.

Libba had dropped her guard for a moment, and Rebecca Wadley saw the pain in her clear blue eyes.

"Sarah Lois, take this exhausted child to her room."

From the sea of faces, one emerged, solicitous, kind. Arresting brown eyes that snapped with intelligence from beneath straight dark brows kept the solemn face from being plain. The eldest daughter, now thirty-two, was the undisputed chatelaine in her mother's stead. Resigned to spinsterhood, she lived through the lives of others. On her twenty-fourth birthday, she had passed the marriageable age, but she had not let being an old maid quell her zest for living. Looking at Libba, she murmured for her to follow.

Libba tried not to stare at the odd lace cap Sarah Lois wore over her severely parted auburn hair. Long lace strips, which hung from each side of the cap and lay in folds on Sarah Lois's broad shoulders, swung as she climbed the stairs. Libba winced as stabs of pain reminded her that she had been thrown from the train.

Sarah Lois opened wide a door. "This is your room."

"Mine?" Libba asked in squeaky-voiced surprise. "You mean a room all to myself?" Timidly, Libba stepped across a cool bare floor of mirror-polished oak.

"Yes, of course. For as long as you—need it. Let me know if I can get you anything." The sweet-faced woman softly closed the door.

Alone! What luxury! For a long moment Libba stood perfectly still, absorbing the quietness. Dominating the room was a bed of rosewood, four-posted, carved in the most exquisite and intricate pineapple design. *It is far too beautiful to sleep on,* she thought. *I ought to lie awake and simply enjoy looking at it.* A matching rosewood dresser and cheval glass stood on either side of the bed. The mirror showed her tiredness.

Removing her drab traveling attire, Libba untied her bustle petticoat with its poufs of muslin which covered the steel hoops of her badly bent bustle. Splashing water into the porcelain bowl from the matching cabbage-rose painted pitcher on the marble-topped washstand, she scrubbed off the grime from the train trip and put on an often-darned muslin gown.

She knelt beside the bed skirts as she had been taught to kneel beside her cot and intoned a prayer with little thought that her words were heard.

Twisting the turquoise ring on her finger, Libba realized that the Wadleys were right: She was thin. Fearing her one treasure would be lost, she placed it on the gold chain about her neck as it had been in her earliest recollection.

Stepping on the needlepoint-covered stool, she climbed onto the bed piled high with a multitude of mattresses. Slightly dizzy, she clung to the top feather mattress, feeling as if she might fall off. She had never slept so high. She lay staring wide-eyed at the white muslin canopy, envisioning the engaging grin of the gentle young man. He had called her plucky. Well, she was used to taking knocks. She had escaped death once more, but for what? Biting her lips, she fought despair and hopelessness of what lay beyond this brief respite.

Her fingers closed on the large Victorian ring. Her thumb rubbed the smooth oval turquoise and pressed one of the carved gold flowers surrounding it. A hidden spring snapped. With blue eyes determinedly tearless, she gazed into the glass-covered compartment which held the only clue to her place in the world.

Chapter 2

Birds singing in the magnolia tree outside her window awakened Libba at daybreak.

"Ohhh-um," she groaned as she tried to turn her aching body in the puff of the feather mattress. Wishing she could bury her head under a goose-down pillow and never get up, she lay for a moment submerged in misery, then, determindly, slid down from the bed.

She must be useful if she were to be welcome here. Summoning every ounce of strength, she pulled her brown calico dress over her stiff shoulders.

Descending down the mahogany-railed staircase, Libba paused uncertainly and looked down from the landing. Everything about the house had an uncluttered elegance, a simple dignity with nothing calculated to impress. Rococo styles were popular, but the Wadleys preferred genuineness.

The rumble of a coffee grinder told Libba someone was up before her. The delicious scent of bacon frying drew her across the hall to the rear of the house.

Stepping into a tremendous kitchen, she blinked, trying to sort out the blur of color and the bustle of activity. Hanging from the exposed rafters of the high ceiling were strings of peppers: red, yellow, green. Drying herbs added nose-twitching aromas. Several women worked busily, laughing, chattering.

"Good morning," said Libba tentatively.

A chorus of welcome greeted her. Mrs. Wadley strode forward and lifted the black curls with which Libba had carefully concealed her forehead.

"How are you feeling, Luther Elizabeth?" she asked as she mashed the purple lump.

"Fine, Ma'am." Libba swallowed pain and curtsied.

Rebecca Wadley's pupils enlarged as she probed Libba's guarded eyes. Without comment, she ladled steaming oatmeal into an earthenware bowl and sprinkled it generously with brown sugar. Handing it to Libba, she said, "Come with me."

Wonderingly, Libba followed outside, down steep steps and across the yard to a small house. Coolness kissed her cheeks as she stepped inside the thick brick walls. They were inside a creamery lined with cold-holding marble shelves keeping pitchers of milk and pans of cream.

Mrs. Wadley dipped a ladle into the thick golden cream and placed a huge dollop on Libba's oatmeal.

Mouth watering, Libba tasted the sweet hot cereal and cool cream. "Delicious! Sheer bliss!"

"Now, I want you to rest and relax all day," Mrs. Wadley commanded.

"No, Ma'am. I'm used to working. Jus' give me a job, and—"

"Tomorrow, maybe. Not today."

As they stepped back into the warm sunshine, Sarah Lois emerged from the other side of the creamery building. Through a heavy iron door that looked like a bank vault, Libba glimpsed a windowless room, dark save for sunbeams slipping through the slits where an occasional brick had been left out to provide ventilation. A huge iron safe hunched in one corner half-hidden by wooden barrels marked Flour and Sugar. Sarah Lois selected a key from the heavy ring she wore dangling from a chain around her waist and carefully locked the door.

They returned to the kitchen where Sarah Lois distributed the measured ingredients to the servants for the day's menu. Mrs. Wadley herself, wiped every breakfast dish.

Libba ate ravenously. As her gnawing stomach began to fill, she nibbled a hot, fluffy biscuit dripping with sticky pear preserves and pondered what she saw. She was not needed here any more than she had been at the orphanage. Because she had graduated as the pupil with the highest honors, she had been appointed as a teacher; but with so many deaths from yellow fever, she had simply become an unwanted mouth to feed. Libba did not know why, seeing her, Miss Rebecca had opened her great heart in compassion and asked her husband to become Libba's guardian. She did know that she was approaching the age when she must find a place for herself.

Screams interrupted her dark thoughts. Squeals, peals of laughter drew her to the center hall. Two small boys and a girl were taking turns riding a throw rug. While the others cheered, one doubled down, took a running start, flopped stomach-down on the rug, and glided down the highly waxed oak floor from the back door to the front.

The freckled-faced girl tugged at Libba's hand. "Come on. Do a belly-whopper."

"I've never seen anything that looked like so much fun." whispered Libba wistfully. She eyed the Tiffany lamp teetering on a marble-topped table in the entry. Chairs marched around the walls with backs as stiff and ramrod straight as the people in this family. "Won't you get in trouble?"

"No. It's allowed," assured a dark-haired boy with a full, sensitive mouth. "But, remember, we can't run anywhere in the house except the hall. Try it."

Libba looked at the portraits on the wall: a stern Colonel Wadley, an imposing General Lee, and a mocking Mona Lisa. Shivering between fear and temptation, she jerked a nod and gathered up her floor-length skirt, which she had only recently started wearing to set her apart from the children. She had not fooled this group. They knew a fellow tomboy when they saw one. Running a few steps, she flopped on the rug. Whizzing down the polished floor past the clapping, yelling children, she raised her head triumphantly just in time to see the front door looming. It opened. The rug sailed across the porch and skidded to a stop at the edge of the stoop.

"Do you try to break that swanlike neck at least once a day?" a deep, virile voice inquired, chuckling.

Mortified, Libba lay facedown, unmoving. She cringed at the sight of two large, well-shined boots. *Maybe if I die they will go away.*

"Are you all right?" The male laughter turned to alarm at her stillness. Strong hands lifted her shoulders.

"Yes, Sir," murmured Libba. "That was a foolish thing to do—especially after yesterday." She threw back her head to look at the dark-haired man. *Why did he have to be the handsomest one in the family who caught me?*

Suddenly she burst out laughing. "It was fun!"

His rich laughter joined hers as he helped her to one of the white wicker porch chairs. "It's a good thing they added the stoop or you'd have gone bumping down the steps like—"

Grasping at the change of subject, Libba replied, "I don't believe I've ever seen a porch with a stoop, Mr. . .I'm so sorry. I met so many of you last night, I've forgotten."

"Paul Morley," he said, looking disappointed that he had not made more of an impression. He sat on the porch swing at one end of the porch and surveyed her. "Paul," he repeated. "Don't call me mister. I'm just kinfolk—here for a visit. But to answer your question, Cousin William is of Puritan ancestery. Now, Cousin Rebecca is a daughter of the Old South." His brown eyes twinkled as he tweaked his dark mustache and smiled with calculated charm.

"When they moved here after the war and began remodeling this old house, Cousin William assembled the family and asked if they wanted a Southern porch or a Northern stoop. The vote was a tie, so he built both. The house is a strange mix. Perhaps we all are, too."

Libba had feared that her silly display would make him think her a child, but as the swing rocked, he roamed his eyes up and down her with the motion, clearly assessing her a woman. Her insides jerked and bumped like a train zigzagging down a crooked track.

Oooummmm! The shattering whistle seemed a part of her emotions, but it brought a clattering of footsteps. Children tumbled off the stoop and galloped down the lane.

"They're catching the train to school," Paul explained, relaxing his spell upon her. "And I'd better get to work. I'm designing a system to give the house running water—you can come and see if you like."

Unaccustomed to talking with a man at all, much less one this handsome, Libba felt relief at the interruption. Cautioning herself that she must be better armed for his overwhelming virility, she refused. "Thank you, no, but perhaps tomorrow." She fanned back her thick lashes from her clear blue eyes and gave him her most charming smile. "For now, I'm going to obey Miss Rebecca's command and rest."

Paul grinned agreeably. "Good idea. Why don't you help yourself to the library?" He tipped a wide-brimmed straw hat and went down the steps two at a time.

Libba went back into the house, empty now, quiet. From the library's well-stocked shelves, she selected a slim volume of poetry, *Sonnets from the Portuguese.* The oak-paneled library seemed as imposing as Colonel Wadley himself, and Libba hoped it was permitted to take the books from the room. A door opening on a side porch provided escape.

Pale sunshine filtered the mists of a sky that looked like scrubbed pewter. The breeze was cool, refeshing after the steaming heat of summer in Savannah. Here in the hills of middle Georgia, summer-parched earth had been revived by September gales, and lush green overflowed the yard and meadow beyond. In the distance, she could see cotton fields white unto harvest.

The pungent smell of boxwood invited Libba toward a formal garden. For a moment she stood at the entrance and looked down a series of terraces. A flower bed several levels down seemed alive with bobbing heads of surprise lilies awakened by the recent rains. Popped up on their nearly invisible, leafless stems, they looked like so many red spiders suspended knee-high. Libba was tempted to follow the walk which wound into mysterious, unseen depths. Intrigued, she wanted to explore; but a terrible weakness, a feeling that she had been beaten by a heavy rod, made her decide to wait.

A prickling sensation that she was not alone made her glance overhead. A girl about her own age lay entwined along a smooth, flat limb of a mimosa tree with her nose in a book. Moving softly lest she disturb her, Libba turned away toward the kitchen yard.

A tall, turbaned woman was sweeping the red clay with a broom made of branches from wild dog fennel bushes. Libba greeted her pleasantly. "Good morning."

The servant returned her "Good morning" sympathetically, but as soon as Libba passed, the woman began to talk as though the girl could not hear with her back turned.

"Po' little critter. So thin and hongry a puff o' wind could blow her away."

"Humph. A lot you know," a man's voice replied. "She eats a sight. So much it makes her po' to tote it."

Squaring her shoulders, Libba marched up a hill toward a hammock strung between two elms. The hillcrest was a delightful suspension between inhabited yard and the meadow rolling away in every direction with an open invitation to roam, to lie among the daisies, and to dream. Away on the next rise, a vaulted brick tower stood guarding the meadow. For what strange purpose? It excited Libba's imagination, but aching legs made her stop at the hammock.

She stretched out luxuriously. Swinging gently, lulled by birdsongs, she let the joy, the peace of the atmosphere soothe her troubled spirit. For a few moments she would allow herself to pretend she was somebody, a real person who belonged on this beautiful plantation, isolated from the world's harsh reality.

Idly, she read a few pages, but her eyelids became heavy. Drifting into dream-troubled sleep, she tossed, wrestled, and set the hammock wildly rocking.

"No!" she screamed. "Don't let them see you. They'll kill us—or worse!" She flung the book. The ringing of hammers, the penetrating smell of turpentine, the grotesque image of iron rails knotted around the pine trees, the searing heat of a roaring fire: All of her nightmare returned.

With a sudden bump, Libba awakened. Dumped on her bustle again, she sat with the netting of the hammock wrapped about her head. Struggling free, she looked about furtively. The ringing of the hammers was real. Workman were adding a wing, apartments for William Oconius Wadley and his family while they built a home.

No one seemed to have witnessed her latest tumble. Getting up gingerly, she started for the house.

The book! She limped back. Her welcome would certainly be revoked if she left that fine leather volume on the ground.

She took refuge in her room. At noon there was a knock on her door. Sarah Lois peered in, wearing, as usual, her odd lace cap and her enigmatic smile. "I brought you a tray," she said. "Endine told me you took another fall. You just stay in bed all afternoon until you get over being shaky."

"You're too kind to me," Libba protested. She sipped a swallow of buttermilk and attacked the laden plate. Who was Endine and which show of stupidity had she witnessed?

Her stomach full, she began to read Elizabeth Barrett Browning's Sonnet I:

And a voice said in mastery while I strove, . . .
　　"Guess now who holds thee?"—"Death," I said.
But there,
　　The silver answer rang. . . "Not Death, but Love."

She envisioned a tousled head, a pair of gray-blue eyes brimming with concern. She cupped her hand around her cheek and felt again a gentle touch, hearing a warm voice saying, "It's over. Forgive. Forget."

A bittersweet longing made her wish that she could laugh with the good-natured clowning of that interesting young man. She realized that he had been awed when the prominent Wadleys greeted her familiarly. He had retreated. Sighing, Libba commanded herself to stop dreaming. She would never see him again.

When the afternoon shadows stretched across the shining floor, Libba's natural determination gained victory over her shakiness. She slid down from the high bed.

Silk was not in her wardrobe. Her Sunday gingham with its crotcheted collar hung alone in the vastness of the mahogany armoire. Brushing her black curls furiously, she left them as wild a tumble as if she had been running in the wind.

Stepping into the hall, she encountered the girl she had seen reading in the mimosa. Her hair was as faded as pink, as fine and frizzy as a mimosa blossom; her face as freckled as if it had been pasted with the big brown seeds. Because she had neither the beauty nor the dignity of the other family members, Libba dropped her guard, smiled, admiring one who did not think herself too old or too grand to climb a tree. "Hello. You're. . . ?"

"Endine," the girl answered.

"Ahn—"

"Deen. It's spelled E-n-d-i-n-e, but it's pronounced like a doctor told you to say ah, then sneeze." She laughed.

Happiness warmed Libba. This was Paul's sister. Perhaps she had found a friend.

"My name is Elizabeth, but there was a child who could only lisp out Libba and it stuck."

Endine linked Libba's arm through hers and guided her through the back hall to join the rest of the family assembling in the large, stiffly formal dining room. Although the ladies had not dressed elaborately, they were fresh, clean, smelling of lavender sachet. Each one held her carefully groomed head in a certain way as she walked gracefully across the room and seated herself properly into her chair by a rule which escaped Libba. As Paul held back a chair for her, Libba fumbled, forgetting which side of the chair to enter.

Looking up and down the long table, Libba tried to identify the rest of the family, sons and daughters and their families with numerous children named for their grandparents. All of the Wadleys were tall and had patrician noses, masses of auburn hair, and eyes that arrested one with a glance. Oh, she would never keep them straight, especially since there were so many of them carrying on the important family names.

Nervously watching Mrs. Wadley to see which fork to take, Libba ate something that she guessed was an artichoke. Under the butler's scrutiny, she determined not to eat piggishly as she had done the night before. She jumped when she heard her name.

"Libba's trying to break every bone in her body," Endine said. "She fell out of the hammock screaming about pretzels."

Pinioned by Endine's yellow eyes, Libba clutched the ring dangling on its golden chain about her neck. A forced laugh gurgled in her throat. "I have an unexplainable nightmare. It's impossible, but railroad tracks are twisted around pine trees, and. . ." Her voice trailed away.

Brown eyes in blank faces stared at her from motionless bodies up and down the long table.

Endine's freckles seemed to stand out from her face as she curled her thin lip in a sneer. "Just who are you, anyway?"

Chapter 3

Biting the turquoise ring, Libba shrank from Endine's unexpected enmity. Suddenly, she threw back her dark cloud of hair and stared, unblinking, at her freckle-faced challenger.

"I can't really say." Her voice cracked, but she continued. "I know I'm a Southerner because I'll always hate blue cloth!"

"I know Libba's a Southern lady because she has such tiny feet," Paul said, kicking his sister's large shoe. "Did you know the Chinese marry a little-footed girl and then take a big-footed wife to be her slave?"

The others made a show of eating, but Colonel Wadley put down his fork and fixed his piercing eyes upon Endine. At first the girl glared back at him in defiance, but as his lower lip protruded sternly, she mumbled a halfhearted apology.

Wadley's handsome face remained set in its usual grave expression, but his hazel eyes softened with kindness as he turned to Libba, who was angrily crumbling a piece of corn bread.

"I've seen your nightmare."

Heedlessly dropping her bread, Libba stared at him.

Wadley continued in his crisp, terse twang. "I recall the rails looped around pines like pretzels. I still feel the heat of anger." His mouth twisted bitterly. "It's no wonder a child would be permanently marked by such horror."

All eyes turned toward him. With a self-conscious laugh, he resumed speaking in a gentler tone.

"Sometimes when the source of a nightmare is explained, the dream will cease." He settled back in his chair with laced fingers resting on his vest. "When the unfortunate War Between the States ended, this family was, of course, heartbroken, penniless, destitute of clothing save for the coarsest homespun. We were living in Louisiana at the time. Life was a shambles. No work. The finances of the Vicksburg, Shreveport, and Texas Railroad Company did not admit of repairing the ruined road."

Libba shifted. What had all this to do with her dreams? Could he really help her find herself?

"A man of fifty-two with seven children, I was without a dollar. I decided to seek refuge from the United States rule by moving us to Brazil to rehabilitate my fortunes.

"Then on the hottest day in July—it was 1865—I was working in my blacksmith shop when Mr. Courvoisie arrived from Savannah bearing a letter asking me to return to Georgia to restore the ruined railroad. It was nothing but twisted track and burned bridges."

Mrs. Wadley glowed. "The letter said Mr. Wadley's knowledge, ability, and energy could rebuild the railroads better than anyone."

"Eagerly, I started for Georgia by going on a steamboat down the Mississippi to New Orleans. The South was so utterly devastated it would have taken months to cross it. The quickest way to reach Savannah was by way of Chicago, Niagara Falls, New York City, and thence by steamship to Savannah. I reached there in exactly one month."

"But, Papa!" protested John, reddening because his voice changed. "You haven't explained Libba's nightmare."

"I'm coming to that! What I found in Georgia was this: General Sherman left Atlanta such a burning holocaust that one man said he could read his watch at midnight ten miles away. The Yankees marched across Georgia to the sea. Sherman's 'bummers' destroyed everything in their path, but their special prey was the Georgia damage of $100,000,000 with $20,000,000 advantage to Union forces and the rest waste and destruction."

Tension crackled as the older ones relived the anguish.

Wadley's voice seemed to echo into the silence. "Luther Elizabeth, don't you remember anything about what happened to you? Where your home was located?"

A sad-eyed waif, Libba shook her head, unable to speak.

"I hazard you witnessed the destruction of the rails. With fiendish glee, Sherman's troops built bonfires of crossties, heated the middle of the rails red hot, and twisted them around the trees. They destroyed three hundred miles of railroad."

Clenching her fists against her face to stifle a scream, Libba thought, *Three hundred miles? It's hopeless! I'll never find my home!* Bereavement drained her as if she had just been dealt the wrenching.

Rebecca Wadley's understanding softened her plain features. She got up and walked around the table to embrace Libba's hunched shoulders. "You have a home now, Dear—and a family."

Libba longed to throw herself against Mrs. Wadley and sob out her wretchedness, but Endine's cold glare made her swallow the ache in her throat and renew her vow: *I'll never let myself cry.*

"Come, everyone!" Sarah Lois spoke in a voice that commanded attention. "What Libba needs is fun! Let's all go into the parlor and play—"

"Charades!"

"Funny recitations!"

"Dumb crambo!"

Libba struggled to smile as grandchildren sprang to life with happy shouting and good-natured shoving for supremacy. A tingle of warmth penetrated her misery, and she looked up through a fan of dark lashes at Paul bending over her.

His spreading smile slowed, slipping into an expression of beguilement at her piquancy. With urging fingers on her elbow, he drew her up. "Come," he said in a voice meant only for her ears, "I'll teach you to play backgammon."

With a stiff shoulder toward Endine's sly looks, Libba preceded Paul into the parlor. Before he could unfold the wooden game board, sixteen-year-old John claimed her attention.

"I wanted to show you something." John smiled shyly and thrust a brass-bound mahogany tube into Libba's hand.

"What?" Libba began wonderingly. The foot-long piece was beautifully made, but she could not fathom its use.

"You've never seen a kaleidoscope?" John asked gleefully. "They are the latest rage in parlor entertainment."

"But what—"

Both men vied to clasp their hands over hers around the cyclinder and tilt it toward the lamp.

Libba peeped into the end as they indicated. Sparkling, multicolored bits reflected by mirrors formed a many-faceted design. Fascinated, she turned the kaleidoscope as directed and watched the tumbling pieces patterning endlessly.

John leaned adoringly over her shoulder. His hollow-cheeked face glowed red with the pleasure of making her smile. Paul reared back with his hands behind his head and heaved a sophisticated snort of boredom as the children began to clap and chant.

"Auntie, do 'Miss Fanny,' do 'Miss Fanny.' "

The dignified, austere Sarah Lois stood in the center of the parlor and recited a dialogue, changing her voice and making broad gestures which jiggled the white lace streamers of her house cap.

The children screamed and shouted at the solemn old maid aunt who was jumping up and down and grabbing her legs against an imaginary whipping.

"Yes'm, Mama. Yes'm, Mama. I'm going back to church every Sunday," she screeched in a high-pitched voice. She danced from more blows of an almost visibly flapping strap.

"Yes'm, Mama. I'm gon' to read my Bible from lid to lid."

Waiting for the giggling to die down, she delivered the anticipated climax in the voice of the mother. "I tell you, Miss Fanny, I can make more Christians out of sinners with my old trunk strap than a preacher can in forty lebben years."

Applause filled the room. Endine jumped up to take center stage. With tossing pink hair, she recited:

Whatever I do; whatever I say,
Aunt Sophie says it isn't the way.
When she was a girl (forty summers ago);
Aunt Sophie says they never did so.

Endine shook her meaningful finger at Libba sandwiched between John and Paul and continued:

If I take a lad's arm—just for safety, you know—
Aunt Sophie says they never did so. . .

Self-consciously, Libba drew away from the cousins. The changing voices and gestures of the recitations brought back an image of the young man at the wreck. She did wish she had thanked him.

Bong! Bong! The grandfather clock in the hall was striking then, bedtime.

Mounting the stairs, Libba reached the turning and looked down as Endine's red head came conspiratorially close to Paul.

"You're as cow-eyed over her as John," Endine hissed. "You're the most eligible bachelor in the state of Georgia. Don't get mixed up with a nobody!"

Tears stung Libba's eyes, but she blinked them back. In the orphanages, everyone had suffered from the war. They had never talked about what was past. She had never allowed herself to think about who she might be. She had sought only to make each day as bright as possible for the children in her charge and work herself tired enough to sleep without her nightmare. Now Endine's needling prickled her very soul.

Squeezing her ring, she stood in the shadows until everyone had drifted away. Summoning every ounce of her courage, she stole back down the stairs.

Because the dignified gentleman had not joined his children in the parlor games, Libba had assumed Colonel Wadley must have retired to the solitude of his study. Her timid knock went unanswered. Raking her hair away from her face, she drew a tremulous breath and rapped smartly.

"Come."

The terse voice weakened her knees. Wanting to bolt, Libba resolutely opened the door.

The air was redolent of richly oiled leathers. The room spoke one word: railroads. Lining the walls were lithographs of locomotives, beginning with the first crude 1820s steam machines pulling carriages and ending with the contemporary, handsomely painted engines and coal cars of the 1870s. In a prominent place was a picture of the W. M. Wadley. A kerosene lamp cast a yellow glow over the man who looked splendid even at this hour in his white, winged collar and dark suit. He cocked one appraising eye from the report he was reading and fastened it sharply upon the slender girl who swayed like a milkweed pod poised before a puff of wind.

Libba cleared her throat. "Colonel Wadley, Sir. I. . .I don't mean to bother you, Sir. You've probably saved my life bringing me here, but. . .but. . ." She whacked the heel of her hand at the back of her black curls tumbling in her eyes and winced as she mashed the bruise on her forehead. She felt angry at herself for stammering, but she was not used to talking to men.

"It's probably hopeless to find my home. I've never worried too much before, but. . ." Before her courage left her entirely, she finished in a rush. "Could you, please, help me find out who I am?"

Colonel Wadley's black brows came together. "You are what you make of yourself, young lady." His massive jaws set firmly as he fixed her with piercing eyes. "This is Endine's work. I shall reprimand her."

Lacing his fingers across his muscular chest, he surveyed her. "I came down from New Hampshire with my anvil on my back. I may remark that with nothing but my God-given talent as a blacksmith I rose to an honored position with the railroad. You may, therefore, understand why, when the war destroyed everything any of us owned, I started again."

Libba feared to remind him that even though the late war had opened a few jobs for a respectable woman, there was almost no opportunity outside of marriage.

Wadley relaxed his bushy eyebrows and dipped a big finger toward a chair. "Sit. Sit."

Libba obeyed, perching on the edge of the leather seat bending over a rocker.

Wadley forced himself to speak gently. "I do understand what it's like to be fatherless. I liked nothing better than working iron with my father in his blacksmith shop—I made my first pair of pincers at the age of six. But he died when I was thirteen. I became a blacksmith's apprentice."

Libba settled back in the chair as his voice droned.

Wadley told her how he had left New Hampshire in 1833 to seek his fortune in Savannah. He worked for only a few days as a fifty-cents-a day forge striker before he began to rise from one position to the next. With encouragement from his highborn wife, he moved upward to superintendent of the Central Railroad. By 1852, he was Georgia's recognized railroad expert. By 1861, he was accepted as the ablest railroad official in the South.

War came, destroying everything he had built. Recalling this, he sat unmoving.

The ticking of the clock in the hallway intruded into their silence. Libba waited, afraid to breathe until he remembered her again.

"Perhaps you'll understand the reason behind the destruction you witnessed if you know the importance of the railroads," he said at last. "The War Between the States was the first great conflict in which railroads furnished the chief means of transportation. More than that, railroads were one of the chief causes of the war. The firing on Fort Sumter on April 12, 1861, was simply a climax to a long series of quarrels between North and South over interpretation of the Constitution. The North wanted power in the federal government. The South wanted states' rights. The North wanted the federal government to sponsor railroads. Espousing the Confederate cause from principle and feeling, I entered its army, and President Davis appointed me superintendent of railroads.

"It was an impossible task. The North had twice the miles of railroads and industry and mineral resources. We struggled without supplies. As I traveled about trying to keep trains rolling, I looked through cracked car windows and saw my engines standing cold upon the sidings, their wrought-iron tires worn nearly away. Locomotives breathed like consumptives. Rolling stock screamed for lubricating oil and was given only pig grease.

"You must understand that in early days, railroads were owned by states, counties, or municipal interests and built with different gauges of track. Interference from Richmond was feared as a plot from a competitor, so the doctrine of states' rights created problems.

"I pleaded that the power of regulation be vested in the government. At last Congress acted. President Davis signed my railroad law requiring any carrier to devote its facilities to the support of the army and obliging railroads to adhere to schedules prescribed by the government. Congress passed my law, but when the time came for my reappointment, that was denied.

"By 1863, Richmond was ringing with criticism of Yankees in Southern government. I was loyal to the Confederacy but spoke in sharp phrases that rasped on Southern ears. I took on Southern life, but I failed to absorb the Southern flair for diplomacy and tact. At any rate I returned to Louisiana.

"When our cause was lost, my job and my fortune were swept away. Despair made life seem over."

Bong! Bong! The clock struck eleven, reviving the tremendous man and the tiny girl who had sunk beneath the weight of the past.

"I may remark that I do understand your despair—hatred—fear. But with grit and gumption, anyone can begin again. As I told you at dinner, my offer came to return to Georgia, but stiff negotiations were necessary before I was made president of the Central in 1866.

"The only thing I boast of," he concluded, "is that none of my powers have rusted from disuse. Nothing can defeat you as a person except succumbing to bitterness or hopelessness. Be the best you can be whatever the situation. Keep yourself in high esteem."

"Thank you, Sir." Libba rose. "I do appreciate your taking time to tell me this. Good night, Colonel Wad—"

"Wait. Don't ever forget what I've told you. But wait." His stern voice softened. "I do understand that you want to know about your family."

His eyes searched her pale face. "The knowledge could be painful."

She nodded solemnly.

"Do you have any facts?"

"This is my only link."

With trembling fingers, Libba unfastened the chain from around her neck. She removed the turquoise ring. For a long moment she pressed it fearfully against her mouth until a salty taste of blood told her she was biting her tongue.

Her thumb pressed a carved flower. With her hand shaking violently, Libba held out the open ring.

Chapter 4

The ring looked insignificant in Wadley's massive hand. As he gazed into the glassed compartment, his broad shoulders sagged into an uncustomarily hopeless posture.

"This is all you know of your past?"

Libba's throat worked but no sound emerged. She nodded.

"Well!" He laughed shortly. "The impossible simply takes longer. Let's see what the ring tells us. It is a fine Victorian piece of mourning jewelry. This lock of hair preserved under the glass would, most likely, be your mother's."

Libba lifted a black curl and asked, "You think my mother has golden hair?"

"Had, my dear. A mourning ring would have been made for you on the occasion of her death."

"Oh."

"We'll assume, then, that you resemble your father."

Acknowledging his encouragement with a wan smile, Libba said, "There's an inscription."

The lamplight's glow revealed writing on the underside of the compartment lid: Jonathan Ramsey m. Luther Elizabeth King June 6, 1856.

"You know, then, that these are you parents?"

"Yes, Sir. I'm certain of that—and my name."

Snapping the ring shut, Wadley blew his breath against the blue-green stone and polished its gentle luster. His voice was low, musing. "Turquoise is a fashionable gemstone—as fashionable at the moment as hair jewelry. It is a symbol of wealth many people wear; however, I hazard whatever reputation I now have that this particular ring can tell us more. The quality of the gem indicates a fine Persian turquoise. The gold carving and filigree are exquisite."

Endine should be impressed, Libba thought bitterly.

"Yes," Wadley said tersely. "I see a man of wealth and culture in the throes of great grief—perhaps losing a beloved wife in childbirth as so often happens to the frail—having this token of remembrance fashioned for that child in what has long been established as the birthstone for—now, let me see. . ." He drummed his fingers. "Ah! December."

Wadley reared back with his hands behind his head, pleased with himself. Libba huddled in her high-backed chair, fighting through wisps of long-suppressed memories.

At last, she spoke. "I don't know my birthday. I remember a tiny, white-haired woman, thin yet erect. I called her Nannie." Her words came slowly as though from far away. "She kept saying Savannah would be safe. When we got there, I don't know. My mind goes blank. I seem to see a fort, hear loud, loud guns. I remember smelling smoke. I was so scared. So scared. Crying. She said—Nannie said, 'Now you are six. Too old to cry. You must not cry anymore.' "

Libba felt as though her whole body had filled with tears, as though they must drip from her very fingers and toes.

"Probably Fort McAllister." Wadley's voice, too, had a dead sound. "Major-General Sherman took Savannah and telegraphed a message which reached Lincoln on Christmas Eve 1864. Savannah citizens will never forget his words: 'I beg to present you as a Christmas gift the city of Savannah.' "

Colonel Wadley sat capping and uncapping a locomotive-shaped, china inkwell. "If we are correct, you would become eighteen some time this December."

They remained for a long time in silence without realizing that Rebecca Wadley stood watching.

"Tcch, Tcch," she said, clucking her tongue. "Enough sad talk. To bed for you, little one. Tomorrow I'll take you to Macon for tea at Mrs. Johnston's. Her social contacts are wide ranging." She put her arm around Libba's thin shoulders and urged her up.

"I hazard that if Jonathan Ramsey still has property along the railroad, I should be able to find out about him," Colonel Wadley said just a little too heartily.

Libba climbed into bed thinking, *Three hundred miles of railroad!* Mercifully, she slept but did not dream.

Taking her Sunday gingham from the wardrobe the next day when it was time to dress for the trip into Macon, Libba cried out in dismay at the gravy stain on the crocheted collar. The only other thing she owned was a dark skirt and white shirtwaist. If there were a possibility that she might glean information about her family from Mrs. Johnston, she hated to appear meanly dressed.

With a knock and a simultaneous opening of the door, Endine whirled in with three frocks across her arms. "These bodices are too tight for me," she said, throwing out her chest proudly. "They're big enough for you if you want them."

Sensing contrition beneath the arrogance, Libba accepted graciously. "Thank you. I've never had anything so lovely!" She stroked a gold satin dress and held it against her cheek in childlike wonder at the feel of it as part of her.

Endine's smug smile dropped. "Why don't you wear this street dress? It would be more appropriate. The light blue will bring out your beautiful eyes."

Libba smiled radiantly. "Oh, how can I thank you, Endine? I was afraid I would embarrass you and Miss Rebecca with my shabby—"

Endine laughed. "No one would notice your clothes with that milky skin and those eyes like blue luster saucers. But one does feel more confident when dressed in style." She rubbed a thoughtful finger on her freckled cheek. "If you don't mind hand-me-downs, I have lots more things."

"I truly appreciate your generosity."

Endine darted in and out of the room, filling the bureau drawers with cotton stockings, garters, underdrawers, chemises, veils, and gloves. Victorians never showed any skin except that on the face and hands. Dresses in the latest fashion, trimmed with tassels, gimp, fringe, beads, flowers, and bows were hung in the armoire with a dramatic presentation.

"Here is m'lady's breakfast gown, her day gown to go into town, her evening gown for the dinner hour, and her walking gown for the stroll after dinner."

Libba touched the lacy, flounced, white evening gown with hesitant fingers that drew back quickly lest the lovely thing disappear like a froth.

Incredulous that Libba still wore a little girl's corset, Endine laced her tightly into a pear-shaped busk. "You must have a new shape," she said, popping out again, and returning with a horsehair bustle.

After she had donned the corset cover and petticoats, Libba held up her arms as Endine lifted the dress over her head. Smooth, cool, the taffeta slid over her fingers and settled around her. Libba shivered in delight, "Ohhhh," she breathed as she looked over her shoulder in the cheval glass at the tiers of pleats that formed a slight train. She stood very still as Endine wrapped her in an apron of matching blue satin, draping the fullness to accentuate the bustle. Ribbon-bound points floated out behind as Libba strutted about enjoying the sound of the rustling taffeta.

Capturing her hair with a ribbon at the nape of her neck as Endine directed, Libba secured a small blue hat with two long hat pins. The costume was completed by a tiny cape.

"Now you look like a lady going to town. Why don't you rest on the chaise longue while I dress?"

Libba nodded, but she remained standing, gazing into the looking the glass after Endine left. She had never worn this many undergarments at one time. She had never owned this many at one time. She preened, admiring the sophistication of the narrow-skirted silhouette. How did one ever keep up with gloves, fan, and parasol? When she tried to take a deep breath, her corset cinched her waist so tightly that she discovered why Victorian ladies needed fainting couches, but she was too excited to lie down.

Bouncing down the stairs, she paused at the turning. Paul gazed up at her with a look she had never received before. She threw back her shoulders and held her head high lest the precariously perched hat betray her and fall off. Slowing her tomboy gait, she drifted toward him with a regal air, aware of the delightful little cape floating behind. For the first time in her life, she basked in the warmth of male admiration. Was she giddy because of the corset stays or because of Paul's roving eyes and bewitching smile?

With a sweeping bow, Paul touched his forehead to the white lined undersleeve falling over her hand and said, "Your servant, m'lady."

Libba giggled as he continued to press her fingers and brush his mustache across her hand in nibbling kisses. Tremors of sensations she had never known fluttered up from deep within her. Excited by the nearness of this vigorous man, yet frightened because she could not control the beating of her heart, she tried to pull away.

Paul would not release her. He lifted her hand above her head and twirled her in a pirouette, appraising her appearance from all angles. "Nice!"

"It's Endine's. I. . ."

Endine had given her a facade of tantalizing womanhood. She swallowed. Much as she longed for love, she knew she was not schooled in the flirtatious handling of a handsome man. How would she calm herself enough to behave sensibly if he came on the excursion with them?

Part of her wanted to rush back upstairs, to don her little girl's corset and old brown calico, to run—

"It suits you perfectly," Paul was saying.

Fanning her lashes back from innocent blue eyes, Libba looked up at him. He was wearing a work shirt. He had left the collar open, exposing the strong column of his neck, the vein that moved as he smiled. *He is not going.*

"I believe I'll join you. I'm suddenly hungry for afternoon tea."

Startled that he seemed to read her thoughts, Libba jerked her hand away. Trying to take a deep breath past the corset stays, she struggled to regain her composure.

"I can't imagine you holding a tiny teacup in those enormous hands," she said teasingly.

"A long tall glass is more my style," he replied, grinning, "but I do make exceptions, and this—"

"No men allowed," Endine said airily as she clattered down the stairs. With a perfunctory kick in her brother's direction, she moved between Libba and Paul.

Libba's emotions, like the fragmented bits in the kaleidoscope, tumbled, patterning joy, fear, hate, love.

At that moment, Colonel Wadley emerged from his study as his commanding presence filled the hall.

Wadley already had his mind on a boardroom fight he was anticipating with relish. He hurried the women into the carriage. Taking the reins himself, he clucked to the horses.

The village of Bolingbroke was important because Wadley lived there. Tweny-four trains ran through the community in a twenty-four-hour period. Wood was stacked in readiness by the track. On the pond, a pumper was busily filling the tank with water for the next engine. A whistle blew. Around the railroad yard, old men took out pocket watches and checked to see if the train was on time.

Before he left them in the Macon deport, the colonel drew Libba aside. Promising to inquire about Jonathan Ramsey, he said, "Remember what I told you. Grit and gumption, Libba. Gumption and grit."

She smiled at him courageously, but her smile slipped as their hired carriage swung down Mulberry Street and she saw the boulevard lined with mansions. Macon was a city. Finding the young man to thank him would be impossible.

The carriage stopped before a towering, red-brick Italian Renaissance villa. On either side were ginkgo trees with leaves like sparkling golden fans.

Endine laughed at Libba's astonishment. "Hardly expected to have high tea at an Italianate palazzo, did you? It boasts seven stories, counting the cellar, the two-story cupola, and the top belvedere—it has a secret—" Endine's eyes danced mischievously.

Rebecca interrupted. "When Anne and William Johnston honeymooned in Europe, they brought back furnishings and Italian artisans. We were attending a party to celebrate its completion in the spring of 1861 when we heard that the War of Northern Aggression had begun. It's the last great house of antebellum Georgia. I doubt it will ever be surpassed."

Libba climbed white marble stairs and stood on the marble-floored portico in her borrowed finery, thinking what a long way she had come from the Savannah Female Asylum.

Twelve-foot high arched doors swung open on silver hinges. A white-coated butler admitted them.

Mrs. Johnston, attired in a floating green tea gown, hurried into the room as though she were at fault for keeping them waiting even a moment.

"My dear Anne," said Rebecca. "I want you to meet my ward, Luther Elizabeth Ramsey."

"I'm delighted you came to tea." Anne Johnston's refined voice wrapped Libba in hospitable warmth. "Do come into the drawing room and we'll get acquainted."

Mrs. Johnston spoke into a silver tube mounted into the wall. They seated themselves around a gilt tea table, and the butler appeared with a mahogany tea cart.

"What kind of tea would you prefer?" Anne Johnston's eyes twinkled. "Rebecca says my Indian souchong smells as if it were meant for men smoking cigars."

Rebecca laughed. "If you still have that pekoe you brought back from London, that would be delightful. I'm not adventuresome enough to change from China tea to the Assam teas."

"You're not adventuresome enough to try green tea!" Anne winked at Libba. "Do you know tea, my dear?" she asked, then hurried to answer her own question to put the girl at ease. "Different kinds all grow on the same plant. The difference comes from the position of the tea leaves on the stem. It's green if it's left unfermented. To become black tea, the leaves are cured."

Her hands moved deftly, taking loose tea from separate, foil-lined tea caddies and sprinkling it into two porcelain teapots. She added water from a steaming kettle.

"Tea is all the same, yet different. A connoisseur can tell by taste the country, altitude, and climate in which the tea is grown. I rely on Richard Twining and his Golden Lion shop in London's West End where it's been since 1716. He was granted the Royal Warrant by Queen Victoria."

Libba thought her hostess regal, too. She glanced upward at the mouldings beautifully carved with a woman's head. Was it Mrs. Johnston? Libba thought not. The carving was not a unique person, but one of many, like she herself.

Libba decided to try the souchong. The thin china teacup rattled and bumped the saucer as Libba shakily started to sip. She realized others were watching.

"How do you like it?"

"Well, with lem—" Endine nudged her. There was no lemon, only cream and sugar on the silver tray. "P–plain," she stammered. She liked sugar. At the orphanage, they followed the Russian manner of using lemon to prevent scurvy. Libba winked a thank you to Endine. When she took a swallow, her mouth drew. No wonder they added milk. The tea was so pungent and malty it was barely drinkable.

The butler presented a tray of tiny sandwiches. "There are cucumber, watercress, smoked salmon, egg salad."

"I'll have egg salad, please." She took a bite. It was spicy brown, delicious. Everyone else had left their plates on the table. She set hers down and it whacked.

The butler split raisin biscuits. Making sure everyone saw the red sugar rose nestled in clotted cream, he grandly spooned cream unto the biscuits.

From a tray, she took a confection shaped like a swan. The other ladies had made verbal selections and waited for the butler to place their pastries on their plates with tongs.

Oh well, Libba thought. Trying to be nonchalant, she crunched a swan wing.

"Luther Elizabeth is concerned about tracing her family," Rebecca said in a voice which turned the conversation from polite pleasantries to a more serious note. "Her earliest memories indicate that she was in the path of Sherman's infamous march. Since you know all the best families, we hoped you might help. One great heartache of the late war was the children separated from their families—or orphaned."

"I do understand, Dear," said Anne. "Homes have been established all over the South by many of the religious denominations. I have worked with Appleton Church Home for Civil War Orphans. I'll look into any inquiries for lost children, but you must not get your hopes up. We've had little success in reuniting familes."

The butler presented a tiered dish of napoleons and eclairs, but Libba's appetite was waning with her hopes.

"Perhaps your mother attended Wesleyan Female College?"

Libba wondered what in her speech and bearing made them assume her background was of equal rank with theirs. Her lack of expertise at the tea table was demonstrating Endine's assessment of her as a nobody. Not trusting her voice, she removed her ring and showed Mrs. Johnston the inscription.

Anne shook her head. "I'm sorry. The date puts her younger than I. I didn't know her. You must reconcile yourself to their loss. Accept the hospitality of the Wadleys—ah, here is Melrose with our last course. Do have a truffle."

Libba sought comfort in the rich chocolate. She had known this lady would give her no information—just as she had known she would never see the funny young man again. She had no family connections, no past. She must begin right here. . . She blinked. Unpredictable Endine was deliberately smearing cream on her skirt.

"Ohhh, clumsy me!" Endine said. "May I use your washroom, please, Cousin Anne? Do help me, Libba."

Libba followed, but as they started up the stairs, she hissed, "Why did you do that?"

"There are things I want you to see," Endine said airily as she paused on the landing graced by coffin niches set with large Grecian urns. "Do you know who that is in the stained-glass window?"

Libba gasped. Set into the jewel-faceted window was the handsome face of a dark-haired man wearing a white shirt with a daring, open collar. "My goodness! That has to be Lord Byron! How did Mr. Johnston ever let her display that daring picture of such a talked-of romantic man? We weren't even allowed to read his poetry."

Staring at the dark, petulant face and exposed neck, Libba imagined Paul and flushed.

Endine laughed, misunderstanding her blush. "Isn't it scandalous? What with all Lord Byron's love affairs and his tragic death. But Cousin Anne doesn't have to ask anything. She inherited a fortune from her father. She even owns a business."

"Oh, does she run it herself? Is it becoming accepted for a woman to work? I must get a job to support—"

Endine sniffed her freckled nose and flounced up the remaining stairs. "Of course not. It's acceptable for a lady to own a business but certainly not to work! Not out in public!" She grinned conspiratorially. "But forget that. Look at this." She waved her arm at a copper-lined rosewood tub and a water closet. "They built this house in the late 1850s with hot and cold running water!"

While she dabbed at the cream on her skirt, Endine continued her stream of gossip designed to impress Libba.

"During the war, W. B. Johnston was premier of the Confederate States Treasury. This house held the largest gold and silver depository south of Richmond!"

Uneasiness prickled Libba's neck because Endine's every movement was accompanied by giggling.

"You just want to moon over Lord Byron again," Endine taunted as they returned to the landing. She stopped before the stained-glass window, and Libba, following her gaze to the picture, was caught off guard by a studden sharp elbow jabbing her ribs. Libba's shoulder struck the huge porcelain urn in the coffin niche, setting it rocking. Terrified lest she break it, Libba clutched air.

Swaying, she stumbled, fell backward. The very wall failed to support her, melted away. She lay flat on her back again. Stunned, she sniffed a penetrating odor. She wondered if her senses were leaving her. Would her nightmares now invade her days? Fighting panic, she sat up. She was alone in a close, doorless room. How had she gotten into this suffocating place?

"Endine. Endeen! *Endeeen!*"

Chapter 5

Endine! Let me out!" Libba cried. Her prison had a window, but it had no door. The odor of cedar came from shelves laden with linens. Was this the rumored gold depository or simply a linen closet? Why a secret room?

How did I get in here? Disoriented, she struggled to remember. She could see no trapdoor in the ceiling through which she could have fallen. Fuzzily, she recalled a sharp elbow in her ribs. *Endine tricked me into looking at Byron and. . . Yes! She pushed me against the wall. It moved!*

Calmer now, she examined the wall, found concealed hinges. The panel would neither slide nor push. Suddenly it glided noiselessly inward.

"Endine, you rascal, I oughta—" Her words whoosed in her open mouth.

Wearing a stern expressions, Rebecca and Anne stared as the hidden door swung back to reveal the red-faced girl.

Libba stammered, "I–I apologize, Mrs Johnston. I don't know what—I must have leaned—I hope I didn't break. . ."

Endine cackled. "Libba's moony over poets. She swooned into the niche."

"Someone must have left the catch to the linen closet unfastened," Mrs. Johnston said without her usual smile.

The wall matched the one at the opposite end of the landing. There was no telltale crack, no sign of a catch. Obviously, Endine knew the secret of the hidden room.

On the homeward trip as the train chugged its way up the hills of Monroe County, Libba laughed with a nonchalance determined to drench Endine's mirth; but resentment at the embarrassment her spiteful friend had caused smoldered like a burning coal beneath her ribs.

Libba awakened at dawn. Still feeling resentful, she cast aside Endine's pretty garments and put on her old clothes. She slipped out into the misty September morning. Flexing her shoulders, which ached from the tenseness of holding her feelings in check, she was pleased to be the first one up. She wanted to walk enveloped in fog until her swirling emotions cleared.

A wiry little dog trotted down the path. Behind him followed an old man carrying a bucket. As he came toward her, she saw it was filled with foaming milk, bubbling over, running down the side. Libba nodded, but the man ignored her.

She recoiled as if from a blow. Had her escapade been told? Would even the servants ostracize her?

When his sliding steps came even with her, she sniffed at her inflated sense of importance. She was not worth everyone talking about her, of course. This man was blind.

"Good morning!"

He stopped, sloshing milk. "Morning. Who be you?"

"Libba Ramsey. I thought I was the first one up."

"Heh, heh, heh, you ain't never gonna beat Miss Sarah."

Amazed at the way the terrier was leading, Libba fell into step. "That certainly is a smart dog."

"Heh, heh, heh." He laughed again. "They thought when old Henry went blind, he'd have to give over the milking, but they had another thunk comin'. Old Rags, he teached hisself to take Henry where he needs to go."

In the brick dairy, Sarah Lois greeted Libba warmly. She took the milk, folded a clean cloth over the bucket's lip, and poured an aerating steam over a cornucopia filled with ice in the center of a tin tub.

"Where do you get ice way out here, Miss Sarah Lois?"

The tall woman considered the little face pinched with distress like the puppy she had saved from a drowning. Tenderness softened her plain features. "Why don't you call me 'Auntie' like all children do?"

"Yes, Ma'am!" Libba's face glowed. "Thank you."

"The ice comes on the train once a week. We put it in a croaker sack and bury it in a hole lined with sawdust. Since you're ambitious enough to be up, you may wash this bucket."

Chores finished, they started out. The door to the other half of the building stood open. Kneeling before the steel safe was Paul.

Libba wished she had not let anger at Endine keep her from putting on one of the pretty frocks.

Paul folded money into a leather wallet and flashed a grin at her. "You are an early bird."

Libba smiled, too tongue-tied to talk. *You are certainly not the idle rich I have heard about,* she thought.

"I'm hungry as a bear," he said, leering at her and popping his teeth. "Are you ready for breakfast?"

The boisterous family enjoyed a hearty breakfast before scattering in all directions for various pursuits. After helping with the last task, Libba tucked the small volume of poetry into her pocket and headed outdoors.

The pungency of the black-green boxwoods drew her toward the formal garden. Sentinels of tall, thin cypress brought, Auntie had told her, directly from Italy stood watch at the perimeter. Libba stepped through the entrance onto a granite-lined path. Before her descended a panorama of boxwood-bordered terraces. The upper level brimmed with chrysanthemums waving pink daisy blooms. Rock steps led down each terrace level into—what? Everywhere boxwood concealed and revealed, making the depths unseen, mysterious.

Down below, the surprise lilies beckoned her again, This time she succumbed. Apprehensively at first, she stepped downward, timidly examining each layer.

Suddenly she stepped into a fairyland like an artist's painting of autumn joy. Swamp sunflowers reigned, towering over Libba's head. Artemisia waved its fronds of silver lace. Fat, pink heads of sedum bowed at her feet. And, oh, the asters, tumbling everywhere! She plucked one bright blue blossom and tucked it into her hair. Knowing it matched her eyes, she longed to meet Paul, feared to meet Paul.

As she continued downward, her heedless footsteps pressed thyme and mint, releasing clean, fresh fragrance. In the middle of the garden was a paved circle with granite benches ringing a sculpture of a slender youth. With broad-brimmed hat and sandals adorned with small wings, Hermes paused in his flight over land and sea.

Libba tapped the caduceus in his hand. "Do you bear a message for me?" Liking the Greek messenger's company, she sat on a bench and took out Elizabeth Barrett Browning's book. She read the plaintive lines from the invalid wife to her tender, supportive husband:

What can I give thee back, O liberal
And princely giver, who hast brought the gold
And purple of thine heart, unstained, untold,
And laid them on the outside of the wall
For such as I to take or leave withal,
In unexpected largesse? Am I cold,
Ungrateful, that for these most manifold
High gifts, I render nothing back at all?
No so; not cold,—but very poor instead.

She thought of her helpmate at the train and winced at her rudeness. He could not have guessed at her vow never to cry. She had treated him with unforgivable coldness.

Would that she could pen a note to him as Mrs. Browning had done to her Robert.

Words flitted through her brain, teased her, vanished behind a worry bush before she could capture them into a line of poetry.

She shook herself. She should go back, inquire if there were other chores. But the air felt fresh against her cheek. The breeze stilled, then flaunted the leaves, tempting her. The path wound intriguingly downward. She followed.

Now the garden became forest. Ferns and wood's violets nestled in brown leaves that rustled as squirrels scampered to a creek where laughing water leapt over rocks, kissed yearning ferns, dashed heedlessly on.

Click-chug! Click-chug! Click-chug! In the green stillness, the sharp staccato sounded a startling note. Alarmed, she drew back. The sound ceased. Voices drifted upstream. Paul! With lightened footsteps, she picked her way around a bending.

Below a waterfall, several men were working.

"Hello!" Paul called out. "Exploring Auntie's garden?"

"Yes. It's the most enchanted spot I've ever seen."

"Come and see what we're doing. I'm designing a system to give running water for the house and livestock." He took her hand to help her over a fallen log.

Trembling with delight at his touch, Libba watched him adoringly. He showed her how the weight of the water flowing over a lever clicked the valve shut and the recoil hurled the water against an inner valve, opening it.

Libba did not understand his explanation of hydraulic machinery. "You must be the smartest man in the world to make water pump itself with no other source of energy."

"The principle was discovered in the seventeenth century by a Frenchman named Pascal. I've only adapted it. With a plentiful flow of water and a fall of only a foot and a half, the ram pump can lift the supply 250 feet," he explained. "Water is forced in this pipe and up the hill to a cistern. The water in the holding tank will have strong pressure from gravity—but come—let me show you." He pointed the way up the hill.

With clasped hands swinging between them, they crossed the open meadow. Before them stood the tower that had aroused Libba's interest, a grand, round column of brick encompassing the water tank. Architecturally beautiful, it had a high-arched doorway and, inside, a spiraling staircase.

Libba saw the strength and permanence of this great family symbolized in the brick outbuildings. No makeshifts or simple log structures were here, no simple country people. Dwarfed, Libba dragged back on Paul's hand. She gazed up at the turret—the transported tip of a fairy castle?

Looking at the high round window, she whispered, "I expect to see Rapunzel letting down her hair."

Paul gave a deep-throated laugh. "Umm-huh. Come see." Slipping his arm around her wispy waist, Paul made a show of helping her up the steep spiral.

Tremors of fear tickled Libba's spine as he guided her up the narrow staircase. She should not be here unchaperoned. Her footsteps faltered. She should turn back.

Caught in the winding circle of stairs, she stopped breathing as he wrapped both arms around her. He brushed his mustache back and forth across her cheek. Suddenly he pressed his mouth upon her innocent lips.

A clattering of boots preceded John's head up the steps. "Paul? Oh, there you are. Hello, Libba. Is Paul showing you Captain Raoul's water system?"

"Yes." Libba could barely recognize her voice over the buzzing in her ears as she drew away. Fearing her face was painted with guilt, she stared out of the fairy-tale window. She had longed dreamed of the poetry of a first kiss. Placing a finger to her lips, she could not bring to memory that snatched moment. She felt only embarrassment and fear.

Libba's infatuation, fueled by the fact that Paul had left the plantation on business, grew more giddy with each passing day. She spent long hours leaning Rapunzel-like from her window, enjoying feeling sad and singing songs of parted lovers.

Saturday at midmorning, Auntie decided to make sweet potato pies. Removing a key from her ring at her waist, she sent Libba to bring her some brown sugar.

Humming to herself, Libba lifted the key to the door of the creamery. Ajar, it moved.

Paul! He had returned! He was opening the safe, and he merely nodded as she went by him timidly and slid back the top from the brown sugar barrel. The hair on the back of her neck prickled as she stood on tiptoe to scoop sugar into her bowl.

The safe slammed shut. Paul stepped behind her, circled his arm around her, and reached into the barrel.

"The best sugar is this that's stuck around the rim." He pulled off a hunk of the crystallized sugar and popped it into her mouth. Leaning against her, he reached again and took a handful for himself, focusing his dark eyes on her as he crunched.

With candy sweet upon her tongue, she lifted her eager lips, knowing his kiss would be as sweet. His mouth came down to meet her lips. His hand stroked her hair, pulled down, forced her head back. His mustache tickled her throat.

Frightened by what was happening, she dropped the bowl into the sugar barrel. He grasped both her wrists. She struggled. "No, Paul. Stop!"

The heavy door creaked, swung open. Libba saw Endine's pulsating freckles and gaping mouth. Behind her a tousle of gray-streaked hair jerked back in surprise. A round, boyish face peered with wide, blinking eyes.

Libba snatched the blue bowl from the barrel and thrust it between her and Paul. Primly she marched out into the sunlight's glare.

Endine was nearly as flustered as Libba. "This gentleman, uh—came looking for you."

"My name is Daniel Marshall," he said quickly. "I didn't mean to intrude, but—"

"No, no," Libba stammered. "I'm so glad you. . .came. I. . .you were so kind, and I was so rude that I've been. . ." She clung to the bowl, stared down at it, suddenly saw it. "Oh! Auntie will be waiting for this. Please excuse me. I'll be right back."

Without looking at any of them, Libba fled toward the kitchen. She could hear Paul, self-possessed, the perfect host making the visitor welcome.

In the dim hall, Libba leaned against the wall until her breathing became normal. Auntie had grown impatient, but she excused Libba when the red-faced girl explained about the young man who had come.

When she returned to the yard, Endine and Paul had led her guest to the scuppernong arbor. They were strolling beneath it, reaching up to pluck the bronze scuppernongs.

Daniel turned, blinked his eyes. A smile spread over his candid face infecting Libba.

"However did you find me?"

Daniel wondered how to begin. Why had he been so foolish as to think himself welcome here? He could hardly tell her that from the first moment he saw her he had thought of nothing else. "You know the Chinese—" He laughed and changed to a tone that poked fun at his own lack of knowledge. "Or is it the Indians? Anyway. They believe that if you save a life, you are responsible for it. So you see. . ." He shrugged. "I had to find you and be sure you were all right."

Libba met his gaze, and it seemed as if he could see some of her fears receding. What had he witnessed between her and Paul? Paul was more handsome than any man had a right to be. *She does seem happy to see me.*

"I'm fine," she said at last. "Be ye Chinese or Indian, I thank you for saving me. It's nice to have a friend!"

"Speaking of Indians," Endine interrupted. "I have a marvelous idea! Why don't you stay for dinner, Mr. Marshall? Then, this afternoon we could all go explore the old Ocmulgee fields and have a picnic!"

"I'd be honored, Miss Endine," Daniel said with a bow. "Perhaps, if we all keep close watch over little Libba here, she won't hurt herself again."

"Now, wait a minute," Libba protested, laughing. "Maybe you've found out too much about me."

When the plantation bell clanged noon, they found that Auntie had already added a plate.

Daniel took hardy helpings. He was famished, but it was difficult to eat this close to Libba. Endine, on his other side, talked steadily.

"You never did say how you traced me," Libba said softly when Endine paused for breath.

"Easy," he replied. "Everyone knows the Wadleys and Great Hill Place. I thought you were part of the family 'til I learned they all have dark eyes and red hair." He gestured down the family table. "No one could forget those innocent blue eyes of yours. And then I recalled—" His cheeks went slack.

He had remembered her putting her hand over a patch. If she were also destitute, she might not think little of him because his fortune vanished in the war.

Willie Wadley, host in his father's absence, spoke into the sudden silence. "Tell us about yourself, Mr. Marshall."

"Well, Sir," Daniel cleared his throat. "My father was Morrison Marshall. He was a member of the Macon Guards. He was killed at Gettysburg."

"I've heard of him," replied Willie. "You may be proud that he died a hero."

"Thank you, Sir. My mother and I still live at Morrison Hall." He paused. It was unnecessary to explain the conditions. He had no need to let the Wadleys' wealth intimidate him. He finished simply. "I teach at Mercer University."

"Admirable. Admirable," said Willie.

After they demolished the pies, Daniel went out with the men while the women prepared for the picnic.

Insisting that Libba must be attired in the proper sportswear, Endine brought her a gray, textured silk that had a pleated underskirt which allowed freedom in walking.

"Ohhh! We're going to have such fun!" Endine exclaimed. "You won't believe all the strange things you're going to see! An excursion to Brown's Mount is everyone's favorite."

The party included John and Auntie. Libba could hardly believe the good fortune of a safely chaperoned outing with Paul and a suitor for Endine.

The jaunty rhythm of the clacking rails played accompaniment to the merriment of the group. The train trip into Macon was all too short. There they piled into carriages and rode across the bridge spanning the Ocmulgee River.

They were in the famous old Ocmulgee fields, the rich low area that had been Indian cropland and ceremonial grounds with beginnings lost in antiquity. They reined the horses beneath a red oak tree and climbed down to show Libba the site of Fort Hawkins, built in 1806 as a trading post with the Creeks.

"During the War Between the States, the Yankees took this old fort and prepared to invade Macon," Daniel said, with his eyes shooting sparks as he launched into his favorite tale. "The enemy battery fired one shot that fell into the heart of the city. I was a lad at the time, and—"

"Oh, Daniel," Libba protested. "Let's don't talk about Yankees. I'd rather hear about Indians."

Daniel's face dropped. Libba turned away.

John was calling her. "Come on, Libba. I'll show you about Indians. Come this way." He pointed to a winding trail.

At the end of the woodland trail, Paul lifted a branch. Stepping out into the clearing, Libba gasped at the strange sight. Straight-sided mounds of earth rose to lofty heights from the level plane of the Macon plateau.

"What?" Libba whispered, staring at the tremendous flattened cones. "How strange! How eerie! The precise form seems to indicate they are man-made, but that seems impossible given their gigantic size! What are they?"

"Indian mounds," replied Paul. "The smaller mounds were heaped up in honor of the dead," he explained. "But this larger one was the temple mound."

"Who built the mounds?" Libba inquired. "When?"

"No one knows," said Daniel, stepping quickly to her side to capture her attention. He hurried to press his advantage. "All of the Indians in recorded history say the mounds were here when their tribe conquered the area. Even the records of DeSoto in 1540 remarked upon the antiquity."

They showed her where the mound had been cut through when the track was laid for the Central Railroad in 1842.

"A number of Indian relics were exhumed," Paul said.

"The exciting thing to me," Daniel said, claiming Libba's interest, "was layers used by tribes who perhaps had no knowledge of each other."

"Enough scientific talk," interrupted Endine. "Let's climb up and see the view."

Stronger, more agile, Endine moved ahead of Libba and reached the top. Looking down at the pale girl panting for breath, she called mockingly, "Come on, you can make it to the top. It's magnificent!"

The breeze had died down. The sun had burned away the morning mists. It beamed hot on Libba's back. Raking sticky curls from her perspiring forehead, she wondered how much farther she had to climb. Two hands reached down for her, Paul's strong, brown, beckoning fingers and Daniel's eager, gentle, uplifting palm.

Chapter 6

Light-headed, Libba allowed both men to pull her up. Breathing heavily as she reached the flat summit of the Indian mound, which rose fifty feet above the plateau, she wavered, feeling as if she might fall off the top of the world.

"I know it's too wide to fall off—but it feels strange."

"You'll adjust in a minute," Daniel said soothingly.

"You're hardly on a pinnacle," said Paul, laughing at her. "The top of the mound is one hundred eighty feet north and south and two hundred feet east and west."

"Should we be here—on their burial place? Isn't walking on centuries of graves sacrilege?"

"No," replied Daniel. "This is where they worshiped."

"The sun? Were they trying to reach the sun?"

"No." He smiled at her. "The Muscogee Indians who were here when the British took possession of this country—the British renamed them Creeks because of the small streams or creeks they lived along—anyway, those Indians believed in God, the Great Spirit, the giver and taker away of the breath of life. Their high moral standards prepared for an afterlife in warm and flowery savannas."

"It makes me feel insignificant," whispered Libba.

"Not me," said Endine. "I feel powerful up here. You can see forever. Stop being so introspective." She wrinkled her freckled nose at Libba. "Enjoy the view."

Paul grabbed Libba by the shoulders and shoved her toward the sheer drop on the southwest. She shrieked as he pretended to cast her over the side.

"Paul, behave yourself," called Auntie.

"No, look," he said, laughing as Libba hid her face. "Look how far you can see. Can't you imagine an Indian waving his blanket over his signal fire?"

"The great view is from this side," called Daniel, summoning them to where he and Endine stood overlooking the red-stained waters of the Ocmulgee River.

"Above Macon the Ocmulgee is rocky, unnavigable. Macon became a shipping point when steamboating began. It draws trade from cotton fields from all directions."

"But the railroads brought affluence," boasted Paul. "The Central Railroad arrived here from Savannah in 1843, making Macon the 'queen inland city of the South' at the head of the 'longest railroad in the world built and owned by one company.' "

"I'm impressed," said Libba.

Endine turned her toward the city with its parkways and mansions resembling Greek temples.

"Perfection," agreed Libba. "This scene makes me think of Keats's line, 'A thing of beauty is a joy forever.' "

"Enough tour. Let's eat," interrupted Paul. "Auntie's fried pies may not be a thing of beauty, but they are a joy forever." He smacked his lips.

"Now, what's wrong with the way my pies look?" inquired Auntie tartly.

Joking their way back to the carriages, they rode to Brown's Mount. The road wound gently upward beneath spreading oaks whose cool, damp shade gave welcome relief from the September sun.

They stopped to show Libba the first of many curiosities, a stone wall four feet high and four feet thick.

Paul guided Libba into the ditch behind the wall. "From here the defenders were protected from the shafts of their assailants. These ancient fortifications at one time encircled the entire top of the mount." He underscored his words by circling his arm around her shoulder and squeezing.

Libba smiled up at him coquettishly.

Daniel clenched his teeth. Deftly he stepped to Libba's other side, took her elbow, and left Paul empty-handed. He lifted her back into the carriage, telling her interesting details.

"I wish I could study more and become an enthusiastic teacher like you," she said.

The carriage rolled around a bend. A deer, drinking from a pond of water lilies, quivered for a timeless moment. Her liquid brown eyes rolled back in fright. She leaped, barely missing the carriage.

In a glade, they spread quilts on the ground and set out crusty fried chicken, huge, fluffy, soda-smelling biscuits, deviled eggs, and Auntie's watermelon rind pickles.

They were reclining and nibbling the pies, bite by ever slower bite, when Daniel said, "I can speak Indian."

Derisive hoots sounded.

"No, really." He jumped up, folded his arms, tucked his chin, and spoke gutturally. "Tobesofkee Ocmulgee." Then he sat down closer to Libba. "See. Told you."

"Oh, that's not speaking Indian," she said. "You just muttered the name of the creek and the river."

"It's speaking a language if you know what the words mean." He feigned a hurt expression. His mobile face changed to a triumphant grin. "Ocmulgee is Muscogee origin. Oc signifies 'water' and mulgee means 'bubbling' water. An Indian was crossing the creek in his canoe and lost his provisions, tobe means 'I have lost.' Sofskee is a dish prepared with ground corn."

Eyes twinkling, he intoned, "Tobesofkee Ocmulgee. Translated: I have spilled my grits in the bubbling water."

Libba laughed and threw a biscuit at Daniel. Happiness was seeping into all of the cold, secret corners of her small, thin body.

John poked Paul. "You're getting fat. Let's play catch."

Paul groaned, but he complied.

Endine and Auntie moved into the shade.

Libba found herself virtually alone with Daniel, not knowing what to say. He began a light conversation, and gradually she realized that talking with Daniel was easy. She did not stammer as she did with most men. His blue eyes rested gently upon her, unlike Paul's darting, probing gaze which excited yet frightened her. As unaccustomed to being in the presence of a friend as she was to being satiated with food, Libba relaxed as she caught Daniel's contagious smile.

"The Wadleys are a wonderful family," he said quietly. "Not affected. Wealth and power don't seem to. . ." His voice trailed away. He looked directly into her face.

"They're genuinely kind," Libba agreed. "I thought Colonel Wadley was bringing me to be a governess. But Auntie teaches the smaller children and the older ones go into Forsyth." She shrugged. "I guess Mrs. Wadley was really moved with compassion when she found me in the orphanage."

She turned the subject from herself. "Did you say you're a teacher at the university?"

"Yes," Daniel replied. "I'm at Mercer University. There are many fine schools here. Perhaps you could—"

"I doubt I have enough teaching credentials."

"There are two orphans' homes—"

"No!" She shook her black curls vigorously. "I don't have the heart to ever, ever return to an orphanage."

Suddenly Libba's story poured forth as she had never shared with anyone. Daniel listened as she told of her pinch-faced childhood. She had been starved for affection, destitute for clothing, hungry for sufficient food during the terrible Reconstruction Era when even the most charitable Southerners had nothing to give to the little lost orphans of the war.

"The Wadleys are wonderful," she finished. "But still, I feel I have no place. I'm nobody. Oh, if only I knew the truth!"

Daniel caught her flailing hands in both of his. "A little while ago you quoted Keats. Remember his 'Ode on a Grecian Urn'? 'Beauty is truth, truth beauty—that is all ye know on earth, and all ye need to know.' You are a beautiful young woman. And you are beautiful on the inside. That is all the truth you need."

Libba pulled her hands away and hid her face.

Softly Daniel continued, "Don't worry about who your family was. God is your Father. He created you as a very special person. You can do or be anything you strive—"

"That's fine for you to say," Libba flung out bitterly. "You're a hypocrite."

Daniel blanched as if she had slapped him.

"What did you do when Willy asked who you were?" She shook her finger before his blinking eyes. "I remember. You told who and what your father was, where your home was. Last of all, your job. First—first, your family connection—as all good Southerners do."

Chagrined, Daniel stared at Libba at a loss for words.

With her hurting heart spreading open before this stranger, Libba turned away. She groped blindly for her shawl. Slanting rays from the brilliant sunset turned dogwood leaves to flickering red flames like her twitching, burning cheeks. A warning of impending night in the quickening breeze chilled the dampness of her forehead as her very marrow seemed chilled.

As if signaled by the plummeting sun, everyone assembled, had one last morsel, packed, and loaded.

Libba turned her back on Daniel and flashed a smiling facade toward Paul. "You worked that down, and you're eating again?" She forced a laugh.

"I'm thirsty," Paul replied, cutting his eyes at her as he took her arm to help her climb back down from the lofty world of the hilltop. "There are four springs issuing from the four faces of Brown's Mount. On the paths leading to the springs, the Indians built stone walls and partially covered walkways. Let's get a drink of the best water you've ever tasted."

"Oh, no!" Auntie intervened. "You won't be taking little Libba looking for hidden passageways. I do declare, Paul Morley, it's men like you who keep a chaperone on her toes."

Paul winked at Libba, but he acquiesced to Auntie.

The interlude ended. They were back in Macon at the depot. Daniel slipped a folded paper into Libba's hand.

"The Indians believe in circles," he whispered. "They believe nature and men were created by God as brothers. A proverb clings to the Ocmulgee mounds. Chief Seattle wrote, 'All things are connected.' There's a place and time for all things to happen. Maybe someday—" He squeezed her hand.

Libba watched with stinging eyes as he bounded away.

Too keyed-up to sleep, Libba put on a flannel wrapper over her gown and crept downstairs. Thirsty, she thought of how Paul would have stolen a kiss had he taken her to the spring.

On the back porch, an oaken bucket of well water was kept on a high shelf. She filled the gourd dipper and drank.

The deep timbre of a voice echoed in the hall. Paul! The gourd shook, dribbling water down the blue robe. His footsteps were coming toward the porch. For him to catch her dressed like this would be scandalous.

"Paul, wait." The slight nasal twang was Auntie's voice.

"Yes, Ma'am?"

"I must speak with you. You must stop toying with little Libba. You will break her heart."

Paul laughed lightly. "Now, Auntie, a little flirtation never hurt anyone. I—"

"Exactly! A flirtation to you, but to her—she looks at you like a puppy who has been spanked and is begging for love."

Libba shrank against the porch wall and berated herself for letting her love for Paul show.

"You are the first handsome man who's ever smiled at her. The thrill may soon pass. Worse, she may remain in love with you. Your parents expect you to marry Victoria Landingham."

Paul's easy laughter became a harsh snort. "I'm well familiar with keeping blood blue and combining fortunes to build empires. Just because Victoria is the richest girl in the county—aw, Auntie, you know how affected she is because she's named for the queen. Could I ever satisfy Queen Victoria?"

Libba stumbled down the porch steps. Paul's voice penetrated the roaring in her ears.

"Besides, I'm not sure I'm toying with Libba. There's something about our sad-eyed little waif that tugs at my heart. Maybe I'm a little in love with her. Who's to say I wouldn't be happier with Little Miss Nobody?"

Libba began to run. Her feet found blind Henry's path. She ran past the milking barn, out across the meadow.

Wrenching breaths came in great, dry sobs as she fell on the ground and beat her fists. *Little. Little. Little.*

Calmer at last, she lay looking up at the brick arch of the water tower. Only fairy tales ended happily ever after. She must escape again. Tomorrow. She must leave tomorrow. But where would she go? She had nowhere to run.

Chapter 7

Libba scowled at her reflection in the mirror. Her eyes were swollen with unshed tears. Her hair stuck out wildly, giving evidence of her night spent tossing about. She attacked her unruly curls angrily, brushing them away from her scalp which seemed to bulge over thoughts wrestling, tumbling, falling over each other. Her body hurt as if Paul and Auntie's words had been blows.

She must escape this house she had hoped would be home.

Paul thought of her as little. Still, he had said he might love her. *But what will happen if he loves me? Would his parents permit our marriage?*

Leaving seemed the only answer. But how?

Daniel. The only person in the world she could truly trust. How could she turn to him? It would be improper. She laughed, imagining the face he would make at that word.

Daniel Marshall
Morrison Hall
College Street
Macon, Georgia

If you ever need a friend.

But how could she ask his help? She had lashed out at him simply because she had allowed him—as no one ever had before—to glimpse inside her soul.

When she trudged down the stairs to breakfast, Auntie greeted her with loving warmth. Libba shuttered her eyes and turned away. Could she trust her? Her face was always set in a smile as enigmatic as the parlor painting of Mona Lisa. She had thought Auntie loved her. That she did not love her hurt, perhaps, worst of all.

Colonel Wadley had returned and was sitting at the head of the table. His sharp eyes penetrated her defenses.

"Libba, after breakfast come into my study."

Fear lodged in her throat, restricting food.

Timidly, Libba knocked on the study door. It pushed open ever so slightly, and she could hear Colonel Wadley dictating a letter to Sarah Lois. She drew back, waiting.

"Father," said Sarah Lois when he ended the letter, "must you travel to Alabama? You are ill."

"I shall have a commissary car fitted up so that I can have privacy. I must look at the Montgomery and Eufaula Railroad. Eufaula has long been an important shipping point for steamboats on the Chattahoochee. Railroads are becoming important there now. I may remark, one day railroads will supplant steamboats, and I must be ready. Ill or not, I must go to Eufaula."

Sarah Lois left frowning. Libba entered fearfully and sank into a chair.

"I have located Jonathan Ramsey's homeplace."

"Ohhh!" Libba sprang to life.

"No. No. It is not good news."

Libba shrank into a hard little knot.

"A Jonathan Ramsey is—or was—the owner of a large cotton plantation, Magnolia Springs along the Ogeechee River in Bulloch County, Georgia. This must be the same Ramsey. This would have placed you in the vicinity of Savannah. I began searching by backtracking up the railroad from the city."

His terse twang echoed in her ears. Mute, she waited for him to explain in his measured way.

"I'm sorry to tell you this. The land is idle. I may remark, the deeds have never been transferred from Ramsey's name. The property is lying with taxes unpaid."

"The house?" Libba squeaked hoarsely.

"Burned. Your hatred of Sherman is well-founded. Everything was destroyed."

The acrid juices of her mouth could not be swallowed. If her father was alive, how could he have left her with no trace? Was her only legacy a burned-out plantation on which money was owed? As surely as the steamboats were stopped by the rocks above Macon, she could go no farther upstream.

Wadley broke the bitter silence. "This knowledge makes no difference to Mrs. Wadley and me. We knew only your name when we asked you into our home. Mrs. Wadley saw something in you that she wanted to nurture."

Tears rushed to the surface. Libba had never been so near to uncontrollable weeping. She looked at the kindly man and wished she could climb into his lap and cry and be comforted as she had seen his grandchildren do.

Have I repaid your kindness by causing conflict within your family? Libba wondered desparately. *Has Sarah Lois spoken to you about Paul?* John merely had a boyish crush on her. It was a fleeting thing. Was Auntie right? Would her passionate love for Paul also fade? Frightened at the hopelessness of her situation, she knew only one thing to do: run.

"Colonel Wadley, I—" Her voice broke; she tried again. "Your family has been wonderful to me. I. . .hope to remain welcome, but I should. . . Perhaps, my place is teaching orphans. I understand there are two orphanages in Macon." The words seared her tongue, but she could imagine no alternative. "If you could secure me a position to pay for my living, and. . .and I could still come here to visit. I love your family so much. . ." Her voice jerked in a snuffling sob.

Wadley considered her for a long time. "If that is what you wish, I will see what I can do."

Overnight the wind had banished September's misty warmth. Crisp air snapped; the sky gleamed clear, bright, heartbreakingly blue. Libba sighed as she took one last look at the dogwood. Yesterday's jolly, red-gold leaves, somber now, were like great drops of blood. With one foot on the carriage step, she gazed longingly back at the house. How she regretted her decision to leave! How could she return to an orphanage after tasting of family and home?

Sarah Lois accompanied her and Colonel Wadley on the silent journey into Macon. By carriage they continued up College Hill and stopped before a tremendous pink brick building. Massive white pillars marched across the front, setting off the recessed center porch. The imposing structure had three stories in each wing, four in the center surmounted by a parapet. This magnificent building could hardly be a charity home. Colonel Wadley must have business here. She drew back in a corner.

Colonel Wadley reached for her hand to help her down.

Libba did not stir. "This can't be the orphanage!"

Sarah Lois's plain face broke into a smile at her astonishment. "No. We all agreed our little girl had had enough of sad places. This is Wesleyan Female College. Here you can gain confidence as well as knowledge, polish as well as culture."

"But—surely, I'm too old to be a student—even if I had the pedigree to qualify. I'm not good enough to teach."

"Father has thought of everything." Auntie patted her.

In gentle tones reserved for his towheaded grandchildren, he explained. "My good friend, the Reverend Capers Bass, who is president, offered the perfect solution. He found a vacancy in the preparatory department. You see, the young ladies come here from over several states, and they are unevenly prepared. Some must be brought up to a common level of performance before they begin the college classes. This is especially true of the group who grew up during the war when so many of the British governesses fled from the plantation schools to return to safety in England."

"I suggested," interposed Auntie, "that you might enjoy teaching the course in orthography and English grammar. I know you love poetry, and your records from Savannah indicated. . ."

Stunned, Libba followed through an iron fence, climbed the stairs, and stepped reverently through the door into the hushed solemn halls.

Libba could scarcely believe that she was in the "Mother of Female colleges," the first in the entire world to grant the same honors, degrees, and licenses to women as those conferred on men. Her hands were clammy as she curtsied before President Bass. His bald pate shone in the flickering gaslight, and his white mustache and goatee worked up and down as he surveyed her assessingly. Libba was afraid to breathe.

"Welcome to Wesleyan, my dear. Colonel Wadley assures me you will fit well into our program."

"As a favor to Colonel Wadley," Bass continued, "you will be allowed to audit some of the postgraduate courses of Shakespeare, Dickens, Thackery—when you have no duties."

"Thank you, Sir!" Her enthusiasm overcame her fear.

Libba followed Auntie down a long, dim hallway to a door marked: Housemother, Miss Cornelia Burt.

Before the tall, handsome woman's penetrating gaze, Libba felt that she was shrinking like Alice. Miss Burt briefed her on the statutes of the college, internal regulations, and the strict regimen.

Summoning a willowy woman, Miss Clifford Cotton, to show Libba to her quarters, Miss Burt laughed.

"I declare, Miss Ramsey, I shall have difficulty distinguishing you from your pupils; you are so small!"

Sarah Lois accompanied Libba to the large room she was to share.

Clifford Cotton went at once to the chandelier in the middle of the room. Producing a matchbox, she lifted the chimney and turned up the wick. "You see, the trick is to strike your match and light the gas without smoking up the chimney," she said, laughing, "like I just did. Now, I'll leave you to your good-byes."

Sarah Lois put her arm around Libba's unforgiving shoulders. "You must write to me. If you're not happy here, let me know immediately! Always remember, I am your friend."

Libba's thoughts tumbled. Was Auntie her friend? Or were they separating her from Paul?

Throughout the long dark night, the question nagged. The massive iron fence locked her way away from Paul, away from the world, less rigidly than the rules.

Regulations allowed no visiting on the Sabbath. Only lady visitors and near relatives were permitted during the week at such hours as did not conflict with college duties. Gentlemen friends were never allowed to call. Even correspondence with young men was forbidden.

Special permission of the president was required for any student to visit outside the college. Homesick for a home that was not really hers, Libba lay thinking of the shining halls of Great Hill Place ringing with laughter. In that wonderful home, one could be surrounded by love or be alone. Three other teachers slept in this lofty-ceilinged room. She had reveled in having her own bedroom for such a short time. Why had she panicked and fled?

Gradually, Libba began to feel more at home. She had no worry about her wardrobe. Rules interdicted the use of jewelry and required simplicity of dress.

The bell rang each day at sunrise summoning them to the chapel for prayer. They were expected to study until breakfast and then have recreation until nine o'clock when the bell rang for morning prayer which preceded recitations. It was a choice thing to ring the bell on the front porch. They went, two girls at a turn, the only time they were let out in public.

In the dining hall, all ate at the same tables. Food was plain, healthful fare with no rich condiments such as meats and cakes. Libba let her mouth remember the taste of cream as Auntie dolloped it on her oatmeal. . .of brown sugar. . .of—no. She must not let herself dream of candied brown sugar from the barrel, the sweetness of Paul's lips upon hers.

There was little time for daydreams. As busy days passed, Libba worried less about who she had been and wondered more about who she might become if she only strove. Taking pleasure in helping young pupils, she also learned.

Late one afternoon, when Libba was immersed in reading Longfellow, a tap sounded at her door.

"Miss Ramsey," said Miss Cotton with an enigmatic smile, "you have a caller in the parlor. Your brother."

Chapter 8

"You didn't say good-bye," Paul said, holding out his hand.

Libba skimmed across the parlor with her feet barely touching the floor.

"Paul! I—" Her voice echoed—too animated to be greeting her brother. Red spots of guilt quivered in her cheeks.

"How is the family?" she asked loudly. "Auntie? Miss Rebecca?" Covertly, she watched the huge Chippendale mirror until Miss Cotton left. "You left first—without saying good-bye," she said, bristling.

"That's different." Paul frowned. "I had to work."

Around them the hum of voices ceased. Down the long parlor, arranged with chairs grouped around oil portraits, families stopped their visiting to stare.

Libba pointed him to a Sheraton sofa slightly secluded by a potted palm.

"Why did you leave? Did I really frighten you on the Indian Mound? I was only playing. . ."

Libba fanned back her lashes, and her throat pulsed as she questioned herself. Was he only playing at love? She could not ask about Victoria.

"Paul, I—" Her voice squeaked. Angry at herself, she whispered huskily, "Has it occurred to you that Colonel Wadley sent you on business to keep you away from me?"

Surprised, Paul snorted a rueful laugh. "Maybe. That doesn't matter. They offered you a home and they meant it. Come back! You know I'm attracted to you, and I know you are to me." He smirked and devoured her with his eyes.

Longing for his touch, Libba was glad for the chaperones. She might not have had the strength for refusal.

"I can't come back now," she whispered. "Later. Maybe. Your family is wonderful, but. . .I'm too rough a stone among all those jewels."

"You have a delicate beauty. Auntie could polish you to whatever luster—"

"I have no dowry at all!"

Paul opened his mouth, closed it. After an uncomfortable silence, he said, "We need time to know each other."

"Yes. I need time to learn— to grow."

His voice rose. "We can't get to know each other in this. . .this nunnery."

"Shhh. It's not that bad. You're here, aren't you?"

"But not for long."

It was sunset. Someone appeared to light the gaslights, signaling the end of the visitation. Parents were kissing their daughters good-bye. Paul's handsome face clouded with a bad-tempered scowl.

Suddenly strong, wrapped in Miss Burt's protective rules, Libba could get to know Paul without the frightening whirl of physical excitement scattering her brains. Standing tall, she extended her hand in a grand gesture of farewell that would have done Miss Burt credit.

"Do come again, Brother. Tell the family that in this wonderful atmosphere I'm learning to appreciate things of worth and beauty." She laughed. "Did you notice I even descend a staircase properly?"

"I liked the tomboy tumbling down the stairs," Paul grumbled. "Is it true you can't even come home for Christmas?"

Her resolve shook at the thought of a real Christmas at Great Hill Place. Wavering, she reached toward him.

The doors were opening, closing. Paul was gone.

On Sundays Libba's duty was to escort rows of girls marching en masse down the hill to the church. Small and innocent as a student, she did little to deter the Mercer boys. They pranced alongside, trying to speak to the Wesleyannes.

In the darkened sanctuary of the old church, Libba sat centered amid her pupils.

The organ's solemn strains indicated heads should bow in prayer, but a scuffling in the pew behind the girls pricked Libba's ears. A hoarse whisper cajoled the Mercer boys to exchange seats. Each in turn grunted refusal. She peeped back.

Daniel perched at the end of the pew. Rolling his eyes, he pulled his lips over his teeth, forcing Libba into a fit of coughing to cover her laughter.

Being a teacher-chaperone for a solemn occasion made it funnier. Giggles escaped. Swallowing her laughter, Libba hiccuped. Miss Burt leaned over and frowned.

Folding her hands as if in prayer, Libba pinched her nose and tried to concentrate on the pastor as he intoned, "Judge not, and ye shall not be judged: condemn not, and ye shall not be condemned: forgive, and ye shall be forgiven."

Suddenly sober, Libba remembered all of the things she could not forgive and merely wanted to forget.

When worship ended, Miss Burt with strength of character no one dared challenge, stationed herself to block the pew. Motioning for the girls to file out, she instructed Libba, "Keep the girls moving smartly. The rules of the trustees allow no fraternizing with Mercer boys."

Staunchly remaining, Miss Burt greeted friends, keeping the boys chafing.

Libba glimpsed Daniel's bouncing head but saw him no more. Throughout the long, quiet Sabbath, she thought of Daniel and giggled.

The next Sunday as Libba led her girls through the iron gates, she could feel their anticipation. Eveyone sensed Daniel liked the challenge of the ironclad rules. A gaggle of boys waiting beneath the trees across College Street swooped down upon them, matching their marching steps. Strutting like a gander, Daniel tipped a stylish, round hat.

Libba nodded curtly. Holding her chin straight ahead, she cut her eyes at him. His normal attire, clean but rumpled with mismatched colors and missing buttons, was replaced by a new gray jacket that swung open to reveal a double-breasted, plaid waistcoat strung with a gold watch chain.

Eyes darting mischievously, mouth twitching, he started to speak, but she cut him short.

"Daniel Marshall, you'll get me thrown out of school!"

With a droll, contrite expression, he doubled the pace of the girls and marched smartly ahead. Tipping his hat to each row in turn, he descended around the curve and disappeared.

Regretting her curtness, Libba reckoned without Daniel's determination. Mercer boys waited in the churchyard. Deftly they took the pew behind the girls. With scuffling and mock refusals to exchange seats, Daniel negotiated one place at a time. At last behind Libba, he warmed her back with his eyes.

Standing for a hymn, Daniel dropped a paper over her shoulder. Unfolding it surreptitously inside the hymnbook, she read, "Forgive this humble hypocrite."

She nodded.

"I must see you," he whispered, breath against her hair before she could sit.

Libba whispered back, "Rules."

The watchful Miss Burt circumvented further contact.

On Tuesday a letter arrived, wrinkled, bearing an ink blot; it could only be from Daniel.

Miss Burt had said correspondence with young men was forbidden, but they never inspected the pupils' letters.

Teachers' letters either, I hope. Libba giggled guiltily and scurried to her room.

She felt Daniel's energy bouncing around her as she read his opening lines. "I'm happy to think of you living and learning in the romantic atmosphere of Wesleyan." She laughed. Daniel must know this to be the most carefully chaperoned place in the world. She had locked herself away from romance. A thought echoed: *Love always finds a way.*

She savored his long, warm letter. He told her of the romance of his mother's cousin, Mary Day, and Sidney Lanier who were among refugees who boarded at Wesleyan during the bitter months after Macon was surrendered to the Yankees.

He is a poet, novelist, teacher, and musician par excellence. I hope to introduce you to them. You share another kinship with him because, like you, he bears the scars of the war with great courage.

Libba sat reading the poems he had included. Strengthened, encouraged, she took hope that Daniel counted her a friend and thought her worthy to meet so great a man as Lanier.

A few days later, another letter came, smooth, clean, and bearing the Great Hill Place crest. Paul! She ripped it open.

Rebecca's handwriting. She clapped her hand over her mouth to smother a shriek as she read the chatty letter about the engagement party she and Mrs. Landingham were planning for Victoria and Paul.

Clutching her shawl about her shaking shoulders, Libba ran down the stairs to the basement. Like a caged animal, she stalked up and down the dark corridors between the practice cubicles. Sawing violins, scaling voices, and jangling pianos pelted her raw nerves. How many ghostly girls still practiced their lessons in this hall, wringing their hands? In this cacophany of music, would anyone notice if she screamed?

After an endless night, daylight came. The thought remained: *Couldn't Paul care enough for me to wait?*

Numbly, Libba stumbled through her day. That afternoon, a pupil came to tell her there was a lady waiting in the parlor. She stared at the calling card unable to comprehend what her eyes read: Mrs. Daniel Marshall.

Chapter 9

Daniel's wife? Can he be married? Am I so starved for affection that I mis-read the simple kindness he offered?

Libba could think of no way to escape the interview. Blindly, she descended the stairs and peeped into the parlor.

A wisp of a woman glimpsed Libba and smiled. She moved across the room with her back ramrod straight, her chin up, and her head held as if her snow-white hair were a crown. Extending both black-gloved hands, palm upward, she said, "You must be Libba."

"Yes, Ma'am." Libba knees bent, and she prepared to curtsy, but she felt engulfed by the woman's graciousness, and instead, placed her hands on the out-stretched palms. The fragile-looking woman gave her fingers a warm squeeze.

If I could be that beautiful with age, I wouldn't mind growing old, Libba thought, noting the older woman's tissuelike skin, aristocratic Roman nose and fine, high cheekbones.

"I'm Dorothea Marshall," she said. "My son asked me to make you welcome."

"Thank you." Libba sighed. How foolish she had been to let anxiety con-fuse her into thinking this would be Daniel's wife!

They sat down on a pair of corset-backed chairs positioned for a tête-à-tête.

"I'm glad Daniel asked me to come." Mrs. Marshall's eyes sparkled with fun. Her lower lip pressed ever so slightly on her upper teeth as if to suppress ripples of laughter. "I wanted to see the girl who got him to buy new clothes. Now my Morrison. . ."

While she chattered about her husband as if he had only momentarily left the room, Libba relaxed and appraised her. Although the pert little hat perched at an angle over her forehead was fashionable, her black dress was rusty, and the gored skirt and bustle had evidently been refashioned from an old, prewar hoop skirt.

The interesting, vital woman drew Libba into a lively exchange, and when her call was over, Libba felt that she had found a friend.

But in the darkness of the night, loneliness blanketed her cot. She dreamed of Paul waiting just beyond reach. Achingly awake, she promised that she would never again expose herself to the hurt of falling in love. Worthlessness overwhelmed her.

When the invitation to Paul's engagement party arrived, Miss Cotton watched Libba thrust it away as if it burned her fingers. Confessing her troubles to the sympathetic woman, Libba finished by saying, "How can I not go when they have been so kind?"

"Don't worry," said Miss Cotton. "I'm certain Miss Burt will say that the rules of the trustees forbid getting out of school for engagement parties."

"How could the trustees have thought of so many rules?"

"Don't you know? There are no rules for students in the trustees' minutes. Whenever a girl is tempted by something she should not do, Miss Burt makes up a rule on the spot."

Libba laughed. Relieved, she hurried to her duty of supervising day students in the study room. Unable to free her mind of Paul, she was daydreaming over a stack of papers that needed grading when a student timidly interrupted her.

"Your brother is here."

Dumbfounded, Libba looked at the calling card—actually a scrap of paper—with the scrawled initials, "P. M."

Libba upset her bottle of ink. Spreading black stains inched over the papers, obliterating everything.

"Here, I'll clean it up," the girl offered. "You must go." She whispered, "It's your young man."

My young man! Libba dabbed at the ink. *Oh, Paul! Do you really love me after all?*

Forgetting everything, she tumbled down the stairs. Silhouetted against the glow from the fireplace, a tousled gray-streaked head bobbed back and forth in rhythm to a tune he was hummng while he waited. Drawing back into a shadow, Libba pulled the scrap of paper from her pocket. The hoped-for P was a D with an inky tail.

Forgetting how relieved she had been that Mrs. Marshall was Daniel's mother, not his wife, she now felt exasperated.

"Daniel! You'll get us both in trouble," she reprimanded. "They'll know you're not my brother."

"Neither is Paul."

"How—"

"Oh, I have my ways. His eyebrows went up at the bridge of his nose making a mournful expression. Then he relaxed his features and showed his white teeth in a grin that made him handsome. "Anyway, I had to see you. Mama said you looked unhappy. We Indians have our responsibilities, you know."

Libba laughed in spite of herself, but the painful lump at the base of her throat refused to dislodge. She could not allow herself disappointment that this was not Paul.

Huddled in a cold little lump, she looked at her clenched hands while Daniel chattered. He sat on the edge of the seat with his vibrant body turned so that he could face her. Ducking his head, Daniel sought her downcast eyes.

Momentarily, she lifted her gaze to meet his. Tenderness, flowing over her, begged to warm her very soul. She caught a tremulous breath and retreated behind thick lashes.

Daniel was leaving. She held out her hand, mumbled good-bye. Trudging up the stairs, she rubbed her aching head and wondered dully what he had said, what she had replied. His vulnerable face swam before her eyes, but she willed it away. She wallowed in the misery of Paul's conversation with Sarah Lois. She pictured a scene where she made her presence known to them and flung out bitter, unforgiving words. All night long, resentment festered.

A few days later as Libba entered the dining hall, President Bass stopped her.

"I have a request for your presence, Miss Ramsey. Mrs. Dorothea Marshall has petitioned a special privilege that you be allowed to attend luncheon with her tomorrow. Her servant will call for you."

"Yes, Sir. Thank you, Sir."

The old gentleman gave her a courtly bow. "Do accord me the honor of joining me at my table this evening."

Libba's reply came out a swallowed squeak. Students always sat with a teacher at the head of each table because dining ranked as one of the fine arts, but Libba had never sat with an eminent professor. In a society with no traditional aristocracy, manners delineated class and status. Libba was struggling to learn, but she wished she had more time before coming under President Bass's scrutiny.

President Bass explained that Mrs. Marshall's father had been one of Wesleyan's Trustees; she was denied nothing.

Libba watched as he selected a pointed orange spoon from the array of silver and dipped it into an orange. Trying to dip out the fruit without upsetting the footed orange cup, Libba half listened to the conversation.

"Did anyone read about the steamboat race on the Chattahoochee?" President Bass asked.

"How is that possible?" asked one of the professors. "It's too narrow a river for two boats to race side by side."

"It's a race against time. The *Columbus Enquirer* stated that the *Mignonne Wingate* left the Columbus docks at 8:00 A.M. November 3, to rendezvous with a Liverpool-bound ship in Apalachicola Bay at dawn on the fifth."

"That's entirely too fast!" One of the ladies spoke up indignantly. "Speed is dangerous on a river with so many sandbars and rocks! The Chattahoochee is well named the longest graveyard in the state of Georgia."

"It's hard to believe a well-known captain like Harrison Wingate would attempt anything so foolhardy!"

"Still, steamboats must begin to keep schedules and make better time or the railroads will put them out of business," said President Bass, pulling his goatee thoughtfully.

"The pilot is an inexperienced young whippersnapper named Foy Edwards. . . ," someone volunteered. "The engineer was in the navy, though, Jonathan. . . What's his name? One of the men injured when the gunboat *Chattahoochee* exploded. . ."

Libba had been watching carefully as the orange cups were removed and everyone wiped their fingers on doilies—small, fringed napkins used to protect the dinner napkins from fruit stains. She wiped her hands. The race did not concern her.

Libba dressed carefully, excited at the prospect of luncheon with Daniel's mother. Would he be there?

A servant called for her. They walked up College Street to a templelike, white house. Libba stared in amazement. Thick, round columns towering to the flat, balustraded roof, marched eight strong across the front porch. Mrs. Marshall stood waiting. She clasped Libba's hand in both of hers.

"You like my house?" She smiled at Libba's astonishment. "When Morrison was building it for me as a bride thiry years ago, I casually mentioned that I'd always dreamed of a house with white columns." She grinned impishly. "I really didn't dream he'd grant my whim. This was one of the first Greek Revival houses in the area."

"It's magnificent!"

Libba's exalted feeling continued as she stepped into the spacious entrance hall. To her disappointment, people filled the entertaining rooms. She was part of a crowd—a crowd which did not include Daniel.

Uncomprehendingly acknowledging introductions, Libba allowed herself to be seated at the place of honor by her hostess's right hand. Delicate bone china, gleaming coin-silver flatware, and a dozen centerpieces of colorful fruit in cut glass compotes arrayed the long table.

The butler served a multicoursed meal of elegant food enhanced by delicate French sauces.

"Libba, dear," Mrs. Marshall said as she lifted a whole roast squab to her plate. "Daniel tells me you're interested in poetry."

"Yes, Ma'am." Libba struggled to use the serving spoon and fork in the same way. "And he tells me you are related to Sidney Lanier. His words make you see and hear his images. They seem to sing."

Mrs. Marshall's smile was a gift, making everyone feel happy in her presence. Libba thought, *She possesses the perception and humor I so love in Daniel.*

Dessert was savored slowly. Finger bowls like blue lotus buds were set before the guests. Libba rubbed her fingertips on the floating orange leaf and dried them on the doily. With compliments on the meal, everyone rose.

While her hostess mingled a moment, Libba stood in a corner trying to take deep breaths against her corset stays. The richness of the food and the opulence of the setting contradicted the mother and son's personal attire. Suddenly Libba saw details she had not noticed: The table linens were discreetly patched; the upholstery was split on several chairs; the paint was scrubbed thin. When Mrs. Marshall spoke close by her elbow, she jumped.

"You're too pale, my dear. Let's take a constitutional."

"Oh, I couldn't take you away from your guests!"

Mrs. Marshall studied Libba for a moment. "They are quite at home. You didn't know? They are boarders."

Libba looked at her incredulously.

"Paying guests. Since the war, one does what one must."

Setting a brisk pace through the streets lined with sun-burnished red oaks and hickories glittering to pure gold, Mrs. Marshall told how her husband's fortune had been swept away by war. To save Morrison Hall she had taken paying guests, many of whom had been refugees to Macon when Sherman burned their plantations.

Bitterly, Libba related her own tale of Sherman's advancing army and the terror of her flight.

Mrs. Marshall bit her lips and murmured unintelligible sounds. She could share Libba's pain, but could she ease it?

Their heels clicked as they walked swiftly, exorcising their passion.

"How was Sherman generous enough to spare Macon?"

"Hardly that!" Mrs. Marshall snorted a laugh. "We battled for our town. Macon was filled with six thousand disabled troops crowding our hospitals—a number equal to the population of women and children. We escaped a raid until the last summer of the war. I was separated from Daniel when the shelling started, and I was frantic."

Daniel! Libba's heart leapt. Suddenly she wanted to hear his mother tell about his childhood.

"Our protectors were a company of aged gentlemen, the Silver Grays, plus hospital convalescents, and so on. The enemy placed a battery on the east side of the river." She gestured. "Near the Indian Mounds."

Libba nodded.

"I was working with the Ladies Soldiers' Relief Society. Daniel was coming along here. He was ten. A cute little freckle-faced lad. Wide-eyed. Curious."

Libba smiled at the image.

"He and some other children had been helping pack cartridges. Suddenly, a shot from Stoneman's artillery fell right here on Mulberry Street. Daniel and six-year-old William Sims Payne were playing on the sidewalk when a cannonball struck the sand. It bounced, went up through that column, entered the parlor of Judge Holt's house, and landed unexploded in the hall." She laughed. "After the enemy was routed, Mrs. Holt presented the cannonball to the Macon Volunteers."

"But how did you hold them off with no troops?"

"A battalion of Tennesseans, who were heading toward the battle for Atlanta, passed here in time to join Findlay's Georgia Reserves. They spread so wide and yelled so loud that the enemy thought there was an army and retreated."

"And Daniel. Was he hurt when the cannonball fell?"

"No." Mrs. Marshall's eyes crinkled and she pressed her lower lip up on her teeth, then burst into laugher. "But you should have seen him telling the tale."

Libba felt a pang of remorse. She enjoyed the animated way Daniel related stories, but she had rudely stopped him at Fort Hawkins when he had tried to tell her this story.

They reached the gates of Rose Hill Cemetery. Mrs. Marshall showed her rows of markers for Confederate dead and told how the ladies defied bayonet rule by placing flowers on the graves with Federal officers watching them.

"We had a true Memorial Day after the troops had been removed. Sidney Lanier made the address." Libba sensed the scruting of her gaze.

"The bitterness of the times did not tarnish dear Sidney's soul even though he had been in a Yankee prison. He said to bear our load of wrong and injury with the tranquil dignity that becomes those who would be great in misfortune. I remember his exact words: 'Today we are here for love and not for hate. Today we are here for harmony and not for discord. Today we are risen immeasurably above all vengeance. Today, standing upon the serene heights of forgiveness, our souls choir together the enchanting music of harmonious Christian civilization.' "

They sat in silence. Gradually Libba's numbness tingled into realization. Daniel had shared with his mother how hatred of Sherman and bitterness toward her father strangled her. She blinked back tears.

"Forgiveness is a freeing thing. Unforgiveness eats at the soul until it shrinks away instead of growing. Only as we forgive can we feel the cleansing of God's forgiveness."

Seeing the caring face of this sensitive woman so like her son, Libba thought, *Daniel must love me if has taken my problems to his mother.*

Paul's virility had ignited girlish fantasies, inflamed youthful passions, made her spurn Daniel's tender, infinitely caring advances. When last he called, she had coldly turned him away again. Could he forgive her?

With heaviness of soul, she thought, *I have been blind, far more blind than poor old Henry!*

Chapter 10

Clapping hands, stamping feet, cheering male voices erupted in solemn Pierce Chapel as the Mercer boys applauded the Wesleyan girls' Christmas program. Libba faced the stage, but her smile flickered. After weeks of seeing him only from afar, she was in the same room with him.

It was over. Libba could turn, free her radiant smile to cross the aisle. There with his students sat Daniel.

He mouthed unmistakably, "I love you."

Not caring if her pupils had seen, Libba accompanied them into the dining hall, secure, knowing that Daniel would seek her.

The girls knew all. She had become as foolish as they, leaning out of the third-story window to watch through falling leaves for glimpses of Daniel. Often, he waited across the street, eager to return her wave. Afraid he would break the rule by coming to visit, she felt deflated that he did not. Once, on a moonlit winter night, the giggling girls were drawn to the window by the plinking of banjos, the strumming of guitars. Libba leaned far out, not wanting to miss a word of Daniel's serenade.

Boldly she had written to him, begging forgiveness for her rudeness. No need to apologize, he had said. Of course, he understood. His daily letters were warm, funny, yet tender. Their friendship had blossomed through their correspondence, and now, here he was threading his way across the crowded room.

"Mr. Marshall," Libba said, formally extending her hand. "How nice of you to bring your group to our program."

Correctly, Daniel clicked his heels and bowed before her. Lifting her hand to his lips, he kissed it warmly. "An excellent recital, Miss Ramsey. I apologize for the overzealousness of my men." He was still holding her fingertips. Before he released her, he bent again. Covertly, he pressed his lips against her palm.

Libba nodded mutely, cupping her hand to her cheek, knowing she would never forget the moment of that kiss.

Daniel found a secluded corner.

With their heads inclined toward each other, their eyes meeting over the punch cups, they needed no other food. Voices flowed around them like melodies plucked from violins. They stood at the center of the sound sharing a delicious silence.

All too soon he was gone. She was back in her room wondering when she would see him again. She had promised herself after her bittersweet pain from loving Paul that she would shut up her heart. She and Daniel would only be friends. Now, as if seeing him for the first time, she knew. He was rescuer/friend no longer. She had fallen in love with Daniel.

Christmas was two days of quiet worship before the girls returned to classes. Then, startling news swept though the dormitory. Smallpox!

With a girl in the infirmary diagnosed, an epidemic threatened. School was dismissed for a fortnight.

Sarah Lois came to get Libba, and she was once again enveloped in the warmth of home.

The next day, Daniel arrived with plans carefully laid. He had brought Zachary Jones, whom he introduced to Endine. Patting her mimosa hair, Endine took Zachary off down the stone steps of Auntie's garden, already embroiled in debate.

Blissfully alone, suddenly shy, Daniel and Libba descended slowly.

He whispered, "I've read and reread every word you've written to me. Between the lines I suspect the soul of a poet—if you'd but open your heart and let your words flow from within."

Libba shook her head. "I could never be good enough to write poetry. Sometimes, I think of a line, but I never have the courage to write it. Someone might see—and laugh."

"I wouldn't laugh. *With* you, of course. But never *at* you."

Libba memorized Daniel's honest face. She knew there was no place in his soul for derision. Understanding and tenderness flowed from his smile, wrapped round her.

They paused in their descent and turned aside onto a terrace devoted to beautiful winter plants. Pristine white narcissus bloomed. Daniel snapped off a stem of the delicate, clustered blossoms. Solemnly, he presented it to Libba as though it represented great worth. Accepting it in kind, she buried her face in the fragrance.

Daniel gently put his arms around Libba. Twining her hands about his neck, standing on tiptoe, she lifted her yearning lips.

"My darling little Libba, I love you. I want to take care of you. I. . ." He nuzzled her cloud of black hair, brushed her cheek, kissed her.

Wondrous at the flood of long-pent emotions his lips conveyed, Libba joyfully returned his kiss.

They lingered as long as they dared, each vowing silently never to forget this moment of beauty.

Rejoining the others at the pagoda-like shelter over the well, they laughed and drank of the fresh, cold water. Nothing in Libba's life had ever tasted so sweet.

Daniel looked at Zachary, lifting the corners of his mobile eyebrows into question marks. Receiving an eager nod, he cleared his throat.

"Ahem! Ladies, I have the pleasure to announce that we are here on an important mission." He made a fist-trumpet.

"Ta-toot-ta-too! We wish to formally invite you to our neighborhood New Year's Eve ball. We offer ourselves as your humble escorts."

"Ohhh," Endine squealed. "That sounds like fun!"

"A. . .ball? What would I wear? Oh, I couldn't. Where will it be? Who. . . ?"

"Oh, Libba, don't be so skittish. I've lots of gowns. Of course you could."

Daniel panicked, floundered. "I want to show you to our friends. It's one of the oldest houses in town. Belonged to a cotton farmer named Joseph Bond. Now his daughter, Mary Lockett—but never mind, Mother will be there to welcome you."

"Shouldn't we ask someone's permission?" Libba asked.

"We'll ask Auntie."

Sarah Lois assured Libba that attending this ball should not endanger her position at Wesleyan's academy. She insisted that she wanted to buy Libba a ball gown all her own.

With their invitation accepted, the gentlemen left amid a great deal of jollity. In the marvelous privacy of her room, Libba pressed her narcissus between the pages of a book.

She'd keep it forever, but she needed no remembrance. She would never forget Daniel's first kiss.

Auntie and Libba had decided upon blue to match Libba's eyes. After a great deal of nipping to make the dress drape gracefully over Libba's fragile figure, Sarah Lois declared the ball gown ready.

Libba stood looking in the cheval glass. Her eyes illuminated her delicate face as she stroked the lustrous satin. The back cascaded from her tiny waist into a short train bursting with intricate puffs captured here and there by fluttering bows. *Can I manage all of this on the dance floor? Dare I trust Endine's waltz instructions?*

Carefully, she placed the turquoise ring on her finger, over the elbow-length, white-kid gloves. *In so large a gathering might someone notice it and know who I am?*

Endine's mature figure was encased in apricot satin, making an asset of her hair. She took charge of making the foursome merry, and all went well until they reached Macon.

The carriage ascended a hill toward a magnificent site overlooking the city.

Libba's eyes widened in fear. "Daniel!" she exclaimed. "You said a cotton farmer. A party at your neighbor's old house! This looks like we're climbing the Acropolis! Is that the Parthenon?"

Endine laughed. "What did you expect? For all his acting the buffoon, Daniel is somebody."

"Yes, but—no, I. . .nothing so grand as this!"

Brilliantly lighted, the two-storied, Greek Revival mansion had massive, towering columns marching across the front and around the side porticoes. Imposing in scale, the house looked down upon Macon.

"Joseph Bond was a cotton man," supplied Zachary. "In his day, he was the largest cotton grower in the state. While the Federal troops occupied Macon, the Yankee General Wilson took this house for his."

"I don't wonder," murmured Libba.

Libba managed the introductions gracefully. Her tensions mounted as she followed Endine up a beautiful, free-hanging staircase spiraling upward past the second floor through the third floor to the attic to be capped by a glass-domed cupola. Twinkling stars seemed an arm's length above them.

She took off her wrap and pinched color into her cheeks, but foreboding tickled its way up her spine. She forced herself to lift her chin and march out of the sanctuary.

Daniel, handsome in white tie and tails, waited patiently at the foot of the stairs.

The ballroom, a porch stretching across the rear of the house, was a fairy garden of rubber trees in brass containers and potted palms in cachepots of Oriental porcelain. The orchestra had not begun to play, but a slender girl sat strumming a large harp. Libba's cares floated away on the quivering notes of ethereal music plucked from the strings.

"Ohh," she whispered to Daniel. "This is probably as near to heaven as I'll ever get."

Intent upon hearing every note, she sat close to the harpist, whose music was lost in the babble of the room filled with partygoers. While Daniel went for punch, Libba watched gentlemen and their bejeweled ladies greet one another with outstretched hands, cheek kisses, and excited cries. Shrinking into the corner, an observer, she was not part of the scene.

Her breathing ceased. Paul! Incredibly handsome in formal attire, he stood looking about. An elegant, dark-haired beauty wearing emeralds slithered up to take his arm. The fabled Victoria. Even as Libba winced, she felt only a twinge for Paul. Seeing them did not truly hurt.

Daniel brought a plate of food too pretty to eat. He hovered protectively. She nibbled, fearing the music. Should she merely watch the others dance?

Daniel gave her no choice. When the orchestra burst into the lilting music of Strauss, he led her to the floor. His arms tightened around her. Swaying, whirling, she was waltzing!

The world receded. There was only music and Daniel.

Cheeks glowing, Libba reveled in the strength of Daniel's embrace as they swayed to the three-quarter time. The mirrors over the mantels were angled, reflecting the dancers. Libba smiled at herself, a part of the group.

Next, a brisk cotillion set her mind spinning as she tried to keep up with the changing patterns. With elbows entwining partner to partner, she reeled. Different men smiled and flirted and squeezed, enjoying the opportunity, because dancing was the only time deemed proper for a girl to be in a man's arms. Each time she rotated to Daniel, Libba tingled anew. It was only the feel of Daniel's arms, the sound of his voice whispering in her ear that made her heart sing. She wanted to dance with him forever.

Light-headed, Libba at last cried, "Enough," and Daniel took her outside. Many couples were enjoying the garden.

"I must show you the view," he said in a husky voice.

They stood at the top of the world, shouldering the stars, looking down upon the flickering lights of the city, down upon the rushing river. Suspended in beauty beyond reality, she nestled into the curve of Daniel's arm.

"Libba, my love," he whispered against her hair.

"Daniel, I. . .I. . ." She felt afraid her heart would burst.

Leading her into an Oriental summerhouse that looked like wooden lace, Daniel kissed her gently but with a great deal of affection.

Surprise fluttered through her. Paul's stolen kisses had been fraught with excitement, fear. Daniel's lips conveyed a passion springing from love. Libba responded with deep stirrings she had never known existed.

Seating her on the bench, he dropped to one knee before her. "My darling Miss Ramsey, I love you with all my heart. Will you do me the honor of becoming my wife?"

"Oh, Daniel. I love you. I do!" She began to shake with dry sobs. Her voice, a stranger's voice, was hollow in her ears. "It's you and you only that I'll ever love." Her breath came in wrenching hiccups. "But I cannot marry you."

Daniel fell back on his heels in shock. His mobile face went slack. "You can't mean that!" he said. "If you love me, that's all that matters. Of course, you can marry me!"

"No!" Near hysteria, Libba trembled violently. "Oh, I should not have led you on. You're so much fun to be with—and I do love you. . .but, oh, I'm so miserable." She buried her face in her hands.

Mystified, Daniel tried to pry away her fingers. "Tell me what's wrong. Let me help!" His hands dropped; his voice harshened. "Is it Paul?"

"No, no," she shrieked, flailing out her hands, thumping her ring against the scrollwork of the summerhouse. "It's being up here—so high above. . .all of the prominent families. . .your mother."

"Mama! She was proud of you when I brought you into the ball. She loves you. Libba, you're not making sense."

"It's this!" Snatching off the ring, she touched the hidden lock, shook it under his nose. "This is all I know about Libba Ramsey. Your mother maintains her dignity, her station in life in spite of all her tragedy. She knows who she is. To all these people, genealogy is—everything. They can tell you every branch—every acorn—on their family trees. They have their heirlooms to remind them that no matter how hard the future might be, they have a past to build on. Don't you see? I can't marry you not knowing who I am. I never allowed myself to dream you might ask me to marry you. It seemed too remote a possibility. As Endine reminded me, you are somebody. When you proposed, it hit me like a hammer that I have no father to walk me down the aisle."

"Is that all?" Daniel laughed in relief, but the sound strangled to a gurgle as she raised her head and he could see her face twisted with anguish.

"It's not just that—or because I have no dowry—"

"Not a bit of that matters! You're not waiting to see if Paul—"

"Oh, Daniel!" Realizing his distress, she pulled him to the bench and cupped his face in her hands. She kissed the drooping corner of his mouth and forced herself to consider him. Calming, she spoke in more normal tones.

"Forget Paul. I have. I was just a girl—in love with the idea of being in love. Yes, I was attracted to Paul—you've had crushes, maybe been in love before?" She pressed her fingers over his mouth and laughed shakily. "No, I don't want to hear about it."

"What about me? Do you love me at all?"

"At first, I only thought I liked you—and I do still like you more than any person I have ever known. Love for you has grown every time I've seen you, every time I've read your letters. You must remember that I've never had anyone to love me. I've only read books. I guess I thought love was only feelings of excitement. And pain when you weren't loved. You've shown me what love really is."

Humor drained from Daniel's face. He blew out his cheeks and spoke in cold, measured tones. "Then you're saying that I'm comfortable and safe, but Paul excited you. Libba, you've stirred my heart from the moment I saw you, but I'll quit bothering you if you don't feel the same."

"No, no, you've got it all wrong. It's just the opposite!" Libba blushed demurely. "When you kissed me just now, I became a woman. You stirred feelings I didn't know existed. I'm scared. When you proposed marriage, I realized there would be children. Not knowing where I come from frightens me. What kinds of traits might I pass on?"

"My darling." Daniel raised her wringing hands to his lips and kissed them tenderly. "I love you for yourself alone. That's all I need to know."

He tried to take her in his arms as if the matter were settled. She struggled against him.

"No. It's not fair to marry you. I'm not a whole person."

His arms dropped as dead weight. Sadness leadened his voice. "I thought I'd been patient. I've tried to give you time. I was waiting for this special spot. Our time. Our place."

The strains of "Auld Lang Syne" drifted from the house as the partygoers rang in 1877 with the words, "Should old acquaintance be forgot and never brought to mind?"

Down below lights winked out; the restless river rushed on in its endless search for the sea.

Even the stars seemed to dim as their carriage descended from the top of the world.

In the blackness of the night, Libba lay staring upward at the protective muslin canopy of her bed at Great Hill Place. It had felt so good for this brief time to be childlike and wrapped in the arms of kindness, of love. Now a wild restlessness surged within her breast.

The words of the old Scottish melody which had ended the ball beat upon her brain. "Auld Lang Syne" meant "old long since." What old long since did she have? She rubbed the cold turquoise of her ring. Loneliness had been her way of life.

Growing up in the orphanage, each child by mutual consent had let death of family remain a wound scabbed over, never discussed. Now as she had found out what family and love could mean, her boil festered, burst. Seared with the pain, she agonized to become a part of someone in the past, to find out what she had missed.

She pressed the spring and the ring flew open. She sat bolt upright, strengthened with sudden resolve. She must take the meager clues concealed within the heart of the stone. Impossible as the quest might be, Libba now knew she would never be a whole woman until she searched for her past.

Chapter 11

Stiff-backed, Libba fought the lurching as the train rattled over zigzagging rails.

Emerging from the forest of the Piedmont, the track plunged onto Georgia's flat coastal plain. These tracks held no memories for Libba. She saw nothing familiar, no friendly face at rural crossings. The tenseness which had gripped her through the wet winter and spring as the very elements had wept out her misery would not abate even though June had come at last and she had begun her trek.

She had forced herself to go back to Wesleyan to fulfill her commitment even though she had longed to begin her search.

Daniel had not been allowed for parlor visits because everyone knew he was not her brother. Their only contact had been when Dorothea Marshall arranged for her to visit Morrison Hall. Daniel had spent these occasions looking about the room at everything except Libba as she sat wringing her hands in stony silence. He tried to dissuade her from her intention to look for her father. When he saw that he could not, he offered to take her on her quest.

"No. It wouldn't be proper for us to travel together."

"It would be if you married me," he responded eagerly. "I promise we'd spend the summer searching. . ."

She had been adamant. She could not marry him without knowing who she was. Pleas exhausted, Daniel had agreed to wait, to release her until she accepted the impossibility of the task she had set for herself.

The train jerked. She tried to forget Daniel's unhappy face and instead focus on the cotton fields passing slowly like an unfolding fan. Sturdy, bright green plants, dotted with big blossoms which opened pure white and faded rose pink in the summer sun, spread before her. Jonathan Ramsey had owned such a plantation in Bulloch County, but he had not returned after the war. It lay idle, a hopeless dead end. She gave in to the tiring motion of the train fighting its way over the endless tracks. Why had she thought she could find anything about a man and woman who were merely names inscribed in the gold of her ring?

The whistle whined a warning. Libba jumped, and a startled baby at the end of the coach bellowed. A liver-spotted hound at the muddy crossroad planted his feet firmly, bristled his hair, and barked at the intruding train.

Libba laughed at him approvingly. Jutting her chin, she determined to stay armed with courage. She intended to search.

A billow of black smoke floated beside the train, and an ash of charred wood blew into Libba's eye. She turned to Auntie for assistance with the cinder, glad that the competent woman was with her. She knew how to take care of everything. In a time when ordinary people remained in one county from birth until death, the Wadleys were at home on this railroad track.

Auntie produced a clean, white handkerchief and captured the cinder. "It's not much farther. I'm glad you decided not to go all the way to Savannah."

Libba grinned crookedly. "Unless we find a trail in Bulloch County, there's no use in going on. All they know at the orphanage in Savannah is that I was with refugees fleeing Sherman's bummers, I was totally exhausted, and my satin dress was hanging in rags. All I had was the ring under my clothes on a chain about my neck."

Auntie nodded. "It's time to get off. For the last thirty miles the railroad has been running along the Ogeechee River. Father thought we should start our inquiries at the county seat of Bulloch County, Statesboro. We'll find something here," she said just a shade too heartily.

With a screeching of steel against steel, the locomotive turned its wheels into a long curve. *Ssst!* Steam released. The train rattled, slowed. With a jerk it jolted to a stop.

The elegantly uniformed conductor helped them down from the high step and waved good-bye. The train whistled, was swallowed up by the dark pine forest.

Left in the clearing beside the lonely railroad tracks, Libba clutched her carpetbag and wailed, "I thought we were at Statesboro. There's nothing here. This is wilderness!"

"We are at Statesboro," said Sarah Lois, laughing. "Or almost. The railroad planners meant to run through Statesboro, but someone told the people that sparks from the woodburning engine would burn up the county. They made the railroad go around Bulloch. The area has remained isolated, entirely agricultural."

Undaunted, Sarah Lois hired the services of an old man with a mule and two-seated wagon. Opening their trunk, she took out long, linen dusters to protect their gray wool-serge traveling suits. Dignity intact, Auntie climbed onto the high seat, opened a black umbrella to protect them from the sun, and nodded to the white-haired man to proceed.

The wagon squeaked and bumped into a forest of towering pines. Libba's spirits plummeted, and her bonnet ribbons seemed weighted with lead.

"It's hopeless to find a trace in such an unsettled area!"

"Don't let your courage flag. We've got clues to follow."

"What clues?"

"First, we know that you're the daughter of a planter rather than a yeoman farmer."

Blue eyes wide, Libba thought, *There she goes again, assuming I am something more than I feel myself to be.* Aloud she said, "How can you say that? This ring might not even be mine."

Sarah Lois pursed her prim lips. "Even if I grant you that, you have one thing no one could take away."

Libba raised questioning eyebrows.

"Your speech. You have a soft Southern drawl, a well-modulated voice, correct grammar that you learned at someone's knee when you learned to talk—before you were six when the orphanage took you in. That tells me you were born beneath a hickory, not a pine."

Sparks flashed from Libba's eyes. She threw back her head angrily. Sarah Lois was being irritatingly cryptic. Suddenly she grinned, realizing her spine was stiff, her spunk renewed.

"All right. I trust your wisdom." She lifted cupped palms. "What's the answer to your riddle?"

"That's better. Bulloch County settlers on the oak and hickory lands along the Ogeechee River built plantations with many workmen. The owners were designated as planters. On the other hand, settlers in the piney woods built cabins and put cattle out to feed on the wire grass. These yeomen led a simple, rugged life. Getting to and from market was difficult. They had little or no education. Many could not read or write. You don't have their singsong 'geechee' dialect." She bent one eyebrow toward their driver as an example. "The matron at the orphanage said when you came you could read and write your name." Point proved, she gave a self-satisfied nod.

"All right. Where do we begin?"

The dusty road had widened into a street. The wagon lurched to a stop in front of a dwelling with gray clapboards showing through a thin coat of whitewash. A lopsided sign proclaimed: WHITE HOUSE TRAVELER'S REST. A log grocery store and whiskey shop comprised the business section. In the center of town was a square, barren except for a gnarled walnut tree beside the ramshackle courthouse.

A one-armed man who sat on a bench beneath the walnut tree was eyeing them suspiciously. Auntie cut an astonishing figure. Tall and imposing, she wore a fashionable, high-crowned Gainsborough hat lavishly trimmed with mauve taffeta ribbons and huge ostrich plumes that fluttered as she swept along. The wide brim of the black velvet hat dipped low over one snapping, dark eye and gave her a sardonic expression. With Libba, the sad-eyed waif, they made a pair to arouse curiosity.

Libba nodded at the man. He struck his whittling knife against a stick in a sharp gesture that said he had no truck with strangers. Marshaling her courage, she crossed to him.

"Good afternoon, Sir."

He looked at her with watery blue eyes. Disarmed by her smile, he spoke. "Howdy, little lady. You look 'bout as disgusted with our town as the Yankee who rode up to Charnock Fletcher's gate—" he pointed with his knife— "and asked, 'How far to Statesboro?' "

"I thought this was States—"

"It is." He guffawed. "He was smack-ka-dab in the heart of town—three buildings and a walnut tree." He thrust his tobacco into his cheek and spat. "Patui."

Libba forced a smile. "I'm no Yankee," she replied sweetly. "I was born here. I'm Luther Elizabeth Ramsey come to look in the old courthouse records for my family. I was hoping you—I'll bet you knew my father, Jonathan Ramsey?"

"Easy enough to know everyone. Ain't but twenty-five folks here. Countin' pigs and chickens."

Once started he was hard to stop. Libba repeated firmly, "Jonathan Ramsey?"

The old man rubbed his hand over the pink skin of his bald head. "Ramsey? I recollect 'im before th' war. High and mighty he wuz. Allus chasing the almighty dollar. But the old courthouse ain't here no more. Dadburned Yankees burnt it plum to the ground."

Libba's taut smile twisted into a grimace.

"In the winter of '64, them fightin' Yankees come in here like the whole world was full of bluecoats. The southern column of Sherman's plundering army. . ." His voice faded to a growl in his throat. "Folks round here didn't leave. They stayed to protect what was their'en. Charnock Fletcher organized hisself a army of thirty old men too old to go to the regular army. He wuz going to protect the homes, but old Sherman had fifty thousand men. Ask Obadiah, here." He motioned to a bent old man who had hobbled up. "Obadiah clumb that there walnut tree—seed 'em coming. Got so skeered, he stayed up there three days."

"Zeke, you're always telling lies on me," Obadiah protested. He removed his hat and bowed. "Don't let him upset you, Ma'am. They burnt the old courthouse, but Ordinary Beasley had hidden most of the records. You'll find them in the new courthouse."

"Thank you," Libba murmured, afraid to ask for another opinion of her father.

When they went inside, the ordinary gave Libba eager attention while she explained her situation.

"Are you come to pay the taxes and reclaim the land?"

"No," Libba said ruefully. "Why is the land unclaimed after all these years?"

"It's been twelve years, yes. But we're still suffering real want. Folks hereabouts are far too needy to buy land, and seed, and guano. Don't know if we'll ever recover. You see, Sherman's two colums swarmed over a ten-mile swath of the county like locusts, destroying everything. Anything they couldn't pile into their wagons, they put to the torch. The Ramsey ground is still there—the dirt—I'll show you the plat. But the value. . ." He threw out expressively empty hands.

The farm was, as Sarah Lois had said, in the oak and hickory lands along the river. Libba poured over the census of 1850, even reveling in numbers of bales of cotton and pounds of rice Jonathan Ramsey had grown. The tax digest of 1861 showed her father among the top four landholders with 2,890 acres valued at $12,000.

Endine should see that, she thought. Her heart was beating a rapid staccato. Her father had had money, but was the old man right about his character?

Ramsey's taxes had been paid in December 1863. Here the trail ended.

They perused the dusty muster of rolls for the Toombs Guards.

Names were given and sometimes places of death. They read lists of four other companies but found no Jonathan Ramsey. Did he not serve in the Confederacy? Had he been a traitor to his heritage? Had he been a profiteer?

Dejected, Libba left the courthouse. Auntie had gone ahead to hire a driver.

As they bumped along in the wagon, Libba read and reread the date of her parents' marriage and, glorious, glorious, her birthday. "December 14, 1858. Can you imagine knowing my birthday!"

With a singing in her blood that told her they were coming close to discovery, Libba leaned forward, not noticing the lurching of the wagon. They were moving toward higher ground beneath a canopy of overarching live oaks.

"This be the Ramsey place," said their guide.

Stretching before them was a long, damp, mossy lane. Magnolia trees, planted close together, formed an allée of black-green leaves. Creamy blossoms, wide as dinner plates, exuded heavy sweetness that filled Libba with sadness.

Sobered into silence, unbroken save for the squeaking of the wagon and the *clop-clop-clop* of hooves, they stopped expectantly at a break in the ground-sweeping magnolias where a shrub garden marked a path.

Climbing down slowly, Libba stopped to pick up a leaf and hold it against her cheek. She started down the holly-and-boxwood-defined trail that led through the woods, willing Auntie and the guide to let her walk it alone. A brick wall warned her of what was to come.

The family cemetery housed many well-marked graves, but her attention focused immediately upon the granite obelisk at the center.

With her fists clenched against her mouth, she read:

LUTHER ELIZABETH RAMSEY
WELL-BELOVED WIFE OF
JONATHAN RAMSEY
BORN SAVANNAH FEBRUARY 12, 1840
DIED BULLOCH COUNTY
DECEMBER 14, 1858

Grief overwhelmed Libba. She had found her mother only to lose her so quickly. Gooseflesh prickled her cold arms. She felt rather than saw Sarah Lois standing outside the wall.

"My. . .mother. . .died the day I was born. Oh, Auntie, do you think she even saw me? Did she hold me in her arms—even once?"

"Oh, she must have." Tears streamed down her plain face.

Steeling herself, Libba glanced over the markers which commemorated her forebears, here a Salzburger seeking religious freedom, there a Revolutionary War hero. She would come back and commune with them. For now she must deal with the grief of seeing her mother's grave. Whatever had happened to Jonathan, he did not lie beside his wife.

Summoning all her strength, Libba retraced her steps to the road and pressed on down the dark avenue. Stark against the sky, brick chimneys towered two stories high, standing on either end of a blackened pile of rubble that had been Magnolia Springs. Within the lumpy mass of sooty ashes, a piece of metal arched grotesquely. Stepping over the crumbled foundation, Libba surveyed her home, struggling to remember what her mind still blocked out. Stirring a sour smell as she kicked through the ashes, she picked up a pottery bird. It meant nothing. Auntie found a cast-iron skillet.

Near the fireplace—a fragment. Libba pounced upon it. The flesh on her thighs turned cold, seemingly sloughed from her bones. The porcelain head, cracked, burnt blue-black, stared at her with black eyes and pursed red lips.

"Sudie!"

Groping for support, Libba's hands slid down the chimney, slashing on the rough bricks. Face in the ashes, she sank into the blackness.

Chapter 12

Black smoke plumed against the winter sky above the towering chimneys on each end of Magnolia Springs. Panting, Libba ran toward the house as fast as her stubby, five-year-old legs would carry her. The terrifying sound of drums beat louder, louder. She dropped Sudie, tripped, fell flat.

With her breath knocked out, she lay dazed. Up ahead her playmate turned. His chubby black face became all eyes, white, rounded with horror. He ran back, tugged at her limp arm.

"G'up, Libba," Joshua lisped. "Wun!"

Scampering for the safety of the log kitchen behind the tall white house, the children did not understand what sort of demons were behind them. They only knew that for three weeks distant drumming had sent the grown folks scurrying about hiding things, hauling bales of cotton to the swamp, burying barrels of syrup in holes in the ground as they whispered fearfully of some strange monsters called, "Sherman's bummers."

Outrunning Libba into the steamy kitchen, Joshua flung himself against his mother, rooting beneath the canopy of her white apron. Libba followed him, and the long-limbed woman cuddled her equally close.

"Hush yo' crying, chirrun. Old France won't let nothing harm you."

Bustling into the kitchen, a tiny wisp of a woman with thinning white hair drawn back severely from her fine-boned, transparently pink skin, bent to kiss Libba. Patting the child absently, she spoke in a breathless voice.

"Do you have the rotten eggs ready, France?"

"Yes, Miss Nannie."

Libba followed her grandmother into the chicken yard. Looking about furtively to make sure her movements were concealed, Nannie went inside the rickety fowl house and dug a hole in one corner. Surreptitiously, she slipped an ebony and ivory box from the folds of her black taffeta skirt. Libba stood on tiptoe to watch as she opened it. She loved to look at the twinkling jewels.

Nannie took out a turquoise ring. "You've seen this ring before. Your father had it specially made for you. Watch me now. I want you to remember its secret." She pressed a carved gold flower. The ring popped open. Pointing to the plaited hair preserved beneath glass, she said, "This is a lock of your mother's hair. She was my daughter. And, see. Your mother and father's names."

With her lips clamped firmly together and her eyes forced wide to hold back tears, Nannie threaded a gold chain through the ring and fastened it about Libba's neck.

"Keep this hidden beneath your dress. It, and the teaching I've given you, might be your only legacy."

Nannie put the jewel case in the hole. Packing the earth, she covered the spot with straw, made a hen nest, and added the rotten eggs. She grabbed the feet of her maddest setting hen and plopped her on top to guard. Brushing off her hands with a self-satisfied smile, Nannie put a finger to her lips.

"Shhh, Libba. Don't tell a soul. Now. We must get you cleaned up. We shall look like Southern ladies when our guests arrive and trust that our dignity. . ."

They went upstairs where Nannie scrubbed Libba's freckled nose. Libba stubbornly insisted upon brushing her hair herself. Suddenly, she heard Nannie's intake of breath and ran to stand beside her looking down into the yard.

Horsemen in blue coats rode through the gate, brandishing swords and firing pistols into the air. They demanded of old Augustus, the man-of-all-work, the whereabouts of the Rebs. Screaming and yelling, they rode round and round, tearing down the chicken yard palings and the split-rail fence that kept the cows out of the corn.

Trembling, Libba clung to Nannie through the deathly stillness after they had gone. Suddenly, the yard filled with another group, quieter, wearing blue coats with gold braid.

With her back ramrod straight, her head proudly erect, Nannie greeted the men with dignity. They stamped up on the porch with their saber scabbards dragging, scarring.

"Good evening, officers, may I give you directions?"

"You can save yourself the trouble, old woman, if you hand over your valuables and make us a good meal."

A redheaded man came around the corner of the house. Grinning and holding out a silver tray and tea service, he said. "Lookee here! This little feller showed me what grows in rose gardens these days."

"It seems you found my valuables," Nannie said regally. "If you care to wash up—and clean your boots. . .I will fix your supper."

"Here." The red-haired man shoved the tray at Nannie. "You serve it yourself and on our tray." He laughed and spit on the porch, splattering Nannie and Libba with slimy, brown tobacco juice.

Libba stamped her foot and whispered loudly, "Joshua, you shouldn't tell! These are Yankees!"

Bewilderment sagged his cheeks. He had obeyed. He dragged his toe in the dirt.

Noticing Libba for the first time, the ruddy soldier grabbed her. Instantly, her pet goose hissed, darted across the yard with his long neck extended.

Swooshing toward the offending hand, he pecked.

Screaming, the man fell back in surprise. Honking, the goose attacked him. The soldier kicked out with his heavy boot.

"No. Nooo!" Libba screamed, throwing herself on the enemy. "Gandy's my friend!"

Flinging Libba away, he kicked, kicked, kicked. Expelling air in a plaintive honk, the goose fell dead.

France appeared, scooped shrieking Libba under one arm and dumbfounded Joshua under the other. The terrified woman ran with the struggling children to the sanctuary of the kitchen.

Libba hid behind the velvet draperies in the dining room angrily watching the rude men make Nannie wait on them herself instead of sitting at the head of her own table. Hugging the soft rag body of her doll, she rubbed Sudie's cold porcelain head against her hot cheek and immersed herself in the fury of hating every man dressed in blue cloth. With Gandy gone, Sudie was her only friend because there sat Joshua on the Yankee's knee.

Nannie had returned outside the kitchen and France had come in with a tureen of stewed chicken—or was it Gandy? The soldiers suddenly focused their attention upon the tall woman. With her head wound up in a bright red turban, France wore her best dress, a stylish hoop-skirted black satin.

"You there!" The soldier stopped France. "Your mistress put you in her dress to save it, didn't she?"

"No, Sir. This is my Sunday-go-to-meeting."

"You lie!" Whipping his knife from his belt, he lashed out, slashing the satin dress.

The porcelain tureen crashed to the floor spilling its contents—whatever they were—across the Oriental rug. Screaming protests, France danced in frenzy with the satin fluttering, shredding from the flashing knife.

Nannie flew into the room. The tiny woman pulled back her servant who towered over her. Furious but without hysteria, Nannie said, "I demand that in my house, you behave yourself like gentlemen."

Mumbling about showing uppity little Rebs a thing or two, the soldiers prepared to leave.

Old Uncle Augustus was commanded to drive a mule in their wagon train. Taking a fancy to Joshua, saying he could fetch and carry for them, the red-haired man swung the stunned little boy up in the wagon and drove away.

France's screams terrified Libba. She clapped her hands over her ears, but she could not shut out the chanting wails.

In the blackness of the night, a candle flickering, a furtive whispering awakened Libba. Tiptoeing across the hall, she peeped in. Nannie and France were folding back the feather bed. They laid a shivering Joshua on top of the hard-packed cotton mattress. Commanding him to lie still, they flung the pliant feather bed over him. Carefully, they spread the sheets and counterpane so that the bed looked smooth.

Libba padded into the room, dragging Sudie.

Nannie jumped at the sound. "Shhh, Libba. Joshua ran away when the soldiers weren't watching. My guess is, they'll come looking for him. You stay in bed and pretend you are asleep. Nothing looks as innocent as a sleeping child, and. . .France, go back to your quarters. Just cry so much you can't tell them a word."

Lying immobile, Libba clung to Sudie. She clenched her teeth as the sound of heavy boots, of crashing furniture, and breaking china rang through the big house. From the yard, chickens squawked, pigs squealed, shots echoed.

In the morning dead chickens sprawled everywhere. Strewn hog carcasses lay spoiling with only the hams cut out.

But the exhaused little boy still slept, made up into the feather bed.

Nightmares and daylight hours merged. More bluecoats came, demanded food, took valuables until there was nothing, nothing.

Libba sat in the parlor close beside the smoldering fire talking to Sudie. A rock hit the floor beside her with splinters of crackling glass. The lace curtain flamed. Terrifed, the child dropped her doll and ran screaming. Voices drew her to the veranda where Nannie stood demanding, cajoling, pleading with men who threatened her with flaming torches.

Torches flung through windows turned furniture into flambeaux. Nannie snatched Libba roughly, ran, dragging her away from the roaring inferno that had been home.

Tears streamed down Libba's face as she struggled to free herself from Nannie's grip. "Sudie. I left Sudie."

"Hush, Darling. Oh, where are France and Joshua? She's too handsome a woman for her own good. We must run. Don't cry. We'll go to Miss Nicy's. Surely the Yankees will spare so fine a house as Bird's Nest."

They stumbled along the shortcut path to their nearest neighbor. In the darkness, they collided with a fleeing servant. Cyrus reported that the courthouse in Statesboro had been burned. Men with torches were circling Bird's Nest.

"We must—run for the river," Nannie gasped in short breaths that gulped air. "With no bridges across the Ogeechee—maybe the river will stop the wagon trains. If they cross, it will be at Rocky Ford. It's so dark! Cyrus, can you find the place where the mail is rowed across from Screven County?"

"Yes'm."

Libba felt herself being lifted in the hard-muscled arms of the tall man she could hardly see in the darkness. With her head bumping his shoulder, she fell asleep. She awakened as he laid her in a rowboat. She looked up at exposed tree roots dangling grotesquely from the high bank over her head and whimpered. Nannie's arms tightened comfortingly around her. Libba could feel the thudding of Nannie's heart.

Cyrus carefully dipped the oars, and the boat slipped silently beneath boughs of dark green live oaks. Gray beards of Spanish moss, hanging nearly to the water, brushed their faces with hairy tendrils.

A beam of moonlight riding the middle of the river had to be crossed. All three held their breaths until the boat was once again hidden by the lush vegetation on the opposite shore.

"Thank you, Cyrus," Nannie said. Pressing her hand against her chest, Nannie panted, "I can't go—any farther—but even Sherman's army can't be—everywhere. We should be safe in Screven County. In the morning—we'll find the railroad."

Cyrus cleared a sheltered spot in the thick forest, and before he left them built a small fire against the cold of the December night.

Libba wept for Sudie. Lacking the doll's comfort, she found her thumb. Sucking noisily, she went to sleep.

Awakening, Libba looked into Nannie's face, pinched and blue, but smiling in determination as she combed her white hair with her fingers.

"We must make ourselves presentable before we get on the train," she said in a determinedly cheerful voice. "The Central line is not far. I'm sure Wheeler's Cavalry is protecting it. All of the Southern newspapers say that Sherman's men are ruined and lost, fleeing for their lives to the safety of their fleet on the seacoast."

Gauging their position as the red ball of the sun broke through the eastern mist, Nannie headed due north toward the rail. Struggling for breath, she had to stop for rest. The sturdy child watched her with frowning, slant-eyed glances.

A cloud of black smoke billowing above the treetops made Nannie clap her hands in glee. "We're safe, Libba. What did I tell you? The train has stopped to wood up."

Eagerly, they hurried forward. Voices drifted on the still morning air. Strange, clipped voices, some speaking in foreign tongues, startled Nannie; and she clasped her hand over Libba's mouth lest she give their presence away. Trying not to cry, the snuffling child could not understand what had suddenly struck her courageous grandmother with terror.

On hands and knees, they peeped from beneath a bush. The smell of turpentine burned Libba's nose. Black smoke, sinking in the oppressive air, swirled low. Bluecoat infantry clustered along one side of the railroad track that was to have taken them to Savannah, to safety. Libba heard a shout of command.

As one man, they lifted the line of the rail and ties as high as their shoulders. At another command, they let it drop heavily, shaking loose many of the spikes and the chairs from the rail joints. The men seized the loosened rails and used them as levers to pry off the rest. Piling crossties like kindling wood, they set fire blazing.

Tears streamed down Nannie's cheeks, and she retched violently.

With frightening fascination, Libba watched the men lay the iron rails crisscrossed over the fire. They stood back, wiping sweat until the rails gleamed red hot in the middle. Gleefully, they lifted the ends and twisted rails into great iron knots. Other men, shouting to better this, carried the rails to wayside pines. Laughing raucously, they wrapped the hot rails around the slender trees, skinning, searing, causing turpentine to drip.

Nannie lay weak, sick. Libba shut her eyes. Still she could see the pine trees with rails looped around them like pretzels. The backs of her eyes burned with the fearsome image.

Too terrified to cry, Libba wiped Nannie's face. Nannie's teeth chattered. Libba pressed her warm little body over her in an effort to stop Nannie's shivering. Warming, they remained in each other's arms until a shout roused them.

"General Sherman is coming!"

"Hey, there's Uncle Billy himself!"

They peered out. The soldiers snapped to attention as Major-General William Sherman, a man with hard, cold eyes and a cropped beard, dismounted from his horse. His orderly handed him a flask of whiskey. He took a long pull.

"Well done, men. I congratulate you. We have devoured the land. The people retire before us. Desolation is behind. To realize what war is, one should follow our tracks. War is hell."

Nannie and Libba crawled away.

"That snake-eyed Sherman!" Nannie spat out the words with hatred. "I'm afraid his funeral pyres of our railroads are also the death biers of our noble cause."

The child could not understand her grandmother's words or her reaction of defeat, but watching her, Libba seemed to see Nannie's spark go out. Kissing her blue-veined hand, Libba sensed that she was the stronger and determined to help Nannie.

When they stopped to rest, Nannie promised safety in Savannah. "We have friends and relatives there, Libba. We'll get a message to your father. You'll like Savannah. It's beautiful—fine houses—parks—spreading live oaks. We'll be happy again. Keep that little chin up. You'll see." Lulled, they slept in a warm spot of sunshine.

Libba awakened screaming. Smelling turpentine until she tasted it, seeing railroad tracks twisted around pine trees like pretzels, she thrashed wildly.

With trembling hands, Nannie comforted her from her dream.

The nightmare returned each time she slept. Images blurred, tumbled, merged over long miles. Nightmare and daydream became indistinguishable. Running in the wrong direction, seeing the whole horizon lit with campfires, seeing wagon trains with men throwing on stacks of fodder or kicking in cribs of corn without even stopping, seeing the conquering army crossing their river on pontoon trains, they despaired.

They joined a group of refugees, women and children, moving toward the haven of Savannah. Libba had to feed Nannie because she could not reach her mouth with her shaking hand. Near the mouth of the Ogeechee River, they hid in a rice mill huddled together, silent except for babies crying.

"Libba." Nannie drew her close with cold, cold hands. "I'm confused. I've lost track, but it must be near your birthday. You will be six years old. A big girl. You must be a big girl. You must not cry anymore!"

"Yes, Nannie." She nodded her curly black hair. Solemnly she rubbed the blue hands. Pulling rice straw around her, she repeated, "I'm six now. I won't ever cry again."

The night was suddenly bright with rockets.

When morning came, the refugees could see Fort McAllister plainly across the marsh. The Confederate flag was fluttering in the breeze above the earthen-work fortification. The weary women cheered.

Their voices choked midword. Shot rained from Parrott guns across the river toward the fort. Heavy shot fired back across the marsh. Then all became quiet as a Sabbath.

A blue-coated signal officer, waving his flag from a platform on the ridgepole of the rice mill on the left bank, made them remain hidden. They heard a commotion in the fort, musket skirmishing in the woods, then quiet.

The sun was fading, and Libba piled more straw over Nannie.

Signal flags wigwagged. Troops rushed out of the fringe of the woods that encompassed the fort. The lines, dressed as on parade with colors flying, moved forward.

Fort McAllister came alive with big guns belching forth dense smoke enveloping the the assaulting lines. One color went down, but it was up in a moment.

Libba's nose burned from the sulfurous smoke. There was a pause, a cessation of fire. Smoke cleared away. The parapets were blue with swarming men firing muskets in the air, shouting so that the watchers heard, or felt they did, that Fort McAllister had fallen.

Libba crept back to Nannie. How could she have gone to sleep in all that noise? Libba wrapped her small arms around Nannie and tried in vain to warm her cold, still body.

"I love you, Nannie," she whispered innocently against the waxen cheek. "I promise I won't ever cry again. But I wish I had Sudie!"

Chapter 13

The chimney wavered drunkenly in Libba's bleary glaze. Lying in the sour ashes beside the brick pillar, she shivered even though the summer sun beat down upon her. Cold water touched her lips. A strange woman was bathing her face with water from a shard of pottery. Who? Libba brushed aside cobwebs of memory. Something was in her hand, a cold, hard object. Straining to lift her jelly-muscled arm, she held it up, squinting.

"Sudie," she whimpered.

"You frightened me," said Sarah Lois. "You've been in a faint a long time."

Strength did not return. Libba responded numbly as they helped her to the wagon. Dozing, fainting, she ran from dreams. Voices penetrated her darkness. Hands lifting. Funny dream. The hard wagon had become a soft feather bed; the cold springwater, steaming herb tea.

Strengthened, she fluttered thick lashes, gazed myopically at the canopied bed.

"What. . . ? Where?"

"Shhh. Just rest," Auntie whispered. "I sought aid at a neighbor's house. She was your mother's friend. Sleep. She'll tell you all you need to know in the morning."

June sunlight streamed across Libba's bed, but she remained in a cold fog of taunting, teasing dreams. At last she forced herself to move. Immediately, a maid appeared with steaming coffee and buttered toast.

When she felt sufficiently fortified and presentable, Libba descended the stairs. Auntie and a plump woman sat chatting as cozily as two old friends.

"Good morning," Libba said.

Their hostess turned and her soft cheeks lifted in a smile of delight. "Good morning, my dear. Refreshed?"

"Libba, this is Mrs. Nicy Bird. We are her guests in her home, Bird's Nest."

"How do you do? Thank you so much for your kindness."

"Not at all. You have brought excitement to the summer doldrums. Do sit down. My, my, you don't have Jonathan's big nose, thank goodness, but you have his hair. Black, unruly curls always fell over his forhead. See, there! He had the same habit of raking them back."

Libba stayed the involuntary motion. This voluble lady would bring her family to life. She pushed a footstool close to Mrs. Bird's feet and sat cupped, waiting.

Mrs. Bird described the young couple, so much in love, the dark curls and the fine blond hair bending to cut the wedding cake.

"Leaving for their honeymon, they followed the tradition of crossing the river at Rocky Ford. It was legendary for the girl to feign fear of her horse stumbling so that the one she loved could take her in his arms, and step by step, from rock to rock, carry her to the opposite bank. Many couples have known the thrill of crossing upon the rocks of the Ogeechee."

Libba clapped her hands in delight. Throughout the recital of stories, she interrupted only once to ask, "Did my mother live to see me?"

"Yes, Dear. She would not let us take you from her all day. She kept kissing your fuzzy head. She nursed you even though her strength was waning. The doctor could not stop her hemorrhaging. That night she slipped from us. Jonathan was wild with grief, inconsolable. France Handshaw became your wet nurse. You grew up with her Joshua as a playmate. Betty's mother, Amanda King, came to raise you."

Nannie. Libba cherished the memories that had come pouring over her amid the ashes of Magnolia Springs. She held back the rushing flood of tears because the woman's voice was babbling on.

"Jonathan became another person. He had been a Christian lad as a youth, but he fairly worshiped his beautiful wife and took too much pride in his home. When she died, material possessions became his god. He threw himself into raising tremendous crops of Sea Island Cotton, which grows only along this coast and is highly priced in world markets.

"Money came easily. It didn't satisfy. Oh, he was still charming, laughing, using funny old sayings, but his heart was hollow. He turned to humanism, thinking he had no need of God. He indulged himself, traveling restlessly."

"What you're avoiding saying. . ." Libba swallowed a bitter taste rising in her throat, "is that he had no love at all left for me. Did he blame me for my mother's death?"

"I don't think he blamed you as much as he blamed God."

Libba had drunk too much of pain. Her heart seemed to fill and swell and ache within her chest until it could hold no more. At least Nannie had loved her. Nannie's great heart must have strained like this until it simply could pump no more. Nannie had left her saying, "You're a big girl now. Never cry." Libba gritted her teeth and tossed back her hair, but the room reeled. She felt weak, sick with all the remembering.

Mrs. Bird sensed her sorrow. "Enough talk. Let's walk in the garden. The daisies will lift your spirits."

As they strolled around the old house, Sarah Lois asked, "How were you lucky enough to escape?"

"Sherman's bummers demanded I leave the house, but I refused to get out of bed, telling them I had just borne twins who had died and been buried. Someone torched the house with me in it while others dug in the fresh dirt thinking I was lying and had hidden valuables. When they uncovered the bodies of my babies, they were remorseful enough to come back and extinguish the fire. But, oh, they left the little graves uncovered!"

Libba's hatred boiled, spilled over, caught flame. How could her father have been so callous that he left her with only her frail grandmother in such a dangerous place? Enmity for Sherman became an enmity for Jonathan Ramsey.

"If only we had run this way! Nannie might not have died if we hadn't been running in the wrong direction."

"There was no way to know. There was a sea of bluecoats between us."

Libba could not rest. Over their protests, she returned to Magnolia Springs.

Walking over land that should have been her legacy, Libba longed for her home. Rampant with weeds, diminished by encroaching forest, the fields, nevertheless, held promise in their rich loam. She was surprised at the intensity of feeling the smell of this earth, the greenness of these trees evoked.

Paul, defending her against Endine, had marked her as a Southerner. Looking pridefully at Magnolia Springs, Libba knew she had a trait of which she had not been aware. She possessed that fundamental Southernness: love for the land.

Little good it will do me. Brooding, she poked and searched among the ashes of her past.

Later, over the supper table, they tried to speak of pleasantries, but the question that had chewed at the edges of Libba's heart could remain unanswered no longer.

"Was my father a traitor?" she blurted. "We did not find him listed in the local army companies."

"No. You've gotten the wrong impression. He was away when the war began. He wrote Nannie that he realized too late that he had neglected you. He had a part in organizing the Confederate Navy. He was a blockade-runner—and he wrote once about some new thing—iron ships which would change all the navies of the world."

"Didn't you ever see him again?"

"No. Well—I believe it was the summer of '61. He sent for a ruby necklace and ring that had belonged to his mother. He hoped Nannie would understand that he'd fallen in love with a woman who reminded him of Betty. He wanted an engagement gift—said he'd come home before he married."

"And. . .and he never did?"

"We never heard from him again. No, wait. That spring after Lee surrendered, a private detective came 'round. Said Jonathan had been wounded in an explosion. They had to amputate a foot. Said he'd been sent to search for you. Of course, you and Nannie were gone without a trace."

The clacking of the train along the track filled Libba's ears and muted the voices from her past until she found the strength to consider them. A faint smile lifted her cheek as she visualized the much-loved young girl who had been her mother. She kissed the turquoise ring. Its hidden lock of hair now became her pearl. Staring unseeingly out of the window as Georgia's sandy, low country became rich, red clay hills, Libba cherished her newfound remembrance of Nannie. Mercifully, her mind still blotted out the moment of her realization of Nannie's death and the strangers who had taken her from her dead grandmother's arms. Her eyes filled and her chin trembled.

Sarah Lois patted her hand. "I could teach that Nicy Bird a thing or two about tact."

"She painted my father as having no love for me. But how could he have left me in the path of—"

"No, now. He thought you were safe and well-cared-for. No one dreamed the war would take that course, and—"

"But she made him sound a reprobate. She finally did remember he survived the war—but with an amputation. With what she said, I feel I am also less than a whole person."

"You're forgetting onc important fact. He sent someone searching for you."

"Yes." It was a small sound. Libba turned her face to the window. Night was falling. Flickering lights along the way filtered through the mist. Suddenly it was dark, and the glass mirrored her drained face. The coach hurled through blackness as if it were a separate entity from the present world.

Behind her the hum of voices rose to a chatter. Passengers who had traveled all day stiffly ignoring the strangers around them reacted to the darkness, reaching out to one another, needing friendly talk. Shrinking from her need, Libba withdrew into her own cold depths. At last, she let the clacking rhythm of the rails carry her from pain toward sleep.

Great Hill Place welcomed them home. The boisterous family enveloped them. Realizing Libba needed time with her grief, they let her spend several days in quietude.

Finally the sunshine beckoned her. Seeking seclusion, she descended the granite-lined path. She plucked a fragile flower and buried her face in the spicy-sweet perfume. *It smells like orange blossoms,* she mused. The thought opened Pandora's box. Around her swarmed Daniel's promises that she kept locked in the back corner of her mind.

She had reached the paved circle in the center of the garden. Sinking to a bench beside the sculpture of the winged Greek messenger, she yearned more for Daniel as she listened to a bird calling across the still air. The lonely sound received a joyous answer from some dark corner of the forest.

"Oh, Hermes," she said to the statue paused in flight. "Can't you wing a message to Daniel?"

"Perhaps he did, for here I am!"

Startled, Libba wondered if in her fanciful mood she was dream-wishing Daniel's voice. Half-afraid, she turned.

Daniel stood there. Unaware of his own manliness and charm, he warmed her with a smile that lit his face with love. Running into his outstretched arms, Libba burrowed against him in childlike need for comfort.

They sat on the bench, and Libba told him of her search. Unburdening her heart of the hurtful details which she had been able to share with no one else, she ended with a wail, "Oh, if we hadn't been always running in the wrong direction, I might have Nannie now to love and care for."

"But aren't you glad you remembered something of her love?" Daniel kissed her clenched fingers. He tried to draw her closer. "I don't mean to press you, my beloved, but aren't you ready now to marry me—to let me care for you?"

"No, Daniel!" She pulled her hands away. "My heart is too hollow. My family came to my life only to die. I feel as if I have been to a funeral."

Daniel saw that she needed to weep and release her grief. As he had done that first day they met, he pulled his face into a mask of tragedy and spoke in comic register. "You'll feel better if you cry."

"No," she snapped, jumping to her feet. "No! I told you of my vow to Nannie."

"You know she didn't mean. . ." As Libba turned her back and isolated herself, Daniel pounded his fist against his thigh. Frustated, he flung out, "Don't be foolish, Libba."

"Don't call me foolish!" Wringing her hands, she cried out in misery, "I hate Sherman, and oh, Daniel, I know it is heretical, but I hate my father!"

"But don't hate me!" The tragedy of Daniel's drooping eyes and mouth were no longer a mask. "Don't shut me out." He held out his arms. "Let me love you!"

She could hear a sharp edge in his voice warning her that even Daniel Marshall's infinite patience was wearing thin, but she eluded his reaching arms.

"I can't forgive my father for not loving me. What—oh, Daniel, what if we had a child, and I couldn't love it? You can't marry me. I'm only half a person!"

"Nonsense. Oh, Libba, think! Think about the love you and Nannie shared. You've had a tragic experience, but many people have suffered. God did not promise that we would not suffer, but that He could turn the suffering to—don't run away from me," he pleaded, hurting as badly as she.

"Libba," he called after her as she plunged up the stone steps. "Don't keep running in the wrong direction!"

Chapter 14

Running from Daniel, fleeing from herself, Libba was overtaken by a rigor that rattled her teeth. In her emotionally weakened condition, she could not fight a severe case of grippe. To her nightmares was added a fevered dream of stumbling through a maze, always bumping against a dead end. She burrowed beneath the quilts and railed at Daniel's God. Her hate-hardened heart blocked out His reply.

Auntie dosed her with Farmer's Fever Pills and herb tea. At last, Libba was able to sit by the window and look outward for the first time in weeks. Against the verdancy of a June day, a cardinal cocked a merry eye from the bough of a creamy rose. Senses quickening, Libba tried to capture the image, but poetry would not come. She thought only of blood and snow.

When Auntie came in, Libba shared her decision to remain an old maid devoted to teaching.

"You're fulfilled with the life of a spinster."

Auntie pursed her prim mouth. "Yes, but I enjoy my position as chatelaine of Great Hill Place. I feel valuable to my father—" Embarassed, she shook the streamers of her cap.

"I imagine when one's father is a great man, it's impossible to find a suitor who can measure up," said Libba.

Auntie's dark eyes snapped. "Libba! You're placing too much import on who and what your father might be! God made each person unique. He gave us the freedom of choice in what we shall become. You are special. Don't shut yourself away. Daniel loves you—Paul, too, I suspect."

Libba's blue eyes clouded. Daniel had not returned. She was not vain enough to think Paul had postponed his engagement because of her, even though the discovery of her background made her an eligible catch.

When Libba was well enough, she was summoned to Colonel Wadley's study.

"I have been making inquiries from your neighbor's facts."

What facts? Libba wondered.

"I may remark that I have made a check of the East Coast, but no one knew a blockade-runner named Jonathan Ramsey. Since Mrs. Bird mentioned iron ships, I went to Hampton Roads, Virginia."

Libba blinked uncomprehendingly.

"It was there that the important battle was fought between the ironclads, the *Merrimack* and the *Monitor*.

"Yes, Sir."

"Ramsey's name wasn't recorded as having served in the Confederate Navy along the East Coast. This means that your search should now be—"

"Forgotten?" It came out in a squeak. "Oh, I can't, Sir. I must keep trying."

He smiled approvingly. "Forgotten? No, indeed, but I may remark that you seem to have acquired gumption and grit."

Grinning, Libba tossed back her sooty curls. "Yes, Sir! What do you suggest?"

"That you write inquiries about Confederate naval officers."

"Thank you, Sir."

Each day, Libba posted more requests. Each mail brought disappointment. Weak with despair, she threw up her chin and began again.

When Wadley returned and discovered Libba had received no information, he said, "What you need, young lady, is a trip. We shall take a family excursion to Columbus."

Libba thought, *At least I can put off facing Daniel.* Columbus's factories had supplied the Confederacy. Perhaps she might find information about her father. Quickened hopes as quickly died. Second only to Sherman's holocaust of Atlanta had been Wilson's burning of Columbus.

Colonel Wadley had sent Paul to work in the office in Columbus. What if Daniel thought she was leaving him and going to Paul?

The exuberant Wadley family filled the train to the nearby town. They remained in a state of secret excitement until the next morning when they went to the wharf on the Chattahoochee River.

A sparkling white steamboat waited on the building ways. Emblazoned on the hubs of the paddle wheel was the name *Rebecca*. All was in readiness for the launching of this addition to the Central line, the largest and most beautiful ever built to ply the Chattahoochee.

Happy at Miss Rebecca's pleased smile, Libba wondered why the surprise included her. She had seen dry-docked, oceangoing ships with deep-draft, curved bottoms. This riverboat was flat. Realization crept over her. Boats were different. Water was different, but they all meant sailors. What if her father had been in the navy here?

Hopes fell as she looked around. Everything was too new. She could see the building of the Eagle and Phoenix Mill with its white phoenix rising symbolically.

After much ado, Captain Whitesides shouted through a megaphone, "Ready for launching. Cut the ropes!" He broke a bottle of wine over her bow as the *Rebecca* slid swiftly down the building ways.

Paul appeared and pinched Libba's arm. "Now we've completed business.

It's time for your surprise, little one."

"What do you mean?" Libba drew away.

"Iron ships," Paul said cryptically. Laughing at her blank face, he explained, "The navy yard in Columbus constructed—among other things—the *Muscogee,* an ironclad ram."

"Ships of iron!" exclaimed Libba, suddenly luminescent.

"Catesby Jones, hero on the *Merrimack,* came here to command the CSS *Chattahoochee,* and. . . Anyway, I'll take you to the newspaper office to see what we can find in the files."

They turned through page after page of yellow, musty newspapers until they came to a *Columbus Daily Enquirer* article which told of the ill-fated attempt at launching the ironclad *Muscogee*. It made no mention of Ramsey. An aside in the story described the *Chattahoochee* as being at the wharf for repairs.

"Perhaps your father merely saw the *Muscogee* but served on the *Chattahoochee?* " said a reporter who was helping. "Here's another story: 'The ram was launched December 22, 1864, but when the Union cavalry laid waste to Columbus on April 16, 1865, the Yankees set her afire. She burned to her waterline.' The gunboat, *Chattahoochee,* escaped. Her crew set fire to her to keep her out of the enemies hands."

"Then that's a dead end, too," said Libba sadly.

"Not necessarily, Ma'am," the reporter said. "The *Chattahoochee* led two lives. Earlier in the war the gunboat exploded and sank. She was raised and repaired. Let's look farther back in the files."

The horrifying story leaped from the pages of the June 7, 1863, *Columbus Daily Sun*.

> "Pandemonium followed on the *Chattahoochee*. Fourteen men were killed in the blast or died immediately afterward. Those who had been scalded ran about the deck frantic with pain, leaving the impression of their bleeding feet and sometimes the entire flesh, the nails and all, behind them."

With her fist against her mouth, pressing back nausea, Libba read the names of those killed. Jonathan Ramsey's name was not listed.

" 'The graves of these men are in the town of Chattahoochee, Florida. Wounded were transported to the hospital in Columbus,' " she read.

Libba wiped her sweating face. She felt weak and ill from her constantly fluctuating emotions.

"Names of the wounded aren't given, but I have another idea," said Paul. "Let's go to the city clerk's office."

"But if the town burned, wouldn't the records be gone?"

"Some enterprising soul usually remains calm enough to save the records." In the post registrar of sick and wounded soldiers, they found names of the patients in eight hospitals.

"Oh!" Libba wailed. "The web is just too tangled."

Paul whooped. "Listen to this! 'On May 21, 1861, the Ladies Soldiers' Society organized. They operated the Soldiers' Wayside Home at the center of Broad and Thomas Streets. When the gunboat *Chattahoochee* exploded, the victims were brought here to be cared for.' There's a list!"

"Jonathan Ramsey!" they chorused.

No information was furnished on recoveries, but the clerk told them the dead had been buried in Linwood Cemetery.

There in the southwest corner of the graveyard they found markers for the victims of the explosion. Libba knelt to read the tombstones.

Chapter 15

Daniel Marshall had never felt so unsure of himself. Walking through the sun-dappled woodland that led to Great Hill Place, he tried to let the quietness seep into his soul. He enjoyed being alone with nature and with God, but his attempts at prayer about Libba had become strivings.

Listening to the callings of birds, his heart yearned for Libba. He would never have wealth like the Wadleys to bestow upon her, but he could take care of her. He was ready to make a home, to begin life with Libba.

Waiting on the stoop of Great Hill Place, he saw her at last! His eyes sought hers beyond the span of assorted Wadleys noisily returning home.

Libba looked so tiny, alone in their midst. Daniel's jaw twitched over clenched teeth. Paul was handing her down from the carriage.

She lifted her chin in that endearing gesture of courage and caught the tenderness, the pain on Daniel's face before he could mask it. Moving shyly toward him, she held out her hesitant fingers, coming short of touching him. She spoke huskily. "Hello, Daniel."

Auntie, perceptive as always, shooed the children pawing at Daniel for a story and said firmly, "Libba, why don't you take your guest into the garden while we all get settled?"

Walking stiffly apart, they started down the stone steps. The memory of how she had run away from him blocked words; they could think of nothing to say.

Daniel, struggling not to rush her, held himself in check until they reached the center of the garden before he spoke. "Did you find a record of your father's service?"

"Yes." It was a small, dead sound. "He was wounded when the *Chattahoochee* exploded. We saw some graves. There wasn't a tombstone with his name. We plan to look in a graveyard at Chattachoochee, Florida, where the accident happened."

Her words, her coldness, were shutting Daniel out. "We," she had said. She and Paul? Would it be best if he went and left her alone? Leaning over her, feeling more anguish than all the trying experiences his life had brought him, Daniel struggled to understand her pain.

"But Libba. . .why graveyards? Mrs. Bird said that a detective looked for you after the war. That would mean—"

Libba blinked. "Yes, I suppose he survived the war. I've felt so miserable, I forgot about her saying that. I did bring back some names to write, but—oh, Daniel, I don't know that I care to keep trying." Her hand waved toward his chest.

Relief, joy spread over Daniel's face. "You know it doesn't matter to me!" He opened welcoming arms for her.

Shrugging away from his grasp, she stepped backward. "I do remember Mrs. Bird said he didn't love me. I can't forgive that."

Daniel threw back his head in exasperation and rolled his eyes heavenward. He dropped to one knee before her. Tilting her pointed little chin with one finger so that she must meet his eyes, he spoke softly, patiently as to a child.

"Libba, you are judging your father. The Bible says we must not judge. You don't know his side. If he's a reprobate, that doesn't matter. It doesn't change who you are. What matters is you are letting unforgiveness poison your soul."

She tried to twist away, but he held firm.

"No! Listen to me. Jesus said, 'Judge not, and ye shall not be judged: condemn not, and ye shall not be condemned: forgive, and ye shall be forgiven."

"Don't preach me a sermon! You're judging me!"

Daniel rocked back on his heels and waited. Praying for her, bathing her in the warmth of his love, hoping God's words would sink into her soul, he rejoiced when her face softened. Slowly, she raised her arms toward him.

"You're right, Daniel. You are right! There is no room in my heart for love. I have to forgive!"

With a passion she had never before released, Libba flung herself into Daniel's waiting embrace. He buried his face in her dark cloud of hair, then held her back to search her eyes.

"Yes, Daniel. I love you. I do."

Laughing, he caressed her face. Libba returned his kisses. Keeping his arm around her lest she flee, he fumbled in his pocket.

"How did you know I would be back today?"she asked.

"I didn't. I've been coming on the noon train every day. It made me feel closer to you. I've been afraid that Paul would beat my time—"

"I told you there was no need to be jealous of Paul."

"Then it's time I marked my claim, Woman!" Daniel said in a bass voice that was meant to be funny and strong, but shook. He took out a large, square-cut diamond. "I'd be honored if you'd wear my grandmother's ring."

"Ohhh! It's beautiful. I love it! I love you. But I'm still—I'm just afraid—I'm not ready—"

Daniel placed a finger on her lips. "I wish we were married this instant—but I love you too much to press you. Just wear my ring. Say we're betrothed. Let me help with your search."

Unable to speak, Libba extended her hand. Tenderly, Daniel slipped the ring onto her finger and kissed her hand. His laughing eyes met hers and locked. He gathered her into his arms for a kiss that sealed his commitment.

Letters coming in answer to Libba's inquiries to former members of the Ladies' Soldiers' Friend Society of Columbus plucked her tightly strung nerves.

At last she opened one from a Mrs. David Hudson that read in part:

> *Many of the worst patients were transferred to the gangrene hospital in Eufaula, Alabama. Perhaps Dr. Hamilton Weedon of that city would remember, although he treated a sad multitude of cases.*

Mrs. Bird had mentioned an amputation, but it seemed useless to write to a harried doctor. This was probably another dead end.

The letter she had saved until last bore the signature, Mrs. Daniel Morrison Marshall. She recalled her panic when first she received a note from Daniel's mother. She was not ready to be badgered about an engagement party with this obsession for finding her father, and she ripped open the envelope with her temper at the ready. The brief note said: "I must see you at once. Come as soon as possible."

When Libba arrived at Morrison Hall, she found Mrs. Marshall's quiet manner replaced by jumpiness. Without preamble, she led Libba to stand before an oil painting depicting a sailboat on the building ways. Libba cocked her head to one side as she stared uncomprehendingly.

"It's luminous. The silvery gray shines like opal, but—"

Mrs. Marshall tapped the signature. "It's here. The key. It was here all along. Cowles Myles Collier. Your father's friend. Oh, what a mystery it is how our lives entwine if only we take the time to notice how we touch others!"

Libba's mind was blank.

"Myles Collier. A navy man. There when the *Chattahoochee* was being built. Oh, I apologize for not thinking of it sooner. One thinks of oceans and not rivers when one thinks of navies. I don't know the extent of Collier's service, but—" She burst out laughing. "I'm babbling. Wait! Here comes my neighbor from High Street. She can explain it all!"

Libba turned to meet a woman with masses of auburn hair.

"May I present Mrs. Richard Hines, the former Miss Georgie Shackelford."

"I'm delighted to be of help," Georgie bubbled. "I knew Jonathan well."

Libba brushed back her tumbling black curls in amazement.

Georgie clapped her hands. "That was his habit, too. You are his daughter! You look like him instead of your mother."

"You knew my mother?"

"No. I knew Emma Edwards who was in love with him. Emma, a willowy blond, confided in me that Jonathan said she was exactly like his dead wife, all pink and blue and gold."

Libba winced at the thought of her father in love with another woman, but she drank in the details of the story this gracious lady related.

"Our plantation, The Pines, was a haven during the dreadful times of war. The gunboat *Chattahoochee* was being built at the Saffold navy yard in Early County, Georgia, and the officers visited us frequently. My twin, Hannah, married Myles. I married Richard."

"And Jonathan? Did he marry Emma?"

"He kept saying they'd marry as soon as the South won the war. He seemed to recover from the wound he received in the explosion. Evidently the infection was deep in the bone. The last I heard, the sickness had returned, and gangrene had set in."

Pieces were beginning to fit. Libba did not know if she could face the picture they made. Twisting her hands, she thought of dear Colonel Wadley. *Grit and gumption, Libba,* she said to herself. *Gumption and grit.*

Georgie fumbled in her reticule. "I wrote to Hannah and Myles because he and Jonathan were close friends. Ah, here it is!" She extracted a letter.

Libba skimmed Collier's kind words about her father. At least someone thought well of him. He wrote about Jonathan's daredevil adventures as a blockade-runner at the gulf port:

> *When the war ended, Jonathan was being cared for by Emma Edwards in her home, Barbour Hall, which had been converted into a hospital. He refused to have his foot amputated. I regret that I haven't kept in touch with Jonathan. Ellen and George moved to California, but they would have written me if Jonathan had died. I'm certain you'll find him in Eufaula.*

Georgie smiled sweetly. "Captain Harrison Wingate and his vivacious wife, Lily, Emma's niece, were also our guests at The Pines. The Wingates are prominent in Eufaula society. Perhaps you read the newspaper accounts last fall about the race of the steamboat named for their daughter, Mignonne?"

Libba felt numb. "I recall the excitement. Everyone was talking about it. I had no way of knowing that my father—"

"And every day," Mrs. Marshall broke in, "I saw Myles Collier's sailboat and did not connect him with the navy."

Daniel arrived. He bounced around the room unable to contain his excitement. "You'll write to Eufaula?"

"No. I cannot bear another letter. I must go. See him for myself. The Wadleys are going to Columbus for the trial run of the *Rebecca.* Colonel Wadley mentioned business in Eufaula. Everything is pointing there."

"I am going with you!"

September gales had raised the river. The Chattahoochee tumbled over the falls at Columbus in its rush to the sea. Daniel realized that the water lapping beneath the gangway to the *Rebecca* was making Libba dizzy on the springing plank. He reached to steady her, but Paul, on the deck, pulled her aboard.

The *Rebecca* was a floating palace. Three stairstep decks turreted by a glassed pilothouse were adorned with wooden-lace trimming on every available overhang. The dazzling boat commanded the attention of everyone on the wharf.

"Will we get to Eufaula today?"

"No, little one," Paul said. "We came on board to test the new electric lights. We will lie at the wharf tonight. Eufaula is eighty-five miles south. It will only take thirteen or fourteen hours to get there."

While the others toured the boat, Libba sank down on a velvet settee in the grand saloon, pleading a headache.

"Alone at last," said Daniel. "I had thought a romantic river cruise would make you fall so madly in love with me that you'd succumb and be ready to marry." He gave her the look of a sad-eyed puppy. "I'm beginning to have my doubts."

"Oh, Daniel! You promised not to press. I really have a headache, and being on this elegant boat makes me feel so insignificant. I'm terrified. I don't want to see my father. And. . .what if he's dying? You know that the alternatives of gangrene are amputation or death."

"Darling, you'll feel better if—"

"Don't you dare say if I cry!"

"No. No. If you'll find your father and forgive him. You'll never be satisfied if you turn your back now."

"But how can I endure it until we get under way?"

Daniel slid a comforting arm around her shoulders, but Libba remained as hard and unyielding as the stiff-backed sofa.

Dinner was a multicoursed meal served with flourish. Colonel and Mrs. Wadley dined with the ship's master, while the younger group was hosted by the mate.

When the warm September night was dark, the party went on deck to witness the test of the new electric lights.

Daniel stood back in the shadows watching. The gray streaks in his dark hair stood awry in little plumes like the pinfeathers of a ruffled bird. Libba's eyes, like those of everyone else, had fastened on Paul.

Conscious of the crowd's attention, Paul dramatically turned on the switch that pulled apart the hard-carbon sticks in the arc lamp. An arc of brillant white flame formed between them.

"Ahhh!" came an intake of breath from the crowd as the night became bright. In contrast to the brilliant white glow, light from the kerosene lamps in the cabin and the gaslights on the street corner faded into nothingness.

"That was the Brush light," Paul announced. "Next is the light of the United States Electric Company, a bull's-eye, the same as used on locomotives."

After a long discussion, it was decided that the streamer would use both. Even though the inventor had not declared it perfected, the Brush light would be tried in the place of the flambeaux which had been used when landing or loading. This would prevent danger of sparks setting the cotton afire.

With the test over, Libba bid Daniel a hurried good night and disappeared into the stateroom.

Daniel had anticipated a stroll in the moonlight after those infernal electric lights were out. He told himself her indifference was merely trying to block out the pain of tomorrow's discovery. Pacing the darkened decks alone, he wondered if she had been judging the two men. Surely she could see that his love and Paul's were not the same.

Chapter 16

Darkness smothered Libba, blacker than ever after the brilliancy of the electric lights. She fell into exhausted sleep only to awaken to empty silence. Having abandoned her childish nighttime prayers, she felt utterly alone.

She had nearly found Jonathan Ramsey. Why should he want to meet her? She'd be of no interest to him. Worse. A bother. Probably she deserved the treatment she had received. Torturing herself throughout the night, Libba looked out as dawn broke over the Georgia shore. They were still at the wharf. She had hoped the journey had passed in the night and she would have less to endure.

After breakfast, Daniel led Libba to the deck and produced a banjo. He sang a funny ballad about a maiden on her maiden voyage on the fabled steamboat, *Rebecca*. As the group gathered around them, leaning in to harmonize, Daniel twanged his voice, twisted his eyebrows, and launched into the disaster song, "Lost on the Steamer Stonewall."

Laughing, everyone leaned in close to harmonize on the popular song which immortalized the steamboat disaster.

By nightfall, the *Rebecca* was still far from her destination. The merry group dressed in elaborate evening attire. After a sumptuous meal, they danced in the mahogany-floored ballroom. Paul claimed a waltz with Libba, but she was relieved when Daniel took her on deck and she no longer had to keep up a false smile.

"Oh, Daniel, how much farther?"

"Have patience, my dearest. Tomorrow."

"What if my knees are too weak to walk the gangplank?"

"I'll be with you every step of the way. You can always know that for the rest of your life."

Libba gazed at Daniel's dear face in wonderment. She moved into his arms and lifted her lips to kiss him with gratitude.

In the stillness of Sunday afternoon, the steamboat glided into the wharf at Eufaula, Alabama. Libba and Daniel hired a carriage with Sarah Lois as their chaperone.

Libba had not wanted to consult the Wingates or look for Barbour Hall and the blond woman unless forced. Dr. Weedon would be easiest to find.

As they rode down Randolph Avenue, Libba felt intimidated by the grandeur of the mansions. "I've never seen such houses. They go up, up, up."

"Can't you picture ladies on those widow's walks watching the river for wayward husbands? Ah, that sounds like a song." Daniel plinked an imaginary banjo.

Climbing the steps to the Weedon house, Libba's knees shook. Daniel and Auntie both supported her.

A man with a graying mustache assessed them with snapping eyes. "Bring her right into my office."

"Oh, no, Sir." Libba's voice was a husky rasp. "I'm not a patient—" She realized there was swelling around her eyes. Her hands and ankles were puffy. She spoke strongly. "I'm sorry to disturb your Sabbath rest, but I'm seeking information about a naval officer wounded on the *Chattahoochee*. I'm told he was sent to the gangrene hospital here—"

"You must realize the blockade had cut us off from supplies, and we were treating dying men with herbs and bark and using carpenter's tools for surgical instruments."

He called his wife. "Mary, these people are tracing a naval officer who was my patient. I'm trying to warn them—whom did you say you—"

"Oh, I'm sorry," Libba said quickly. "This is Miss Wadley and Mr. Marshall and I am Elizabeth Ramsey. My father was Jonathan Ram—"

"Can it be?" Mary Weedon exclaimed. "Those black curls. It must. . ."

Wordlessly, Libba snapped open her ring and held it out.

Mary Weedon clapped her hands. "Of course, we know him. I must run and tell them immediately."

Paling, Libba shouted, "No! Please!"

"Wait, Mary!" Dr. Weedon said. "Jonathan's detective found no trace. They assumed you dead. This will be a shock. We must prepare him."

"Yes, please. I'm not ready to see him. I doubted he was alive. I'd heard he was dying—refusing amputation."

"Yes, he was dying. Hatred and pride were poisoning his soul even as the infection in his foot was poisoning his blood. He was willing himself to die."

Mary broke in. "With Emma's love and prayers, he let God into his life. With her as his wife, he's a changed man."

"When he allowed me to amputate, his health became good."

"Last summer he felt God calling him to preach." Mary consulted the watch pinned to her bodice. "He'll be preaching soon. Do let me tell him before he leaves for the church."

"No! Promise me you won't tell him. He may not want to see me." Libba began to wring her hands.

"Of course he does," said Mary, wiping tears.

Daniel spoke in his professor's voice. "The man wouldn't be able to preach after such a shock. If you'll kindly direct us to the church, we'll slip in. Libba can get accustomed to seeing him before she introduces herself."

Before he let her go, Dr. Weedon pressed his stethoscope, a short wooden rod, against Libba's chest. He pulled around her eyes and examined her cold fingers.

"Young lady, you are suffering from a case of simple stress. You are bottling your emotions within you. The most beneficial thing I could prescribe would be a good cry."

They waited in the churchyard until the services had begun. They slipped into the back pew, and Libba cowered behind the man in front of her. Only when Jonathan Ramsey began his sermon did she move to see the man whose presence she was trying to shut out.

Dark laughing eyes swept over her as he included the strangers in a humorous remark. He raked back a tumble of black curls, sending waves of emotion vibrating through her.

Daniel stretched his arm along the back of the seat in a message of his surrounding love. She smiled wanly and forced herself to look back at the man in the pulpit.

The preacher was not handsome. He had a bulbous, red nose. His face was heavily lined but pleasantly set as though he took joy in his religion. The silly man was talking about how to boil a frog. For a moment she let herself listen to his jovial voice.

"If you throw a frog into hot water, he will jump out. To boil a frog you place him in cold water. Make him comfortable. Then warm the water just a tad. He won't notice. Add more heat—more heat. He accepts it. Suddenly the water is boiling. It's too late!"

The congregation laughed.

"It's the same way with sin. We. . ."

Libba followed his glance to a placid woman with silver streaks in her pale blond hair. Precious Emma? *How could he marry someone else who looks like my mother?*

The woman tapped a wiggling lad of about ten. Her child. His! The black curls were unmistakable.

My half brother. She tried to summon feelings of love, joy. Guilt overwhelmed her. All she could feel was jealousy. Jonathan cared for his son, lived with his son. He did not love his daughter. He had blamed his daughter for her mother's death. He had left her. Beads of sweat crawled on her upper lip.

Music. Closing hymn, people standing.

Libba fled.

Daniel found her retching beneath a giant oak tree.

"Do you want me to speak to him first?"

"No! I can't speak to him. I can't forgive him. Take me back to the boat."

Chapter 17

Libba lay in her bunk shaking.

Auntie spoke tartly. "For two days I have let you wallow in misery. You should be the happiest girl in the world. Drink this tea. Then go out and speak with Daniel. He is stricken that you've refused to see him."

"I should send him away forever," Libba stormed. "Don't you see? He's so gentle—has so much love to give. He deserves someone better. My heart is too cold."

"Nonsense! This tea will warm you."

Swallowing the bitter stuff, Libba longed to see Daniel, yearned for the comfort of his arms. If only they were married. Part of her wanted to be his wife, to bear his children, but something was missing. She had no joy. Demoralized by the aching void that her father did not love her, she felt unable to function. She'd leave Eufaula. She had seen him. Wasn't that enough? She'd return Daniel's ring—she loved him too much to hurt him. *I'll devote my life to teaching. I'll prove myself worthwhile to some student.*

Sarah Lois filled the cabin with the strength of her presence. Helping Libba to dress, she pushed her on deck.

Daniel saw Libba's swollen eyes and little blotched face and bounded to her. His gray eyes were big, round hollows. His voice was liquid emotion. "Let's go up on the hurricane deck."

The top deck afforded privacy. Hurting for her, Daniel tried to shelter her in his embrace. Her stiffness made him drop his hands. She did not need him as he needed her.

"Libba, I know this is hard, but you make me want to shake you. I understand that growing up unloved is tough. But you must know that early neglect, whether real or imagined, is not insurmountable. It can build character—as it has in your case. We all admire you so much."

He turned away, hurting so badly he did not want her to see. His voice dropped until it was nearly blown away on the breeze. "You were doing well until I asked you to marry me. Do you find me so distasteful? Do you want me to release you from our engagement? To go away and leave you alone?"

"Yes, I've been thinking that would be best."

Without looking back, he walked away.

Libba ran down the deck and hurled herself against his hunched back.

"No. Daniel. No! I couldn't bear life without you. I love you. I do."

He looked at her with a grave, vacant face, waiting.

"I needed to know who I am. I've found Jonathan Ramsey. It doesn't help. My insides are torn, bleeding. He's a hypocrite! Preaching about love when he ran off and left his daughter. A silly sermon. Boiling a frog, indeed!"

"I liked it—and him. There's truth in his humor." He kissed her gently on the forehead. He wanted to be more than her mentor, but he saw that he must restrain his passion and try to give her love. "Perhaps he's not the knight you hoped to find. But you're lucky. Most orphans of the war will never know who or what their fathers were. Even we with fathers find that earthly fathers often fail."

"He gave up searching for me!"

"But God never gives up on us. He sent His Son, reaching out, searching for each one of us to be part of His family. You haven't found peace. . .because it is your heavenly Father you must find and accept."

Libba wriggled free of his grasp. "I was baptized as a child," she snapped, "but God doesn't care any more than Mr. Ramsey does." She jutted a defiant chin. He did not reply, and at last she relented. "All right. How do I find your God?"

"The first step is confronting your father, forgiving him."

She gripped the rail. From this pedestal, she looked across the treetops, down to the rushing water. "I'm confused. Where are we? Which way are we going? Back to Columbus?"

"Not yet. We headed downriver making adjustments on the machinery. Now we're heading back to Eufaula. We should reach there Wednesday afternoon." *Oh, Libba,* he thought, *I'm confused, too. Which way are you and I going?*

"Probably he'll have prayer service. Will you take me back?"

"You know you must speak to him this time?"

"I know." Libba faced into the wind.

The turquoise ring shone on Libba's finger as she walked into the church and took a seat halfway down. All of her ill feelings tumbled about, bumping, pulling, exhausting her.

The service was over at last. People were standing. Libba sat. Swallowing, she feared she would be sick. Daniel's hands, strong, sustaining, lifted her, guided her toward the door.

The preacher was shaking hands. He wavered before her as a bright blue blur.

Why did he have to wear blue cloth like those Yankee fiends he left me and Nannie to face alone?

Suddenly she could see the image of the enemy soldier kicking, kicking,

kicking until Gandy lay dead.

Daniel would not let her flee. The moment had come.

Libba stood face-to-face with Jonathan Ramsey.

Coldness froze her heart. There was no forgiveness in her.

She could not speak. She could not lift her hand.

She sagged against Daniel. Surely he would speak, bridge this silent gap. She waited. No one could do this for her but her, herself, yet she was too weak.

She prayed, *God, if You're out there. If You really do care, help me! At least I can take his hand and speak, but I don't have any feeling. Help!*

Her hand moved. It met the big, callused grip of the man who had stood waiting. A wonderful warmth gave healing power to her body. She lifted her face, smiled.

Jonathan's hand pressed her ring. His red face crumpled as he gazed at her in wonderment. He turned her hand over, touched the carved gold flower that released the mourning ring's secret. The turquoise opened. Jonathan kissed the blue glass-covered lock of plaited golden hair. Tears streamed over the ridges of his face. He smothered Libba with a hug.

Dry-eyed, stiff-backed, she said, "My name is Luther Elizabeth Ramsey."

Everyone was crowding around, patting, hugging, talking without being heard.

Numb, Libba nodded acknowledgment to introductions. The blond woman, Emma. Plain! What did she think? That placid expression concealed her emotions. She spoke in a quiet voice as she introduced her son, Wingate Ramsey. Handsome Captain Harrison Wingate; his twinkly-eyed wife, Lily; Harrison Junior, and the black-haired, porcelain-skinned Mignonne were presented as family. Libba was being transported to a place called Barbour Hall.

The carriages rolled up the drive to an Italianate mansion crowned by a glassed belvedere. Painted brown velvet and ermine, Barbour Hall sat like a comfortable dowager with a welcoming look.

The double doors were thrown open. Like a picture framed by the glowing sidelights, a beautiful woman with a dazzling cascade of red-gold hair stood waiting. Her beauty was enhanced by an inner glow of contentment. Near to bearing a child, she rested her hand on her protuding stomach with obvious joy.

Adrianna Edwards greeted Libba warmly. "I'm delighted to have you all." Her words lifted with a rising inflection that carried the sound of her smile.

The extended family swirled about Libba ready to pour out love, but she stood isolated, lonely.

Daniel was asking Foy and Harrison Wingate about the big race won by their steamboat, *Mignonne Wingate,* as the group gathered around the dining table.

After they had eaten supper, someone voiced the question in all their minds. "Where have you been all these years?"

Libba began her soliloquy in a whisper which caused them to lean forward as she related the events of the enemy's capture of Magnolia Springs and her subsequent flight. She enunciated every heart-rending detail, feeling grim satisfaction when Jonathan wiped tears and pushed away his bowl of peach cobbler. She sat back, relieved of the lump in her throat, and ate the sharp, juicy pie with relish.

"It's a miracle you survived," Ramsey said. "I had given you up for dead. I wasn't physically able to go myself—and somehow I could not bear to see Magnolia Springs. I hired a detective who found no trace. I had given up all hope."

Libba thought, *You had given me up long before that.*

"And now you have made our family circle complete!" The lilting voice belonged to Lily Edwards Wingate, Foy's sister, Emma's niece. "Since Foy and Adrianna have so beautifully restored our parents' home—and now the promise of an heir to carry on the name—only this part of Emma and Jonathan was lacking." Lily's face glowed with contentment from being cherished by the handsome man who sat with his hand upon her shoulder.

Libba's troubled eyes met hers, and Lily, perceptive to the needs of others, added quickly, "We've claimed you for our own. We haven't given you a moment alone. Why don't you and Jonathan walk in the garden?"

Relief and fear dueled. Libba nodded mute thanks to Lily. Trailing her fingers over Daniel's sleeve in reluctant parting, she followed her father to the back porch.

Jonathan negotiated the steep steps stiff-legged, struggling with his cane. Libba stood back, waiting. He led her to the summerhouse. "Let's sit," he said gruffly. "My knees don't want to carry me."

For the first time, Libba forced herself to look at the stump of her father's leg. He walked on a wooden peg fastened below the calf with leather straps. Fighting to suppress a shudder, she said, "I was afraid you might not want me to interfere with your new life."

"How could you think that?"

"You didn't check the orphanage."

"At the war's end, I was out of my mind with illness from this foot. It was Emma who thought of hiring a detective—she longed to have you as our daughter. Most orphanages had not been built. Churches began building them to care for the orphans left by the war."

"Bethesda Orphanage was there since 1740."

"But I heard that orphanage suffered loss to Sherman and was in ruins until Colonel Wadley took charge—"

"You know Colonel Wadley?"

"Everyone knows of his reputation. No one dreamed an old woman and a child could travel that far. I reckoned without the backbone of Amanda King. I'm proud to see that you've inherited her determination. This could not have been an easy task."

"No."

"You're disappointed in what you've found. You're not ready to claim me as your father. What proof—"

Libba pushed back her unruly curls with their shared habit. She laughed ruefully. "It's not proof. I couldn't forgive your not searching for me. I see now I was wrong. Daniel has asked me to marry him. First, I had to know about you—about who I am."

"You have no memory of me nor I of you. I couldn't forgive myself for that either. I loved your mother possessively. Had tremendous pride in her beauty and my home. I worshiped money. Things it would do for her. I won't lie about my character to make you proud. When I was a child, I accepted the fact that Jesus died for my sins, but when I reached my teens, I fell into what I thought were good times. I let material possessions become my god. When my Betty died, I lost everything."

"You had me. Did you blame me for her dying?"

"No. You were a bundle in a blanket that my grieved mind didn't think about. I blamed God. Sometimes with grief there is terrible anger. A frustrating, futile anger. I didn't have a wife anymore. So I had nothing. I turned to humanism, indulging myself.

"I was yearning for spiritual things that I couldn't possess. My soul was panting, but it could not rest. I was seeking but never finding, journeying yet never arriving." Tears trickled over his rough cheeks.

"And you never thought of me at all?"

A strained silence stretched between them.

"When I came to Eufaula, my life began to change. Mignonne, a beautiful baby, was the center of everyone's love. I began to long for you, to plan to marry Emma and take her back to Magnolia Springs as a mother for you."

Eyeing him doubtfully, Libba said nothing.

"Then came the war, and the world was turned upside down. Our cause was lost, my home burned, my child dead. I planned suicide."

"Suicide?"

"I almost threw myself into the Chattahoochee."

"What changed your mind?"

"Emma's love. Emma's prayers. When I let Jesus into the ship of my life, I was immediately at the land whither I went. My searching was over. A new life had begun."

"So you became a preacher?"

"Not then. God had work to do on me. Last summer, I saw Adrianna struggling for direction and realized that many people need to turn back to the Bible as a guide for living. I felt the call to preach."

Daniel's caring face was framed in the arch of the gazebo.

"I'm sorry to interrupt, but everyone wants to go back with us to see the *Rebecca*."

The Wingates and Edwardses offered her so much love that Libba felt more guilty at her resentment of Jonathan Ramsey's son, Win.

Colonel Wadley welcomed everyone aboard and invited Libba's new family to get acquainted with her by being his guests for a cruise.

Everyone agreed as enthusiastically as if they had never ridden a boat.

Chapter 18

Uhmmm! Uhm! Uhmmm! The *Rebecca*'s whistle echoed and reechoed as she prepared to leave Eufaula. Steam *chu-chooing*, black smoke billowing, the steamboat quivered with the thrill of departure. On the bottom deck, standees ranged around and on nine hundred bales of cotton. Lifted high above them on the stateroom deck, one hundred twenty passengers filled to capacity this maiden voyage in regular trade. Businessmen strutting with black coattails flapping, women clutching spreading hats abloom with flowers, and children costumed with richly adorned clothing like minature adults waved at those unfortunates left ashore.

The Wadleys had returned home, but with Libba and Daniel at the rail were Lily Wingate, Mignonne, and Beau; Jonathan, his wife, and his boy. Instead of joy, Libba felt she must endure the cruise. Then she would return to teaching.

The stern-wheel swished, turned, lifted a spray of water. Faster, faster it caught the rhythm, propelled them forward. Libba's emotions churned like the waterwheel.

Piercing music from the calliope on the hurricane deck peaked the enthusiasm of the throng. From across the water, another steam organ played a shrill staccato. The sleek *Mignonne Wingate* shot smoothly forward tootling a competitive battle of the calliopes. The group on the *Mignonne* began to sing. The *Rebecca*'s passengers, hanging over her rails, screamed the champion roar.

Scrunching her shoulders against the noise, Libba a witnessed private scene. Lily blew a kiss to her husband in the *Mignonne*'s pilothouse. As he saluted her, love linked them, making them one, at peace above the chaos. Their tangible warmth made Libba long for the fire of such love. Why had she kept denying Daniel? Her hand groped for his but found nothing.

Daniel was gone. Passengers dispersed. Libba was alone.

She could no longer put off facing Jonathan Ramsey's blond wife and his black-haired son. She joined them on the front deck.

Eagerly, Emma made a place for her.

"How nice of the Wadleys to give us this trip to get acquainted," Emma said, soothing the situation. "It's special for us to go back where we courted. We'll show you."

Libba did not want to hear, but Emma's including smile made her relent.

They reminisced about the Shackelford twins being wooed by Myles and Richard, and Libba explained how Daniel's mother made the connection betwen Collier's painting, her neighbor, Georgie, and the Ramseys.

"When people take the trouble of loving and caring about one another, things connect in a marvelous way," agreed Emma.

"Why, you've almost quoted an Indian proverb Daniel shared with me. 'All things are connected,' " Libba said.

Jonathan nodded sagely. "The rains fall, the rivers rush to the sea, evaporate, and begin again. All the waters of the world connect. When they don't—when they're blocked—disaster reigns. Life changed when we could not go beyond this river. We were getting barefooted as a bunch of yard dogs when our plantations were shut off from England's factories by the Yankees. Let me tell you about my daring blockade-runner days."

When Libba returned to the stateroom she shared with Mignonne, she wrote down what her father had said.

"Waters of the world connect."

A line in search of a poem, she thought. She sifted her brain for words, images. None came. *I'm beginning to feel better toward him—them. Can he forgive and accept me?*

Libba chose her blue ball gown. Mignonne helped her tame her curls into a fashionable coiffure.

"Daniel and Paul will be overwhelmed with your beauty, and your father will be proud!"

For the first time in her life, Libba felt pretty. Maybe at last she could please those who had rejected her.

Libba entered the grand saloon eager to see—and be seen by—Daniel. Descending the steps of the ornate staircase, Libba glanced about. She had not seen Daniel since they came aboard. Was he avoiding her? With the guilt she carried for all the wrongs she felt she had caused, had she driven him away? Was he jealous because Paul Morley was arrogantly asserting his authority as representative of the steamboat line?

"The penalty for being punctual is that one must always wait for others who are late." Lily joined her unbidden.

"I guess I'm constantly waiting to be punished."

Lily's smile did not fade. "You were raised in a strict, legalistic atmosphere with a strong sense of right and wrong. Sometimes people like that watch themselves, thinking they must work to achieve perfection and forgiveness, but God is not like that. He reached down for us in love when He sent His Son to achieve our forgiveness. All we need to do is accept the gift. Let Jesus into your heart, and He will take away your burdens and fill your life with joy."

Lily's insight brought tears flooding to the surface. Wanting to pour out her heart, Libba could not. Dr. Weedon was right—and Daniel. She needed to cry. But she had held her tears too long; she could not let them go.

Uninvited, Lily said no more.

Diners were drifting in, and Daniel appeared at last. With his hair neatly cut and combed and his black formal evening clothes immaculate, he was more handsome than Libba had ever seen him. He smiled at her as if she were the most beautiful delicacy of all.

Course after course was served. From a tea cart laden with sweets, Libba chose a napoleon and swapped Daniel a bite for a taste of his eclair.

To walk off the meal before dancing began, Libba and Daniel strolled the deck, oblivious to other passengers. From the hurricane deck, the sobbing of a gypsy violin sent shivers of music trembling over the water.

A discordant note set Libba's teeth on edge. Emitting from within the heart of the great boat, a mournful sawing and scraping twanged a quivering foreboding.

"We've stopped," she gasped.

"Yes, my lovely one." Daniel laughed. "Even a floating palace must stop for wood to fire those monstrous furnaces. And to pick up freight to pay the bills." He pointed to the stevedores lifting more bales to add to the lower deck.

"More? The boat is loaded already. Look how tattered those bales are. The cotton's wasting." She leaned over the rail. "See? Locks are floating down the stream like little ducks."

"Some old farmer has been saving those shabby bales, waiting for a rainy day. It's amazing how the new electric lamps flood the river with light. They say people who see the boat approaching think she's afire."

Libba stiffened with alarm.

Daniel cuffed her chin. "It's safe. The machines for generating the lamps fluid are worked by steam from the boilers. The electric light does away with the danger from flaming torches. There'll be no more fires in this age of electricity."

The orchestra began playing the summer's most popular song, "Whisper You'll Be Mine, Love." Daniel hoped the moment for romance had come. "May I have the honor of this waltz?"

They stepped into the ballroom. Dancers made a kaleidoscope of colors as they swirled.

Paul came striding toward her. Grasping her bare shoulder, he gave her a knowing wink and whirled her away over the waxen floor before Daniel could protest.

Libba awakened sweating. Bolting upright, blinking in the blackness, she smelled smoke. Probably her old nightmare. But there had been no railroad tracks knotted like pretzels. Of course, there was smoke above a steamboat.

Trying to relax, she relived the passion of Daniel's kiss stolen in the shadow of a lifeboat before he walked her to her stateroom. He had urged her to postpone their marriage no longer, to give him a definite answer. Why had she not?

Mignonne groaned. Something was bothering her, too.

Libba stood up. Smoke! Black! Thick, hot! Real smoke!

She opened the door. "Fire!" The dreaded word, the curse of steamboats. Bells clanged. Whistles shrieked.

Grabbing their wraps, Libba pulled at the sleep-drugged Mignonne. "We must save our parents. Our brothers. You get Lily and the boys. I must help my father. He can't run." She choked on smoke that smelled like burning rags. Eyes smarting, she stumbled toward her father's stateroom. Swirling smoke confused her. Lost, she sank to her knees to get a clearer breath.

Scrubbing at her streaming eyes, she suddenly released a flow of cleansing, long-pent tears. *Oh, God, I am lost.*

And suddenly she knew. They had all loved her so much, had tried to help her, to bring her face-to-face with God. The moment had come. Only she, herself, could do the rest. Only she could remove the cold, hard stone she had placed over her heart and open the secret place.

Crying for mercy and forgiveness, she prayed. *Oh, God, I know now I can never be good enough to come to One so holy, but You have come in to me. Strengthen me now. Help me to save my papa. Oh, my heavenly Father, save Daniel.*

A quietness came over her. Her mind cleared to think.

Count the doors. Third from the corner. She banged on the door. Jonathan answered. Flinging herself into the cabin, she fell upon him sobbing.

"Oh, Papa, I was lost. I couldn't find you in the smoke. I thought I'd never find you!"

Her father's tears mingled with hers as he kissed her tenderly. "My little daughter. How I've needed you!"

Weeping, they held each other. Nothing else mattered.

Emma's arms encircled them, urging them up. From her deep reserve of inner strength, she murmured words of direction.

Flames were spreading. Nothing could be saved. There was no time to find and strap on the wooden leg.

Sharing the burden of the crippled man, the two women timed their strides so that he could swing between them. Steady, calm amid people rushing madly by, they gained the deck. Gale winds blew fresh air to anxious faces, relieved stricken lungs. The winds fanned the flames, sending them leaping across the cotton bales on the deck below, consuming everything. Captain Whitesides, running with an ax preparing to scuttle his boat, suddenly dropped it in despair. The fire had gained too great a headway.

"The cargo can't be saved," he shouted to his crew. "Save the passengers!"

People were rushing from the cabins, jumping into the river, piling upon those who had been standees on the freight deck. The mass of humanity struggled to swim and keep themselves afloat.

The dry cotton, burning like powder, sent flames leaping up to the cabin deck, threatening the huddled family.

"Looks like Judgment Day," Jonathan said with a laugh as one of the officers handed him a cork life preserver.

Libba stared at her father, then laughed. Freed by forgiveness, warmed by love for him, she knew that now she could leave everything to God's judgment. Circumstances and the natural failings of humanity had driven her father. She would no longer judge him. She would love him and remember that her own character was as it was because of what he had been.

Screams glanced off her as she moved with the surging crowd. Feeling the turquoise ring, she knew her father had loved her without knowing it. Even in his grief, he had given her this first clue that had enabled her to search.

Libba helped her father and Emma into a lifeboat and turned back into the blaze crying out for Daniel. She had put him on a pedestal, fearing she could never be good enough for him. Now she understood he loved her just as she was, in spite of her shortcomings. She stumbled toward his cabin.

Oh, Daniel. I wish I had not put off marrying you. Dear God, don't let it be too late!

Daniel found Libba's stateroom engulfed in flames. Wild with grief, he covered his face to plunge in, but something tugged at his brain, telling him her door was open. She must be out! Crawling to Jonathan's door, he found it open. Fiery timbers were dropping around him.

Daniel stood up, ready to run. A falling rafter grazed his cheek. Stunned, he fell, fighting for his senses. He had brought Libba to Jonathan. Was his mission ended? He had hoped to bring her to God. He had hoped—but everything was collasping.

Beyond a wall of flames, Libba collided with the young purser. He pushed her onto the deck. "Hurry, Miss. The pilot's ramming the boat ashore. When it strikes the bank, jump!"

"No!" she twisted away. "I can't go without Daniel." She searched a sea of smudged faces, shrieking, "Daniel!"

Flames leaped above the roof, met over the pilothouse. High in the air as if he were floating above them, the brave pilot remained at his post. The steamboat struck the bank. Libba slammed to her knees.

Commands to jump ashore. Noise, confusion. Lily, Mignonne, Beau, her brother, Win. Hands picking Libba up, forcing her to make the terrifying leap.

Splashing, Libba hit cold water. Her hands went down, sank into oozing, muddy slime. All around her stunned passengers sat, crouched, knelt, in black swamp water. Wide-eyed, they stared in helpless fascination at the flames engulfing the beautiful *Rebecca*. Hissing, sputtering, leaping, the fire consumed the boat to the water's edge.

In minutes, light, heat were gone. People were picking themselves up from the swamp, wading down the river toward a higher ground, shivering, suddenly realizing they were wet and cold.

The Chattahoochee was a solid sea of charred remnants. Fragmentary bales of burned cotton bobbed crazily in the currents. One bale washed ashore bearing a number of small coins, a bunch of keys, and three fingers of a human hand.

Horrified, Libba covered her face. A splashing in the dark water brought a relieved sigh from close beside her.

"Thank you, dear Lord," Lily Wingate prayed. "The officers are swimming to shore. I'm glad my Harrison wasn't with us. Captains always think they must save everyone or go down with their vessels."

Eyes straining, Libba leaned forward. Unable to breathe, she tried to distinguish the men rising like phoenixes from the ash-laden water.

Cheers rang out because Pilot Lapham had managed to jump at the last minute. Captain Whitesides—the engineer—Paul, humbly accepting praise for heroism. Behind him a smaller man. The way he moved. It had to be. Daniel. Oh, yes! Daniel!

Blinded by tears, Libba struggled through the crowd. He was reaching out. His hands, his dear sweet, funny face bore angry burns.

"Daniel!" She flung herself at him.

"Libba. Oh, my love!" He wrapped her in his arms as if he would never let her go. "I couldn't find you. I searched. So many staterooms separated us."

"Too many things have separated us!"

They drank in each other's aliveness, not worrying about the decorum or people around them. Suddenly, Libba became aware that she and her clothes were wet and dirty, covered in mud. Embarrassed, she drew away from Daniel.

Paul touched her shoulder. "Thank God you're all right."

Wagons arrived from the Fitzgerald plantation, alerted by the glow from the holocaust. David Fitzgerald opened his home to all. Physicians came to help the many who were burned.

The remains of the hull had sunk, and none of the missing were found. After questioning his crew, the captain discovered that the globe had broken on the arc light. A spark from the electric light had ignited a ragged bale. Instead of smoldering, the tatters had been fanned into flames by the wind.

Libba listened through a haze of exhaustion. Her head nodded and her chin fell on her chest. She dozed, dreaming not of this fire but of turpentine and pine trees with railroad tracks twisted around them like pretzels.

"Libba."

She jerked upright. It was Paul standing before her. Somehow he had changed. His handsome face, his carriage had lost self-absorption, had taken on new manhood.

"Yes, Paul?"

"I wanted to be certain you were all right before I left. Captain Whitesides and I are going to walk upriver and catch the train. I must telegraph the office. They will send another steamboat to fill the place of the *Rebecca*. The Chattahoochee has always been death for steamboats, but this disaster foreshadows the end of an era. The importance of the steamboat is breaking beneath the swift, sure power of the railroads. Progress will win over romance." He took her hands with a rueful smile.

Libba wondered at the working of his face, the stiffening of his jaw as he shouldered responsibility. "I'm proud of you, Paul." Impulsively, she stood on tiptoe and kissed him good-bye.

Daniel, watching from across the way where a doctor was applying salve to his burns, saw only the kiss and thought forlornly, *She did not pull away from him. Libba has chosen Paul.*

Chapter 19

Sunlight burst through the mists of morning and streamed in the dormer window of Jonathan Ramsey's cottage in Eufaula where Libba sat writing. She turned words over on her tongue. With a sudden inspiration, she dipped her pen in the crystal inkwell.

> Your tears that fall to share my grief and shame
> Say waters of the world connect, and tears,
>   of one must cleanse another's pain.

She added the date, September 20, 1877. So much had happened in the past year. Yet everything that mattered had begun a few days ago. How exciting it was to express the freeing that forgiveness had brought her! She would make a gift of her poem to her father.

Probably she would never be a great poet, but this was the first step. Daniel's mother might even introduce her to Sidney Lanier.

Her heart was full of love to share. She wanted to spend time with her brother, to find out the ways he was different from and the ways he was a part of her, before she returned to Georgia. Everyone had invited her to stay in Eufaula, but she needed to share all that happened with Miss Rebecca and Colonel Wadley and dear, dear Auntie.

Whistling drew her back to the window. Daniel was swinging through the gate carrying a mysterious package.

Scampering down the stairs, Libba flung open the door and dragged him into the parlor.

She wanted to throw her arms around him and kiss him. She had so much to tell him, but the way the outside corners of his eyebrows had gone up from his little-boy eyes made her stand back looking at him curiously.

"What have you brought me?"

Twisting his mobile face into a mocking expression, he spoke in a funny accent. "Who said this is for you?"

Libba stood on tiptoe to capture the brown-paper package he waved over her head. She untied the strings and blinked at a boxful of glazed German biscuits—pretzels.

"What?"

"I had a crazy idea. You'll think my parting gift silly, but I wanted to give you a good dream." He rubbed his hand over his hair, standing gray strands in all directions. Libba had changed. She no longer looked weak and sick. Her eyes were like sparkling sunlight on water. She did not need to lean on him now. He longed to continue to hold her, but if he loved her enough to seek what was best for her, he must be ready to let her go. But how could he bear trusting her care to Paul? He must speak his piece and leave as quickly as possible.

Libba realized that Daniel was hurting. Why was he not sharing her happiness? She sat quietly waiting.

"I wanted to leave you with a different image of pretzels. A reminder to help you find the peace of forgiveness." He reddened. "People see pretzels as knots because they've forgotten their origin. Monks in southern Europe made them to reward children who learned their prayers. They represent a child's arms crossed in prayer. That's all you must do. Become as a child. Ask for forgiveness and give it—"

Libba stayed his words with a kiss. "You are a wonderful, caring man. I won't worry any more about deserving you. I'll just be thankful for being blessed." She laughed because he was puzzled. "You don't understand, but how could you?"

Quickly she told Daniel about her experience during the fire. Beside him, she knew that all her searching was ended.

"Hatred and unforgiveness were blocking my heart, stopping my love from flowing. Now I know I loved you from the first moment you pulled me from the train wreck."

"Me? What about—I thought you'd decided on Paul!"

"Paul! How could you? Oh! You saw me kiss him good-bye. But I didn't think you'd think. . .I was only congratulating him on growing up at last—and bidding him farewell. My darling, what I felt for Paul—before I really knew you, remember? That was only what some sage long ago termed puppy love."

Libba kissed Daniel with a passion that convinced him.

"Marry me now. There's a preacher in the other room."

Libba laughed shakily. "I'm sorry I've kept you waiting so long. But please. Just a little more patience. I promise to make the fastest wedding plans. . . All of my best clothes burned, but I'll gather the quickest trousseau."

Suddenly love made her hungry. She bit a pretzel. "I won't forget what these mean."

A mischievous look crossed her face. "Can I still hate Sherman a little?"

Daniel grinned and tousled her hair. "All sane men hate war. But just mentally. Don't let hatred and unforgiveness obsess you again. And after all, Sherman didn't defeat you. You and that spunky spirit rose up from the ashes the strong little person I could aways see in there fighting. If you ever should have a nightmare again, you will be safely—" he knotted his arms around her—"wrapped in my love."

Libba and Daniel gazed from the windows of the belvedere of Barbour

Hall for one last look across Eufaula and beyond the searching river.

Lily had wanted them to see the view from the widow's walk where she had watched for Harrison Wingate's steamboat, *Wave,* during that long-ago time when the river had separated them. Libba smiled at Lily gratefully. Such a short while ago, these people had been strangers, but her stepmother Emma's nieces and nephews had included her in the circle of their love and now—glorious, glorious—she had a family.

Following Adrianna and Foy back down the winding stairs to the second floor, Libba and Daniel tiptoed into the nursery and stood over the cradle of Foy Edwards, Junior, in silent awe at the wonder of love. Libba reached out to touch Daniel's cheek with promise.

Libba leaned out the window of her bedroom at Great Hill Place. The sky was as clear and blue as only an October day could be. There remained no trace of September's fog. A train whistle floated across the peaceful woodland from Bolingbroke.

Endine flounced into the room. "The last of the guests have arrived. I never expected to see such a crowd of distinguished folks at the wedding of a couple of nobodies!"

Libba laughed. Secure now in her own identity, she could no longer be wounded by Endine. She was sorry that the girl was jealous. Her freckles had fairly stood out on stems since Libba's family jewels had been recovered. By piecing Papa's knowledge of the henhouse with Libba's remembrance of the jewel box's burial, they had been able to find the treasure and pay the taxes on Magnolia Springs. Papa joked that a burned-out plantation was a poor wedding gift, but Libba and Daniel knew that rich land waited for them to put down roots and grow.

Endine adjusted Libba's train, cascading like a waterfall of satin and Chantilly lace. Scallops of lace fell softly from her hands to reveal her treasured turquoise ring.

A tap sounded at the door. Colonel Wadley waited, stern-faced, but with love enough to spare for widows and orphans to be a father to her. Libba tried to express her thanks, but he shook his head and offered her his arm.

They descended the stone steps into the fragrant garden where Auntie had turned Hermes's secret place into a wedding bower.

Through a blur Libba saw Lily, Captain Wingate, Beau, and the lovely Mignonne. Happily, she smiled at Emma and Win, at Dorothea Marshall. Now the pathway had brought her at last to Daniel.

Unquestioningly, they stepped before Jonathan Ramsey.

"Dearly beloved, we are gathered in the sight of God and these witnesses to join this man and this woman. . ."

Daniel lifted the mists of her veil to kiss his bride. Her face was wet. Unashamed, Libba wept tears of joy.

Acknowledgments

When readers asked for another book in my river series to tell what happened to Jonathan Ramsey's baby, it seemed impossible. How could I reunite them in an era when people rarely moved from their birthplaces? Although my main characters live only for my readers and me, my backgrounds are factual.

My search for the story was as circuitous as Libba's. Edward Mueller, author of *Perilous Journeys: A History of Steamboating on the Chattahoochee, Apalachicola, and Flint Rivers,* 1828–1928, told me the *Rebecca Everingham,* the grandest steamboat on the Chattahoochee, was named for a lady in Bolingbroke, Georgia. Kitty Oliver of the Middle Georgia Historical Society, introduced me to Rebecca Everingham Wadley's great-granddaughter, Mrs. Henry Dillon Worship. Anne Winship took me to Great Hill Place and made the era come alive. She entrusted me with Sarah Lois Wadley's diary, *A Brief Record of the Life of William Wadley.*

Libba's fiction and Wadley's fact melded. He oversaw the orphanage and did all I mentioned and much more. At a time when others of his era manipulated railroads to build wealth and power, Wadley worked on fixed principles of right and wrong that placed his company above his private interest. A bronze statue of Wadley, at Mulberry and Third in Macon, overlooks the railroads and river. With eyes seeming to snap and coattails seeming to flap, he remains a monument to railroading and to integrity.

I also thank poet Julia Evatt, who enticed me with the line, "Waters of the world connect." My excitement mounted at Ocmulgee National Monument with its use of words attributed to Chief Seattle: "All things are connected." Thanks to Sibbald Smith, Sam Lawson, and Sylvia Flowers. Thanks to Macon historian Calder W. Payne; Mrs. George G. Felton, Jr.; the Hay House Museum, which was Anne Johnson's home; and *Historical Record of Macon and Central Georgia* by Butler.

Thanks also go to *The First Hundred Years of Wesleyan College, 1836–1936* by Samuel Akers; to his widow, Elizabeth Akers, as well as to Miss Cornelia Shiver, Mrs. Schley Gatewood, Sr., and Joanne Weaver; to the Cowles Myles Collier Gallery at Wesleyan; to *Hope Bids Me Onward* by Castlen for the Shackelford story; to Libba Smith; to *The Story of Bulloch County;* to *War Is Hell, Sherman;* to Mary Burton Carson, who related my great-grandmother

Rebecca Slaughter King's eyewitness account of the soldiers at Magnolia Springs; to Birdville Plantation; to Harriet Bates, Lake Blackshear Regional Library; to Marty Willett and Nancy Gaston; to Glenda Calhoun; to Barbara Manger; to Carlene McPherson; and to Endine Hart.

The *Rebecca Everingham,* launched in 1880 and burned in 1884, signaled the end of the steamboat era on the Chattahoochee, but the romance of riverboats will never die.

A Letter to Our Readers

Dear Readers:

In order that we might better contribute to your reading enjoyment, we would appreciate you taking a few minutes to respond to the following questions. When completed, please return to the following: Fiction Editor, Barbour Publishing, Inc., P.O. Box 719, Uhrichsville, OH 44683.

1. Did you enjoy reading *Magnolias?*
   - ❑ Very much. I would like to see more books like this.
   - ❑ Moderately. I would have enjoyed it more if ______________

____

____

2. What influenced your decision to purchase this book? (Check those that apply.)
   - ❑ Cover ❑ Back cover copy ❑ Title ❑ Price
   - ❑ Friends ❑ Publicity ❑ Other

3. Which story was your favorite?
   - ❑ *The River Between* ❑ *River of Fire*
   - ❑ *The Wind Along the River* ❑ *Beyond the Searching River*

4. Please check your age range:
   - ❑ Under 18 ❑ 18–24 ❑ 25–34
   - ❑ 35–45 ❑ 46–55 ❑ Over 55

5. How many hours per week do you read? ________________

Name ____

Occupation ____________________________________

Address ______________________________________

City ______________ State ________ Zip ________